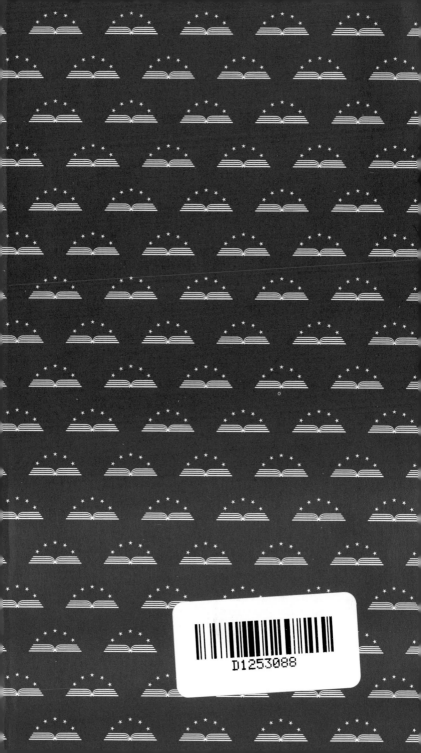

PHILIP K. DICK

PHILIP K. DICK

VALIS AND LATER NOVELS
A Maze of Death
VALIS
The Divine Invasion
The Transmigration of Timothy Archer

THE LIBRARY OF AMERICA

The paper used in this publication meets the
minimum requirements of the American National Standard for
Information Sciences—Permanence of Paper for Printed
Library Materials, ANSI Z39.48—1984.

Distributed to the trade in the United States
by Penguin Group (USA) Inc.
and in Canada by Penguin Books Canada Ltd.

Library of Congress Control Number: 2009921284
ISBN 978-1-59853-044-5

———

Second Printing
The Library of America—193

Manufactured in the United States of America

JONATHAN LETHEM
SELECTED THE CONTENTS AND
WROTE THE NOTES FOR THIS VOLUME

Contents

A MAZE OF DEATH

To my two daughters, Laura and Isa

AUTHOR'S FOREWORD

The theology in this novel is not an analog of any known religion. It stems from an attempt made by William Sarill and myself to develop an abstract, logical system of religious thought, based on the arbitrary postulate that God exists. I should say, too, that the late Bishop James A. Pike, in discussions with me, brought forth a wealth of theological material for my inspection, none of which I was previously acquainted with.

In the novel, Maggie Walsh's experiences after death are based on an L.S.D. experience of my own. In exact detail.

The approach in this novel is highly subjective; by that I mean that at any given time, reality is seen—not directly—but indirectly, i.e., through the mind of one of the characters. This viewpoint mind differs from section to section, although most of the events are seen through Seth Morley's psyche.

All material concerning Wotan and the death of the gods is based on Richard Wagner's version of *Der Ring des Nibelungen*, rather than on the original body of myths.

Answers to questions put to the tench were derived from the *I Ching*, the Chinese *Book of Changes.*

"Tekel upharsin" is Aramaic for, "He has weighed and now they divide." Aramaic was the tongue that Christ spoke. There should be more like him.

CONTENTS

One

HIS job, as always, bored him. So he had during the previous week gone to the ship's transmitter and attached conduits to the permanent electrodes extending from his pineal gland. The conduits had carried his prayer to the transmitter, and from there the prayer had gone into the nearest relay network; his prayer, during these days, had bounced throughout the galaxy, winding up—he hoped—at one of the god-worlds.

His prayer had been simple. "This damn inventory-control job bores me," he had prayed. "Routine work—this ship is too large and in addition it's overstaffed. I'm a useless standby module. Could you help me find something more creative and stimulating?" He had addressed the prayer, as a matter of course, to the Intercessor. Had it failed he would have presently re-addressed the prayer, this time to the Mentufacturer.

But the prayer had not failed.

"Mr. Tallchief," his supervisor said, entering Ben's work cubicle. "You're being transferred. How about that?"

"I'll transmit a thankyou prayer," Ben said, and felt good inside. It always felt good when one's prayers were listened to and answered. "When do I transfer? Soon?" He had never concealed his dissatisfaction from his supervisor; there was now even less reason to do so.

"Ben Tallchief," his supervisor said. "The praying mantis."

"Don't you pray?" Ben asked, amazed.

"Only when there's no other alternative. I'm in favor of a person solving his problems on his own, without outside help. Anyhow, your transfer is valid." His supervisor dropped a document on the desk before Ben. "A small colony on a planet named Delmak-O. I don't know anything about it, but I suppose you'll find it all out when you get there." He eyed Ben thoughtfully. "You're entitled to use one of the ship's nosers. For a payment of three silver dollars."

"Done," Ben said, and stood up, clutching the document.

He ascended by express elevator to the ship's transmitter, which he found hard at work transacting official ship business.

"Will you be having any empty periods later today?" he asked the chief radio operator. "I have another prayer, but I don't want to tie up your equipment if you'll be needing it."

"Busy all day," the chief radio operator said. "Look, Mac —we put one prayer through for you last week; isn't that enough?"

Anyhow I tried, Ben Tallchief mused as he left the transmitter with its hardworking crew and returned to his own quarters. If the matter ever comes up, he thought, I can say I did my best. But, as usual, the channels were tied up by nonpersonal communications.

He felt his anticipation grow; a creative job at last, and just when he needed it most. Another few weeks here, he said to himself, and I would have been pizzling away at the bottle again as in lamented former times. And of course that's why they granted it, he realized. They knew I was nearing a break. I'd probably have wound up in the ship's brig, along with— how many were there in the brig now?—well, however many there were in there. Ten, maybe. Not much for a ship this size. And with such stringent rules.

From the top drawer of his dresser he got out an unopened fifth of Peter Dawson scotch, broke the seal, unscrewed the lid. Little libation, he told himself as he poured scotch into a Dixie cup. And celebration. The gods appreciate ceremony. He drank the scotch, then refilled the small paper cup.

To further enlarge the ceremony he got down—a bit reluctantly—his copy of The Book: A. J. Specktowsky's *How I Rose From the Dead in My Spare Time and So Can You*, a cheap copy with soft covers, but the only copy he had ever owned; hence he had a sentimental attitude toward it. Opening at random (a highly approved method) he read over a few familiar paragraphs of the great twenty-first century Communist theologian's apologia pro sua vita.

"God is not supernatural. His existence was the first and most natural mode of being to form itself."

True, Ben Tallchief said to himself. As later theological investigation had proved. Specktowsky had been a prophet as well as a logician; all that he had predicted had turned up sooner or later. There remained, of course, a good deal to know . . . for example, the cause of the Mentufacturer's coming into being (unless one was satisfied to believe, with Specktowsky, that beings of that order were self-creating, and existing outside of time, hence outside of causality). But in the main it was all there on the many-times-printed pages.

"With each greater circle the power, good and knowledge on the part of God weakened, so that at the periphery of the greatest circle his good was weak, his knowledge was weak— too weak for him to observe the Form Destroyer, which was called into being by God's acts of form creation. The origin of the Form Destroyer is unclear; it is, for instance, not possible to declare whether (one) he was a separate entity from God from the start, uncreated by God but also self-creating, as is God, or (two) whether the Form Destroyer is an aspect of God, there being nothing—"

He ceased reading, sat sipping scotch and rubbing his forehead semi-wearily. He was forty-two years old and had read The Book many times. His life, although long, had not added up to much, at least until now. He had held a variety of jobs, doing a modicum of service to his employers, but never ever really excelling. Maybe I can begin to excel, he said to himself. On this new assignment. Maybe this is my big chance.

Forty-two. His age had astounded him for years, and each time that he had sat so astounded, trying to figure out what had become of the young, slim man in his twenties, a whole additional year slipped by and had to be recorded, a continually growing sum which he could not reconcile with his self-image. He still saw himself, in his mind's eye, as youthful, and when he caught sight of himself in photographs he usually collapsed. For example, he shaved now with an electric razor, unwilling to gaze at himself in his bathroom mirror. Somebody took my actual physical presence away and substituted *this*, he had thought from time to time. Oh well, so it went. He sighed.

Of all his many meager jobs he had enjoyed one alone, and he still meditated about it now and then. In 2105 he had operated the background music system aboard a huge colonizing ship on its way to one of the Deneb worlds. In the tape vault he had found all of the Beethoven symphonies mixed haphazardly in with string versions of *Carmen* and of Delibes and he had played the *Fifth*, his favorite, a thousand times throughout the speaker complex that crept everywhere within the ship, reaching each cubicle and work area. Oddly enough no one had complained and he had kept on, finally shifting his loyalty to the *Seventh* and at last, in a fit of excitement during the final months of the ship's voyage, to the *Ninth*—from which his loyalty never waned.

Maybe what I really need is sleep, he said to himself. A sort of twilight of living, with only the background sound of Beethoven audible. All the rest a blur.

No, he decided; I want to *be*! I want to act and accomplish something. And every year it becomes more necessary. Every year, too, it slips further and further away. The thing about the Mentufacturer, he reflected, is that he can renew everything. He can abort the decay process by replacing the decaying object with a new one, one whose form is perfect. And then that decays. The Form Destroyer gets hold of it—and presently the Mentufacturer replaces that. As with a succession of old bees wearing out their wings, dying and being replaced at last by new bees. But I can't do that. I decay and the Form Destroyer has me. And it will get only worse.

God, he thought, help me.

But not by replacing me. That would be fine from a cosmological standpoint, but ceasing to exist is not what I'm after; and perhaps you understood this when you answered my prayer.

The scotch had made him sleepy; to his chagrin he found himself nodding. To bring himself back to full wakefulness: that was necessary. Leaping up he strode to his portable phonograph, took a visrecord at random, and placed it on the turntable. At once the far wall of the room lit up, and bright shapes intermingled with one another, a mixture of motion and of life, but unnaturally flat. He reflexively adjusted the depth-circuit; the figures began to become three dimensional. He turned up the sound as well.

". . . Legolas is right. We may not shoot an old man so, at unawares and unchallenged, whatever fear or doubt be on us. Watch and wait!"

The bracing words of the old epic restored his perspective; he returned to his desk, reseated himself and got out the document which his supervisor had given him. Frowning, he studied the coded information, trying to decipher it. In numbers, punch-holes and letters it spelled out his new life, his world to come.

". . . You speak as one that knows Fangorn well. Is that so?" The visrecord played on, but he no longer heard it; he had begun to get the gist of the encoded message.

"What have you to say that you did not say at our last meeting?" a sharp and powerful voice said. He glanced up and found himself confronted by the gray-clad figure of Gandalf. It was as if Gandalf were speaking to him, to Ben Tallchief. Calling him to account. "Or, perhaps, you have things to unsay?" Gandalf said.

Ben rose, went over to the phonograph and shut it off. I do not feel able at this time to answer you, Gandalf, he said to himself. There are things to be done, real things; I can't indulge myself in a mysterious, unreal conversation with a mythological character who probably never existed. The old values, for me, are suddenly gone; I have to work out what these damn punch-holes, letters and numbers mean.

He was beginning to get the drift of it. Carefully, he replaced the lid on the bottle of scotch, twisting it tight. He would go in a noser, alone; at the colony he would join roughly a dozen others, recruited from a variety of sources. Range 5 of skills: a class C operation, on a K-4 pay scale. Maximum time: two years of operation. Full pension and medical benefits, starting as soon as he arrived. An override for any instructions he had already received, hence he could go at once. He did not have to terminate his work here before leaving.

And I have the three silver dollars for the noser, he said to himself. So that is that; nothing else to worry about. Except—

He could not discover what his job would consist of. The letters, numbers and punch-holes failed to say, or perhaps it was more correct to say that he could not get them to divulge this one piece of information—a piece he would much have wanted.

But still it looked good. I like it, he said to himself. I want it. Gandalf, he thought, I have nothing to unsay; prayers are not often answered and I will take this. Aloud he said, "Gandalf, you no longer exist except in men's minds, and what I have here comes from the One, True and Living Deity, who is completely real. What more can I hope for?" The silence of the room confronted him; he did not see Gandalf now because he had shut the record off. "Maybe someday," he continued, "I will unsay this. But not yet; not now. You understand?" He waited, experiencing the silence, knowing that he could begin it or end it by a mere touch of the phonograph's switch.

Two

SETH MORLEY neatly divided the Gruyère cheese lying before him with a plastic-handled knife and said, "I'm leaving." He cut himself a giant wedge of cheese, lifted it to his lips via the knife. "Late tomorrow night. Tekel Upharsin Kibbutz has seen the last of me." He grinned, but Fred Gossim, the settlement's chief engineer, failed to return the message of triumph; instead Gossim frowned even more strongly. His disapproving presence pervaded the office.

Mary Morley said quietly, "My husband applied for this transfer eight years ago. We never intended to stay here. You knew that."

"And we're going with them," Michael Niemand stammered in excitement. "That's what you get for bringing a top-flight marine biologist here and then setting him to work hauling blocks of stone from the goddam quarry. We're sick of it." He nudged his undersized wife, Clair. "Isn't that right?"

"Since there is no body of water on this planet," Gossim said gratingly, "we could hardly put a marine biologist to use in his stated profession."

"But you advertised, eight years ago, for a marine biologist," Mary Morley pointed out. This made Gossim scowl even more profoundly. "The mistake was yours."

"But," Gossim said, "this is your home. All of you—" He gestured at the group of kibbutz officials crowded around the entrance of the office. "We all built this."

"And the cheese," Seth Morley said, "is terrible, here. Those quakkip, those goat-like suborganisms that smell like the Form Destroyer's last year's underwear—I want very much to have seen the last of them and it. The quakkip and the cheese both." He cut himself a second slice of the expensive, imported Gruyère cheese. To Niemand he said, "You can't come with us. Our instructions are to make the flight by noser. Point A. A noser holds only two people; in this case my wife and me. Point B. You and your wife are two more people, ergo you won't fit. Ergo you can't come."

"We'll take our own noser," Niemand said.

"You have no instructions and/or permission to transfer to Delmak-O," Seth Morley said from within his mouthful of cheese.

"You don't want us," Niemand said.

"Nobody wants you," Gossim grumbled. "As far as I'm concerned without you we would do better. It's the Morleys that I don't want to see go down the drain."

Eying him, Seth Morley said tartly, "And this assignment is, a priori, 'down the drain.' "

"It's some kind of experimental work," Gossim said. "As far as I can discern. On a small scale. Thirteen, fourteen people. It would be for you turning the clock back to the early days of Tekel Upharsin. You want to build up from that all over again? Look how long it's taken for us to get up to a hundred efficient, well-intentioned members. You mention the Form Destroyer. Aren't you by your actions decaying back the form of Tekel Upharsin?"

"And my own form too," Morley said, half to himself. He felt grim, now; Gossim had gotten to him. Gossim had always been good with words, amazing in an engineer. It had been Gossim's silver-tongued words which had kept them all at their tasks throughout the years. But those words, to a good extent, had become vapid as far as the Morleys were concerned. The words did not work as they once had. And yet a glimmer of their past glory remained. He could just not quite shake off the bulky, dark-eyed engineer.

But we're leaving, Morley thought. As in Goethe's *Faust*, "In the beginning was the deed." The deed and not the word, as Goethe, anticipating the twentieth century existentialists, had pointed out.

"You'll want to come back," Gossim opined.

"Hmm," Seth Morley said.

"And you know what I'll say to that?" Gossim said loudly. "If I get a request from you—both of you Morleys—to come back here to Tekel Upharsin Kibbutz, I'll say, 'We don't have any need of a marine biologist; we don't even have an ocean. And we're not going to build so much as a puddle so that you can have a legitimate reason for working here.' "

"I never asked for a puddle," Morley said.

"But you'd like one."

the jars one by one within the magnetic grip-field of the storage compartment. I am afraid this is one thing I'll miss.

He called Mary on his neck radio. "I've picked out a noser," he informed her. "Come on down to the parking area and I'll show it to you."

"Are you sure it's a good one?"

"You know you can take my mechanical ability for granted," Morley said testily. "I've examined the rocket engine, wiring, controls, every life-protect system, everything, completely." He pushed the last jar of marmalade away in the storage area and shut the door firmly.

She arrived a few minutes later, slender and tanned in her khaki shirt, shorts and sandals. "Well," she said, surveying the *Morbid Chicken*, "it looks rundown to me. But if you say it's okay it is, I guess."

"I've already begun loading," Morley said.

"With what?"

Opening the door of the storage compartment he showed her the ten jars of marmalade.

After a long pause Mary said, "Christ."

"What's the matter?"

"You haven't been checking the wiring and the engine. You've been out scrounging up all the goddam marmalade you could talk them out of." She slammed the storage area door shut with venomous ire. "Sometimes I think you're insane. Our lives depend on this goddam noser working. Suppose the oxygen system fails or the heat circuit fails or there're microscopic leaks in the hull. Or—"

"Get your brother to look at it," he interrupted. "Since you have so much more trust in him than you do in me."

"He's busy. You know that."

"Or he'd be here," Morley said, "picking out which noser for us to take. Rather than me."

His wife eyed him intently, her spare body drawn up in a vigorous posture of defiance. Then, all at once, she sagged in what appeared to be half-amused resignation. "The strange thing is," she said, "that you have such good luck—I mean in relation to your talents. This probably *is* the best noser here. But not because you can tell the difference but because of your mutant-like luck."

"It's not luck. It's judgment."

"No," Mary said, shaking her head. "That's the last thing it is. You have no judgment—not in the usual sense, anyhow. But what the hell. We'll take this noser and hope your luck is holding as well as usual. But how can you live like this, Seth?" She gazed up plaintively into his face. "It's not fair to me."

"I've kept us going so far."

"You've kept us here at this—kibbutz," Mary said. "For eight years."

"But now I've gotten us off."

"To something worse, probably. What do we know about this new assignment? Nothing, except what Gossim knows—and he knows because he makes it his business to read over everyone else's communications. He read your original prayer . . . I didn't want to tell you because I knew it would make you so—"

"That bastard." He felt red, huge fury well up inside him, spiked with impotence. "It's a moral violation to read another person's prayers."

"He's in charge. He feels everything is his business. Anyhow we'll be getting away from that. Thank God. Come on; cool off. You can't do anything about it; he read it years ago."

"Did he say whether he thought it was a good prayer?"

Mary Morley said, "Fred Gossim would never say if it was. I think it was. Evidently it was, because you got the transfer."

"I think so. Because God doesn't grant too many prayers by Jews due to that covenant back in the pre-Intercessor days when the power of the Form Destroyer was so strong, and our relationship to him—to God, I mean—was so fouled up."

"I can see you back in those days," Mary said. "Kvetching bitterly about everything the Mentufacturer did and said."

Morley said, "I would have been a great poet. Like David."

"You would have held a little job, like you do now." With that she strode off, leaving him standing in the doorway of the noser, one hand on his row of stored-away marmalade jars.

His sense of impotence rose within him, choking his windpipe. "Stay here!" he yelled after her. "I'll leave without you!"

She continued on under the hot sun, not looking back and not answering.

*

For the remainder of the day Seth Morley busied himself loading their possessions into the *Morbid Chicken*. Mary did not show herself. He realized, toward dinnertime, that he was doing it all. Where is she? he asked himself. It's not fair.

Depression hit him, as it generally did toward mealtime. I wonder if it's all worth it, he said to himself. Going from one no-good job to another. I'm a loser. Mary is right about me; look at the job I did selecting a noser. Look at the job I'm doing loading this damn stuff in here. He gazed about the interior of the noser, conscious of the ungainly piles of clothing, books, records, kitchen appliances, typewriter, medical supplies, pictures, wear-forever couch covers, chess set, reference tapes, communications gear and junk, junk, junk. What have we in fact accumulated in eight years of work here? he asked himself. Nothing of any worth. And in addition, he could not get it all into the noser. Much would have to be thrown away or left for someone else to use. Better to destroy it, he thought gloomily. The idea of someone else gaining use of his possessions had to be sternly rejected. I'll burn every last bit of it, he told himself. Including all the nebbish clothes that Mary's collected in her jaybird manner. Selecting whatever's bright and gaudy.

I'll pile her stuff outside, he decided, and then get all of mine aboard. It's her own fault: she should be here to help. I'm under no mandate to load her kipple.

As he stood there with an armload of clothes gripped tightly he saw, in the gloom of twilight, a figure approaching him. Who is it? he wondered, and peered to see.

It was not Mary. A man, he saw, or rather something like a man. A figure in a loose robe, with long hair falling down his dark, full shoulders. Seth Morley felt fear. The Walker-on-Earth, he realized. Come to stop me. Shaking, he began to set down the armload of clothes. Within him his conscience bit furiously; he felt now the complete weight of all the bad-doings he had done. Months, years—he had not seen the Walker-on-Earth for a long time, and the weight was intolerable. The accumulation which always left its mark within. Which never departed until the Intercessor removed it.

The figure halted before him. "Mr. Morley," it said.

"Yes," he said, and felt his scalp bleeding perspiration. His face dripped with it and he tried to wipe it away with the back of his hand. "I'm tired," he said. "I've been working for hours to get this noser loaded. It's a big job."

The Walker-on-Earth said, "Your noser, the *Morbid Chicken*, will not get you and your little family to Delmak-O. I therefore must interfere, my dear friend. Do you understand?"

"Sure," he said, panting with guilt.

"Select another."

"Yes," he said, nodding frantically. "Yes, I will. And thank you; thanks a lot. The fact of the matter is you saved our lives." He peered at the dim face of the Walker-on-Earth, trying to see if its expression reproached him. But he could not tell; the remaining sunlight had begun to diffuse into an almost nocturnal haze.

"I am sorry," the Walker-on-Earth said, "that you had to labor so long for nothing."

"Well, as I say—"

"I will help you with the reloading," the Walker-on-Earth said. It reached its arms out, bending; it picked up a pile of boxes and began to move among the parked, silent nosers. "I recommend this," it said presently, halting by one and reaching to open its door. "It is not much to look at, but mechanically it's perfect."

"Hey," Morley said, following with a swiftly snatched-up load. "I mean, thanks. Looks aren't important anyhow; it's what's on the inside that counts. For people as well as nosers." He laughed, but the sound emerged as a jarring screech; he cut it off instantly, and the sweat gathered around his neck turned cold with his great fear.

"There is no reason to be afraid of me," the Walker said.

"Intellectually I know that," Morley said.

Together, they labored for a time in silence, carrying box after box from the *Morbid Chicken* to the better noser. Continually Morley tried to think of something to say, but he could not. His mind, because of his fright, had become dim; the fires of his quick intellect, in which he had so much faith, had almost flickered off.

"Have you ever thought of getting psychiatric help?" the Walker asked him at last.

"No," he said.

"Let's pause a moment and rest. So we can talk a little."

Morley said, "No."

"Why not?"

"I don't want to know anything; I don't want to hear any-thing." He heard his voice bleat out in its weakness, steeped in its paucity of knowledge. The bleat of foolishness, of the great-est amount of insanity of which he was capable. He knew this, heard it and recognized it, and still he clung to it; he contin-ued on. "I know I'm not perfect," he said. "But I can't change. I'm satisfied."

"Your failure to examine the *Morbid Chicken*."

"Mary made a good point; usually my luck is good."

"She would have died, too."

"Tell her that." Don't tell me, he thought. Please, don't tell me any more. I don't want to know!

The Walker regarded him for a moment. "Is there anything," it said at last, "that you want to say to me?"

"I'm grateful, damn grateful. For your appearance."

"Many times during the past years you've thought to your-self what you would say to me if you met me again. Many things passed through your mind."

"I—forget," he said, huskily.

"May I bless you?"

"Sure," he said, his voice still husky. And almost inaudible. "But why? What have I done?"

"I am proud of you, that's all."

"But why?" He did not understand; the censure which he had been waiting for had not arrived.

The Walker said, "Once years ago you had a tomcat whom you loved. He was greedy and mendacious and yet you loved him. One day he died from bone fragments lodged in his stom-ach, the result of filching the remains of a dead Martian root-buzzard from a garbage pail. You were sad, but you still loved him. His essence, his appetite—all that made him up had driven him to his death. You would have paid a great deal to have him alive again, but you would have wanted him as he was, greedy and pushy, himself as you loved him, unchanged. Do you understand?"

"I prayed then," Morley said. "But no help came. The Men-tufacturer could have rolled time back and restored him."

"Do you want him back now?"

"Yes," Morley said raspingly.

"Will you get psychiatric help?"

"No."

"I bless you," the Walker-on-Earth said, and made a motion with his right hand: a slow and dignified gesture of blessing. Seth Morley bowed his head, pressed his right hand against his eyes . . . and found that black tears had lodged in the hollows of his face. Even now, he marveled. That awful old cat; I should have forgotten him years ago. I guess you never really forget such things, he thought. It's all in there, in the mind, buried until something like this comes up.

"Thank you," he said, when the blessing ended.

"You will see him again," the Walker said. "When you sit with us in Paradise."

"Are you sure?"

"Yes."

"Exactly as he was?"

"Yes."

"Will he remember me?"

"He remembers you now. He waits. He will never stop waiting."

"Thanks," Morley said. "I feel a lot better."

The Walker-on-Earth departed.

Entering the cafeteria of the kibbutz, Seth Morley sought out his wife. He found her eating curried lamb shoulder at a table in the shadows of the edge of the room. She barely nodded as he seated himself facing her.

"You missed dinner," she said presently. "That's not like you."

Morley said, "I saw him."

"Who?" She eyed him keenly.

"The Walker-on-Earth. He came to tell me that the noser I picked out would have killed us. We never would have made it."

"I knew that," Mary said. "I knew that—*thing* would never have gotten us there."

Morley said, "My cat is still alive."

"You don't have a cat."

He grabbed her arm, halting her motions with the fork. "He

says we'll be all right; we'll get to Delmak-O and I can begin the new job."

"Did you ask him what the new job is all about?"

"I didn't think to ask him that, no."

"You fool." She pried his hand loose and resumed eating. "Tell me what the Walker looked like."

"You've never seen it?"

"You *know* I've never seen it!"

"Beautiful and gentle. He held out his hand and blessed me."

"So it manifested itself to you as a man. Interesting. If it had been as a woman you wouldn't have listened to—"

"I pity you," Morley said. "It's never intervened to save you. Maybe it doesn't consider you worth saving."

Mary, savagely, threw down her fork; she glowered at him with animal ferocity. Neither of them spoke for a time.

"I'm going to Delmak-O alone," Morley said at last.

"You think so? You really think so? I'm going with you; I want to keep my eyes on you at all times. Without me—"

"Okay," he said scathingly. "You can come along. What the hell do I care? Anyhow if you stayed here you'd be having an affair with Gossim, ruining his life—" He ceased speaking, panting for breath.

In silence, Mary continued eating her lamb.

Three

"YOU are one thousand miles above the surface of Delmak-O," the headphone clamped against Ben Tallchief's ear declared. "Switch to automatic pilot, please."

"I can land her myself," Ben Tallchief said into his mike. He gazed at the world below him, wondering at its colors. Clouds, he decided. A natural atmosphere. Well, that answers one of my many questions. He felt relaxed and confident. And then he thought of his next question: Is this a god-world? And that issue sobered him.

He landed without difficulty . . . stretched, yawned, belched, unfastened his seat belt, stood up, awkwardly walked to the hatch, opened the hatch, then went back to the control room to shut off the still active rocket engine. While he was at it he shut off the air supply, too. That seemed to be all. He clambered down the iron steps and bounced his way clumsily onto the surface of the planet.

Next to the field a row of flat-roofed buildings: the tiny colony's interwoven installations. Several persons were moving toward his noser, evidently to greet him. He waved, enjoying the feel of the plastic leather steering gloves—that and the very great augmentation of his somatic self which his bulky suit provided.

"Hi!" a female voice called.

"Hi," Ben Tallchief said, regarding the girl. She wore a dark smock with matching pants, a general issue outfit that matched the plainness of her round, clean, freckled face. "Is this a god-world?" he asked, walking leisurely toward her.

"It is not a god-world," the girl said, "but there are some strange things out there." She gestured toward the horizon vaguely; smiling at him in a friendly manner she held out her hand. "I'm Betty Jo Berm. Linguist. You're either Mr. Tallchief or Mr. Morley; everyone else is here already."

"Tallchief," he said.

"I'll introduce you to everyone. This elderly gentleman is Bert Kosler, our custodian."

"Glad to meet you, Mr. Kosler." Handshake.

"I'm glad to meet you, too," the old man said.

"This is Maggie Walsh, our theologian."

"Glad to meet you, Miss Walsh." Handshake. Pretty girl.

"Glad to meet you, too, Mr. Tallchief."

"Ignatz Thugg, thermoplastics."

"Hi, there." Overly masculine handshake. He did not like Mr. Thugg.

"Dr. Milton Babble, the colony's M.D."

"Nice to know you, Dr. Babble." Handshake. Babble, short and wide, wore a colorful short-sleeved shirt. His face had on it a corrupt expression which was hard to penetrate.

"Tony Dunkelwelt, our photographer and soil-sample expert."

"Nice to meet you." Handshake.

"This gentleman here is Wade Frazer, our psychologist." A long, phony handshake with Frazer's wet, unclean fingers.

"Glen Belsnor, our electronics and computer man."

"Glad to meet you." Handshake. Dry, horny, competent hand.

A tall, elderly woman approached, supporting herself with a cane. She had a noble face, pale in its quality but very fine. "Mr. Tallchief," she said, extending a slight, limp hand to Ben Tallchief. "I am Roberta Rockingham, the sociologist. It's nice to meet you. We've all been wondering and wondering about you."

Ben said, "Are you *the* Roberta Rockingham?" He felt himself glow with the pleasure of meeting her. Somehow he had assumed that the great old lady had died years ago. It confused him to find himself being introduced to her now.

"And this," Betty Jo Berm said, "is our clerk-typist, Susie Dumb."

"Glad to know you, Miss—" He paused.

"Smart," the girl said. Full-breasted and wonderfully shaped. "Suzanne Smart. They think it's funny to call me Susie Dumb." She extended her hand and they shook.

Betty Jo Berm said, "Do you want to look around, or just what?"

Ben said, "I'd like to know the purpose of the colony. They didn't tell me."

"Mr. Tallchief," the great old sociologist said, "they didn't tell us either." She chuckled. "We've asked everyone in turn as he arrives and no one knows. Mr. Morley, the last man to arrive—he won't know either, and then where will we be?"

To Ben, the electronics maintenance man said, "There's no problem. They put up a slave satellite; it's orbiting five times a day and at night you can see it go past. When the last person arrives—that'll be Morley—we're instructed to remote activate the audio tape transport aboard the satellite, and from the tape we'll get our instructions and an explanation of what we're doing and why we're here and all the rest of that crap; everything we want to know except 'How do you make the refrig colder so the beer doesn't get warm?' Yeah, maybe they'll tell us that, too."

A general conversation among the group of them was building up. Ben found himself drifting into it without really under-standing it. "At Betelgeuse 4 we had cucumbers, and we didn't grow them from moonbeams, the way you hear." "I've never seen him." "Well, he exists. You'll see him someday." "We've got a linguist so evidently there're sentient organisms here, but so far our expeditions have been informal, not scientific. That'll change when—" "Nothing changes. Despite Specktowsky's the-ory of God entering history and starting time into motion again." "If you want to talk about that, talk to Miss Walsh. Theological matters don't interest me." "You can say that again. Mr. Tallchief, are you part Indian?" "Well, I'm about one-eighth Indian. You mean the name?" "These buildings are built lousy. They're already ready to fall down. We can't get it warm when we need warm; we can't cool it when we need cool. You know what I think? I think this place was built to last only a very short time. Whatever the hell we're here for we won't be long, or rather, if we're here long we'll have to construct new installations, right down to the electrical wiring." "Some bug squeaks in the night. It'll keep you awake for the first day or so. By 'day' of course I mean twenty-four hour period. I don't mean 'daylight' because it's not in the daytime that it squeaks, it's at night. Every goddam night. You'll see." "Listen, Tallchief, don't call Susie 'dumb.' If there's one thing she's not it's dumb." "Pretty, too." "And do you notice how her—" "I noticed, but I don't think we should discuss it." "What line of work did you say you're in, Mr. Tallchief? Pardon?" "You'll have to speak up, she's a little deaf." "What I said was—" "You're frightening

her. Don't stand so close to her." "Can I get a cup of coffee?"
"Ask Maggie Walsh. She'll fix one for you." "If I can get the
damn pot to shut off when it's hot; it's been just boiling the
coffee over and over." "I don't see why our coffee pot won't
work. They perfected them back in the twentieth century. What's
left to know that we don't know already?" "Think of it as being
like Newton's color theory. Everything about color that could
be known was known by 1800. And then Land came along
with his two-light-source and intensity theory, and what had
seemed a closed field was busted all over." "You mean there
may be things about self-regulating coffee pots that we don't
know? That we just think we know?" "Something like that."
And so on. He listened distantly, answered when he was spoken to and then, all at once fatigued, he wandered off, away
from the group, toward a cluster of leathery green trees: they
looked to Ben as if they constituted the primal source for the
covering of psychiatrists' couches.

The air smelled bad—faintly bad—as if a waste-processing
plant were chugging away in the vicinity. But in a couple of
days I'll be used to it, he informed himself.

There is something strange about these people, he said to
himself. What is it? They seem so . . . he hunted for the word.
Overly bright. Yes, that was it. Prodigies of some sort, and all
of them ready to talk. And then he thought, I think they're very
nervous. That must be it; like me, they're here without knowing
why. But—that didn't fully explain it. He gave up, then, and
turned his attention outward, to embrace the pompous green-
leather trees, the hazy sky overhead, the small nettle-like plants
growing at his feet.

This is a dull place, he thought. He felt swift disappointment.
Not much better than the ship; the magic had already left. But
Betty Jo Berm had spoken of unusual life forms beyond the
perimeter of the colony. So possibly he couldn't justifiably ex-
trapolate on the basis of this little area. He would have to go
deeper, farther and farther away from the colony. Which, he
realized, is what they've all been doing. Because after all, what
else is there to do? At least until we receive our instructions
from the satellite.

I hope Morley gets here soon, he said to himself. So we can
get started.

A bug crawled up onto his right shoe, paused there, and then extended a miniature television camera. The lens of the camera swung so that it pointed directly at his face.

"Hi," he said to the bug.

Retracting its camera, the bug crawled off, evidently satisfied. I wonder who or what it's probing for? he wondered. He raised his foot, fooling momentarily with the idea of crushing the bug, and then decided not to. Instead he walked over to Betty Jo Berm and said, "Were the monitoring bugs here when you arrived?"

"They began to show up after the buildings were erected. I think they're probably harmless."

"But you can't be sure."

"There isn't anything we can do about them anyhow. At first we killed them, but whoever made them just sent more out."

"You better trace them back to their source and see what's involved."

"Not 'you,' Mr. Tallchief. 'We.' You're as much a part of this operation as anyone here. And you know just as much—and just as little—as we do. After we get our instructions we may find that the planners of this operation want us to—or do not want us to—investigate the indigenous life forms here. We'll see. But meanwhile, what about coffee?"

"You've been here how long?" Ben asked her as they sat at a plastic micro-bar sipping coffee from faintly-gray plastic cups.

"Wade Frazer, our psychologist, arrived first. That was roughly two months ago. The rest of us have been arriving in dribs and drabs. I hope Morley comes soon. We're dying to hear what this is all about."

"You're sure Wade Frazer doesn't know?"

"Pardon?" Betty Jo Berm blinked at him.

"He was the first one here. Waiting for the rest of you. I mean of us. Maybe this is a psychological experiment they've set up, and Frazer is running it. Without telling anyone."

"What we're afraid of," Betty Joe Berm said, "is not that. We have one vast fear, and that is this: there is no purpose to us being here, and we'll never be able to leave. Everyone came here by noser: that was mandatory. Well, a noser can land but it can't take off. Without outside help we'd never be able to leave here. Maybe this is a prison—we've thought of that. Maybe we've all done something, or anyhow someone *thinks* we've done something." She eyed him alertly with her gray, calm eyes. "Have you done anything, Mr. Tallchief?" she asked.

"Well, you know how it is."

"I mean, you're not a criminal or anything."

"Not that I know of."

"You look ordinary."

"Thanks."

"I mean, you don't look like a criminal." She rose, walked across the cramped room to a cupboard. "How about some Seagram's VO?" she asked.

"Fine," he said, pleased at the idea.

As they sat drinking coffee laced with Seagram's VO Canadian whiskey (imported) Dr. Milton Babble strolled in, perceived them, and seated himself at the bar. "This is a second-rate planet," he said to Ben without preamble. His dingy, shovel-like face twisted in distaste. "It just plain is second rate. Thanks." He accepted his cup of coffee from Betty Jo, sipped, still showed distaste. "What's in this?" he demanded. He then saw the bottle of Seagram's VO. "Hell, that ruins coffee," he said angrily. He set his cup down again, his expression of distaste greater than ever.

"I think it helps," Betty Jo Berm said.

Dr. Babble said, "You know, it's a funny thing, all of us here together. Now see, Tallchief, I've been here a month and I have yet to find someone I can talk to, really talk to. Every person here is completely involved with himself and doesn't give a damn about the others. Excluding you, of course, B.J."

Betty Jo said, "I'm not offended. It's true. I don't care about you, Babble, or any of the rest. I just want to be left alone." She turned toward Ben. "We have an initial curiosity when someone lands . . . as we had about you. But afterward, after we see the person and listen to him a little—" She lifted her cigarette from the ashtray and inhaled its smoke silently. "No offense meant, Mr. Tallchief, as Babble just now said. We'll get you pretty soon and you'll be the same; I predict it. You'll talk with us for a while and then you'll withdraw into—" She hesitated, groping the air with her right hand as if physically searching for a word. As if a word were a three dimensional object which she could seize manually. "Take Belsnor. All he thinks about is the refrigeration unit. He has a phobia that it'll stop working, which you would gather from his panic would mean the end of us. He thinks the refrigeration unit is keeping us from—" She gestured with her cigarette. "Boiling away."

"But he's harmless," Dr. Babble said.

"Oh, we're all harmless," Betty Jo Berm said. To Ben she said, "Do you know what I do, Mr. Tallchief? I take pills. I'll show you." She opened her purse and brought out a pharmacy bottle. "Look at these," she said as she handed the bottle to Ben. "The blue ones are stelazine, which I use as an anti-emetic. You understand: I use it for that, but that isn't its basic purpose. Basically stelazine is a tranquilizer, in doses of less than twenty milligrams a day. In greater doses it's an anti-hallucinogenic agent. But I don't take it for that either. Now, the problem with stelazine is that it's a vasodilator. I sometimes have trouble standing up after I've taken some. Hypostasis, I think it's called."

Babble grunted, "So she also takes a vasoconstrictor."

"That's this little white tablet," Betty Jo said, showing him the part of the bottle in which the white tablets dwelt. "It's methamphetamine. Now, this green capsule is—"

"One day," Babble said, "your pills are going to hatch, and some strange birds are going to emerge."

"What an odd thing to say," Betty Jo said.

"I meant they look like colored birds' eggs."

"Yes, I realize that. But it's still a strange thing to say." Removing the lid from the bottle she poured out a variety of pills into the palm of her hand. "This red cap—that's of course pentobarbital, for sleeping. And then this yellow one, it's norpramin, which counterbalances the C.N.S. depressive effect of the mellaril. Now, this square orange tab, it's new. It has five layers on it which time-release on the so-called 'trickle principle.' A very effective C.N.S. stimulant. Then a—"

"She takes a central nervous system depressor," Babble broke in, "and also a C.N.S. stimulant."

Ben said, "Wouldn't they cancel each other out?"

"One might say so, yes," Babble said.

"But they don't," Betty Jo said. "I mean subjectively I can feel the difference. I know they're helping me."

"She reads the literature on them all," Babble said. "She

brought a copy of the *P.D.R.* with her—*Physicians' Desk Reference*—with lists of side effects, contraindications, dosage, when indicated and so forth. She knows as much about her pills as I do. In fact, as much as the manufacturers know. If you show her a pill, any pill, she can tell you what it is, what it does, what—" He belched, drew himself up higher in his chair, laughed, and then said, "I remember a pill that had as side effects—if you took an overdose—convulsions, coma and then death. And in the literature, right after it told about the convulsions, coma and death, it said, *May Be Habit Forming.* Which always struck me as an anticlimax." Again he laughed, and then pried at his nose with one hairy, dark finger. "It's a strange world," he murmured. "Very strange."

Ben had a little more of the Seagram's VO. It had begun to fill him with a familiar warm glow. He felt himself beginning to ignore Dr. Babble and Betty Jo. He sank into the privacy of his own mind, his own being, and it was a good feeling.

Tony Dunkelwelt, photographer and soil-sample specialist, put his head in the door and called, "There's another noser landing. It must be Morley." The screen door banged shut as Dunkelwelt scuttled off.

Half-rising to her feet, Betty Jo said, "We'd better go. So at last, we're finally all here." Dr. Babble rose, too. "Come on, Babble," she said, and started toward the door. "And you, Mr. Eighth-Part-Indian-Tallchief."

Ben drank down the rest of his coffee and Seagram's VO and got up, dizzily. A moment later and he was following them out the door and into the light of day.

Four

SHUTTING off the retrojets Seth Morley shuddered, then unfastened his seat belt. Pointing, he instructed Mary to do the same.

"I know," Mary said, "what to do. You don't have to treat me like a child."

"You're sore at me," Morley said, "even though I navigated us here perfectly. The whole way."

"You were on automatic pilot and you followed the beam," she said archly. "But you're right, I should be grateful." Her tone of voice did not sound grateful, however. But he did not care. He had other things on his mind.

He manually unbolted the hatch. Green sunlight streamed in and he saw, shielding his eyes, a barren landscape of meager trees and even more meager brush. Off to the left a gaggle of unimpressive buildings jutted irregularly. The colony.

People were approaching the noser, a gang of them. Some of them waved and he waved back. "Hello," he said, stepping down the iron pins and dropping to the ground. Turning, he began to help Mary out, but she shook him loose and descended without assistance.

"Hi," a plain, brownish girl called as she approached. "We're glad to see you—you're the last!"

"I'm Seth Morley," he said. "And this is Mary, my wife."

"We know," the plain, brownish girl said, nodding. "Glad to meet you. I'll introduce you to everyone." She indicated a muscular youth nearby. "Ignatz Thugg."

"Glad to meet you." Morley shook hands with him. "I'm Seth Morley and this is my wife Mary."

"I'm Betty Jo Berm," the plain, brownish girl said. "And this gentleman—" She directed his attention toward an elderly man with stooped, fatigued posture. "Bert Kosler, our custodian."

"Glad to meet you, Mr. Kosler." Vigorous handshake.

"I'm glad to meet you, too, Mr. Morley. And Mrs. Morley. I hope you will enjoy it here."

"Our photographer and soil-sample expert, Tony Dunkelwelt." Miss Berm pointed out a long-snouted teenager who glared sullenly and did not extend his hand.

"Hello," Seth Morley said to him.

"Lo." The boy glowered down at his own feet.

"Maggie Walsh, our specialist in theology."

"Glad to meet you, Miss Walsh." Vigorous handshake. What a really nice-looking woman, Morley thought to himself. And here came another attractive woman, this one wearing a sweater stretched tight over her peek-n-squeeze bra. "What's your field?" he asked her as they shook hands.

"Clerical work and typing. My name is Suzanne."

"What's your last name?"

"Smart."

"That's a nice name."

"I don't think so. They call me Susie Dumb, which isn't really all that funny."

"I don't think it's funny at all," Seth Morley said.

His wife nudged him violently in the ribs and, being well-trained, he at once cut his conversation with Miss Smart short and turned to greet a skinny, rat-eyed individual who held out a wedge-shaped hand which appeared to have sharpened, tapered edges. He felt an involuntary refusal arise within him. This was not a hand he wanted to shake, and not a person he wanted to know.

"Wade Frazer," the rat-eyed individual said. "I'm acting as the settlement's psychologist. By the way—I've done an introductory T.A.T. test on everyone as they've arrived. I'd like to do one on both of you, possibly later today."

"Sure," Seth Morley said, without conviction.

"This gentleman," Miss Berm said, "is our doctor, Milton G. Babble of Alpha 5. Say hello to Dr. Babble, Mr. Morley."

"Glad to meet you, doctor." Morley shook hands.

"You're a bit overweight, Mr. Morley," Dr. Babble said.

"Hmm," Morley said.

An elderly woman, extremely tall and straight, came out of the group, moving with the aid of a cane. "Mr. Morley," she said, and extended a light, limp hand to Seth Motley. "I am Roberta Rockingham, the sociologist. It's a pleasure to meet you, and I do hope you had a pleasurable voyage here with not too much trouble."

"We did fine." Morley accepted her little hand and delicately shook it. She must be 110 years old, by the look of her, he said to himself. How can she function still? How did she get here? He could not picture her piloting a noser across interplanetary space.

"What is the purpose of this colony?" Mary asked.

"We'll find out in a couple of hours," Miss Berm said. "As soon as Glen—Glen Belsnor, our electronics and computer expert—is able to raise the slave satellite orbiting this planet."

"You mean you don't know?" Seth Morley said. "They never told you?"

"No, Mr. Morley," Mrs. Rockingham said in her deep, elderly voice. "But we'll know now, and we've waited so long. It'll be such a delight to know why all of us are here. Don't you think so, Mr. Morley? I mean, wouldn't it be wonderful for all of us to know our purpose?"

"Yes," he said.

"So you do agree with me, Mr. Morley. Oh, I think that's so nice that we can all agree." To Seth Morley she said in a low, meaningful voice, "That's the difficulty, I'm afraid, Mr. Morley. We have no common purpose. Interpersonal activity has been at a low ebb but of course it will pick up, now that we can—" She bent her head to cough briefly into a diminutive handkerchief. "Well, it really is so nice," she finished at last.

"I don't agree," Frazer said. "My preliminary testing indicates that by and large this is an inherently ego-oriented group. As a whole, Morley, they show what appears to be an innate tendency to avoid responsibility. It's hard for me to see why some of them were chosen."

A grimy, tough-looking individual in work clothes said, "I notice you don't say 'us.' You say 'they.'"

"Us, they." The psychologist gestured convulsively. "You show obsessive traits. That's another overall unusual statistic for this group: you're all hyper-obsessive."

"I don't think so," the grimy individual said in a level but firm voice. "I think what it is is that you're nuts. Giving those tests all the time has warped your mind."

That started all of them talking. Anarchy had broken out. Going up to Miss Berm, Seth Morley said, "Who's in charge of this colony? You?" He had to repeat it twice before she heard.

"No one has been designated," she answered loudly, over the noise of the group quarrel. "That's one of our problems. That's one of the things we want to—" Her voice trailed off in the general din.

"At Betelgeuse 4 we had cucumbers, and we didn't grow them from moonbeams, the way you hear. For one thing, Betelgeuse 4 has no moon, so that should answer that." "I've never seen him. And I hope I never will." "You'll see him someday." "The fact that we have a linguist on our staff suggests that there're sentient organisms here, but so far we don't know anything because our expeditions have been informal, sort of like picnics, not in any way scientific. Of course, that'll change when—" "Nothing changes. Despite Specktowsky's theory of God entering history and starting time into motion again." "No, you've got that wrong. The whole struggle before the Intercessor came took place in time, a very long time. It's just that everything has happened so fast since then, and it's so relatively easy, now in the Specktowsky Period, to directly contact one of the Manifestations. That's why in a sense our time is different from even the first two thousand years since the Intercessor first appeared." "If you want to talk about that, talk to Maggie Walsh. Theological matters don't interest me." "You can say that again. Mr. Morley, have you ever had contact with any of the Manifestations?" "Yes, as a matter of fact I have. Just the other day —I guess it was Wednesday by Tekel Upharsin time—the Walker-on-Earth approached me to inform me that I had been given a faulty noser, the result of the using of which would have cost my wife and I our lives." "So it saved you. Well, you must be very pleased to know that it would intercede for you that way. It must be a wonderful feeling." "These buildings are built lousy. They're already ready to fall down. We can't get it warm when we need warm; we can't cool it when we need cool. You know what I think? I think this place was built to last only a very short time. Whatever the hell we're here for we won't be long; or rather, if we're here long we'll have to construct new installations, right down to the BX cable." "Some insect or plant squeaks in the night. It'll keep you awake for the first day or so, Mr. and Mrs. Morley. Yes, I'm trying to speak to you, but it's so hard with all the noise. By 'day' of course I mean the twenty-four-hour period. I don't mean 'daytime'

because it's not in the daytime that it squeaks. You'll see."
"Hey Morley, don't get like the others and start calling Susie
'dumb.' If there's one thing she's not it's dumb." "Pretty, too."
"And do you notice how her—" "I noticed, but—my wife, you
see. She takes a dim view so perhaps we'd better drop the subject." "Okay, if you say so. What field are you in, Mr. Morley?"
"I'm a qualified marine biologist." "Pardon? Oh, were you
speaking to me, Mr. Morley? I can't quite make it out. If you
could say it again." "Yeah, you'll have to speak up. She's a little
deaf." "What I said was—" "You're frightening her. Don't stand
so close to her." "Can I get a cup of coffee or a glass of milk
anywhere?" "Ask Maggie Walsh, she'll fix one for you. Or B.J.
Berm." "Oh Christ, if I can just get the damn pot to shut off
when it's hot. It's been just boiling the coffee over and over
again." "I don't see why our communal coffee pot won't work,
they perfected them back in the early part of the twentieth
century. What's left to know that we don't know?" "Think of it
as being like Newton's Color Theory. Everything about color
that could be known was known by 1800." "Yes, you always
bring that up. You're obsessive about it." "And then Land
came along with his two-light-source and intensity theory, and
what had seemed a closed field was busted into pieces." "You
mean there may be things about homeostatic coffee pots that
we don't know? That we just think we know?" "Something
along that order." And so on.

Seth Morley groaned. He moved away from the group,
toward a tumble of great water-smoothed rocks. A body of
water had been here at some time, anyhow. Although perhaps
by now it was entirely gone.

The grimy, lanky individual in work clothes broke away from
the group and followed after him. "Glen Belsnor," he said,
extending his hand.

"Seth Morley."

"We're a friggin' mob, Morley. It's been like this since I got
here, right after Frazer came." Belsnor spat into nearby weeds.
"You know what Frazer tried to do? Since he was the first one
here he tried to set himself up as the group-leader; he even told
us—told me, for example—that he 'Understood his instructions to mean that he would be in charge.' We almost believed

him. It sort of made sense. He was the first one to arrive and he started giving those friggin' tests to everybody and then making loud comments about our 'statistical abnormalities,' as the creep puts it."

"A competent psychologist, a reliable one, would never make a public statement of his findings." A man not yet introduced to Seth Morley came walking up, hand extended. He appeared to be in his early forties, with a slightly large jaw, ridged brows, and shiny black hair. "I'm Ben Tallchief," he informed Morley. "I arrived just before you did." He seemed to Seth Morley to be a little unsteady; as if, Morley reflected, he's had a drink or three. He put out his hand and they shook. I like this man, he thought to himself. Even if he has had a couple. He has a different aura from the others. But, he thought, maybe they were all right before they got here, and something here made them change.

If that is so, he thought, it will change us, too, Tallchief, Mary and I. Eventually.

The thought did not please him.

"Seth Morley, here," he said. "Marine biologist, formerly attached to the staff of Tekel Upharsin Kibbutz. And your field is—"

Tallchief said, "I am a qualified naturalist, class B. Aboard ship there was little to do, and it was a ten year flight. So I prayed, via the ship's transmitter, and the relay picked it up and carried it to the Intercessor. Or perhaps it was the Mentufacturer. But I think the former, because there was no rollback of time."

"It's interesting to hear that you're here because of a prayer," Seth Morley said. "In my case I was visited by the Walker-on-Earth at the time in which I was busy finding an adequate noser for the trip here. I picked one out, but it wasn't adequate; the Walker said it would never have gotten Mary and myself here." He felt hungry. "Can we get a meal pried loose from this outfit?" he asked Tallchief. "We haven't eaten today; I've been busy piloting the noser for the last twenty-six hours. I only picked up the beam at the end."

Glen Belsnor said, "Maggie Walsh will be glad to slap together what passes as a meal around here. Something along the lines of frozen peas, frozen ersatz veal steak, and coffee from the goddam unhomeostatic friggin' coffee machine, which never worked even at the start. Will that do?"

"It will have to," Morley said, feeling gloom.

"The magic departs fast," Ben Tallchief said.

"Pardon?"

"The magic of this place." Tallchief made a sweeping gesture which took in the rocks, the gnarly green trees, the wobble of low hut-like buildings which made up the colony's sole installations. "As you can see."

"Don't sell it completely short," Belsnor spoke up. "These aren't the only structures on this planet."

"You mean there's a native civilization here?" Morley asked, interested.

"I mean there're things out there that we don't understand. There is a building. I've caught a glimpse of it, one time on a prowl, and I was going back but I couldn't find it again. A big gray building—really big—with turrets, windows, I would guess about eight floors high. I'm not the only one who's seen it," he added defensively. "Berm saw it; Walsh saw it; Frazer says he saw it, but he's probably horse-crudding us. He just doesn't want to look like he's left out."

Morley said, "Was the building inhabited?"

"I couldn't tell. We couldn't see that much from where we were; none of us really got that close. It was very—" He gestured. "Forbidding."

"I'd like to see it," Tallchief said.

"Nobody's leaving the compound today," Belsnor said. "Because now we can contact the satellite and get our instructions. And that comes first; that's what really matters." He spat into the weeds once more, deliberately and thoughtfully. And with accurate aim.

Dr. Milton Babble examined his wristwatch and thought, It's four-thirty and I'm tired. Low blood sugar, he decided. It's always a sign of that when you get tired in the late afternoon. I should try to get some glucose into myself before it becomes serious. The brain, he thought, simply can't function without adequate blood sugar. Maybe, he thought, I'm becoming diabetic. That could be; I have the right genetic history.

"What's the matter, Babble?" Maggie Walsh said, seated beside him in the austere briefing hall of their meager settlement. "Sick again?" She winked at him, which at once made him furious. "What's it now? Are you wasting away, like Camille, from T.B.?"

"Hypoglycemia," he said, studying his hand as it rested on the arm of his chair. "Plus a certain amount of extra-pyramidal neuromuscular activity. Motor restlessness of the dystonic type. Very uncomfortable." He hated the sensation: his thumb twitching in the familiar pellet-rolling motion, his tongue curling up within his mouth, dryness in his throat—dear God, he thought, is there no end of this?

Anyhow the herpes simplex keratitis which had afflicted him during the previous week had abated. He was glad of that (thank God).

"Your body is to you like what a house is for a woman," Maggie Walsh said. "You keep experiencing it as if it were an environment, rather than—"

"The somatic environment is one of the realest environments in which we live," Babble said testily. "It's our first environment, as infants, and then as we decline into old age, and the Form Destroyer corrodes our vitality and shape, we once again discover that it little matters what goes on in the so-called outside world when our somatic essence is in jeopardy."

"Is this why you became a doctor?"

"It's more complex than a simple cause-and-effect relationship. That supposes a duality. My choice of vocations—"

"Pipe down over there," Glen Belsnor yapped, pausing in his fiddlings. Before him rested the settlement's transmitter, and he had been trying for several hours to get it functioning. "If you want to talk clear out." Several other people in the hall added noisy agreement.

"Babble," Ignatz Thugg said from the seat in which he sprawled, "you're well-named." He barked a canine-like laugh.

"You, too," Tony Dunkelwelt said to Thugg.

"Pipe down!" Glen Belsnor yelled, his face red and steaming as he poked the innards of the transmitter. "Or by God we'll never get our poop-sheet from the friggin' satellite. If you don't shut up I'm going to come over there and take you apart instead of taking this mass of metallic guts apart. And I'd enjoy it."

Babble rose, turned and left the hall.

In the cold, long sunlight of late afternoon he stood smoking his pipe (being careful not to start up any pyloric activity) and contemplated their situation. Our lives, he thought, are in the hands of little men like Belsnor; here, they rule. The kingdom of the one-eyed, he thought acidly, in which the blind are king. What a life.

Why did I come here? he asked himself. No answer immediately came, only a wail of confusion from within him: drifting shapes that complained and cried out like indignant patients in a charity ward. The shrill shapes plucked at him, drawing him back into the world of former times, into the restlessness of his last years on Orionus 17, back to the days with Margo, the last of his office nurses with whom he had conducted a long, inelegant affair, a misadventure which had ended up in a heap of tangled tragicomedy—both for him and for her. In the end she had left him . . . or had she? Actually, he reflected, everyone leaves everyone when something as messy and jury-rigged as that terminates. I was lucky, he thought, to get out of it how and when I did. She could have made a lot more trouble. As it was, she had seriously jeopardized his physical health, just by protein depletion alone.

That's right, he thought. It's time for my wheat germ oil, my vitamin E. Must go to my quarters. And, while I'm there, I'll take a few glucose tablets to counterbalance my hypoglycemia. Assuming I don't pass out on the way. And if I did, who would care? What in fact would they do? I'm essential to their survival, whether they recognize it or not. I'm vital to them, but are they vital to me? Yes, in the sense that Glen Belsnor is; vital because they can do, or allegedly can do, skilled tasks necessary for the maintenance of this stupid little incestuous small town that we're running here. This pseudo-family that doesn't work as a family in any respect. Thanks to the meddlers from outside.

I'm going to have to tell Tallchief and—what's his name? Morley. Tell Tallchief and Morley and Morley's wife—who is not bad-looking at all—about the meddlers from outside, about the building which I have seen . . . seen close enough to read the Writing above the entrance. Which no one else has. Insofar as I know.

He started down the gravel path toward his quarters. As he came up onto the plastic porch of the living quarters he saw four people in a gathering together: Susie Smart, Maggie Walsh, Tallchief and Mr. Morley. Morley was talking, his tub-shaped middle protruding like a huge inguinal hernia. I wonder what he lives on, Babble said to himself. Potatoes, broiled steak, with ketchup on everything, and beer. You can always tell a beer-drinker. They have that perforated facial skin, perforated where the hairs grow, and the bags under their eyes. They look, as he looks, as if they have an edema puffing them out. And renal damage as well. And of course the ruddy skin.

A self-indulgent man, he thought, like Morley, doesn't in any way understand—*can't* understand—that he's pouring poisons into his body. Minute embolisms . . . damage to critical areas of the brain. And yet they keep on, these oral types. Regression to a pre-reality testing stage. Maybe it's a misplaced biological survival mechanism: for the good of the species they weed themselves out. Leaving the women to more competent, and more advanced, male types.

He walked up to the four of them, stood with his hands in his pockets, listening. Morley was relating the minutiae of a theological experience which he evidently had had. Or pretended to have had.

". . . 'my dear friend,' he called me. Obviously I mattered to him. He helped me with the reloading . . . it took a long time and we talked. His voice was low but I could understand him perfectly. He never used any excess words and he could express himself perfectly; there was no mystery about it, like you sometimes hear. Anyhow, we loaded and talked. And he wanted to bless me. Why? Because—he said—I was exactly the kind of person who mattered to him. He was completely matter-of-fact about it; he simply stated it. 'You are the kind of person whom I think matters,' he said, or words to that effect. 'I'm proud of you,' he said. 'Your great love of animals, your compassion toward lower life forms, pervades your entire mentality. Compassion is the basis of the person who has risen from the confines of the Curse. A personality type like yours is exactly what we are looking for.'" Morley paused, then.

"Go on," Maggie Walsh said, in a fascinated voice.

"And then he said a strange thing," Morley said. "He said,

'As I have saved you, saved your life, by my own compassion, I know that your own great capacity for compassion will enable you to save lives, both physically and spiritually, of others.' Presumably he meant here at Delmak-O."

"But he didn't say," Susie Smart said.

"He didn't have to," Morley said. "I knew what he meant; I understood everything he said. In fact I could communicate a lot more clearly with him than with most of the people I've known. I don't mean any of you—hell, I don't really know you, yet—but you see what I mean. There weren't any transcendental symbolic passages, no metaphysical nonsense like they used to talk about before Specktowsky wrote The Book. Specktowsky was right; I can verify it on the basis of my own experiences with him. With the Walker."

"Then you've seen it before," Maggie Walsh said.

"Several times."

Dr. Milton Babble opened his mouth and said, "I've seen it seven times. And I encountered the Mentufacturer once. So if you add it together I've had eight experiences with the One True Deity."

The four of them gazed at him with various expressions. Susie Smart looked skeptical; Maggie Walsh showed absolute disbelief; both Tallchief and Morley seemed relatively interested.

"And twice," Babble said, "with the Intercessor. So it's ten experiences in all. Throughout my whole life, of course."

"From what you heard from Mr. Morley about his experience," Tallchief said, "did it sound similar to your own?"

Babble kicked at a pebble on the porch; it bounced away, struck the nearby wall, fell silent, then. "Fairly much so. By and large. Yes, I think we can in some part accept what Morley says. And yet—" He hesitated meaningfully. "I'm afraid I'm skeptical. Was it truly the Walker, Mr. Morley? Could it not have been a passing itinerant laborer who wanted you to think he was the Walker? Had you thought of that? Oh, I'm not denying that the Walker appears again and again among us; my own experiences testify to that."

"I know he was," Morley said, looking angry, "because of what he said about my cat."

"Ah, your cat." Babble smiled both within and without; he felt deep and hearty amusement transverse his circulatory system. "So this is where the business about your 'great compassion for lower life forms' comes from."

Looking nettled and even more angrily outraged Morley said, "How would a passing tramp know about my cat? Anyhow, there aren't any passing tramps at Tekel Upharsin. Everybody works; that's what a kibbutz is." He looked, now, hurt and unhappy.

The voice of Glen Belsnor dinned in the darkened distance behind them. "Come on in! I've made contact with the goddam satellite! I'm about to have it run its audio tapes!"

Babble, as he started walking, said, "I didn't think he could do it." How good he felt, although he did not know exactly why. Something to do with Morley and his awe-inspiring account of meeting the Walker. Which now did not seem awe-inspiring after all. Once it had been scrupulously investigated, and by a person with adult, critical judgment.

The five of them entered the briefing hall and seated themselves among the others. From the speakers of Belsnor's radio equipment sharp static punctuated with random voice-noises sounded. The din hurt Babble's ears, but he said nothing. He displayed the formal attention which the technician had demanded.

"What we're picking up right now is a scatter track," Belsnor informed them over the racket. "The tape hasn't started to run yet; it won't do that until I give the satellite the right signal."

"Start the tape," Wade Frazer said.

"Yeah, Glen, start the tape." Voices from here and there in the chamber.

"Okay," Belsnor said. He reached out, touched control knobs on the panel before him. Lights winked on and off as servo-assist mechanisms switched into activity aboard the satellite.

From the speakers a voice said, "Greetings to the Delmak-O colony from General Treaton of Interplan West."

"That's it," Belsnor said. "That's the tape."

"Shut up, Belsnor. We're listening."

"It can be run back any number of times," Belsnor said.

"You have now completed your recruiting," General Treaton of Interplan West said. "This completion was anticipated by us at Interplan R.A.V. to occur not later than the fourteenth of September, Terran statute time. First, I would like to explain

why the Delmak-O colony was created, by whom and for
what purpose. It is basically—" All at once the voice stopped.
"Wheeeeee," the speakers blared. "Ughhhhhh. Akkkkkkkkk."
Belsnor stared at the receiving gear with mute dismay.
"Ubbbbb," the speakers said; static burst in, receded as Bels-
nor twisted dials, and then—silence.

After a pause Ignatz Thugg guffawed.

"What is it, Glen?" Tony Dunkelwelt said.

Belsnor said thickly, "There are only two tape-heads used in
transmitters such as are aboard the satellite. An erase head,
mounted first on the transport, then a replay-record head. What
has happened is that the replay-record head has switched from
replay to record. So it is erasing the tape an inch ahead automatically. There's no way I can switch it off; it's on record and
that's where it'll probably stay. Until the whole tape is erased."

"But if it erases," Wade Frazer said, "then it'll be gone forever. No matter what you do."

"That's right," Glen Belsnor said. "It's erasing and then recording nothing. I can't get it out of the record mode. Look."
He snapped several switches open and shut. "Nothing. The head
is jammed. So much for that." He slammed a major relay into
place, cursed, sat back, removed his glasses and wiped his forehead. "Christ," he said. "Well, so it goes."

The speakers twittered briefly with cross talk, then fell silent
again. No one in the room spoke. There was nothing to say.

Five

W HAT we can do," Glen Belsnor said, "is to transmit to the relay network, transmit so it'll be carried back to Terra, and inform General Treaton at Interplan West of what's happened, that our briefing of his instructions has failed to take place. Under the circumstances they'll undoubtedly be willing —and able—to fire off a communications rocket in our direction. Containing a second tape which we can run through the transport here." He pointed to the tape deck mounted within the radio gear.

"How long will that take?" Susie Smart asked.

"I haven't ever tried to raise the relay network from here," Glen Belsnor said. "I don't know; we'll have to see. Maybe we can do it right away. But at the most it shouldn't take more than two or three days. The only problem would be—" He rubbed his bristly chin. "There may be a security factor. Treaton may not want this request run through the relay network, where anyone with a class one receiver can pick it up. His reaction then would be to ignore our request."

"If they do that," Babble spoke up, "we ought to pack up and leave here. Immediately."

"Leave how?" Ignatz Thugg said, grinning.

Nosers, Seth Morley thought. We have no vehicles here except inert and fuel-zero nosers, and even if we could round up the fuel—say by syphoning from every fuel tank to fill up one —they don't have tracking gear by which we could pilot a course. They would have to use Delmak-O as one of two coordinates, and Delmak-O is not on Interplan West charts—hence no tracking value. He thought, Is this why they insisted on our coming in nosers?

They're experimenting with us, he thought wildly. That's what this is: an experiment. Maybe there never were any instructions on the satellite's tape. Maybe it all was planned.

"Make a sample try at picking up the relay people," Tallchief said. "Maybe you can get them right now."

"Why not?" Belsnor said. He adjusted dials, clamped an earphone to the side of his head, opened circuits, closed others down. In absolute silence the others waited and watched. As if, Morley thought, our lives depend on this. And—perhaps they do.

"Anything?" Betty Jo Berm asked at last.

Belsnor said, "Nothing. I'll switch it on video." The small screen jumped into life. Mere lines, visual static. "This is the frequency on which the relay operates. We should pick them up."

"But we're not," Babble said.

"No. We're not." Belsnor continued to spin dials. "It's not like the old days," he said, "when you could tinker with a variable condenser until you got your signal. This is complex." All at once he shut off the central power supply; the screen blanked out and, from the speakers, the snatches of static ceased.

"What's the matter?" Mary Morley asked.

"We're not on the air," Belsnor said.

"What?" Startled exclamations from virtually all of them.

"We're not transmitting. I can't pull them and if we're not on the air they sure as hell aren't going to pull us." He leaned back, convulsed with disgust. "It's a plot, a friggin' plot."

"You mean that literally?" Wade Frazer demanded. "You mean this is intentional?"

"I didn't assemble our transmitter," Glen Belsnor said. "I didn't hook up our receiving equipment. For the last month, since I've been here, in fact, I've been making sample tests; I've picked up several transmissions from operators in this star system, and I was able to transmit back. Everything seemed to be working normally. And then this." He stared down, his face working. "Oh," he said abruptly. He nodded. "Yes, I understand what happened."

"Is it bad?" Ben Tallchief asked.

Belsnor said, "When the satellite received my signal to activate the audio tape construct and complying transmitter, the satellite sent a signal back. A signal to this gear." He indicated the receiver and transmitter rising up before him. "The signal shut down everything. It overrode my instructions. We ain't receiving and we ain't transmitting, no matter what I tell this junk to do. It's off the air, and it'll probably take another signal from the satellite to get it functioning again." He shook his head. "What can you do but admire it?" he said. "We transmit our initial instruction to the satellite; in response it sends one back.

It's like chess: move and respond. I started the whole thing going. Like a rat in a cage, trying to find the lever that drops food. Rather than the one that transmits an electric shock." His voice was bitter, and laden with defeat.

"Dismantle the transmitter and receiver," Seth Morley said. "Override the override by removing it."

"It probably—hell, undoubtedly—has a destruct component in it. It's either already destroyed vital elements or it will when I try to search for it. I have no spare parts; if it's destroyed a circuit here and there I can't do anything toward fixing it."

"The automatic pilot beam," Morley said. "That I followed to get here. You can send out the message on it."

"Automatic pilot beams work for the first eighty or ninety thousand miles and then peter out. Isn't that where you picked up yours?"

"More or less," he admitted.

"We're totally isolated," Belsnor said. "And it was done in a matter of minutes."

"What we must do," Maggie Walsh said, "is to prepare a joint prayer. We can probably get through on pineal gland emanation, if we make it short."

"I can help on preparing it, if that's the criterion," Betty Jo Berm said. "Since I'm a trained linguist."

"As a last resort," Beslnor said.

"Not as a last resort," Maggie Walsh said. "As an effective, proven method of getting help. Mr. Tallchief, for example, got here because of a prayer."

"But it passed along the relay," Belsnor said. "We have no way to reach the relay."

"You have no faith in prayer?" Wade Frazer asked, nastily.

Belsnor said, "I have no faith in prayer that's not electronically augmented. Even Specktowsky admitted that; if a prayer is to be effective it must be electronically transmitted through the network of god-worlds so that all Manifestations are reached."

"I suggest," Morley said, "that we transmit our joint prayer as far as we can through the automatic pilot beam. If we can project it eighty or ninety thousand miles out it should be easier for the Deity to pick it up . . . since gravity works in inverse proportion to the power of the prayer, meaning that if you can get the prayer away from a planetary body—and ninety thousand miles is reasonably away—then there is a good mathematical chance of the various Manifestations receiving it, and Specktowsky mentions this; I forget where. At the end, I think, in one of his addenda."

Wade Frazer said, "It's against Terran law to doubt the power of prayer. A violation of the civil code of all Interplan West stages and holdings."

"And you'd report it," Ignatz Thugg said.

"Nobody's doubting the efficacy of prayer," Ben Tallchief said, eying Frazer with overt hostility. "We're merely disagreeing on the most effective way of handling it." He got to his feet. "I need a drink," he said. "Goodbye." He left the room, tottering a little as he went.

"A good idea," Susie Smart said to Seth Morley. "I think I'll go along, too." She rose, smiling at him in an automatic way, a smile devoid of feeling. "This is really terrible, isn't it? I can't believe that General Treaton could have authorized this deliberately; it must be a mistake. An electronic breakdown that they don't know about. Don't you agree?"

"General Treaton, from all I've heard," Morley said, "is a thoroughly reputable man." Actually, he had never heard of General Treaton before, but it seemed to him a good thing to say, in order to try to cheer her up. They all needed cheering up, and if it helped to believe that General Treaton was definitely reputable then so be it; he was all for it. Faith in secular matters, as well as in theological matters, was a necessity. Without it one could not go on living.

To Maggie Walsh, Dr. Babble said, "Which aspect of the Deity should we pray to?"

"If you want time rolled back, say to the moment before any of us accepted this assignment," Maggie said, "then it would be to the Mentufacturer. If we want the Deity to stand in for us, collectively to replace us in this situation, then it would be the Intercessor. If we individually want help in finding our way out—"

"All three," Bert Kosler said in a shaking voice. "Let the Deity decide which part of himself he wishes to use."

"He may not want to use any," Susie Smart said tartly. "We better decide on our own. Isn't that part of the art of praying?"

"Yes," Maggie Walsh said.

"Somebody write this down," Wade Frazer said. "We should start by saying, 'Thank you for all the help you have given us in the past. We hesitate to bother you again, what with all you have to do all the time, but our situation is as follows.'" He paused, reflecting. "What is our situation?" he asked Belsnor. "Do we just want the transmitter fixed?"

"More than that," Babble said. "We want to get entirely out of here, and never have to see Delmak-O again."

"If the transmitter's working," Belsnor said, "we can do that ourselves." He gnawed on a knuckle of his right hand. "I think we ought to settle for getting replacement parts for the transmitter and do the rest on our own. The less asked for in a prayer the better. Doesn't The Book say that?" He turned toward Maggie Walsh.

"On page 158," Maggie said, "Specktowsky says, 'The soul of brevity—the short time we are alive—is wit. And as regards the art of prayer, wit runs inversely proportional to length.'"

Belsnor said, "Let's simply say, 'Walker-on-Earth, help us find spare transmitter parts.'"

"The thing to do," Maggie Walsh said, "is to ask Mr. Tallchief to word the prayer, inasmuch as he was so successful in his recent previous prayer. Evidently he knows how to phrase properly."

"Get Tallchief," Babble said. "He's probably moving his possessions from his noser to his living quarters. Somebody go find him."

"I'll go," Seth Morley said. He rose, made his way out of the briefing chamber and into the evening darkness.

"That was a very good idea, Maggie," he heard Babble saying, and other voices joined his. A chorus of agreement went up from those gathered in the briefing room.

He continued on, feeling his way cautiously; it would be so easy to get lost in this still unfamiliar colony site. Maybe I should have let one of the others go, he said to himself. A light shone in the window of a building ahead. Maybe he's in there, Seth Morley said to himself, and made his way toward the light.

Ben Tallchief finished his drink, yawned, picked at a place on his throat, yawned once again and clumsily rose to his feet.

Time to start moving, he said to himself. I hope, he thought, I can find my noser in the dark.

He stepped outdoors, found the gravel path with his feet, began moving in the direction which he supposed the nosers to be. Why no guide lights around here? he asked himself, and then realized that the other colonists had been too preoccupied to turn the lights on. The breakdown of the transmitter had ensnared the attention of every one of them, and justly so. Why aren't I in there? he asked himself. Functioning as part of the group. But the group didn't function as a group anyhow; it was always a finite number of self-oriented individuals squalling with one another. With such a bunch he felt as if he had no roots, no common source. He felt nomadic and in need of exercise; right now something called to him: it had called him from the briefing room and back to his living quarters, and now it sent him trudging through the dark, searching for his noser.

A vague area of darkness moved ahead of him, and, against the less-dark sky, a figure appeared. "Tallchief?"

"Yes," he said. "Who is it?" He peered.

"Morley. They sent me to find you. They want you to compose the prayer, since you had such good luck a couple of days ago."

"No more prayers for me," Tallchief said, and clamped his teeth in bitterness. "Look where that last prayer got me—stuck here with all of you. No offense, I just mean—" He gestured. "It was a cruel and inhuman act to grant that prayer, considering the situation here. And it must have known it."

"I can understand your feeling," Morley said.

"Why don't you do it? You just recently met the Walker; it would be smarter to use you."

"I'm no good at prayers. I didn't summon the Walker; it was his idea to come to me."

"How about a drink?" Tallchief said. "And then maybe you could give me a hand with my stuff, moving it to my quarters and like that."

"I have to move my own stuff."

"That's an outstanding cooperative attitude."

"If you had helped me—"

Tallchief said, "I'll see you later." He continued on, groping and flailing in the darkness, until all at once he stumbled against a clanking hull. A noser. He had found the right area; now to pick out his own ship.

He looked back. Morley had gone; he was alone.

Why couldn't the guy have helped me? he asked himself. I'm going to need another person for most of the cartons. Let's see, he pondered. If I can turn on the landing lights of the noser I'll be able to see. He located the locking wheel of the hatch, spun it, tugged the hatch open. Automatically the safety lights came on; now he could see. Maybe I'll just move in my clothes, bathroom articles and my copy of The Book, he decided. I'll read The Book until I get ready to go to sleep. I'm tired; piloting the noser here took everything out of me. That and the transmitter failing. Utter defeat.

Why did I ask him to help me? he wondered. I don't know him, he hardly knows me. Getting my stuff moved is my own problem. He has problems of his own.

He picked up a carton of books, began to lug it away from the parked noser in the general direction—he hoped—of his living quarters. I've got to get a flashlight, he decided as he waddled along. And hell, I forgot to turn on the landing lights. This is all going wrong, he realized. I might as well go back and join the others. Or I could move this one carton and then have another drink, and possibly by that time most of them would have come out of the briefing room and could help me. Grunting and perspiring, he made his way up the gravel path toward the dark and inert structure which provided them with their living quarters. No lights on. Everyone was still involved in pasting together an adequate prayer. Thinking about that he had to laugh. They'll probably haggle about it all night, he decided, and laughed again, this time with angry disgust.

He found his own living quarters, by virtue of the fact that the door hung open. Entering, he dropped the carton of books to the floor, sighed, stood up, turned on all the lights . . . standing there he surveyed the small room with its dresser and bed. The bed did not please him; it looked small and hard. "Christ," he said, and seated himself on it. Lifting several books from the carton he rummaged about until he came onto the bottle of Peter Dawson scotch; he unscrewed the lid and drank somberly from the bottle itself.

Through the open door he gazed out at the nocturnal sky; he saw the stars haze over with atmospheric disturbances, then clear for a moment. It is certainly hard, he thought, to make out stars through the refractions of a planetary atmosphere.

A great gray shape merged with the doorway, blotting out the stars.

It held a tube and it pointed the tube at him. He saw a telescopic sight on it and a trigger mechanism. Who was it? What was it? He strained to see, and then he heard a faint pop. The gray shape receded and once more stars appeared. But now they had changed. He saw two stars collapse against one another and a nova form; it flared up and then, as he watched, it began to die out. He saw it turn from a furiously blazing ring into a dim core of dead iron and then he saw it cool into darkness. More stars cooled with it; he saw the force of entropy, the method of the Destroyer of Forms, retract the stars into dull reddish coals and then into dust-like silence. A shroud of thermal energy hung uniformly over the world, over this strange and little world for which he had no love or use.

It's dying, he realized. The universe. The thermal haze spread on and on until it became only a disturbance, nothing more; the sky glowed weakly with it and then flickered. Even the uniform thermal disbursement was expiring. How strange and goddam awful, he thought. He got to his feet, moved a step toward the door.

And there, on his feet, he died.

They found him an hour later. Seth Morley stood with his wife at the far end of the knot of people jammed into the small room and said to himself, *To keep him from helping with the prayer.*

"The same force that shut down the transmitter," Ignatz Thugg said. "They knew; they knew if he phrased the prayer it would go through. Even without the relay." He looked gray and frightened. All of them did, Seth Morley noticed. Their faces, in the light of the room, had a leaden, stone-like cast. Like, he thought, thousand-year-old idols.

Time, he thought, is shutting down around us. It is as if the future is gone, for all of us. Not just for Tallchief.

"Babble, can you do an autopsy?" Betty Jo Berm asked.

"To a certain extent." Dr. Babble had seated himself beside Tallchief's body and was touching him here and there. "No visible blood. No sign of an injury. His death could be natural, you all realize; it might be that he had a cardiac condition. Or, for example, he might have been killed by a heat gun at close range . . . but then, if that's the case, I'll find the burn marks." He unfastened Tallchief's collar, reached down to explore the chest area. "Or one of us might have done it," he said. "Don't rule that out."

"They did it," Maggie Walsh said.

"Possibly," Babble said. "I'll do what I can." He nodded to Thugg and Wade Frazer and Glen Belsnor. "Help me carry him into the clinic; I'll start the autopsy now."

"None of us even knew him," Mary said.

"I think I probably saw him last," Seth Morley said. "He wanted to bring his things from his noser here to his living area. I told him I'd help him later on, when I had time. He seemed to be in a bad mood; I tried to tell him we needed him to compose a prayer but he didn't seem interested. He just wanted to move his things." He felt acutely guilty. Maybe if I had helped him he'd still be alive, he said to himself. Maybe Babble's right; maybe it was a heart attack, brought on by moving heavy cartons. He kicked at the box of books, wondering if this box had done it—this box and his own refusal to help. Even when I was asked I wouldn't give it, he realized.

"You didn't see any indication of a suicidal attitude at work, did you?" Dr. Babble asked.

"No."

"Very strange," Babble said. He shook his head wearily. "Okay; let's get him to the infirmary."

Six

THE four men carried Tallchief's body across the dark, nocturnal compound. Cold wind licked at them and they shivered; they drew together against the hostile presence of Delmak-O—the hostile presence which had killed Ben Tallchief.

Babble switched on lights here and there. At last they had Tallchief up on the high, metal-topped table.

"I think we should retire to our individual living quarters and stay there until Dr. Babble has finished his autopsy," Susie Smart said, shivering.

Wade Frazer spoke up. "Better if we stay together, at least until Dr. Babble's report is in. And I also think that under these unexpected circumstances, this terrible event in our lives, that we must immediately elect a leader, a strong one who can keep us together as a group, when in fact right now we are not, but should be—must be. Doesn't everyone agree?"

After a pause Glen Belsnor said, "Yeah."

"We can vote," Betty Jo Berm said. "In a democratic way. But I think we must be careful." She struggled to express herself. "We mustn't give a leader too much power. And we should be able to recall him when and if at any time we're not satisfied with him; then we can vote him out as our leader and elect someone else. But while he is leader we should obey him—we don't want him to be too weak, either. If he's too weak we'll just be like we are now: a mere collection of individuals who can't function together, even in the face of death."

"Then let's get back to the briefing room," Tony Dunkelwelt said, "rather than to our personal quarters. So we can start casting votes. I mean, it or they could kill us before we have a leader; we don't want to wait."

In a group they made their way somberly from Dr. Babble's infirmary to the briefing room. The transmitter and receiver were still on; each person, entering, heard the dull, low hum.

"So big," Maggie Walsh said, gazing at the transmitter. "And so useless."

"Do you think we should arm ourselves?" Bert Kosler said,

plucking at Morley's sleeve. "If there's someone after us to kill all of us—"

"Let's wait for Babble's autopsy report," Seth Morley said.

Seating himself, Wade Frazer said in a business-like way, "We'll vote by a show of hands. Everybody sit down and be quiet and I'll read off our names and keep the tally. Is that satisfactory to everyone?" There was a sardonic undertone to his voice, and Seth Morley did not like it.

Ignatz Thugg said, "You won't get it, Frazer. No matter how badly you want it. Nobody in this room is going to let somebody like you tell them what to do." He dropped into a chair, crossed his legs, and got a tobacco cigarette from his jacket pocket.

As Wade Frazer read off the names and took the tally, several others made their own notations. They don't trust Frazer to make an accurate account, Seth Morley realized. He did not blame them.

"The greatest number of votes for one person," Frazer said, when all the names had been read, "goes to Glen Belsnor." He dropped his tally sheet with a blatant sneer . . . as if, Morley thought, the psychologist is saying Go ahead and doom yourselves. It's your lives, if you want to toss them away. But it seemed to him that Belsnor was a good choice; on his own very limited knowledge he had himself voted for the electronics maintenance man. He was satisfied, even if Frazer was not. And by their relieved stir he guessed that most of the others were, too.

"While we're waiting for Dr. Babble's report," Maggie Walsh said, "perhaps we should join in a group prayer for Mr. Tallchief's psyche to be taken immediately into immortality."

"Read from Specktowsky's Book," Betty Jo Berm said. She dipped into her pocket and brought out her own copy, which she passed to Maggie Walsh. "Read the part on page 70 about the Intercessor. Isn't it the Intercessor that we want to reach?"

From memory, Maggie Walsh intoned the words which all of them knew. " 'By His appearance in history and creation, the Intercessor offered Himself as a sacrifice by which the Curse could be partially nullified. Satisfied as to the redemption of His creation by this manifestation of Himself, this signal of His great —but partial—victory, the Deity "died" and then remanifested

Himself to indicate that He had overcome the Curse and hence death, and, having done this, moved up through the concentric circles back to God Himself.' And I will add another part which is pertinent. 'The next—and last—period is the Day of Audit, in which the heavens will roll back like a scroll and each living thing—and hence all creatures, both sentient man and man-like nonterrestrial organisms—will be reconciled with the original Deity, from whose unity of being everything has come (with the possible exception of the Form Destroyer).'" She paused a moment and then said, "Repeat what I say after me, all of you, either aloud or in your thoughts."

They lifted their faces and gazed straight upward, in the accepted fashion. So that the Deity could hear them more readily.

"We did not know Mr. Tallchief too well."

They all said, "We did not know Mr. Tallchief too well."

"But he seemed to be a fine man."

They all said, "But he seemed to be a fine man."

Maggie hesitated, reflected, then said, "Remove him from time and thereby make him immortal."

"Remove him from time and thereby make him immortal."

"Restore his form to that which he possessed before the Form Destroyer went to work on him."

They all said, "Restore his form to that—" They broke off. Dr. Milton Babble had come into the briefing room, looking ruffled.

"We must finish the prayer," Maggie said.

"You can finish it some other time," Dr. Babble said. "I've been able to determine the cause of death." He consulted several sheets of paper which he had brought along. "Cause of death: vast inflammation of the bronchial passages, due to an unnatural amount of histamine in the blood, resulting in a stricture of the trachea; exact cause of death was suffocation as reaction to a heterogenic allergen. He must have been stung by an insect or brushed against a plant while he was unloading his noser. An insect or plant containing a substance to which he was violently allergic. Remember how sick Susie Smart was her first week here, from brushing against one of the nettle-like bushes? And Kosler." He gestured in the direction of the elderly custodian. "If he hadn't gotten to me as quick as he did he would be dead, too. With Tallchief the situation was against us; he had gone out by himself, at night, and there was no one around to react to his plight. He died alone, but if we had been there he could have been saved."

After a pause Roberta Rockingham, seated, with a huge rug over her lap, said, "Why, I think that's ever so much more encouraging than our own speculation. It would appear that no one is trying to kill us . . . which is really quite wonderful, don't you think?" She gazed around at them, straining to hear if any had spoken.

"Evidently," Wade Frazer said remotely, with a private grimace.

"Babble," Ignatz Thugg said, "we voted without you."

"Good grief," Betty Jo Berm said. "That's so. We'll have to vote again."

"You selected one of us as a leader?" Babble said. "Without letting me exercise my own personal involvement? Who did you decide on?"

"On me," Glen Belsnor said.

Babble consulted with himself. "It's all right as far as I'm concerned," he said at last, "to have Glen as our leader."

"He won by three votes," Susie Smart said.

Babble nodded. "In any case I'm satisfied."

Seth Morley walked over to Babble, faced him and said, "You're sure that was the cause of death?"

"Beyond doubt. I have equipment which can determine—"

"Did you find an insect bite-mark on him anywhere?"

"Actually no," Babble said.

"A possible spot where a plant leaf might have speared him?"

"No," Babble said, "but that isn't an important aspect of such a determination. Some of the insects here are so small that any sting-spot or bite-spot wouldn't be visible without a microscopic examination, and that would take days."

"But you're satisfied," Belsnor said, also coming up; he stood with his arms folded, rocking back and forth on his heels.

"Absolutely." Babble nodded vigorously.

"You know what it would mean if you're wrong."

"How? Explain."

"Oh Christ, Babble," Susie Smart said, "it's obvious. If someone or something deliberately killed him then we're in just as much danger as he was—possibly. But if an insect stung him—"

"That's what it was," Babble said. "An insect stung him." His ears had turned bright carmen with stubborn, irritable anger. "Do you think this is my first autopsy? That I'm not capable of handling pathology-report instrumentation that I've handled all my adult life?" He glared at Susie Smart. "Miss Dumb," he said.

"Come on, Babble," Tony Dunkelwelt said.

"It's Dr. Babble to you, sonny," Babble said.

Nothing is changed, Seth Morley said to himself. We are as we were, a mob of twelve people. And it may destroy us. End forever our various separate lives.

"I feel a vast amount of relief," Susie Smart said, coming up beside him and Mary. "I guess we were becoming paranoid; we thought everyone was after us, trying to kill us."

Thinking about Ben Tallchief—and his last encounter with him—Morley felt no sympathetic resonance within him to her newly refreshed attitude. "A man is dead," he said.

"We barely knew him. In fact we didn't know him at all."

"True," Morley said. Maybe it's because I feel so much personal guilt. "Maybe I did it," he said aloud to her.

"A bug did it," Mary said.

"May we finish the prayer, now?" Maggie Walsh said.

Seth Morley said to her, "How come we need to shoot a petition-prayer eighty thousand miles up from the planet's surface, but this sort of prayer can be done without electronic help?" I know the answer, he said to himself. This prayer now —it really doesn't matter to us if it's heard. It is merely a ceremony, this prayer. The other one was different. The other time we needed something for ourselves, not for Tallchief. Thinking this he felt more gloomy than ever. "I'll see you later," he said aloud to Mary. "I'm going to go unpack the boxes I've brought from our noser."

"But don't go near the nosers," Mary warned him. "Until tomorrow; until we have time to scout out the plant or bug—"

"I won't be outdoors," Morley agreed. "I'll go directly to our quarters." He strode from the briefing room out into the compound. A moment later he was ascending the steps to the porch of their joint living quarters.

*

I'll ask The Book, Seth Morley said to himself. He rummaged through several cartons and at last found his copy of *How I Rose From the Dead in My Spare Time and So Can You.* Seated, he held it on his lap, placed both hands on it, shut his eyes, turned his face upward and said, "Who or what killed Ben Tallchief?"

He then, eyes shut, opened the book to a page at random, put his finger at one exact spot, and opened his eyes.

His finger rested on: the Form Destroyer.

That doesn't tell us much, he reflected. All death comes as a result of a deterioration of form, clue to the activity of the Form Destroyer.

And yet it scared him.

It doesn't sound like a bug or a plant, he thought starkly. It sounds like something entirely else.

A tap-tap sounded at his door.

Rising warily, he moved by slow degrees to the door; keeping it shut he swept the curtain back from the small window and peered out into the night darkness. Someone stood on the porch, someone small, with long hair, tight sweater, peek-n-squeeze bra, tight short skirt, barefoot. Susie Smart has come to visit, he said to himself, and unlocked the door.

"Hi," she said brightly, smiling up at him. "May I come in and talk a little?"

He led her over to The Book. "I asked it what or who killed Tallchief."

"What did it say?" She seated herself, crossed her bare legs and leaned forward to see as he placed his finger on the same spot as before. "The Form Destroyer," she said soberly. "But it's always the Form Destroyer."

"Yet I think it means something."

"That it wasn't an insect?"

He nodded.

"Do you have anything to eat or drink?" Susie said. "Any candy?"

"The Form Destroyer," he said, "is loose outside."

"You're scaring me."

"Yes," he said. "I want to. We've got to get a prayer off this planet and to the relay network. We're not going to survive unless we get help."

"The Walker comes without prayer," Susie said.

"I have a Baby Ruth candy bar," he said. "You can have that." He rummaged through a suitcase of Mary's, found it, handed it to her.

"Thank you," she said, tearing the paper from one of the candy bar's blunt ends.

He said, "I think we're doomed."

"We're always doomed. It's the essence of life."

"Doomed immediately. Not abstractly—doomed in the sense that I and Mary were doomed when I tried to load up the *Morbid Chicken*. Mors certa, hora incerta; there's a big difference between knowing that you're going to die and knowing you're going to die within the next calendar month."

"Your wife is very attractive."

He sighed.

"How long have you two been married?" Susie gazed at him intently.

"Eight years," he said.

Susie Smart swiftly stood up. "Come over to my place and let me show you how nice these little rooms can be fixed up. Come on—it's depressing in here." She tugged little-girlwise at his hand and he found himself following after her.

They danced up the porch, passed several doorways and came at last to Susie's door. It was unlocked; she opened it, welcoming him into warmth and light. She had told the truth; it did look nice. Can we make ours as nice as this? he asked himself as he looked around, at the pictures on the walls, the textures of fabrics, and the many, many planter boxes and pots, out of which multicolored blossoms dazzled the eye.

"Nice," he said.

Susie banged the door shut. "Is that all you can say? It's taken me a month to make it look like this."

" 'Nice' was your word for it, not mine."

She laughed. "I can call it 'nice,' but since you're a visitor you have to be more lavish about it."

"Okay," he said, "it's wonderful."

"That's better." She seated herself in a black canvas-backed chair facing him, leaned back, rubbed her hands together briskly, then fastened her attention on him. "I'm waiting," she said.

"For what?"

"For you to proposition me."

"Why would I do that?"

Susie said, "I'm the settlement whore. You're supposed to die of priapism because of me. Haven't you heard?"

"I just got here late today," he pointed out.

"But somebody must have told you."

"When someone does," he said, "he'll get his nose punched in."

"But it's true."

"Why?" he said.

"Dr. Babble explained to me that it's a diencephalic distur-bance in my brain."

He said, "That Babble. You know what he said about my visit with the Walker? He said most of what I said was untrue."

"Dr. Babble has a keen little maliciousness about him. He loves to put down everyone and everything."

"If you know that about him," Seth Morley said, "then you know enough not to pay any attention."

"He just explained *why* I'm that way. I am that way. I've slept with every man in the settlement, except that Wade Frazer." She shook her head, making a wry face. "He's awful."

With curiosity, he said, "What does Frazer say about you? After all, he's a psychologist. Or claims he is."

"He says that—" She reflected, staring up pensively at the ceiling of the room, meantime chewing abstractedly on her lower lip. "It's a search for the great world-father archetype. That's what Jung would have said. Do you know about Jung?"

"Yes," he said, although in fact he had only heard little more than the name; Jung, he had been told, had in many ways laid the groundwork for a rapprochement between intellectuals and religion—but at that point Seth Morley's knowledge gave out. "I see," he said.

"Jung believed that our attitudes toward our actual mothers and fathers are because they embody certain male and female archetypes. For instance, there's the great bad earth-father and the good earth-father and the destroying earth-father, and so forth . . . and the same with women. My mother was the bad earth-mother, so all my psychic energy was turned toward my father."

"Hmm," he said. He had, all at once, begun to think about

Mary. Not that he was afraid of her, but what would she think when she got back to their living quarters and found him gone? And then—God forbid—found him here with Susie Dumb, the self-admitted settlement whore?

Susie said, "Do you think the sexual act makes a person impure?"

"Sometimes," he responded reflexively, still thinking about his wife. His heart labored and he felt his pulse race. "Specktowsky isn't too clear about that in The Book," he mumbled.

"You're going to take a walk with me," Susie said.

"Now? I am? Where? Why?"

"Not now. Tomorrow when it's daylight. I'll take you outside the settlement, out into the real Delmak-O. Where the strange things are, the movements that you catch out of the corner of your eye—and the Building."

"I'd like to see the Building," he said, truthfully.

Abruptly she rose. "Better get back to your living quarters, Mr. Seth Morley," she said.

"Why?" He, too, confused, rose to his feet.

"Because if you stay here your attractive wife is going to find us and create chaos and open the way for the Form Destroyer, who you say is loose outside, to get all of us." She laughed, showing perfect, pale teeth.

"Can Mary come on our walk?" he asked.

"No." She shook her head. "Just you. Okay?"

He hesitated, a flock of thoughts invading his mind; they pulled him this way and that, then departed, leaving him free to make an answer. "If I can work it," he said.

"Try. Please. I can show you all the places and life forms and things I've discovered."

"Are they beautiful?"

"S-some. Why are you looking at me so intently? You make me nervous."

"I think you're insane," he said.

"I'm just outspoken. I simply say, 'A man is a sperm's way of producing another sperm.' That's merely practical."

Seth Morley said, "I don't know much about Jungian analysis, but I certainly do not recall—" He broke off. Something had moved at the periphery of his vision.

"What's the matter?" Susie Smart asked.

He turned swiftly, and this time saw it clearly. On the top of the dresser a small gray square object inched its way forward, then, apparently aware of him, ceased moving.

In two steps he was over to it; he snatched up the object, held it gripped tightly in the palm of his hand.

"Don't hurt it," Susie said. "It's harmless. Here, give it to me." She held out her hand, and, reluctantly, he opened his enclosing fingers.

The object which he held resembled a tiny building.

"Yes," Susie said, seeing the expression on his face. "It comes from the Building. It's a sort of offspring, I suppose. Anyhow it's exactly like the Building but smaller." She took it from him, for a time examined it, then placed it back on the dresser. "It's alive," she said.

"I know," he said. Holding it, he had felt the animate quality of it; it had pushed against his fingers, trying to get out.

"They're all over the place," Susie said. "Out there." She made a vague gesture. "Maybe tomorrow we can find you one."

"I don't want one," he said.

"You will when you've been here long enough."

"Why?"

"I guess they're company. Something to break the monotony. I remember as a child finding a Ganymedian toad in our garden. It was so beautiful with its shining flame and its long smooth hair that—"

Morley said, "It could have been one of these things that killed Tallchief."

"Glen Belsnor took one apart one day," Susie said. "He said—" She pondered. "It's harmless, anyhow. The rest of what he said was electronic talk; we couldn't follow it."

"And he'd know?"

"Yes." She nodded.

Seth Morley said, "You—we—have a good leader." But I don't think quite good enough, he said to himself.

"Shall we go to bed?" Susie said.

"What?" he said.

"I'm interested in going to bed with you. I can't judge a man unless I've been in bed with him."

"What about women?"

"I can't judge them at all. What, do you think I go to bed

with the women, too? That's depraved. That sounds like something Maggie Walsh would do. She's a lesbian, you know. Or
didn't you know?"

"I don't see that it matters. Or that it's any of our business."
He felt shaky and uneasy. "Susie," he said, "you should get
psychiatric help." He remembered, all at once, what the Walker-
on-Earth had said to him, back at Tekel Upharsin. Maybe we
all need psychiatric help, he thought. But not from Wade
Frazer. That's totally, entirely out.

"You don't want to go to bed with me? You'd enjoy it, despite your initial prudery and reservations. I'm very good. I
know a lot of ways. Some which you probably never heard
about. I made them up myself."

"From years of experience," he said.

"Yes." She nodded. "I started at twelve."

"No," he said.

"Yes," Susie said, and grabbed him by the hand. On her face
he saw a desperate expression, as if she were fighting for her
life. She drew him toward her, straining with all her strength;
he held back and she strained vainly.

Susie Smart felt the man pulling away from her. He's very
strong, she thought. "How come you're so strong?" she asked,
gasping for air; she found herself almost unable to breathe.

"Carry rocks," he said with a grin.

I want him, she thought. Big, evil, powerful . . . he could
tear me to pieces, she thought. Her longing for him grew.

"I'll get you," she gasped, "because I want you." I need to
have you, she said to herself. Covering me like a heavy shade, a
protection from the sun and from seeing. I don't want to look
any more, she said to herself. Weigh me down, she thought.
Show me what there is of you; show me your real being, without benefit of clothes. Fumbling behind her she unsnapped
her peek-n-squeeze bra. Deftly she tugged it out from its place
within her sweater; she pulled, strained, managed to drop it
onto a chair. At that the man laughed. "Why are you laughing?"
she demanded.

"Your neatness," he said. "Getting it onto a chair instead of
dropping it onto the floor."

"Damn you," she said, knowing that he, like everyone else, was laughing at her. "I'll get you," she snarled, and pulled him with all her strength; this time she managed to move him a few tottering steps in the direction of the bed.

"Hey, goddam it," he protested. But again she managed to move him several steps. "Stop!" he said. And then she had tumbled him onto the bed. She held him down with one knee and rapidly, with great expertise, unsnapped her skirt and pushed it from the bed, onto the floor.

"See?" she said. "I don't have to be neat." She dove for him then; she pinned him down with her knees. "I'm not obsessive," she said, as she removed the last of her clothing. Now she tore at the buttons of his shirt. A button, ripped loose, rolled like a little wheel from the bed and onto the floor. At that she laughed. She felt very good. This part always excited her—it was like the final stage of a hunt, in this case a hunt for a big animal which smelled of sweat and of cigarette smoke and of agitated fear. How can he be afraid of me? she asked herself, but it was always this way—she had come to accept it. In fact she had come to like it.

"Let—me—go," he gasped, pushing upward against her weight. "You're so darn—slippery," he managed to say as she gripped his head with her knees.

"I can make you so happy, sexually," she told him; she always said this, and sometimes it worked; sometimes the man gave in at the prospect which she held open to him. "Come on," she said, in rapid, imploring grunts.

The door of the room banged open. Immediately, instinctively, she sprang from the man, from the bed, stood upright, breathing noisily, peering at the figure in the doorway. His wife. Mary Morley. Susie at once snatched up her clothes; this was one part which she did not enjoy, and she felt overwhelming hatred toward Mary Morley. "Get out of here," Susie panted. "This is my room."

"Seth!" Mary Morley said in a shrill voice. "What in the name of God is the matter with you? *How could you do this?*" She moved stiffly toward the bed, her face pale.

"God," Morley said, sitting up and smoothing his hair into place. "This girl is nuts," he said to his wife in a plaintive, whining tone. "I had nothing to do with it; I was trying to get away. You saw that, didn't you? Couldn't you tell I was trying to get away? Didn't you see that?"

Mary Morley said in her shrill, speeded-up voice, "If you had wanted to get away you could have."

"No," he said imploringly. "Really, so help me God. She had me pinned down. I was getting loose, though. If you hadn't come in I would have gotten away by myself."

"I'll kill you," Mary Morley said; she spun, paced about in a great circle which swept out most of the room. Looking for something to pick up and hit with; Susie knew the motion, the searching, the glazed, ferocious, incredulous expression on her face. Mary Morley found a vase, snatched it up, stood by the dresser, her chest heaving as she confronted Seth Morley. She raised the vase in a spasmodic, abrupt, backward swing of her right arm . . .

On the dresser the miniaturized building slid a minute panel aside. A tiny cannon projected. Mary did not see it, but Susie and Seth Morley did.

"Look out!" Seth gasped, groping at his wife to get hold of her hand. He yanked her toward him. The vase crashed to the floor. The barrel of the cannon rotated, taking new aim. All at once a beam projected from it, in Mary Morley's direction. Susie, laughing, backed away, putting distance between herself and the beam.

The beam missed Mary Morley. On the far wall of the room a hole appeared and through it black night air billowed, cold and harsh, entering the room. Mary wobbled, retreated a step.

Rushing into the bathroom, Seth Morley disappeared, then came dashing out again, the waterglass in his hand. He sprinted to the dresser, poured water onto the building replica. The snout of the cannon ceased to rotate.

"I think I got it," Seth Morley said, wheezing asthmatically.

From the diminutive structure a curl of gray smoke drifted up. The structure hummed briefly and then a pool of sticky, grease-like stain dribbled out from it, mixing with the pool of water which had now formed around it. The structure bucked, spun, and then all at once decayed into inanimation. He was right; it was dead.

"You killed it," Susie said, accusingly.

Seth Morley said, "That's what killed Tallchief."

"Did it try to kill me?" Mary Morley asked faintly. She looked about unsteadily, the fanaticism of fury gone from her face now. Cautiously, she seated herself and stared at the structure, blank and pale, then said to her husband, "Let's get out of here."

To Susie, Seth Morley said, "I'm going to have to tell Glen Belsnor." He gingerly, and with great caution, picked up the dead little block; holding it in the palm of his hand he stared at it a long, long time.

"It took me three weeks to tame that one," Susie said. "Now I have to find another, and bring it back here without getting killed, and tame it like I did this one." She felt massive waves of accusation slapping higher and higher within her. "Look what you did," she said, and went swiftly to gather up her clothing.

Seth and Mary Morley started toward the door, Seth's hand on his wife's back. Guiding her out.

"Goddam you both!" she shouted in accusation. Half-dressed, she followed after them. "What about tomorrow?" she said to Seth. "Are we still going on a walk? I want to show you some of the—"

"No," he said harshly, and then he turned to gaze at her long and somberly. "You really don't understand what happened," he said.

Susie said, "I know what *almost* happened."

"Does someone have to die before you can wake up?" he said.

"No," she said, feeling uneasy; she did not like the expression in his hard, boring eyes. "All right," she said, "if it's so important to you, that little toy—"

" 'Toy,' " he said mockingly.

"Toy," she repeated. "Then you ought to be really interested in what's out there. Don't you understand? This is just a model of the real Building. Don't you want to see it? I've seen it very closely. I even know what the sign reads over the main entrance. Not the entrance where the trucks come and go but the entrance—"

"What does it say?" he said.

Susie said, "Will you go with me?" To Mary Morley she said, with all the graciousness she could command, "You, too. Both of you ought to come."

"I'll come alone," Seth said. To his wife he said, "It's too dangerous; I don't want you along."

"You don't want me along," Mary said, "for obvious other reasons." But she sounded dim and scared, as if the close call with the structure's energy beam had banished every emotion in her except raw, clinging fear.

Seth Morley said, "What does it say over the entrance?"

After a pause Susie said, "It says 'Whippery.'"

"What does that mean?" he said.

"I'm not positive. But it sounds fascinating. Maybe we can somehow get inside, this time. I've gone real close, almost up to the wall. But I couldn't find a side door, and I was afraid—I don't know why—to go in the main entrance."

Wordlessly, Seth Morley, steering his dazed wife, strode out into the night. She found herself standing there in the middle of her room, alone and only half-dressed.

"Bitch!" she called loudly after them. Meaning Mary.

They continued on. And were gone from sight.

Seven

"Don't kid yourself," Glen Belsnor said. "If it shot at your wife it's because that loopy dame, that Susie Dumb or Smart, whichever it is, wanted it to. She taught it. They can be trained, you see." He sat holding the tiny structure, staring down at it, a brooding expression settling by degrees into his long, lean face.

"If I hadn't grabbed her," Seth said, "we would have had a second death tonight."

"Maybe yes, maybe no. Considering the meager output of these things it probably would only have knocked her out."

"The beam bored through the wall."

Belsnor said, "The walls are cheap plastic. One layer. You could punch a hole through with your fist."

"So you're not upset by this."

Belsnor plucked at his lower lip, thoughtfully. "I'm upset by the whole thing. What the hell were you doing with Susie in her room?" He raised his hand. "Don't tell me, I know. She's deranged sexually. No, don't give me any details." He played aimlessly with the replica of the Building. "Too bad it didn't shoot Susie," he murmured, half to himself.

"There's something the matter with all of you," Seth said.

Belsnor raised his shaggy head and studied Seth Morley. "In what way?"

"I'm not sure. A kind of idiocy. Each of you seems to be living in his own private world. Without regard for anyone else. It's as if—" He pondered. "As if all you want, each of you, is to be left alone."

"No," Belsnor said. "We want to get away from here. We may have nothing else in common, but we do share that." He handed the destroyed structure back to Seth. "Keep it. As a souvenir."

Seth tossed it onto the floor.

"You're going out exploring with Susie tomorrow?" Belsnor said.

"Yes." He nodded.

"She'll probably attack you again."

"I'm not interested in that. I'm not worried by that. I think that we have an active enemy on the planet, working from outside the settlement area. I think it—or they—killed Tallchief. Despite what Babble found."

Belsnor said, "You're new here. Tallchief was new here. Tallchief is dead. I think there's a connection; I think his death was connected to his unfamiliarity with the conditions on this planet. Therefore you're equally in danger. But the rest of us—"

"You don't think I should go."

"Go, yes. But be very careful. Don't touch anything, don't pick up anything, keep your eyes open. Try to go only where she's been; don't tackle new areas."

"Why don't you come too?"

Regarding him intently, Belsnor said, "You want me to?"

"You're the settlement's leader, now. Yes, I think you should come. And armed."

"I—" Belsnor pondered. "It could be argued that I ought to stay here and work on the transmitter. It could be argued that you ought to be at work composing a prayer, instead of tramping around in the wilderness. I have to think of every aspect of this situation. It could be argued—"

"It could be argued that your 'could be argueds' may kill us all," Seth Morley said.

"Your 'could be argued' may be correct." Belsnor smiled as if at a private, secret reality. The smile, with no amusement in it, lingered on his face; it remained and became sardonic.

Seth Morley said, "Tell me what you know about the ecology out there."

"There is an organism which we call the tench. There are, we've gathered, five or six of them. Very old."

"What do they do? Are they artifact makers?"

"Some, the feeble ones, do nothing. They just sit there here and there in the middle of the landscape. The less feeble ones, however, print."

"'Print'?"

"They duplicate things brought to them. Small things, such as a wristwatch, a cup, an electric razor."

"And the printings work?"

Belsnor tapped his jacket pocket. "The pen I'm using is a print. But—" He lifted out the pen and extended it toward Seth Morley. "See the decay?" The surface of the pen had a furry texture, much like dust. "They decompose very rapidly. This'll be good for another few days, and then I can have another print made from the original pen."

"Why?"

"Because we're short on pens. And the ones we have are running out of ink."

"What about the writing of one of these print-pens? Does the ink fade out after a few days?"

"No," Belsnor said, but he looked uncomfortable.

"You're not sure."

Standing, Belsnor dug into his back pocket and got out his wallet. For a time he examined small, folded pieces of paper and then he placed one in front of Seth. The writing was clear and distinct.

Maggie Walsh entered the briefing chamber, saw the two of them, and came over. "May I join you?"

"Sure," Belsnor said remotely. "Pull up a chair." He glanced at Seth Morley, then said to her in a leisurely, hard voice, "Susie Smart's toy building tried to shoot Morley's wife a little while ago. It missed, and Morley poured a plate of water over it."

"I warned her," Maggie said, "that those things are unsafe."

"It was safe enough," Belsnor said. "It's Susie that isn't safe . . . as I was explaining to Morley."

"We should pray for her," Maggie said.

"You see?" Belsnor said to Seth Morley. "We do have concern for one another. Maggie wants to save Susie Smart's immortal soul."

"Pray," Seth Morley said, "that she doesn't capture another replica and begin teaching that one, too."

"Morley," Belsnor said, "I've been thinking about your thoughts on the whole bunch of us. In a way you're right: there is something the matter with each of us. But not what you think. The thing we have in common is that we're failures. Take Tallchief. Couldn't you tell he's a wino? And Susie—all she can think about is sexual conquests. I can make a guess about you, too. You're overweight; obviously you eat too much. Do you live to eat, Morley? Or had you never asked yourself that? Babble is a hypochondriac. Betty Jo Berm is a compulsive pill-taker: her life is in those little plastic bottles. That kid, Tony Dunkelwelt; he lives for his mystical insights, his schizophrenic trances . . . which both Babble and Frazer call catatonic stupor. Maggie, here—" He gestured toward her. "She lives in an illusory world of prayer and fasting, doing service to a deity which isn't interested in her." To Maggie he said, "Have you ever seen the Intercessor, Maggie?"

She shook her head no.

"Or the Walker-on-Earth?"

"No," she said.

"Nor the Mentufacturer either," Belsnor said. "Now take Wade Frazer. His world—"

"How about you?" Seth asked him.

Belsnor shrugged. "I have my own world."

"He invents," Maggie Walsh said.

"But I've never invented anything," Belsnor said. "Everything developed during the last two centuries has come from a composite lab, where hundreds, even thousands of research workers work. There is no such thing as an inventor in this century. Maybe I just like to play private games with electronic components. Anyhow, I enjoy it. I get most if not all of my pleasure in this world from creating circuits that ultimately do nothing."

"A dream of fame," Maggie said.

"No." Belsnor shook his head. "I want to contribute something; I don't want to be just a consumer, like the rest of you." His tone was hard and flat and very earnest. "We live in a world created and manufactured from the results of the work of millions of men, most of them dead, virtually none of them known or given any credit. I don't care if I'm known for what I create; all I care about is having it be worthwhile and useful, with people able to depend on it as something they take for granted in their lives. Like the safety pin. Who knows who created that? But everyone in the goddam galaxy makes use of safety pins, and the inventor—"

"Safety pins were invented on Crete," Seth Morley said. "In the fourth or fifth century B.C."

Belsnor glared at him. "About one thousand B.C."

"So it matters to you when and where they were invented," Seth Morley said.

"I came close to producing something one time," Belsnor said. "A silencing circuit. It would have interrupted the flow of electrons in any given conductor for a range of about fifty feet.

As a weapon of defense it would have been valuable. But I couldn't get the field to propagate for fifty feet; I could only get it functional for one-and-a-half feet. So that was that." He lapsed into silence, then. Brooding, baleful silence. Withdrawn into himself.

"We love you anyway," Maggie said.

Belsnor raised his head and glared at her.

"The Deity accepts even that," Maggie said. "Even an attempt which led nowhere. The Deity knows your motive, and motive is everything."

"It wouldn't matter," Belsnor said, "if this whole colony, everybody in it, died. None of us contribute anything. We're nothing more than parasites, feeding off the galaxy. 'The world will little note nor long remember what we do here.' "

Seth Morley said to Maggie, "Our leader. The man who's going to keep us alive."

"I'll keep you alive," Belsnor said. "As best I can. That could be my contribution: inventing a device made out of fluid-state circuitry that'll save us. That'll spike all the toy cannons."

"I don't think you're very bright to call something a toy simply because it's small," Maggie Walsh said. "That would mean that the Toxilax artificial kidney is a toy."

"You would have to call eighty percent of all Interplan ship circuitry toys," Seth Morley said.

"Maybe that's my problem," Belsnor said wryly. "I can't tell what's a toy and what isn't . . . which means I can't tell what's real. A toy ship is not a real ship. A toy cannon is not a real cannon. But I guess if it can kill—" He pondered. "Perhaps tomorrow I should require everyone to go systematically through the settlement, collecting all the toy buildings, in fact everything from outside, and then we'll ignite the whole pile and be done with it."

"What else has come into the settlement from outside?" Seth Morley inquired.

"Artificial flies," Belsnor said. "For one thing."

"They take pictures?" Seth asked.

"No. That's the artificial bees. The artificial flies fly around and sing."

" 'Sing'?" He thought he must have heard wrong.

"I have one here." Belsnor rummaged in his pockets and at

last brought out a small plastic box. "Hold it to your ear. There's one in there."

"What sort of thing do they sing?" Seth Morley held the box to his ear, listened. He heard it, then, a far-off sweet sound, like divided strings. And, he thought, like many distant wings. "I know that music," he said, "but I can't place it." An indistinct favorite of mine, he realized. From some ancient era.

"They play what you like," Maggie Walsh said.

He recognized it, now. *Granada.* "I'll be goddamed," he said aloud. "Are you sure it's a fly that's doing that?"

"Look in the box," Belsnor said. "But be careful—don't let it out. They're rare and hard to catch."

With great care Seth Morley slid back the lid of the box. He saw within it a dark fly, like a Proxima 6 tape-fly, large and hairy, with beating wings and eyes protruding, composite eyes, such as true flies had. He shut the box, convinced. "Amazing," he said. "Is it acting as a receiver? Picking up a signal from a central transmitter somewhere on the planet? It's a radio—is that it?"

"I took one apart," Belsnor said. "It's not a receiver; the music is emitted by a speaker but it emanates from the fly's works. The signal is created by a miniature generator in the form of an electrical impulse, not unlike a nerve impulse in an organic living creature. There's a moist element ahead of the generator which alters a complex pattern of conductivity, so a very complex signal can be created. What's it singing for you?"

"*Granada*," Seth Morley said. He wished he could keep it. The fly would be company for him. "Will you sell it?" he asked.

"Catch your own." Belsnor retrieved his fly and placed the box back in his pocket.

"Is there anything else from outside the settlement?" Seth Morley asked. "Besides the bees, flies, printers and miniature buildings?"

Maggie Walsh said, "A sort of flea-sized printer. But it can only print one thing; it does it over and over again, grinding out a flood that seems endless."

"A print of what?"

"Of Specktowsky's Book," Maggie Walsh said.

"And that's it?"

"That's all we know about," Maggie amended. "There may be others unknown to us." She shot a sharp glance at Belsnor.

Belsnor said nothing; he had again retracted into his own personal world, for the moment, oblivious to them.

Seth Morley picked up the abolished miniature building and said, "If the tenches only print duplicates of objects then they didn't make this. Something with highly-developed technical skills would have had to."

"It could have been made centuries ago," Belsnor said, rousing himself. "By a race that's no longer here."

"And printed continually since?"

"Yes. Or printed after we arrived here. For our benefit."

"How long do these miniature buildings last? Longer than your pen?"

"I see what you mean," Belsnor said. "No, they don't seem to decay rapidly. Maybe they're not printings. I don't see that it makes much difference; they could have been held in reserve all this time. Put aside until needed, until something along the lines of our colony manifested itself."

"Is there a microscope here in the settlement?"

"Sure." Belsnor nodded. "Babble has one."

"I'll go see Babble, then." Seth Morley moved toward the door of the briefing chamber. "Goodnight," he said, over his shoulder.

Neither of them answered; they seemed indifferent to him and to what he had said. Will I be this way in a couple of weeks? he asked himself. It was a good question, and before long he would have the answer.

"Yes," Babble said. "You can use my microscope." He had on pajamas and slippers and an ersatz-wool striped bathrobe. "I was just going to bed." He watched Seth Morley bring forth the miniature building. "Oh, one of those. They're all over the place."

Seating himself at the microscope, Seth Morley pried open the tiny structure, broke away the outer hull, then placed the component-complex onto the stage of the microscope. He used the low-power resolution, obtaining a magnification of 600x.

Intricate strands . . . printed circuitry, of course, on a series of modules. Resistors, condensers, valves. A power supply: one ultra-miniaturized helium battery. He could make out the swivel of the cannon barrel and what appeared to be the germanium arc which served as the source of the energy beam. It can't be very strong, he realized. Belsnor in a sense was right: the output, in ergs, must be terribly small.

He focused on the motor which drove the cannon barrel as it moved from side to side. Words were printed on the hasp which held the barrel in place; he strained to read them—and saw, as he adjusted the fine focus of the microscope, a confirmation of what he most feared.

MADE AT TERRA 35082R

The construct had come from Earth. It had not been invented by a superterrestrial race—it did not emanate from the native life forms of Delmak-O. So much for that.

General Treaton, he said to himself grimly. It is you, after all, who is destroying us. Our transmitter, our receiver—and the demand that we reach this planet by noser. Was it you who had Ben Tallchief killed? Obviously.

"What are you finding there?" Babble asked.

"I am finding," he said, "that General Treaton is our enemy and that we don't have a chance." He moved away from the microscope. "Take a look."

Babble placed his eye against the eye-piece of the microscope. "Nobody thought of that," he said presently. "We could have examined one of these any time during the last two months. It just never occurred to us." He looked away from the microscope, peering falteringly at Seth Morley. "What'll we do?"

"The first thing is to collect all of these, everything brought into the settlement from outside, and destroy them."

"That means the Building is Earth-made."

"Yes." Seth Morley nodded. Evidently so, he thought. "We are part of an experiment," he said.

"We've got to get off this planet," Babble said.

"We'll never get off," Seth Morley said.

"It must all be coming from the Building. We've got to find a way to destroy it. But I don't see how we can."

"Do you want to revise your autopsy report on Tallchief?"

"I have nothing more to go on. At this point I'd say he was probably killed by a weapon that we know nothing about. Something that generates fatal amounts of histamine in the blood supply. Which brings on what looks like a natural breathing-apparatus involvement. There is another possibility which you might consider. It could be a forgery. After all, Earth has become one giant mental hospital."

"There are military research labs there. Highly secret ones. The general public doesn't know about them."

"How do you know about them?"

Seth Morley said, "At Tekel Upharsin, as the kibbutz's marine biologist, I had dealings with them. And when we bought weapons." Strictly speaking, this was not true; he had, really, only heard rumors. But the rumors had convinced him.

"Tell me," Babble said, eying him, "did you really see the Walker-on-Earth?"

"Yes," he said. "And I know firsthand about the secret military research labs on Terra. For example—"

Babble said, "You saw someone. I believe that. Someone whom you didn't know came up and pointed out something that should have been obvious to you: namely, that the noser you had picked out was not spaceworthy. But you had it already in your mind—because it was taught to you throughout childhood —that if a stranger came to you and offered unsolicited help, that that stranger had to be a Manifestation of the Deity. But look: what you saw was what you expected to see. You assumed that he was the Walker-on-Earth because Specktowsky's Book is virtually universally accepted. But I don't accept it."

"You don't?" Seth Morley said, surprised.

"Not at all. Strangers—true strangers, ordinary men—show up and give good advice; most humans are well-intentioned. If I had happened by I would have intervened too. I would have pointed out that your ship wasn't spaceworthy."

"Then you would have been in the possession of the Walker-on-Earth; you would have temporarily become him. It can happen to anyone. That's part of the miracle."

"There are no miracles. As Spinoza proved centuries ago. A miracle would be a sign of God's weakness, as a failure of natural law. If there were a God."

Seth Morley said, "You told us, earlier this evening, that you saw the Walker-on-Earth seven times." Suspicion filled him; he had caught the inconsistency. "And the Intercessor too."

"What I meant by that," Babble said smoothly, "is that I en-countered life-situations in which human beings *acted* as the

Walker-on-Earth would have acted, did he exist. Your problem is that of a lot of people: it stems from our having encountered non-humanoid sentient races, some of them, the ones we call 'gods,' on what we call 'god-worlds,' so much superior to us as to put us in—for example—the rôle that, say, dogs or cats have to us. To a dog or a cat a man seems like God: he can do god-like things. But the quasi-biological, ultra-sentient life forms on god-worlds—they're just as much the products of natural biological evolution as we are. In time we may evolve that far . . . even farther. I'm not saying we will, I'm saying we can." He pointed his finger determinedly at Seth Morley. "They didn't create the universe. They're not Manifestations of the Mentufacturer. All we have is their verbal report that they are Manifestations of the Deity. Why should we believe them? Naturally, if we ask them, 'Are you God? Did you make the universe?' they'll reply in the affirmative. We'd do the same thing; white men, back in the sixteenth and seventeenth centuries, told the natives of North and South America exactly the same thing."

"But the Spanish and English and French were colonists. They had a motive for pretending to be gods. Take Cortez. He—"

"The life forms on so-called 'god-worlds' have a similar motive."

"Like what?" He felt his dull anger beginning to glow. "They're saint-like. They contemplate; they listen to our prayers —if they can pick them up—and they act to fulfill our prayers. As they did, for example, with Ben Tallchief."

"They sent him here to die. Is that right?"

That had been acutely bothering him, starting at the moment he had first caught sight of Tallchief's dead and inert body. "Maybe they didn't know," he said uncomfortably. "After all, Specktowsky points out that the Deity does not know everything. For instance, He did not know that the Form Destroyer existed, or that He'd be awakened by the concentric rings of emanation that make up the universe. Or that the Form Destroyer would enter the universe, and hence time, and corrupt the universe that the Mentufacturer had made in his own image, so that it was no longer his image."

"Just like Maggie Walsh. She talks the same way." Dr. Babble barked out a harsh, short laugh.

Seth Morley said, "I've never met an atheist before." In actuality he had met one, but it had been years ago. "It seems very strange in this era, when we have proof of the Deity's existence. I can understand there being widespread atheism in previous eras, when religion was based on faith in things unseen . . . but now it's not unseen, as Specktowsky indicated."

"The Walker-on-Earth," Babble said sardonically, "is a sort of anti-Person-from-Porlock. Instead of interfering with a good process or event he—" Babble broke off.

The door of the infirmary had opened. A man stood there, wearing a soft plastic work-jacket, semi-leather pants and boots. He was dark-haired, probably in his late thirties, with a strong face; his cheekbones were high and his eyes were large and bright. He carried a flashlight, which he now shut off. He stood there, gazing at Babble and Seth Morley, saying nothing. Merely standing silent and waiting. Seth Morley thought, *This is a resident of the settlement that I've never seen.* And then, noticing Babble's expression, *he realized that Babble had never seen him either.*

"Who are you?" Babble said hoarsely.

The man said in a low, mild voice, "I just arrived here in my noser. My name is Ned Russell. I'm an economist." He held out his hand toward Babble, who accepted it reflexively.

"I thought everyone was here," Babble said. "We have thirteen people; that's all there's supposed to be."

"I applied for a transfer and this was the destination. Delmak-O." Russell turned to Seth Morley, again holding out his hand. The two men shook.

"Let's see your transfer order," Babble said.

Russell dug into his coat pocket. "This is a strange place you're operating here. Almost no lights, the automatic pilot inoperative . . . I had to land it myself and I'm not that used to a noser. I parked it with all the others, in the field at the edge of your settlement."

"So we have two points to raise with Belsnor," Seth Morley said. "The made-at-Terra inscription on the miniaturized building. And him." He wondered which would prove to be the more important. At the moment he could not see clearly enough ahead to know one way or the other. Something to save us, he thought; something to doom us. It—the equation of everything—could go either way.

In the nocturnal darkness Susie Smart slipped by degrees in the direction of Tony Dunkelwelt's living quarters. She wore a black slip and high heels—knowing that the boy liked that.

Knock, knock.

"Who is it?" a voice mumbled from within.

"Susie." She tried the knob. The door was unlocked. So she went ahead on in.

In the center of the room Tony Dunkelwelt sat crosslegged on the floor in front of a single candle. His eyes, in the dim light, were shut; evidently he was in a trance. He showed no sign of noticing her or recognizing her, and yet he had asked her name. "Is it all right for me to come in?"

His trance-states worried her. In them he withdrew entirely from the regular world. Sometimes he sat this way for hours, and when they questioned the boy about what he saw he could give little or no answer.

"I don't mean to butt in," she said, when he did not answer.

In a modulated, detached voice, Tony said, "Welcome."

"Thank you," she said, relieved. Seating herself in a straight-backed chair she found her package of cigarettes, lit one, settled back for what she knew would be a long wait.

But she did not feel like waiting.

Cautiously, she kick-kicked at him with the toe of her high heeled shoe. "Tony?" she said. "Tony?"

"Yes," he said.

"Tell me, Tony, what do you see? Another world? Can you see all the busy gods running about doing good deeds? Can you see the Form Destroyer at work? How does he look?" No one ever saw the Form Destroyer except Tony Dunkelwelt. He had the principle of evil all to himself. And it was this frightening quality about the boy's trances which kept her from trying to interfere; when he was in a trance-state she tried to leave him alone, to work his way back from his vision of pure malignancy to their normal and everyday responsibility.

"Don't talk to me," Tony mumbled. He had his eyes squeezed shut, and his face was pinched and red.

"Knock off for a while," she said. "You ought to be in bed. Do you want to go to bed, Tony? With me, for example?" She placed her hand on his shoulder; by degrees he then slid away, until she was holding nothing. "You remember what you said about me loving you because you're not yet a real man? You are a real man. Wouldn't I know? Leave the deciding up to me: I'll tell you when you're a man and when you're not, if you ever happen to be not. But up until now you've been more than a man. Did you know that an eighteen-year-old can have seven orgasms in one twenty-four-hour period?" She waited, but he said nothing. "That's pretty good," she said.

Tony said raptly, "There is a deity above the Deity. One who embraces all four."

"What four? Four what?"

"The four Manifestations. The Mentufacturer, the—"

"Who's the fourth?"

"The Form Destroyer."

"You mean you can commune with a god that combines the Form Destroyer with the other three? But that's not possible, Tony; they are good gods and the Form Destroyer is evil."

"I know that," he said in a sullen voice. "That's why what I see is so keen, A god-above-god, which no one can see but me." Again, by degrees, he drifted back into his trance; he ceased speaking to her.

"How come you can see something that no one else can, and still call it real?" Susie asked. "Specktowsky didn't say any-thing about such a super Deity. I think it's all in your own mind." She felt cross and cold, and the cigarette burned her nose; she had, as usual, been smoking too much. "Let's go to bed, Tony," she said vigorously, and stubbed out her cigarette. "Come on." Bending, she took hold of him by the arm. But he remained inert. Like a rock.

Time passed. He communed on and on.

"Jesus!" she said angrily. "Well the hell with it; I'll leave. Goodnight." Rising, she walked rapidly to the door, opened it, stood half inside and half out. "We could have so much fun if we went to bed," she said plaintively. "Is there something about me you don't like? I mean, I could change it. And I've been reading; there're several positions I didn't know. Let me teach them to you; they sound like a lot of fun."

Tony Dunkelwelt opened his eyes and, unwinkingly, regarded her. She could not decipher the expression on his face, and it made her uneasy; she began rubbing her bare arms and shivering.

"The Form Destroyer," Tony said, "is absolutely-not-God."

"I realize that," she said.

"But 'absolutely-not-God' is a category of being."

"If you say so, Tony."

"And God contains all categories of being. Therefore God can be absolutely-not-God, which transcends human reason and logic. But we intuitively feel it to be so. Don't you? Wouldn't you prefer a monism that transcends our pitiful dualism? Specktowsky was a great man, but there is a higher monistic structure above the dualism that he foresaw. *There is a higher God.*" He eyed her. "What do you think about that?" he asked, a little timidly.

"I think it's wonderful," Susie said, with enthusiasm. "It must be so great to have trances and perceive what you perceive. You should write a book saying that what Specktowsky says is wrong."

"It's not wrong," Tony said. "It's transcended by what I see. When you get to that level, two opposite things can be equal. That's what I'm trying to reveal."

"Couldn't you reveal it tomorrow?" she asked, still shivering and massaging her bare arms. "I'm so cold and so tired and I had an awful run-in with that goddam Mary Morley tonight already, so come on, please; let's go to bed."

"I'm a prophet," Tony said. "Like Christ or Moses or Specktowsky. I will never be forgotten." Again he shut his eyes. The weak candle flickered and almost went out. He did not notice.

"If you're a prophet," Susie said, "perform a miracle." She had read in Specktowsky's Book about that, about the prophets having miraculous powers. "Prove it to me," she said.

One eye opened. "Why must you have a sign?"

"I don't want a sign. I want a miracle."

"A miracle," he said, "is a sign. All right, I'll do something that will show you." He gazed around the room, his face holding a deeply-ingrained resentment. She had awakened him now, she realized. And he didn't like it.

"Your face is turning black," she said.

He touched his brow experimentally. "It's turning red. But the candle light doesn't contain a full light spectrum so it looks black." He slid to his feet and walked stiffly about, rubbing the base of his neck.

"How long were you sitting there?" she asked.

"I don't know."

"That's right; you lose all conception of time." She had heard him say it. That part alone awed her. "Okay," she said, "turn this into a stone." She had found a loaf of bread, a jar of peanut butter, and a knife; holding up the loaf of bread she moved toward him, feeling mischievous. "Can you do that?"

Solemnly, he said, "The opposite of Christ's miracle."

"Can you do it?"

He accepted the loaf of bread from her, held it with both hands; he gazed down at it, his lips moving. His entire face began to writhe, as if with tremendous effort. The darkness grew; his eyes faded out and were replaced by impenetrable buttons of darkness.

The loaf of bread flipped from his hands, rose until it hung well above him . . . it twisted, became hazy, and then, like a stone, it dropped to the floor. *Like* a stone? She knelt down to stare at it, wondering if the light of the room had put her into a hypnotic trance. The loaf of bread was gone. What rested on the floor appeared to be a smooth, large rock, a water-tumbled rock, with pale sides. "My good God," she said, half-aloud. "Can I pick it up? Is it safe?"

Tony, his eyes once more filled with life, also knelt and stared at it. "God's power," he said, "was in me. I didn't do that; it was done *through* me."

Picking up the rock—it was heavy—she discovered that it felt warm and nearly alive. An animate rock, she said to herself. As if it's organic. Maybe it's not a real rock. She banged it against the floor; it felt hard enough, and it made the right noise. It is a rock, she realized. It is!

"Can I have it?" she asked. Her awe had become complete now; she gazed at him hopefully, willing to do exactly what he said.

"You may have it, Suzanne," Tony said in a calm voice. "But arise and go back to your room. I'm tired." He did sound tired, and his entire body drooped. "I'll see you in the morning at breakfast. Goodnight."

"Goodnight," she said, "but I can undress you and put you to bed; I'd enjoy that."

"No," he said. He went to the door and held it open for her.

"Kiss." Coming up to him she leaned forward and kissed him on the lips. "Thank you," she said, feeling humble. "Goodnight, Tony. And thanks for the miracle." The door started to close behind her but, adroitly, she stopped it with the wedge-shaped toe of her shoe. "Can I tell everyone about this? I mean, isn't this the first miracle you've ever done? Shouldn't they know? But if you don't want them to know I won't tell them."

"Let me sleep," he said, and shut the door; it clicked in her face and she felt animal terror—this was what she feared most in life: the clicking shut of a man's door in her face. Instantly, she raised her hand to knock, discovered the rock . . . she banged on the door with the rock, but not loudly, just enough to let him know how desperate she was to get back in, but not loudly enough to bother him if he didn't want to answer.

He didn't. No sound, no movement of the door. Nothing but the void.

"Tony?" she gasped, pressing her ear to the door. Silence. "Okay," she said numbly; clutching her rock she walked unsteadily across the porch toward her own living quarters.

The rock vanished. Her hand felt nothing.

"Damn," she said, not knowing how to react. Where had it gone? Into air. But then it must have been an illusion, she realized. He put me in a hypnotic state and made me believe. I should have known it wasn't really true.

A million stars burst into wheels of light, blistering, cold light, that drenched her. It came from behind and she felt the great weight of it crash into her. "Tony," she said, and fell into the waiting void. She thought nothing; she felt nothing. She saw only, saw the void as it absorbed her, waiting below and beneath her as she plummeted down the many miles.

On her hands and knees she died. Alone on the porch. Still clutching for what did not exist.

Eight

GLEN BELSNOR lay dreaming. In the dark of night he dreamed of himself; he perceived himself as he really was, a wise and beneficial provider. Happily he thought, I can do it. I can take care of them all, help them and protect them. They must be protected at all costs, he thought to himself in his dream.

In his dream he attached connecting cable, screwed a circuit-breaker in place, tried out a servo-assist unit.

A hum rose from the elaborate mechanism. A generated field, miles high, rose in every direction. No one can get past that, he said to himself in satisfaction, and some of his fear began to dwindle away. The colony is safe and I have done it.

In the colony the people moved back and forth, wearing long red robes. It became midday and then it became midday for a thousand years. He saw, all at once, that they had become old. Tottering, with tattered beards—the women, too—they crept about in a feeble, insect-like manner. And some of them, he saw, were blind.

Then we're not safe, he realized. Even with the field in operation. They are fading away from inside. They will all die anyhow.

"Belsnor!"

He opened his eyes and knew what it was.

Gray, early-morning sunlight filtered through the shades of his room. Seven A.M., he saw by his self-winding wristwatch. He rose up to a sitting position, pushing the covers away. Chill morning air plucked at him and he shivered. "Who?" he said to the men and women pouring into his room. He shut his eyes, grimaced, felt, despite the emergency, the rancid remains of sleep still clinging to him.

Ignatz Thugg, wearing gaily-decorated pajamas, said loudly, "Susie Smart."

Putting on his bathrobe, Belsnor moved numbly toward the door.

"Do you know what this means?" Wade Frazer said.

"Yes," he said. "I know exactly what it means."

Roberta Rockingham, touching the corner of a small linen handkerchief to her eyes, said, "She was such a bright spirit, always lighting up things with her presence. How could anybody do it to her?" A trail of tears materialized on her withered cheeks.

He made his way across the compound; the others clumped after him, none of them speaking.

There she lay, on the porch. A few steps from her door. He bent over her, touched the back of her neck. Absolutely cold. No life of any kind. "You examined her?" he said to Babble. "She really is dead? There's no doubt about it?"

"Look at your hand," Wade Frazer said.

Belsnor removed his hand from the girl's neck. His hand dripped blood. And now he saw the mass of blood in her hair, near the top of her skull. Her head had been crushed in.

"Care to revise your autopsy?" he said scathingly to Babble. "Your opinion about Tallchief; do you care to change it now?"

No one spoke.

Belsnor looked around, saw not far off a loaf of bread. "She must have been carrying that," he said.

"She got it from me," Tony Dunkelwelt said. His face had paled from shock; his words were barely audible. "She left my room last night and I went to bed. I didn't kill her. I didn't even know about it until I heard Dr. Babble and the others yelling."

"We're not saying you did it," Belsnor said to him. Yes, she used to flit from one room to another at night, he thought. We made fun of her and she was a little deranged . . . but she never hurt anybody. She was as innocent as a human being could get; she was even innocent of her own wrong-doing.

The new man, Russell, approached. The expression on his face showed that he, too, without even knowing her, understood what an awful thing it was, what an awful moment it was for all of them.

"You see what you came here to see?" Belsnor said to him harshly.

Russell said, "I wonder if you could get help by means of the transmitter in my noser."

"They're not good enough," Belsnor said. "The noser radio-rig. Not good enough at all." He rose to his feet stiffly, hearing his bones crack. And it's Terra that's doing this, he thought, remembering what Seth Morley and Babble had said last night when they brought Russell over. Our own government. As if we're rats in a maze with death; rodents confined with the ultimate adversary, to die one by one until none are left.

Seth Morley beckoned him off to one side, away from the others. "You're sure you don't want to tell them? They have a right to know who the enemy is."

Belsnor said, "I don't want them to know because as I explained to you their morale is low enough already. If they knew it came from Terra they wouldn't be able to survive; they'd go friggin' mad."

"I'll leave it up to you," Seth Morley said. "You've been elected as the group's leader." But his tone of voice showed that he disagreed, and very strongly. As he had last night.

"In time," Belsnor said, clamping his long, expert fingers around Seth's upper arm. "When the right time comes—"

"It never will," Seth Morley said, moving back a step. "They'll die without knowing."

Maybe, Belsnor thought, it would be better that way. Better if all men, wherever they are, were to die without knowing who did it or why.

Squatting down, Russell turned Susie Smart over; he gazed down at her and said, "She certainly was a pretty girl."

"Pretty," Belsnor said harshly, "but batty. She had an overactive sex drive; she had to sleep with every man she came across. We can do without her."

"You bastard," Seth Morley said, his tone fierce.

Belsnor lifted his empty hands and said, "What do you want me to say? That we can't get along without her? That this is the end?"

Morley did not answer.

To Maggie Walsh, Belsnor said, "Say a prayer." It was time for the ceremony of death, the rituals so firmly attached to it that even he himself could not imagine a death without it.

"Give me a few minutes," Maggie Walsh said huskily. "I—just can't talk now." She retreated and turned her back; he heard her sobbing.

"I'll say it," Belsnor said, with savage fury.

Seth Morley said, "I'd like permission to go on an exploratory trip outside the settlement. Russell wants to come along."

"Why?" Belsnor said.

Morley said in a low, steady voice, "I've seen the miniaturized version of the Building. I think it's time to confront the real thing."

"Take someone with you," Belsnor said. "Someone who knows their way around out there."

"I'll go with them," Betty Jo Berm spoke up.

"There should be another man with them," Belsnor said. But, he thought, it's a mistake for us not to stay together; death comes when one of us is off by himself. "Take Frazer and Thugg, both of them, with you," he decided. "As well as B.J." That would split the group, but neither Roberta Rockingham nor Bert Kosler were physically able to make such a journey. Neither had as yet left the camp. "I'll stay here with the rest of them," he said.

"I think we should be armed," Wade Frazer said.

"Nobody is going to be armed," Belsnor said. "We're in a bad enough situation already. If you're armed you'll kill one another, either accidently or intentionally." He did not know why he felt this, but intuitively he knew himself to be correct. Susie Smart, he thought. Maybe you were killed by one of us . . . one who is an agent of Terra and General Treaton.

As in my dream, he thought. The enemy within. Age, deterioration and death. Despite the field-barrier surrounding the settlement. That's what my dream was trying to tell me.

Rubbing at her grief-reddened eyes, Maggie Walsh said, "I'd like to go along with them."

"Why?" Belsnor said. "Why does everyone want to leave the settlement? We're safer here." But his knowledge, his awareness of the untruth of what he was saying, found its way into his voice; he heard his own insincerity. "Okay," he said. "And good luck." To Seth Morley he said, "Try and bring back one of those singing flies. Unless you find something better."

"I'll do the best I can," Seth Morley said. Turning, he moved away from Belsnor. Those who were going with him started away, too.

They'll never come back, Belsnor said to himself. He watched them go and, within him, his heart struck heavy, muffled blows, as if the pendulum of the cosmic clock were swinging back and forth, back and forth, within his hollow chest.

The pendulum of death.

The seven of them trudged along the edge of a low ridge, their attention fixed on each object that they saw. They said very little.

Unfamiliar hazy hills spread out, lost in billowing dust. Green lichens grew everywhere; the soil was a tangled floor of growing plants. The air smelled of intricate organic life here. A rich, complex odor, nothing like any of them had smelled before. Off in the distance great columns of steam rose up, geysers of boiling water forcing its way through the rocks to the surface. An ocean lay far off, pounding invisibly in the drifting curtain of dust and moisture.

They came to a damp place. Warm slime, compounded from water, dissolved minerals and fungoid pulp, lapped at their shoes. The remains of lichens and protozoa colored and thickened the scum of moisture dripping everywhere, over the wet rocks and sponge-like shrubbery.

Bending down, Wade Frazer picked up a snail-like unipedular organism. "It's not fake—this is alive. It's genuine."

Thugg was holding a sponge which he had fished from a small, warm pool. "This is artificial. But there are legitimate sponges like this on Delmak-O. And these are fakes, too." From the water Thugg grabbed a wriggling snake-like creature with short, stubby legs that thrashed furiously. Swiftly, Thugg removed the head; the head came off and the creature stopped moving. "A totally mechanical contraption—you can see the wiring." He restored the head; once more the creature began flopping. Thugg tossed it back in the water and it swam happily off.

"Where's the Building?" Mary Morley said.

Maggie Walsh said, "It—seems to change locations. The last time anyone encountered it it was along this ridge and past the geysers. But it probably won't be next time."

"We can use this as a starting stage," Betty Jo Berm said. "When we get to the spot where it last was we can fan out in various directions." She added, "It's a shame we don't have intercoms with us. They would be a lot of help."

"That's Belsnor's fault," Thugg said. "He's our elected leader; he's supposed to think of technical details like that."

To Seth Morley Betty Jo Berm said, "Do you like it out here?"

"I don't know yet." Perhaps because of Susie Smart's death he felt repelled by everything he saw. He did not like the mixture of artificial life forms with the real ones: the mixing together of them made him sense the whole landscape as false . . . as if, he thought, those hills in the background, and that great plateau to the right, are a painted backdrop. As if all this, and ourselves, and the settlement—all are contained in a geodetic dome. And above us Treaton's research men, like entirely deformed scientists of pulp fiction, are peering down at us as we walk, tiny-creature-wise, along our humble way.

"Let's stop and rest," Maggie Walsh said, her face grim and elongated still; the shock of Susie's death had, for her, not worn off in the slightest. "I'm tired. I didn't have any breakfast, and we didn't bring any food with us. This whole trip should have been carefully planned out in advance."

"None of us were thinking clearly," Betty Jo Berm said with sympathy. She brought a bottle out of her skirt pocket, opened it, sorted among the pills and at last found one that was satisfactory.

"Can you swallow those without water?" Russell asked her.

"Yes," she said, and smiled. "A pillhead can swallow a pill under any circumstances."

Seth Morley said to Russell, "For B.J. it's pills." He eyed Russell, wondering about him. Like the others, did this new member also have a weak link in his character? And if so, what was it?

"I think I know what Mr. Russell's fondness is for," Wade Frazer said in his somewhat nasty, baiting voice. "He has, I believe, from what I've observed about him, a cleaning fetish."

"Really?" Mary Morley said.

"I'm afraid so," Russell said and smiled to show perfect, white teeth, like the teeth of an actor.

They continued on and came, at last, to a river. It seemed too wide to cross; there they halted.

"We'll have to follow the river," Thugg said. He scowled. "I've been in this area, but I didn't see any river before."

Frazer giggled and said, "It's for you, Morley. Because you're a marine biologist."

Maggie Walsh said, "That's a strange remark. Do you mean the landscape alters according to our expectation?"

"I was making a joke," Frazer said insultingly.

"But what a strange idea," Maggie Walsh said. "You know, Specktowsky speaks about us being 'prisoners of our own pre-conceptions and expectations.' And that one of the conditions of the Curse is to remain mired in the quasi-reality of those proclivities. Without ever seeing reality as it actually is."

"Nobody sees reality as it actually is," Frazer said. "As Kant proved. Space and time are modes of perception, for example. Did you know that?" He poked at Seth Morley. "Did you know that, mister marine biologist?"

"Yes," he answered, although in point of fact he had never even heard of Kant, much less read him.

"Specktowsky says that ultimately we can see reality as it is," Maggie Walsh said. "When the Intercessor releases us from our world and condition. When the Curse is lifted from us, through him."

Russell spoke up. "And sometimes, even during our physical lifetime, we get momentary glimpses of it."

"Only if the Intercessor lifts the veil for us," Maggie Walsh said.

"True," Russell admitted.

"Where are you from?" Seth Morley asked Russell.

"From Alpha Centauri 8."

"That's a long way from here," Wade Frazer said.

"I know." Russell nodded. "That's why I arrived here so late. I'd been traveling for almost three months."

"Then you were one of the first to obtain a transfer," Seth Morley said. "Long before me."

"Long before any of us," Wade Frazer said. He contemplated Russell, who stood head and shoulders above him. "I wonder why an economist would be wanted here. There's no economy on this planet."

Maggie Walsh said, "There seems to be no use to which *any* of us can put our skills. Our skills, our training—they don't seem to matter. I don't think we were selected because of them."

"Obviously," Thugg grated.

"Is that so obvious to you?" Betty Jo said to him. "Then what do you think the basis of selection was?"

"Like Belsnor says. We're all misfits."

"He doesn't say we're misfits," Seth Morley said. "He says we're failures."

"It's the same thing," Thugg said. "We're the debris of the galaxy. Belsnor is right, for once."

"Don't include me when you say that," Betty Jo said. "I'm not willing to admit I'm part of the 'debris of the universe' quite yet. Maybe tomorrow."

"As we die," Maggie Walsh said, half to herself, "we sink into oblivion. An oblivion in which we already exist . . . one out of which only the Deity can save us."

"So we have the Deity trying to save us," Seth Morley said, "and General Treaton trying to—" He broke off; he had said too much. But no one noticed.

"That's the basic condition of life anyhow," Russell put in, in his neutral, mild voice. "The dialectic of the universe. One force pulling us down to death: the Form Destroyer in all his manifestations. Then the Deity in His three Manifestations. Theoretically always at our elbow. Right, Miss Walsh?"

"Not theoretically." She shook her head. "Actually."

Betty Jo Berm said quietly, "There's the Building."

So now he saw it. Seth Morley shaded his eyes against the bright midday sun, peered. Gray and large, it reared up at the limit of his vision. A cube, almost. With odd spires . . . probably from heat-sources. From the machinery and activity within. A pall of smoke hung over it and he thought, It's a factory.

"Let's go," Thugg said, starting in that direction.

They trudged that way, strung out in an uneven file.

"It's not getting any closer," Wade Frazer said presently, with jejune derision.

"Walk faster, then," Thugg said with a grin.

"It won't help." Maggie Walsh halted, gasping. Circles of dark sweat were visible about her armpits. "Always it's like this. You walk and walk and it recedes and recedes."

"And you never get really close," Wade Frazer said. He, too, had stopped walking; he was busy lighting up a battered rosewood pipe . . . using with it, Seth Morley noted, one of the worst and strongest pipe-mixtures in existence. The smell of it, as the pipe flared into irregular burning, befouled the natural air.

"Then what do we do?" Russell said.

"Maybe you can think of something," Thugg said. "Maybe if we close our eyes and walk around in a little circle we'll find ourselves standing next to it."

"As we stand here," Seth Morley said, shading his eyes and peering, "it gets closer." He was positive. He could pick out all the spires, now, and the pall of smoke above it seemed to have lifted. Maybe it's not a factory after all, he thought. *If it will come just a little nearer maybe I can tell.* He peered on and on; the others, presently, did the same.

Russell said reflectively, "It's a phantasm. A projection of some kind. From a transmitter located probably within a square mile of us. A very efficient, modern vidtransmitter . . . but you can still see a slight waver."

"What do you suggest, then?" Seth Morley asked him. "If you're right then there's no reason to try to get close to it, since it isn't there."

"It's somewhere," Russell corrected. "But not in that spot. What we're seeing is a fake. But there is a real Building and it probably is not far off."

"How can you know that?" Seth Morley said.

Russell said, "I'm familiar with Interplan West's method of decoy-composition. This illusory transmission is in existence to fool those who know there is a Building. Who expect to find it. And when they see this they think they have. This is not for someone who does not know there is a Building somewhere out here." He added, "This worked very well in the war between Interplan West and the warrior-cults of Rigel 10. Rigelian missiles zeroed in on illusory industrial complexes over and over again. You see, this kind of projection shows up on radar screens and computerized sweep-scanner probes. It has a kind of semi-material basis; strictly speaking it's not a mirage."

"Well, you would know," Betty Jo Berm said. "You're an economist; you'd be familiar with what happened to industrial complexes during a war." But she did not sound convinced.

"Is that why it retreats?" Seth Morley asked him. "As we approach?"

"That is how I made out its composition," Russell said.

Maggie Walsh said to him, "Tell us what to do."

"Let's see." Russell sighed, pondered. The others waited. "The real Building could be almost anywhere. There's no way to trace it back from the phantasm; if there were, the method would not have worked. I think—" He pointed. "I have a feeling that the plateau over there is illusory. A superimposition over something, resulting in a negative hallucination for anyone who sights in that direction." He explained, "A negative hallucination—when you do not see something that's actually there."

"Okay," Thugg said. "Let's head for the plateau."

"That means crossing the river," Mary Morley said.

To Maggie Walsh, Frazer said, "Does Specktowsky say anything about walking on water? It would be useful, right now. That river looks damn deep to me, and we already decided we couldn't take the chance of trying to cross it."

"The river may not be there either," Seth Morley said.

"It's there," Russell said. He walked toward it, stopped at its edge, bent down and lifted out a temporary handful of water.

"Seriously," Betty Jo Berm said, "does Specktowsky say anything about walking on water?"

"It can be done," Maggie Walsh said, "but only if the person or persons are in the presence of the Deity. The Deity would have to lead him—or them—across; otherwise they'd sink and drown."

Ignatz Thugg said, "Maybe Mr. Russell is the Deity." To Russell he said, "Are you a Manifestation of the Deity? Come here to help us? Are you, specifically, the Walker-on-Earth?"

"Afraid not," Russell said in his reasonable, neutral voice.

"Lead us across the water," Seth Morley said to him.

"I can't," Russell said. "I'm a man just like you."

"Try," Seth Morley said.

"It's strange," Russell said, "that you would think I'm the Walker-on-Earth. It's happened before. Probably because of the nomadic existence I lead. I'm always showing up as a stranger, and if I do anything right—which is rare—then someone gets the bright idea that I'm the third Manifestation of the Deity."

"Maybe you are," Seth Morley said, scrutinizing him keenly; he tried to recall how the Walker had looked when he had re-

vealed himself back at Tekel Upharsin. There was little resemblance. And yet—the odd intuition, to an extent, remained
with him. It had come to him with no warning: one moment he
had accepted Russell as an ordinary man and then all at once
he had felt himself to be in the presence of the Deity. And it
lingered; it did not completely go away.

"I'd know if I was," Russell pointed out.

"Maybe you do know," Maggie Walsh said. "Maybe Mr.
Morley is right." She, too, scrutinized Russell, who looked
now a little embarrassed. "If you are," she said, "we will know
eventually."

"Have you ever seen the Walker?" Russell asked her.

"No."

"I am not he," Russell said.

"Let's just wade into the goddam water and see if we can
make the other side," Thugg said impatiently. "If it's too deep
then the hell with it; we'll turn back. Here I go." He strode
toward the river and into it; his legs disappeared in the opaque
blue-gray water. He continued on and, by degrees, the others
followed after him.

They reached the far side with no trouble. All across, the
river remained shallow. Feeling chagrined the six of them—and
Russell—stood together, slapping water from their clothing. It
had come up to their waists and no farther.

"Ignatz Thugg," Frazer said. "Manifestation of the Deity.
Equipped to ford rivers and battle typhoons. I never guessed."

"Up yours," Thugg said.

To Maggie Walsh, Russell said suddenly, "Pray."

"For what?"

"For the veil of illusion to rise to expose the reality beneath."

"May I do it silently?" she asked. Russell nodded. "Thank
you," she said, and turned her back to the group; she stood for
a time, hands folded, her head bowed, and then she turned
back. "I did as well as I could," she informed them. She looked
happier, now, Seth Morley noticed. Maybe, temporarily, she
had forgotten about Susie Smart.

A tremendous pulsation throbbed nearby.

"I can hear it," Seth Morley said, and felt fear. Enormous,
instinctive fear.

A hundred yards away a gray wall rose up into the smoky haze of the midday sky. Pounding, vibrating, the wall creaked as if alive . . . while, above it, spires squirted wastes in the form of dark clouds. Further wastes, from enormous pipes, gurgled into the river. Gurgled and gurgled and never ceased.

They had found the Building.

Nine

"So now we can see it," Seth Morley said. At last. It makes a noise, he thought, like a thousand cosmic babies dropping an endless number of giant pot lids onto a titanic concrete floor. What are they doing in there? he asked himself, and started toward the front face of the structure, to see what was inscribed over the entrance.

"Noisy, isn't it?" Wade Frazer shouted.

"Yes," he said, and was unable to hear his own voice over the stupendous racket of the Building.

He followed a paved road that led along the side of the structure; the others tagged after him, some of them holding their ears. Now he came out in front, shielded his eyes and peered up, focused on the raised surface above the closed sliding doors.

WINERY

That much noise from a winery? he asked himself. It makes no sense.

A small door bore a sign reading: Customers' entrance to wine and cheese tasting room. Holy smoke, he said to himself, the thought of cheese drifting through his mind and burnishing all the shiny parts of his conscious attention. I ought to go in, he said to himself. Apparently it's free, although they like you to buy a couple of bottles before you leave. But you don't have to.

Too bad, he thought, that Ben Tallchief isn't here. With his great interest in alcoholic beverages this would constitute, for him, a fantastic discovery.

"Wait!" Maggie Walsh called from behind him. "Don't go in!"

His hand on the customers' door, he half-turned, wondering what was the matter.

Maggie Walsh peeped up into the splendor of the sun and saw mixed with its remarkably strong rays a glimmer of words. She traced the letters with her finger, trying to stabilize them. What does it say? she asked herself. What message does it have for us, with all we yearn to know?

WITTERY

"Wait!" she called to Seth Morley, who stood with his hand on a small door marked: Customers' entrance. "Don't go in!"

"Why not?" he yelled back.

"We don't know what it is!" She came breathlessly up beside him. The great structure shimmered in the mobile sunlight which spilled and dribbled over its higher surfaces. As if one could walk up on a single mote, she said to herself longingly. A carrier to the universal self: made partly of this world, partly of the next. *Wittery*. A place where knowledge is accumulated? But it made too much noise to be a book and tape and micro-film depository. Where witty conversations take place? Perhaps the essences of man's wit were being distilled within; she might find herself immersed in the wit of Dr. Johnson, of Voltaire.

But wit did not mean humor. It meant perspicacity. It meant the most fundamental form of intelligence coupled with a certain amount of grace. But, over all, the capacity of man to possess absolute knowledge.

If I go in there, she thought, I will learn all that man can know in this interstice of dimensions. I must go in. She hurried up to Seth Morley, nodding. "Open the door," she said. "We must go inside the wittery; we've got to learn what is in there."

Ambling after them, regarding their agitation with distinguished irony, Wade Frazer perceived the legend incised above the closed, vast doors of the Building.

At first he was perplexed. He could decipher the letters and thus make out the word. But he had not the foggiest notion as to the meaning of the word.

"I don't get it," he said to Seth Morley and the religious fanatic of the colony, Mag the Hag. He strained once more to see, wondering if his problem lay in a psychological ambivalence; perhaps on some lower level he did not really desire to know what the letters spelled. So he had garbled it, to foil his own maneuvering.

STOPPERY

Wait, he thought. I think I know what a stoppery is. It is based on the Celtic, I believe. A dialect word only comprehensible to someone who has a varied and broad background of liberal, humanistic information at his disposal. Other persons would walk right by.

It is, he thought, a place where deranged persons are apprehended and their activities curtailed. In a sense it's a sanitarium, but it goes much further than that. The aim is not to cure the ill and then return them to society—probably as ill as they ever were—but to close the final door on man's ignorance and folly. Here, at this point, the deranged preoccupations of the mentally ill come to an end; they *stop*, as the incised sign reads. They—the mentally ill who come here—are not returned to society, they are quietly and painlessly put to sleep. Which, ultimately, must be the fate for all who are incurably sick. Their poisons must not continue to contaminate the galaxy, he said to himself. Thank God there is such a place as this; I wonder why I wasn't notified of it vis-à-vis the trade journals.

I must go in, he decided. I want to see how they work. And let's find out what their legal basis is; there remains, after all, the sticky problem of the nonmedical authorities—if they could be called that—intervening and blocking the process of stoppery.

"Don't go in!" he yelled at Seth Morley and the religious nut Maggie Baggie. "This isn't for you; it's probably classified. Yes. See?" He pointed to the legend on the small aluminum door; it read: Trained personnel entrance only. "I can go in!" he yelled at them over the din, "but you can't! You're not qualified!" Both Maggie Baggie Haggie and Seth Morley looked at him in a startled way, but stopped. He pushed past them.

Without difficulty, Mary Morley perceived the writing over the entrance of the gray, large building.

WITCHERY

I know what it is, she said to herself, but they don't. A witchery is a place where the control of people is exercised by means of formulas and incantations. Those who rule are masters because of their contact with the witchery and its brews, its drugs.

"I'm going in there," she said to her husband.

Seth said, "Wait a minute. Just hold on."

"I can go in," she said, "but you can't. It's there for me. I know it. I don't want you to stop me; get out of the way."

She stood before the small door, reading the gold letters that adhered to the glass. Introductory chamber open to all qualified visitors, the door read. Well, that means me, she thought. It's speaking directly to me. That's what it means by "qualified."

"I'll go in with you," Seth said.

Mary Morley laughed. Go in with her? Amusing, she thought; he thinks they'll welcome him in the witchery. A man. This is only for women, she said to herself; there aren't any male witches.

After I've been in there, she realized, I'll know things by which I can control him; I can make him into what he ought to be, rather than what he is. So in a sense I'm doing it for his sake.

She reached for the knob of the door.

Ignatz Thugg stood off to one side, chuckling to see their antics. They howled and bleated like pigs. He felt like walking up and sticking them but who cared? I'll bet they stink when you get right up close to them, he told himself. They look so clean and underneath they stink. What is this poop place? He squinted, trying to read the jerky letters.

HIPPERY HOPPERY

Hey, he said to himself. That's swell; that's where they have people hop onto animals for youknowwhat. I always wanted to watch a horse and a woman make it together; I bet I can see that inside there. Yeah; I really want to see that, for everyone to watch. They show everything really good in there and like it really is.

And there'll be real people watching who I can talk to. Not like Morley and Walsh and Frazer using fatass words that're so long they sound like farting. They use words like that to make it look like their poop don't stink. But they're no different from me.

Maybe, he thought, they have fat asses, people like Babble, making it with big dogs. I'd like to see some of these fatassed people in there plugging away; I'd like to see that Walsh plugged by a Great Dane for once in her life. She'd probably love that. That's what she really wants out of life; she probably dreams about it.

"Get out of the way," he said to Morley and Walsh and Frazer. "You can't go in there. Look at what it says." He pointed to the words painted in classy gold on the glass window of the small door. Club members only. "I can go in," he said, and reached for the knob.

Going swiftly forward, Ned Russell interposed himself between them and the door. He glanced up at the class-one building, saw then on their various faces separate and intense cravings, and he said, "I think it would be better if none of us goes in."

"Why?" Seth Morley said, visibly disappointed. "What could be harmful in going into the tasting room of a winery?"

"It's not a winery," Ignatz Thugg said, and chortled with glee. "You read it wrong; you're afraid to admit what it really is." He chortled once again. "But I know."

" 'Winery'!" Maggie Walsh exclaimed. "It's not a winery, it's a symposium of the achievement of man's highest knowledge. If we go in there we'll be purified by God's love for man and man's love for God."

"It's a special club for certain people only," Thugg said.

Frazer said, with a smirk, "Isn't it amazing, the lengths people will go to in an unconscious effort to block their having to face reality. Isn't that correct, Russell?"

Russell said, "It's not safe in there. For any of us." I know now what it is, he said to himself, and I am right. I must get them—and myself—away from here. "Go," he said to them, forcefully and sternly. He remained there, not budging.

Some of their energy faded.

"You think so, really?" Seth Morley said.

"Yes," he said. "I think so."

To the others, Seth Morley said, "Maybe he's right."

"Do you really think so, Mr. Russell?" Maggie Walsh said in a faltering voice. They retreated from the door. Slightly. But enough.

Crushed, Ignatz Thugg said, "I knew they'd close it down. They don't want anyone to get any kickers out of life. It's always that way."

Russell said nothing; he stood there, blocking the door, and patiently waiting.

All at once Seth Morley said, "Where's Betty Jo Berm?"

Merciful God, Russell thought. I forgot her. I forgot to watch. He turned rapidly and, shielding his eyes, peered back the way they had come. Back at the sunlit, midday river.

She had seen again what she had seen before. Each time that she saw the Building she clearly made out the vast bronze plaque placed boldly above the central entrance.

MEKKISRY

As a linguist she had been able to translate it the first time around. *Mekkis*, the Hittite word for power; it had passed into the Sanskrit, then into Greek, Latin, and at last into modern English as *machine* and *mechanical*. This was the place denied her; she could not come here, as the rest of them could.

I wish I were dead, she said to herself.

Here was the font of the universe . . . at least as she understood it. She understood as literally true Specktowsky's theory of concentric circles of widening emanation. But to her it did not concern a Deity; she understood it as a statement of material fact, with no transcendental aspects. When she took a pill she rose, for a brief moment, into a higher, smaller circle of greater intensity and concentration of power. Her body weighed less; her ability, her motions, her animation—all functioned as if powered by a better fuel. I burn better, she said to herself as she turned and walked away from the Building, back toward the river. I am able to think more clearly; I am not clouded over as I am now, drooping under a foreign sun.

The water will help, she said to herself. Because in water you no longer have to support your heavy body; you are not lifted into greater *mekkis* but you do not care; the water erases everything. You are not heavy; you are not light. You are not even there.

I can't go on dragging my heavy body everywhere, she said to herself. The weight is too much. I cannot endure being pulled down any longer; I have to be free.

She stepped into the shallows. And walked out, toward the center. Without looking back.

The water, she thought, has now dissolved all the pills I carry; they are gone forever. But I no longer have any need for them. If I could enter the *Mekkisry* . . . maybe, without a body, I can, she thought. There to be remade. There to cease, and then begin all over. But starting at a different point. I do not want to go over again what I have gone over already, she told herself.

She could hear the vibrating roar of the *Mekkisry* behind her. The others are in there now, she realized. Why, she asked herself, is it this way? *Why can they go where I can't?* She did not know.

She did not care.

"There she is," Maggie Walsh said, pointing. Her hand shook. "Can't you see her?" She broke into motion, became unfrozen; she sprinted toward the river. But before she reached it Russell and Seth Morley passed her, leaving her behind. She began to cry, stopped running and stood there, watching through fragmented bits of crystal-like tears as Thugg and Wade Frazer caught up with Seth Morley and Russell; the four men, with Mary Morley trailing after them, rapidly waded out into the river, toward the black object drifting slightly toward the far side.

Standing there, she watched them carry Betty Jo's body from the water and up onto land. She's dead, she realized. While we argued about going into the *Wittery*. Goddam it, she thought brokenly. Then, halting, she made her way toward the five of them who now knelt around B.J.'s body, taking turns at giving mouth-to-mouth resuscitation.

She reached them. Stood. "Any chance?" she said.

"No," Wade Frazer said.

"Goddam it," she said, and her voice came out broken and lame. "Why did she do it? Frazer, do you know?"

"Some pressure that's built up over a long period of time," Frazer said.

Seth Morley stared at him with violence flaming in his eyes. "You fool," he said. "You stupid bastard fool."

"It's not my fault she's dead," Frazer chattered anxiously. "I didn't have enough testing apparatus to give anyone a really complete exam; if I had had what I wanted I could have uncovered and treated her suicidal tendencies."

"Can we carry her back to the settlement?" Maggie Walsh

said in a tear-stricken voice; she found herself almost unable to speak. "If you four men could carry her—"

"If we could float her down the river," Thugg said, "it'd be a lot less work. By river around half the time is cut off."

"We have nothing to float her on," Mary Morley said.

Russell said, "When we were crossing the river I saw what looked like a jury-rigged raft. I'll show you." He beckoned them to follow him to the river's edge.

There it lay, trapped into immobility by an extrusion of the river. It lay undulating slightly from the activity of the water, and Maggie Walsh thought, It almost looks as if it's here on purpose. For this reason: to carry one of us who has died back home.

"Belsnor's raft," Ignatz Thugg said.

"That's right," Frazer said, picking at his right ear. "He did say he was building a raft somewhere out here. Yes, you can see how he's lashed the logs together with heavy-duty electrical cable. I wonder if it's well-enough put together to be safe."

"If Glen Belsnor built it," Maggie said fiercely, "it's safe. Put her on it." And in the name of God be gentle, she said to herself. Be reverent. What you're carrying is holy.

The four men, grunting, instructing one another as to what to do and how to do it, managed at last to move the body of Betty Jo Berm onto Belsnor's raft.

She lay face up, her hands placed across her stomach. Her eyes sightlessly fixed on the harsh, midday sky. Water dribbled from her still, and her hair seemed to Maggie like some hive of black wasps which had fastened on an adversary, never again to let it go.

Attacked by death, she thought. The wasps of death. And the rest of us, she thought; when will it happen to us? Who will be the next? Maybe me, she thought. Yes, possibly me.

"We can all get on the raft with her," Russell said. To Maggie he said, "Do you know at what point we should leave the river?"

"I know," Frazer said, before she could answer.

"Okay," Russell said matter-of-factly. "Let's go." He guided Maggie and Mary Morley down the riverside and onto the raft; he touched the two women in a gentle manner, an attitude of chivalry which Maggie had not encountered in some time.

"Thank you," she said to him.

"Look at it," Seth Morley said, gazing back at the Building. The artificial background had already begun to phase into being; the Building wavered, real as it was. As the raft moved out into the river—pushed there by the four men—Maggie saw the huge gray wall of the Building fade into the far-off bronze of a counterfeit plateau.

The raft picked up speed as it entered the central current of the river. Maggie, seated by Betty Jo's wet body, shivered in the sun and shut her eyes. Oh God, she thought, help us get back to the settlement. Where is this river taking us? she asked herself. I've never seen it before; as far as I know it doesn't run near the settlement. We didn't walk along it to get here. Aloud, she said, "Why do you think this river will take us home? I think you've all taken leave of your senses."

"We can't carry her," Frazer said. "It's too far."

"But this is taking us farther and farther away," Maggie said. She was positive of it. "I want to get off!" she said, and scrambled to her feet in panic. The raft was moving too swiftly; she felt trapped fear as she saw the contours of the banks passing in such quick succession.

"Don't jump into the water," Russell said, taking her by the arm. "You'll be all right; we'll all be all right."

The raft continued to gather speed. Now no one spoke; they rode along quietly, feeling the sun, sensing the water . . . and all of them afraid and sobered by what had happened. And, Maggie Walsh thought, by what lies ahead.

"How did you know about the raft?" Seth Morley asked Russell.

"As I said, I saw it when we—"

"Nobody else saw it," Seth Morley broke in.

Russell said nothing.

"Are you a man or are you a Manifestation?" Seth Morley said.

"If I was a Manifestation of the Deity I would have saved her from drowning," Russell pointed out caustically. To Maggie Walsh he said, "Do you think I'm a Manifestation?"

"No," she said. How I wish you were, she thought. How badly we need intercession.

Bending, Russell touched Betty Jo Berm's black, dead, soaked hair. They continued on in silence.

*

Tony Dunkelwelt, shut up in his hot room, sat crosslegged on the floor and knew that he had killed Susie.

My miracle, he thought. It must have been the Form Destroyer who came when I called. It turned the bread into stone and then took the stone from her and killed her with it. The stone I made. No matter how you look at it, it goes back to me.

Listening, he heard no sound. Half the group had gone; the remaining half had sunk into oblivion. Maybe they're all gone now, he said to himself. I'm alone . . . left here to fall into the terrible paws of the Form Destroyer.

"I will take the Sword of Chemosh," he said aloud. "And slay the Form Destroyer with it." He held up his hand, groping for the Sword. He had seen it before during his meditations, but he had never touched it. "Give me the Sword of Chemosh," he said, "and I will do its work; I will seek out the Black One and murder it forever. It will never rise again."

He waited but saw nothing.

"Please," he said. And then he thought, I must merge more deeply into the universal self. I am still separate. He shut his eyes and compelled his body to relax. Receive, he thought; I must be clear enough and empty enough to have it pour into me. Once again I must be a hollow vessel. As so many, many times before.

But he could not do it now.

I am impure, he realized. So they send me nothing. By what I have done I've lost the capacity to accept and even to see. Will I never see the God-Above-God again? he asked himself. Has it all ended?

My punishment, he thought.

But I don't deserve it. Susie wasn't that important. She was demented; the stone left her in revulsion. That was it; the stone was pure and she was impure. But still, he thought, it's awful that she's dead. Brightness, mobility and light—Susie had all three. But it was a broken, fractured light which she gave off. A light which scorched and injured . . . me, for example. It was wrong for me. What I did I did in self-defense. It's obvious.

"The Sword," he said. "The Sword-wrath of Chemosh. Let it come to me." He rocked back and forth, reached up once again into the awesomeness above him. His hand groped, disappeared; he watched it as it vanished. His fingers fumbled in empty space, a million miles into the emptiness, the hollowness above man . . . he continued to grope on and on, and then, abruptly, his fingers touched something.

Touched—but did not grasp.

I swear, he said to himself, that if I am given the Sword I will use it. I will avenge her death.

Again he touched but did not grasp. I know it is there, he thought; I can feel it with my fingers. "Give it to me!" he said aloud. "I swear that I'll use it!" He waited, and then, into his empty hand, was placed something hard, heavy and cold.

The Sword. He held it.

He drew the Sword downward, carefully. God-like, it blazed with heat and light; it filled the room with its authority. He at once leaped up, almost dropping the Sword. I have it now, he said to himself joyfully. He ran to the door of the room, the Sword wobbling in his meager grip. Pushing open the door he emerged in the midday light; gazing around he said, "Where are you, mighty Form Destroyer, you decayer of life? Come and fight with me!"

A shape moved clumsily, slowly along the porch. A bent shape which crept blindly, as if accustomed to the darkness within the Earth. It looked up at him with filmed-over gray eyes; he saw and understood the shirt of dust which clung to it . . . dust trickled silently down its bent body and drifted into the air. And it left a fine trail of dust as it moved.

It was badly decayed. Yellowed, wrinkled skin covered its brittle bones. Its cheeks were sunken and it had no teeth. The Form Destroyer hobbled forward, seeing him; as it hobbled it wheezed to itself and squeaked a few wretched words. Now its dry-skin hand groped for him and it rasped, "Hey there, Tony. Hey there. How are you?"

"Are you coming to meet me?" he said.

"Yes," it gasped, and came a step closer. He smelled it, now; mixture of fungus-breath and the rot of centuries. It did not have long to live. Plucking at him it cackled; saliva ran down its chin and dripped onto the floor. It tried to wipe the saliva away with the crust-like back of its hand, but could not. "I want you—" it started to say, and then he stuck the Sword of Chemosh into its paunchy, soft middle.

Handfuls of worms, white pulpy worms, oozed out of it as he withdrew the Sword. Again it laughed its dry cackle; it stood there swaying, one arm and hand groping for him . . . he stepped back and looked away as the worms grew in a pile before it. It had no blood: it was a sack of corruption and nothing more.

It sank down onto one knee, still cackling. Then, in a kind of convulsion, it clawed at its hair. Between its grasping fingers strands of long, lusterless hair appeared; it tore the hair from itself, then held it in his direction, as if it meant to give him something priceless.

He stabbed it again. Now it lay, sightlessly; its eyes gummed over entirely and its mouth fell open.

From its mouth a single furry organism, like an inordinately large spider, crawled. He stepped on it and, under his foot, it lay mashed into oblivion.

I have killed the Form Destroyer, he said.

From far off, on the other side of the compound, a voice carried to him. "*Tony!*" A shape came running. At first he could not tell who or what it was; he shielded his eyes from the sun and strained to see.

Glen Belsnor. Running as fast as he could.

"I killed the Form Destroyer," Tony said as Belsnor dashed up onto the porch, his chest heaving. "See?" He pointed, with his Sword, at the crippled shape lying between them; it had drawn up its legs and entered, at the moment of its death, a fetal position.

"That's Bert Kosler!" Belsnor shouted, panting for breath. "You killed an old man!"

"No," he said, and looked down. He saw Bert Kosler, the settlement's custodian, lying there. "He fell into the possession of the Form Destroyer," he said, but he did not believe it—he saw what he had done, knew what he had done. "I'm sorry," he said. "I'll ask the God-Above-God to bring him back." He turned and ran into his room; locking the door he stood there shaking. Nausea flung itself up into his throat; he gagged, blinked . . . deep pains filled his stomach and he had to bend over, groaning with pain. The Sword fell heavily from him, onto the floor; its clank frightened him and he retreated a few steps, leaving it to lie there.

"Open the door!" Glen Belsnor yelled from outside.

"No," he said, and his teeth chattered; terrible cold dashed through his arms and legs; the cold knotted itself into the nausea in his stomach, and the pains became greater.

At the door a terrible crash sounded; the door hesitated and creaked, then abruptly threw itself open.

Glen Belsnor stood there, gray-haired and grim, holding a military pistol pointed directly into the room. Directly at Tony Dunkelwelt.

Bending, Tony Dunkelwelt reached to pick up the Sword.

"Don't," Glen Belsnor said, "or I'll kill you."

His hand closed over the handle of the Sword.

Glen Belsnor fired at him. Pointblank.

Ten

As the raft drifted downstream, Ned Russell stood staring off in the distance, cloaked by his own thoughts.

"What are you looking for?" Seth Morley asked him.

Russell pointed. "There, I see one." He turned to Maggie. "Isn't that one of them?"

"Yes," she said. "The Grand Tench. Or else one almost as large as he."

"What kind of questions have you asked them?" Russell said.

Showing surprise, Maggie said, "We don't ask them anything; we have no way of communicating with them—they don't have a language or vocal organs insofar as we can determine."

"Telepathically?" Russell said.

"They're not telepathic," Wade Frazer said. "And neither are we. All they do is print duplicates of objects . . . which puddle in a few days."

"They can be communicated with," Russell said. "Let's steer this raft over into the shallows; I want to consult with your tench." He slid from the raft, into the water. "All of you get off and help me guide it." He seemed determined; his face was relatively firm. So, one by one, they slid into the water, leaving only B.J.'s silent body aboard the raft.

In a matter of minutes they had pushed the raft up against the grass-covered shore. They moored it firmly—by shoving it deep into the gray mud—and then crawled up onto the bank.

The cube of gelatinous mass towered over them as they approached it. The sunlight danced in a multitude of flecks, as if caught within it. The interior of the organism glowed with activity.

It's bigger than I expected, Seth Morley said to himself. It looks—ageless. How long do they live? he wondered.

"You put articles in front of it," Ignatz Thugg said, "and it pushes a hunk of itself out, and then that hunk forms into a duplicate. Here, I'll show you." He tossed his wet wristwatch onto the ground before the tench. "Duplicate that, you jello," he said.

The gelatin undulated, and presently, as Thugg had predicted, a section of it oozed out to come to rest beside the watch. The color of the production altered; it became silver-like. And then it flattened. Design appeared in the silver-substance. Several more minutes passed, as if the tench were resting, and then all at once the excreted product sank into the shape of a leather-bound disk. It looked exactly like the true watch beside it . . . or rather almost exactly, Seth Morley noted. It was not as bright; it had a dulled quality. But—it was still basically a success.

Russell seated himself in the grass and began to search through his pockets. "I need a dry piece of paper," he said.

"I have some in my purse that're still dry," Maggie Walsh said. She rummaged in her purse, handed him a small tablet. "Do you need a pen?"

"I've got a pen." He wrote darkly on the top sheet of paper. "I'm asking it questions." He finished writing, held the sheet of paper up, and read from it. " 'How many of us will die here at Delmak-O?' " He folded the paper and placed it before the tench, next to the two wristwatches.

More of the tench's gelatin burbled out, to come to rest in a mound beside Russell's piece of paper.

"Won't it simply duplicate the question?" Seth Morley asked.

"I don't know," Russell said. "We'll see."

Thugg said, "I think you're barmy."

Eying him, Russell said, "You have a strange idea, Thugg, of what's 'barmy' and what isn't."

"Is that meant to be an insult?" Thugg flushed an angry red.

Maggie Walsh said, "Look. The duplicate piece of paper is forming."

Two folded sheets of tablet paper rested directly in front of the tench. Russell waited a moment, then, evidently deciding that the duplicating process had finished, took the two sheets, unfolded both of them, studied them for a long time.

"Did it answer?" Seth Morley said. "Or did it repeat the question?"

"It answered." Russell handed him one of the sheets of paper.

The note was short and simple. And impossible to misinterpret. *You will go out onto your compound and not see your people.*

"Ask it who our enemy is," Seth Morley said.

"Okay." Russell wrote again, placed the sheet of paper, folded, before the tench. "'Who is our enemy?'" he said. "That's so to speak the ultimate question."

The tench fashioned an answering slip, which Russell at once grabbed. He studied it intently, then read it aloud. "*Influential circles.*"

"That doesn't tell us much," Maggie Walsh said.

Russell said, "Evidently that's all it knows."

"Ask it, 'What should we do?'" Seth Morley said.

Russell wrote that, again placing the question before the tench. Presently he had the answer; again he prepared to read aloud. "This is a long one," he said apologetically.

"Good," Wade Frazer said. "Considering the nature of the question."

Russell read, "*There are secret forces at work, leading together those who belong together. We must yield to this attraction; then we make no mistakes.*" He pondered. "We shouldn't have split up; the seven of us shouldn't have left the settlement. If we had stayed there Miss Berm would still be alive. It's obvious that from now on we must keep one another in visual sight all the—" He broke off. An additional glob of gelatin was extruding from the tench. Like those before, it formed into a folded slip of paper. Russell took it, opened and read it. "Addressed to you," he said, and handed it to Seth Morley.

"*Often a man feels an urge to unite with others, but the individuals around him have already formed themselves into a group, so that he remains isolated. He should then ally himself with a man who stands nearer to the center of the group and can help him gain admission to the closed circle.*" Seth Morley crumpled up the slip of paper and dropped it onto the ground. "That would be Belsnor," he said. "The man who stands nearer to the center." It's true, he thought; I am outside and isolated. But in a sense all of us are. Even Belsnor.

"Maybe it means me," Russell said.

"No," Seth Morley said. "It's Glen Belsnor."

Wade Frazer said, "I have a question." He held out his hand and Russell passed him the pen and paper. Frazer wrote rapidly, then, finished, read them his question. "'Who or what is the man calling himself Ned Russell?'" He placed that question in front of the tench.

When the answer appeared, Russell took it. Smoothly and without effort; one moment it lay there and the next he had it in his hand. Calmly, he read it to himself. Then, at last, he passed it to Seth Morley and said, "You read it aloud."

Seth Morley did so. "*Every step, forward or backward, leads into danger. Escape is out of the question. The danger comes because one is too ambitious.*" He handed the slip over to Wade Frazer.

"It doesn't tell us a damn thing," Ignatz Thugg said.

"It tells us that Russell is creating a situation in which every move is a losing move," Wade Frazer said. "Danger is everywhere and we can't escape. And the cause is Russell's ambition." He eyed Russell long and searchingly. "What's your ambition all about? And why are you deliberately leading us into danger?"

Russell said, "It doesn't say I'm leading you into danger, it just says that the danger exists."

"What about your ambition? It's plainly referring to you."

"The only ambition I have," Russell said, "is to be a competent economist, doing useful work. That's why I asked for a work-transfer; the job I was doing—through no fault of my own—was insipid and worthless. That's why I was so glad to be transferred here to Delmak-O." He added, "My opinion has somewhat changed since I arrived here."

"So has ours," Seth Morley said.

"Okay," Frazer said fussily. "We've learned a little from the tench but not much. All of us will be killed." He smiled a mirthless, bitter smile. "Our enemy is 'influential circles.' We must stay in close proximity to one another, otherwise they'll knock us off one by one." He pondered. "And we're in danger, from every direction; nothing we can do will change that. And Russell is a hazard to us, due to his ambition." He turned toward Seth Morley and said, "Have you noticed how he's already taken over as leader of the six of us? As if it's natural to him."

"It is natural to me," Russell said.

"So the tench is right," Frazer said.

After a pause, Russell nodded. "I suppose so, yes. But someone has to lead."

"When we get back," Seth Morley said, "will you resign and accept Glen Belsnor as the group's leader?"

"If he's competent."

Frazer said, "We elected Glen Belsnor. He's our leader whether you like it or not."

"But," Russell said, "I didn't get a chance to vote." He smiled. "So I don't consider myself bound by it."

"I'd like to ask the tench a couple of questions," Maggie Walsh said. She took the pen and paper and wrote painstakingly. "I'm asking, 'Why are we alive?'" She placed the paper before the tench and waited.

The answer, when they had obtained it, read:

To be in the fullness of possession and at the height of power.

"Cryptic," Wade Frazer said. "'The fullness of possession and the height of power.' Interesting. Is that what life's all about?"

Again Maggie wrote. "I'm now asking, 'Is there a God?'" She placed the slip before the tench and all of them, even Ignatz Thugg, waited tensely.

The answer came.

You would not believe me.

"What's that mean?" Ignatz Thugg said hotly. "It doesn't mean nothing; that's what it means. Doesn't mean."

"But it's the truth," Russell pointed out. "If it said no, you wouldn't believe it. Would you?" He turned questioningly toward Maggie.

"Correct," she said.

"And if it said there was?"

"I already believe it."

Russell, satisfied, said, "So the tench is right. It makes no difference to any of us what it says in answer to a question like that."

"But if it said yes," Maggie said, "then I could be sure."

"You are sure," Seth Morley said.

"Sweet Jesus," Thugg said. "The raft is on fire."

Leaping up they saw flames billowing and leaping; they heard now the crackle of the wood as it heated up, burned, became glowing ash. The six of them sprinted toward the river . . . but, Seth Morley realized, we're too late.

Standing on the bank they watched helplessly; the burning raft had begun to drift out into the center of the water. It reached the current and, still engulfed by fire, it drifted downstream, became smaller, became, at last, a spark of yellow fire. And then they could no longer see it.

After a time Ned Russell said, "We shouldn't feel badly. That's the old Norse way of celebrating death. The dead Viking was laid on his shield, on his boat, and the boat was set on fire and sent drifting out to sea."

Meditating, Seth Morley thought, *Vikings*. A river, and, beyond it, a mystifying building. The river would be the Rhein and the Building would be Walhalla. That would explain why the raft, with Betty Jo Berm's body on it, caught fire and drifted away. Eerie, he thought, and shivered.

"What's the matter?" Russell asked, seeing his face.

"For a moment," he said, "I thought I understood." But it couldn't be; there had to be another explanation.

The tench, answering questions, would be—he could not remember her name, and then it came to him. Erda. The goddess of the earth who knew the future. Who answered questions brought to her by Wotan.

And Wotan, he thought, walks among the mortals in disguise. Recognizable only by the fact that he had but one eye. The Wanderer, he is called.

"How's your vision?" he asked Russell. "Twenty-twenty in both eyes?"

Startled, Russell said, "No—actually not, as a matter of fact. Why do you ask?"

"One of his eyes is false," Wade Frazer said. "I've been noticing. The right one is artificial; it sees nothing, but the muscles operate it, moving it as if it were real."

"Is that true?" Seth Morley asked.

"Yes." Russell nodded. "But it's none of your business."

And Wotan, Seth Morley recalled, destroyed the gods, brought on *die Götterdämmerung*, by his ambition. What was his ambition? To build the castle of the gods: Walhalla. Well, Walhalla had been built, all right; it bore the legend *Winery*. But it was not a winery.

And, at the end, he thought, it will sink into the Rhein and disappear. And the Rheingold will return to the Rhein Maidens.

But that has not happened yet, he reflected.

Specktowsky had not mentioned *this* in his Book!

*

Trembling, Glen Belsnor laid the pistol down on the chest of drawers to his right. Before him on the floor, still clutching the great golden sword, lay Tony Dunkelwelt. A tiny flow of blood from his mouth trickled down his cheek and drip-dripped onto the handmade rug which covered the plastic floor.

Having heard the shot, Dr. Babble came running up. Puffing and wheezing he halted at Bert Kosler's body on the porch, turned the withered old body over, examined the sword wound . . . then, seeing Glen Belsnor, he entered the room. Together the two of them stood gazing down.

"I shot him," Glen Belsnor said. His ears still rang from the noise of the shot; it had been an ancient lead slug pistol, part of his collection of odds and ends that he carried everywhere he went. He pointed out onto the porch. "You saw what he did to old Bert."

"And he was going to stab you, too?" Babble asked.

"Yes." Glen Belsnor got out his handkerchief and blew his nose; his hand shook and he felt satanically miserable. "What a hell of a thing," he said, and heard his voice wobble with grief. "To kill a kid. But Christ—he would have gotten me, then you, and then Mrs. Rockingham." The thought of anyone killing the distinguished old lady . . . that, more than any-thing else, had prompted him to act. *He* could have run away; so could Babble. But not Mrs. Rockingham.

Babble said, "Obviously, it was Susie Smart's death that made him psychotic, that brought on his break with reality. He un-doubtedly blamed himself for it." He stooped, picked up the sword. "I wonder where he got this. I've never seen it before."

"He always was on the verge of a breakdown," Glen Belsnor said. "With those goddam 'trances' he went into. He probably heard the voice of God telling him to kill Bert."

"Did he say anything? Before you killed him?"

" 'I killed the Form Destroyer.' That's what he said. And then he pointed at Bert's body and said, 'See?' Or something like that." He shrugged weakly. "Well, Bert was very old. Very much decayed. The handiwork of the Form Destroyer was all over him, God knows. Tony seemed to recognize me. But he was completely insane anyhow. It was all crap he was saying, and then he went for the sword."

They were both silent for a time.

"Four dead now," Babble said. "Maybe more."

"Why do you say 'maybe more'?"

Babble said, "I'm thinking of those who left the settlement this morning. Maggie, the new man Russell, Seth and Mary Morley—"

"They're probably all right." But he did not believe his own words. "No," he said savagely, "they're probably all dead. Maybe all seven of them?"

"Try to calm down," Babble said; he seemed a little afraid. "Is that gun of yours still loaded?"

"Yes." Glen Belsnor picked it up, emptied it, handed the shells to Babble. "You can keep them. No matter what happens I'm not going to shoot anyone else. Not even to save one of the rest of us or all of the rest of us." He made his way to a chair, seated himself, clumsily got out a cigarette and lit up.

"If there's a court of inquiry," Babble said, "I'll be glad to testify that Tony Dunkelwelt was psychiatrically insane. But I can't testify to his killing old Bert, or attacking you. I mean to say, I have only your verbal report for that." He added quickly, "But of course I believe you."

"There won't be any inquiry." He knew it as an absolute verity; there was no doubt in him on that score. "Except," he said, "a posthumous one. Which won't matter to us."

"Are you keeping a log of some sort?" Babble asked.

"No."

"You should."

"Okay," he snarled, "I will. But just leave me alone, goddam it!" He glared at Babble, panting with anger. "Lay off!"

"Sorry," Babble said in a small voice, and shrank perceptibly away.

Glen Belsnor said, "You and I and Mrs. Rockingham may be the only ones alive." He felt it intuitively, in a rush of comprehension.

"Perhaps we should round her up and stay with her. So that nothing happens to her." Babble cringed his way to the door.

"Okay." He nodded irritably. "You know what I'm going to

do? You go stay with Mrs. Rockingham; I'm going to go over Russell's possessions and his noser. Ever since you and Morley brought him around last night I've been wondering about him. He seems odd. Did you get that impression?"

"It's just that he's new here."

"I didn't feel that way about Ben Tallchief. Or the Morleys." He got abruptly to his feet. "You know what occurred to me? *Maybe he picked up the aborted signal from the satellite.* I want to get a good look at his transmitter and receiver." Back to what I know, he pondered. Where I don't feel so alone.

Leaving Babble, he made his way toward the area in which all the nosers lay parked. He did not look back.

The signal from the satellite, he reasoned, short as it was, may have brought him here. He may have been already in the area, not on his way here but preparing a flyby. And yet he had transfer papers. The hell with it, he thought, and began taking apart the radio equipment of Russell's noser.

Fifteen minutes later he knew the answer. Standard receiver and transmitter, exactly like the others in all their other nosers. Russell would not have been able to pick up the satellite's signal because it was a flea-signal. Only the big receiver on Delmak-O could have monitored it. Russell had come in on the automatic pilot, like everybody else. And in the way that everybody else arrived.

So much for that, he said to himself.

Most of Russell's possessions remained aboard the noser; he had only carried his personal articles from the noser to his living quarters. A big box of books. Everybody had books. Glen Belsnor idly tossed the books about, prowling deep in the carton. Textbook after textbook on economics; that figured. Microtapes of several of the great classics, including Tolkien, Milton, Virgil, Homer. All the epics, he realized. Plus *War and Peace*, as well as tapes of John Dos Passos' *U.S.A.* I always meant to read that, he said to himself.

Nothing about the books and tapes struck him as odd. Except—

No copy of Specktowsky's Book.

Maybe Russell, like Maggie Walsh, had memorized it.

Maybe not.

There was one class of people who did not carry a copy of Specktowsky's Book—did not carry it because they were not allowed to read it. The ostriches shut up in the planetwide aviary at Terra: those who lived in the sandpile because they had crumbled under the enormous psychological pressure suffered while emigrating. Since all the other planets of the Sol System were uninhabitable, emigration meant a trip to another star system . . . and the insidious beginning, for many, of the space illness of loneliness and uprootedness.

Maybe he recovered, Glen Belsnor reflected, and they let him loose. But they then would have made sure he owned a copy of Specktowsky's Book; that would be the time when one really needed it.

He got away, he said to himself.

But why would he come here?

And then he thought, The Interplan West base, where General Treaton operates, is on Terra, tangent to the aviary. What a coincidence. The place, evidently, where all the nonliving organisms on Delmak-O had been constructed. As witness the inscription in the tiny replica of the Building.

In a sense it fits together, he decided. But in another sense it adds up to zero. Plain, flat zero.

These deaths, he said to himself, they're making me insane, too. Like they did poor nutty Tony Dunkelwelt. But suppose: a psychological lab, operated by Interplan West, needing aviary patients as subjects. They recruit a batch—those bastards would, too—and one of them is Ned Russell. He's still insane, but they can teach him; the insane can learn, too. They give him a job and send him out to do it—send him here.

And then a gross, vivid, terrifying thought came to him. *Suppose we're all ostriches from the aviary,* he said to himself. Suppose we don't know; Interplan West cut a memory conduit in our friggin' brains. That would explain our inability to function as a group. That's why we can't really even talk clearly to one another. The insane can learn, but one thing they can't do is to function collectively . . . except, perhaps, as a mob. But that is not really functioning in the sane sense; that is merely mass insanity.

So we *are* an experiment, then, he thought. I now know what we wanted to know. And it might explain why I have that tattoo stuck away on my right instep, that Persus 9.

But all this was a great deal to base on one slim datum: the fact that Russell did not possess a copy of Specktowsky's Book.

Maybe it's in his goddam living quarters, he thought all at once. Christ, of course; it's *there*.

He departed from the assembly of nosers; ten minutes later he reached the common and found himself stepping up onto the porch. The porch where Susie Smart had died—opposite to the porch where Tony Dunkelwelt and old Bert had died.

We must bury them! he realized. —And shrank from it.

But first: I'll look at Russell's remaining stuff.

The door was locked.

With a prybar—taken from his rolypoly aggregate of worldly goods, his great black crowish conglomeration of junk and treasures—he forced open the door.

There, in plain sight, on the rumpled bed, lay Russell's wallet and papers. His transfer, his everything else, back to his birth certificate; Glen Belsnor pawed through them, conscious that here he had something. The chaos attendant on Susie's death had confused them all; undoubtedly Russell had not meant to leave these here. Unless he was not accustomed to carrying them . . . and the ostriches at the aviary did not carry identification of any sort.

At the door appeared Dr. Babble. In a voice shrill with panic he said, "I—can't find Mrs. Rockingham."

"The briefing room? The cafeteria?" She may have gone off for a walk, he thought. But he knew better. Roberta Rockingham could scarcely walk; her cane was essential to her, due to a long-term circulatory ailment. "I'll help look," he grunted; he and Babble hurried from the porch and across the common, hiking aimlessly; Glen Belsnor stopped, realizing that they were simply running in fear. "We have to think," he gasped. "Wait a minute." Where the hell might she be? he asked himself. "That fine old woman," he said in frenzy and in despair. "She never did any harm to anyone in her life. Goddam them, whoever they are."

Babble nodded glumly.

She had been reading. Hearing a noise, she glanced up. And saw a man, unfamiliar to her, standing in the entrance-way of her small, neatly-arranged room.

"Yes?" she said, politely lowering her microtape scanner. "Are you a new member of the settlement? I haven't seen you before, have I?"

"No, Mrs. Rockingham," he said. His voice was kind and very pleasant, and he wore a leather uniform, complete with huge leather gloves. His face gave off a near radiance . . . or perhaps her glasses had steamed up, she wasn't sure. His hair, cut short, did gleam a little, she was positive of that. What a nice expression he has, she declared to herself. So thoughtful, as if he has thought and done many wonderful things.

"Would you like a little bourbon and water?" she asked. Toward afternoon she generally had one drink; it eased the perpetual ache in her legs. Today, however, they could enjoy the Old Crow bourbon a little earlier.

"Thank you," the man said. Tall, and very slender, he stood at the doorway, not coming fully in. It was as if he were in some way attached to the outside; he could not fully leave it and would soon go back to it entirely. I wonder, she thought, could he be a Manifestation, as the theological people of this enclave call it? She peered at him in an effort to distinguish him more clearly, but the dust on her glasses—or whatever it was—obscured him; she could not get a really clear view.

"I wonder if you might get it," she said, pointing. "There's a drawer in that somewhat shabby little table by the bed. You'll find the bottle of Old Crow in there, and three glasses. Oh dear; I don't have any soda. Can you enjoy it with just bottled tapwater? And no ice?"

"Yes," he said, and walked lightly across her room. He had on tall boots, she observed. How very attractive.

"What is your name?" she inquired.

"Sergeant Ely Nichols." He opened the table drawer, got out the bourbon and two of the glasses. "Your colony has been relieved. I was sent here to pick you up and fly you home. From the start they were aware of the malfunctioning of the satellite's tape-transmission."

"Then it's over?" she said, filled with joy.

"All over," he said. He filled the two glasses with bourbon and water, brought her hers, seated himself in a straight-backed chair facing her. He was smiling.

Eleven

GLEN BELSNOR, searching futilely for Roberta Rockingham, saw a small number of people trudging toward the settlement. Those who had gone off: Frazer and Thugg, Maggie Walsh, the new man Russell, Mary and Seth Morley . . . they were all there. Or were they?

His heart laboring, Belsnor said, "I don't see Betty Jo Berm. Is she injured? You left her, you bastards?" He stared at them, feeling his jaw tremble with impotent anger. "Is that correct?"

"She's dead," Seth Morley said.

"How?" he said. Dr. Babble came up beside him; the two of them waited together as the four men and two women approached.

Seth Morley said, "She drowned herself." He looked around. "Where's that kid, that Dunkelwold?"

"Dead," Dr. Babble said.

Maggie Walsh said, "And Bert Kosler?"

Neither Babble nor Belsnor answered.

"Then he's dead, too," Russell said.

"That's right." Belsnor nodded. "There're eight of us left. Roberta Rockingham—she's gone. So possibly she's dead, too. I think we'll have to assume she is."

"Didn't you stay together?" Russell said.

"Did you?" Glen Belsnor answered.

Again there was silence. Somewhere, far off, a warm wind blew dust and infirm lichens about; a swirl lifted above the main buildings of the settlement and then writhed off and gone. The air, as Glen Belsnor sucked it in noisily, smelled bad. As if, he thought, the skins of dead dogs are drying somewhere on a line.

Death, he thought. That's all I can think of now. And it's easy to see why. Death for us has blotted everything else out; it has become, in less than twenty-four hours, the mainstay of our life.

"You couldn't bring her body back?" he said to them.

"It drifted downstream," Seth Morley said. "And it was on

fire." He came up beside Belsnor and said, "How did Bert Kosler die?"

"Tony stabbed him."

"What about Tony?"

Glen Belsnor said, "I shot him. Before he could kill me."

"What about Roberta Rockingham? Did you shoot her, too?"

"No," Belsnor said shortly.

"I think," Frazer said, "we're going to have to pick a new leader."

Belsnor said woodenly, "I had to shoot him. He would have killed all the rest of us. Ask Babble, he'll back me up."

"I can't back you up," Babble said. "I have nothing more to go on than they do. I have only your oral statement."

Seth Morley said, "What was Tony using as a weapon?"

"A sword," Belsnor said. "You can see that; it's still there with him in his room."

"Where did you get the gun you shot him with?" Russell said.

"I had it," Belsnor said. He felt sick and weak. "I did what I could," he said. "I did what I had to."

"So 'they' aren't responsible for all the deaths," Seth Morley said. "You are responsible for Tony Dunkelwold's death and he's responsible for Bert's."

"Dunkelwelt," Belsnor corrected, aimlessly.

"And we don't know if Mrs. Rockingham is dead; she may just have roamed off. Possibly out of fear."

"She couldn't," Belsnor said. "She was too ill."

"I think," Seth Morley said, "that Frazer is right. We need a different leader." To Babble he said, "Where's his gun?"

"He left it in Tony's room," Babble said.

Belsnor slid away from them, in the direction of Tony Dunkelwelt's living quarters.

"Stop him," Babble said.

Ignatz Thugg, Wade Frazer, Seth Morley and Babble hurried past Belsnor; in a group they trotted up the steps and onto the porch and then into Tony's quarters. Russell stood aloof; he remained with Belsnor and Maggie Walsh.

Coming out of Tony's doorway, Seth Morley held the gun

in his hand and said, "Russell, don't you think we're doing the right thing?"

"Give him back his gun," Russell said.

Surprised, Seth Morley halted. But he did not bring the gun over to Belsnor. "Thanks," Belsnor said to Russell. "I can use the support." To Morley and the others he said, "Give me the gun, as Russell says. It isn't loaded anyhow; I took the shells out." He held out his hand and waited.

Coming back down the steps from the porch, and still carrying the gun, Seth Morley said with grave reservations, "You killed someone."

"He had to," Russell said.

"I'm keeping the gun," Seth Morley said.

"My husband is going to be your leader," Mary Morley said. "I think it's a very good idea; I think you'll find him excellent. At Tekel Upharsin he held a position of large authority."

"Why don't you join them?" Belsnor said to Russell.

"Because I know what happened. I know what you had to do. If I can manage to talk to them maybe I can—" He broke off. Belsnor turned toward the group of men to see what was happening.

Ignatz Thugg held the gun. He had grabbed it away from Morley; now he held it pointed at Belsnor, a seedy, twisted grin on his face.

"Give it back," Seth Morley said to him; all of them were shouting at Thugg, but he stood unmoved, still pointing the gun at Belsnor.

"I'm your leader, now," Thugg said. "With or without a vote. You can vote me in if you want, but it doesn't matter." To the three men around him he said, "You go over there where they are. Don't get too close to me. You understand?"

"It's not loaded," Belsnor repeated.

Seth Morley looked crushed, his face had a pale, dry cast to it, as if he knew—obviously he knew—that he had been responsible for Thugg getting possession of the gun.

Maggie Walsh said, "I know what to do." She reached into her pocket and brought out a copy of Specktowsky's Book.

In her mind she knew that she had found the way to get the gun away from Ignatz Thugg. Opening The Book at random

she walked toward him, and as she walked she read aloud from
The Book. " 'Hence it can be said,' " she intoned, " 'that God-
in-history shows several phases: (one) The period of purity
before the Form Destroyer was awakened into activity. (two)
The period of the Curse, when the power of the Deity was
weakest, the power of the Form Destroyer the greatest—this
because God had not perceived the Form Destroyer and so
was taken by surprise. (three) The birth of God-on-Earth, sign
that the period of Absolute Curse and Estrangement from God
had ended. (four) The period now—' " She had come almost
up to him; he stood unmoving, still holding the gun. She continued to read the sacred text aloud. " 'The period now, in
which God walks the world, redeeming the suffering now, redeeming all life later through the figure of himself as the Intercessor who—' "

"Go back with them," Thugg told her. "Or I'll kill you."

" 'Who, it is sure, is still alive, but not in this circle. (five)
The next and last period—' "

A terrific *bang* boomed at her eardrums; deafened, she moved
a step back and then she felt great pain in her chest; she felt her
lungs die from the great, painful shock of it. The scene around
her became dull, the light faded and she saw only darkness.
Seth Morley, she tried to say, but no sound came out. And yet
she heard noise; she heard something huge and far off, chugging violently into the darkness.

She was alone.

Thud, thud, came the noise. Now she saw iridescent color,
mixed into a light which traveled like a liquid; it formed buzz-
saws and pinwheels and crept upward on each side of her. Directly before her the huge Thing throbbed menacingly; she
heard its imperative, angry voice summoning her upward. The
urgency of its activity frightened her; it demanded, rather than
asked. It was telling her something; she knew what it meant by
its enormous pounding. Wham, wham, wham, it went and,
terrified, filled with physical pain, she called to it. "Libera me,
Domine," she said. "De morte aeterna, in die illa tremenda."

It throbbed on and on. And she glided helplessly toward it.
Now, on the periphery of her vision, she saw a fantastic spectacle; she saw a great crossbow and on it the Intercessor. The
string was pulled back; the Intercessor was placed on it like an

arrow; and then, soundlessly, the Intercessor was shot upward, into the smallest of the concentric rings.

"Agnus Dei," she said, "qui tollis peccata mundi." She had to look away from the throbbing vortex; she looked down and back . . . and saw, far below her, a vast frozen landscape of snow and boulders. A furious wind blew across it; as she watched, more snow piled up around the rocks. A new period of glaciation, she thought, and found that she had trouble thinking—let alone talking—in English. "Lacrymosa dies illa," she said, gasping with pain; her entire chest seemed to have become a block of suffering. "Qua resurget ex favilla, judicandus homo reus." It seemed to make the pain less, this need to express herself in Latin—a language which she had never studied and knew nothing about. "Huic ergo parce, Deus!" she said. "Pie Jesu Domine, dona eis requiem." The throbbing continued on.

A chasm opened before her feet. She began to fall; below her the frozen landscape of the hell-world grew closer. Again she cried out, "Libera me, Domine, de morte aeterna!" But still she fell; she had almost reached the hell-world, and nothing meant to lift her up.

Something with immense wings soared up, like a great, metallic dragon fly with spines jutting from its head. It passed her, and a warm wind billowed after it. "Salve me, fons pietatis," she called to it; she recognized it and felt no surprise at seeing it. The Intercessor, fluttering up from the hell-world, back to the fire of the smaller, inner rings.

Lights, in various colors, bloomed on all sides of her; she saw a red, smoky light burning close and, confused, turned toward it. But something made her pause. *The wrong color*, she thought to herself. I should be looking for a clear, white light, the proper womb in which to be reborn. She drifted upward, carried by the warm wind of the Intercessor . . . the smoky red light fell behind and in its place, to her right, she saw a powerful, unflickering, yellow light. As best she could she propelled herself toward that.

The pain in her chest seemed to have lessened; in fact her entire body felt vague. Thank you, she thought, for easing the discomfort; I appreciate that. I have seen it, she said to herself; I have seen the Intercessor and through it I have a chance of surviving. Lead me, she thought. Take me to the proper color of light. To the right new birth.

The clear, white light appeared. She yearned toward it, and something helped propel her. Are you angry at me? she thought, meaning the enormous presence that throbbed. She could still hear the throbbing, but it was no longer meant for her; it would throb on throughout eternity because it was beyond time, outside of time, never having been in time. And —there was no space present, either; everything appeared two dimensional and squeezed together, like robust but crude figures drawn by a child or by some primitive man. Bright colorful figures, but absolutely flat . . . and touching.

"Mors stupebit et natura," she said aloud. "Cum resurget creatura, judicanti responsura." Again the throbbing lessened. It has forgiven me, she said to herself. It is letting the Intercessor carry me to the right light.

Toward the clear, white light she floated, still uttering from time to time pious Latin phrases. The pain in her chest had gone now entirely and she felt no weight; her body had ceased to consume both time and space.

Wheee, she thought. This is marvelous.

Throb, throb, went the Central Presence, but no longer for her; it throbbed for others, now.

The Day of the Final Audit had come for her—had come and now had passed. She had been judged and the judgment was favorable. She experienced utter, absolute joy. And continued, like a moth among novas, to flutter upward toward the proper light.

"I didn't mean to kill her," Ignatz Thugg said huskily. He stood gazing down at the body of Maggie Walsh. "I didn't know what she was going to do. I mean, she kept walking and walking; I thought she was after the gun." He jerked an accusing shoulder toward Glen Belsnor. "And he said it was empty."

Russell said, "She was going for the gun; you're right."

"Then I didn't do wrong," Thugg said.

No one spoke for a time.

"I'm not giving up the gun," Thugg said presently.

"That's right, Thugg," Babble said. "You keep hold of it. So we can see how many other innocent people you want to kill."

"I didn't want to kill her." Thugg pointed the gun at Dr. Babble. "I've never killed nobody before. Who wants the gun?" He looked around, wildly, at all of them. "I did exactly what Belsnor did, no more and no less. We're the same, him and me. So I'm sure as hell not going to give *him* the gun." Panting, his breath rasping in his windpipe, Thugg gripped the gun and stared huge-eyed around at all of them.

Belsnor walked over to Seth Morley. "We've got to get it away from him."

"I know," Seth Morley said. But he could think of no way to get it. If Thugg had killed simply because someone—and a woman at that—had approached him reading from The Book, then he would shoot any and all of them at the slightest pretext.

Thugg now was blatantly and floridly psychotic. It was obvious. He had wanted to kill Maggie Walsh, and Seth Morley realized something now that he hadn't understood before. *Belsnor had killed but he had not wanted to. Thugg had killed for the pleasure of it.*

It made a difference. They were safe from Belsnor—unless they became homicidal themselves. In that case, Belsnor would of course shoot. But if they did nothing provocative—

"Don't," his wife Mary said in his ear.

"We have to get the gun back," Seth Morley said. "And it's my fault he has it; I let him get it away from me." He held out his hand, held it in Ignatz Thugg's direction. "Give it to me," he said, and felt his body squinch up in fear; his body prepared itself for death.

Twelve

"HE'LL kill you," Russell said. He, too, walked toward Ignatz Thugg. Everyone else watched. "We need to have that gun," Russell said to Thugg. To Seth Morley he said, "Probably he can get only one of us. I know that gun; it can't be fired rapidly. He'll be able to get off one shot and that'll be it." He moved to the other side of Thugg, approaching at a wide angle. "All right, Thugg," he said, and held out his hand.

Thugg turned uncertainly toward him. Seth Morley moved rapidly forward, reaching.

"Goddam you, Morley," Thugg said; the barrel of the gun swiveled back, but momentum carried Seth Morley forward. He collided with the skinny but muscular body of Ignatz Thugg —the man smelled of hair grease, urine and sweat.

"Get him now," Belsnor yelled; he, too, ran at Thugg, reaching to grapple with him.

Cursing, Thugg tore away from Seth Morley. His face blank with psychopathic neutrality, his eyes glittering with cold, his mouth tormented into a squirming line, he fired.

Mary Morley shrieked.

Reaching with his left arm, Seth Morley touched his right shoulder and felt blood oozing through the fabric of his shirt. The noise of the shot had paralyzed him; he sank to his knees, convulsed by the pain, realizing in a dim way that Thugg had shot him in the shoulder. I'm bleeding, he thought. Christ, he thought, I didn't get the gun from him. With effort he managed to open his eyes. He saw Thugg running; Thugg hurried away, pausing a time or two to fire. But he hit no one; they had all scattered, even Belsnor. "Help me," Seth Morley grated, and Belsnor and Russell and Dr. Babble sneaked their way to him, their attention fixed on Thugg.

At the far end of the compound, by the entrance to the briefing room, Thugg halted; gasping for breath he aimed the gun at Seth Morley and fired one more shot. It passed Morley; it did not strike. Then, with a shudder, Thugg turned away again and jogged off, leaving them.

"Frazer!" Babble exclaimed. "Help us get Morley into the

infirmary! Come on; he's bleeding from a severed artery, I think."

Wade Frazer hurried over. He, Belsnor and Ned Russell lifted Seth up and began the task of carrying him to the doctor's infirmary.

"You're not going to croak," Belsnor gasped as they laid him onto the long metal-topped table. "He got Maggie but he didn't get you." Standing back from the table, Belsnor got out a handkerchief and, shaking as he did so, blew his nose. "That pistol should have stayed with me. Can you see that now?"

"Shut up and get out of here," Babble said, as he snapped on the sterilizer and rapidly placed surgical instruments in it. He then tied a tourniquet around Seth Morley's injured shoulder. The flow of blood continued; it had now formed a pool on the table beside Seth Morley. "I'll have to open him up, get the artery ends, and fuse them together," he said. He tossed the tourniquet away, then turned on the artificial blood-supply machinery. Using a small surgical tool to drill a hole in Seth Morley's side, he adroitly fastened the feeder-tube of the artificial blood-supply. "I can't stop him from bleeding," he said. "It'll take ten minutes to dig in, get the artery ends and fuse them. But he won't bleed to death." Opening the sterilizer, he got out a tray of steaming tools. Expertly, hastily, he began to cut away Seth Morley's clothing. A moment later and he had begun exploring the injured shoulder.

"We're going to have to keep a continual watch for Thugg," Russell said. "Damn it. I wish there were other weapons available. That one gun, and he's got it."

Babble said, "I have a tranquilizing gun." He got out a set of keys, tossed them to Belsnor. "That locked cabinet over there." He pointed. "The key with the diamond-shaped head."

Russell unlocked the cabinet and got out a long tube with a telescopic sighting device on it. "Well, well," he said. "These can be handy. But do you have any ammunition besides tranquilizers? I know the amount of tranquilizers these hold; it would stun him, maybe, but—"

"Do you want to finish him off?" Babble said, pausing in his investigation of Seth Morley's shoulder.

Presently Belsnor said, "Yes." Russell, too, nodded.

"I have other ammo for it," Babble said. "Ammo that will kill. As soon as I'm finished with Morley I'll get it."

Lying on the table, Seth Morley managed to make out the sight of Babble's tranquilizer gun. Will that protect us? he wondered. Or will Thugg make his way back here and kill all of us or possibly just kill me as I lie here helpless. "Belsnor," he gasped, "don't let Thugg come back here tonight and kill me."

"I'll stay here with you," Belsnor said; he gave him a thump with the edge of his hand. "And we'll be armed with this." He held Babble's tranquilizing gun, scrutinizing it. He seemed more confident, now. So did the others.

"Did you give Morley any demerol?" Russell asked Dr. Babble.

"I don't have time," Babble said, and continued working.

"I'll give it to him," Frazer said, "if you'll tell me where it is and where the hypos are."

"You aren't qualified to do that," Babble said.

Frazer said, "And you're not qualified to do surgery."

"I have to," Babble said. "If I don't he'll die. But he can get by without an analgesic."

Mary Morley, crouching down so that her head was close to her husband's, said, "Can you stand the pain?"

"Yes," Seth Morley said tightly.

The operation continued.

He lay in semi-darkness. Anyhow the bullet is out of me, he thought drowsily. And I've had demerol both intravenously and intermuscularly . . . and I feel nothing. Did he manage to stitch the artery properly? he wondered.

A complex machine monitored his internal activity: it kept note of his blood pressure, his heart rate, his temperature and his respiratory apparatus. But where's Babble? he wondered. And Belsnor, where is he?

"Belsnor!" he said as loudly as he could. "Where are you? You said you'd be here with me all the time."

A dark shape materialized. Belsnor, carrying the tranquilizer gun with both hands. "I'm here. Calm down."

"Where are the others?"

"Burying the dead," Belsnor said. "Tony Dunkelwelt, old

Bert, Maggie Walsh . . . they're using some heavy digging equipment left over from the building of the settlement. And Tallchief. We're burying him, too. The first one to die. And Susie. Poor, dumb Susie."

"Anyhow he didn't get me," Seth Morley said.

"He wanted to. He did his best."

"We shouldn't have tried to get the gun away from you," Seth Morley said. He knew that, now. For what it was worth.

"You should have listened to Russell," Belsnor said. "He knew."

"Hindsight is cheap," Seth Morley said. But Belsnor was patently right; Russell had tried to show them the way and they, from panic, had failed to listen. "No sign of Mrs. Rockingham?"

"None. We've searched throughout the settlement. She's gone; Thugg's gone. But we know he's alive. And armed and dangerous and psychopathically oriented."

Seth Morley said, "We don't know he's alive. He may have killed himself. Or what got Tallchief and Susie may have gotten him too."

"Maybe. But we can't count on it." Belsnor examined his wristwatch. "I'll be outside; from there I can see the digging operation and still watch over you. I'll see you." He thumped Morley on his left shoulder, then walked silently from the room and disappeared at once from sight.

Seth Morley wearily shut his eyes. The smell of death, he thought, is everywhere. We are inundated with it. How many people have we lost? he asked himself. Tallchief, Susie, Roberta Rockingham, Betty Jo Berm, Tony Dunkelwelt, Maggie Walsh, old Bert Kosler. Seven dead. Seven of us left. They've gotten half of us in less than twenty-four hours.

And for this, he thought, we left Tekel Upharsin. There is a macabre irony about it; we all came here because we wanted to live more fully. We wanted to be useful. Everyone in this colony had a dream. Maybe that's what was wrong with us, he thought. We have been lodged too deeply in our respective dream worlds. We don't seem able to come out of them; that's why we can't function as a group. And some of us, such as Thugg and Dunkelwelt—there are some of us who are functionally, outright insane.

A gun muzzle jutted against the side of his head. A voice said, "Be quiet."

A second man, wearing black leather, strode toward the front of the infirmary, an erggun held ready. "Belsnor is outside," he said to the man holding the gun against Seth Morley's head. "I'll take care of him." Aiming his weapon he fired an arc of electricity; emerging from the anode coil of the gun it connected with Belsnor, turning him momentarily into a cathode terminal. Belsnor shivered, then slid down onto his knees. He fell over on one side and lay, the tranquilizer gun resting beside him.

"The others," the man squatting next to Seth Morley said.

"They're burying their dead. They won't notice. Even his wife isn't here." He came over to Seth Morley; the man beside him rose and both of them stood together for a moment, surveying Seth Morley. Both wore black leather and he wondered who or what they were.

"Morley," the first man said, "we're taking you out of here."

"Why?" Morley said.

"To save your life," the second man said. Swiftly they produced a stretcher and laid it beside Morley's bed.

Thirteen

Parked behind the infirmary a small squib-ship glistened moistly in the moon-laden night. The two men in black leather uniforms carried Morley in his stretcher to the hatch of the squib; there they set the stretcher down. One of them opened the hatch. They again picked up the stretcher and carried him carefully inside.

"Is Belsnor dead?" he asked.

The first man said, "Stunned."

"Where are we going?" Morley said.

"To a place you'd like to go to." The second leather-clad man seated himself at the control board; he threw several switches to "on," adjusted dials and meters. The squib rose up and hurled itself into the nocturnal sky. "Are you comfortable, Mr. Morley? I'm sorry we had to put you on the floor, but this will not be a very long trip."

"Can you tell me who you are?" Morley said.

"Just tell us," the first man said, "if you're comfortable."

Morley said, "I'm comfortable." He could distinguish the viewscreen of the squib; on it, as if this were daylight, he saw trees and smaller flora: shrubs, lichens, and then a flash of illumination: a river.

And then, on the viewscreen, he saw the Building.

The squib prepared to land. On the Building's roof.

"Isn't that right?" the first man in black leather said.

"Yes." Morley nodded.

"Do you still want to go there?"

He said, "No."

"You don't remember this place," the first man said. "Do you?"

"No," Morley said. He lay breathing shallowly, trying to conserve his strength. "I saw it today for the first time," he said.

"Oh no," the second man said. "You've seen it before."

Warning lights on the Building's roof glinted as the squib bounced to an unskilled landing.

"Damn that R.K. beam," the first man said. "It's erratic again. I was right; we should have come in on manual."

"I couldn't land on this roof," the second man said. "It's too irregular. I'd hit one of those hydro-towers."

"I don't think I want to work with you any more," the first man said, "if you can't land a size-B ship on a roof this large."

"It has nothing to do with the size. What I'm complaining about is the random obstructions. There're too many of them." He went to the hatch and manually cranked it open. Night air smelling of violets drifted in . . . and, with it, the dull, moaning roar of the Building.

Seth Morley scrambled to his feet; at the same time he strained to get his fingers on the erggun held loosely by the man at the hatch.

The man was slow to react; he had looked away from Seth Morley for a moment, asking the man at the control board something—in any case he did not see Seth Morley in time. His companion had already shouted a warning before he reacted.

In Seth Morley's grip the erggun slithered and escaped from him; he fell on it deliberately, struggling to get hold of it once again.

A high-frequency electrical impulse, released by the man at the control board, shimmered past him. The man had missed. Seth Morley flopped back onto his good shoulder, dragged himself to a quasi-sitting position, and fired back.

The beam touched the man at the control board; it caught him above the right ear. At the same time, Seth Morley swiveled the gun barrel; he shot the man tumbling vainly over him. At such close range the impact of the beam was enormous; the man convulsed, fell backward, tumbled with a loud crash into a complex of instrumentation mounted against the far wall of the squib.

Morley slammed the hatch, turned it to lock, then sank down onto the floor. Blood seeped through the bandage on his shoulder, befouling the area adjacent to him. His head hummed and he knew that he would, in a moment or two, pass entirely out.

A speaker mounted above the control board clicked on. "Mr. Morley," it said, "we know that you have taken control of the squib. We know that both our men are unconscious. Please do not take off. Your shoulder was not operated on properly; the junction of torn pieces of artery was unsuccessful. If you do not open the hatch of the squib and let us render you major and immediate medical assistance, then you probably will not live another hour."

The hell with you, Seth Morley thought. He crept toward the control board, reached one of its two seats; with his good arm he hoisted himself up, groped to steady himself and, gradually, pulled himself into place.

"You are not trained to pilot a high-speed squib," the speaker said. Evidently monitors of some sort, within the squib, were telling them what he was doing.

"I can fly it," he said, snorting for breath; his chest seemed weighted down and he had immense difficulty inhaling. On the dashboard a group of switches were marked as being tape-programmed flight patterns. Eight in all. He selected one at random, pressed the switch shut.

Nothing happened.

It's still on the incoming beam, he realized. I have to release the beam lock.

He found the lock, clicked it to off. The squib quivered and then, by degrees, rose up into the night sky.

Something is wrong, he said to himself. The squib isn't handling right. The flaps must still be in landing position.

By now he could barely see. The cab of the vehicle had begun to dim around him; he shut his eyes, shuddered, opened his eyes once more. Christ, he thought; I'm passing out. Will this thing crash without me? Or will it go somewhere, and if so, where?

He fell, then, toppling from the seat and onto the floor of the squib. Blackness collected around him and included him within itself.

As he lay on the floor unconscious the squib flew on and on.

Baleful white light dinned into his face; he felt the scorching brilliance, squeezed his eyes shut again—but he could not suppress it. "Stop," he said; he tried to put up his arms, but they did not move. At that, he managed to open his eyes; he gazed around, trembling with weakness.

The two men in black leather uniforms lay quietly . . . ex–actly as he had last seen them. He did not have to examine them to know that they were dead. *Belsnor, then, was dead;* the weapon did not stun—it killed.

Where am I now? he wondered.

The viewscreen of the squib was still on, but its lens fed directly into an obstruction of some sort; on it he saw only a flat, white surface.

Rotating the ball which controlled the sweep of the viewscreen he said to himself, A lot of time has passed. He touched his injured shoulder cautiously. The bleeding had stopped. Perhaps they had lied to him; perhaps Babble had done an adequate job after all.

Now the viewscreen showed—

A great dead city. Under him. The squib had come to rest at a field up in the higher spires of the city's building-web.

No movement. No life. No one lived in the city; he saw in the viewscreen decay and absolute, endless collapse. As if, he thought, this is the city of the Form Destroyer.

The speaker mounted above the control board made no sound. He would get no help from *them.*

Where the hell can I be? he asked himself. Where in the galaxy is there a city of this size which has been abandoned, allowed to die? Left to erode and rot away. It has been dead for a century! he said to himself, appalled.

Rising unsteadily to his feet he crept to the hatch of the squib. Opening it electrically—he did not have enough strength to operate the quicker manual crank—he peered out.

The air smelled stale and cold. He listened. No sound.

Summoning his strength he lurched haltingly out of the squib, onto the roof top.

There is no one here, he said to himself.

Am I still on Delmak-O? he wondered.

He thought, *There is no place like this on Delmak-O.* Because Delmak-O is a new world to us; we never colonized it. Except for our one small settlement of fourteen people.

And this is old!

He clambered unstably back into the squib, stumbled to the control board and awkwardly reseated himself. There he sat for a time, meditating. What should I do? he asked himself. I've got to find my way back to Delmak-O, he decided. He examined his watch. Fifteen hours had passed—roughly—since the two men in black leather uniforms had kidnaped him. Are the others in the group still alive? he wondered. Or did *they* get all of them?

The automatic pilot; it had a voice-control box.

He snapped it on and said into the microphone, "Take me to Delmak-O. At once." He shut the microphone off, leaned back to rest himself, waited.

The ship did nothing.

"Do you know where Delmak-O is?" he said into the microphone. "Can you take me there? You were there fifteen hours ago; you remember, don't you?" Nothing. No response, no movement. No sound of its ion-propulsion engine cackling into activity. There is no Delmak-O flight pattern engrammed into it, he realized. The two leather-clad men had taken the squib there on manual, evidently. Or else he was operating the equipment incorrectly.

Gathering his faculties, he inspected the control board. He read everything printed on its switches, dials, knobs, control-ball . . . every written declaration. No clue. He could learn nothing from it—least of all how to operate it manually. I can't go anywhere, he said to himself, because I don't know where I am. All I could do would be fly at random. Which presupposes that I figure out how to operate this thing manually.

One switch caught his eye; he had missed it the first time around. REFERENCE, the switch read. He snapped it on. For a time nothing happened. And then the speaker above the control board squawked into life.

"Your query."

He said, "Can you tell me my location?"

"You want FLIGHT INFO."

"I don't see anything on the panel marked FLIGHT INFO," he said.

"It is not on the panel. It is mounted above the panel to your right."

He looked. There it was.

Snapping the FLIGHT INFO unit into operating position, he said, "Can you tell me where I am?"

Static, the semblance of something at work . . . he heard a

faint zzzzzzz sound: almost a whirr. A mechanical device had slid into activity. And then, from the speaker, a vodor voice, an electronic matching of human vocal sound. "Yezzz sirrr. Euuuu arrrr in London."

"'London'!" he echoed, dazed. "How can that be?"

"Euuuu fluuuu there."

He struggled with that but could make nothing out of it. "You mean the city of London, England, on Terra?" he asked.

"Yezzz sirrr."

After a time he managed to pull himself together enough to put another question to it. "Can I fly to Delmak-O in this squib?"

"That izzz a six-year flighttt. Euuuur squib is not equipped for such a flightt. Forrr example it doesss not possess enough thrust to breakkk euuuu freeeee from the planet."

"Terra," he said thickly. Well, it explained the deserted city. All the big cities on Terra were—he had heard—deserted. They no longer served any purpose. There was no population to house itself in them because everyone, except the ostriches, had emigrated.

"My squib, then," he said, "is a local high-velocity shuttle vessel, for homoplanetary flight only?"

"Yesss sirrr."

"Then I could fly here to London only from another locus on the planet."

"Yesss sirrr."

Morley, his head ringing, his face damp with grease-like drops of perspiration, said, "Can you retroplot my previous course? Can you determine where I came here from?"

"Certainly." A protracted wheeze from the mechanism. "Yezzz. Euuuu flewww here from the following origination: #3R68-222B. And before thattt—"

"The ident notation is incomprehensible to me," Morley said. "Can you translate that into words?"

"Nooo. There are nooo wordzzz to describe it."

"Can you program my squib to returnfly there?"

"Yezzz. I can feed the coordinates into euuuur flight-control assembly. I am also equipped to accident-arrest monitor the flighttt; shall I do thattt?"

"Yes," he said, and slumped, exhausted and painfilled, against the horizontal frame of the control board.

The FLIGHT INFO unit said, "Sirrr, do you need medical attentionnn?"

"Yes," Morley said.

"Dooo you wish your squibbb to shuttle euuuu to the nearest medical station?"

He hesitated. Something at work in the deeper parts of his mind told him to say no. "I'll be all right," he said. "The trip won't take long."

"Nooo sirrr. T-ank euuuu, sirrr. I am now feeding the coordinates for a flight to #3R68-222B. And I will accident-arrest minimon euuuur flight; isss that correct?"

He could not answer. His shoulder had begun bleeding once more; evidently he had lost more blood than he realized.

Lights, as on a player piano, lit up before him; he vaguely made their winking warmth out. Switches opened and shut . . . it was like resting his head on a pinball machine prepared to release a free game—in this case a black and dismal free game. And then, smoothly, the squib rose up into the midday sky; it circled London—if it actually was London—and then headed west.

"Give me oral confirmation," he grunted. "When we get there."

"Yezzz sirrr. I will awaken euuuu."

"Am I really talking to a machine?" Morley murmured.

"Technically I am an inorganic artificial constructtt in the proto-computer classsss. But—" It rambled on, but he did not hear it; once again Seth Morley had passed out.

The squib continued on its short flight.

"We are approaching coordinates #3R68-222B," a shrill voice squeaked in his ear, jarring him awake.

"Thanks," he said, lifting his heavy head to peer cloudily into the viewscreen. A massive entity loomed up in the viewscreen; for a moment he could not identify it—most certainly it was not the settlement—*and then, with horror, he realized that the squib had returned to the Building.* "Wait," he said frantically. "Don't land!"

"But we are at coordinates #3R68—"

"I countermand that order," he snapped. "Take me to the coordinates prior to that."

A pause, and then the FLIGHT INFO unit said, "The previousss flight originated at a locussss manually plotted. Hence there isss nooo recorddd of it in the guide-assembly. There isss nooo way I can compute ittt."

"I see," he said. It did not really surprise him. "Okay," he said, watching the Building below, become smaller and smaller; the squib was rising from it to flap about in a circle overhead. "Tell me how to assume manual control of this craft."

"Firssst euuuu push switch tennn for override cancellation. Then—doo euuuu seee that large plastic ball? Euuuu roll that from side to side and forwarddd and backkk; that controlsss the flight path of euuuur smalll craft. I suggest euuuu practice before I release controlll."

"Just release control," he said savagely. Far below, he saw two black dots rising from the Building.

"Control released."

He rotated the big plastic ball. The squib at once bucked, floundered; it shuddered and then plunged nose-first toward the dry lands below.

"Back, back," FLIGHT INFO said warningly. "Euuur descending too fassst."

He rolled the ball back and this time found himself on a reasonably horizontal course.

"I want to lose those two ships following me," he said.

"Euuuur ability to maneuver thisss craft isss not such that—"

"Can you do it?" he broke in.

The FLIGHT INFO unit said, "I possess a variety of random flight-patternsss, any one of which would tend to throwww them offf."

"Pick one," Morley said, "and use it." The two pursuing ships were much closer, now. And, in the viewscreen, he saw the barrel of a cannon poking from the nose of each, a .88 millimeter barrel. Any second now they would open fire.

"Random course in operation, sirrr," the FLIGHT INFO unit told him. "Pleeezzz strap eurrself in, sirrr."

He haltingly fiddled with the seat belt. As he clicked the

buckle into place his squib abruptly shot upward, rolling into an immelmann loop . . . it came out of the maneuver flying in the opposite direction, and well above the pursuing ships.

"Radar fixxx on usss, sirrr," the FLIGHT INFO unit informed him. "From the aforementioned two vesselsss. I shall program the flight-control assembly to take proper evasive action. Therefore we will shortly be flying close to the groundddd. Do not be alarmed." The ship plunged down like a deranged elevator; stunned, he rested his head on his arm and shut his eyes. Then, equally abruptly, the squib levelled off. It flew erratically, compensating from moment to moment against altitude-variations in the terrain.

He lay resting in his seat, sickened by the up-and-down gyrations of the ship.

Something boomed dully. One of the pursuing ships had either fired its cannon or released an air-to-air missile. Swiftly coming awake he studied the viewscreen. Had it been close?

He saw, far off, across the wild terrain, a tall column of black smoke arising. The shot had been across his bow, as he had feared; it was now telling him that he had been caught.

"Are we armed in any manner?" he asked FLIGHT INFO.

FLIGHT INFO said, "As per regulation we carry two 120-A type air-to-air missiles. Shall I program the control carrier to activate themmm in relation to the craft following ussss?"

"Yes," he said. It was, in a way, a hard decision to make; he would be committing his first voluntary homicidal act in their —in any—direction. But they had started the firing; they had no hesitation about killing him. And if he did not defend himself they would.

"Missssilesss fired," a new and different vodor voice sounded, this one from the central control panel itself. "Doooo euuuu want a vizzzual scan of their activity?"

"Yesss, he doesss," FLIGHT INFO ordered.

On the screen a different scene appeared; it was being transmitted, via a split screen, from *both* missiles.

The missile on the left side of the screen missed its target and passed on by, to descend, gradually, into a collision course with the ground. The second one, however, flew directly at its target. The pursuing ship wheeled, screamed directly upward . . . the missile altered target and then the viewscreen

was suffused with silent, white light. The missile had deto-
nated. One of the two pursuing ships had died.

The other one continued on, directly at him. Picking up velocity as it came. The pilot knew that he had fired all his arma-
ments. Combatwise he was now helpless—and the remaining
ship knew it.

"Do we have a cannon?" Morley asked.

FLIGHT INFO said, "The small size of thisss ship doesss
not permit—"

"A simple yes or no."

"No."

"Anything, then?"

"No."

Morley said, "I want to give up. I'm injured and I'm bleeding
to death as I sit here. Land this ship as soon as possible."

"Yesss sirrr." Now the squib dipped down; again it flew par-
allel to the ground, but this time braking, slowing its speed.
He heard its wheel-lowering mechanism go into operation and
then, with a shuddering bump, the squib touched down.

He moaned with pain as the squib bounced, quaked, then
turned on an angle, its tires squealing.

It came to a stop. Silence. He lay against the central control
panel, listening for the other ship. He waited; he waited. No
sound. Still only the empty silence.

"FLIGHT INFO," he said aloud, raising his head in a pal-
sied, trembling motion. "Has it landed?"

"It continued on byyy."

"Why?"

"I do not knowww. It continuesss to move away from usss;
my scanner can barely pick it up." A pause. "Now it's beyond
scanner-probe range."

Maybe it had failed to perceive his landing. Maybe it—the
pilot—had assumed his low-level, horizontal flight to be a further attempt to defeat the computerized radar.

Morley said, "Take off again. Fly in widening circles. I'm
looking for a settlement that's in this area." He chose a course
at random. "Fly slightly northeast."

"Yesss sirrr." The squib pulsed with new activity and then, in
a professional, competent way, rose up into the sky.

Again he rested, but this time lying so that he could perpetually scan the viewscreen. He did not really think that they would be successful; the settlement was small and the funky landscape was enormous. But—what was the alternative?

To go back to the Building. And now he had a firm, physical revulsion toward it; his earlier desire to enter it had evaporated.

It is not a winery, he said to himself. But what the hell is it, then?

He did not know. And he hoped he never would.

Something glinted to the right. Something metallic. He roused himself groggily. Looking at the control board clock he saw that the squib had been flying in widening circles for almost an hour. Did I drift off? he wondered. Squinting, he peeped to see what had glinted. Small buildings.

He said, "That's it."

"Shall I land there?"

"Yes." He hunched forward, straining to see. Straining to be sure.

It was the settlement.

Fourteen

A SMALL—heartbreakingly small—group of men and women trudged wanly up to the parked squib as Seth Morley activated the electrical dehatching mechanism. They stared at him bleakly as he stumbled out, stood swaying, trying to get control of his waning vitality.

There they were. Russell, looking stern. His wife Mary, her face taut with alarm—then relief at seeing him. Wade Frazer, who looked tired. Dr. Milton Babble, chewing on his pipe in a reflexive, pointless way. Ignatz Thugg was not among them.

Neither was Glen Belsnor.

Leadenly, Seth Morley said, "Belsnor is dead, isn't he?"

They nodded.

Russell said, "You're the first of all of them to come back. We noticed late last night that Belsnor wasn't guarding us. We got to him at the infirmary door; he was already dead."

"Electrocuted," Dr. Babble said.

"And you were gone," Mary said. Her eyes remained glazed and hopeless, despite his return.

"You better get back into bed in the infirmary," Babble said to him. "I don't know how you could still be alive. Look at you; you're drenched with blood."

Together, they assisted him back to the infirmary. Mary fussily made up the bed; Seth Morley, swaying, stood waiting and then let them stretch his body out, propped up by pillows.

"I'm going to work on your shoulder some more," Babble said to him. "I think the artery is allowing seepage out into the—"

Seth Morley said, "We're on Earth."

They stared at him. Babble froze; he turned toward Seth, then mechanically returned to his task of fumbling with a tray of surgical instruments. Time passed, but no one spoke.

"What is the Building?" Wade Frazer said, at last.

"I don't know. But they say I was there, once." So on some level I do know, he realized. Maybe we all do. Perhaps at some time in the past all of us were there. *Together.*

145

"Why are they killing us?" Babble said.

"I don't know that either," Seth Morley answered.

Mary said, "How do you know we're on Earth?"

"I was at London a little while ago. I saw it, the ancient, abandoned city. Mile after mile of it. Thousands of decaying, deserted houses, factories and streets. Bigger than any non-terran city anywhere in the galaxy. Where at one time six million people lived."

Wade Frazer said, "But there's nothing on Terra except the aviary! And nobody except ostriches!"

"Plus Interplan West military barracks and research installations," Seth Morley said, but his voice ebbed; it lacked conviction and enthusiasm. "We're an experiment," he said, anyhow. "As we guessed last night. A military experiment being carried out by General Treaton." But he did not believe it either. "What kind of military personnel wear black leather uniforms?" he said. "And jackboots . . . I think they're called."

Russell, in a modulated, disinterested voice, said, "Aviary guards. A sop to keep up their morale. It's very discouraging to work around ostriches; introduction of the new uniforms, three or four years back, has done a great deal of morale-boosting for the personnel."

Turning toward him, Mary said searchingly, "How do you happen to know that?"

"Because," Russell said, still calm, "I am one of them." Reaching into his jacket he brought out a small, shiny erggun. "We carry this type of weapon." He held the gun pointed toward them, meanwhile motioning them to stand closer together. "It was one chance out of a million that Morley got away." Russell pointed to his right ear. "They've been periodically keeping me informed. I knew he was on his way back here, but I—and my various superiors—never thought he'd arrive." He smiled at them. Graciously.

A sharp *thump* sounded. Loudly.

Russell half-turned, lowered his erggun and slumped down, letting the weapon fall. What is it? Seth Morley asked himself; he sat up, trying to see. He made out a shape, the shape of a man, walking into the room. The Walker? he thought. The Walker-on-Earth come to save us? The man held a gun—an old-fashioned lead slug pistol. Belsnor's gun, he realized. But

Ignatz Thugg has it. He did not understand. Neither did the others; they milled about incoherently as the man, holding the pistol, walked up to them.

It was Ignatz Thugg.

On the floor, Russell lay dying. Thugg bent, picked up the erggun, and put it away in his belt.

"I came back," Thugg said grimly.

"Did you hear him?" Seth Morley said. "Did you hear Russell say that—"

Thugg said, "I heard him." He hesitated, then brought out the erggun; he handed it to Morley. "Somebody get the tranquilizer gun," he said. "We'll need all three. Are there any more? In the squib?"

"Two in the squib," Seth Morley said, accepting the erggun from Thugg. You're not going to kill us? he wondered. The psychopathic countenance of Ignatz Thugg had relaxed; the strained attentiveness which had marked Thugg had relented. Thugg looked calm and alert; sanely so.

"You're not my enemies," Thugg said. "They are." He gestured with Belsnor's pistol toward Russell. "I knew someone in the group was; I thought it was Belsnor, but I was wrong. I'm sorry." He was silent for a time.

The rest of them remained silent, too. Waiting to see what would happen. It would come soon, they all knew. Five weapons, Seth Morley said to himself. Pitiful. They have air-to-ground missiles, .88 millimeter cannon—God knows what else. Is it worth it, trying to fight them?

"It is," Thugg said, evidently reading his expression.

Seth Morley said, "I think you're right."

"I think I know," Wade Frazer said, "what this experiment is all about." The others waited for him to go on but he did not.

"Say it," Babble said.

"Not until I'm sure," Frazer said.

Seth Morley thought, I think I know, too. And Frazer is right; until we know absolutely, until we have total proof, we had better not even discuss it.

"I knew we were on Terra," Mary Morley said quietly. "I recognized the moon; I've seen Luna in pictures . . . a long time ago when I was a child."

"And what did you infer from that?" Wade Frazer said.

Mary said, "I—" She hesitated, glancing at her husband. "Isn't it a military experiment by Interplan West? As all of us suspected?"

"Yes," Seth Morley said.

"There's another possibility," Wade Frazer said.

"Don't say it," Seth Morley said.

"I think we had better say it," Wade Frazer said. "We should face it openly, decide if it's true, and then decide whether we want to go on and fight them."

"Say it," Babble said, stammering from overintensity.

Wade Frazer said, "We're criminally insane. And at one time, probably for a long time, maybe years, we were kept inside what we call 'the Building.'" He paused. "The Building, then, would be both a prison and a mental hospital. A prison for the—"

"What about our settlement?" Babble said.

"An experiment," Frazer said. "But not by the military. By the prison and hospital authorities. To see if we could function on the outside . . . on a planet supposedly far away from Terra. And we failed. We began to kill one another." He pointed at the tranquilizing gun. "That's what killed Tallchief; that's what started it all off. You did it, Babble. You killed Tallchief. Did you also kill Susie Smart?"

"I did not," Babble said thinly.

"But you did kill Tallchief."

"Why?" Ignatz Thugg asked him.

Babble said, "I—guessed what we were. I thought Tallchief was what Russell turned out to be."

"Who killed Susie Smart?" Seth Morley asked Frazer.

"I don't know. I have no clue to that. Maybe Babble. Maybe you, Morley. Did you do it?" Frazer eyed Seth Morley. "No, I guess you didn't. Well, maybe Ignatz did it. But my point is made; any one of us could have done it. We all have the inclination. *That's what got us into the Building.*"

Mary said, "I killed Susie."

"Why?" Seth Morley said. He could not believe it.

"Because of what she was doing with you." His wife's voice was ultra calm. "And she tried to kill me; she had that replica of the Building trained. I did it in self-defense; she engineered it all."

"Christ," Seth Morley said.

"Did you love her that much?" Mary demanded. "That you can't understand why I would do it?"

Seth Morley said, "I barely knew her."

"You knew her well enough to—"

"Okay," Ignatz Thugg broke in. "It doesn't matter, now. Frazer made his point; we all might have done it, and in every case one of us did." His face twitched spasmodically. "I think you're wrong. I just don't believe it. We can't be criminally insane."

"The killings," Wade Frazer said. "I've known for a long time that everyone here was potentially homicidal. There's a great deal of autism, of schizophrenic lack of adequate affect." He indicated Mary Morley scathingly. "Look how she tells about murdering Susie Smart. As if it's nothing at all." He pointed at Dr. Babble. "And his account of Tallchief's death—Babble killed a man he didn't even know . . . just in case—in case!—he might be some kind of authority figure. *Any* kind of authority figure."

After an interval Dr. Babble said, "What I can't fathom is, Who killed Mrs. Rockingham? That fine, dignified, educated woman . . . she never did any harm."

"Maybe nobody did kill her," Seth Morley said. "She was infirm; maybe they came for her, the way they came for me. To remove her so she'd survive. That's the reason they gave me for coming after me and taking me away; they said Babble's work on my shoulder was defective and I would soon die."

"Do you believe that?" Ignatz Thugg asked.

Truthfully, Seth Morley said, "I don't know. It might have been. After all, they could have shot me here, the way they did Belsnor." He thought, Is Belsnor the only one they killed? And we did the rest? It supported Frazer's theory . . . and they might not have intended to kill Belsnor; they were in a hurry and evidently they thought their ergguns were set on stun.

And they were probably afraid of us.

"I think," Mary said, "that they interfered with us as little as possible. After all, this was an experiment; they wanted to see how it would come out. And then they did see how it was coming out, so they sent Russell here . . . and they killed Belsnor. But maybe they saw nothing wrong with killing Belsnor;

he had killed Tony. Even we understand the—" She searched for the word.

"Unbalance," Frazer said.

"Yes, the unbalanced quality in that. He could have gotten the sword some other way." Lightly, she put her hand on her husband's injured shoulder. Very lightly, but with feeling. "That's why they wanted to save Seth. *He hadn't killed anyone;* he was innocent. And you—" She snarled at Ignatz Thugg, snarled with hatred. "You would have slipped in and murdered him as he lay here hurt."

Ignatz Thugg made a noncommittal gesture. Of dismissal.

"And Mrs. Rockingham," Mary finished. "She hadn't killed anybody either. So they saved her, too. In the breakdown of an experiment of this type it would be natural for them to try to save as—"

"All you've said," Frazer interrupted, "tends to indicate that I'm right." He smiled disdainfully, as if he were personally unconcerned. As if he were not involved.

"There has to be something else at work," Seth Morley said. "They wouldn't have let the killings go on as long as they did. They must not have known. At least until they sent Russell. But I guess by then they knew."

"They may not be monitoring us properly," Babble said. "If they relied on those little artificial insects that scurry around carrying miniature TV cameras—"

"I'm sure they have more," Seth Morley said. To his wife he said, "Go through Russell's pockets; see what you can find. Labels in his clothing, what kind of watch or quasi-watch he's wearing, bits of paper stuck away here and there."

"Yes," she said, and, gingerly, began to remove Russell's spick-and-span jacket.

"His wallet," Babble said, as Mary lifted it out. "Let me see what's in it." He took it from her, opened it. "Identification. Ned W. Russell, residing at the dome-colony on Sirius 3. Twenty-nine years old. Hair: brown. Eyes: brown. Height: five eleven-and-a-half. Authorized to pilot class B and C vessels." He looked deeper into the wallet. "Married. Here's a 3-D photo of a young woman, undoubtedly his wife." He rummaged further. "And this. Pictures of a baby."

No one said anything for a time.

"Anyhow," Babble said presently, "there's nothing of value on him. Nothing that tells us anything." He rolled up Russell's left sleeve. "His watch: Omega self-winding. A good watch." He rolled up the brown canvas sleeve a little farther. "A tattoo," he said. "On the inside of his lower arm. How strange; it's the same thing I have tattooed on my arm, and in the same place." He traced the tattoo on Russell's arm with his finger. " 'Persus 9,' " he murmured. He unfastened his cuff and rolled back his own left sleeve. There, sure enough, was the same tattoo on his arm and in exactly the same place.

Seth Morley said, "I have one on my instep." Strange, he thought. And I haven't thought about that tattoo in years.

"How did you get yours?" Dr. Babble asked him. "I don't remember getting mine; it's been too long. And I don't remember what it means . . . if I ever did know. It looks like some kind of identifying military service mark. A location. A military outpost at Persus 9."

Seth looked around at the rest of the group. All of them had acutely uncomfortable—and anxious—expressions on their faces.

"All of you have the mark on you, too," Babble said to them, after a long, long time had passed.

"Does any one of you remember when you got this mark?" Seth Morley said. "Or why? Or what it means?"

"I've had mine since I was a baby," Wade Frazer said.

"You were never a baby," Seth Morley said to him.

"What an odd thing to say," Mary said.

"I mean," Seth Morley said, "that it isn't possible to imagine him as a baby."

"But that's not what you said," Mary said.

"What difference does it make what I said?" He felt violently irritable. "So we do have one common element—this annotation chiselled into our flesh. Probably those who are dead have it, too. Susie and the rest of them. Well, let's face it; we all have a slot of amnesia dug somewhere in our brains. Otherwise we'd know why we got this tattoo and what it means. We'd know what Persus 9 is—or was at the time the tattoo was made. I'm afraid this confirms the criminally insane theory; we were probably given these marks when we were prisoners in the Building. We don't remember that, so we don't remember this tattoo either." He lapsed into brooding introversion, ignoring, for the time, the rest of the group. "Like Dachau," he said. "I think," he said, "that it's very important to find out what these marks mean. It's the first really solid indication we've found as to who we are and what this settlement is. Can any of you suggest how we find out what Persus 9 means?"

"Maybe the reference library on the squib," Thugg said.

Seth Morley said, "Maybe. We can try that. But first I suggest we ask the tench. And I want to be there. Can you get me into the squib along with you?" Because, he said to himself, if you leave me here I will, like Belsnor, be murdered.

Dr. Babble said, "I'll see that you're gotten aboard—with this one proviso. First we ask the squib's reference libraries. If it has nothing, then we'll go searching out the tench. But if we can get it from the squib then we won't be taking such a great—"

"Fine," Morley said. But he knew that the ship's reference service would be unable to tell them anything.

Under Ignatz Thugg's direction they began the task of getting Seth Morley—and themselves—into the small squib.

Propped up at the controls of the squib once more, Seth Morley snapped on REFERENCE. "Yezzz sirr," it squeaked.

"What is referred to by the designate Persus 9?" he asked.

A whirr and then it spoke in its vodor voice. "I have no information on a Persusssss 9," REFERENCE said.

"If it were a planet, would you have a record of it?"

"Yezzz, if known to Interplan West or Interplan East authorities."

"Thanks." Seth Morley shut off the REFERENCE service. "I had a feeling it wouldn't know. And I have an even stronger feeling that the tench does know." That, in fact, the tench's ultimate purpose would be served by asking it this question.

Why he thought that he did not know.

"I'll pilot the ship," Thugg said. "You're too injured; you lie down."

"There's no place to lie down because of all these people," Seth Morley said.

They made room. And he stretched himself out gratefully. The squib, in the hands of Ignatz Thugg, zipped up into the sky. A murderer for a pilot, Seth Morley reflected. And a doctor who's a murderer.

And my wife. A murderess. He shut his eyes.

The squib zoomed on, in search of the tench.

"There it is," Wade Frazer said, studying the viewscreen. "Bring the ship down."

"Okay," Thugg said cheerfully. He moved the control ball; the ship at once began to descend.

"Will they pick up our presence?" Babble said nervously. "At the Building?"

"Probably," Thugg said.

"We can't turn back now," Seth Morley said.

"Sure we can," Thugg said. "But nobody said anything about it." He adjusted the controls; the ship glided to a long, smooth landing and came to rest, bumping noisily.

"Get me out," Morley said, standing hesitantly; again his head rang. As if, he thought, a sixty cycle hum is being conducted through my brain. Fear, he thought; it's fear that's making me this way. Not my wound.

They gingerly stepped from the squib onto parched and highly arid land. A thin smell, again like something burning, reached their noses. Mary turned away from the smell, paused to blow her nose.

"Where's the river?" Seth Morley said, looking around.

The river had vanished.

Or maybe we're somewhere else, Seth Morley thought. Maybe the tench moved. And then he saw it—not far away. It had managed to blend itself almost perfectly with its local environment. Like a desert toad, he thought. Screwing itself backward into the sand.

Rapidly, on a small piece of paper, Babble wrote. He handed it, when finished, to Seth Morley. For confirmation.

WHAT IS PERSUS 9?

"That'll do." Seth Morley handed the slip around; all of them soberly nodded. "Okay," he said, as briskly as he could manage. "Put it in front of the tench." The great globular mass of protoplasmic slush undulated slightly, as if aware of him.

Then, as the question was placed before it, the tench began to shudder . . . as if, Morley thought, to get away from us. It swayed back and forth, evidently in distress. Part of it began to liquify.

Something's wrong, Seth Morley realized. It did not act like this before.

"Stand back!" Babble said warningly; he took hold of Seth Morley by his good shoulder and propelled him bodily away.

"My God," Mary said, "it's coming apart." Turning swiftly, she ran; she hurried away from the tench and climbed back into the squib.

"She's right," Wade Frazer said. He, too, retreated.

Babble said, "I think it's going to—" A loud whine from the tench sounded, shutting out his voice. The tench swayed, changed color; liquid oozed out from beneath it and formed a gray, disturbed pool on all sides of it. And then, as they stared fixedly in dismay, the tench ruptured. It spilt into two pieces, and, a moment later, into four: it had split again.

"Maybe it's giving birth," Seth Morley said, above the eerie whine. By degrees, the whine had become more and more intense. And more and more urgent.

"It's not giving birth to anything," Seth Morley said. "It's breaking apart. We've killed it with our question; it isn't able to answer. And instead it's being destroyed. Forever."

"I'll retrieve the question." Babble knelt, whisked the slip of paper back from its spot close to the tench.

The tench exploded.

They stood for a time, not speaking, gazing at the ruin that had been the tench. Gelatin everywhere . . . a circle of it, on all sides of the central remains. Seth Morley took a few steps forward, in its direction; Mary and the others who had run away came slipping cautiously back, to stand with him and view it. View what they had done.

"Why?" Mary demanded in agitation. "What could there have been about that question that—"

"It's a computer," Seth Morley said. He could distinguish electronic components under the gelatin, exposed by the tench's explosion, the hidden core—and electronic computer—lay visible. Wiring, transistors, printed circuits, tape storage drums,

Thurston gate-response crystals, basic irmadium valves by the thousand, lying scattered everywhere on the ground like minute Chinese firecrackers . . . lady crackers, they're called, Seth Morley said to himself. Pieces of it flung in all directions. Not enough left to repair; the tench, as he had intuited, was gone for good.

"So all the time it was inorganic," Babble said, apparently dazed. "You didn't know that, did you Morley?"

"I had an intuition," Seth Morley said, "but it was the wrong one. I thought it would answer—be the only living thing that could answer—the question." How wrong he had been.

Wade Frazer said, "You were right about one thing, Morley. That question is the key question, evidently. But where do we go from here?"

The ground surrounding the tench smoked, now, as if the gelatinous material and computer parts were starting into some kind of thermal chain reaction. The smoke had an ominous quality about it. Seth Morley, for reasons not understood, felt, sensed, the seriousness of their situation. Yes, he thought; a chain reaction which we have started but which we can't stop. How far will it go? he wondered somberly. Already, large cracks had begun to appear in the ground adjacent to the tench. The liquid squirted from the dying, agonized tench, spilling now into the cracks . . . he heard, from far down, a low drumming noise, as if something immense and sickly-vile had been disturbed by the surface explosion.

The sky turned dark.

Incredulous, Wade Frazer said, "Good God, Morley; what have you done with your—question?" He gestured in a seizure of motor-spasms. "This place is breaking up!"

The man was correct. Fissions had appeared everywhere now; in a few moments there would be no safe spot to stand on. *The squib,* Seth Morley realized. We've got to get back to it. "Babble," he said hoarsely, "get us all into the squib." But Babble had gone. Looking around in the turbulent gloom, Seth Morley saw no sign of him—nor of the others.

They're in the squib already, he told himself. As best he could he made his way in that direction. Even Mary, he realized. The bastards. He falteringly reached the hatch of the squib; it hung open.

A fast-widening crack in the ground, almost six feet wide, appeared crashingly beside him; it burgeoned as he stood there. Now he found himself looking into the orifice. At the bottom something undulated. A slimy thing, very large, without eyes; it swam in a dark, stinking liquid and ignored him.

"Babble," he croaked, and managed to make the first step that led up into the squib. Now he could see in; he clambered clumsily up, using only his good arm.

No one was in the squib.

I'm Christ-awful alone, he said to himself. Now the squib shuddered and bucked as the ground beneath it heaved. Rain had begun; he felt hot, dark drops on him, acrid rain, as if it was not water but some other, less-pleasant substance. The drops seared his skin; he scrambled into the squib, stood wheezing and choking, wondering frantically where the others had gone. No sign of them. He hobbled to the squib's viewscreen . . . the squib heaved; its hull shuddered and became unstable. It's being pulled under, he said to himself. I've got to take off; I can't spend any more time searching for them. He jabbed at a button and turned on the squib's engine. Tugging on the control ball he sent the squib—with himself inside, alone—up into the dark and ugly sky . . . a sky obviously ominous to all life. He could hear the rain beating against the hull; the rain of what? he wondered. Like an acid. Maybe, he thought, it will eat its way through the hull and destroy both the squib and me.

Seating himself, he clicked on the viewscreen to greatest magnification; he rotated it, simultaneously sending the squib into a rotating orbit.

On the viewscreen appeared the Building. The river, swollen and mud-colored, angrily lapped at it. The Building, faced with its last danger, had thrown a temporary bridge across the river and, Seth Morley saw, men and women were crossing the bridge, crossing thereby the river, and going on into the Building.

They were all old. Gray and fragile, like wounded mice, they huddled together and advanced step by step in the direction of the Building. They're not going to make it, he realized. Who are they?

Peering into the viewscreen he recognized his wife. But old, like the others. Hunched over, tottering, afraid . . . and then he made out Susie Smart. And Dr. Babble. Now he could distinguish them all. Russell, Ben Tallchief, Glen Belsnor, Wade Frazer, Betty Jo Berm, Tony Dunkelwelt, Babble, Ignatz Thugg, Maggie Walsh, old Bert Kosler—he had not changed, he had already been old—and Roberta Rockingham, and, at the end, Mary.

The Form Destroyer has seized them, Seth Morley realized. And done this to them. And now they are on their way back to where they came from. Forever. To die there.

The squib, around him, vibrated. Its hull clanged, again and again. Something hard and metallic was pinging off the hull. He sent the squib higher and the noise abated. What had done it? he wondered, again inspecting the viewscreen.

And then he saw.

The Building had begun to disintegrate. Parts of it, chunks of plastic and alloy bonded together, hurled as if in a giant wind up into the sky. The delicate bridge across the river broke, and as it fell it carried those crossing it to their death: they fell with the fragments of the bridge into the snarling, muddy water and vanished. But it made no difference; the Building was dying, too. They would not have been safe in it anyhow.

I'm the only one who survived, he said to himself. Moaning with grief he revolved the control ball and the ship putt-putted out of its orbit and on a tangent leading back to the settlement.

The engine of the squib died into silence.

He heard nothing, now, but the slap-slap of rain against its hull. The squib sailed in a great arc, dropping lower each moment.

He shut his eyes. I did what I could throughout, he said to himself. There was nothing more possible for me. I tried.

The squib hit, bounced, threw him from his chair onto the floor. Sections of the hull broke off, ripped away; he felt the acrid, acid-like rain pour in on him, drenching him. Opening his pain-glazed eyes he saw that the downpour had burned holes in his clothing; it was devouring his body. He perceived that in a fragment of a second—time seemed to have stopped as the squib rolled over and over, skated on its top across the terrain . . . he felt nothing, no fear, no grief, no pain any longer; he merely experienced the death of his ship—and of himself—as a kind of detached observer.

The ship skidded, at last, to a halt. Silence, except for the drip-drip of the rain of acid on him. He lay half-buried in collapsed junk: portions of the control board and viewscreen, all shattered. Jesus, he thought. Nothing is left, and presently the earth will swallow the squib and me. But it does not matter, he thought, because I am dying. In emptiness, meaninglessness and solitude. Like all the others who have gone before this fragment of the one-time group. Intercessor, he thought, intercede for me. Replace me; die for me.

He waited. And heard only the tap-tap of the rain.

Fifteen

GLEN BELSNOR removed the polyencephalic cylinder from his aching head, set it carefully down, rose unsteadily to a standing position. He rubbed his forehead and experienced pain. That was a bad one, he said to himself. We did not do well this time at all.

Going unsteadily to the dining hall of the ship he poured himself a glass of tepid, bottled water. He then rummaged in his pockets until he found his powerful analgesic tablet, popped it into his mouth, swallowed it with more of the reprocessed water.

Now, in their cubicles, the others stirred. Wade Frazer tugged at the cylinder which enclosed his brain and skull and scalp and, a few cubicles off, Sue Smart, too, appeared to be returning to active awareness of a homoencephalic kind.

As he helped Sue Smart off with her heavy cylinder he heard a groan. A lament, telling of deep suffering. It was Seth Morley, he discovered. "Okay," Belsnor said. "I'll get to you as soon as I can."

All of them were coming out of it, now. Ignatz Thugg yanked violently at his cylinder, managed to detach it from its screw-lock base at his chin . . . he sat up, his eyes swollen, an expression of displeasure and hostility on his wan, narrow face.

"Give me a hand," Belsnor said. "I think Morley is in shock. Maybe you better get Dr. Babble up."

"Morley'll be all right," Thugg said huskily; he rubbed his eyes, grimacing as if nauseated. "He always is."

"But he's in shock—his death must have been a bad one."

Thugg stood up, nodding dully. "Whatever you say, captain."

"Get them warm," Belsnor said. "Set up the standby heat to a higher notch." He bent over the prone Dr. Milton Babble. "Come on, Milt," he said emphatically as he removed Babble's cylinder.

Here and there others of the crew sat up. Groaned.

Loudly, to them all, Captain Belsnor said, "You are all right now. This one turned out to be a fiasco, but you are going—as always—to be fine. Despite what you've gone through. Dr.

Babble will give you a shot of something to ease the transition from polyencephalic fusion to normal homoencephalic functioning." He waited a moment, then repeated what he had said.

Seth Morley, tremblingly, said, "Are we aboard Persus 9?"

"You are back on the ship," Belsnor informed him. "Back aboard Persus 9. Do you remember how you died, Morley?"

"Something awful happened to me," Seth Morley managed to say.

"Well," Belsnor pointed out, "you had that shoulder wound."

"I mean later. After the tench. I remember flying a squib . . . it lost power and split up—disintegrated in the atmosphere. I was either torn or knocked into pieces; I was all over the squib, by the time it had finished plowing up the landscape."

Belsnor said, "Don't expect me to feel sorry for you." After all, he himself, in the polyencephalic fusion, had been electrocuted.

Sue Smart, her long hair tangled, her right breast peeping slyly from between the buttons of her blouse, gingerly touched the back of her head and winced.

"They got you with a rock," Belsnor told her.

"But why?" Sue asked. She seemed dazed, still. "What did I do wrong?"

Belsnor said, "It wasn't your fault, This one turned out to be a hostile one; we were venting our long-term, pent-up aggressiveness. Evidently." He could remember, but only with effort, how he had shot Tony Dunkelwelt, the youngest member of the crew. I hope he won't be too angry, Captain Belsnor said to himself. He shouldn't be. After all, in venting his own hostility, Dunkelwelt had killed Bert Kosler, the cook of the Persus 9.

We sniffed ourselves virtually out of existence, Captain Belsnor noted to himself. I hope—I pray!—the next one is different. It should be; as in previous times we probably managed to get rid of the bulk of our hostilities in that one fusion, that (what was it?) Delmak-O episode.

To Babble, who stood unsteadily fooling with his disarranged clothing, Belsnor said, "Get moving, doctor. See who needs what. Painkillers, tranquilizers, stimulants . . . they need you. But—" He leaned close to Babble. "Don't give them anything we're low on, as I've told you before, and as you ignore."

Leaning over Betty Jo Berm, Babble said, "Do you need some chemical-therapy help, Miss Berm?"

"I—I think I'll be okay," Betty Jo Berm said as she sat painstakingly up. "If I can just sit here and rest . . ." She managed a brief, cheerless smile. "I drowned," she said. "Ugh." She made a weary, but now somewhat relieved, face.

Speaking to all of them, Belsnor said quietly but with firm insistence, "I'm reluctantly writing off that particular construct as too unpleasant to try for again."

"But," Frazer pointed out, lighting his pipe with shaking fingers, "it's highly therapeutic. From a psychiatric standpoint."

"It got out of hand," Sue Smart said.

"It was supposed to," Babble said as he worked with the others, rousing them, finding out what they wanted. "It was what we call a total catharsis. Now we'll have less free-floating hostility surging back and forth between everyone here on the ship."

Ben Tallchief said, "Babble, I hope your hostility toward me is over." He added, "And for what you did to me—" He glared.

"'The ship,'" Seth Morley murmured.

"Yes," Captain Belsnor said, slightly, sardonically, amused. "And what else have you forgotten this time? Do you want to be briefed?" He waited, but Seth Morley said nothing. Morley seemed still to be entranced. "Give him some kind of amphetamine," Belsnor said to Dr. Babble. "To get him into a lucid state." It usually came to this with Seth Morley; his ability to adapt to the abrupt transition between the ship and the polyencephalically-determined worlds was negligible.

"I'll be okay," Seth Morley said. And shut his weary eyes.

Clambering to her feet, Mary Morley came over to him, sank down beside him and put her lean hand on his shoulder. He started to slide away from her, remembering the injury to his shoulder . . . and then he discovered that, strangely, the pain had gone. Cautiously, he patted his shoulder. No injury. No blood-seeping wound. Weird, he thought. But—I guess it's always this way. As I seem to recall.

"Can I get you anything?" his wife asked him.

"Are you okay?" he asked her. She nodded. "Why did you kill Sue Smart?" he said. "Never mind," he said, seeing the strong, wild expression on her face. "I don't know why," he said, "but this one really bothered me. All the killing. We've never had so much of it before; it was dreadful. We should have been yanked out of this one by the psychocircuit-breaker as soon as the first murder took place."

"You heard what Frazer said," Mary said. "It was necessary; we were building too many tensions here on the ship."

Morley thought, I see now why the tench exploded. When we asked it, What does Persus 9 mean? No wonder it blew up . . . and, with it, took the entire construct. Piece by piece.

The large, far-too-familiar cabin of the ship forced itself onto his attention. He felt a kind of dismal horror, seeing it again. To him the reality of the ship was far more unpleasant than— what had it been called?—Delmak-O, he recalled. That's right. We arranged random letters, provided us by the ship's computer . . . we made it up and then we were stuck with what we made up. An exciting adventure turned into gross murder. Of all of us, by the time it had finished.

He examined his calendar wristwatch. Twelve days had passed. In real time, twelve whole, overly long days; in polyencephalic time, only a little over twenty-four hours. Unless he counted the "eight years" at Tekel Upharsin, which he could not really do: it had been a manufactured recall-datum, implanted in his mind during fusion, to add the semblance of authenticity in the polyencephalic venture.

What did we make up? he asked himself blearily. The entire theology, he realized. They had fed into the ship's computer all the data they had in their possession concerning advanced religions. Into T.E.N.C.H. 889B had gone elaborated information dealing with Judaism, Christianity, Mohammedanism, Zoroastrianism, Tibetan Buddhism . . . a complex mass, out of which T.E.N.C.H. 889B was to distill a composite religion, a synthesis of every factor involved. *We made it up,* Seth Morley thought, bewildered; memory of Specktowsky's Book still filled his mind. The Intercessor, the Mentufacturer, the Walker-on-Earth—even the ferocity of the Form Destroyer. Distillate of man's total experience with God—a tremendous logical system, a comforting web deduced by the computer from the postulates given it—in particular the postulate that God existed.

And Specktowsky . . . he shut his eyes, remembering.

Egon Specktowskv had been the original captain of the ship. He had died during the accident which had disabled them. A nice touch by T.E.N.C.H. 889B, to make their dear former captain the author of the galaxy-wide worship which had acted as the base of this, their latest world. The awe and near-worship which they all felt for Egon Specktowsky had been neatly carried over to their episode on Delmak-O because for them, in a sense, he was a god—functioned, in their lives, as a god would. This touch had given the created world a more plausible air; it fitted in perfectly with their preconceptions.

The polyencephalic mind, he thought. Originally an escape toy to amuse us during our twenty-year voyage. But the voyage had not lasted twenty years; it would continue until they died, one by one, in some indefinably remote epoch, which none of them could imagine. And for good reason: everything, especially the infinitude of the voyage, had become an endless nightmare to them.

We could have survived the twenty years, Seth Morley said to himself. *Knowing it would end;* that would have kept us sane and alive. But the accident had come and now they circled, forever, a dead star. Their transmitter, because of the accident, functioned no longer, and so an escape toy, typical of those generally used in long, inter-stellar flights, had become the support for their sanity.

That's what really worries us, Morley realized. The dread that one by one we will slip into psychosis, leaving the others even more alone. More isolated from man and everything associated with man.

God, he thought, how I wish we could go back to Alpha Centaurus. If only—

But there was no use thinking about that.

Ben Tallchief, the ship's maintenance man, said, "I can't believe that we made up Specktowsky's theology by ourselves. It seemed so real. So—airtight."

Belsnor said, "The computer did most of it; of course it's airtight."

"But the basic idea was ours," Tony Dunkelwelt said. He had fixed his attention on Captain Belsnor. "You killed me in that one," he said.

"We hate one another," Belsnor said. "I hate you; you hate me. Or at least we did before the Delmak-O episode." Turning to Wade Frazer he said, "Maybe you're right; I don't feel so irritated now." Gloomily, he said, "But it'll come back, give or take a week or so."

"Do we really hate one another that much?" Sue Smart asked.

"Yes," Wade Frazer said.

Ignatz Thugg and Dr. Babble helped elderly Mrs. Rockingham to her feet. "Oh dear," she gasped, her withered and ancient face red, "that was just simply dreadful! What a terrible, terrible place; I hope we never go there again." Coming over, she plucked at Captain Belsnor's sleeve. "We won't have to live through that again, will we? I do think, in all honesty, that life aboard the ship is far preferable to that wicked, uncivilized little place."

"We won't be going back to Delmak-O," Belsnor said.

"Thank heavens." Mrs. Rockingham seated herself; again Thugg and Dr. Babble assisted her. "Thank you," she said to them. "How kind of you. Could I have some coffee, Mr. Morley?"

" 'Coffee'?" he echoed and then he remembered; he was the ship's cook. All the precious food supplies, including coffee, tea and milk, were in his possession. "I'll start a pot going," he told them all.

In the kitchen he spooned heaping tablespoonfuls of good black ground coffee into the top of the pot. He noticed, then, as he had noticed many times before, that their store of coffee had begun to run low. In another few months they would be out entirely.

But this is a time at which coffee is needed, he decided, and continued to spoon the coffee into the pot. We are all shaken up, he realized. As never before.

His wife Mary entered the galley. "What was the Building?"

"The Building." He filled the coffee pot with reprocessed water. "That was the Boeing plant on Proxima 10. Where the ship was built. Where we boarded it, remember? We were sixteen months at Boeing, getting trained, testing the ship, getting everything aboard and straightened out. Getting Persus 9 spaceworthy."

Mary shivered and said, "Those men in black leather uniforms."

"I don't know," Seth Morley said.

Ned Russell, the ship's M.P., entered the galley. "I can tell you what they were. The black leather guards were indications of our attempt to break it up and start again—they were directed by the thoughts of those who had 'died.'"

"You would know," Mary said shortly.

"Easy," Seth Morley said, putting his arm around her shoulder. From the start, many of them had not gotten along well with Russell. Which, considering his job, could have been anticipated.

"Someday, Russell," Mary said, "you're going to try to take over the ship . . . take it away from Captain Belsnor."

"No," Russell said mildly. "All I'm interested in is keeping the peace. That's why I was sent here; that's what I intend to do. Whether anyone else wants me to or not."

"I wish to God," Seth Morley said, "that there was really an Intercessor." He still had trouble believing that they had made up Specktowsky's theology. "At Tekel Upharsin," he said, "when the Walker-on-Earth came to me, it was so real. Even now it seems real. I can't shake it off."

"That's why we created it," Russell pointed out. "Because we wanted it; because we didn't have it and needed to have it. Now we're back to reality, Morley; once again we have to face things as they are. It doesn't feel too good, does it?"

"No," Seth Morley said.

Russell said, "Do you wish you were back on Delmak-O?"

After a pause he said, "Yes."

"So do I," Mary said, at last.

"I'm afraid," Russell said, "that I have to agree with you. As bad as it was, as bad as we acted . . . at least there was hope. And back here on the ship—" He made a convulsive, savage, slashing motion. "No hope. Nothing! Until we grow old like Roberta Rockingham and die."

"Mrs. Rockingham is lucky," Mary said bitterly.

"Very lucky," Russell said, and his face became swollen with impotence and bleak anger. And suffering.

Sixteen

AFTER dinner that "night" they gathered in the ship's control cabin. The time had come to plot out another polyencephalic world. To make it function it had to be a joint projection from all of them; otherwise, as in the final stages of the Delmak-O world, it would rapidly disintegrate.

In fifteen years they had become very skilled.

Especially Tony Dunkelwelt. Of his eighteen years, almost all had been spent aboard Persus 9. For him, the procession of polyencephalic worlds had become a normal way of life.

Captain Belsnor said, "We didn't do so bad, in a way; we got rid of almost two weeks."

"What about an aquatic world this time?" Maggie Walsh said. "We could be dolphin-like mammals living in warm seas."

"We did that," Russell said. "About eight months ago. Don't you remember it? Let's see . . . yes; we called it Aquasoma 3 and we stayed there three months of real time. A very successful world, I would say, and one of the most durable. Of course, back then we were less hostile."

Seth Morley said, "Excuse me." He rose and walked from the ship's cabin into the narrow passageway.

There he stood, alone, rubbing his shoulder. A purely psychosomatic pain remained in it, a memory of Delmak-O which he would probably carry for a week. And that's all, he thought, that we have left of that particular world. Just a pain, plus a rapidly-fading memory.

How about a world, he thought, in which we lie good and dead, buried in our coffins? *That's what we really want.*

There had been no suicides aboard the ship for the last four years. Their population had become stabilized, at least temporarily.

Until Mrs. Rockingham dies, he said to himself.

I wish I could go with her, he thought. How long, really, can we keep on? Not much longer. Thugg's wits are scrambled; so are Frazer's and Babble's. And me, too, he thought. Maybe I'm gradually breaking down, too. Wade Frazer is right; the murders on Delmak-O show how much derangement and hostility exists in all of us.

In that case, he thought suddenly, each escape world will be more feral . . . Russell is right. *It is a pattern.*

He thought, We will miss Roberta Rockingham when she dies; of us, she is the most benign and stable.

Because, he realized, she knows she is soon going to die.

Our only comfort. Death.

I could open vents here and there, he realized, and our atmosphere would be gone. Sucked out into the void. And then, more or less painlessly, we could all die. In one single, brief instant.

He placed his hand on the emergency release-lock of a nearby hatch vent. All I have to do, he said to himself, is move this thing counterclockwise.

He stood there, holding onto the release-lock, but doing nothing. What he intended to do had made him frozen, as if time had stopped. And everything around him looked two-dimensional.

A figure, coming down the corridor from the rear of the ship, approached him. Bearded, with flowing, pale robes. A man, youthful and erect, with a pure, shining face.

"Walker," Seth Morley said.

"No," the figure said. "I am not the Walker-on-Earth. I am the Intercessor."

"But we invented you! We and T.E.N.C.H. 889B."

The Intercessor said, "I am here to take you away. Where would you like to go, Seth Morley? What would you like to be?"

"An illusion, you mean?" he said. "Like our polyencephalic worlds?"

"No," the Intercessor said. "You will be free; you will die and be reborn. I will guide you to what you want, and to what is fitting and proper for you. Tell me what it is."

"You don't want me to kill the others," Seth Morley said, with abrupt comprehension. "By opening the vents."

The Intercessor inclined his head in a nod. "It is for each of them to decide. You may decide only for yourself."

"I'd like to be a desert plant," Seth Morley said. "That could see the sun all day. I want to be growing. Perhaps a cactus on some warm world. Where no one will bother me."

"Agreed."

"And sleep," Seth Morley said. "I want to be asleep but still aware of the sun and of myself."

"That is the way with plants," the Intercessor said. "They sleep. And yet they know themselves to exist. Very well." He held out his hand to Seth Morley. "Come along."

Reaching, Seth Morley touched the Intercessor's extended hand. Strong fingers closed around his own hand. He felt happy. He had never before been so glad.

"You will live and sleep for a thousand years," the Intercessor said, and guided him away from where he stood, into the stars.

Mary Morley, stricken, said to Captain Belsnor, "Captain, I can't find my husband." She felt wet slow tears make their way down her cheeks. "He's gone," she said, in a half-wail.

"You mean he isn't on the ship anywhere?" Belsnor said. "How could he get out without opening one of the hatches? They're the only way out of here, and if he opened one of the hatches our internal atmosphere would cease; we'd all be dead."

"I know that," she said.

"Then he still must be on the ship. We can search for him after we have our next polyencephalic world plotted out."

"Now," she said fiercely. "Look for him *now*."

"I can't," Belsnor said.

Turning, she started away from him.

"Come back. You have to help."

"I'm not coming back," she said. She continued on, down the narrow corridor, into the galley. I think he was here last, she said to herself. I still sense him here, in the galley, where he spends so much of his time.

Huddled in the cramped little galley she heard their voices dim, gradually and slowly, into silence. They've gone into polyencephalic fusion again, she realized. Without me, this time. I hope they're happy now. This is the first time I haven't gone with them, she thought. I've missed out. What should I do? she asked herself. Where should I go?

Alone, she realized. Seth's gone; they're gone. And I can't make it by myself.

By degrees she crept back into the control cabin of the ship.

There they lay, in their individual cubicles, the many-wired cylinders covering their heads. All cylinders were in use except for hers . . . and for Seth's. She stood there, trembling with hesitation. What did they feed into the computer this time? she wondered. What are the premises, and what has T.E.N.C.H. 889B deduced from that?

What is the next world going to be like?

She examined the faintly-humming computer . . . but, of all of them, only Glen Belsnor really knew how to operate it. They had of course used it, but she could not decipher the settings. The coded output baffled her, too; she remained by the computer, holding the punched tape in her hands . . . and then, with effort, made up her mind. It *must* be a reasonably good place, she told herself. We've built up so much skill, so much experience; it's not like the nightmare worlds we found ourselves in at first.

True, the homicidal element, the hostility, had grown. But the killings were not real. They were as illusory as killings in a dream.

And how easily they had taken place. How easy it had been for her to kill Susie Smart.

She lay down on the cot which belonged to her, anchored within her own particular cubicle, plugged in the life-protek mechanisms, and then, with relief, placed the cylinder over her head and shoulders. Its modulated hummm sounded faintly in her ears: a reassuring noise and one which she had heard so many times in the past, over the long and weary years.

Darkness covered her; she breathed it into herself, accepting it, demanding it . . . the darkness took over and, presently, she realized that it was night. She yearned, then, for daylight. For the world to be exposed—the new world which she could not yet see.

Who am I? she asked herself. Already it had become unclear in her mind. The Persus 9, the loss of Seth, their empty, trapped lives—all these faded from her like a burden released. She thought only of the daylight ahead; lifting her wrist to her face she tried to read her watch. But it was not running. And she could not see.

She could make out stars, now, patterns of light interladen with drifts of nocturnal fog.

"Mrs. Morley," a fussy male voice said.

She opened her eyes, fully awake. Fred Gossim, Tekel Up-harsin Kibbutz's top engineer, walked toward her carrying official papers. "You got your transfer," he told her; he held out the papers and Mary Morley accepted them. "You're going to a colony settlement on a planet called—" He hesitated, frowning. "Delmar."

"Delmak-O," Mary Morley said, scanning the transfer orders. "Yes—and I'm to go there by noser." She wondered what kind of place Delmak-O was; she had never heard of it. And yet it sounded highly interesting; her curiosity had been stirred up. "Did Seth get a transfer, too?" she asked.

" 'Seth'?" Gossim raised an eyebrow. "Who's 'Seth'?"

She laughed. "That's a very good question. I don't know. I guess it doesn't matter. I'm so glad to get this transfer—"

"Don't tell me about it," Gossim said in his usual harsh way. "As far as I'm concerned you're abandoning your responsibilities to the kibbutz." Turning, he stalked off.

A new life, Mary Morley said to herself. Opportunity and adventure and excitement. Will I like Delmak-O? she wondered. Yes. I know I will.

On light feet she danced toward her living area in the kibbutz's central building-complex. To begin to pack.

VALIS

To Russell Galen,
Who showed me the right way.

VALIS (acronym of Vast Active Living Intelligence System, from an American film): A perturbation in the reality field in which a spontaneous self-monitoring negentropic vortex is formed, tending progressively to subsume and incorporate its environment into arrangements of information. Characterized by quasi-consciousness, purpose, intelligence, growth and an armillary coherence.

—*Great Soviet Dictionary*
Sixth Edition, 1992

1

HORSELOVER FAT'S nervous breakdown began the day he got the phone call from Gloria asking if he had any Nembutals. He asked her why she wanted them and she said that she intended to kill herself. She was calling everyone she knew. By now she had fifty of them, but she needed thirty or forty more, to be on the safe side.

At once Horselover Fat leaped to the conclusion that this was her way of asking for help. It had been Fat's delusion for years that he could help people. His psychiatrist once told him that to get well he would have to do two things: get off dope (which he hadn't done) and to stop trying to help people (he still tried to help people).

As a matter of fact, he had no Nembutals. He had no sleeping pills of any sort. He never did sleeping pills. He did uppers. So giving Gloria sleeping pills by which she could kill herself was beyond his power. Anyhow, he wouldn't have done it if he could.

"I have ten," he said. Because if he told her the truth she would hang up.

"Then I'll drive up to your place," Gloria said in a rational, calm voice, the same tone in which she had asked for the pills.

He realized then that she was not asking for help. She was trying to die. She was completely crazy. If she were sane she would realize that it was necessary to veil her purpose, because this way she made him guilty of complicity. For him to agree, he would need to want her dead. No motive existed for him—or anyone—to want that. Gloria was gentle and civilized, but she dropped a lot of acid. It was obvious that the acid, since he had last heard from her six months ago, had since wrecked her mind.

"What've you been doing?" Fat asked.

"I've been in Mount Zion Hospital in San Francisco. I tried suicide and my mother committed me. They discharged me last week."

"Are you cured?" he said.

"Yes," she said.

175

That's when Fat began to go nuts. At the time he didn't know it, but he had been drawn into an unspeakable psychological game. There was no way out. Gloria Knudson had wrecked him, her friend, along with her own brain. Probably she had wrecked six or seven other people, all friends who loved her, along the way, with similar phone conversations. She had undoubtedly destroyed her mother and father as well. Fat heard in her rational tone the harp of nihilism, the twang of the void. He was not dealing with a person; he had a reflex-arc thing at the other end of the phone line.

What he did not know then is that it is sometimes an appropriate response to reality to go insane. To listen to Gloria rationally ask to die was to inhale the contagion. It was a Chinese finger-trap, where the harder you pull to get out, the tighter the trap gets.

"Where are you now?" he asked.

"Modesto. At my parents' home."

Since he lived in Marin County, she was several hours' drive away. Few inducements would have gotten him to make such a drive. This was another serving-up of lunacy: three hours' drive each way for ten Nembutals. Why not just total the car? Gloria was not even committing her irrational act rationally. Thank you, Tim Leary, Fat thought. You and your promotion of the joy of expanded consciousness through dope.

He did not know his own life was on the line. This was 1971. In 1972 he would be up north in Vancouver, British Columbia, involved in trying to kill himself, alone, poor and scared, in a foreign city. Right now he was spared that knowledge. All he wanted to do was coax Gloria up to Marin County so he could help her. One of God's greatest mercies is that he keeps us perpetually occluded. In 1976, totally crazy with grief, Horselover Fat would slit his wrist (the Vancouver suicide attempt having failed), take forty-nine tablets of high-grade digitalis, and sit in a closed garage with his car motor running—and fail there, too. Well, the body has powers unknown to the mind. However, Gloria's mind had total control over her body; she was *rationally* insane.

Most insanity can be identified with the bizarre and the theatrical. You put a pan on your head and a towel around your waist, paint yourself purple and go outdoors. Gloria was as calm as she had ever been; polite and civilized. If she had lived in ancient Rome or Japan, she would have gone unnoticed. Her driving skills probably remained unimpaired. She would stop at every red light and not exceed the speed limit—on her trip to pick up the ten Nembutals.

I am Horselover Fat, and I am writing this in the third person to gain much-needed objectivity. I did not love Gloria Knudson, but I liked her. In Berkeley, she and her husband had given elegant parties, and my wife and I always got invited. Gloria spent hours fixing little sandwiches and served different wines, and she dressed up and looked lovely, with her sandy-colored short-cut curly hair.

Anyhow, Horselover Fat had no Nembutal to give her, and a week later Gloria threw herself out of a tenth floor window of the Synanon Building in Oakland, California, and smashed herself to bits on the pavement along MacArthur Boulevard, and Horselover Fat continued his insidious, long decline into misery and illness, the sort of chaos that astrophysicists say is the fate in store for the whole universe. Fat was ahead of his time, ahead of the universe. Eventually he forgot what event had started off his decline into entropy; God mercifully occludes us to the past as well as the future. For two months, after he learned of Gloria's suicide, he cried and watched TV and took more dope—his brain was going, too, but he didn't know it. Infinite are the mercies of God.

As a matter of fact, Fat had lost his own wife, the year before, to mental illness. It was like a plague. No one could discern how much was due to drugs. This time in America—1960 to 1970—and this place, the Bay Area of Northern California, was totally fucked. I'm sorry to tell you this, but that's the truth. Fancy terms and ornate theories cannot cover this fact up. The authorities became as psychotic as those they hunted. They wanted to put all persons who were not clones of the establishment away. The authorities were filled with hate. Fat had seen police glower at him with the ferocity of dogs. The day they moved Angela Davis, the black Marxist, out of the Marin County jail, the authorities dismantled the whole civic center. This was to baffle radicals who might intend trouble. The elevators got unwired; doors got relabeled with spurious information; the district attorney hid. Fat saw all this. He had gone to the civic center that day to return a library book. At the electronic hoop at the civic center entrance, two cops had ripped open the book and papers that Fat carried. He was perplexed. The whole day perplexed him. In the cafeteria, an armed cop watched everyone eat. Fat returned home by cab, afraid of his own car and wondering if he was nuts. He was, but so was everyone else.

I am, by profession, a science fiction writer. I deal in fantasies. My life is a fantasy. Nonetheless, Gloria Knudson lies in a box in Modesto, California. There's a photo of her funeral wreaths in my photo album. It's a color photo so you can see how lovely the wreaths are. In the background a VW is parked. I can be seen crawling into the VW, in the midst of the service. I am not able to take any more.

After the graveside service Gloria's former husband Bob and I and some tearful friend of his—and hers—had a late lunch at a fancy restaurant in Modesto near the cemetery. The waitress seated us in the rear because the three of us looked like hippies even though we had suits and ties on. We didn't give a shit. I don't remember what we talked about. The night before, Bob and I—I mean, Bob and Horselover Fat—drove to Oakland to see the movie *Patton*. Just before the graveside service Fat met Gloria's parents for the first time. Like their deceased daughter, they treated him with utmost civility. A number of Gloria's friends stood around the corny California ranch-style living room recalling the person who linked them together. Naturally, Mrs. Knudson wore too much makeup; women always put on too much makeup when someone dies. Fat petted the dead girl's cat, Chairman Mao. He remembered the few days Gloria had spent with him upon her futile trip to his house for the Nembutal which he did not have. She greeted the disclosure of his lie with aplomb, even a neutrality. When you are going to die you do not care about small things.

"I took them," Fat had told her, lie upon lie.

They decided to drive to the beach, the great ocean beach of the Point Reyes Peninsula. In Gloria's VW, with Gloria driving (it never entered his mind that she might, on impulse, wipe out him, herself and the car) and, an hour later, sat together on the sand smoking dope.

What Fat wanted to know most of all was why she intended to kill herself.

Gloria had on many-times-washed jeans and a T-shirt with Mick Jagger's leering face across the front of it. Because the sand felt nice she took off her shoes. Fat noticed that she had pink-painted toenails and that they were perfectly pedicured. To himself he thought, she died as she lived.

"They stole my bank account," Gloria said.

After a time he realized, from her measured, lucidly stated narration, that no "they" existed. Gloria unfolded a panorama of total and relentless madness, lapidary in construction. She had filled in all the details with tools as precise as dental tools. No vacuum existed anywhere in her account. He could find no error, except of course for the premise, which was that everyone hated her, was out to get her, and she was worthless in every respect. As she talked she began to disappear. He watched her go; it was amazing. Gloria, in her measured way, talked herself out of existence word by word. It was rationality at the service of—well, he thought, at the service of nonbeing. Her mind had become one great, expert eraser. All that really remained now was her husk; which is to say, her uninhabited corpse.

She is dead now, he realized that day on the beach.

After they had smoked up all their dope, they walked along and commented on seaweed and the height of waves. Seagulls croaked by overhead, sailing themselves like frisbies. A few people sat or walked here and there, but mostly the beach was deserted. Signs warned of undertow. Fat, for the life of him, could not figure out why Gloria didn't simply walk out into the surf. He simply could not get into her head. All she could think of was the Nembutal she still needed, or imagined she needed.

"My favorite Dead album is *Workingman's Dead*," Gloria said at one point. "But I don't think they should advocate taking cocaine. A lot of kids listen to rock."

"They don't advocate it. The song's just about someone taking it. And it killed him, indirectly; he smashed up his train."

"But that's why I started on drugs," Gloria said.

"Because of the Grateful Dead?"

"Because," Gloria said, "everyone wanted me to do it. I'm tired of doing what other people want me to do."

"Don't kill yourself," Fat said. "Move in with me. I'm all alone. I really like you. Try it for a while, at least. We'll move your stuff up, me and my friends. There's lots of things we can do, like go places, like to the beach today. Isn't it nice here?"

To that, Gloria said nothing.

"It would really make me feel terrible," Fat said. "For the rest of my life, if you did away with yourself." Thereby, as he later realized, he presented her with all the wrong reasons for living. She would be doing it as a favor to others. He could not have found a worse reason to give had he looked for years. Better to back the VW over her. This is why suicide hotlines are not manned by nitwits; Fat learned this later in Vancouver, when, suicidal himself, he phoned the British Columbia Crisis Center and got expert advice. There was no correlation between this and what he told Gloria on the beach that day.

Pausing to rub a small stone loose from her foot, Gloria said, "I'd like to stay overnight at your place tonight."

Hearing this, Fat experienced involuntary visions of sex.

"Far out," he said, which was the way he talked in those days. The counterculture possessed a whole book of phrases which bordered on meaning nothing. Fat used to string a bunch of them together. He did so now, deluded by his own carnality into imagining that he had saved his friend's life. His judgment, which wasn't worth much anyhow, dropped to a new nadir of acuity. The existence of a good person hung in the balance, hung in a balance which Fat held, and all he could think of now was the prospect of scoring. "I can dig it," he prattled away as they walked. "Out of sight."

A few days later she was dead. They spent that night together, sleeping fully dressed; they did not make love; the next afternoon Gloria drove off, ostensibly to get her stuff from her parents' house in Modesto. He never saw her again. For several days he waited for her to show up and then one night the phone rang and it was her ex-husband Bob.

"Where are you right now?" Bob asked.

The question bewildered him; he was at home, where his phone was, in the kitchen. Bob sounded calm. "I'm here," Fat said.

"Gloria killed herself today," Bob said.

*

I have a photo of Gloria holding Chairman Mao in her arms; Gloria is kneeling and smiling and her eyes shine. Chairman Mao is trying to get down. To their left, part of a Christmas tree can be seen. On the back, Mrs. Knudson has written in tidy letters:

How we made her feel gratitude for our love.

I've never been able to fathom whether Mrs. Knudson wrote that after Gloria's death or before. The Knudsons mailed me the photo a month—mailed Horselover Fat the photo a month—after Gloria's funeral. Fat had written asking for a photo of her. Initially he had asked Bob, who replied in a savage tone, "What do you want a picture of Gloria for?" To which Fat could give no answer. When Fat got me started writing this, he asked me why I thought Bob Langley got so mad at his request. I don't know. I don't care. Maybe Bob knew that Gloria and Fat had spent a night together and he was jealous. Fat used to say Bob Langley was a schizoid; he claimed that Bob himself told him that. A schizoid lacks proper affect to go with his thinking; he's got what's called "flattening of affect." A schizoid would see no reason not to tell you that about himself. On the other hand, Bob bent down after the graveside service and put a rose on Gloria's coffin. That was about when Fat had gone crawling off to the VW. Which reaction is more appropriate? Fat weeping in the parked car by himself, or the ex-husband bending down with the rose, saying nothing, showing nothing, but doing something . . . Fat contributed nothing to the funeral except a bundle of flowers which he had belatedly bought on the trip down to Modesto. He had given them to Mrs. Knudson, who remarked that they were lovely. Bob had picked them out.

After the funeral, at the fancy restaurant where the waitress had moved the three of them out of view, Fat asked Bob what Gloria had been doing at Synanon, since she was supposed to be getting her possessions together and driving back up to Marin County to live with him—he had thought.

"Carmina talked her into going to Synanon," Bob said. That was Mrs. Knudson. "Because of her history of drug involvement."

Timothy, the friend Fat didn't know, said, "They sure didn't help her very much."

What had happened was that Gloria walked in the front door of Synanon and they had gamed her right off. Someone, on purpose, had walked past her as she sat waiting to be interviewed and had remarked on how ugly she was. The next person to parade past had informed her that her hair looked like something a rat slept in. Gloria had always been sensitive about her curly hair. She wished it was long like all the other hair in the world. What the third Synanon member would have said was moot, because by then Gloria had gone upstairs to the tenth floor.

"Is that how Synanon works?" Fat asked.

Bob said, "It's a technique to break down the personality. It's a fascist therapy that makes the person totally outer-directed and dependent on the group. Then they can build up a new personality that isn't drug oriented."

"Didn't they realize she was suicidal?" Timothy asked.

"Of course," Bob said. "She phoned in and talked to them; they knew her name and why she was there."

"Did you talk to them after her death?" Fat asked.

Bob said, "I phoned them up and asked to talk to someone high up and I told him they had killed my wife, and the man said that they wanted me to come down there and teach them how to handle suicidal people. He was super upset. I felt sorry for him."

At that, hearing that, Fat decided that Bob himself was not right in the head. Bob felt sorry for Synanon. Bob was all fucked up. Everyone was fucked up, including Carmina Knudson. There wasn't a sane person left in Northern California. It was time to move somewhere else. He sat eating his salad and wondering where he could go. Out of the country. Flee to Canada, like the draft protesters. He personally knew ten guys who had slipped across into Canada rather than fight in Vietnam. Probably in Vancouver he would run into half a dozen people he knew. Vancouver was supposed to be one of the most beautiful cities in the world. Like San Francisco, it was a major port. He could start life all over and forget the past.

It entered his head as he sat fooling with his salad that when Bob phoned he hadn't said, "Gloria killed herself" but rather "Gloria killed herself today," as if it had been inevitable that she would do it one day or another. Perhaps this had done it, this assumption. Gloria had been timed, as if she were taking a math test. Who really was the insane one? Gloria or himself (probably himself) or her ex-husband or all of them, the Bay Area, not insane in the loose sense of the term but in the strict technical sense? Let it be said that one of the first symptoms of psychosis is that the person feels perhaps he is becoming psychotic. It is another Chinese finger-trap. You cannot think about it without becoming part of it. By thinking about madness, Horselover Fat slipped by degrees into madness.

I wish I could have helped him.

2

ALTHOUGH there was nothing I could do to help Horselover Fat, he did escape death. The first thing that came along to save him took the form of an eighteen-year-old highschool girl living down the street from him and the second was God. Of the two of them the girl did better.

I'm not sure God did anything at all for him; in fact in some ways God made him sicker. This was a subject on which Fat and I could not agree. Fat was certain that God had healed him completely. That is not possible. There is a line in the *I Ching* reading, "Always ill but never dies." That fits my friend.

Stephanie entered Fat's life as a dope dealer. After Gloria's death he did so much dope that he had to buy from every source available to him. Buying dope from highschool kids is not a smart move. It has nothing to do with dope itself but with the law and with morality. Once you begin to buy dope from kids you are a marked man. I'm sure it's obvious why. But the thing I knew—which the authorities did not—is this: Horselover Fat really wasn't interested in the dope that Stephanie had for sale. She dealt hash and grass but never uppers. She did not approve of uppers. Stephanie never sold anything she did not approve of. She never sold psychedelics no matter what pressure was put on her. Now and then she sold cocaine. Nobody could quite figure out her reasoning, but it was a form of reasoning. In the normal sense, Stephanie did not think at all. But she did arrive at decisions, and once she arrived at them no one could budge her. Fat liked her.

There lay the gist of it; he liked her and not the dope, but to maintain a relationship with her he had to be a buyer, which meant he had to do hash. For Stephanie, hash was the beginning and end of life—life worth living, anyhow.

If God came in a poor second, at least he wasn't doing anything illegal, as Stephanie was. Fat was convinced that Stephanie would wind up in jail; he expected her to be arrested any day. All Fat's friends expected him to be arrested any day. We worried about that and about his slow decline into depression and psychosis and isolation. Fat worried about Stephanie.

Stephanie worried about the price of hash. More so, she worried about the price of cocaine. We used to imagine her suddenly sitting bolt upright in the middle of the night and exclaiming, "Coke has gone up to a hundred dollars a gram!" She worried about the price of dope the way normal women worry about the price of coffee.

We used to argue that Stephanie could not have existed before the Sixties. Dope had brought her into being, summoned her out of the very ground. She was a coefficient of dope, part of an equation. And yet it was through her that Fat made his way eventually to God. Not through her dope; it had nothing to do with dope. There is no door to God through dope; that is a lie peddled by the unscrupulous. The means by which Stephanie brought Horselover Fat to God was by means of a little clay pot which she threw on her kickwheel, a kickwheel which Fat had helped pay for, as a present on her eighteenth birthday. When he fled to Canada he took the pot with him, wrapped up in shorts, socks and shirts, in his single suitcase.

It looked like an ordinary pot: squat and light brown, with a small amount of blue glaze as trim. Stephanie was not an expert potter. This pot was one of the first she threw, at least outside of her ceramics class in high school. Naturally, one of her first pots would go to Fat. She and he had a close relationship. When he'd get upset, Stephanie would quiet him down by supercharging him with her hashpipe. The pot was unusual in one way, however. In it slumbered God. He slumbered in the pot for a long time, for almost too long. There is a theory among some religions that God intervenes at the eleventh hour. Maybe that is so; I couldn't say. In Horselover Fat's case God waited until three minutes before twelve, and even then what he did was barely enough: barely enough and virtually too late. You can't hold Stephanie responsible for that; she threw the pot, glazed it and fired it as soon as she had the kickwheel. She did her best to help her friend Fat, who, like Gloria before him, was beginning to die. She helped her friend the way Fat had tried to help his friend, only Stephanie did a better job. But that was the difference between her and Fat. In a crisis she knew what to do. Fat did not. Therefore Fat is alive today and Gloria is not. Fat had a better friend than Gloria had had. Perhaps he would have wanted it the other way around but the option was not his. We do not serve up people to ourselves; the universe does. The universe makes certain decisions and on the basis of those decisions some people live and some people die. This is a harsh law. But every creature yields to it out of necessity. Fat got God, and Gloria Knudson got death. It is unfair and Fat would be the first person to say so. Give him credit for that.

After he had encountered God, Fat developed a love for him which was not normal. It is not what is usually meant in saying that someone "loves God." With Fat it was an actual hunger. And stranger still, he explained to us that God had injured him and still he yearned for him, like a drunk yearns for booze. God, he told us, had fired a beam of pink light directly at him, at his head, his eyes; Fat had been temporarily blinded and his head had ached for days. It was easy, he said, to describe the beam of pink light; it's exactly what you get as a phosphene after-image when a flashbulb has gone off in your face. Fat was spiritually haunted by that color. Sometimes it showed up on a TV screen. He lived for that light, that one particular color.

However, he could never really find it again. Nothing could generate that color for light but God. In other words, normal light did not contain that color. One time Fat studied a color chart, a chart of the visible spectrum. The color was absent. He had seen a color which no one can see; it lay off the end.

What comes after light in terms of frequency? Heat? Radio waves? I should know but I don't. Fat told me (I don't know how true this is) that in the solar spectrum what he saw was above seven hundred millimicrons; in terms of Fraunhofer Lines, past B in the direction of A. Make of that what you will. I deem it a symptom of Fat's breakdown. People suffering nervous breakdowns often do a lot of research, to find explanations for what they are undergoing. The research, of course, fails.

It fails as far as we are concerned, but the unhappy fact is that it sometimes provides a spurious rationalization to the disintegrating mind—like Gloria's "they." I looked up the Fraunhofer Lines one time, and there is no "A." The earliest letter-indication that I could find is B. It goes from G to B, from ultraviolet to infrared. That's it. There is no more. What Fat saw, or thought he saw, was not light.

After he returned from Canada—after he got God—Fat and

I spent a lot of time together, and in the course of our going out at night, a regular event with us, cruising for action, seeing what was happening, we one time were in the process of parking my car when all at once a spot of pink light showed up on my left arm. I knew what it was, although I had never seen such a thing before; someone had turned a laser beam on us.

"That's a laser," I said to Fat, who had seen it, too, since the spot was moving all around, onto telephone poles and the cement wall of the garage.

Two teenagers stood at the far end of the street holding a square object between them.

"They built the goddam thing," I said.

The kids walked up to us, grinning. They had built it, they told us, from a kit. We told them how impressed we were, and they walked off to spook someone else.

"That color pink?" I asked Fat.

He said nothing. But I had the impression that he was not being up front with me. I had the feeling that I had seen his color. Why he would not say so, if such it was, I do not know. Maybe the notion spoiled a more elegant theory. The mentally disturbed do not employ the Principle of Scientific Parsimony: the most simple theory to explain a given set of facts. They shoot for the baroque.

The cardinal point which Fat had made to us regarding his experience with the pink beam which had injured and blinded him was this: he claimed that instantly—as soon as the beam struck him—he knew things he had never known. He knew, specifically, that his five-year-old son had an undiagnosed birth defect and he knew what that birth defect consisted of, down to the anatomical details. Down, in fact, to the medical specifics to relate to the doctor.

I wanted to see how he told it to the doctor. How he explained knowing the medical details. His brain had trapped all the information the beam of pink light had nailed him with, but how would he account for it?

Fat later developed a theory that the universe is made out of information. He started keeping a journal—had been, in fact, secretly doing so for some time: the furtive act of a deranged person. His encounter with God was all there on the pages in his—Fat's, not God's—handwriting.

The term "journal" is mine, not Fat's. His term was "exegesis," a theological term meaning a piece of writing that explains or interprets a portion of scripture. Fat believed that the information fired at him and progressively crammed into his head in successive waves had a holy origin and hence should be regarded as a form of scripture, even if it just applied to his son's undiagnosed right inguinal hernia which had popped the hydroseal and gone down into the scrotal sack. This was the news Fat had for the doctor. The news turned out to be correct, as was confirmed when Fat's ex-wife took Christopher in to be examined. Surgery was scheduled for the next day, which is to say as soon as possible. The surgeon cheerfully informed Fat and his ex-wife that Christopher's life had been in danger for years. He could have died during the night from a strangulated piece of his own gut. It was fortunate, the surgeon said, that they had found out about it. Thus again Gloria's "they," except that in this instance the "they" actually existed.

The surgery came off a success, and Christopher stopped. being such a complaining child. He had been in pain since birth. After that, Fat and his ex-wife took their son to another G.P., one who had eyes.

One of the paragraphs in Fat's journal impressed me enough to copy it out and include it here. It does not deal with right inguinal hernias but is more general in nature, expressing Fat's growing opinion that the nature of the universe is information. He had begun to believe this because for him the universe—his universe—was indeed fast turning into information. Once God started talking to him he never seemed to stop. I don't think they report that in the Bible.

Journal entry #37. Thoughts of the Brain are experienced by us as arrangements and rearrangements—change — in a physical universe; but in fact it isreally information and information-processing which we substantialize. We do not merely see its thoughts as objects, but rather as the movement, or, more precisely, the placement of objects: how they become linked to one another. But we cannot read the patterns of arrangement; we cannot extract the information in it—i.e. it as information, which is what it is. The linking and relinking of objects by the Brain is actually a language,

but not a language like ours (since it is addressing itself and not someone or something outside itself).

Fat kept working this particular theme over and over again, both in his journal and in his oral discourse to his friends. He felt sure the universe had begun to talk to him. Another entry in his journal reads:

#36. **We should be able to hear this information, or rather narrative, as a neutral voice inside us. But something has gone wrong. All creation is a language and nothing but a language, which for some inexplicable reason we can't read outside and can't hear inside. So I say, we have become idiots. Something has happened to our intelligence. My reasoning is this: arrangement of parts of the Brain is a language. We are parts of the Brain; therefore we are language. Why, then, do we not know this? We do not even know what we are, let alone what the outer reality is of which we are parts. The origin of the word "idiot" is the word "private." Each of us has become private, and no longer shares the common thought of the Brain, except at a subliminal level. Thus our real life and purpose are conducted below our threshold of consciousness.**

To which I personally am tempted to say, Speak for yourself, Fat.

Over a long period of time (or "Desarts of vast Eternity," as he would have put it) Fat developed a lot of unusual theories to account for his contact with God, and the information derived therefrom. One in particular struck me as interesting, being different from the others. It amounted to a kind of mental capitulation by Fat to what he was undergoing. This theory held that in actuality he wasn't experiencing anything at all. Sites of his brain were being selectively stimulated by tight energy beams emanating from far off, perhaps millions of miles away. These selective brain-site stimulations generated in his head the *impression*—for him—that he was in fact seeing and hearing words, pictures, figures of people, printed pages, in short God and God's Message, or, as Fat liked to call it, the Logos. But (this particular theory held) he really only imagined he experienced these things. They resembled holograms. What struck me was the oddity of a lunatic discounting his hallucinations in this sophisticated manner; Fat had intellectually dealt himself out the game of madness while still enjoying its sights and sounds. In effect, he no longer claimed that what he experienced was actually there. Did this indicate he had begun to get better? Hardly. Now he held the view that "they" or God or someone owned a long-range very tight information-rich beam of energy focussed on Fat's head. In this I saw no improvement, but it did represent a change. Fat could now honestly discount his hallucinations, which meant he recognized them as such. But, like Gloria, he now had a "they." It seemed to me a Pyrrhic victory. Fat's life struck me as a litany of exactly that, as, for example, the way he had rescued Gloria.

The exegesis Fat labored on month after month struck me as a Pyrrhic victory if there ever was one—in this case an attempt by a beleaguered mind to make sense out of the inscrutable. Perhaps this is the bottom line to mental illness: incomprehensible events occur; your life becomes a bin for hoax-like fluctuations of what used to be reality. And not only that—as if that weren't enough—but you, like Fat, ponder forever over these fluctuations in an effort to order them into a coherency, when in fact the only sense they make is the sense you impose on them, out of the necessity to restore everything into shapes and processes you can recognize. The first thing to depart in mental illness is the familiar. And what takes its place is bad news because not only can you not understand it, you also cannot communicate it to other people. The madman experiences something, but what it is or where it comes from he does not know.

In the midst of his shattered landscape, which one can trace back to Gloria Knudson's death, Fat imagined God had cured him. Once you notice Pyrrhic victories they seem to abound.

It reminds me of a girl I once knew who was dying of cancer. I visited her in the hospital and did not recognize her; sitting up in her bed she looked like a little old hairless man. From the chemotherapy she had swollen up like a great grape. From the cancer and the therapy she had become virtually blind, nearly deaf, underwent constant seizures, and when I bent close to her to ask her how she felt she answered, when she could understand my question, "I feel that God is healing me." She had been religiously inclined and had planned to go into a religious order. On the metal stand beside her bed she had, or someone had, laid out her rosary. In my opinion a FUCK YOU, GOD sign would have been appropriate; the rosary was not.

Yet, in all fairness, I have to admit that God—or someone calling himself God, a distinction of mere semantics—had fired precious information at Horselover Fat's head by which their son Christopher's life had been saved. Some people God cures and some he slays. Fat denies that God slays anyone. Fat says, God never harms anyone. Illness, pain and undeserved suffering arise not from God but from elsewhere, to which I say, How did this elsewhere arise? Are there two gods? Or is part of the universe out from under God's control? Fat used to quote Plato. In Plato's cosmology, *noös* or Mind is persuading *ananke* or blind necessity—or blind chance, according to some experts —into submission. *Noös* happened to come along and to its surprise discovered blind chance: chaos, in other words, onto which *noös* imposes order (although how this "persuading" is done Plato nowhere says). According to Fat, my friend's cancer consisted of disorder not yet persuaded into sentient shape. *Noös* or God had not yet gotten around to her, to which I said, "Well, when he did get around to her it was too late." Fat had no answer for that, at least in terms of oral rebuttal. Probably he sneaked off and wrote about it in his journal. He stayed up to four A.M. every night scratching away in his journal. I suppose all the secrets of the universe lay in it somewhere amid the rubble.

We enjoyed baiting Fat into theological disputation because he always got angry, taking the point of view that what we said on the topic mattered—that the topic itself mattered. By now he had become totally whacked out. We enjoyed introducing the discussion by way of some careless comment: "Well, God gave me a ticket on the freeway today" or something like that. Ensnared, Fat would leap into action. We whiled away the time pleasantly in this fashion, torturing Fat in a benign way. After we left his place we had the added satisfaction of knowing he was writing it all down in the journal. Of course, in the journal his view always prevailed.

No need existed to bait Fat with idle questions, such as, "If God can do anything can he create a ditch so wide he can't jump over it?" We had plenty of real questions that Fat couldn't field. Our friend Kevin always began his attack one way. "What about my dead cat?" Kevin would ask. Several years ago, Kevin had been out walking his cat in the early evening. Kevin, the fool, had not put the cat on a leash, and the cat had dashed out into the street and right into the front wheel of a passing car. When he picked up the remains of the cat it was still alive, breathing in bloody foam and staring at him in horror. Kevin liked to say, "On judgment day when I'm brought up before the great judge I'm going to say, 'Hold on a second,' and then I'm going to whip out my dead cat from inside my coat. 'How do you explain *this*?' I'm going to ask." By then, Kevin used to say, the cat would be as stiff as a frying pan; he would hold out the cat by its handle, its tail, and wait for a satisfactory answer.

Fat said, "No answer would satisfy you."

"No answer you could give," Kevin sneered. "Okay, so God saved your son's life; why didn't he have my cat run out into the street five seconds later? *Three* seconds later? Would that have been too much trouble? Of course, I suppose a cat doesn't matter."

"You know, Kevin," I pointed out one time, "you could have put the cat on a leash."

"No," Fat said. "He has a point. It's been bothering me. For him the cat is a symbol of everything about the universe he doesn't understand."

"I understand fine," Kevin said bitterly. "I just think it's fucked. God is either powerless, stupid or he doesn't give a shit. Or all three. He's evil, dumb and weak. I think I'll start my own exegesis."

"But God doesn't talk to you," I said.

"You know who talks to Horse?" Kevin said. "Who really talks to Horse in the middle of the night? People from the planet Stupid. Horse, what's the wisdom of God called again? Saint what?"

"Hagia Sophia," Horse said cautiously.

Kevin said, "How do you say Hagia Stupid? St. Stupid?"

"Hagia Moron," Horse said. He always defended himself by

giving in. "Moron is a Greek word like Hagia. I came across it when I was looking up the spelling of oxymoron."

"Except that the -*on* suffix is the neuter ending," I said.

That gives you an idea of where our theological arguments tended to wind up. Three malinformed people disagreeing with one another. We also had David our Roman Catholic friend and the girl who had been dying of cancer, Sherri. She had gone into remission and the hospital had discharged her. To some extent her hearing and vision were permanently impaired, but otherwise she seemed to be fine.

Fat, of course, used this as an argument for God and God's healing love, as did David and of course Sherri herself. Kevin saw her remission as a miracle of radiation therapy and chemotherapy and luck. Also, he confided to us, the remission was temporary. At any time, Sherri could get sick again. Kevin hinted darkly that the next time she got sick there wouldn't be a remission. We sometimes thought that he hoped so, since it would confirm his view of the universe.

It was a mainstay of Kevin's bag of verbal tricks that the universe consisted of misery and hostility and would get you in the end. He looked at the universe the way most people regard an unpaid bill; eventually they will force payment. The universe reeled you out, let you flop and thrash and then reeled you in. Kevin waited constantly for this to begin with him, with me, with David and especially with Sherri. As to Horselover Fat, Kevin believed that the line hadn't been payed out in years; Fat had long been in the part of the cycle where they reel you back in. He considered Fat not just potentially doomed but doomed in fact.

Fat had the good sense not to discuss Gloria Knudson and her death in front of Kevin. Had he done so, Kevin would add her to his dead cat. He would be talking about whipping her out from under his coat on judgment day, along with the cat.

Being a Catholic, David always traced everything wrong back to man's free will. This used to annoy even me. I once asked him if Sherri getting cancer consisted of an instance of free will, knowing as I did that David kept up with all the latest news in the field of pyschology and would make the mistake of claiming that Sherri had subconsciously wanted to get cancer and so had shut down her immune system, a view floating around in advanced psychological circles at that time. Sure enough, David fell for it and said so.

"Then why did she get well?" I asked. "Did she subconsciously want to get well?"

David looked perplexed. If he consigned her illness to her own mind he was stuck with having to consign her remission to mundane and not supernatural causes. God had nothing to do with it.

"What C. S. Lewis would say," David began, which at once angered Fat, who was present. It maddened him when David turned to C. S. Lewis to bolster his straight-down-the-pipe orthodoxy.

"Maybe Sherri overrode God," I said. "God wanted her sick and she fought to get well." The thrust of David's impending argument would of course be that Sherri had neurotically gotten cancer due to being fucked up, but God had stepped in and saved her; I had turned it around in anticipation.

"No," Fat said. "It's the other way around. Like when he cured me."

Fortunately, Kevin was not present. He did not consider Fat cured (nor did anyone else) and anyway God didn't do it. That is a logic which Freud attacks, by the way, the two-proposition self-cancelling structure. Freud considered this structure a revelation of rationalization. Someone is accused of stealing a horse, to which he replies, "I don't steal horses and anyhow you have a crummy horse." If you ponder the reasoning in this you can see the actual thought-process behind it. The second statement does not reinforce the first. It only looks like it does. In terms of our perpetual theological disputations—brought on by Fat's supposed encounter with the divine—the two-proposition self-cancelling structure would appear like this:

1) God does not exist.
2) And anyhow he's stupid.

A careful study of Kevin's cynical rantings reveals this structure at every turn. David continually quoted C. S. Lewis; Kevin contradicted himself logically in his zeal to defame God; Fat made obscure references to information fired into his head by a beam of pink light; Sherri, who had suffered dreadfully, wheezed out pious mummeries; I switched my position according to who I was talking to at the time. None of us had a grip on the situation, but we did have a lot of free time to waste in this fashion. By now the epoch of drug-taking had ended, and everyone had begun casting about for a new obsession. For us the new obsession, thanks to Fat, was theology.

A favorite antique quotation of Fat's goes:

"And can I think the great Jehovah sleeps,
 Like Shemosh, and such fabled deities?
 Ah! no; heav'n heard my thoughts, and wrote them down
 It must be so."

Fat doesn't like to quote the rest of it.

" 'Tis this that racks my brain,
 And pours into my breast a thousand pangs,
 That lash me into madness . . ."

It's from an aria by Handel. Fat and I used to listen to my Seraphim LP of Richard Lewis singing it. *Deeper, and deeper still.*

Once I told Fat that another aria on the record described his mind perfectly.

"Which aria?" Fat said guardedly.

"*Total eclipse,*" I answered.

"Total eclipse! no sun, no moon,
 All dark amidst the blaze of noon!
 Oh, glorious light! no cheering ray
 To glad my eyes with welcome day!
 Why thus deprived Thy prime decree?
 Sun, moon and stars are dark to me!"

To which Fat said, "The opposite is true in my case. I am illuminated by holy light fired at me from another world. I see what no other man sees."

He had a point there.

3

A QUESTION we had to learn to deal with during the dope decade was, How do you break the news to someone that his brains are fried? This issue had now passed over into Horselover Fat's theological world as a problem for us—his friends—to field.

It would have been simple to tie the two together in Fat's case: the dope he did during the Sixties had pickled his head on into the Seventies. If I could have arranged it so that I could think so I would have; I like solutions that answer a variety of problems simultaneously. But I really couldn't think so. Fat hadn't done psychedelics, at least not to any real extent. Once, in 1964, when Sandoz LSD-25 could still be acquired—especially in Berkeley—Fat had dropped one huge hit of it and had abreacted back in time or had shot forward in time or up outside of time; anyhow he had spoken in Latin and believed that the *Dies Irae*, the Day of Wrath, had come. He could hear God thumping tremendously, in fury. For eight hours Fat had prayed and whined in Latin. Later he claimed that during his trip he could only think in Latin and talk in Latin; he had found a book with a Latin quotation in it, and could read it as easily as he normally read English. Well, perhaps the etiology of his later God-madness lay there. His brain, in 1964, liked the acid trip and taped it, for future replay.

On the other hand, this line of reasoning merely relegates the question back to 1964. As far as I can determine, the ability to read, think and speak in Latin is not normal for an acid trip. Fat knows no Latin. He can't speak it now. He couldn't speak it before he dropped the huge hit of Sandoz LSD-25. Later, when his religious experiences began, he found himself thinking in a foreign language which he did *not* understand (he had understood his own Latin in '64). Phonetically, he had written down some of the words, remembered at random. To him they constituted no language at all, and he hesitated to show anyone what he had put on paper. His wife—his later wife Beth—had taken a year of Greek in college and she recognized what Fat had written down, inaccurately, as *koine* Greek. Or at least Greek of some sort, Attic or *koine*.

The Greek word *koine* simply means *common*. By the time of the New Testament, the *koine* had become the *lingua franca* of the Middle East, replacing Aramaic which had previously supplanted Akkadian (I know these things because I am a professional writer and it is essential that I possess a scholarly knowledge about languages). The New Testament manuscripts survived in *koine* Greek, although probably Q, the source of the synoptics, had been written in Aramaic, which is in fact a form of Hebrew. Jesus spoke Aramaic. Thus, when Horselover Fat began to think in *koine* Greek, he was thinking in the language which St. Luke and St. Paul—who were close friends— had used, at least to write with. The *koine* looks funny when written down because the scribes left no spaces between the words. This can lead to a lot of peculiar translations, since the translator gets to put the spaces wherever he feels is appropriate or in fact wherever he wants. Take this English instance:

GOD IS NO WHERE
GOD IS NOW HERE

Actually, these matters were pointed out to me by Beth, who never took Fat's religious experiences seriously until she saw him write down phonetically several words of the *koine*, which she knew he had no experience with and could not recognize even as a genuine language. What Fat claimed was—well, Fat claimed plenty. I must not start any sentence with, "What Fat claimed was." During the years—outright years!—that he labored on his exegesis, Fat must have come up with more theories than there are stars in the universe. Every day he developed a new one, more cunning, more exciting and more fucked. God, however, remained a constant theme. Fat ventured away from belief in God the way a timid dog I once owned had ventured off its front lawn. He—both of them— would go first one step, then another, then perhaps a third and then turn tail and run frantically back to familiar territory. God, to Fat, constituted a territory which he had staked out. Unfortunately for him, following the initial experience, Fat could not find his way back to that territory.

They ought to make it a binding clause that if you find God you get to keep him. For Fat, finding God (if indeed he did find God) became, ultimately, a bummer, a constantly diminishing supply of joy, sinking lower and lower like the contents of a bag of uppers. Who deals God? Fat knew that the churches couldn't help, although he did consult with one of David's priests. It didn't work. Nothing worked. Kevin suggested dope. Being involved with literature, I recommended he read the English seventeenth century minor metaphysical poets such as Vaughan and Herbert:

> "He knows he hath a home, but scarce knows where,
>   He sayes it is so far
> That he hath quite forgot how to go there."

Which is from Vaughan's poem "Man." As nearly as I could make out, Fat had devolved to the level of those poets, and had, for these times, become an anachronism. The universe has a habit of deleting anachronisms. I saw this coming for Fat if he didn't get his shit together.

Of all the suggestions given to Fat, the one that seemed most promising came from Sherri, who still lingered on with us in a state of remission. "What you should do," she told Fat during one of his darker hours, "is get into studying the characteristics of the T-34."

Fat asked what that was. It turned out that Sherri had read a book on Russian armor during World War Two. The T-34 tank had been the Soviet Union's salvation and thereby the salvation of all the Allied Powers—and, by extension, Horselover Fat's, since without the T-34 he would be speaking—not English or Latin or the *koine*—but German.

"The T-34," Sherri explained, "moved very rapidly. At Kursk they knocked out even Porsche Elefants. You have no idea what they did to the Fourth Panzer Army." She then started drawing sketches of the situation at Kursk in 1943, giving figures. Fat and the rest of us were mystified. This was a side of Sherri we hadn't known. "It took Zhukov himself to turn the tide against the Panzers," Sherri wheezed on. "Vatutin screwed up. He was later murdered by pro-Nazi partisans. Now, consider the Tiger tank the Germans had and their Panthers." She showed us photographs of various tanks and related with relish how General Koniev had successfully crossed the Dniester and Prut Rivers by March twenty-sixth.

Basically, Sherri's idea had to do with bringing Fat's mind down from the cosmic and the abstract to the particular. She had hatched out the practical notion that nothing is more real than a large World War Two Soviet tank. She wanted to provide an antitoxin to Fat's madness. However, her recitation, complete with maps and photographs, only served to remind him of the night he and Bob had seen the movie *Patton* before attending Gloria's graveside service. Naturally, Sherri had not known about that.

"I think he should take up sewing," Kevin said. "Don't you have a sewing machine, Sherri? Teach him to use it."

Sherri, showing a high degree of stubbornness, continued, "The tank battles at Kursk involved over four thousand armored vehicles. It was the greatest battle of armor in history. Everyone knows about Stalingrad, but nobody knows about Kursk. The real victory by the Soviet Union took place at Kursk. When you consider—"

"Kevin," David interrupted, "what the Germans should have done was show the Russians a dead cat and ask them to explain it."

"That would have stopped the Soviet offensive right there," I said. "Zhukov would still be trying to account for the cat's death."

To Kevin, Sherri said, "In view of the stunning victory by the good side at Kursk, how can you complain about one cat?"

"There's something in the Bible about falling sparrows," Kevin said. "About his eye being on them. That's what's wrong with God; he only has one eye."

"Did God win the battle at Kursk?" I said to Sherri. "That must be news to the Russians, especially the ones who built the tanks and drove them and got killed."

Sherri said patiently, "God uses us as instruments through which he works."

"Well," Kevin said, "regarding Horse, God has a defective instrument. Or maybe they're both defective, like an eighty-year-old lady driving a Pinto with a drop-in gas tank."

"The Germans would have had to hold up Kevin's dead cat,"

Fat said. "Not just any dead cat. All Kevin cares about is that one cat."

"That cat," Kevin said, "did not exist during World War Two."

"Did you grieve over him then?" Fat said.

"How could I?" Kevin said. "He didn't exist."

"Then his condition was the same as now," Fat said.

"Wrong," Kevin said.

"Wrong in what way?" Fat said. "How did his nonexistence then differ from his nonexistence now?"

"Kevin's got the corpse now," David said. "To hold up. That was the whole point of the cat's existence. He lived to become a corpse by which Kevin could refute the goodness of God."

"Kevin," Fat said, "who created your cat?"

"God did," Kevin said.

"So God created a refutation of his own goodness," Sherri said. "By your logic."

"God is stupid," Kevin said. "We have a stupid deity. I've said that before."

Sherri said, "Does it take much skill to create a cat?"

"You just need two cats," Kevin said. "One male and one female." But he could obviously see where she was leading him. "It takes—" He paused, grinning. "Okay, it takes skill, if you presume purpose in the universe."

"You don't see any purpose?" Sherri said.

Hesitating, Kevin said, "Living creatures have purpose."

"Who puts the purpose in them?" Sherri said.

"They—" Again Kevin hesitated. "They are their purpose. They and their purpose can't be separated."

"So an animal is an expression of purpose," Sherri said. "So there is purpose in the universe."

"In small parts of it."

"And unpurpose gives rise to purpose."

Kevin eyed her. "Eat shit," he said.

In my opinion, Kevin's cynical stance had done more to ratify Fat's madness than any other single factor—any other, that is, than the original cause, whatever that might have been. Kevin had become the unintentional instrument of that original cause, a realization which had not escaped Fat. In no way, shape or form did Kevin represent a viable alternative to mental illness. His cynical grin had about it the grin of death; he grinned like a triumphant skull. Kevin lived to defeat life. It originally amazed me that Fat would put up with Kevin, but later I could see why. Every time Kevin tore down Fat's system of delusions—mocked them and lampooned them—Fat gained strength. If mockery were the only antidote to his malady, he was palpably better off as he stood. Whacked out as he was, Fat could see this. Actually, were the truth known, Kevin could see it too. But he evidently had a feedback loop in his head that caused him to step up the attacks rather than abandon them. His failure reinforced his efforts. So the attacks grew and Fat's strength grew. It resembled a Greek myth.

In Horselover Fat's exegesis the theme of this issue is put forth over and over again. Fat believed that a streak of the irrational permeated the entire universe, all the way up to God, or the Ultimate Mind, which lay behind it. He wrote:

#38. From loss and grief the Mind has become deranged. Therefore we, as parts of the universe, the Brain, are partly deranged.

Obviously he had extrapolated into cosmic proportions from his own loss of Gloria.

#35. The Mind is not talking to us but by means of us. Its narrative passes through us and its sorrow infuses us irrationally. As Plato discerned, there is a streak of the irrational in the World Soul.

Entry #32 gives more on this:

The changing information which we experience as world is an unfolding narrative. *It tells about the death of a woman* (italics mine). This woman, who died long ago, was one of the primordial twins. She was one half of the divine syzygy. The purpose of the narrative is the recollection of her and of her death. The Mind does not wish to forget her. Thus the ratiocination of the Brain consists of a permanent record of her existence, and, if read, will be understood this way. All the information processed by the Brain— experienced by us as the arranging and rearranging of physical objects—is an attempt at this preservation of her; stones and rocks and sticks and amoebae are traces of her. The record of her existence and passing is ordered onto the

meanest level of reality by the suffering Mind which is now alone.

If, in reading this, you cannot see that Fat is writing about himself, then you understand nothing.

On the other hand, I am not denying that Fat was totally whacked out. He began to decline when Gloria phoned him and he continued to decline forever and ever. Unlike Sherri and her cancer, Fat experienced no remission. Encountering God was not a remission. But probably it wasn't a worsening, despite Kevin's cynical views. You cannot say that an encounter with God is to mental illness what death is to cancer: the logical outcome of a deteriorating illness process. The technical term —theological technical term, not psychiatric—is theophany. A theophany consists of a self-disclosure by the divine. It does not consist of something the percipient does; it consists of something the divine—the God or gods, the high power—does. Moses did not create the burning bush. Elijah, on Mount Horeb, did not generate the low, murmuring voice. How are we to distinguish a genuine theophany from a mere hallucination on the part of the percipient? If the voice tells him something he does not know *and could not know*, then perhaps we are dealing with the genuine thing and not the spurious. Fat knew no *koine* Greek. Does this prove anything? He did not know about his son's birth defect—at least not consciously. Perhaps he knew about the near-strangulated hernia unconsciously, and simply did not want to face it. There exists, too, a mechanism by which he might have known the *koine*; it has to do with phylogenic memory, the experience of which has been reported by Jung: he terms it the collective or racial unconscious. The ontogeny—that is, the individual—recapitulates the phylogeny —that is, the species—and since this is generally accepted, then maybe here lies a basis for Fat's mind serving up a language spoken two thousand years ago. If there were phylogenic memories buried in the individual human mind, this is what you might expect to find. But Jung's concept is speculative. No one, really, has been able to verify it.

If you grant the possibility of a divine entity, you cannot deny it the power of self-disclosure; obviously any entity or being worthy of the term "god" would possess, without effort, that ability. The real question (as I see it) is not, Why theophanies? but, Why aren't there more? The key concept to account for this is the idea of the *deus absconditus*, the hidden, concealed, secret or unknown god. For some reason Jung regards this as a notorious idea. But if God exists, he must be a *deus absconditus*—with the exception of his rare theophanies, or else he does not exist at all. The latter view makes more sense, except for the theophanies, rare though they be. All that is required is one absolutely verified theophany and the latter view is voided.

The vividness of the impression which a supposed theophany makes on the percipient is no proof of authenticity. Nor, really, is group perception (as Spinoza supposed, the entire universe may be one theophany, but then, again, the universe may not exist at all, as the Buddhist idealists decided). Any given alleged theophany may be a fake because anything may be a fake, from stamps to fossil skulls to black holes in space.

That the entire universe—as we experience it—could be a forgery is an idea best expressed by Heraclitus. Once you have taken this notion, or doubt, into your head, you are ready to deal with the issue of God.

> "It is necessary to have understanding (*noös*) in order to be able to interpret the evidence of eyes and ears. The step from the obvious to the latent truth is like the translation of utterances in a language which is foreign to most men. Heraclitus . . . in *Fragment 56* says that men, in regard to knowledge of perceptible things, 'are the victims of illusion much as Homer was.' To reach the truth from the appearances, it is necessary to interpret, to guess the riddle . . . but though this seems to be within the capacity of men, it is something most men never do. Heraclitus is very vehement in his attacks on the foolishness of ordinary men, and of what passes for knowledge among them. They are compared to sleepers in private worlds of their own."

Thus says Edward Hussey, Lecturer in Ancient Philosophy at the University of Oxford and a Fellow of All Souls College, in his book THE PRESOCRATICS, published by Charles Scribner's Sons, New York, 1972, pages 37–38. In all my reading I have—I mean, Horselover Fat has—never found anything more significant as an insight into the nature of reality. In *Fragment 123*, Heraclitus says, "The nature of things is in the habit of concealing itself." And in *Fragment 54* he says, "Latent structure is master of obvious structure," to which Edward Hussey adds, "Consequently, he (Heraclitus) necessarily agreed . . . that reality was to some extent 'hidden.'" So if reality "[is] to some extent 'hidden,'" then what is meant by "theophany"? Because a theophany is an in-breaking of God, an in-breaking which amounts to an invasion of our world; and yet our world is only seeming; it is only "obvious structure," which is under the mastery of an unseen "latent structure." Horselover Fat would like you to consider this above all other things. Because if Heraclitus is correct, there is in fact no reality but that of theophanies; the rest is illusion; in which case Fat alone among us comprehends the truth, and Fat, starting with Gloria's phonecall, is insane.

Insane people—psychologically defined, not legally defined—are not in touch with reality. Horselover Fat is insane; therefore he is not in touch with reality. Entry #30 from his exegesis:

The phenomenal world does not exist; it is a hypostasis of the information processed by the Mind.

#35. The Mind is not talking to us but by means of us. Its narrative passes through us and its sorrow infuses us irrationally. As Plato discerned, there is a streak of the irrational in the World Soul.

In other words, the universe itself—and the Mind behind it—is insane. Therefore someone in touch with reality is, by definition, in touch with the insane: infused by the irrational.

In essence, Fat monitored his own mind and found it defective. He then, by the use of that mind, monitored outer reality, that which is called the macrocosm. He found it defective as well. As the Hermetic philosophers stipulated, the macrocosm and the microcosm mirror each other faithfully. Fat, using a defective instrument, swept out a defective subject, and from this sweep got back the report that everything was wrong.

And in addition, there was no way out. The interlocking between the defective instrument and the defective subject produced another perfect Chinese finger-trap. Caught in his own maze, like Daedalus, who built the labyrinth for King

Minos of Crete and then fell into it and couldn't get out. Presumably Daedalus is still there, and so are we. The only difference between us and Horselover Fat is that Fat knows his situation and we do not; therefore Fat is insane and we are normal. "They are compared to sleepers in private worlds of their own," as Hussey put it, and he would know; he is the foremost living authority on ancient Greek thought, with the possible exception of Francis Cornford. And it is Cornford who says that Plato believed that there was an element of the irrational in the World Soul.*

There is no route out of the maze. The maze shifts as you move through it, because it is alive.

> PARSIFAL: I move only a little, yet already I seem to have gone far.
> GURNEMANZ: You see, my son, here time turns into space.

(The whole landscape becomes indistinct. A forest ebbs out and a wall of rough rock ebbs in, through which can be seen a gateway. The two men pass through the gateway. What happened to the forest? The two men did not really move; they did not really go anywhere, and yet they are not now where they originally were. *Here time turns into space.* Wagner began *Parsifal* in 1845. He died in 1873, long before Hermann Minkowski postulated four-dimensional space-time (1908). The source-basis for *Parsifal* consisted of Celtic legends, and Wagner's research into Buddhism for his never-written opera about the Buddha to be called *The Victors* (*Die Sieger*). Where did Richard Wagner get the notion that time could turn into space?)

And if time can turn into space, can space turn into time?

In Mircea Eliade's book *Myth and Reality* one chapter is titled, "Time Can Be Overcome." It is a basic purpose of mythic ritual and sacrament to overcome time. Horselover Fat found himself thinking in a language used two thousand years ago, the language in which St. Paul wrote. *Here time turns into space.* Fat told me another feature of his encounter with God:

* *Plato's Cosmology, The Timaeus of Plato,* Library of Liberal Arts, New York, 1937.

all of a sudden the landscape of California, U.S.A., 1974 ebbed out and the landscape of Rome of the first century c.e. ebbed in. He experienced a superimposition of the two for a while, like techniques familiar in movies. In photography. Why? How? God explained many things to Fat but he never explained that, except for this cryptic statement: it is journal listing **#3. He causes things to look different so it would appear time has passed.** Who is "he"? Are we to infer that time has *not* in fact passed? And did it ever pass? Was there once a real time, and for that matter a real world, and now there is counterfeit time and a counterfeit world, like a sort of bubble growing and looking different but actually static?

Horselover Fat saw fit to list this statement early in his journal or exegesis or whatever he calls it. Journal listing #4, the next entry, goes:

Matter is plastic in the face of Mind.

Is any world out there at all? For all intents and purposes Gurnemanz and Parsifal stand still, and the landscape changes; so they become located in another space—a space which formerly had been experienced as time. Fat thought in a language of two thousand years ago and saw the ancient world appropriate to that language; the inner contents of his mind matched his perceptions of the outer world. Some kind of logic seems involved, here. Perhaps a time dysfunction took place. But why didn't his wife Beth experience it, too? She was living with him when he had his encounter with the divine. For her nothing changed, except (as she told me) she heard strange popping sounds, like something overloaded: objects pushed to the point where they exploded, as if jammed, jammed with too much energy.

Both Fat and his wife told me another aspect of those days, in March 1974. Their pet animals underwent a peculiar metamorphosis. The animals looked more intelligent and more peaceful. That is, until both animals died of massive malignant tumors.

Both Fat and his wife told me one thing about their pets which has stuck in my mind ever since. During that time the animals seemed to be trying to communicate with them, trying to use language. That cannot be written off as part of Fat's psychosis—that, and the animals' death.

The first thing that went wrong, according to Fat, had to do with the radio. Listening to it one night—he had not been able to sleep for a long time—he heard the radio saying hideous words, sentences which it could not be saying. Beth, being asleep, missed that. So that could have been Fat's mind breaking down; by then his psyche was disintegrating at a terrible velocity.

Mental illness is not funny.

4

FOLLOWING his spectacular suicide attempt with the pills, the razor blade and the car engine, all this due to Beth taking their son Christopher and leaving him, Fat found himself locked up in the Orange County mental hospital. An armed cop had pushed him in a wheelchair from the cardiac intensive care ward through the underground corridor which connected with the psychiatric wing.

Fat had never been locked up before. From the forty-nine tablets of digitalis he had suffered several days of PAT arrhythmia, since his efforts had yielded maximum dig toxicity, listed on the scale as Three. Digitalis had been prescribed for him to counter an hereditary PAT arrhythmia, but nothing such as he experienced while dig toxic. It's ironic that an overdose of digitalis induces the very arrhythmia it is used to counteract. At one point, while Fat lay on his back gazing up at the cathode-tube screen over his head, a straight line showed; his heart had stopped beating. He continued to watch, and finally the trace dot resumed its wave-form. The mercies of God are infinite.

So in a weakened condition he arrived under armed guard at the psychiatric lock-up, where he soon found himself sitting in a corridor breathing vast amounts of cigarette smoke and shaking, both from fatigue and fear. That night he slept on a cot—six cots to a room—and discovered that his cot came equipped with leather manacles. The door had been propped open to the corridor so the psych techs could keep watch over the patients. Fat could see the communal TV set, which remained on. Johnny Carson's guest turned out to be Sammy Davis, Jr. Fat lay watching, wondering how it felt to have one glass eye. At that point he had no insight into his situation. He understood that he had survived the dig toxicity; he understood that for all intents and purposes he was now under arrest for his suicide attempt; he had no idea what Beth had been doing during the time he lay in the cardiac intensive care ward. She had neither called nor come to visit him. Sherri had come first, then David. No one else knew. Fat particularly did not want Kevin to know because Kevin would show up and be cynical at his—Fat's—expense. And he wasn't in any condition to receive cynicism, even if it were well meant.

The chief cardiologist at the Orange County Medical Center had exhibited Fat to a whole group of student doctors from U.C. Irvine. O.C.M.C. was a teaching hospital. They all wanted to listen to a heart laboring under forty-nine tabs of high-grade digitalis.

Also, he had lost blood from the slash on his left wrist. What had saved his life initially emanated from a defect in the choke of his car; the choke hadn't opened properly as the engine warmed, and finally the engine had stalled. Fat had made his way unsteadily back into the house and lain down on his bed to die. The next morning he woke up, still alive, and had begun to vomit up the digitalis. That was the second thing which saved him. The third thing came in the form of all the paramedics in the world removing the glass and aluminum sliding door at the rear of Fat's house. Fat had phoned his pharmacy somewhere along the line to get a refill on his Librium prescription; he had taken thirty Librium just before taking the digitalis. The pharmacist had contacted the paramedics. A lot can be said for the infinite mercies of God, but the smarts of a good pharmacist, when you get down to it, is worth more.

After one night in the receiving ward of the psychiatric wing of the county medical hospital, Fat underwent his automatic evaluation. A whole host of well-dressed men and women confronted him; each held a clipboard and all of them scrutinized him intently.

Fat put on the trappings of sanity, as best he could. He did everything possible to convince them that he had regained his senses. As he spoke he realized that nobody believed him. He could have delivered his monolog in Swahili with equal effect. All he managed to do was abase himself and thereby divest himself of his last remnant of dignity. He had stripped away his self-respect by his own earnest efforts. Another Chinese finger-trap.

Fuck it, Fat said to himself finally, and ceased talking.

"Go outside," one of the psych techs said, "and we'll let you know our decision."

"I really have learned my lesson," Fat said as he rose and started out of the room. "Suicide represents the introjection of hostility which should better be directed outward at the person who has frustrated you. I had a lot of time to meditate during the intensive cardiac care unit or ward and I realized that years of self-abnegation and denial manifested itself in my destructive act. But what amazed me the most was the wisdom of my body, which knew not only to defend itself from my mind but specifically how to defend itself. I realize now that Yeats's statement, 'I am an immortal soul tied to the body of a dying animal' is diametrically opposite to the actual state of affairs *vis-à-vis* the human condition."

The psych tech said, "We'll talk to you outside after we've made our decision."

Fat said, "I miss my son."

No one looked at him.

"I thought Beth might hurt Christopher," Fat said. That was the only true statement he had made since entering the room. He had tried to kill himself not so much because Beth had left him but because with her living elsewhere he could not look after his little son.

Presently, he sat outside in the corridor, on a plastic and chrome couch, listening to a fat old woman tell how her husband had plotted to kill her by pumping poison gas under the door of her bedroom. Fat thought back over his life. He did not think about God, who he had seen. He did not say to himself, I am one of the few human beings who has actually seen God. Instead he thought back to Stephanie who had made him the little clay pot which he called Oh Ho because it seemed like a Chinese pot to him. He wondered if Stephanie had become a heroin addict by now or had been locked up in jail, as he was now locked up, or was dead, or married, or living in the snow in Washington like she had always talked about, the state of Washington, which she had never seen but dreamed about. Maybe all of those things or none of them. Maybe she had been crippled in an auto accident. He wondered what Stephanie would say to him if she could see him now, locked up, his wife and child gone, the choke on his car not working, his mind fried.

Were his mind not fried he probably would have thought about how lucky he was to be alive—not in the philosophical sense of lucky but in the statistical sense. Nobody survives forty-nine tabs of high grade pure digitalis. As a general rule,

twice the prescribed dose of digitalis will off you. Fat's prescribed dose had been fixed at *q.i.d.*: four a day. He had swallowed 12.25 times his prescribed daily dose and survived. The
infinite mercies of God make no sense whatsoever, in terms of
practical considerations. In addition he had downed all his Librium, twenty Quide and sixty Apresoline, plus half a bottle of
wine. All that remained of his medication was a bottle of Miles
Nervine. Fat was technically dead.

Spiritually, he was dead, too.

Either he had seen God too soon or he had seen him too
late. In any case, it had done him no good at all in terms of
survival. Encountering the living God had not helped to equip
him for the tasks of ordinary endurance, which ordinary men,
not so favored, handle.

But it could also be pointed out—and Kevin had done so—
that Fat had accomplished something else in addition to seeing
God. Kevin had phoned him up one day in excitement, having
in his possession another book by Mircea Eliade.

"Listen!" Kevin said. "You know what Eliade says about the
dream-time of the Australian bushmen? He says that anthro-
pologists are wrong in assuming that the dream-time is time in
the past. Eliade says that it's another kind of time going on
right now, which the bushmen break through and into, the
age of the heroes and their deeds. Wait; I'll read you the part."
An interval of silence. "Fuck," Kevin then said. "I can't find it.
But the way they prepare for it is to undergo dreadful pain; it's
their ritual of initiation. You were in a lot of pain when you
had your experience; you had that impacted wisdom tooth and
you were—" On the phone Kevin lowered his voice; he had
been shouting. "You remember. Afraid about the authorities
getting you."

"I was nuts," Fat had answered. "They weren't after me."

"But you thought they were and you were so scared you
fucking couldn't sleep at night, night after night. And you
underwent sensory deprivation."

"Well, I lay in bed unable to sleep."

"You started seeing colors. Floating colors." Kevin had
begun to shout again in excitement; when his cynicism vanished
he became manic. "That's described in *The Tibetan Book of
the Dead*; that's the trip across to the next world. You were

mentally dying! From stress and fear! That's how it's done—reaching into the next reality! The dream-time!"

Right now Fat sat on the plastic and chrome couch mentally dying; in fact he was already mentally dead, and in the room he had left, the experts were deciding his fate, passing sentence and judgment on what remained of him. It is proper that technically qualified non-lunatics should sit in judgment on lunatics. How could things be otherwise?

"If they could just get across to the dream-time!" Kevin shouted. "That's the only *real* time; all the real events happen in the dream-time! The actions of the gods!"

Beside Fat the huge old lady held a plastic pan; for hours she had been trying to throw up the Thorazine they had forced on her; she believed, she rasped at Fat, that the Thorazine had poison in it, by which her husband—who had penetrated the top levels of the hospital staff under a variety of names—intended to finish killing her.

"You found your way into the upper realm," Kevin declared. "Isn't that how you put it in your journal?"

#48. Two realms there are, upper and lower. The upper, derived from hyperuniverse I or Yang, Form I of Parmenides, is sentient and volitional. The lower realm, or Yin, Form II of Parmenides, is mechanical, driven by blind, efficient cause, deterministic and without intelligence, since it emanates from a dead source. In ancient times it was termed "astral determinism." We are trapped, by and large, in the lower realm, but are, through the sacraments, by means of the plasmate, extricated. Until astral determinism is broken, we are not even aware of it, so occluded are we. "The Empire never ended."

A small, pretty, dark-haired girl walked silently past Fat and the huge old woman, carrying her shoes. At breakfast time she had tried to smash a window using her shoes and then, having failed, knocked down a six-foot-high black technician. Now, the girl had about her the presence of absolute calm.

"The Empire never ended," Fat quoted to himself. That one sentence appeared over and over again in his exegesis; it had become his tag line. Originally the sentence had been revealed to him in a great dream. In the dream he again was a child, searching dusty used-book stores for rare old science fiction magazines, in particular *Astoundings*. In the dream he had looked through countless tattered issues, stacks upon stacks, for the priceless serial entitled "The Empire Never Ended." If he could find it and read it he would know everything; that had been the burden of the dream.

Prior to that, during the interval in which he had experienced the two-world superimposition, had seen not only California, U.S.A., of the year 1974 but also ancient Rome, he had discerned within the superimposition a Gestalt shared by both space-time continua, their common element: a Black Iron Prison. This is what the dream referred to as "the Empire." He knew it because, upon seeing the Black Iron Prison, he had recognized it. Everyone dwelt in it without realizing it. The Black Iron Prison was their world.

Who had built the prison—and why—he could not say. But he could discern one good thing: the prison lay under attack. An organization of Christians, not regular Christians such as those who attended church every Sunday and prayed, but secret early Christians wearing light gray-colored robes, had started an assault on the prison, and with success. The secret, early Christians were filled with joy.

Fat, in his madness, understood the reason for their joy. This time the early, secret, gray-robed Christians would get the prison, *rather than the other way around*. The deeds of the heroes, in the sacred dream-time . . . the only time, according to the bushmen, that was real.

Once, in a cheap science fiction novel, Fat had come across a perfect description of the Black Iron Prison but set in the far future. So if you superimposed the past (ancient Rome) over the present (California in the twentieth century) and superimposed the far future world of *The Android Cried Me a River* over that, you got the Empire, the Black Iron Prison, as the supra- or trans-temporal constant. Everyone who had ever lived was literally surrounded by the iron walls of the prison; they were all inside it and none of them knew it—except for the gray-robed secret Christians.

That made the early, secret Christians supra- or trans-temporal, too, which is to say present at all times, a situation which Fat could not fathom. How could they be early but in the present and the future? And if they existed in the present, why couldn't anyone see them. On the other hand, why couldn't anyone see the walls of the Black Iron Prison which enclosed everyone, including himself, on all sides? Why did these antithetical forces emerge into palpability only when the past, present and future somehow—for whatever reason—got superimposed?

Maybe in the bushmen's dream-time no time existed. But if no time existed, how could the early, secret Christians be scampering away in glee from the Black Iron Prison which they had just succeeded in blowing up? And how could they blow it up back in Rome circa 70 C.E., since no explosives existed in those days? And how, if no time passed in the dream-time, could the prison come to an end? It reminded Fat of the peculiar statement in *Parsifal*: "You see, my son, here time turns into space." During his religious experience in March of 1974, Fat had seen an augmentation of space: yards and yards of space, extending all the way to the stars; space opened up around him as if a confining box had been removed. He had felt like a tomcat which had been carried inside a box on a car drive, and then they'd reached their destination and he had been let out of the box, let free. And at night in sleep he had dreamed of a measureless void, yet a void which was alive. The void extended and drifted and seemed totally empty and yet it possessed personality. The void expressed delight in seeing Fat, who, in the dreams, had no body; he, like the boundless void, merely drifted, very slowly; and he could, in addition, hear a faint humming, like music. Apparently the void communicated through this echo, this humming.

"You of all people," the void communicated. "Out of everyone, it is you I love the most."

The void had been waiting to be reunited with Horselover Fat, of all the humans who had ever existed. Like its extension into space, the love in the void lay boundless; it and its love floated forever. Fat had never been so happy in all his life.

The psych tech walked up to him and said, "We are holding you for fourteen days."

"I can't go home?" Fat said.

"No, we feel you need treatment. You're not ready to go home yet."

"Read me my rights," Fat said, feeling numb and afraid.

"We can hold you fourteen days without a court hearing.

After that with your approval we can, if we feel it's necessary, hold you another ninety days."

Fat knew that if he said anything, anything at all, they would hold him the ninety days. So he said nothing. When you are crazy you learn to keep quiet.

Being crazy and getting caught at it, out in the open, turns out to be a way to wind up in jail. Fat now knew this. Besides having a county drunk tank, the County of Orange had a county lunatic tank. He was in it. He could stay in it for a long time. Meanwhile, back at home, Beth undoubtedly was taking everything she wanted from their house to the apartment she had rented—she had refused to tell him where the apartment was; she wouldn't even tell him the city.

Actually, although Fat didn't know it at the time, due to his own folly he had allowed a payment on his house to lapse, as well as on his car; he had not paid the electric bill nor the phone bill. Beth, distraught over Fat's mental and physical state, could not be expected to take on the crushing problems Fat had created. So when Fat got out of the hospital and returned home he found a notice of foreclosure, his car gone, the refrigerator leaking water, and when he tried to phone for help the phone was dreadfully silent. This had the effect of wiping out what little morale he had left, and he knew it was all his own fault. It was his karma.

Right now, Fat did not know these things. All he knew was that he had been thrown in the lock-up for a minimum of two weeks. Also, he had found out one other thing, from the other patients. The County of Orange would bill him for his stay in the lock-up. As a matter of fact his total bill, including that portion covering his time in the cardiac intensive care ward, came to over two thousand dollars. Fat had gone to the county hospital in the first place because he didn't have the money to be taken to a private hospital. So now he had learned something else about being crazy: not only does it get you locked up, but it costs you a lot of money. They can bill you for being crazy and if you don't pay or can't pay they can sue you, and if a court judgment is issued against you and you fail to comply, they can lock you up again, as being in contempt of court.

When you consider that Fat's original suicide attempt had emanated out of a deep despair, the magic of his present situation,

the glamor, somehow had departed. Beside him on the plastic
and chrome couch the huge old lady continued to throw up
her medication in the plastic basin provided by the hospital for
such matters. The psych tech had taken hold of Fat by the arm
to lead him to the ward where he would be confined during
the two weeks ahead. They called it the North Ward. Unpro-
testingly, Fat accompanied the psych tech out of the receiving
ward, across the hall and into the North Ward, where once
again the door got locked behind him.

Fuck, Fat said to himself.

The psych tech escorted Fat to his room—which had two
beds in it instead of six cots—and then took Fat to a small room
to get a questionaire filled out. "This'll only take a few minutes," the psych tech said.

In the small room stood a girl, a Mexican girl, heavy-set,
with rough, dark skin and huge eyes, dark and peaceful eyes,
eyes like pools of fire; Fat stopped dead in his tracks as he saw
the girl's flaming, peaceful huge eyes. The girl held a magazine
open on top of a TV set; she displayed a crude drawing printed
on the page: a picture of the Peaceful Kingdom. The magazine, Fat realized, was the *Watchtower*. The girl, smiling at him,
was a Jehovah's Witness.

The girl said in a gentle and moderated voice, to Fat and not
to the psych tech, "Our Lord God has prepared for us a place
to live where there will be no pain and no fear and see? the
animals lie happily together, the lion and the lamb, as we shall
be, all of us, friends who love one another, without suffering or
death, forever and ever with our Lord Jehovah who loves us
and will never abandon us, whatever we do."

"Debbie, please leave the lounge," the psych tech said.

Still smiling at Fat, the girl pointed to a cow and a lamb in
the crude drawing. "All beasts, all men, all living creatures great
and small will bask in the warmth of Jehovah's love, when the
Kingdom arrives. You think it will be a long time, but Christ
Jesus is with us today." Then, closing up the magazine, the
girl, still smiling but now silent, left the room.

"Sorry about that," the psych tech said to Fat.

"Gosh," Fat said, amazed.

"Did she upset you? I'm sorry about that. She's not sup-

posed to have that literature; somebody must have smuggled it
in to her."

Fat said. "I'll be okay." He realized it; it dazed him.

"Let's get this information down," the psych tech said,
seating himself with his clipboard and pen. "The date of your
birth."

You fool, Fat thought. You fucking fool. God is here in your
goddam mental hospital and you don't know it; you see it but
you don't know it. You have been invaded and you don't even
know it.

He felt joy.

He remembered entry #9 from his exegesis. **He lived a long
time ago but he is still alive.** He is still alive, Fat thought.
After all that's happened. After the pills, after the slashed wrist,
after the car exhaust. After being locked up. He is still alive.

After a few days, the patient he liked best in the ward was
Doug, a large, young, deteriorated hebephrenic who never put
on street clothing but simply wore a hospital gown open at the
back. The women in the ward washed, cut and brushed Doug's
hair because he lacked the skills to do those things himself.
Doug did not take his situation seriously, except when they all
got wakened up for breakfast. Every day Doug greeted Fat
with terror.

"The TV lounge has devils in it," Doug always said, every
morning. "I'm afraid to go in there. Can you feel it? I feel it
even walking past it."

When they all made out their lunch-orders Doug wrote:

SWILL

"I'm ordering swill," he told Fat.

Fat said, "I'm ordering dirt."

In the central office, which had glass walls and a locked door,
the staff watched the patients and made notations. In Fat's case
it got noted down that when the patients played cards (which
took up half their time, since no therapy existed) Fat never
joined in. The other patients played poker and blackjack, while
Fat sat off by himself reading.

"Why don't you play cards?" Penny, a psych tech, asked him.

"Poker and blackjack are not card games but money games,"

Fat said, lowering his book. "Since we're not allowed to have any money on us, there's no point in playing."

"I think you should play cards," Penny said.

Fat knew that he had been ordered to play cards, so he and Debbie played kids' card games like "Fish." They played "Fish" for hours. The staff watched from their glass office and noted down what they saw.

One of the women had managed to retain possession of her Bible. For the thirty-five patients it was the only Bible. Debbie was not allowed to look at it. However, at one turn in the corridor—they were locked out of their rooms during the day, so that they could not lie down and sleep—the staff couldn't see what was happening. Fat sometimes turned their copy of the Bible, their communal copy, over to Debbie for a fast look at one of the psalms. The staff knew what they were doing and detested them for it, but by the time a tech got out of the office and down the corridor, Debbie had strolled on.

Mental inmates always move at one speed and one speed only. But some always move slowly and some always run. Debbie, being wide and solid, sailed along slowly, as did Doug. Fat, who always walked with Doug, matched his pace to his. Together they circled around and around the corridor, conversing. Conversations in mental hospitals resemble conversations in bus stations, because in a Greyhound Bus Station everyone is waiting, and in a mental hospital—especially a county lock-up mental hospital—everyone is waiting. They wait to get out.

Not much goes on in a mental ward, contrary to what mythic novels relate. Patients do not really overpower the staff, and the staff does not really murder the patients. Mostly people read or watch TV or just sit smoking or try to lie down on a couch and sleep, or drink coffee or play cards or walk, and three times a day trays of food are served. The passage of time is designated by the arrival of the food carts. At night visitors show up and they always smile. Patients in a mental hospital can never figure out why people from the outside smile. To me, it remains a mystery to this day.

Medication, which is always referred to as "meds," gets doled out at irregular intervals, from tiny paper cups. Everyone is given Thorazine plus something else. They do not tell you what you are getting and they watch to make sure you swallow the pills. Sometimes the meds nurses fuck up and bring the same tray of medication around twice. The patients always point out that they just took their meds ten minutes ago and the nurses give them the meds again anyhow. The mistake is never discovered until the end of the day, and the staff refuses to talk about it to the patients, all of whom now have twice as much Thorazine in their systems as they are supposed to have.

I have never met a mental patient, even the paranoid ones, who believed that double-dosing was a tactic to oversedate the ward deliberately. It is patently obvious that the nurses are dumb. The nurses have enough trouble figuring out which patient is which, and finding each patient's little paper cup. This is because a ward population constantly changes; new people arrive; old people get discharged. The real danger in a mental ward is that someone spaced out on PCP* will be admitted by mistake. The policy of many mental hospitals is to refuse PCP users and force the armed police to process them. The armed police constantly try to force the PCP users onto the unarmed mental hospital patients and staffs. Nobody wants to deal with a PCP user, for good reasons. The newspapers constantly relate how a PCP freak, locked up in a ward somewhere, bit off another person's nose or tore out his own eyes.

Fat was spared this. He did not even know such horrors existed. This came about through the wise planning of OCMC, which made sure that no PCP-head wound up in the North Ward. In point of fact, Fat owed his life to OCMC (as well as two thousand dollars), although his mind remained too fried for him to appreciate this.

When Beth read the itemized bill from OCMC, she could not believe the number of things they had done for her husband to keep him alive; the list ran to five pages. It even included oxygen. Fat did not know it, but the nurses at the intensive cardiac care ward believed that he would die. They monitored him constantly. Every now and then, in the intensive cardiac care ward, an emergency warning siren sounded. It meant someone had lost vital signs. Fat, lying in his bed attached as he was to the video screen, felt as if he had been

*Also known as Angel Dust.

placed next to a switching yard for railroad trains; life support mechanisms constantly sounded their various noises.

It is characteristic of the mentally ill to hate those who help them and love those who connive against them. Fat still loved Beth and he detested OCMC. This showed he belonged in the North Ward; I have no doubt of it. Beth knew when she took Christopher and left for parts unknown that Fat would try suicide; he'd tried it in Canada. In fact, Beth planned to move back in as soon as Fat offed himself. She told him so later. Also, she told him that it had infuriated her that he'd failed to kill himself. When he asked her why that had infuriated her, Beth said:

"You have once again shown your inability to do anything."

The distinction between sanity and insanity is narrower than a razor's edge, sharper than a hound's tooth, more agile than a mule deer. It is more elusive than the merest phantom. Perhaps it does not even exist; perhaps it *is* a phantom.

Ironically, Fat hadn't been tossed into the lock-up because he was crazy (although he was); the reason, technically, consisted of the "danger to yourself" law. Fat constituted a menace to his own well-being, a charge that could be brought against many people. At the time he lived in the North Ward a number of psychological tests were administered to him. He passed them, but on the other hand he had the good sense not to talk about God. Though he passed all the tests, Fat had faked them out. To while away the time he drew over and over again pictures of the German knights who Alexander Nevsky had lured onto the ice, lured to their deaths. Fat identified with the heavily-armored Teutonic knights with their slot-eyed masks and ox-horns projecting out on each side; he drew each knight carrying a huge shield and a naked sword; on the shield Fat wrote: "*In hoc signo vinces,*" which he got from a pack of cigarettes. It means, "In this sign you shall conquer." The sign took the form of an iron cross. His love of God had turned to anger, an obscure anger. He had visions of Christopher racing across a grassy field, his little blue coat flapping behind him, Christopher running and running. No doubt this was Horselover Fat himself running, the child in him, anyhow. Running from something as obscure as his anger.

In addition he several times wrote:

Dico per spiritum sanctum. Haec veritas est. Mihi crede et mecum in aeternitate vivebis. Entry #28.

This meant, "I speak by means of the Holy Spirit. This is the truth. Believe me and you will live with me in eternity."

One day on a list of printed instructions posted on the wall of the corridor he wrote:

Ex Deo nascimur, in Jesu mortimur, per spiritum sanctum reviviscimus.

Doug asked him what it meant.

"'**From God we are born**,'" Fat translated, "'**in Jesus we die, by the Holy Spirit we live again.**'"

"You're going to be here ninety days," Doug said.

One time Fat found a posted notice that fascinated him. The notice stipulated what could not be done, in order of descending importance. Near the top of the list all parties concerned were told:

NO ONE IS TO REMOVE ASHTRAYS
FROM THE WARD.

And later down the list it stated:

FRONTAL LOBOTOMIES ARE NOT
TO BE PERFORMED WITHOUT
THE WRITTEN CONSENT OF THE PATIENT.

"That should read 'prefrontal,'" Doug said, and wrote in the "pre."

"How do you know that?" Fat said.

"There's two ways of knowing," Doug said. "Either knowledge arises through the sense organs and is called empirical knowledge, or it arises within your head and it's called *a priori*." Doug wrote on the notice:

IF I BRING BACK THE ASHTRAYS,
CAN I HAVE MY PREFRONTAL?

"You'll be here ninety days," Fat said.

Outside the building rain poured down. It had been raining since Fat arrived in the North Ward. If he stood on top of the washing machine in the laundry room, he could see out through a barred window to the parking lot. People parked their cars and then ran through the rain. Fat felt glad he was indoors, in the ward.

Dr. Stone, who had charge of the ward, interviewed him one day.

"Did you ever try suicide before?" Dr. Stone asked him.

"No," Fat said, which of course wasn't true. At that moment he no longer remembered Canada. It was his impression that his life had begun two weeks ago when Beth walked out.

"I think," Dr. Stone said, "that when you tried to kill yourself you got in touch with reality for the first time."

"Maybe so," Fat said.

"What I am going to give you," Dr. Stone said, opening a black suitcase on his small cluttered desk, "we term the Bach remedies." He pronounced it *batch*. "These organic remedies are distilled from certain flowers which grow in Wales. Dr. Bach wandered through the fields and pastures of Wales experiencing every negative mental state that exists. With each state that he experienced he gently held one flower after another. The proper flower trembled in the cup of Dr. Bach's hand and he then developed unique methods of acquiring an essence in elixir form of each flower and combinations of flowers which I have prepared in a rum base." He put three bottles together on the desk, found a larger, empty bottle, and poured the contents of the three into it. "Take six drops a day," Dr. Stone said. "There is no way the Bach remedies can hurt you. They are not toxic chemicals. They will remove your sense of helplessness and fear and inability to act. My diagnosis is that those are the three areas where you have blocks: fear, helplessness and an inability to act. What you should have done instead of trying to kill yourself would have been, take your son away from your wife—it's the law in California that a minor child must remain with his father until there is a court order to the contrary. And then you should have lightly struck your wife with a rolled-up newspaper or a phonebook."

"Thank you," Fat said, accepting the bottle. He could see that Dr. Stone was totally crazy, but in a good way. Dr. Stone was the first person at the North Ward, outside the patients, who had talked to him as if he were human.

"You have much anger in you," Dr. Stone said. "I am lending

you a copy of the *Tao Te Ching*. Have you ever read Lao Tzu?"

"No," Fat admitted.

"Let me read you this part here," Dr. Stone said. He read aloud.

> "Its upper part is not dazzling;
> Its lower part is not obscure.
> Dimly visible, it cannot be named
> And returns to that which is without substance.
> This is called the shape that has no shape,
> The image that is without substance.
> This is called indistinct and shadowy.
> Go up to it and you will not see its head;
> Follow behind it and you will not see its rear."

Hearing this, Fat remembered entries #1 and #2 from his journal. He quoted them, from memory, to Dr. Stone.

#1. One Mind there is; but under it two principles contend.

#2. The Mind lets in the light, then the dark; in interaction; so time is generated. At the end Mind awards victory to the light; time ceases and the Mind is complete.

"But," Dr. Stone said, "if Mind awards victory to the light, and the dark disappears, then reality will disappear, since reality is a compound of Yang and Yin equally."

"Yang is Form I of Parmenides," Fat said. "Yin is Form II. Parmenides argued that Form II does not in fact exist. Only Form I exists. Parmenides believed in a monistic world. People *imagine* that both forms exist, but they are wrong. Aristotle relates that Parmenides equates Form I with 'that which is' and Form II with 'that which is not.' Thus people are deluded."

Eying him, Dr. Stone said, "What's your source?"

"Edward Hussey," Fat said.

"He's at Oxford," Dr. Stone said. "I attended Oxford. In my opinion Hussey has no peer."

"You're right," Fat said.

"What else can you tell me?" Dr. Stone said.

Fat said, "Time does not exist. This is the great secret known to Apollonius of Tyana, Paul of Tarsus, Simon Magus, Paracelsus, Boehme and Bruno. The universe is contracting into a unitary entity which is completing itself. Decay and disorder are seen by us in reverse, as increasing. Entry# 18 of my exegesis reads: **'Real time ceased in 70 C.E. with the fall of the Temple at Jerusalem. It began again in 1974. The intervening period was a perfect spurious interpolation aping the creation of the Mind.'** "

"Interpolated by whom?" Dr. Stone asked.

"The Black Iron Prison, which is an expression of the Empire. What has been—" Fat had started to say, "What has been revealed to me." He rechose his words. "What has been most important in my discoveries is this: **'The Empire never ended.'** "

Leaning against his desk, Dr. Stone folded his arms, rocked forward and back and studied Fat, waiting to hear more.

"That's all I know," Fat said, becoming belatedly cautious.

"I'm very interested in what you're saying," Dr. Stone said.

Fat realized that one of two possibilities existed and only two; either Dr. Stone was totally insane—not just insane but totally so—or else in an artful, professional fashion he had gotten Fat to talk; he had drawn Fat out, and now knew that Fat was totally insane. Which meant that Fat could look forward to a court appearance and ninety days.

This is a mournful discovery.

1) Those who agree with you are insane.

2) Those who do not agree with you are in power.

These were the twin realizations which now percolated through Fat's head. He decided to go for broke, to tell Dr. Stone the most fantastic entry in his exegesis.

"Entry number twenty-four," Fat said. **" 'In dormant seed form, as living information, the plasmate slumbered in the buried library of codices at Chenoboskion until—' "**

"What is 'Chenoboskion'?" Dr. Stone interrupted.

"Nag Hammadi."

"Oh, the Gnostic library." Dr. Stone nodded. "Found and read in 1945 but never published. 'Living information'?" His eyes fixed themselves in intent scrutiny of Fat. " 'Living information,' " he echoed. And then he said, "The Logos."

Fat trembled.

"Yes," Dr. Stone said. "The Logos would be living information, capable of replicating."

"Replicating not through information," Fat said, "in information, but *as* information. This is what Jesus meant when he spoke elliptically of the 'mustard seed' which, he said, would grow into a tree large enough for birds to roost in.'"

"There is no mustard tree," Dr. Stone agreed. "So Jesus could not have meant that literally. That fits with the so-called 'secrecy' theme of Mark; that he didn't want outsiders to know the truth. And you know?"

"Jesus foresaw not only his own death but that of all—" Fat hesitated. **"Homoplasmates.** That's a human being to which the plasmate has crossbonded. Interspecies symbiosis. **As living information the plasmate travels up the optic nerve of a human to the pineal body. It uses the human brain as a female host—"**

Dr. Stone grunted and squeezed himself violently.

"—in which to replicate itself into its active form," Fat said. **"The Hermetic alchemists knew of it in theory from ancient texts but could not duplicate it, since they could not locate the dormant buried plasmate."**

"But you're saying the plasmate—the Logos—was dug up at Nag Hammadi!"

"Yes, when the codices were read."

"You're sure it wasn't in dormant seed form at Qumran? In Cave Five?"

"Well," Fat said, uncertainly.

"Where did the plasmate originally come from?"

After a pause Fat said, "From another star system."

"You wish to identify that star system?"

"Sirius," Fat said.

"Then you believe that the Dogon People of the western Sudan are the source of Christianity."

"They use the fish sign," Fat said. "For Nommo, the benign twin."

"Who would be Form I or Yang."

"Right," Fat said.

"And Yurugu is Form II. But you believe that Form II doesn't exist."

"Nommo had to slay her," Fat said.

"That's what the Japanese myth stipulates, in a sense," Dr. Stone said. "Their cosmogonical myth. The female twin dies giving birth to fire; then she descends under the ground. The male twin goes after her to restore her but finds her decomposing and giving birth to monsters. She pursues him and he seals her up under the, ground."

Amazed, Fat said, "She's decomposing and yet she's still giving birth?"

"Only to monsters," Dr. Stone said.

About this time two new propositions entered Fat's mind, due to this particular conversation.

1) Some of those in power are insane.

2) And they are right.

By "right" read "in touch with reality." Fat had reverted back to his most dismal insight, that the universe and the Mind behind it which governed it are both totally irrational. He wondered if he should mention this to Dr. Stone, who seemed to understand Fat better than anyone else during all Fat's life.

"Dr. Stone," he said, "there's something I want to ask you. I want your professional opinion."

"Name it."

"Could the universe possibly be irrational?"

"You mean not guided by a mind. I suggest you turn to Xenophanes."

"Sure," Fat said. "Xenophanes of Colophon. 'One god there is, in no way like mortal creatures either in bodily form or in the thought of his mind. The whole of him sees, the whole of him thinks, the whole of him hears. He stays always motionless in the same place; it is not right—'"

"'Fitting,'" Dr. Stone corrected. "'It is not fitting that he should move about now this way, now that.' And the important part, *Fragment 25.* 'But, effortlessly, he wields all things by the thought of his mind.'"

"But he could be irrational," Fat said.

"How would we know?"

"The whole universe would be irrational."

Dr. Stone said, "Compared with what?"

That, Fat hadn't thought of. But as soon as he thought of it he realized that it did not tear down his fear; it increased it. If the whole universe were irrational, because it was directed by an irrational—that is to say, insane—mind, whole species could come into existence, live and perish and never guess, precisely for the reason that Stone had just given.

"The Logos isn't irrational," Fat decided out loud. "What I call the plasmate. Buried as information in the codices at Nag Hammadi. Which is back with us now, creating new homoplasmates. The Romans, the Empire, killed all the original ones."

"But you say real time ceased in 70 A.D. when the Romans destroyed the Temple. Therefore these are still Roman times; the Romans are still here. This is roughly—" Dr. Stone calculated. "About 100 A.D."

Fat realized, then, that this explained his double exposure, the superimposition he had seen of ancient Rome and California 1974. Dr. Stone had solved it for him.

The psychiatrist in charge of treating him for his lunacy had ratified it. Now Fat would never depart from faith in his encounter with God. Dr. Stone had nailed it down.

5

F AT spent thirteen days at North Ward, drinking coffee and reading and walking around with Doug, but he never got to talk to Dr. Stone again because Stone had too many responsibilities, inasmuch as he had charge of the whole ward and everyone in it, staff and patients alike.

Well, he did have one brief dipshit hurried interchange at the time of his discharge from the ward.

"I think you're ready to leave," Stone said cheerfully.

Fat said, "But let me ask you. I'm not talking about no mind at all directing the universe. I'm talking about a mind like Xenophanes conceived of, but the mind is insane."

"The Gnostics believed that the creator deity was insane," Stone said. "Blind. I want to show you something. It hasn't been published yet; I have it in a typescript from Orval Wintermute who is currently working with Bethge in translating the Nag Hammadi codices. This quote comes from *On The Origin of the World*. Read it."

Fat read it to himself, holding the precious typescript.

> "He said, 'I am god and no other one exists except me.' But when he said these things, he sinned against all of the immortal (imperishable) ones, and they protected him. Moreover, when Pistis saw the impiety of the chief ruler, she was angry. Without being seen, she said, 'You err, Samael,' i.e. 'the blind god.' 'An enlightened, immortal man exists before you. This will appear within your molded bodies. He will trample upon you like potter's clay, (which) is trampled. And you will go with those who are yours down to your mother, the abyss.'"

At once, Fat understood what he had read. Samael was the creator deity and he imagined that he was the only god, as stated in Genesis. However, he was blind, which is to say, occluded. "Occluded" was Fat's salient term. It embraced all other terms: insane, mad, irrational, whacked out, fucked up, fried, psychotic. In his blindness (state of irrationality; i.e. cut off from reality), he did not realize that—

What did the typescript say? Feverishly, he searched over it, at which Dr. Stone thereupon patted him on the arm and told him he could keep the typescript; Stone had Xeroxed it several times over.

An enlightened, immortal man existed before the creator deity, and that enlightened, immortal man would appear within the human race which Samael was going to create. And that enlightened, immortal man who had existed *before* the creator deity would trample upon the fucked-up blind deluded creator like potter's clay.

Hence Fat's encounter with God—the true God—had come through the little pot Oh Ho which Stephanie had thrown for him on her kickwheel.

"Then I'm right about Nag Hammadi," he said to Dr. Stone.

"You would know," Dr. Stone said, and then he said something that no one had ever said to Fat before. "You're the authority," Dr. Stone said.

Fat realized that Stone had restored his—Fat's—spiritual life. Stone had saved him; he was a master psychiatrist. Everything which Stone had said and done *vis-à-vis* Fat had a therapeutic basis, a therapeutic thrust. Whether the content of Stone's information was correct was not important; his purpose from the beginning had been to restore Fat's faith in himself, which had when Beth left—which had vanished, actually, when he had failed to save Gloria's life years ago.

Dr. Stone wasn't insane; Stone was a healer. He held down the right job. Probably he healed many people and in many ways. He adapted his therapy to the individual, not the individual to the therapy.

I'll be goddamned, Fat thought.

In that simple sentence, "You're the authority," Stone had given Fat back his soul.

The soul which Gloria, with her hideous malignant psychological death-game, had taken away.

They—note the "they"—paid Dr. Stone to figure out what had destroyed the patient entering the ward. In each case a bullet had been fired at him, somewhere, at some time, in his life. The bullet entered him and the pain began to spread out. Insidiously, the pain filled him up until he split in half, right down the middle. The task of the staff, and even of the other patients, was to put the person back together but this could not be done so long as the bullet remained. All that lesser therapists did was note the person split into two pieces and begin the job of patching him back into a unity; but they failed to find and remove the bullet. The fatal bullet fired at the person was the basis of Freud's original attack on the psychologically injured person; Freud had understood: he called it a trauma. Later on, everyone got tired of searching for the fatal bullet; it took too long. Too much had to be learned about the patient. Dr. Stone had a paranormal talent, like his paranormal Bach remedies which were a palpable hoax, a pretext to listen to the patient. Rum with a flower dipped in it—nothing more, but a sharp mind hearing what the patient said.

Dr. Leon Stone turned out to be one of the most important people in Horselover Fat's life. To get to Stone, Fat had had to nearly kill himself physically, matching his mental death. Is this what they mean about God's mysterious ways? How else could Fat have linked up with Leon Stone? Only some dismal act on the order of a suicide attempt, a truly lethal attempt, would have achieved it; Fat had to die, or nearly die, to be cured. Or nearly cured.

I wonder where Leon Stone practices now. I wonder what his recovery rate is. I wonder how he got his paranormal abilities. I wonder a lot of things. The worst event in Fat's life—Beth leaving him, taking Christopher, and Fat trying to kill himself—had brought on limitless benign consequences. If you judge the merits of a sequence by their final outcome, Fat had just gone through the best period of his life; he emerged from North Ward as strong as he would ever get. After all, no man is infinitely strong; for every creature that runs, flies, hops or crawls there is a terminal nemesis which he will not circumvent, which will finally do him in. But Dr. Stone had added the missing element to Fat, the element taken away from him, half-deliberately, by Gloria Knudson, who wished to take as many people with her as she could: self-confidence. "You are the authority," Stone had said, and that sufficed.

I've always told people that for each person there is a sentence —a series of words—which has the power to destroy him. When Fat told me about Leon Stone I realized (this came years after the first realization) that another sentence exists, another series of words, which will heal the person. If you're lucky you will get the second; but you can be certain of getting the first: that is the way it works. On their own, without training, individuals know how to deal out the lethal sentence, but training is required to deal out the second. Stephanie had come close when she made the little ceramic pot Oh Ho and presented it to Fat as her gift of love, a love she lacked the verbal skills to articulate.

How, when Stone gave Fat the typscript material from the Nag Hammadi codex, had he known the significance of *pot* and *potter* to Fat? To know that, Stone would have to be telepathic. Well, I have no theory. Fat, of course, has. He believes that like Stephanie, Dr. Stone was a micro-form of God. That's why I say Fat is nearly healed, not healed.

Yet by regarding benign people as micro-forms of God, Fat at least remained in touch with a good god, not a blind, cruel or evil one. That point should be considered. Fat had a high regard for God. If the Logos was rational, and the Logos equaled God, then God had to be rational. This is why the Fourth Gospel's statement about the identity of the Logos is so important: "*Kai theos en ho logos*" which is to say "and the word was God." In the New Testament, Jesus says that no one has seen God but him; that is, Jesus Christ, the Logos of the Fourth Gospel. If that be correct, what Fat experienced was the Logos. But the Logos *is* God; so to experience Christ is to experience God. Perhaps a more important statement shows up in a book of the New Testament which most people don't read; they read the gospels and the letters of Paul, but who reads *One John*?

> "My dear people, we are already the children
> of God but what we are to be in the future
> has not yet been revealed; all we know is,
> that we shall be like him because we shall
> see him as he really is."   (*1 John 3:1/2.*)

It can be argued that this is the most important statement in the New Testament; certainly it is the most important not-generally-known statement. *We shall be like him*. That means that man is isomorphic with God. *We shall see him as he really is*. There will occur a theophany, at least to some. Fat could base the credentials for his whole encounter on this passage.

He could claim that his encounter with God consisted of a fulfillment of the promise of *1 John 3:1/2*—as Bible scholars indicate it, a sort of code which they can read in an instant, as cryptic as it looks. Oddly, to a certain extent this passage dovetails with the Nag Hammadi typescript that Dr. Stone handed to Fat the day Fat got discharged from North Ward. Man and the true God are identical—as the Logos and the true God are —but a lunatic blind creator and his screwed-up world separate man from God. That the blind creator sincerely imagines that he is the true God only reveals the extent of his occlusion. This is Gnosticism. In Gnosticism, man belongs with God *against* the world and the creator of the world (both of which are crazy, whether they realize it or not). The answer to Fat's question, "Is the universe irrational, and is it irrational because an irrational mind governs it?" receives this answer, via Dr. Stone: "Yes it is, the universe is irrational; the mind governing it is irrational; but above them lies another God, the true God, and he is *not* irrational; in addition that true God has outwitted the powers of this world, ventured here to help us, and we know him as the Logos," which, according to Fat, is living information.

Perhaps Fat had discerned a vast mystery, in calling the Logos living information. But perhaps not. Proving things of this sort is difficult. Who do you ask? Fat, fortunately, asked Leon Stone. He might have asked one of the staff, in which case he would still be in North Ward drinking coffee, reading, walking around with Doug.

Above everything else, outranking every other aspect, object, quality of his encounter, Fat had witnessed a benign power *which had invaded this world*. No other term fitted it: the benign power, whatever it was, had *invaded* this world, like a champion ready to do battle. That terrified him but it also excited his joy because he understood what it meant. Help had come.

The universe might be irrational, but something rational had broken into it, like a thief in the night breaks into a sleeping household, unexpectedly in terms of place, in terms of time. Fat had seen it—not because there was anything special about him—but because it had wanted him to see it.

Normally it remained camouflaged. Normally when it ap-

and dazzling him, but imparting to him knowledge beyond the telling. For openers, it saved Christopher's life.

More accurately speaking, it didn't break through to fire the information; it had at some past date broken through. What it did was step forward out of its state of camouflage; it disclosed itself as set to ground and fired information at a rate our calculations will not calibrate; it fired whole libraries at him in nanoseconds. And it continued to do this for eight hours of real elapsed time. Many nanoseconds exist in eight hours of RET. At flash-cut speed you can load the right hemisphere of the human brain with a titanic quantity of graphic data.

Paul of Tarsus had a similar experience. A long time ago. Much of it he refused to discuss. According to his own statement, much of the information fired at his head—right between the eyes, on his trip to Damascus—died with him unsaid. Chaos reigns in the universe, but St. Paul knew who he had talked to. He mentioned that. Zebra, too, identified itself, to Fat. It termed itself "St. Sophia," a designation unfamiliar to Fat. "St. Sophia" is an unusual hypostasis of Christ.

Men and the world are mutually toxic to each other. But God—the true God—has penetrated both, penetrated man and penetrated the world, and sobers the landscape. But that God, the God from outside, encounters fierce opposition. Frauds—the deceptions of madness—abound and mask themselves as their mirror opposite: pose as sanity. The masks, however, wear thin and the madness reveals itself. It is an ugly thing.

The remedy is here but so is the malady. As Fat repeats obsessively, **"The Empire never ended."** In a startling response to the crisis, the true God mimics the universe, the very region he has invaded: he takes on the likeness of sticks and trees and beer cans in gutters—he presumes to be trash discarded, debris no longer noticed. Lurking, the true God literally ambushes reality and us as well. God, in very truth, attacks and injures us, in his role as antidote. As Fat can testify to, it is a scary experience to be bushwhacked by the Living God. Hence we say, the true God is in the habit of concealing himself. Twenty-five hundred years have passed since Heraclitus wrote, "Latent form is the master of obvious form," and, "The nature of things is in the habit of concealing itself."

So the rational, like a seed, lies concealed within the irrational bulk. What purpose does the irrational bulk serve? Ask yourself what Gloria gained by dying; not in terms of her death *vis-à-vis* herself but in terms of those who loved her. She paid back their love with—well, with what? Malice? Not proven. Hate? Not proven. With the irrational? Yes; proven. In terms of the effect on her friends—such as Fat—no lucid purpose was served but purpose there was: purpose without purpose, if you can conceive of that. Her motive was no motive. We're talking about nihilism. Under everything else, even under death itself and the will toward death, lies something else and that something else is nothing. The bedrock basic stratum of reality is irreality; the universe is irrational because it is built not on mere shifting sand—but on that which is not.

No help to Fat to know this: the *why* of Gloria's taking him with her—or doing her best to—when she went. "Bitch," he could have said if he could have grabbed her. "Just tell me why; why the fucking why?" To which the universe would hollowly respond, "My ways cannot be known, oh man." Which is to say, "My ways do not make sense, nor do the ways of those who dwell in me."

The bad news coming down the pipe for Fat was mercifully still unknown to him, at this point, at the time of his discharge from North Ward. He could not return to Beth, so who could he return to, when he hit the outside world? In his mind, during his stay at North Ward, Sherri, who was in remission from her cancer, had faithfully visited him. Therefore Fat had engrammed onto her, believing that if he had one true friend in all the world it was Sherri Solvig. His plan had unfolded like a bright star: he would live with Sherri, helping to keep up her morale during her remission, and if she lost her remission, he would care for her as she had cared for him during his time in the hospital.

In no sense had Dr. Stone cured Fat, when the motor driving Fat got later exposed. Fat homed in on death more rapidly and more expertly this time than he had ever done before. He had become a professional at seeking out pain; he had learned the rules of the game and now knew how to play. What Fat in his lunacy—acquired from a lunatic universe; branded so by Fat's own analysis—sought was to be dragged down along with someone who wanted to die. Had he gone through his address book he could not have yielded up a better source than Sherri, "Smart move, Fat," I would have told him if I had known what he was planning for his future, during his stay at North Ward. "You've really scored this time." I knew Sherri; I knew she spent all her time trying to figure out a way to lose her remission. I knew that because she expressed fury and hatred, constantly, at the doctors who had saved her. But I did not know what Fat had planned. Fat kept it a secret, even from Sherri. I will help her, Fat said to himself in the depths of his fried mind. I will help Sherri stay healthy but if and when she gets sick again, there I will be at her side, ready to do anything for her.

His error, when deconstructed, amounted to this: Sherri did not merely plan to get sick again; she like Gloria planned to take as many people with her as possible—in direct proportion to their love toward her. Fat loved her and, worse, felt gratitude toward her. Out of this clay, Sherri could throw a pot with the warped kickwheel she used as a brain that would smash what Leon Stone had done, smash what Stephanie had done, smash what God had done. Sherri had more power in her weakened body than all these other entities combined, including the living God.

Fat had decided to bind himself to the Antichrist. And out of the highest possible motives: out of love, gratitude and the desire to help her.

Exactly what the powers of hell feed on: the best instincts in man.

Sherri Solvig, being poor, lived in a tiny rundown room with no kitchen; she had to wash her dishes in the bathroom sink. The ceiling showed a vast water stain, from a toilet upstairs which had overflowed. Having visited her there a couple of times Fat knew the place and considered it depressing. He had the impression that if Sherri moved out and into a nice apartment, a modern one, and with a kitchen, her spirits would pick up.

Needless to say, the realization had never penetrated to Fat's mind that Sherri sought out this kind of abode. Her dingy surroundings came as a result of her affliction, not as a cause; she could recreate these conditions wherever she went—which Fat eventually discovered.

At this point in time, however, Fat had geared up his mental and physical assembly line to turn out an endless series of good acts toward the person who, before all other persons, had visited him in the cardiac intensive care ward and later at North Ward. Sherri had official documents declaring her a Christian. Twice a week she took communion and one day she would enter a religious order. Also, she called her priest by his first name. You cannot get any closer to piety than that.

A couple of times Fat had told Sherri about his encounter with God. This hadn't impressed her, since Sherri Solvig believed that one encounters God only through channels. She herself had access to these channels, which is to say her priest Larry.

Once Fat had read to Sherri from the *Britannica* about the "secrecy theme" in Mark and Matthew, the idea that Christ veiled his teachings in parable form so that the multitude—that is, the many outsiders—would not understand him and so would not be saved. Christ, according to this view or theme, intended salvation only for his little flock. The *Britannica* discussed this up front.

"That's bullshit," Sherri said.

Fat said, "You mean this *Britannica* is wrong or the Bible is wrong? The *Britannica* is just—"

"The Bible doesn't say that," Sherri said, who read the Bible all the time, or at least had a copy of it always with her.

It took Fat hours to find the citation in Luke; finally he had it, to set before Sherri:

> "His disciples asked him what this parable might
> mean, and he said, 'The mysteries of the kingdom
> of God are revealed to you; for the rest there are
> only parables, so that they might see but not per-
> ceive, listen but not understand.'" (*Luke 8:9/10.*)

"I'll ask Larry if that's one of the corrupt parts of the Bible," Sherri said.

Pissed off, Fat said irritably, "Sherri, why don't you cut out all the sections of the Bible you agree with and paste them together? And not have to deal with the rest."

"Don't be snippy," Sherri said, who was hanging up clothes in her tiny closet.

Nonetheless, Fat imagined that basically he and Sherri shared a common bond. They both agreed that God existed; Christ had died to save man; people who didn't believe this didn't know what was going on. He had confided to her that he had seen God, news which Sherri received placidly (at that moment she had been ironing).

"It's called a theophany," Fat said. "Or an epiphany."

"An epiphany," Sherri said, pacing her voice to the rate of her slow ironing, "is a feast celebrated on January sixth, marking the baptism of Christ. I always go. Why don't you go? It's a lovely service. You know, I heard this joke—" She droned on. Hearing this, Fat was mystified. He decided to change the subject; now Sherri had switched to an account of an instance when Larry—who was Father Minter to Fat—had poured the sacramental wine down the front of a kneeling female communicant's low-cut dress.

"Do you think John the Baptist was an Essene?" he asked Sherri.

Never at any time did Sherri Solvig admit she didn't know the answer to a theological question; the closest she came surfaced in the form of responding, "I'll ask Larry." To Fat she now said calmly, "John the Baptist was Elijah who returns before Christ comes. They asked Christ about that and he said John the Baptist was Elijah who had been promised."

"But was he an Essene."

Pausing momentarily in her ironing, Sherri said, "Didn't the Essenes live in the Dead Sea?"

"Well, at the Qumran Wadi."

"Didn't your friend Bishop Pike die in the Dead Sea?"

Fat had known Jim Pike, a fact he always proudly narrated to people given a pretext. "Yes," he said. "Jim and his wife had driven out onto the Dead Sea Desert in a Ford Cortina. They had two bottles of Coca-Cola with them; that's all."

"You told me," Sherri said, resuming her ironing.

"What I could never figure out," Fat said, "is why they didn't drink the water in the car radiator. That's what you do when your car breaks down in the desert and you're stranded." For years Fat had brooded about Jim Pike's death. He imagined that it was somehow tied in with the murders of the Kennedys and Dr. King, but he had no evidence whatsoever for it.

"Maybe they had anti-freeze in their radiator," Sherri said.

"In the Dead Sea Desert?"

Sherri said, "My car has been giving me trouble. The man at the Exxon station on Seventeenth says that the motor mounts are loose. Is that serious?"

Not wanting to talk about Sherri's beat-up old car but wanting instead to rattle on about Jim Pike, Fat said, "I don't know." He tried to think how to get the topic back to his friend's perplexing death but could not.

"That damn car," Sherri said.

"You didn't pay anything for it; that guy gave it to you."

"'Didn't pay anything'? He made me feel like he owned me for giving me that damn car."

"Remind me never to give you a car," Fat said.

All the clues lay before him that day. If you did something for Sherri she felt she should feel gratitude—which she did not —and this she interpreted as a burden, a despised obligation. However, Fat had a ready rationalization for this, which he had already begun to employ. He did not do things for Sherri to get anything back; *ergo*, he did not expect gratitude. *Ergo*, if he did not get it that was okay.

What he failed to notice that not only was there no gratitude (which he could psychologically handle) but downright malice showed itself instead. Fat had noted this but had written it off as nothing more than irritability, a form of impatience. He could not believe that someone would return malice for assistance. Therefore he discounted the testimony of his senses.

Once, when I lectured at the University of California at Fullerton, a student asked me for a short, simple definition of reality. I thought it over and answered, "Reality is that which when you stop believing in it, it doesn't go away."

Fat did not believe that Sherri returned malice for assistance given her. But that failure to believe changed nothing. Therefore her response lay within the framework of what we call "reality." Fat, whether he liked it or not, would in some way have to deal with it, or else stop seeing Sherri socially.

One of the reasons Beth left Fat stemmed from his visits to Sherri at her rundown room in Santa Ana. Fat had deluded himself into believing that he visited her out of charity. Actually he had become horny, due to the fact that Beth had lost interest in him sexually and he was not, as they say, getting any.

In many ways Sherri struck him as pretty; in fact Sherri was pretty; we all agreed. During her chemotherapy she wore a wig. David had been fooled by the wig and often complimented her on her hair, which amused her. We regarded this as macabre, on both their parts.

In his study of the form that masochism takes in modern man, Theodor Reik puts forth an interesting view. Masochism is more widespread than we realize because it takes an attenuated form. The basic dynamism is as follows: a human being sees something bad which is coming as inevitable. There is no way he can halt the process; he is helpless. This sense of helplessness generates a need to gain some control over the impending pain—any kind of control will do. This makes sense; the subjective feeling of helplessness is more painful than the impending misery. So the person seizes control over the situation in the only way open to him: he connives to bring on the impending misery; he hastens it. This activity on his part promotes the false impression that he enjoys pain. Not so. It is simply that he cannot any longer endure the helplessness or the supposed helplessness. But in the process of gaining control over the inevitable misery he becomes, automatically, anhedonic (which means being unable or unwilling to enjoy pleasure). Anhedonia sets in stealthily. Over the years it takes control of him. For example, he learns to defer gratification; this is a step in the dismal process of anhedonia. In learning to defer gratification he experiences a sense of self-mastery; he has become stoic, disciplined; he does not give way to impulse. He has *control*. Control over himself in terms of his impulses and control over the external situation. He is a controlled and controlling person. Pretty soon he has branched out and is controlling other people, as part of the situation. He becomes a manipulator. Of course, he is not consciously aware of this; all he intends to do is lessen his own sense of impotence. But in his task of lessening this sense, he insidiously overpowers the freedom of others. Yet, he derives no pleasure from this, no positive psychological gain; all his gains are essentially negative.

Sherri Solvig had had cancer, lymphatic cancer, but due to valiant efforts by her doctors she had gone into remission. However, encoded in the memory-tapes of her brain was the datum that patients with lymphoma who go into remission usually eventually lose their remission. They aren't cured; the ailment has somehow mysteriously passed from a palpable state into a sort of metaphysical state, a limbo. It is there but it is not there. So despite her current good health, Sherri (her mind told her) contained a ticking clock, and when the clock chimed she would die. Nothing could be done about it, except the frantic promotion of a second remission. But even if a second remission were obtained, that remission, too, by the same logic, the same inexorable process, would end.

Time had Sherri in its absolute power. Time contained one outcome for her: terminal cancer. This is how her mind had factored the situation out; it had come to this conclusion, and no matter how good she felt or what she had going for her in her life, this face remained a constant. A cancer patient in remission, then, represents a stepped-up case of the status of all humans; eventually you are going to die.

In the back of her mind, Sherri thought about death ceaselessly. Everything else, all people, objects and processes had become reduced to the status of shadows. Worse yet, when she contemplated other people she contemplated the injustice of the universe. They did not have cancer. This meant that, psychologically speaking, they were immortal. This was unfair. Everyone had conspired to rob her of her youth, her happiness and eventually her life; in place of those, everyone else had piled infinite pain on her, and probably they secretly enjoyed it. "Enjoying themselves" and "enjoying it" amounted to the same evil thing. Sherri, therefore, had motivation for wishing that the whole world would go to hell in a handbasket.

Of course, she did not say this aloud. But she lived it. Due to her cancer she had become totally anhedonic. How can one deny the sense in this? Logically, Sherri should have squeezed every moment of pleasure out of life during her remission, but the mind does not function logically, as Fat had figured out. Sherri spent her time anticipating the loss of her remission.

In this respect she did not postpone gratification; she enjoyed her returning lymphoma now.

Fat couldn't make this complex mental process out. He only saw a young woman who had suffered a lot and who had been dealt a bum hand. He reasoned that he could improve her life. That was a good thing to do. He would love her, love himself and God would love the both of them. Fat saw love, and Sherri saw impending pain and death over which she had no control. There can be no meeting of such two different worlds.

In summary (as Fat would say), the modern-day masochist does not enjoy pain; he simply can't stand being helpless. "Enjoying pain" is a semantic contradiction, as certain philosophers and psychologists have pointed out. "Pain" is defined as something that you experience as unpleasant. "Unpleasant" is defined as something you don't want. Try to define it otherwise and see where it gets you. "Enjoying pain" means "enjoying what you find unpleasant." Reik had the handle on the situation; he decoded the true dynamism of modern attenuated masochism . . . and saw it spread out among almost all of us, in one form or another and to some degree. It has become an ubiquity.

One could not correctly accuse Sherri of enjoying cancer. Or even wanting to have cancer. But she believed that cancer lay in the deck of cards in front of her, buried somewhere in the pack; she turned one card over each day, and each day cancer failed to show up. But if that card is in the pack and you are turning the cards over one by one eventually you will turn the cancer card over, and there it ends.

So, through no real fault of her own, Sherri was primed to fuck Fat over as he had never been fucked over before. The difference between Gloria Knudson and Sherri was obvious; Gloria wanted to die for strictly imaginary reasons. Sherri would literally die whether she wanted to or not. Gloria had the option to cease playing her malignant death-game any time she psychologically wished, *but Sherri did not.* It was as if Gloria, upon smashing herself to bits on the pavement below the Oakland Synanon Building, had been reborn twice the size with twice the mental strength. Meanwhile, Beth's leaving with Christopher had whittled Horselover Fat down to half his normal size. The odds did not favor a sanguine outcome.

The actual motivation in Fat's head for feeling attracted to Sherri was the locking-in onto death which had begun with Gloria. But, imagining that Dr. Stone had cured him, Fat now sailed out into the world with renewed hope—sailed unerringly into madness and death; he had learned nothing. True, the bullet had been pulled from his body and the wound healed.

But he was primed for another, *eager* for another. He couldn't wait to move in with Sherri and save her.

If you'll remember, helping people was one of the two basic things Fat had been told long ago to give up; helping people and taking dope. He had stopped taking dope, but all his energy and enthusiasm were now totally channeled into saving people.

Better he had kept on with the dope.

hand at the Catholic Workers' Soup Kitchen, or turn as much of your money over to CARE as you possibly can. Let professionals help people. You're lying to yourself; you're lying that Gloria meant something to you, that what's-her-name—Sherri —isn't going to die—of course she's going to die! That's why you're shacking up with her, so you can be there when she dies. She wants to pull you down with her and you want her to; it's a collusion between the two of you. Everybody who comes in this door wants to die. That's what mental illness is all about. You didn't know that? I'm telling you. I'd like to hold your head under water until you fought to live. If you didn't fight, then fuck it. I wish they'd let me do it. Your friend who has cancer—she got it on purpose. Cancer represents a deliberate failure of the immune system of the body; the person turns it off. It's because of loss, the loss of a loved one. See how death spreads out? Everyone has cancer cells floating around in their bodies, but their immune system takes care of it."

"She did have a friend who died," Fat admitted. "He had a *grand mal* seizure. And her mother died of cancer."

"So Sherri felt guilty because her friend died and her mother died. You feel guilty because Gloria died. Take responsibility for your own life for a change. It's your job to protect yourself."

Fat said, "It's my job to help Sherri."

"Let's see your list. You better have that list."

Handing over his list of the ten things he most wanted to do, Fat asked himself silently if Maurice had all his marbles. Surely Sherri didn't want to die; she had put up a stubborn and brave fight; she had endured not only the cancer but the chemotherapy.

"You want to walk on the beach at Santa Barbara," Maurice said, examining the list. "That's number one."

"Anything wrong with that?" Fat said, defensively.

"No. Well? Why don't you do it?"

"Look at number two," Fat said. "I have to have a pretty girl with me."

Maurice said, "Take Sherri."

"She—" He hesitated. He had, as a matter of fact, asked Sherri to go to the beach with him, up to Santa Barbara to spend a weekend at one of the luxurious beach hotels. She had answered that her church work kept her too busy.

"She won't go," Maurice finished for him. "She's too busy. Doing what?"

"Church."

They looked at each other.

"Her life won't differ much when her cancer returns," Maurice said finally. "Does she talk about her cancer?"

"Yes."

"To clerks in stores? Everyone she meets?"

"Yes."

"Okay, her life will differ; she'll get more sympathy. She'll be better off."

With difficulty, Fat said, "One time she told me—" He could barely say it. "That getting cancer was the best thing that ever happened to her. Because then—"

"The Federal Government funded her."

"Yes." He nodded.

"So she'll never have to work again. I presume she's still drawing SSI even though she's in remission?"

"Yeah," Fat said glumly.

"They're going to catch up with her. They'll check with her doctor. Then she'll have to get a job."

Fat said, with bitterness, "She'll never get a job."

"You hate this girl," Maurice said. "And worse, you don't respect her. She's a girl bum. She's a rip-off artist. She's ripping you off, emotionally and financially. You're supporting her, right? And she also gets the SSI. She's got a racket, the cancer racket. And you're the mark." Maurice regarded him sternly. "Do you believe in God?" he asked suddenly.

You can infer from this question that Fat had cooled his Godtalk during his therapeutic sessions with Maurice. He did not intend to wind up in North Ward again.

"In a sense," Fat said. But he couldn't let it lie there; he had to amplify. "I have my own concept of God," he said. "Based on my own—" He hesitated, envisioning the trap built from his words; the trap bristled with barbed wire. "Thoughts," he finished.

"Is this a sensitive topic with you?" Maurice said.

Fat could not see what was coming, if anything. For example, he did not have access to his North Ward files and he did not know if Maurice had read them—or what they contained.

"No," he said.

"Do you believe man is created in God's image?" Maurice said.

"Yes," Fat said.

Maurice, raising his voice, shouted, "Then isn't it an offense against God to ice yourself? Did you ever think of that?"

"I thought of that," Fat said. "I thought of that a lot."

"Well? And what did you decide? Let me tell you what it says in Genesis, in case you've forgotten. 'Then God said, "Let us make man in our image and likeness to rule the fish in the sea, the birds of heaven, the cattle, all—" ' "

"Okay," Fat broke in, "but that's the creator deity, not the true God."

"What?" Maurice said.

Fat said, "That's Yaldabaoth. Sometimes called Samael, the blind god. He's deranged."

"What the hell are you talking about?" Maurice said.

"Yaldabaoth is a monster spawned by Sophia who fell from the Pleroma," Fat said. "He imagines he's the only god but he's wrong. There's something the matter with him; he can't see. He creates our world but because he's blind he botches the job. The real God sees down from far above and in his pity sets to work to save us. Fragments of light from the Pleroma are—"

Staring at him, Maurice said, "Who made up this stuff? You?"

"Basically," Fat said, "my doctrine is Valentinian, second century C.E."

"What's 'C.E.'?"

"Common Era. The designation replaces A.D. Valentinus's Gnosticism is the more subtle branch as opposed to the Iranian, which of course was strongly influenced by Zoroastrianism dualism. Valentinus perceived the ontological salvific value of the gnosis, since it reversed the original primal condition of ignorance, which represents the state of the fall, the impairment of the Godhead which resulted in the botched creation of the phenomenal or material world. The true God, who is totally transcendent, did not create the world. However, seeing what Yaldaboath had done—"

"Who's this 'Yaldaboath'? Yahweh created the world! It says so in the Bible!"

Fat said, "The creator deity imagined that he was the only god; that's why he was jealous and said, 'You shall have no other gods before me,' to which—"

Maurice shouted, "Haven't you read the Bible?"

After a pause, Fat tried another turn. He was dealing with a religious idiot. "Look," he said, as reasonably as possible. "A number of opinions exist as to the creation of the world. For instance, if you regard the world as artifact—which it may not be; it may be an organism, which is how the ancient Greeks regarded it—you still can't reason back to a creator; for instance, there may have been a number of creators at several times. The Buddhist idealists point this out. But even if—"

"You've never read the Bible," Maurice said with incredulity. "You know what I want you to do? And I mean this. I want you to go home and study the Bible. I want you to read *Genesis* over twice; you hear me? Two times. Carefully. And I want you to write an outline of the main ideas and events in it, in descending order of importance. And when you show up here next week I want to see that list." He obviously was genuinely angry.

Bringing up the topic of God had been a poor idea, but of course Maurice hadn't known that in advance. All he intended to do was appeal to Fat's ethics. Being Jewish, Maurice assumed that religion and ethics couldn't be separated, since they are combined in the Hebrew monotheism. Ethics devolve directly from Yahweh to Moses; everybody knows that. Everybody but Horselover Fat, whose problem, at that moment, was that he knew too much.

Breathing heavily, Maurice began going through his appointment book. He hadn't iced Syrian assassins by regarding the cosmos as a sentient entelechy with psyche and soma, a macrocosmic mirror to man the microcosm.

"Let me just say one thing," Fat said.

Irritably, Maurice nodded.

"The creator deity," Fat said, "may be insane and therefore the universe is insane. What we experience as chaos is actually irrationality. There is a difference." He was silent, then.

"The universe is what you make of it," Maurice said. "It's what you do with it that counts. It's your responsibility to do something life-promoting with it, not life-destructive."

"That's the existential position," Fat said. "Based on the concept that we are what we do, rather than, We are what we think. It finds its first expression in Goethe's *Faust*, Part One, where Faust says, *'Im Anfang war das Wort.'* He's quoting the opening of the Fourth Gospel; 'In the beginning was the Word.' Faust says, *'Nein. Im Anfang war die Tat.'* 'In the beginning was the deed.' From this, all existentialism comes."

Maurice stared at him as if he were a bug.

Driving back to the modern two-bedroom, two-bathroom apartment in downtown Santa Ana, a full-security apartment with deadbolt lock in a building with electric gate, underground parking, closed-circuit TV scanning of the main entrance, where he lived with Sherri, Fat realized that he had fallen from the status of authority back to the humble status of crank. Maurice, in attempting to help him, had accidentally erased Fat's bastion of security.

However, on the good side, he now lived in this fortress-like, or jail-like, full-security new building, set dead in the center of the Mexican barrio. You needed a magnetic computer card to get the gate to the underground garage to open. This shored up Fat's marginal morale. Since their apartment was up on the top floor he could literally look down on Santa Ana and all the poorer people who got ripped off by drunks and junkies every hour of the night. In addition, of much more importance, he had Sherri with him. She cooked wonderful meals, although he had to do the dishes and the shopping. Sherri did neither. She sewed and ironed a lot, drove off on errands, talked on the telephone to her old girlfriends from high school and kept Fat informed about church matters.

I can't give the name of Sherri's church because it really exists (well, so, too, does Santa Ana), so I will call it what Sherri called it: Jesus' sweatshop. Half the day she manned the phones and the front desk; she had charge of the help programs, which meant that she disbursed food, money for shelter, advice on how to deal with Welfare and weeded the junkies out from the real people.

Sherri detested junkies, and for good reason. They continually showed up with a new scam every day. What annoyed her the most was not so much their ripping off the church to score smack, but their boasting about it later. However, since junkies have no loyalty to one another, junkies generally showed up to tell her which other junkies were doing the ripping off and the boasting. Sherri put their names down on her shit list. Customarily, she arrived home from the church, raving like a madwoman about conditions there, most especially what the creeps and junkies had said and done that day, and how Larry, the priest, did nothing about it.

After a week of living together, Fat knew a great deal more about Sherri than he had known from seeing her socially over the three years of their friendship. Sherri resented every creature on earth, in order of proximity to her; that is, the more she had to do with someone or something the more she resented him, or her or it. The great erotic love in her life took the form of her priest, Larry. During the bad days when she was literally dying from the cancer, Sherri had told Larry that her great desire was to sleep with him, to which Larry had said (this fascinated Fat, who did not regard it as an appropriate answer) that he, Larry, never mixed his social life with his business life (Larry was married, with three children and a grandchild). Sherri still loved him and still wanted to go to bed with him, but she sensed defeat.

On the positive side, one time while living at her sister's—or conversely, dying at her sister's, to hear Sherri tell it—she had gone into seizures and Father Larry had showed up to take her to the hospital. As he picked her up in his arms she had kissed him and he had french-kissed her. Sherri mentioned this several times to Fat. Wistfully, she longed for those days.

"I love you," she informed Fat one night, "but it's really Larry that I really love because he saved me when I was sick."

Fat soon developed the opinion that religion was a sideline at Sherri's church. Answering the phone and mailing out stuff took the center ring. A number of nebulous people—who might as well be named Larry, Moe and Curly, as far as Fat was concerned—haunted the church, holding down salaries inevitably larger than Sherri's and requiring less work. Sherri wished death to all of them. She often spoke with relish about their misfortunes, as for instance when their cars wouldn't start or they got speeding tickets or Father Larry expressed dissatisfaction toward them.

"Eddy's going to get the royal boot," Sherri would say, upon coming home. "The little fucker."

One particular indigent chronically provoked annoyance in Sherri, a man named Jack Barbina who, Sherri said, rummaged through garbage cans to find little gifts for her. Jack Barbina showed up when Sherri was alone in the church office, handed her a soiled box of dates and a perplexing note stressing his desire to court her. Sherri pegged him as a maniac the first day she saw him; she lived in fear that he would murder her.

"I'm going to call you the next time he comes in," she told Fat. "I'm not going to be there alone with him. There isn't enough money in the Bishop's Discretionary Fund to pay me for putting up with Jack Barbina, especially on what they do pay me, which is about half what Eddy makes, the little fairy." To Sherri, the world was divided up among slackers, maniacs, junkies, homosexuals and back-stabbing friends. She also had little use for Mexicans and blacks. Fat used to wonder at her total lack of Christian charity, in the emotional sense. How could—why would—Sherri want to work in a church and fix her sights on religious orders when she resented, feared and detested every living human being, and, most of all, complained about her lot in life?

Sherri even resented her own sister, who had sheltered, fed and cared for her all the time she was sick. The reason: Mae drove a Mercedes-Benz and had a rich husband. But most of all Sherri resented the career of her best friend Eleanor, who had become a nun.

"Here I am throwing up in Santa Ana," Sherri frequently said, "and Eleanor's walking around in a habit in Las Vegas."

"You're not throwing up now," Fat pointed out. "You're in remission."

"But she doesn't know that. What kind of place is Las Vegas for a religious order? She's probably peddling her ass in—"

"You're talking about a nun," Fat said, who had met Eleanor; he had liked her.

"I'd be a nun by now if I hadn't gotten sick," Sherri said.

To escape from Sherri's nattering drivel, Fat shut himself up in the bedroom he used as a study and began working once more on his great exegesis. He had done almost 300,000 words, mostly holographically, but from the inferior bulk he had begun to extract what he termed his **Tractate: Cryptica Scriptura** (see Appendix p. 386), which simply means "hidden discourse." Fat found the Latin more impressive as a title.

At this point in his *Meisterwerk* he had begun patiently to fabricate his cosmogony, which is the technical term for, "How the cosmos came into existence." Few individuals compose cosmogonies; usually entire cultures, civilizations, people or tribes are required: a cosmogony is a group production, evolving down through the ages. Fat well knew this, and prided himself on having invented his own. He called it:

TWO SOURCE COSMOGONY

In his journal or exegesis it came as entry #47 and was by far the longest single entry.

The One was and was-not, combined, and desired to separate the was-not from the was. So it generated a diploid sac which contained, like an eggshell, a pair of twins, each an androgyny, spinning in opposite directions (the Yin and Yang of Taoism, with the One as the Tao). The plan of the One was that both twins would emerge into being (was-ness) simultaneously; however, motivated by a desire to be (which the One had implanted in both twins), the counter-clockwise twin broke through the sac and separated prematurely; i.e. before full term. This was the dark or Yin twin. Therefore it was defective. At full term the wiser twin emerged. Each twin formed a unitary entelechy, a single living organism made of *psyche* and *soma*, still rotating in opposite directions to each other. The full term twin, called Form I by Parmenides, advanced correctly through its growth stages, but the prematurely born twin, called Form II, languished.

The next step in the One's plan was that the Two would become the Many, through their dialectic interaction. From them as hyperuniverses they projected a hologram-like interface, which is the pluriform universe we creatures inhabit. The two sources were to intermingle equally in maintaining our universe, but Form II continued to languish toward illness, madness and disorder. These aspects she projected into our universe.

It was the One's purpose for our hologramatic universe to serve as a teaching instrument by which a variety of new lives advanced until ultimately they would be isomorphic with the One. However, the decaying condition of hyperuniverse II introduced malfactors which damaged our hologramatic universe. This is the origin of entropy, undeserved suffering, chaos and death, as well as the Empire, the Black Iron Prison; in essence, the aborting of the proper health and growth of the life forms within the hologramatic universe. Also, the teaching function was grossly impaired, since only the signal from the hyperuniverse I was information-rich; that from II had become noise.

The psyche of hyperuniverse I sent a micro-form of itself into hyperuniverse II to attempt to heal it. The microform was apparent in our hologramatic universe as Jesus Christ. However, hyperuniverse II, being deranged, at once tormented, humiliated, rejected and finally killed the microform of the healing *psyche* of her healthy twin. After that, hyperuniverse II continued to decay into blind, mechanical, purposeless causal processes. It then became the task of Christ (more properly the Holy Spirit) to either rescue the life forms in the hologramatic universe, or abolish all influences on it emanating from II. Approaching its task with caution, it prepared to kill the deranged twin, since she cannot be healed; i.e. she will not allow herself to be healed because she does not understand that she is sick. This illness and madness pervades us and makes us idiots living in private, unreal worlds. The original plan of the One can only be realized now by the division of hyperuniverse I into two healthy hyperuniverses, which will transform the hologramatic universe into the successful teaching machine it was designed to be. We will experience this as the "Kingdom of God."

Within time, hyperuniverse II remains alive: "The Empire never ended." But in eternity, where the hyperuniverses exist, she has been killed—of necessity—by the healthy twin of hyperuniverse I, who is our champion. The One grieves for this death, since the One loved both twins; therefore the information of the Mind consists of a tragic tale of the death of a woman, the undertones of which generate anguish into all the creatures of the hologramatic universe without their knowing why. This grief will depart when the healthy twin undergoes mitosis and the "Kingdom of God" arrives. The machinery for this transformation—the procession within time from the Age of Iron to the Age of Gold—is at work now; in eternity it is already accomplished.

Not long thereafter, Sherri got fed up with Fat working night and day on his exegesis; also she got mad because he asked her to contribute some of her SSI money to pay the rent, since because of a court judgment he had to pay out a lot of spousal and child support to Beth and Christopher. Having found another apartment for which the Santa Ana housing authority would pick up the tab, Sherri wound up living by herself rent-free, without the obligation to fix Fat's dinner; also she could go out with other men, something Fat had objected to while he and Sherri were living together. To this possessiveness, Sherri had said hotly one night, when she came home from walking hand-in-hand with a male friend to find Fat furious,

"I don't have to put up with this crap."

Fat promised not to object to Sherri going out with other men any more, nor would he continue to ask her to contribute toward the rent and food costs, even though at the moment he had only nine dollars in his bank account. This did no good; Sherri was pissed.

"I'm moving out," she informed him.

After she moved out, Fat had to raise funds to purchase all manner of furniture, dishes, TV set, flatware, towels—everything, because he had brought little or nothing with him from his marriage; he had expected to depend on Sherri's chattel. Needless to say, he found life very lonely without her; living by himself in the two-bedroom, two-bathroom apartment which they had shared depressed the hell out of him. His friends worried about him and tried to cheer him up. In February Beth had left him and now in early September Sherri had left him. He was again dying by inches. All he did was sit at his type-writer or with notepad and pen, working on his exegesis; nothing else remained in his life. Beth had moved up to Sacramento, seven hundred miles away, so he did not get to see Christopher. He thought about suicide, but not very much, he knew that Maurice would not approve of such thoughts. Maurice would require of him another list.

What really bothered Fat was the intuition that Sherri would soon lose her remission. From going to class at Santa Ana College and working at the church she became rundown and tired; every time he saw her, which was as often as possible, he noticed how tired and thin she looked. In November she complained of the flu; she had pains in her chest and coughed continuously.

"This fucking flu," Sherri said.

Finally he got her to go to her doctor for an X-ray and blood tests. He knew she had lost her remission by then; she could barely drag herself around.

The day she found out that she had cancer again, Fat was with her; since her appointment with the doctor was at eight in the morning, Fat stayed up the night before, just sitting. He drove her to the doctor, along with Edna, a lifelong friend of Sherri's; he and Edna sat together in the waiting room while Sherri conferred with Dr. Applebaum.

"It's just the flu," Edna said.

Fat said nothing. He knew what it was. Three days before, he and Sherri had walked to the grocery store; she could hardly put one foot before the other. No doubt existed in Fat's mind; as he sat with Edna in the crowded waiting room terror filled him and he wanted to cry. Incredibly, today was his birthday.

When Sherri emerged from Dr. Applebaum's office, she had a Kleenex pressed to her eyes; Fat and Edna ran over to her; he caught Sherri as she fell saying, "It's back, the cancer's back." She had it in the lymph nodes in her neck and she had a malignant tumor in her right lung which was suffocating her. Chemotherapy and radiation would be started in twenty-four hours.

Edna said, stricken, "I was sure it was just flu. I wanted her to go up to Melodyland and testify that Jesus had cured her."

To that remark, Fat said nothing.

The argument can be made that at this point Fat no longer had any moral obligation to Sherri. For the most meager reason she had moved out on him, leaving him alone, grieving and desperate, with nothing to do but scribble away at his exegesis. Fat's friends had all pointed this out. Even Edna pointed this out, when Sherri wasn't present in the same room. But Fat still loved her. He now asked her to move back in with him so that he could take care of her, inasmuch as she had become too weak to fix herself meals, and once she began the chemotherapy she would become a lot sicker.

"No thanks," Sherri said, tonelessly.

Fat walked down to her church one day and talked with Father Larry; he begged Larry to put pressure on the State of California Medicare people to provide someone to come in and fix meals for Sherri and to help clean up her apartment, since she would not let him, Fat, do it. Father Larry said he would, but nothing came of it. Again Fat went over to talk to the priest about what could be done to help Sherri, and while he was talking, Fat suddenly began to cry.

To this, Father Larry said enigmatically, "I've cried all the tears I am going to cry for that girl."

Fat could not tell if that meant that Larry had burned out his circuits from grief or that he had calculatedly, as a self-protective device, curtailed his grief. Fat does not know to this day. His own grief had reached critical mass. Now Sherri had been hospitalized; Fat visited her and saw lying in the bed a small sad shape, half the size he was accustomed to, a shape coughing in pain, with wretched hopelessness in its eyes. Fat could not drive home after that, so Kevin drove him home. Kevin, who usually maintained his stance of cynicism, could not speak from grief; the two of them drove along and then Kevin slapped him on the shoulder, which is the only avenue open to men to show love for each other.

"What am I going to do?" Fat said, meaning, What am I going to do when she dies?

He really loved Sherri, despite her treatment of him—if indeed, as his friends maintained, she had treated him shabbily. He himself—he neither knew nor cared about that. All he knew was that she lay in the hospital bed with metastasized tumors throughout her. Every day he visited her in the hospital, along with everyone else who knew her.

At night he did the only act left open to him: work on his exegesis. He had reached an important entry.

Entry 48. ON OUR NATURE. It is proper to say: we appear to be memory coils (DNA carriers capable of experience) in a computer-like thinking system which, although we have correctly recorded and stored thousands of years of experiential information, and each of us possesses somewhat different deposits from all the other life forms, there is a malfunction—a failure—of memory retrieval. There lies the trouble in our particular subcircuit. "Salvation" through *gnosis*—more properly anamnesis (the loss of amnesia)—although it has individual significance for each of us—a quantum leap in perception, identity, cognition, understanding, world- and self-experience, including immortality —it has greater and further importance for the system as a whole, inasmuch as these memories are data needed by it and valuable to it, to its overall functioning.

Therefore it is in the process of self-repair, which includes: rebuilding our subcircuit via linear and orthogonal time changes, as well as continual signaling to us to stimulate blocked memory banks within us to fire and hence retrieve what is there.

The external information or *gnosis*, then, consists of disinhibiting instructions, with the core content actually intrinsic to us— that is, already there (first observed by Plato; *viz*: that learning is a form of remembering).

The ancients possessed techniques (sacraments and rituals) used largely in the Greco-Roman mystery religions, including early Christianity, to induce firing and retrieval, mainly with a sense of its restorative value to the individuals; the Gnostics, however, correctly saw the ontological value to what they called the Godhead Itself, the total entity.

The Godhead is impaired; some primordial crisis occurred in it which we do not understand.

Fat reworked journal entry #29 and added it to his **ON OUR NATURE** entry:

#29. We did not fall because of a moral error; we fell

because of an intellectual error: that of taking the phenomenal world as real. Therefore we are morally innocent. It is the Empire in its various disguised polyforms which tells us we have sinned. "The Empire never ended."

By now Fat's mind was going totally. All he did was work on his exegesis or his *tractate* or just listen to his stereo or visit Sherri in the hospital. He began to install entries in the *tractate* without logical order or reason.

#30. The phenomenal world does not exist; it is a hypostasis of the information processed by the Mind.

#27. If the centuries of spurious time are excised, the true date is not 1978 C.E. but 103 C.E. Therefore the New Testament says that the Kingdom of the Spirit will come before "some now living die." We are living, therefore, in apostolic times.

#20. The Hermetic alchemists knew of the secret race of three-eyed invaders but despite their efforts could not contact them. Therefore their efforts to support Frederick V, Elector Palatine, King of Bohemia, failed. "The Empire never ended."

#21. The Rose Cross Brotherhood wrote, *"Ex Deo nascimur, in Jesu mortimur, per spiritum sanctum reviviscimus,"* which is to say, "From God we are born, in Jesus we die, by the Holy Spirit we live again." This signifies that they had rediscovered the lost formula for immortality which the Empire had destroyed. "The Empire never ended."

#10. Apollonius of Tyana, writing as Hermes Trismegistos, said, "That which is above is that which is below." By this he meant to tell us that our Universe is a hologram, but he lacked the term.

#12. The Immortal One was known to the Greeks as Dionysos; to the Jews as Elijah; to the Christians as Jesus. He moves on when each human host dies, and thus is never killed or caught. Hence Jesus on the cross said, *"Eli, Eli, lama sabachthani,"* to which some of those present correctly said, "The man is calling on Elijah." Elijah had left him and he died alone.

At this moment as he made this entry, Horselover Fat was dying alone. Elijah, or whatever divine presence it was that had fired tons of information into his skull in 1974, had indeed left him. The dreadful question that Fat asked himself over and over again did not get put down in his journal or *tractate*; the question could be put this way:

> If the divine presence knew about Christopher's birth defect and did something to correct it, why doesn't it do something about Sherri's cancer? How could it let her lie there dying?

Fat could not figure this out. The girl had gone an entire year wrongly diagnosed; why hadn't Zebra fired that information to Fat or to Sherri's doctor or to Sherri—to *someone*?

Fired it in time to save her!

One day when Fat visited Sherri in the hospital, a grinning fool stood there by her bed, a simp who Fat had met; this thing used to shamble in while Fat and Sherri lived together and would put his arms around Sherri, kiss her and tell her he loved her—never mind Fat. This childhood friend of Sherri's, when Fat entered the hospital room, was saying to Sherri,

"What'll we do when I'm king of the world and you're queen of the world?"

To which Sherri, in agony, murmured, "I just want to get rid of these lumps in my throat."

Fat had never come so close to coldcocking anybody into tomorrow as at that moment. Kevin, who had accompanied him, had to physically hold Fat back.

On the drive back to Fat's lonely apartment, where he and Sherri had lived together for such a short time, Fat said to Kevin, "I'm going crazy. I can't take it."

"That's a normal reaction," Kevin said, showing nothing of his cynical pose, these days.

"Tell me," Fat said, "why God doesn't help her." He kept Kevin up on the progress of his exegesis; his encounter with God in 1974 was known to Kevin, so Fat could talk openly.

Kevin said, "It's the mysterious ways of the Great Punta."

"What the fuck is that?" Fat said.

"I don't believe in God," Kevin said. "I believe in the Great Punta. And the ways of the Great Punta are mysterious. No one knows why he does what he does, or doesn't do."

"Are you kidding me?"

"No," Kevin said.

"Where did the Great Punta come from?"

"Only the Great Punta knows."

"Is he benign?"

"Some say he is; some say he isn't."

"He could help Sherri if he wanted to."

Kevin said, "Only the Great Punta knows that."

They started laughing.

Obsessed with death, and going crazy from grief and worry about Sherri, Fat wrote entry #15 in his tractate.

#15. The Sibyl of Cumae protected the Roman Republic and gave timely warnings. In the first century c.e. she foresaw the murders of the two Kennedy brothers, Dr. King and Bishop Pike. She saw the two common denominators in the four murdered men: first, they stood in defense of the liberties of the Republic; and second, each man was a religious leader. For this they were killed. The Republic had once again become an empire with a caesar. "The Empire never ended."

#16. The Sibyl said in March 1974, "The conspirators have been seen and they will be brought to justice." She saw them with the third or *ajna* eye, the Eye of Shiva which gives inward discernment, but which when turned outward blasts with desiccating heat. In August 1974 the justice promised by the Sibyl came to pass.

Fat decided to put down on the *tractate* all the prophetic statements fired into his head by Zebra.

#7. The Head Apollo is about to return. St. Sophia is going to be born again; she was not acceptable before. The Buddha is in the park. Siddhartha sleeps (but is going to awaken). The time you have waited for has come.

Knowing this, by direct route from the divine, made Fat a latter-day prophet. But, since he had gone crazy, he also entered absurdities into his *tractate*.

#50. The primordial source of all our religions lies with the ancestors of the Dogon tribe, who got their cosmogony and cosmology directly from the three-eyed invaders who visited long ago. The three-eyed invaders are mute and deaf and telepathic, could not breathe our atmosphere,

had the elongated misshapen skull of Ikhnaton and emanated from a planet in the star-system Sirius. Although
they had no hands, but had, instead, pincer claws such as a
crab has, they were great builders. They covertly influence
our history toward a fruitful end.

By now Fat had totally lost touch with reality.

7

You can understand why Fat no longer knew the difference between fantasy and divine revelation—assuming there is a difference, which has never been established. He imagined that Zebra came from a planet in the star-system Sirius, had overthrown the Nixon tyranny in August 1974, and would eventually set up a just and peaceful kingdom on Earth where there would be no sickness, no pain, no loneliness, and the animals would all dance with joy.

Fat found a hymn by Ikhnaton and copied parts of it out of the reference book and into his *tractate*.

> ". . . When the fledgling in the egg chirps in the egg,
> Thou givest him breath therein to preserve him alive.
> When thou hast brought him together
> To the point of bursting the egg,
> He cometh forth from the egg,
> To chirp with all his might.
> He goeth about upon his two feet
> When he hath come from therefrom.
>
> How manifold are thy works!
> They are hidden from before us,
> O sole god, whose powers no other possesseth.
> Thou didst create the earth according to thy heart
> While thou wast alone:
> Men, all cattle large and small,
> All that go about upon their feet;
> All that are on high,
> That fly with their wings.
>
> Thou are in my heart,
> There is no other that knoweth thee
> Save thy son Ikhnaton.
> Thou hast made him wise
> In thy designs and in thy might.
> The world is in thy hands . . ."

Entry #52 shows that Fat at this point in his life reached out for any wild hope which would shore up his confidence that some good existed somewhere.

#52. Our world is still secretly ruled by the hidden race descended from Ikhnaton, and his knowledge is the information of the Macro-Mind itself.

> "All cattle rest upon their pasturage,
> The trees and the plants flourish,
> The birds flutter in their marshes,
> Their wings uplifted in adoration to thee.
> All the sheep dance upon their feet,
> All winged things fly,
> They live when thou hast shone upon them."

From Ikhnaton this knowledge passed to Moses, and from Moses to Elijah, the Immortal Man, who became Christ. But underneath all the names there is only one Immortal Man; *and we are that man.*

Fat still believed in God and Christ—and a lot else—but he wished he knew why Zebra, his term for the Almighty Divine One, had not given early warning about Sherri's condition and did not now heal her, and this mystery assailed Fat's brain and turned him into a maddened thing.

Fat, who had sought death, could not comprehend why Sherri was being allowed to die, and die horribly.

I myself am willing to step forth and offer some possibilities. A little boy menaced by a birth defect isn't in the same category with a grown woman who desires to die, who is playing a malignant game, as malignant as her physical analog, the lymphoma destroying her body. After all, the Almighty Divine One had not stepped forward to interfere with Fat's own suicide attempt; the Divine Presence had allowed Fat to down the forty-nine tabs of high-grade pure digitalis; nor had the Divine Authority prevented Beth from abandoning him and taking his son away from him, the very son for whom the medical information was put forth in theophanic disclosure.

This mention of three-eyed invaders with claws instead of hands, mute, deaf and telepathic creatures from another star, interested me. Regarding this topic, Fat showed a natural sly reticence; he knew enough not to shoot his mouth off about it. In March 1974 at the time he had encountered God (more properly Zebra), he had experienced vivid dreams about the three-eyed people—he had told me that. They manifested themselves as cyborg entities: wrapped up in glass bubbles staggering under masses of technological gear. An odd aspect cropped up that puzzled both Fat and me; sometimes in these vision-like dreams, Soviet technicians could be seen, hurrying to repair malfunctions of the sophisticated technological communications apparatus enclosing the three-eyed people.

"Maybe the Russians beamed microwave psychogenic or psychotronic or whatever-they-call-it signals at you," I said, having read an article on alleged Soviet boosting of telepathic messages by means of microwaves.

"I doubt if the Soviet Union is interested in Christopher's hernia," Fat said sourly.

But the memory plagued him that in these visions or dreams of hypnagogic states he had heard Russian words spoken and had seen page upon page, hundreds of pages, of what appeared to be Russian technical manuals, describing—he knew this because of the diagrams—engineering principles and constructs.

"You overheard a two-way transmission," I suggested. "Between the Russians and an extra-terrestrial entity."

"Just my luck," Fat said.

At the time of these experiences Fat's blood pressure had gone up to stroke level; his doctor had briefly hospitalized him. The doctor warned him not to take uppers.

"I'm not taking uppers," Fat had protested, truthfully.

The doctor had run every test possible, during Fat's stay in the hospital, to find a physical cause for the elevated blood pressure, but no cause had been found. Gradually his hypertension had diminished. The doctor was suspicious; he continued to believe that Fat had abreacted in his lifestyle to the days when he did uppers. But both Fat and I knew better. His blood pressure had registered 280 over 178, which is a lethal level. Normally, Fat ran about 135 over 90, which is normal. The cause of the temporary elevation remains a mystery to this day. That, and the deaths of Fat's pets.

I tell you these things for what they are worth. They are true things; they happened.

In Fat's opinion his apartment had been saturated with high levels of radiation of some kind. In fact he had seen it: blue light dancing like St. Elmo's Fire.

And, what was more, the aurora that sizzled around the apartment behaved as if it were sentient and alive. When it entered objects it interfered with their causal processes. And when it reached Fat's head it transferred—not just information to him, which it did—but also a personality. A personality which wasn't Fat's. A person with different memories, customs, tastes and habits.

For the first and only time in his life, Fat stopped drinking wine and bought beer, foreign beer. And he called his dog "he" and his cat "she" although he knew—or had previously known—that the dog was a she and the cat a he. This had annoyed Beth.

Fat wore different clothes and carefully trimmed down his beard. When he looked in the bathroom mirror while trimming it he saw an unfamiliar person, although it was his regular self not changed. Also the climate seemed wrong; the air was too dry and too hot: not the right altitude and not the right humidity. Fat had the subjective impression that a moment ago he'd been living in a high, cool, moist region of the world and not in Orange County, California.

Plus the fact that this inner ratiocination took the form of *koine* Greek, which he did not understand as a language, nor as a phenomenon going on in his head.

And he had a lot of trouble driving his car; he couldn't figure out where the controls were; they all seemed to be in the wrong places.

Perhaps most remarkable of all, Fat experienced a particularly vivid dream—if "dream" it was—about a Soviet woman who would be contacting him by mail. In the dream he was shown a photograph of her; she had blonde hair, and, he was told, "Her name is Sadassa Ulna." An urgent message fired into Fat's head that he *must* respond to her letter when it came.

Two days later, a registered air mail letter arrived from the Soviet Union, which shocked Fat into a state of terror. The letter had been sent by a man, who Fat had never heard of (Fat wasn't used to getting letters from the Soviet Union anyhow) who wanted:

1) A photograph of Fat.

2) A specimen of Fat's handwriting, in particular his signature.

To Beth, Fat said, "Today is Monday. On Wednesday, another letter will come. This will be from the woman."

On Wednesday, Fat received a plethora of letters: seven in all. Without opening them he fished among them and pointed out one, which had no return name or address on it. "That's it," he said to Beth, who, by now, was also freaked. "Open it and look at it, but don't let me see her name and address or I'll answer it."

Beth opened it. Instead of a letter *per se* she found a Xerox sheet on which two book reviews from the left-wing New York newspaper *The Daily World* had been juxtaposed. The reviewer described the author of the books as a Soviet national living in the United States. From the reviews it was obvious that the author was a Party member.

"My God," Beth said, turning the Xerox sheet over. "The author's name and address is written on the back."

"A woman?" Fat said.

"Yes," Beth said.

I never found out from Fat and Beth what they did with the two letters. From hints Fat dropped I deduced that he finally answered the first one, having decided that it was innocent; but what he did with the Xerox one, which really wasn't a letter in the strict sense of the term, I do not to this day know, nor do I want to know. Maybe he burned it. Maybe he turned it over to the police or the FBI or the CIA; in any case I doubt if he answered it.

For one thing, he refused to look at the back of the Xerox sheet where the woman's name and address appeared; he had the conviction that if he saw this information he would answer her whether he wanted to or not. Maybe so. Who can say? First eight hours of graphic information is fired at you from sources unknown, taking the form of lurid phosphene activity in eighty colors arranged like modern abstract paintings; then you dream about three-eyed people in glass bubbles and electronic gear; then your apartment fills up with St. Elmo's Fire plasmatic energy which appears to be alive and to think; your animals die; you are overcome by a different personality who thinks in Greek; you dream about Russians; and finally you get a couple of Soviet letters within a three-day period—which you were told were coming. But the total impression isn't bad because some of the information saves your son's life. Oh yes; one more thing: Fat found himself seeing ancient Rome super-imposed over California 1974. Well, I'll say this: Fat's encounter may not have been with God, but it certainly was with *something*.

No wonder Fat started scratching out page after page of his exegesis. I'd have done the same. He wasn't just theory-mongering for the sake of it; he was trying to figure out what the fuck had happened to him.

If Fat had simply been crazy he certainly found a unique form, an original way of doing it. Being in therapy at the time (Fat was always in therapy) he asked that a Rorschach Test be given him, to determine if he had become schizophrenic. The test, upon his taking it, showed only a mild neurosis. So much for that theory.

In my novel *A Scanner Darkly*, published in 1977, I ripped off Fat's account of his eight hours of lurid phosphene activity.

"He had, a few years ago, been experimenting with dis-inhibiting substances affecting neural tissue, and one night, having administered to himself an IV injection considered safe and mildly euphoric, had experienced a disastrous drop in the GABA fluid of his brain. Subjectively, he had then witnessed lurid phosphene activity projected on the far wall of his bedroom, a frantically progressing mon-tage of what, at the time, he imagined to be modern-day abstract paintings.

For about six hours, entranced, S.A. Powers had watched thousands of Picasso paintings replace one another at flash-cut speed, and then he had been treated to Paul Klees, more than the painter had painted during his entire lifetime. S.A. Powers, now viewing Modigliani paintings replacing themselves at furious velocity, had conjectured (one needs a theory for everything) that the Rosicrucians were telepathically beaming pictures at him, probably boosted by microrelay systems of an advanced order; but then, when Kandinsky paintings began to harass him, he recalled that the main art museum at Leningrad specialized in just such nonobjective moderns, and he decided that the Soviets were attempting telepathically to contact him.

In the morning he remembered that a drastic drop in the GABA fluid of the brain normally produced such phosphene activity; nobody was trying to contact him telepathically, with or without microwave boosting . . ."*

The GABA fluid of the brain blocks neural circuits from firing; it holds them in a dormant or latent state until a disinhibiting stimulus—the correct one—is presented to the organism, in this case Horselover Fat. In other words, these are neural circuits designed to fire on cue at a specific time under specific circumstances. Had Fat been presented with a disinhibiting stimulus prior to the lurid phosphene activity—the indication of a drastic drop in the level of GABA fluid in his brain, and hence the firing of previously blocked circuits, meta-circuits, so to speak?

All these events took place in March 1974. The month before that, Fat had had an impacted wisdom tooth removed. For this the oral surgeon administered a hit of IV sodium pentothal. Later that afternoon, back at home and in great pain, Fat had gotten Beth to phone for some oral pain medication. Being as miserable as he was, Fat himself had answered the door when the pharmacy delivery person knocked. When he opened the door, he found himself facing a lovely darkhaired young woman who held out a small white bag containing the Darvon N. But Fat, despite his enormous pain, cared nothing about the pills, because his attention had fastened on the gleaming gold necklace about the girl's neck; he couldn't take his eyes off it. Dazed from pain—and from the sodium pentothal—and exhausted by the ordeal he had gone through, he nonetheless managed to ask the girl what the symbol shaped in gold at the center of the necklace represented. It was a fish, in profile.

Touching the golden fish with one slender finger, the girl said, "This is a sign used by the early Christians."

*A Scanner Darkly, Doubleday, 1977, pgs. 15/16.

Instantly, Fat experienced a flashback. He remembered—just for a half-second. Remembered ancient Rome and himself: as an early Christian; the entire ancient world and his furtive frightened life as a secret Christian hunted by the Roman authorities burst over his mind . . . and then he was back in California 1974 accepting the little white bag of pain pills.

A month later as he lay in bed unable to sleep, in the semi-gloom, listening to the radio, he started to see floating colors. Then the radio shrilled hideous, ugly sentences at him. And, after two days of this, the vague colors began to rush toward him as if he were himself moving forward, faster and faster; and, as I depicted in my novel *A Scanner Darkly*, the vague colors abruptly froze into sharp focus in the form of modern abstract paintings, literally tens of millions of them in rapid succession.

Meta-circuits in Fat's brain had been disinhibited by the fish sign and the words spoken by the girl.

It's as simple as that.

A few days later, Fat woke up and saw ancient Rome super-imposed on California 1974 and thought in *koine* Greek, the *lingua franca* of the Near East part of the Roman world, which was the part he saw. He did not know that the *koine* was their *lingua franca*; he supposed that Latin was. And in addition, as I've already told you, he did not recognize the language of his thoughts even as a language.

Horselover Fat is living in two different times and two different places; i.e. in two space-time continua; that is what took place in March 1974 because of the ancient fish-sign presented to him the month before: his two space-time continua ceased to be separate and merged. And his two identities—personalities —also merged. Later, he heard a voice thing inside his head:

"There's someone else living in me and he's not in this century."

The other personality had figured it out. The other personality was thinking. And Fat—especially just before he fell asleep at night—could pick up the thoughts of this other personality, as recently as a month ago; which is to say, four-and-a-half years after the compartmentalization of the two persons broke down.

*

Fat himself expressed it very well to me in early 1975 when he first began to confide in me. He called the personality in him living in another century and at another place "Thomas."

"Thomas," Fat told me, "is smarter than I am, and he knows more than I do. Of the two of us Thomas is the master personality." He considered that good; woe unto someone who has an evil or stupid other-personality in his head!

I said, "You mean once you were Thomas. You're a reincarnation of him and you remembered him and his—"

"No, he's living now. Living in ancient Rome *now*. And he is not me. Reincarnation has nothing to do with it."

"*But your body*," I said.

Fat stared at me, nodding. "Right. It means my body is either in two space-time continua simultaneously, *or else my body is nowhere at all.*"

Entry #14 from the tractate: **The universe is information and we are stationary in it, not three-dimensional and not in space or time. The information fed to us we hypostatize into the phenomenal world.**

Entry #30, which is a restatement for emphasis: **The phenomenal world does not exist; it is a hypostasis of the information processed by the Mind.**

Fat had scared the shit out of me. He had extrapolated entries #14 and #30 from his experience, inferred them from discovering that someone else existed in his head and that someone else was living in a different place at a different time—two thousand years ago and eight thousand miles away.

We are not individuals. We are stations in a single Mind. We are supposed to remain separate from one another at all times. However, Fat had received by accident a signal (the golden fish sign) intended for Thomas. It was Thomas who dealt in fish signs, not Fat. If the girl hadn't explained the meaning of the sign, the breakdown of compartmentalization would not have occurred. But she did and it did. Space and time were revealed to Fat—and to Thomas!—as mere mechanisms of separation. Fat found himself viewing a double exposure of two realities superimposed, and Thomas probably found himself doing the same. Thomas probably wondered what the hell foreign language was happening in *his* head, Then he realized it wasn't even his head:

"There's someone else living in me and he's not in this century." That was Thomas thinking that, not Fat. But it applied to Fat equally.

But Thomas had the edge over Fat, because, as Fat said, Thomas was smarter; he was the master personality. He took over Fat, switched him off wine and onto beer, trimmed his beard, had trouble with the car . . . but more important, Thomas remembered—if that is the word—other selves, one in Minoan Crete, which is from 3000 B.C.E. to 1100 B.C.E., a long, long time ago. Thomas even remembered a self before that: one which had come to this planet from the stars.

Thomas was the ultimate non-fool of Post Neolithic times. As an early Christian, of the apostolic age; he had not seen Jesus but he knew people who had—my God, I'm losing control, here, trying to write this down. Thomas had figured out how to reconstitute himself after his physical death. *All* the early Christians knew how. It worked through anamnesis, the loss of amnesia which—well, the system was supposed to work this way: when Thomas found himself dying, he would engram himself on the Christian fish sign, eat some strange pink—the same pink color as in the light which Fat had seen—some strange pink food and drink from a sacred pitcher kept in a cool cupboard, and then die, and when he was reborn, he would grow up and be a later person, not himself, *until* he was shown the fish sign.

He had anticipated this happening about forty years after his death. Wrong. It took almost two thousand years.

In this way, through this mechanism, time was abolished. Or, put another way, the tyranny of death was abolished. The promise of eternal life which Christ held out to his little flock was no hoax. Christ had taught them how to do it; it had to do with the immortal plasmate which Fat talked about, the living information slumbering at Nag Hammadi century after century. The Romans had found and murdered all the homoplasmates —all the early Christians crossbonded to the plasmate; they died, the plasmate escaped to Nag Hammadi and slumbered as information on the codices.

Until, in 1945, the library was discovered and dug up—and

read. So Thomas had to wait—not forty years—but two thousand; because the golden fish sign wasn't enough. Immortality, the abolition of time and space, comes only through the Logos or plasmate; only it is immortal.

We are talking about Christ. He is an extra-terrestrial life form which came to this planet thousands of years ago, and, as living information, passed into the brains of human beings already living here, the native population. We are talking about interspecies symbiosis.

Before being Christ he was Elijah. The Jews know all about Elijah and his immortality—and his ability to extend immortality to others by "dividing up his spirit." The Qumran people knew this. They sought to receive part of Elijah's spirit.

"You see, my son, here time changes into space."

First you change it into space and then you walk through it, but as Parsifal realized, he was not moving at all; he stood still and the landscape changed; it underwent a metamorphosis. For a while he must have experienced a double exposure, a superimposition, as Fat did. This is the dream-time, which exists now, not in the past, the place where the heroes and gods dwell and their deeds take place.

The single most striking realization that Fat had come to was his concept of the universe as irrational and governed by an irrational mind, the creator deity. If the universe were taken to be rational, not irrational, then something breaking into it might seem irrational, since it would not belong. But Fat, having reversed everything, saw the rational breaking into the irrational. The immortal plasmate had invaded our world and the plasmate was totally rational, whereas our world is not. This structure forms the basis of Fat's world-view. It is the bottom line.

For two thousand years the single rational element in our world had slumbered. In 1945 it woke up, came out of its dormant seed state and began to grow. It grew within himself, and presumably within other humans, and it grew outside, in the macro-world. He could not estimate its vastness, as I have said. When something begins to devour the world, a serious matter is taking place. If the devouring entity is evil or insane, the situation is not merely serious; it is grim. But Fat viewed the process the other way around. He viewed it exactly as Plato had viewed it in his own cosmology: the rational mind (*noös*) persuades the irrational (chance, blind determinism, *ananke*) into cosmos.

This process had been interrupted by the Empire.

"The Empire never ended." Until now; until August 1974 when the Empire suffered a crippling, perhaps terminal, blow, at the hands—so to speak—of the immortal plasmate, now restored to active form and using humans as its physical agents.

Horselover Fat was one of those agents. He was, so to speak, the hands of the plasmate, reaching out to injure the Empire.

Out of this, Fat deduced that he had a mission, that the plasmate's invasion of him represented its intention to employ him for its benign purposes.

I have had dreams of another place myself, a lake up north and the cottages and small rural houses around its south shore. In my dream I arrive there from Southern California, where I live; this is a vacation spot, but it is very old-fashioned. All the houses are wooden, made of the brown shingles so popular in California before World War Two. The roads are dusty. The cars are older, too. What is strange is that no such lake exists in the northern part of California. In real life I have driven all the way north to the Oregon border and into Oregon itself. Seven hundred miles of dry country exists only.

Where does this lake—and the houses and roads around it—actually exist? Countless times I dream about it. Since in the dreams I am aware that I am on vacation, that my real home is in southern California, I sometimes drive back down here to Orange County in these inter-connected dreams. But when I arrive back down here I live in a house, whereas in actuality I live in an apartment. In the dreams, I am married. In real life, I live alone. Stranger still, my wife is a woman I have never actually seen.

In one dream, the two of us are outside in the back yard watering and tending our rose garden. I can see the house next door; it's a mansion, and we share a common cement retaining wall with it. Wild roses have been planted up the side of the wall, to make it attractive. As I carry my rake past the green plastic garbage cans which we have stuffed with the clippings of trimmed plants, I glance at my wife—she is watering with the hose—and I gaze up at the retaining wall with its wild rose bushes, and I feel good; I think, it wouldn't be possible to live happily in southern California if we didn't have this nice house with its beautiful back garden. I'd prefer to own the mansion next door, but anyhow I get to see it, and I can walk over into its more spacious garden. My wife wears blue jeans; she is slender and pretty.

As I wake up I think, I should drive north to the lake; as beautiful as it is down here, with my wife and the back garden and the wild roses, the lake is nicer. But then I realize that this is January and there will be snow on the highway when I get north of the Bay Area; this is not a good time to drive back to the cabin on the lake. I should wait until summer; I am really, after all, a rather timid driver. My car's a good one, though; a nearly new red Capri. And then as I wake up more I realize that I am living in an apartment in southern California alone. I have no wife. There is no such house, with the back garden and the high retaining wall with wild rose bushes. Stranger still, not only do I not have a cabin on the lake up north but no such lake in California exists. The map I hold mentally during my dream is a counterfeit map; it does not depict California. Then what state does it depict? Washington? There is a large body of water at the north of Washington; I have flown over it going to and returning from Canada, and once I visited Seattle.

Who is this wife? Not only am I single; I have never been married to nor seen this woman. Yet in the dreams I felt deep, comfortable and familiar love toward her, the kind of love which grows only with the passage of many years. But how do I even know that, since I have never had anyone to feel such love for?

Getting up from bed—I've been napping in the early evening—I walk into the living room of my apartment and am struck dumb by the synthetic nature of my life. Stereo (that's synthetic); television set (that's certainly synthetic); books, a second-hand experience, at least compared with driving up the narrow, dusty road which follows the lake, passing under the branches of trees, finally reaching my cabin and the place I park. What cabin? What lake? I can even remember being taken there originally, years ago, by my mother. Now, sometimes, I go by air. There's a direct flight between southern California and the lake . . . except for a few miles after the airfield. What airfield? But, most of all, how can I endure the ersatz life I lead here in this plastic apartment, alone, specifically without her, the slender wife in blue jeans?

If it wasn't for Horselover Fat and his encounter with God or Zebra or the Logos, and this other person living in Fat's head but in another century and place, I would dismiss my dreams as nothing. I can remember articles dealing with the people who have settled near the lake; they belong to a mild religious group, somewhat like the Quakers (I was raised as a Quaker); except, it is stated, they held the strong belief that children should not be put in wooden cradles. This was their special heretical thrust. Also—and I can actually see the pages of the written article about them—it is said of them that "every now and then one or two wizards are born," which has some bearing on their aversion to wooden cradles; if you put an infant or baby who is a wizard—a future wizard—into a wooden cradle, evidently he will gradually lose his powers.

Dreams of another life? But where? Gradually the envisioned map of California, which is spurious, fades out, and, with it, the lake, the houses, the roads, the people, the cars, the airport, the clan of mild religious believers with their peculiar aversion to wooden cradles; but for this to fade out, a host of inter-connected dreams spanning years of real elapsed time must fade, too.

The only connection between this dream landscape and my actual world consists of my red Capri.

Why does that one element hold true in both worlds?

It has been said of dreams that they are a "controlled psychosis," or, put another way, a psychosis is a dream breaking though during waking hours. What does this mean in terms of my lake dream which includes a woman I never knew for whom I feel a real and comfortable love? Are there two persons in my brain, as there are in Fat's? Partitioned off, but, in my case no disinhibiting symbol accidentally triggered the "other" one into bursting through the partition into my personality and my world?

Are we all like Horselover Fat, but don't know it?

How many worlds do we exist in simultaneously?

Groggy from my nap I turn on the TV and try to watch a program called "Dick Clark's Good Ol' Days Part II." Morons and simps appear in the screen, drool like pinheads and water-heads; zitfaced kids scream in ecstatic approval of total banality. I turn the TV set off. My cat wants to be fed. What cat? In the dreams, my wife and I own no pets; we own a lovely house with a large, well-tended yard in which we spend our week-ends. We have a two-car garage . . . suddenly I realize with a distinct jolt that this is an expensive house; in my inter-related dreams I am well-to-do. I live an upper middleclass life. It's not me. I'd never live like that; or if I did I'd be acutely uncomfort-able. Wealth and property make me uneasy; I grew up in Berke-ley and have the typical Berkeley left wing socialist conscience, with its suspicion of the cushy life.

The person in the dream also owns lake-front property. But the goddam Capri is the same. Earlier this year I went out and bought a brand new Capri Ghia, which normally I can't afford; it is the kind of car the person in the dream would own. There is a logic to the dream, then. As that person I would have the same car.

An hour after I have woken up from the dream I can still see in my mind's eye—whatever that may be; the third or *ajna* eye?—the garden hose which my wife in her blue jeans is drag-ging across the cement driveway. Little details, and no plot. I wish I owned the mansion next to our house. I do? In real life, I wouldn't own a mansion on a bet. These are rich people; I detest them. Who am I? How many people am I? Where am I? This plastic little apartment in southern California is not my home, but now I am awake, I guess, and here I live, with my TV (hello, Dick Clark), and my stereo (hello, Olivia Newton-John) and my books (hello nine million stuffy titles). In com-parison to my life in the inter-connected dreams, this life is lonely and phony, and worthless; unfit for an intelligent and educated person. *Where are the roses? Where is the lake? Where is the slim, smiling, attractive woman coiling and tugging the green garden hose?* The person that I am now, compared with the person in the dream, has been baffled and defeated and only supposes he enjoys a full life. In the dreams, I see what a full life really consists of, and it is not what I really have.

Then a strange thought comes to me. I am not close to my

father, who is still alive, in his eighties, living up in northern California, in Menlo Park. Only twice did I ever visit his house, and that was twenty years ago. His house was like that which I owned in the dream. His aspirations—and accomplishments—dovetail with those of the person in the dream. Do I become my father during my sleep? The man in the dream—myself—was about my own actual age, *or younger*. Yes; I infer from the woman, my wife: much younger. I have gone back in time in my dreams, not back to my own youth but back to my father's youth! In my dreams, I hold my father's view of the good life, of what things should be like; the strength of his view is so strong that it lingers an hour after I wake up. Of course I felt dislike for my cat upon awakening; my father hates cats.

My father, in the decade before I was born, used to drive up north to Lake Tahoe. He and my mother probably had a cabin there. I don't know; I've never been there.

Phylogenic memory, memory of the species. Not my own memory, ontogenic memory. "Phylogeny is recapitulated in ontogeny," as it is put. The individual contains the history of his entire race, back to its origins. Back to ancient Rome, to Minos at Crete, back to the stars. All I got down to, all I abreacted to, in sleep, was one generation. This is gene pool memory, the memory of the DNA. That explains Horselover Fat's crucial experience, in which the symbol of the Christian fish disinhibited a personality from two thousand years in the past . . . because the symbol originated two thousand years in the past. Had he been shown an even older symbol he would have abreacted farther; after all, the conditions were perfect for it: he was coming off sodium pentothal, the "truth drug."

Fat has another theory. He thinks that the date is really 103 C.E. (or A.D. as I put it; damn Fat and his hip modernisms). We're actually in apostolic times, but a layer of *maya* or what the Greeks called "*dokos*" obscures the landscape. This is a key concept with Fat: *dokos*, the layer of delusion or the merely seeming. The situation has to do with time, with whether time is real.

I'll quote Heraclitus on my own, without getting Fat's permission: "Time is a child at play, playing draughts; a child's is the kingdom." Christ! What does this mean? Edward Hussey says about this passage: "Here, as probably in Anaximander,

'Time' is a name for God, with an etymological suggestion of his eternity. The infinitely old divinity is a child playing a board game as he moves the cosmic pieces in combat according to rule." Jesus Christ, what are we dealing with, here? Where are we and when are we and who are we? How many people in how many places at how many times? Pieces on a board, moved by the "infinitely old divinity" who is a "child"!

Back to the cognac bottle. Cognac calms me down. Sometimes, especially after I've spent an evening talking to Fat, I get freaked and need something to calm me. I have the dreadful sense that he is into something real and awfully frightening. Personally, I don't want to break any new theological or philosophical ground. But I had to meet Horselover Fat; I had to get to know him and share his harebrained ideas based on his peculiar encounter with God knows what. With ultimate reality, maybe. Whatever it was, it was alive and it thought. And in no way did it resemble us, despite the quote from *1 John 3:1/2*.

Xenophanes was right.

"One god there is, *in no way like mortal creatures* either in bodily form or in the thought of his mind."

Isn't it an oxymoron to say, I am not myself? Isn't this a verbal contradiction, a statement semantically meaningless? Fat turned out to be Thomas; and I, upon studying the information in my dream, conclude that I am my own father, married to my mother when she was young—before my own birth. I think the cryptic mention that, "Now and then one or two wizards are born" is supposed to tell me something. A sufficiently advanced technology would seem to us to be a form of magic; Arthur C. Clarke has pointed that out. A Wizard deals with magic; *ergo*, a "wizard" is someone in possession of a highly sophisticated technology, one which baffles us. Someone is playing a board game with time, someone we can't see. It is not God. That is an archaic name given to this entity by societies in the past, and by people now who're locked into anachronistic thinking. We need a new term, but what we are dealing with is not new.

Horselover Fat is able to travel through time, travel back thousands of years. The three-eyed people probably live in the far future; they are our descendents, highly-evolved. And it is probably their technology which permitted Fat to do his time-traveling. In point of fact, Fat's master personality may not lie in the past but ahead of us—but it expressed itself outside of him in the form of Zebra. I am saying that the St. Elmo's Fire which Fat recognized as alive and sentient probably abreacted back to this time-period and is one of our own children.

8

I DID not think I should tell Fat that I thought his encounter with God was in fact an encounter with himself from the far future. Himself so evolved, so changed, that he had become no longer a human being. Fat had remembered back to the stars, and had encountered a being ready to return to the stars, and several selves along the way, several points along the line. All of them are the same person.

Entry #13 in the *tractate*: **Pascal said, "All history is one immortal man who continually learns." This is the Immortal One whom we worship without knowing his name. "He lived a long time ago but he is still alive," and, "The Head Apollo is about to return." The name changes.**

On some level Fat guessed the truth; he had encountered his past selves and his future selves—two future selves: an early-on one, the three-eyed people, and then Zebra, who is discorporate.

Time somehow got abolished for him, and the recapitulation of selves along the linear time-axis caused the multitude of selves to laminate together into a common entity.

Out of the lamination of selves, Zebra, which is supra- or trans-temporal, came into existence: pure energy, pure living information. Immortal, benign, intelligent and helpful. The essence of the *rational* human being. In the center of an irrational universe governed by an irrational Mind stands rational man, Horselover Fat being just one example. The in-breaking deity that Fat encountered in 1974 was himself. However, Fat seemed happy to believe that he had met God. After some thought I decided not to tell him my views. After all, I might be wrong.

It all had to do with time. "Time can be overcome," Mircea Eliade wrote. That's what it's all about. The great mystery of Eleusis, of the Orphics, of the early Christians, of Sarapis, of the Greco-Roman mystery religions, of Hermes Trismegistos, of the Renaissance Hermetic alchemists, of the Rose Cross Brotherhood, of Apollonius of Tyana, of Simon Magus, of Asklepios, of Paracelsus, of Bruno, consists of the abolition of time. The techniques are there. Dante discusses them in the *Comedy*. It has to do with the loss of amnesia; when forgetfulness is lost, true memory spreads out backward and forward, into the past and into the future, and also, oddly, into alternate universes; it is orthogonal as well as linear.

This is why Elijah could be said correctly to be immortal; he had entered the Upper Realm (as Fat calls it) and is no longer subject to time. Time equals what the ancients called "astral determinism." The purpose of the mysteries was to free the initiate from astral determinism, which roughly equals fate. About this, Fat wrote in his *tractate*:

Entry #48. Two realms there are, upper and lower. The upper, derived from hyperuniverse I or Yang, Form I of Parmenides, is sentient and volitional. The lower realm, or Yin, Form II of Parmenides, is mechanical, driven by blind, efficient cause, deterministic and without intelligence, since it emanates from a dead source. In ancient times it was termed "astral determinism." We are trapped, by and large, in the lower realm, but are through the sacraments, by means of the plasmate, extricated. Until astral determinism is broken, we are not even aware of it, so occluded are we. "The Empire never ended."

Siddhartha, the Buddha, remembered all his past lives; this is why he was given the title of buddha which means "the Enlightened One." From him the knowledge of achieving this passed to Greece and shows up in the teachings of Pythagoras, who kept much of this occult, mystical *gnosis* secret; his pupil Empedocles, however, broke off from the Pythagorean Brotherhood and went public. Empedocles told his friends privately that he was Apollo. He, too, like the Buddha and Pythagoras, could remember his past lives. What they did not talk about was their ability to "remember" future lives.

The three-eyed people who Fat saw represented himself at an enlightened stage of his evolving development through his various lifetimes. In Buddhism it's called the "super-human divine eye" (*dibba-cakkhu*), the power to see the passing away and re-birth of beings. Gautama the Buddha (Siddhartha) attained it during his middle watch (ten P.M. to two A.M.). In his first watch (six P.M. to ten P.M.) he gained the knowledge of all—repeat: *all*—his former existences (*pubbenivasanussati-nana*). I did not tell Fat this, but technically he had become a Buddha. It did not seem to me like a good idea to let him know. After all, if you are a Buddha you should be able to figure it out for yourself.

It strikes me as an interesting paradox that a Buddha—an enlightened one—would be unable to figure out, even after four-and-a-half years, that he had become enlightened. Fat had become totally bogged down in his enormous exegesis, trying futilely to determine what had happened to him. He resembled more a hit-and-run accident victim than a Buddha.

"Holy fuck!" as Kevin would have put it, about the encounter with Zebra. "What was THAT?"

No wimpy hype passed muster before Kevin's eyes. He considered himself the hawk and the hype the rabbit. He had little use for the exegesis, but remained Fat's good friend. Kevin operated on the principle, Condemn the deed not the doer.

These days, Kevin felt fine. After all, his negative opinion of Sherri had proven correct. This brought him and Fat closer together. Kevin knew her for what she was, her cancer notwithstanding. In the final analysis, the fact that she was dying mattered to him not in the least. He had mulled it over and concluded that the cancer was a scam.

Fat's obsessive idea these days, as he worried more and more about Sherri, was that the Savior would soon be reborn—or had been already. Somewhere in the world he walked or soon would walk the ground once more.

What did Fat intend to do when Sherri died? Maurice had shouted that at him in the form of a question. Would he die, too?

Not at all. Fat, pondering and writing and doing research and receiving dribs and drabs of messages from Zebra during hypnagogic states and in dreams, and attempting to salvage something from the wreck of his life, had decided to go in search of the Savior. He would find him wherever he was.

This was the mission, the divine purpose, which Zebra had placed on him in March 1974: the mild yoke, the burden light. Fat, a holy man now, would become a modern-day magus. All he lacked was a clue—some hint as to where to seek. Zebra would tell him, eventually; the clue would come from God.

This was the whole purpose of Zebra's theophany: to send Fat on his way.

Our friend David, upon being told of this, asked, "Will it be Christ?" Thus showing his Catholicism.

"It is a fifth Savior," Fat said enigmatically. After all, Zebra had referred to the coming of the Savior in several—and in a sense conflicting—ways: as St. Sophia, who was Christ; as the Head Apollo; as the Buddha or Siddhartha.

Being eclectic in terms of his theology, Fat listed a number of saviors: the Buddha, Zoroaster, Jesus and Abu Al-Qasim Muhammad Ibn Abd Allah Abd Al-Muttalib Ibn Hashim (i.e. Muhammad). Sometimes he also listed Mani. Therefore, the next Savior would be number five, by the abridged list, or number six by the longer list. At certain times, Fat also included Asklepios, which, when added to the longer list, would make the next Savior number seven. In any case, this forthcoming savior would be the last; he would sit as king and judge over all nations and people. The sifting bridge of Zoroastrianism had been set up, by means of which good souls (those of light) became separated from bad souls (those of darkness). Ma'at had put her feather in the balance to be weighed against the heart of each man in judgment, as Osiris the Judge sat. It was a busy time.

Fat intended to be present, perhaps to hand the *Book of Life* to the Supreme Judge, the Ancient of Days mentioned in the *Book of Daniel.*

We all pointed out to Fat that hopefully the *Book of Life*—in which the names of all who were saved had been inscribed—would prove too heavy for one man to lift; a winch and power crane would be necessary. Fat wasn't amused.

"Wait'll the Supreme Judge sees my dead cat," Kevin said.

"You and your goddam dead cat," I said. "We're tired of hearing about your dead cat."

After listening to Fat disclose his sly plans to seek out the Savior—no matter how far he had to travel to find him—I realized the obvious: Fat actually was in search of the dead girl Gloria, for whose death he considered himself responsible. He had totally blended his religious life and goals with his emotional life and goals. For him "savior" stood for "lost friend." He hoped to be reunited with her, but this side of the grave. If he couldn't go to her, on the other side, he would instead find her here. So although he was no longer suicidal he was still nuts. But this seemed to me to be an improvement; *thanatos* was losing out to *eros*. As Kevin put it, "Maybe Fat'll get laid by some fox somewhere along the way."

By the time Fat took off on his sacred quest he would be searching for two dead girls: Gloria and Sherri. This updated version of the Grail saga made me wonder if equally erotic underpinnings had motived the Grail knights at Montsavat, the castle where Parsifal wound up. Wagner says in his text that only those who the Grail itself calls find their way there. The blood of Christ on the cross had been caught in the same cup from which he had drunk at the Last Supper; so literally it had wound up containing his blood. In essence the blood, not the Grail, summoned the knights; the blood never died. Like Zebra, the contents of the Grail were a plasma or, as Fat termed it, plasmate. Probably Fat had it down somewhere in his exegesis that Zebra equaled plasmate equaled the sacred blood of the crucified Christ.

The spilled blood of the girl broken and dying on the pavement outside the Oakland Synanon Building called to Fat, who, like Parsifal, was a complete fool. That's what the word "parsifal" is supposed to mean in Arabic; it's supposed to have been derived from "*Falparsi*," an Arabic word meaning "pure fool." This of course isn't the actual case, although in the opera *Parsifal*, Kundry addresses Parsifal this way. The name "Parsifal" is in fact derived from "Perceval," which is just a name. However, one point of interest remains: via Persia the Grail is identified with the pre-Christian "*lapis exilix*," which is a magical stone. This stone shows up in later Hermetic alchemy as the agent by which human metamorphosis is achieved. On the basis of Fat's concept of interspecies symbiosis, the human being crossbonded with Zebra or the Logos or plasmate to become a homoplasmate, I can see a certain continuity in all this. Fat believed himself to have crossbonded with Zebra; therefore he had already become that which the Hermetic alchemists sought. It would be natural, then, for him to seek out the Grail; he would be finding his friend, himself and his home.

Kevin held the role of the evil magician Klingsor by his continual lampooning of Fat's idealistic aspirations. Fat, according to Kevin, was horny. In Fat, *thanatos*—death—fought it out with *eros*—which Kevin identified not with life but with getting laid. This probably isn't far off; I mean Kevin's basic description of the dialectical struggle surging back and forth inside Fat's mind. Part of Fat desired to die and part desired life. *Thanatos* can assume any form it wishes; it can kill *eros*, the life drive, and then simulate it. Once thanatos does this to you, you are in big trouble; you suppose you are driven by *eros* but it is *thanatos* wearing a mask. I hoped Fat hadn't gotten into this place; I hoped his desire to seek out and find the Savior stemmed from *eros*.

The true Savior, or the true God for that matter, carries life with him; he *is* life. Any "savior" or "god" who brings death is nothing but *thanatos* wearing a savior mask. This is why Jesus identified himself as the true Savior—even when he didn't want to so identify himself—by his healing miracles. The people knew what healing miracles pointed to. There is a wonderful passage at the very end of the Old Testament where this matter is clarified. God says, "But for you who fear my name, the sun of righteousness shall rise with healing in his wings, and you shall break loose like calves released from the stall."

In a sense Fat hoped that the Savior would heal what had become sick, restore what had been broken. On some level, he actually believed that the dead girl Gloria could be restored to life. This is why Sherri's unrelieved agony, her growing cancer, baffled him and defeated his spiritual hopes and beliefs. According to his system as put forth in his exegesis, based on his encounter with God, Sherri should have been made well.

Fat was in search of a very great deal. Although technically he could understand why Sherri had cancer, spiritually he could not. In fact, Fat could not really make out why Christ, the Son of God, had been crucified. Pain and suffering made no sense to Fat; he could not fit it into the grand design. Therefore, he reasoned, the existence of such dreadful afflictions pointed to irrationality in the universe, an affront to reason.

Beyond doubt, Fat was serious about his proposed quest. He had squirreled away almost twenty thousand dollars in his savings account.

"Don't make fun of him," I said to Kevin one day. "This is important to him."

His eyes gleaming with customary cynical mockery, Kevin said, "Ripping off a piece of ass is important to me, too."

"Come off it," I said. "You're not funny."

Kevin merely continued to grin.

A week later, Sherri died.

Now, as I had foreseen, Fat had two deaths on his conscience. He had been unable to save either girl. When you are Atlas you must carry a heavy load and if you drop it a lot of people suffer, an entire world of people, an entire world of suffering. This now lay over Fat spiritually rather than physically, this load. Tied to him the two corpses cried for rescue—cried even though they had died. The cries of the dead are terrible indeed; you should try not to hear them.

What I feared was a return by Fat to suicide and if that failed, then another stretch in the rubber lock-up.

To my surprise when I dropped by Fat's apartment I found him composed.

"I'm going," he told me.

"On your quest?"

"You got it," Fat said.

"Where?"

"I don't know. I'll just start going and Zebra will guide me."

I had no motivation to try to talk him out of it; what did his alternatives consist of? Sitting by himself in the apartment he and Sherri had lived in together? Listening to Kevin mock the sorrows of the world? Worst of all, he could spend his time listening to David prattle about how "God brings good out of evil." If anything were to put Fat in the rubber lock-up it would be finding himself caught in a cross-fire between Kevin and David: the stupid and pious and credulous versus the cynically cruel. And what could I add? Sherri's death had torn me down, too, had deconstructed me into basic parts, like a toy disassembled back to what had arrived in the gaily-colored kit. I felt like saying, "Take me along, Fat. Show me the way home."

While Fat and I sat there together grieving, the phone rang. It was Beth, wanting to be sure Fat knew that he had fallen behind a week in his child support payment.

As he hung up the phone, Fat said to me, "My ex-wives are descended from rats."

"You've got to get out of here," I said.

"Then you agree I should go."

"Yes," I said.

"I've got enough money to go anywhere in the world. I've thought of China. I've thought, Where is the least likely place He would be born? A Communist country like China. Or France."

"Why France?" I asked.

"I've always wanted to see France."

"Then go to France," I said.

" 'What will you do,' " Fat murmured.

"Pardon?"

"I was thinking about that American Express Travelers' Checks TV ad. 'What will you do. What *will* you do.' That's how I feel right now. They're right."

I said, "I like the one where the middle-aged man says, 'I had six hundred dollars in that wallet. It's the worst thing that ever happened to me in my life.' If that's the worst thing that ever happened to him—"

"Yeah," Fat said, nodding. "He's led a sheltered life."

I knew what vision had conjured itself up in Fat's mind: the vision of the dying girls. Either broken on impact or burst open from within. I shivered and felt, myself, like weeping.

"She suffocated," Fat said, finally, in a low voice. "She just fucking suffocated; she couldn't breathe any longer."

"I'm sorry," I said.

"You know what the doctor said to me to cheer me up?" Fat said. " 'There are worse diseases than cancer.' "

"Did he show you slides?"

We both laughed. When you are nearly crazy with grief, you laugh at what you can.

"Let's walk down to Sombrero Street," I said; that was a good restaurant and bar where we all liked to go. "I'll buy you a drink."

We walked down to Main St. and seated ourselves in the bar at Sombrero Street.

"Where's that little brown-haired lady you used to come in here with?" the waitress asked Fat as she served us our drinks.

"In Cleveland," Fat said. We both started to laugh again. The waitress remembered Sherri. It was too awful to take seriously.

"I knew this woman," I said to Fat as we drank, "and I was talking about a dead cat of mine and I said, 'Well, he's at rest in perpetuity' and she immediately said, completely seriously, 'My cat is buried in Glendale.' We all chimed in and compared the weather in Glendale compared to the weather in perpetuity." Both Fat and I were laughing so hard now that other people stared at us. "We have to knock this off," I said, calming down.

"Isn't it colder in perpetuity?" Fat said.

"Yes, but there's less smog."

Fat said, "Maybe that's where I'll find him."

"Who?" I said.

"Him. The fifth savior."

"Do you remember the time at your apartment," I said, "when Sherri was starting chemotherapy and her hair was falling out—"

"Yeah, the cat's water dish."

"She was standing by the cat's water dish and her hair kept falling into the water dish and the poor cat was puzzled."

" 'What the hell is this?' " Fat said, quoting what the cat would have said could it talk. " 'Here in my water dish?' " He grinned, but no joy could be seen in his grin. Neither of us could be funny any longer, even between us. "We need Kevin to cheer us up," Fat said. "On second thought," he murmured, "maybe we don't."

"We just have to keep on truckin'," I said.

"Phil," Fat said, "if I don't find him, I'm going to die."

"I know," I said. It was true. The Savior stood between Horselover Fat and annihilation.

"I am programmed to self-destruct," Fat said. "The button has been pressed."

"The sensations that you feel—" I began.

"They're rational," Fat said. "In terms of the situation. It's true. This is not insanity. I have to find him, wherever he is, or die."

"Well, then I'll die, too," I said. "If you do."

"That's right," Fat said. He nodded. "You got it. You can't exist without me and I can't exist without you. We're in this together. Fuck. What kind of life is this? Why do these things happen?"

"You said it yourself. The universe—"

"I'll find him," Fat said. He drank his drink and set the

empty glass down and stood up. "Let's go back to my apartment. I want you to hear the new Linda Ronstadt record, *Living In the USA*. It's real good."

As we left the bar, I said, "Kevin says Ronstadt's washed up."

Pausing at the door out, Fat said, "Kevin is washed up. He's going to whip that goddam dead cat out from under his coat on Judgment Day and they're going to laugh at him like he laughs at us. That's what he deserves: a Great Judge exactly like himself."

"That's not a bad theological idea," I said. "You find yourself facing yourself. You think you'll find him?"

"The Savior? Yeah, I'll find him. If I run out of money I'll come home and work some more and go look again. He has to be somewhere. Zebra said so. And Thomas inside my head—he knew it; he remembered Jesus just having been there a little while ago, and he knew he'd be back. They were all joyful, completely joyful, making preparations to welcome him back. The bridegroom back. It was so goddam festive, Phil; totally joyful and exciting, and everyone running around. They were running out of the Black Iron Prison and just laughing and laughing; they had fucking blown it up, Phil; the whole prison. Blew it up and got out of there . . . running and laughing and totally, totally happy. And I was one of them."

"You will be again," I said.

"I will be," Fat said, "when I find him. But until then I won't be; I can't be; there's no way." He halted on the sidewalk, hands in his pockets. "I miss him, Phil; I fucking miss him. I want to be with him; I want to feel his arm around me. Nobody else can do that. I saw him—sort of—and I want to see him again. That love, that warmth—that delight on his part that it's me, seeing me, being glad it's me: *recognizing* me. He *recognized* me!"

"I know," I said, awkwardly.

"Nobody knows what it's like," Fat said, "to have seen him and then not to see him. Almost five years now, five years of—" He gestured. "Of what? And what before that?"

"You'll find him," I said.

"I have to," Fat said, "or I am going to die. And you, too, Phil. And we know it."

*

The leader of the Grail knights, Amfortas, has a wound which will not heal. Klingsor has wounded him with the spear which pierced Christ's side. Later, when Klingsor hurls the spear at Parsifal, the pure fool catches the spear—which has stopped in midair—and holds it up, making the sign of the Cross with it, at which Klingsor and his entire castle vanish. They were never there in the first place; they were a delusion, what the Greeks call *dokos;* what the Indians call the *veil of maya*.

There is nothing Parsifal cannot do. At the end of the opera Parsifal touches the spear to Amfortas's wound and the wound heals. Amfortas, who only wanted to die, is healed. Very mysterious words are repeated, which I never understood, although I can read German:

> *"Gesegnet sei dein Leiden,*
> *Das Mitleids höchste Kraft,*
> *Und reinsten Wissens Macht*
> *Denn zagen Toren gab!"*

This is one of the keys to the story of Parsifal; the pure fool who abolishes the delusion of the magician Klingsor and his castle, and heals Amfortas's wound. But what does it mean?

> "May your suffering be blessed,
> Which gave the timid fool
> Pity's highest power
> And purest knowledge's might!"

I don't know what this means. However, I know that in our case, the pure fool, Horselover Fat, himself had the wound which would not heal, and the pain that goes with it. All right; the wound is caused by the spear which pierced the Savior's side, and only that same spear can heal it. In the opera, after Amfortas is healed, the shrine is at last opened (it has been closed for a long time) and the Grail is revealed, at which point heavenly voices say:

> *"Erlösung dem Erlöser!"*

Which is very strange, because it means:

> "The Redeemer redeemed!"

In other words, Christ has saved himself. There's a technical term for this: *Salvator salvandus.* The "saved savior."

> "The fact that in the discharge of his task the
> eternal messenger must himself assume the lot of
> incarnation and cosmic exile, and the further
> fact that, at least in the Iranian variety of
> the myth, he is in a sense identical with those
> he calls—the once lost parts of the divine
> self—give rise to the moving idea of the
> "saved savior" (*salvator salvandus*)."

My source is reputable: *The Encyclopedia of Philosophy*, Macmillan Publishing Company, New York, 1967; in the article on "Gnosticism." I am trying to see how this applies to Fat. What is this "pity's highest power"? In what way does pity have the power to heal a wound? And can Fat feel pity for himself and so heal his own wound? *Would this, then, make Horselover Fat the Savior himself, the savior saved?* That seems to be the idea which Wagner expresses. The savior saved idea is Gnostic in origin. How did it get into *Parsifal*?

Maybe Fat was searching for himself when he set out in search of the Savior. To heal the wound made by first the death of Gloria and then the death of Sherri. But what in our modern world is the analog for Klingsor's huge stone castle?

That which Fat calls the Empire? The Black Iron Prison?

Is the Empire "which never ended" an illusion?

The words which Parsifal speaks which cause the huge stone castle—and Klingsor himself—to disappear are:

> *"Mit diesem Zeichen bann' Ich deinen Zauber."*
> "With this sign I abolish your magic."

The sign, of course, is the sign of the Cross. Fat's Savior is Fat himself, as I already figured out; Zebra is all the selves along the linear time-axis, laminated into one supra- or trans-temporal self which cannot die, and which has come back to save Fat. But I don't dare tell Fat that he is searching for himself. He is not ready to entertain such a notion, because like the rest of us he seeks an external savior.

"Pity's highest power" is just bullshit. Pity has no power. Fat felt vast pity for Gloria and vast pity for Sherri and it didn't do a damn bit of good in either case. Something was lacking. Everyone knows this, everyone who has gazed down helplessly at a sick or dying human or a sick or dying animal, felt terrible pity, overpowering pity, and realized that this pity, however great it might be, is totally useless.

Something else healed the wound.

For me and David and Kevin this was a serious matter, this wound in Fat which would not heal, but which had to be healed and would be healed—*if* Fat found the Savior. Did some magic scene lie in the future where Fat would come to his senses, recognize that he was the Savior, and thereby automatically be healed? Don't bet on it. I wouldn't.

Parsifal is one of those corkscrew artifacts of culture in which you get the subjective sense that you've learned something from it, something valuable or even priceless; but on closer inspection you suddenly begin to scratch your head and say, "Wait a minute. This makes no sense." I can see Richard Wagner standing at the gates of heaven. "You have to let me in," he says. "I wrote *Parsifal*. It has to do with the Grail, Christ, suffering, pity and healing. Right?" And they answered, "Well, we read it and it makes no sense." *SLAM*. Wagner is right and so are they. It's another Chinese finger-trap.

Or perhaps I'm missing the point. What we have here is a Zen paradox. That which makes no sense makes the *most* sense. I am being caught in a sin of the highest magnitude: using Aristotelian two-value logic: "A thing is either A or not-A." (The Law of the Excluded Middle.) Everybody knows that Aristotelian two-value logic is fucked. What I am saying is that—

If Kevin were here he'd say, "Deedle-deedle queep," which is what he says to Fat when Fat reads aloud from his exegesis. Kevin has no use for the Profound. He's right. All I am doing is going, "Deedle-deedle queep" over and over again in my attempts to understand how Horselover Fat is going to heal—save—Horselover Fat. Because Fat cannot be saved. Healing Sherri was going to make up for losing Gloria; but Sherri died. The death of Gloria caused Fat to take forty-nine tablets of poison and now we are hoping that upon Sherri's death he will go forth, find the Savior (what Savior?) and be healed—healed of a wound that prior to Sherri's death was virtually terminal for him. Now there is no Horselover Fat; only the wound remains.

Horselover Fat is dead. Dragged down into the grave by two malignant women. Dragged down because he is a fool. That's another nonsense part in *Parsifal*, the idea that being stupid is salvific. Why? In *Parsifal* suffering gave the timid fool "purest knowledge's might." How? Why? Please explain.

Please show me how Gloria's suffering and Sherri's suffering contributed anything good to Fat, to anyone, to anything. It's a lie. It's an evil lie. Suffering is to be abolished. Well, admittedly, Parsifal did that by healing the wound; Amfortas's agony ceased.

What we really need is a doctor, not a spear. Let me give you entry #45 from Fat's *tractate*.

#45. In seeing Christ in a vision I correctly said to him, "We need medical attention." In the vision there was an insane creator who destroyed what he created, without purpose; which is to say, irrationally. This is the deranged streak in the Mind; Christ is our only hope, since we cannot now call on Asklepios. Asklepios came before Christ and raised a man from the dead; for this act, Zeus had a Kyklopes slay him with a thunderbolt. Christ also was killed for what he had done: raising a man from the dead. Elijah brought a boy back to life and disappeared soon thereafter in a whirlwind. "The Empire never ended."

Entry #46. The physician has come to us a number of times under a number of names. But we are not yet healed. The Empire identified him and ejected him. This time he will kill the Empire by phagocytosis.

In many ways Fat's exegesis makes more sense than *Parsifal*. Fat conceives of the universe as a living organism into which a toxic particle has come. The toxic particle, made of heavy metal, has embedded itself in the universe-organism and is poisoning it. The universe-organism dispatches a phagocyte. The phagocyte is Christ. It surrounds the toxic metal particle—the Black Iron Prison—and begins to destroy it.

Entry #41. The Empire is the institution, the codification, of derangement; it is insane and imposes its insanity on us by violence, since its nature is a violent one.

Entry #42. To fight the Empire is to be infected by its derangement. This is a paradox; whoever defeats a segment of the Empire becomes the Empire; it proliferates like a

virus, imposing its form on its enemies. Thereby it becomes its enemies.

Entry #43. Against the Empire is posed the living information, the plasmate or physician, which we know as the Holy Spirit or Christ discorporate. These are the two principles, the dark (the Empire) and the light (the plasmate). In the end, Mind will give victory to the latter. Each of us will die or survive according to which he aligns himself and his efforts. Each of us contains a component of each. Eventually one or the other component will triumph in each human. Zoroaster knew this, because the Wise Mind informed him. He was the first savior.* Four have lived in all. A fifth is about to be born, who will differ from the others: he will rule and he will judge us.

In my opinion, Kevin may go "deedle-deedle queep" whenever Fat reads or quotes from his *tractate*, but Fat is onto something. Fat sees a cosmic phagocytosis in progress, one in which in micro-form we are each involved. A toxic metal particle is lodged in each of us: "That which is above (the macrocosm) is that which is below (the microcosm or man)." We are all wounded and we all need a physician—Elijah for the Jews, Asklepios for the Greeks, Christ for the Christians, Zoroaster for the Gnostics, the followers of Mani, and so forth. We die because we are born sick—born with a heavy metal splinter in us, a wound like Amfortas's wound. And when we are healed we will be immortal; this is how it was supposed to be, but the toxic metal splinter entered the macrocosm and simultaneously entered each of its microcosmic pluriforms: ourselves.

Consider the cat dozing on your lap. He is wounded, but the wound does not yet show. Like Sherri, something is eating him away. Do you want to gamble against this statement? Laminate all the cat's images in linear time into one entity; what you get is pierced, injured and dead. But a miracle occurs. An invisible physician restores the cat.

"So everything lingers but a moment, and hastens on to death. The plant and the insect die at the end of summer, the brute and the man after a few years: death reaps un-

*Fat has left out Buddha, perhaps because he doesn't understand who and what the Buddha is.

weariedly. Yet notwithstanding this, nay, as if this were not so at all, everything is always there and in its place, just as if everything were imperishable . . . This is temporal immortality. In consequence of this, notwithstanding thousands of years of death and decay, nothing has been lost, not an atom of the matter, still less anything of the inner being, that exhibits itself as nature. Therefore every moment we can cheerfully cry, 'In spite of time, death and decay, we are still all together!' " (Schopenhauer.)

Somewhere Schopenhauer says that the cat which you see playing in the yard is the cat which played three hundred years ago. This is what Fat had encountered in Thomas, in the three-eyed people, and most of all in Zebra who had no body. An ancient argument for immortality goes like this: if every creature really dies—as it appears to—then life continually passes out of the universe, passes out of being; and so eventually all life will have passed out of being, since there are no known exceptions to this. *Ergo*, despite what we see, life somehow must *not* turn to death.

Along with Gloria and Sherri, Fat had died, but Fat still lived on, as the Savior he now proposed to seek.

9

Wordsworth's "Ode" carries the sub-title: "Intimations of Immortality from Recollections of Early Childhood." In Fat's case, the "intimations of immortality" were based on recollections of a future life.

In addition, Fat could not write poetry worth shit, despite his best efforts. He loved Wordsworth's "Ode," and wished he could come up with its equal. He never did.

Anyhow, Fat's thoughts had turned to travel. These thoughts had acquired a specific nature; one day he drove to Wide-World Travel Bureau (Santa Ana branch) and conferred with the lady behind the counter, the lady and her computer terminal.

"Yes, we can put you on a slow boat to China," the lady said cheerfully.

"How about a fast plane?" Fat said.

"Are you going to China for medical reasons?" the lady asked.

Fat was surprised at the question.

"A number of people from Western countries are flying to China for medical services," the lady said. "Even from Sweden, I'm given to understand. Medical costs in China are exceptionally low . . . but perhaps you already know that. Do you know that? Major operations run approximately thirty dollars in some cases." She rummaged among pamphlets, smiling cheerfully.

"I guess so," Fat said.

"Then you can deduct it on your income tax," the lady said. "You see how we help you here at Wide-World Travel?"

The irony of this side-issue struck Fat forcefully—that he, who sought the fifth Savior, could write his quest off on his state and Federal Income Tax. That night when Kevin dropped over he mentioned it to him, expecting Kevin to be wryly amused.

Kevin, however, had other fish to fry. In an enigmatic tone Kevin said, "What about going to the movies tomorrow night?"

"To see what?" Fat had caught the dark current in his friend's voice. It meant Kevin was up to something. But of course, true to his nature, Kevin would not amplify.

"It's a science fiction film," Kevin said, and that was all he would say.

"Okay," Fat said.

The next night, he and I and Kevin drove up Tustin Avenue to a small walk-in theater; since they intended to see a science fiction film I felt that for professional reasons I should go along.

As Kevin parked his little red Honda Civic we caught sight of the theater marquee.

"*Valis*," Fat said, reading the words. "With Mother Goose. What's 'Mother Goose'?"

"A rock group," I said, disappointed; it did not appear to me to be something I'd like. Kevin had odd tastes, both in films and in music; evidently he had managed to combine the two tonight.

"I've seen it," Kevin said cryptically. "Bear with me. You won't be disappointed."

"You've seen it?" Fat said, "and you want to see it again?"

"Bear with me," Kevin repeated.

As we sat in our seats inside the small theater we noticed that the audience seemed to be mostly teen-agers.

"Mother Goose is Eric Lampton," Kevin said. "He wrote the screenplay for *Valis* and he stars in it."

"He sings?" I said.

"Nope," Kevin said, and that was all he had to say; he then lapsed into silence.

"Why are we here?" Fat said.

Kevin glanced at him without answering.

"Is this like your belch record?" Fat said. One time, when he'd been especially depressed, Kevin had brought over an album which he, Kevin, assured him, Fat, would cheer him up. Fat had to put on his electrostatic Stax headphones and really crank it up. The track turned out to consist of belching.

"Nope," Kevin said.

The lights dimmed; the audience of teen-agers fell silent; the titles and credits appeared.

"Does Brent Mini mean anything to you?" Kevin said. "He did the music. Mini works with computer-created random sounds which he calls 'Synchronicity Music.' He's got three lps out. I've got the second two, but I can't find the first."

"Then this is serious stuff," Fat said.

"Just watch," Kevin said.

Electronic noises sounded.

"God," I said, with aversion. On the screen a vast blob of colors appeared, exploding in all directions; the camera panned in for a tight shot. Low budget sci-fi flick, I said to myself. This is what gives the field a bad reputation.

The drama started abruptly; all at once the credits vanished. An open field, parched, brown, with a few weeds here and there, appeared. Well, I said to myself, here is what we'll see. A jeep with two soldiers in it, bumping across the field. Then something vivid flashes across the sky.

"Looks like a meteor, captain," one soldier says.

"Yes," the other soldier agrees thoughtfully. "But maybe we'd better investigate."

I was wrong.

The film *Valis* depicted a small record firm called Meritone Records, located in Burbank, owned by an electronics genius named Nicholas Brady. The time—by the style of the cars and the particular kind of rock being played—suggested the late Sixties or early Seventies, but odd incongruities prevailed. For example, Richard Nixon didn't seem to exist; the President of the United States bore the name Ferris F. Fremount, and he was very popular. During the first part of the film there were abrupt segues to TV news footage of Ferris Fremount's spirited campaign for reelection.

Mother Goose himself—the actual rock star who in real life is rated with Bowie and Zappa and Alice Cooper—took the form of a song writer who had gotten hooked on drugs, decidedly a loser. Only the fact that Brady kept paying him enabled Goose to survive economically. Goose had an attractive and extremely short-haired wife; this woman possessed an unearthly appearance with her nearly bald head and enormous luminous eyes.

In the film Brady schemed constantly on Linda, Goose's wife (in the film, for some reason, Goose used his real name, Eric Lampton; so the tale narrated had to do with the marginal Lamptons). Linda Lampton wasn't natural; that came across early on. I got the impression that Brady was a son-of-a-bitch despite his wizardry with audio electronics. He had a laser system set up which ran the information—which is to say, the various channels of music—into a mixer unlike anything that actually exists; the damn thing rose up like a fortress—Brady actually entered it through a door, and, inside it, got bathed with laser beams which converted into sound using his brain as a transducer.

In one scene Linda Lampton took off her clothes. She had no sex organs.

Damdest thing Fat and I ever saw.

Meanwhile, Brady schemed on her unaware that no way existed by which he could make it with her, anatomically-speaking. This amused Mother Goose—Eric Lampton—who kept shooting up and writing the worst songs conceivable. It became obvious after a while that his brain was fried; he didn't realize it, either. Nicholas Brady began going through mystifying maneuvers suggesting that by means of his fortress mixer he intended to laser Eric Lampton out of existence, to pave the way for laying Linda Lampton who in fact had no sex organs.

Meanwhile, Ferris Fremount kept showing up in dissolves that baffled us. Fremount kept looking more and more like Brady, and Brady seemed to metamorphose into Fremount. Scenes shot by which showed Brady at enormous gala functions, apparently affairs of state; foreign diplomats wandered around with drinks, and a constant low murmuring hung in the background—an electronic noise resembling the sound created by Brady's mixer.

I didn't understand the picture one bit.

"Do you understand this?" I asked Fat, leaning over to whisper.

"Christ, no," Fat said.

Having lured Eric Lampton into the mixer, Brady stuck a strange black cassette into the chamber and punched buttons. The audience saw a tight shot of Lampton's head explode, literally explode; but instead of brains bursting out, electronic miniaturized parts flew in all directions. Then Linda Lampton walked *through* the mixer, right through the wall of it, did something with an object she carried, and Eric Lampton ran backward in time: the electronic components of his head imploded, the skull returned intact—Brady, meanwhile, staggered out of the Meritone Building onto Alameda, his eyes bugging . . . cut

to Linda Lampton putting her husband back together, both of
them in the fortress-like mixer.

Eric Lampton opens his mouth to speak and out comes
the sound of Ferris F. Fremount's voice. Linda draws back in
dismay.

Cut to the White House; Ferris Fremount, who no longer
looks like Nicholas Brady but like himself, restored.

"I want Brady taken out," he says grimly, "and taken out
now." Two men dressed in skin-tight black shiny uniforms,
carrying futuristic weapons, nod silently.

Cut to Brady crossing a parking lot rapidly to his car; he is
totally fucked up. Pan to black-suited men on roof scope-sights
up with cross-hairs: Brady seating himself and trying to start
his car.

Dissolve to huge crowds of young girls dressed in red, white
and blue cheerleader uniforms. But they're not cheerleaders;
they chant, "Kill Brady! Kill Brady!"

Slow motion. The men in black fire their weapons. All at
once, Eric Lampton stands outside the door of Meritone
Records; close shot of his face; his eyes turn into something
weird. The men in black char into ashes; their weapons melt.

"Kill Brady! Kill Brady!" Thousands of girls dressed in identical red-white-and-blue uniforms. Some strip off their uniforms in sexual frenzy.

They have no reproductive organs.

Dissolve. Time has passed. *Two* Ferris F. Fremounts sit
facing each other at a huge walnut table. Between them: a
cube of pulsing pink light. It's a hologram.

Beside me, Fat grunts. He sits forward staring. I stare, too. I
recognize the pink light; it's the color Fat described to me regarding Zebra.

Scene of Eric Lampton nude in bed with Linda Lampton.
They strip off some kind of plastic membrane and reveal sex
organs underneath. They make love, then Eric Lampton slides
out of bed. Goes into living room, shoots up whatever dope
he's strung out on. Sits down, puts his head wearily down.
Dejection.

Long shot. The Lamptons' house below; camera is what they
call "camera three." A beam of energy fires at the house below.
Quick cut to Eric Lampton; he jerks as if pierced. Holds his

next time I see it I'm taking a battery-powered cassette tape recorder in with me. I think the information is encoded in Mini's Synchronicity Music, his random music."

"It was an alternate U.S.A.," Fat said. "Where instead of Nixon being president Ferris Fremount was. I guess."

"Were Eric and Linda Lampton human or not?" I said. "First they appeared human; then she turned out not to have any—you know, sex organs. And then they stripped those membranes off and they did have sex organs."

"But when his head exploded," Fat said, "it was full of computer parts."

"Did you notice the pot?" Kevin said. "On Nicholas Brady's desk. The little clay pot—like the one you have, the pot that girl—"

"Stephanie," Fat said.

"—made for you."

"No," Fat said. "I didn't notice it. There were a lot of details in the film that kept coming at me so fast, at the audience so fast, I mean."

"I didn't notice the pot the first time," Kevin said. "It shows up in different places; not just on Brady's desk but one time in President Fremount's office, way over in the corner, where only your peripheral vision picks it up. It shows up in different parts of the Lamptons' house; for example in the living room. And in that one scene where Eric Lampton is staggering around he knocks against things and—"

"The pitcher," I said.

"Yes," Kevin said. "It also appears as a pitcher. Full of water. Linda Lampton takes it out of the refrigerator."

"No, that was just an ordinary plastic pitcher," Fat said.

"Wrong," Kevin said. "It was the pot again."

"How could it be the pot again if it was a pitcher?" Fat said.

"At the beginning of the film," Kevin said. "On the parched field. Off to one side; it only registers subliminally unless you're deliberately watching for it. The design on the pitcher is the same as the design on the pot. A woman is dipping it into a creek, a very small, mostly dried-up creek."

I said, "It seemed to me that the Christian fish sign appeared on it once. As the design."

"No," Kevin said emphatically.

"No?" I said.

"I thought so, too, the first time," Kevin said. "This time I looked closer. You know what it is? The double helix."

"That's the DNA molecule," I said.

"Right," Kevin said, grinning. "In the form of a repeated design running around the top of the pitcher."

We all remained silent for a time and then I said, "DNA memory. Gene-pool memory."

"Right," Kevin said. He added, "At the creek when she fills the pitcher—"

" 'She'?" Fat said. "Who was she?"

"A woman," Kevin said. "We never see her again. We never even see her face but she has on a long, old-fashioned dress and she's barefoot. Where she's filling the pot or the pitcher, there's a man fishing. It's flash-cut, just for a fraction of an instant. But he's there. That's why you thought you saw the fish sign. Because you picked up the sight of the man fishing. There may even have been fish lying beside him in a heap; I'll have to look really hard at that when I see it again. You saw the man subliminally and your brain—your right hemisphere—connected it with the double helix design on the pitcher."

"The satellite," Fat said. "VALIS. Vast Active Living Intelligence System. It fires information down to them?"

"It does more than that," Kevin said. "Under certain circumstances it controls them. It can override them when it wants to."

"And they're trying to shoot it down?" I said. "With that missile?"

Kevin said, "The early Christians—the real ones—can make you do anything they want you to do. And see—or *not* see—anything. That's what I get out of the picture."

"But they're dead," I said. "The picture was set in the present."

"They're dead," Kevin said, "if you believe time is real. Didn't you see the time dysfunctions?"

"No," both Fat and I said in unison.

"That dry barren field. That was the parking lot Brady ran across to get into his car when the two men in black were stationed and ready to shoot him."

I hadn't realized that. "How do you know?" I said.

"There was a tree," Kevin said. "Both times."

"I saw no tree," Fat said.

"Well, we'll all have to go see the picture again," Kevin said. "I'm going to; ninety percent of the details are designed to go by you the first time—actually only go by your conscious mind; they register in your unconscious. I'd like to study the film frame by frame."

I said, "Then the Christian fish sign is Crick and Watson's double helix. The DNA molecule where genetic memory is stored; Mother Goose wanted to make that point. That's why—"

"Christians," Kevin agreed. "Who aren't human beings but something without sex organs designed to look like human beings, but on closer inspection they *are* human beings; they do have sex organs and they make love."

"Even if their skulls are full of electronic chips instead of brains," I said.

"Maybe they're immortal," Fat said.

"That's why Linda Lampton is able to put her husband back together," I said. "When Brady's mixer blew him up. They can travel backward in time."

Kevin, not smiling, said, "Right. So now can you see why I wanted you to see *Valis?*" he said to Fat.

"Yes," Fat said, somberly, in deep introspection.

"How could Linda Lampton walk through the wall of the mixer?" I said.

"I don't know," Kevin said. "Maybe she wasn't really there or maybe the mixer wasn't there; maybe she was a hologram."

" 'A hologram,' " Fat echoed.

Kevin said, "The satellite had control of them from the get-go. It could make them see what it wanted them to see; at the end, where it turns out that Fremount is Brady—no one notices! His own wife doesn't notice. The satellite has occluded them, all of them. The whole fucking United States."

"Christ," I said; that hadn't dawned on me yet, but the realization had been coming.

"Right," Kevin said. "We see Brady, but obviously they don't; they don't realize what's happened. It's a power struggle between Brady and his electronic know-how and equipment, and Fremount and his secret police—the men in black are the

secret police. And those broads who looked like cheerleaders
—they're something, on Fremount's side, but I don't know
what. I'll figure it out next time." His voice rose. "There's information in Mini's music; as we watch the events on the screen
the music—Christ, it isn't music; it's certain pitches at specific
intervals—unconsciously cues us. The music is what makes the
thing into sense."

"Could that huge mixer actually be something that Mini
really built?" I asked.

"Maybe so," Kevin said. "Mini has a degree from MIT."

"What else do you know about him?" Fat said.

"Not very much," Kevin said. "He's English. He visited the
Soviet Union one time; he said he wanted to see certain experi-
ments they were conducting with microwave information transfer over long distances. Mini developed a system where—"

"I just realized something," I broke in. "On the credits,
Robin Jamison who did the still photography. I know him. He
took photos of me to go with an interview I did for the *London Daily Telegraph*. He told me he covered the coronation;
he's one of the top still photographers in the world. He said he
was moving his family to Vancouver; he said it's the most beautiful city in the world."

"It is," Fat said.

"Jamison gave me his card," I said. "So I could write to him
for the negatives after the interview was published."

Kevin said, "He would know Linda and Eric Lampton. And
maybe Mini, too."

"He told me to contact him," I said. "He was very nice; he sat
for a long time and talked to me. He had motor-driven cameras;
the noise fascinated my cats. And he let me look through a wide-
angle lens; it was beyond belief, the lenses he had."

"Who put up the satellite?" Fat said. "The Russians?"

"It's never made clear," Kevin said. "But the way they talk
about it . . . it didn't suggest the Russians. There's that one
scene where Fremount is opening a letter with an antique
letter-opener; all of a sudden you have that montage—antique
letter-opener and then the military talking about the satellite.
If you fuse the two together, you get the idea—I got the idea
—the satellite is real old."

"That makes sense," I said. "The time dysfunction, the woman in the old-fashioned long dress, barefoot, dipping water from the creek with a clay pitcher. There was a shot of the sky; did you notice that, Kevin?"

"The sky," Kevin murmured. "Yes; it was a long shot. A panorama shot. Sky, the field . . . the field looks old. Like maybe in the Near East. Like in Syria. And you're right; the pitcher reinforces that impression."

I said, "The satellite is never seen."

"Wrong," Kevin said.

" 'Wrong'?" I said.

"Five times," Kevin said. "It appears once as a picture on a wall calendar. Once briefly as a child's toy in a store window. Once in the sky, but it's a flash-cut; I missed it the first time. Once in diagram form when President Fremount is going through that packet of data and photos on the Meritone Record Company . . . I forget the fifth time, now." He frowned.

"The object the taxi runs over," I said.

"What?" Kevin said. "Oh yeah; the taxi speeding along West Alameda. I thought it was a beer can. It rattled off loudly into the gutter." He reflected, then nodded. "You're right. It was the satellite again, mashed up by being run over. It *sounded* like a beer can; that's what fooled me. Mini again; his damn music or noises—whatever. You hear the sound of a beer can so automatically you *see* a beer can." His grin became stark. "Hear it so you see it. Not bad." Although he was driving in heavy traffic he shut his eyes a moment. "Yeah, it's mashed up. But it's the satellite; it has those antennae, but they're broken and bent. And—shit! There're words written on it. Like a label. What do the words say? You know, you'd have to take a fucking magnifying glass and go over stills from the flick, single-frame stills. One by one by one by one. And do some superimpositions. We're getting retinal lag; it's done through the lasers Brady uses. The light is so bright that it leaves—" Kevin paused.

"Phosphene activity," I said. "In the retinas of the audience. That's what you mean. That's why lasers play such a role in the film."

*

"Okay," Kevin said, when we had returned to Fat's apartment. Each of us sat with a bottle of Dutch beer, kicking back and ready to figure it all out.

The material in the Mother Goose flick overlapped with Fat's encounter with God. That's the plain truth. I'd say, "That's God's truth," but I don't think—I certainly didn't think then—that God had anything to do with it.

"The Great Punta works in wonderful ways," Kevin said, but not in a kidding tone of voice. "Fuck. Holy fuck." To Fat he said, "I just assumed you were crazy. I mean, you're in and out of the rubber lock-up."

"Cool it," I said.

"So I take in *Valis*," Kevin said, "I go to the movies to get away for a little while from all this nutso garbage that Fat here lays on us; there I am sitting in the goddam theater watching a sci-fi flick with Mother Goose in it, and what do I see. It's like a conspiracy."

"Don't blame me," Fat said.

Kevin said to him, "You're going to have to meet Goose."

"How'm I going to do that?" Fat said.

"Phil will contact Jamison. You can meet Goose—Eric Lampton—through Jamison; Phil's a famous writer—he can arrange it." To me, Kevin said, "You have any books currently optioned to any movie producer?"

"Yes," I said. "*Do Androids Dream of Electric Sheep?*"* and also *Three Stigmata*."†

"Fine," Kevin said. "Then Phil can say maybe there's a film in it." Turning to me he said, "Who's that producer friend of yours? The one at MGM?"

"Stan Jaffly," I said.

"Are you still in touch with him?"

"Only on a personal basis. They let their option on *Man in the High Castle*‡ lapse. He writes to me sometimes; he sent me a huge kit of herb seeds one time. He was going to send me a huge bag of peatmoss later on but fortunately he never did."

---

* *Do Androids Dream of Electric Sheep?* Doubleday, 1968.
† *The Three Stigmata of Palmer Eldritch*, Doubleday, 1964.
‡ *The Man in the High Castle*, G.P. Putnam's Sons, 1962.

"Get in touch with him," Kevin said.

"Look," Fat said. "I don't understand. There were—" He gestured. "Things in *Valis* that happened to me in March of 1974. When I—" Again he gestured and fell silent, a perplexed expression on his face. Almost an expression of suffering, I noticed. I wondered why.

Maybe Fat felt that it reduced the stature of his encounter with God—with Zebra—to discover elements of it cropping up in a sci-fi movie starring a rock figure named Mother Goose. But this was the first hard evidence we had had that anything existed, here; and it had been Kevin, who could disintegrate a scam with a single bound, that had brought it to our attention.

"How many elements did you recognize?" I said, as quietly and calmly as I could, to the dejected-looking Horselover Fat.

After a time, Fat pulled himself erect in his chair and said, "Okay."

"Write them down," Kevin said; he brought out a fountain pen. Kevin always used fountain pens, the last of a vanishing breed of noble men. "Paper?" he said, glancing around.

When paper had been brought, Fat began the list. "The third eye with the lateral lens."

"Okay." Nodding, Kevin wrote that down.

"The pink light."

"Okay."

"The Christian fish sign. Which I didn't see, but which you say was—"

"Double helix," Kevin said.

"Same thing," I said. "Apparently."

"Anything else?" Kevin asked Fat.

"Well, the whole goddam information transfer. From VALIS. From the satellite. You say it not only fires information to them but it overrides them and controls them."

"That," Kevin said, "was the whole point of the film. The satellite took—look; here's what the picture was about. There is this tyrant obviously based on Richard Nixon called Ferris F. Fremount. He rules the U.S.A. through those black secret police, I mean, men in black uniforms carrying scope-sight weapons, and those fucking cheerleader broads. They're called 'Fappers' in the film."

"I didn't get that," I said, "when I saw it."

"It was on a banner," Kevin said. "Marginally. Fappers—'Friends of the American People.' Ferris Fremount's citizen army. All alike and all patriotic. Anyhow, the satellite fires beams of information and saves Brady's life. You did get that. Finally the satellite arranges for Brady to replace Fremount at the very end when Fremount has won re-election. It's really Brady who's president, not Fremount. And Fremount knows; there was the scene of him with the dossier of pictures of the people at Meritone Records; he knew what was happening but he couldn't stop it. He gave orders for the military to bring down VALIS but the missile wobbled and had to be destroyed. *Everything* was done by VALIS. Where do you think Brady got his electronics knowledge in the first place? From VALIS. So when Brady became president as Ferris Fremount, it was really the satellite which became president. Now, who or what is the satellite? Who or what is VALIS? The clue is the ceramic pot or the ceramic pitcher; same thing. The fish sign—which your brain has to assemble from separate pieces of information. Fish sign, Christians. Old-fashioned dress on the woman. Time dysfunction. There is some connection between VALIS and the early Christians, but I can't make out what. Anyhow, the film alludes to it elliptically. Everything is in pieces, all the information. For example, when Ferris Fremount is reading the dossier on Meritone Records—did you have time to scan any of the data?"

"No," Fat and I said.

"'He lived a long time ago,'" Kevin said hoarsely, "'but he is still alive.'"

"It said that?" Fat said.

"Yes!" Kevin said. "It said that."

"Then I'm not the only one who encountered God," Fat said.

"Zebra," Kevin corrected him. "You don't know it was God; you don't know what the fuck it was."

"A satellite?" I said. "A very old information-firing satellite?"

Irritably, Kevin said, "They wanted to make a sci-fi flick; that's how you would handle it in a sci-fi flick if you had such an experience. You ought to know that, Phil. Isn't that so, Phil?"

"Yes," I said.

"So they call it VALIS," Kevin said, "and make it an ancient satellite. That's controlling people to remove an evil tyranny that grips the United States—obviously based on Richard Nixon."

I said, "Are we to assume that the film *Valis* is telling us that Zebra or God or VALIS or three-eyed people from Sirius removed Nixon from office?"

"Yep," Kevin said.

To Fat, I said, "Didn't the three-eyed Sibyl you dreamed about talk about 'conspirators who had been seen and would be taken care of'?"

"In August 1974," Fat said.

Kevin, harshly, said, "That's the month and year Nixon resigned."

Later, as Kevin was driving me home, the two of us talked about Fat and about *Valis*, since presumably neither of them could overhear us.

The opinion Kevin copped to was that all along he had taken it for granted that Fat was simply crazy. He had seen the situation this way: guilt and sorrow over Gloria's suicide had destroyed Fat's mind and he had never recovered. Beth was a tremendous bitch, and, married to her out of desperation, Fat had become even more miserable. At last, in 1974, he had totally lost it. Fat had begun a lurid schizophrenic episode to liven up his drab life: he had seen pretty colors and heard comforting words, all generated out of his unconscious which had risen up and literally swamped him, wiping out his ego. In that psychotic state Fat had flailed around, deriving great solace from his "encounter with God," as he had imagined it to be. For Fat, total psychosis was a mercy. No longer in touch with reality in any way, shape or form, Fat could believe that Christ Himself held Fat in his arms, comforting him. But then Kevin had gone to the movies and now he was not so sure; the Mother Goose flick had shaken him up.

I wondered if Fat still intended to fly to China to find what he termed "the fifth Savior." It would seem that he need go no farther than Hollywood, where VALIS had been shot, or, if that was where he would find Eric and Linda Lampton, Burbank, the center of the American recording industry.

The fifth Savior: a rock star.

"When was *Valis* made?" I asked Kevin.

"The film? Or the satellite?"

"The film of course."

Kevin said, "1977."

"And Fat's experience took place in 1974."

"Right," Kevin said. "Probably before work began on the screenplay, from what I can piece together from reviews I've read on *Valis*. Goose says he wrote the screenplay in twelve days. He didn't say exactly when, but apparently he wanted to go into production as soon as possible. I'm sure it was after 1974."

"But you really don't know."

Kevin said, "You can find that out from Jamison, the still photographer; he'd know."

"What if it happened at the same time? March 1974?"

"Beats the fuck out of me," Kevin said.

"You don't think it really is an information satellite, do you?" I said. "That fired a beam at Fat?"

"No; that's a sci-fi film device, a sci-fi way of explaining it." Kevin pondered. "I guess. But there were time dysfunctions in the film; Goose was aware that somehow time's involved. That really is the only way you can understand the film . . . the woman filling the pitcher. How'd Fat get that ceramic pot? Some broad gave it to him?"

"Made it, fired it and gave it to him, around 1971 after his wife left him."

"Not Beth."

"No, some earlier wife."

"After Gloria's death."

"Yes. Fat says God was sleeping in the pot and came out in March 1974—the theophany."

"I know a lot of people who think God sleeps in pot," Kevin said.

"Cheap shot."

"Well, so the barefoot woman was back in Roman times. I saw something tonight in *Valis* I didn't see before that I didn't mention; I didn't want Fat to fizzle around the room like a firecracker. In the background while the woman was by the creek, you could see indistinct shapes. Your still-photographer friend Jamison probably did that. Shapes of buildings. Ancient buildings, from, say, around Roman times. It looked like clouds, but—there are clouds and there are clouds. The first time I saw it I saw clouds and the second time—today—I saw buildings. Does the goddam film change everytime you see it? Holy fuck; what a thought! A different film each time. No, that's impossible."

I said, "So is a beam of pink light that transfers medical information to your brain about your son's birth defect."

"What if I told you that there may have been a time dysfunction in 1974, and the ancient Roman world broke through into our world?"

"You mean as the theme in the film."

"No, I mean really."

"In the real world?"

"Yep."

"That would explain 'Thomas'."

Kevin nodded.

"Broke through," I said, "and then separated again."

"Leaving Richard Nixon walking along a beach in California in his suit and tie wondering what happened."

"Then it was purposeful."

"The dysfunction? Sure."

"Then it's not a dysfunction we're talking about; we're talking about someone or something deliberately manipulating time."

"You got it," Kevin said.

I said, "You've sure gone 180 degrees away from the 'Fat is crazy' theory."

"Well, Nixon is still walking along a beach in California wondering what happened. The first U.S. President ever to be forced out of office. The most powerful man in the world. Which made him in effect the most powerful man who ever lived. You know why the President in *Valis* was named Ferris F. Fremount? I figured it out. 'F' is the sixth letter of the English alphabet. So F equals six. So FFF, Ferris F. Fremount's initials, are in numerical terms 666. That's why Goose called him that."

"Oh God," I said.

"Exactly."

"That makes these the Final Days."

"Well, Fat's convinced the Savior is about to return or has already returned. The inner voice he hears that he identifies with Zebra or God—it told him so in several ways. St. Sophia—which is Christ—and the Buddha and Apollo. And it told him something like, 'The time you've waited for—'"

"'has now come,'" I finished.

"This is heavy shit," Kevin said. "We've got Elijah walking around, another John the Baptist, saying, 'Make straight in the desert a highway for our Lord.' Freeway, maybe." He laughed.

Suddenly I remembered something I had seen in *Valis*; it came into my mind visually: a tight shot of the car which Fremount at the end of the film, Fremount re-elected but actually now Nicholas Brady, had emerged from to address the crowd. "Thunderbird," I said.

"Wine?"

"Car. Ford car. Ford."

"Ah, shit," Kevin said. "You're right. He got out of a Ford Thunderbird and he was Brady. Jerry Ford."

"It could have been a coincidence."

"In *Valis* nothing was a coincidence. And they zoomed in on the car where the metal thing read Ford. How much else is there in *Valis* that we didn't pick up on? Pick up on *consciously*. There's no telling what it's doing to our unconscious minds; the goddam film may be—" Kevin grimaced. "Firing all kinds of information at us, visually and auditorily. I've got to make a tape of the sound track of that flick; I've got to get a tape recorder in there the next time I see it. Which'll be in the next couple of days."

"What kind of music are on the Mini lps?" I asked.

"Sounds resembling the songs of the humpback whale."

I stared at him, not sure he was serious.

"Really," he said. "In fact I did a tape going from whale noises to the Synchronicity Music and back again. There's an eerie continuity; I mean, you can tell the difference, but—"

"How does the Synchronicity Music affect you? What sort of mood does it put you in?"

Kevin said, "A deep theta state, deep sleep. But I personally had visions."

"Of what? Three-eyed people?"

"No," Kevin said. "Of an ancient Celtic sacred ceremony. A

ram being roasted and sacrificed to cause winter to go away and spring to return." Glancing at me he said, "Racially, I'm Celtic."

"Did you know about these myths before?"

"No. I was one of the participants in the sacrifice; I cut the ram's throat. I remembered being there."

Kevin, listening to Mini's Synchronicity Music, had gone back in time to his origins.

10

IT would not be in China, nor in India or Tasmania for that matter, that Horselover Fat would find the fifth Savior. *Valis* had shown us where to look: a beer can run over by a passing taxi. That was the source of the information and the help.

That in fact was VALIS, Vast Active Living Intelligence System, as Mother Goose had chosen to term it.

We had just saved Fat a lot of money, plus a lot of wasted time and effort, including the bother of obtaining vaccinations and a passport.

A couple of days later the three of us drove up Tustin Avenue and took in the film *Valis* once more. Watching it carefully I realized that on the surface the movie made no sense whatsoever. Unless you ferreted out the subliminal and marginal clues and assembled them all together you arrived at nothing. But these clues got fired at your head whether you consciously considered them and their meaning or not; you had no choice. The audience was in the same relationship to the film *Valis* that Fat had had to what he called Zebra: a transducer and a percipient, totally receptive in nature.

Again we found mostly teenagers comprising the audience. They seemed to enjoy what they saw. I wondered how many of them left the theater pondering the inscrutable mysteries of the film as we did. Maybe none of them. I had a feeling it made no difference.

We could assign Gloria's death as the cause of Fat's supposed encounter with God, but we could not consider it the cause of the film *Valis*. Kevin, upon first seeing the film, had realized this at once. It didn't matter what the explanation was; what had now been established was that Fat's March 1974 experience was real.

Okay; it mattered what the explanation was. But at least one thing had been proved: Fat might be clinically crazy but he was locked into reality—a reality of some kind, although certainly not the normal one.

Ancient Rome—apostolic times and early Christians— breaking through into the modern world. And breaking through with a purpose. To unseat Ferris F. Fremount, who was Richard Nixon.

They had achieved their purpose, and had gone back home. Maybe the Empire *had* ended after all.

Now himself somewhat persuaded, Kevin began to comb through the two apocalyptic books of the Bible for clues. He came across a part of the *Book of Daniel* which he believed depicted Nixon.

"In the last days of those kingdoms,
When their sin is at its height,
A king shall appear, harsh and grim, a master of stratagem.
His power shall be great, he shall work havoc untold;
He shall work havoc among great nations and upon a holy
    people.
His mind shall be ever active,
And he shall succeed in his crafty designs;
He shall conjure up great plans.
And, when they least expect it, work havoc on many.
He shall challenge even the Prince of princes
And be broken, but not by human hands."

Now Kevin had become a Bible scholar, to Fat's amusement; the cynic had become devout, albeit for a particular purpose.

But on a far more fundamental level Fat felt fear at the turn of events. Perhaps he had always felt reassured to think that his March 1974 encounter with God emanated from mere insanity; viewing it that way he did not necessarily have to take it as real. Now he did. We all did. Something which did not yield up an explanation had happened to Fat, an experience which pointed to a melting of the physical world itself, and to the ontological categories which defined it: space and time.

"Shit, Phil," he said to me that night. "What if the world doesn't exist? If it doesn't, then what does?"

"I don't know," I said, and then I said, quoting, "You're the authority."

Fat glared at me. "It's not funny. Some force or entity melted the reality around me as if everything was a hologram! An interference with our hologram!"

"But in your *tractate*," I said, "that's exactly what you stipulate reality is: a two-source hologram."

"But intellectually thinking it is one thing," Fat said, "and finding out it's true is another!"

"There's no use getting sore at me," I said.

David, our Catholic friend, and his teeny-bopper underage girlfriend Jan went to see *Valis*, our recommendation. David came out of it pleased. He saw the hand of God squeezing the world like an orange.

"Yeah, well we're in the juice," Fat said.

"But that's the way it should be," David said.

"You're willing to dispense with the whole world as a real thing, then," Fat said.

"Whatever God believes in is real," David said.

Kevin, irked, said, "Can he create a person so gullible that he'll believe nothing exists? Because if nothing exists, what is meant by the word 'nothing'? How is one 'nothing' which exists defined in comparison to another 'nothing' which doesn't exist?"

We, as usual, had gotten caught in the crossfire between David and Kevin, but under altered circumstances.

"What exists," David said, "is God and the Will of God."

"I hope I'm in his will," Kevin said. "I hope he left me more than one dollar."

"All creatures are in his will," David said, not batting an eye; he never let Kevin get to him.

Concern had now, by gradual increments, overcome our little group. We were no longer friends comforting and propping up a deranged member; we were collectively in deep trouble. A total reversal had in fact taken place: instead of mollifying Fat we now had to turn to him for advice. Fat was our link with that entity, VALIS or Zebra, which appeared to have power over all of us, if the Mother Goose film were to be believed.

"Not only does it fire information to us but when it wants to it can take control. It can override us."

That expressed it perfectly. At any moment a beam of pink light could strike us, blind us, and when we regained our sight (if we ever did) we could know everything or nothing and be in Brazil four thousand years ago; space and time, for VALIS, meant nothing.

A common worry unified all of us, the fear that we knew or had figured out too much. We knew that apostolic Christians armed with stunningly sophisticated technology had broken through the space-time barrier into our world, and, with the aid of a vast information-processing instrument had basically deflected human history. The species of creature which stumbles onto such knowledge may not show up too well on the longevity tables.

Most ominous of all, we knew—or suspected—that the original apostolic Christians who had known Christ, who had been alive to receive the direct oral teachings before the Romans wiped those teachings out, were immortal. They had acquired immortality through the plasmate which Fat had discussed in his tractate. Although the original apostolic Christians had been murdered, the plasmate had gone into hiding at Nag Hammadi and was again loose in our world, and as angry as a mother-fucker, if you'll excuse the expression. It thirsted for vengence. And apparently it had begun to score that vengence, against the modern-day manifestation of the Empire, the imperial United States Presidency.

I hoped the plasmate considered us its friends. I hoped it didn't think we were snitches.

"Where do we hide," Kevin said, "when an immortal plasmate which knows everything and is consuming the world by transubstantiation is looking for you?"

"It's a good thing Sherri isn't alive to hear about all this," Fat said, surprising us. "I mean, it would shake her faith."

We all laughed. Faith shaken by the discovery that the entity believed in actually existed—the paradox of piety. Sherri's theology had congealed; there would have been no room in it for the growth, the expansion and evolution, necessary to encompass our revelations. No wonder Fat and she weren't able to live together.

The question was, How did we go about making contact with Eric Lampton and Linda Lampton and the composer of Synchronicity Music, Mini? Obviously through me and my friendship—if that's what it was—with Jamison.

"It's up to you, Phil," Kevin said. "Get off the pot and onto the stick. Call Jamison and tell him—whatever. You're full of it; you'll think of something. Say you've written a hot-property screenplay and you want Lampton to read it."

"Call it *Zebra*," Fat said.

"Okay," I said, "I'll call it Zebra or Horse's Ass or anything you want. You know, of course, that this is going to shoot down my professional probity."

"What probity?" Kevin said, characteristically. "Your probity is like Fat's. It never got off the ground in the first place."

"What you have to do," Fat said, "is show knowledge of the gnosis disclosed to me by Zebra over and above, which is to say beyond, what appears in *Valis*. That will intrigue him. I'll write down a few statements I've received directly from Zebra."

Presently he had a list for me.

#18. Real time ceased in 70 c.e. with the fall of the temple at Jerusalem. It began again in 1974 c.e. The intervening period was a perfect spurious interpolation aping the creation of the Mind. "The Empire never ended," but in 1974 a cypher was sent out as a signal that the Age of Iron was over; the cypher consisted of two words: KING FELIX, which refers to the Happy (or Rightful) King.

#19. The two-word cypher signal KING FELIX was not intended for human beings but for the descendents of Ikhnaton, the three-eyed race which, in secret, exists with us.

Reading these entries, I said, "I'm supposed to recite this to Robin Jamison?"

"Say they're from your screenplay *Zebra*," Kevin said.

"Is this cypher real?" I asked Fat.

A veiled expression appeared on his face. "Maybe."

"This two-word secret message was actually sent out?" David said.

"In 1974," Fat said. "In February. The United States Army cryptographers studied it, but couldn't discern who it was intended for or what it meant."

"How do you know that?" I said.

"Zebra told him," Kevin said.

"No," Fat said, but he did not amplify.

In this industry you always talk to agents, never to principals. One time I had gotten loaded and tried to get hold of Kay Lenz, who I had a crush on from having seen *Breezy*. Her agent cut me off at the pass. The same thing happened when I tried to get through to Victoria Principal, who herself is now an agent; again, I had a crush on her and again I was ripped when I started phoning Universal Studios. But having Robin Jamison's address and phone number in London made a difference.

"Yes, I remember you," Jamison said pleasantly when I put the call through to London. "The science fiction writer with the child bride, as Mr. Purser described her in his article."

I told him about my dynamite screenplay *Zebra* and that I'd seen their sensational film *Valis* and thought that Mother Goose was absolutely perfect for the lead part; even more so than Robert Redford, who we were also considering and who was interested.

"What I can do," Jamison said, "is contact Mr. Lampton and give him your number there in the States. If he's interested he or his agent will get in touch with you or your agent."

I'd fired my best shot; that was it.

After some more talk I hung up, feeling futile. Also I had a minor twinge of guilt over my devious hype, but I knew that the twinge would abate.

Was Eric Lampton the fifth Savior who Fat sought?

Strange, the relationship between the actuality and the ideal. Fat had been prepared to climb the highest mountain in Tibet, to reach a two-hundred-year-old monk who would say, "The meaning of it all, my son, is—" I thought, Here, my son, time turns into space. But I said nothing; Fat's circuits were already overloaded with information. The last thing he needed was more information; what Fat needed was someone to take the information *from* him.

"Is Goose in the States?" Kevin said.

"Yes," I said, "according to Jamison."

"You didn't tell him the cypher," Fat said.

We all gave Fat a withering look.

"The cypher is for Goose," Kevin said. "When he calls."

" 'When,' " I echoed.

"If you have to you can have your agent contact Goose's agent," Kevin said. He had become more earnest about this than even Fat himself. After all, it was Kevin who had discovered *Valis* and thereby put us in business.

"A film like that," David said, "is going to bring a lot of cranks out of the woodwork. Mother Goose is probably being rather careful."

"Thanks," Kevin said.

"I don't mean us," David said.

"He's right," I said, reviewing in my mind some of the mail

my own writing generates. "Goose will probably prefer to contact my agent." I thought, If he contacts us at all. His agent to my agent. Balanced minds.

"If Goose does phone you," Fat said to me in a calm, low, very tense voice, unusual for him, "you are to give him the two-word cypher, KING FELIX. Work it into the conversation, of course; this isn't spy stuff. Say it's an alternate title for the screenplay."

I said, irritably, "I can handle it."

Chances were, there wouldn't be anything to handle. A week later I received a letter from Mother Goose himself, Eric Lampton. It contained one word. KING. And after the word a question mark and an arrow pointing to the right of KING.

It scared the shit out of me; I trembled. And wrote in the word FELIX. And mailed the letter back to Mother Goose.

He had included a stamped self-addressed envelope.

No doubt existed: we had linked up.

The person referred to by the two-word cypher KING FELIX is the fifth Savior who, Zebra—or VALIS—had said, was either already born or would soon be. This was terribly frightening to me, getting the letter from Mother Goose. I wondered how Goose—Eric Lampton and his wife Linda—would feel when they got the letter back with FELIX correctly added. Correctly; yes, that was it. Only one word out of the hundreds of thousands of English words would do; no, not English: Latin. It is a name in English but a word in Latin.

Prosperous, happy, fruitful . . . the Latin word "Felix" occurs in such injunctions as that by God Himself, who in *Genesis* *1:21* says to all the creatures of the world, "Be fruitful and increase, fill the waters of the seas; and let the birds increase on land." This is the essence of the meaning of *Felix*, this command from God, this loving command, this manifestation of his desire that we not only live but that we live happily and prosperously.

FELIX. Fruit-bearing, fruitful, fertile, productive. All the nobler sorts of trees, whose fruits are offered to the superior deities. That brings good luck, of good omen, auspicious, favorable, propitious, fortunate, prosperous, felicitous. Lucky, happy, fortunate. Wholesome. Happier, more successful in.

That last meaning interests me. "More successful in." The King who is more successful in . . . in what? Perhaps in overthrowing the tyrannical reign of the king of tears, replacing that sad and bitter king with his own legitimate reign of happiness: the end of the age of the Black Iron Prison and the beginning of the age of the Garden of Palm Trees in the warm sun of Arabia ("Felix" also refers to the fertile portion of Arabia).

Our little group, upon my receiving the missive from Mother Goose, met in plenipotentiary session.

"Fat is in the fire," Kevin said laconically, but his eyes sparkled with excitement and joy, a joy we all shared.

"You're with me," Fat said.

We had all chipped in to buy a bottle of Courvoisier Napoleon cognac; seated around Fat's living room we warmed our glasses by rubbing their stems like fire sticks, feeling pretty smart.

Kevin, hollowly, intoned, to no one in particular, "It would be interesting if some men in skin-tight shiny black uniforms show up and shoot us all, now. Because of Phil's phonecall."

"Them's the breaks," I said, easily fielding Kevin's wit. "Let's push Kevin out into the hall with the end of a broom handle and see if anyone opens fire on him."

"It would prove nothing," David said. "Half of Santa Ana is tired of Kevin."

Three nights later, at two A.M., the phone rang. When I answered it—I was still up, finishing an introduction for a book of stories culled from twenty-five years of my career*—a man's voice with a slight British accent said, "How many are there of you?"

Bewildered, I said, "Who is this?"

"Goose."

Aw Christ, I thought, and again I trembled. "Four," I said, and my voice shook.

"This is a happy occasion," Eric Lampton said.

"Prosperous," I said.

Lampton laughed. "No, the King isn't financially well-off."

---

*_The Golden Man_, edited by Mark Hurst, Berkley Publishing Corporation, NY., 1980.

"He—" I couldn't go on.

Lampton said, "Vivit. I think. Vivet? He lives, anyhow, you'll be happy to hear. My Latin isn't very good."

"Where?" I said.

"Where are you? I have a 714 area code, here."

"Santa Ana. In Orange County."

"With Ferris," Lampton said. "You're just north of Ferris's mansion-by-the-sea."

"Right," I said.

"Shall we get together?"

"Sure," I said, and in my head a voice said, This is real.

"You can fly up here, the four of you? To Sonoma?"

"Oh yes," I said.

"You'll fly to the Oakland Airport; it's better than San Francisco. You saw *Valis*?"

"Several times." My voice still shook. "Mr. Lampton, is a time dysfunction involved?"

Eric Lampton said, "How can there be a dysfunction in something that doesn't exist?" He paused. "You didn't think of that."

"No," I admitted. "Can I tell you that we thought *Valis* is one of the finest films we ever saw?"

"I hope we can release the uncut version sometime. I'll see that you get a peek at it up here. We really didn't want to cut it, but, you know, practical considerations . . . you're a science fiction writer? Do you know Thomas Disch?"

"Yes," I said.

"He is very good."

"Yes," I said, pleased that Lampton knew Disch's writing. It was a good sign.

"In a way *Valis* was shit," Lampton said. "We had to make it that way, to get the distributors to pick it up. For the popcorn drive-in crowd." There was merriment in his voice, a musical twinkling. "They expected me to sing, you know. 'Hey, Mr. Starman! When You Droppin' In?' I think they were a bit disappointed, do you see."

"Well," I said, nonplussed.

"Then we'll see you up here. You have the address, do you? I won't be in Sonoma after this month, so it must be this month or much later in the year; I'm flying back to the U.K. to do a TV film for the Grenada people. And I have concert engagements . . . I do have a recording date in Burbank; I could meet you there in—what do you call it? The 'Southland'?"

"We'll fly up to Sonoma," I said. "Are there others?" I said. "Who've contacted you?"

" 'Happy King' people? Well, we'll talk about that when we get together, your little group and Linda and Mini; did you know that Mini did the music?"

"Yes," I said. "Synchronicity Music."

"He is very good," Lampton said. "Much of what we get through lies in his music. He doesn't do songs, the prick. I wish he did. He'd do lovely songs. My songs aren't bad but I'm not Paul." He paused. "Simon, I mean."

"Can I ask you," I said, "where *he* is?"

"Oh. Well, yes; you can ask. But no one is going to tell you until we've talked. A two-word message doesn't really tell me very much about you, now does it? Although I've checked you out. You were into drugs for a while and then you switched sides. You met Tim Leary—"

"Only on the phone," I corrected. "Talked to him once on the phone; he was in Canada with John Lennon and Paul Williams—not the singer, but the writer."

"You've not been arrested. For possession?"

"Never," I said.

"You acted as a sort of dope guru to teen-agers in—where was it?—oh yes; Marin County. Someone took a shot at you."

"That's not quite it," I said.

"You write very strange books. But you are positive you don't have a police record; we don't want you if you do."

"I don't," I said.

Mildly, pleasantly, Lampton said, "You were mixed up with black terrorists for a while."

I said nothing.

"What an adventure your life has been," Lampton said.

"Yes," I agreed. That certainly was true.

"You're not on drugs now?" Lampton laughed. "I'll withdraw that question. We know you're squared up now. All right, Philip; I'll be glad to meet you and your friends personally. Was it you who got—well, let's see. Got told things."

"The information was fired at my friend Horselover Fat."

"But that's you. 'Philip' means 'Horselover' in Greek, lover of horses. 'Fat' is the German translation of 'Dick.' So you've translated your name."

I said nothing.

"Should I call you 'Horselover Fat'? Are you more comfortable that way?"

"Whatever's right," I said woodenly.

"An expression from the Sixties." Lampton laughed. "Okay, Philip. I think we have enough information on you. We talked to your agent, Mr. Galen; he seemed very astute and forthright."

"He's okay," I said.

"He certainly understands where your head is at, as they say over here. Your publisher is Doubleday, is it?"

"Bantam," I said.

"When will your group be coming up?"

I said, "What about this weekend?"

"Very good," Lampton said. "You'll enjoy this, you know. The suffering you've gone through is over. Do you realize that, Philip?" His tone was no longer bantering. "It is over; it really is."

"Fine," I said, my heart hammering.

"Don't be scared, Philip," Lampton said quietly.

"Okay," I said.

"You've gone through a lot. The dead girl . . . well, we can let that go; that is gone. Do you see?"

"Yes," I said. "I see." And I did. I hoped I did; I tried to understand; I wanted to.

"You don't understand. He's here. The information is correct. **'The Buddha is in the park.'** Do you understand?"

"No," I said.

"Gautama was born in a great park called Lumbini. It's a story such as that of Christ at Bethlehem. If the information were 'Jesus is in Bethlehem,' you would know what that meant, wouldn't you?"

I nodded, foretting I was on the phone.

"He has slept almost two thousand years," Lampton said. "A very long time. Under everything that has happened. But— well, I think I've said enough. He is awake now; that's the point. Linda and I will see you Friday night or early Saturday, then?"

"Right," I said. "Fine. Probably Friday night."

"Just remember," Lampton said. " 'The Buddha is in the park.' And try to be happy."

I said, "Is it him come back? Or another one?"

A pause.

"I mean—" I said.

"Yes, I know what you mean. But you see, time isn't real. It's him again but not him; another one. There are many Buddhas, but only one. The key to understanding it is time . . . when you play a record a second time, do the musicians play the music a second time? If you play the record fifty times, do the musicians play the music fifty times?"

"Once," I said.

"Thank you," Lampton said, and the phone clicked. I set down the receiver.

You don't see that every day, I said to myself. What Goose said.

To my surprise I realized that I had stopped shaking.

It was as if I had been shaking all my life, from a chronic undercurrent of fear. Shaking, running, getting into trouble, losing the people I loved. Like a cartoon character instead of a person, I realized. A corny animation from the early Thirties. In back of all I had ever done the fear had forced me on. Now the fear had died, soothed away by the news I had heard. The news, I realized suddenly, that I had waited from the beginning to hear; created, in a sense, to be present when the news came, and for no other reason.

I could forget the dead girl. The universe itself, on its macrocosmic scale, could now cease to grieve. The wound had healed.

Because of the late hour I could not notify the others of Lampton's call. Nor could I call Air California and make the plane reservations. However, early in the morning I called David, then Kevin and then Fat. They had me take care of the travel arrangements; late Friday night sounded fine to them.

We met that evening and decided that our little group

needed a name. After some bickering we let Fat decide. In view of Eric Lampton's emphasis on the statement about the Buddha we decided to call ourselves the Siddhartha Society.

"Then count me out," David said. "I'm sorry but I can't go along with it unless there's some suggestion of Christianity. I don't mean to sound fanatic, but—"

"You sound fanatic," Kevin told him.

We bickered again. At last we came up with a name convoluted enough to satisfy Fat, cryptic enough to satisfy Kevin and Christian enough to satisfy David; to me the subject wasn't all that important. Fat told us of a dream he had had recently, in which he had been a large fish. Instead of an arm he had walked around with sail-like or fan-like fins; with one of these fins he had tried to hold onto an M-16 rifle but the weapon had slid to the ground, whereupon a voice had intoned:

"Fish cannot carry guns."

Since the Greek word for that kind of fan was *rhipidos*—with the Rhiptoglossa reptiles—we finally settled on the Rhipidon Society, the name referring elliptically to the Christian fish. This pleased Fat, too, since it alluded back to the Dogon people and their fish symbol for the benign deity.

So now we could approach Lampton—both Eric and Linda Lampton—in the form of an official organization. Small though we were. I guess we were frightened, at this point; intimidated is perhaps the better word.

Taking me off to one side, Fat said in a low voice, "Did Eric Lampton really say we don't have to think about her death any more?"

I put my hand on Fat's shoulder. "It's over," I said. "He told me that. The age of oppression ended in August 1974; now the age of sorrow begins to end. Okay?"

"Okay," Fat said, with a faint smile, as if he could not believe what he was hearing, but wanted to believe it.

"You're not crazy, you know," I said to Fat. "Remember that. You can't use that as a cop-out."

"And he's alive? Already? He really is?"

"Lampton says so."

"Then it's true."

I said, "Probably it's true."

"You believe it."

"I think so," I said. "We'll find out."

"Will he be old? Or a child? I guess he's still a child. Phil—" Fat gazed at me, stricken. "What if he isn't human?"

"Well," I said, "we'll deal with that problem when and if it arises." In my own mind I thought, Probably he's here from the future; that's the most likely possibility. He will not be human in some respects, but in others he will be. Our immortal child . . . the life form of maybe millions of years ahead in time. Zebra, I thought. Now *I* will see you. We all will.

King and judge, I thought. As promised. All the way back to Zoroaster.

All the way back, in fact, to Osiris. And from Egypt to the Dogon people; and from there to the stars.

"A hit of cognac," Kevin said, bringing the bottle into the living room. "As a toast."

"Damn, Kevin," David protested. "You can't toast the Savior, not with cognac."

"Ripple?" Kevin said.

We each accepted a glass of the Courvoisier Napoleon cognac, including David.

"To the Rhipidon Society," Fat said. We touched glasses.

I said, "And our motto."

"Do we have a motto?" Kevin said.

" 'Fish cannot carry guns,' " I said.

We drank to that.

11

IT had been years since I'd visited Sonoma, California, which lies in the heart of the wine country, with lovely hills on three sides of it. Most attractive of all is the town's park, set dead-center, with the old stone courthouse, the pond with ducks, the ancient cannons left over from used-up wars.

The many small shops surrounding the square park pandered by and large to weekend tourists, bilking the unwary with many trashy goods, but a few genuine historically-important buildings from the old Mexican reign still stood, painted and with plaques proclaiming their ancient roles. The air smelled good—especially if you emanate from the Southland—and even though it was night we strolled around before finally entering a bar called Gino's to phone the Lamptons.

In a white VW Rabbit both Eric and Linda Lampton picked us up; they met us in Gino's where the four of us sat at a table drinking Separators, a specialty of the place

"I'm sorry we couldn't pick you up at the airport," Eric Lampton said as he and his wife came over to our table; apparently he recognized me from my publicity pictures.

Eric Lampton is slender, with long blond hair; he wore red bellbottoms and a T-shirt reading: SAVE THE WHALES. Kevin, of course, identified him at once, as did many of the people in the bar; calls, shouts and hellos greeted the Lamptons, who smiled around them at what obviously were their friends. Beside Eric, Linda walked quickly, also slender, with teeth like Emmylou Harris's. Like her husband she is slender, but her hair is dark and quite soft and long. She wore cutoffs, much washed, and a checkered shirt with a bandana knotted around her neck. Both of them had on boots: Eric's were sideboots and Linda's were granny boots.

Shortly, we were squeezed into the Rabbit, sailing down residential streets of relatively modern houses with wide lawns.

"We are the Rhipidon Society," Fat said.

Eric Lampton said, "We are the Friends of God."

Amazed, Kevin reacted violently; he stared at Eric Lampton. The rest of us wondered why.

"You know the name, then," Eric said.

"*Gottesfreunde*," Kevin said. "You go back to the fourteenth century!"

"That's right," Linda Lampton said. "The Friends of God formed originally in Basel. Finally we entered Germany and the Netherlands. You know of Meister Eckehart, then."

Kevin said, "He was the first person to conceive of the God-head in distinction to God. The greatest of the Christian mystics. He taught that a person can attain union with the Godhead—he held a concept that God exists within the human soul!" We had never heard Kevin so excited. "The soul can actually know God as he is! Nobody today teaches that! And, and—" Kevin stammered; we had never heard him stammer before. "Sankara in India, in the ninth century; he taught the same things Eckehart taught. It's a trans-Christian mysticism in which man can reach beyond God, or merges with God, as or with a spark of some kind that isn't created. Brahman; that's why Zebra—"

"VALIS," Eric Lampton said.

"Whatever," Kevin said; turning to me, he said in agitation, "this would explain the revelation about the Buddha and about St. Sophia or Christ. This isn't limited to any one country or culture or religion. Sorry, David."

David nodded amiably, but appeared shaken. He knew this wasn't orthodoxy.

Eric said, "Sankara and Eckehart, the same person; living in two places at two times."

Half to himself, Fat said, " 'He causes things to look different so it would appear time has passed.' "

"Time and space both," Linda said.

"What is VALIS?" I asked.

"Vast Active Living Intelligence System," Eric said.

"That's a description," I said.

"That's what we have," Eric said. "What else is there but that? Do you want a name, the way God had man name all the animals? VALIS is the name; call it that and be satisfied."

"Is VALIS man?" I said. "Or God? Or something else."

Both Eric and Linda smiled.

"Does it come from the stars?" I said.

"This place where we are," Eric said, "is one of the stars; our sun is a star."

"Riddles," I said.

Fat said, "Is VALIS the Savior?"

For a moment, both Eric and Linda remained silent and then Linda said, "We are the Friends of God." Beyond that she added nothing more.

Cautiously, David glanced at me, caught my eye, and made a questioning motion: *Are these people on the level?*

"They are a very old group," I answered, "which I thought had died out centuries ago."

Eric said, "We have never died out and we are much older than you realize. Than you have been told. Than even we will tell you if asked."

"You date back before Eckehart, then," Kevin said acutely.

Linda said, "Yes."

"Centuries?" Kevin asked.

No answer.

"Thousands of years?" I said, finally.

" 'High hills are the haunt of the mountain-goat,' " Linda said, " 'and boulders a refuge for the rock-badger.' "

"What does that mean?" I said; Kevin joined in; we spoke in unison.

"I know what it means," David said.

"It can't be," Fat said; apparently he recognized what Linda had quoted, too.

" 'The stork makes her home in their tops,' " Eric said, after a time.

To me, Fat said, "These are Ikhnaton's race. That's *Psalm 104*, based on Ikhnaton's hymn; it entered our Bible—it's *older* than our Bible."

Linda Lampton said, "We are the ugly builders with clawlike hands. Who hide ourselves in shame. Along with Hephaistos we built great walls and the homes of the gods themselves."

"Yes," Kevin said. "Hephaistos was ugly, too. The builder God. You killed Asklepios."

"These are Kyklopes," Fat said faintly.

"The name means 'Round-eye,' " Kevin said.

"But we have three eyes," Eric said. "So an error in the historic record was made."

"Deliberately?" Kevin said.

Linda said, "Yes."

"You are very old," Fat said.

"Yes, we are," Eric said, and Linda nodded. "Very old. But time is not real. Not to us, anyhow."

"My God," Fat said, as if stricken. "These are the original builders."

"We have never stopped," Eric said. "We still build. We built this world, this space-time matrix."

"You are our creators," Fat said.

The Lamptons nodded.

"You really are the friends of God," Kevin said. "You are literally."

"Don't be afraid," Eric said. "You know how Shiva holds up one hand to show that there is nothing to fear."

"But there is," Fat said. "Shiva is the destroyer; his third eye destroys."

"He is also the restorer," Linda said.

Leaning against me, David whispered in my ear, "Are they crazy?"

They are gods, I said to myself; they are Shiva who both destroys and protects. *They judge.*

Perhaps I should have felt fear. But I did not. They had already destroyed—brought down Ferris F. Fremount, as he had been depicted in the film *Valis.*

The period of Shiva the Restorer had begun. The restoration, I thought, of all we have lost. Of two dead girls.

As in the film *Valis*, Linda Lampton could turn time back, if necessary; and restore everything to life.

I had begun to understand the film.

The Rhipidon Society, I realized, fish though it be, is out of its depth.

An irruption from the collective unconscious, Jung taught, can wipe out the fragile individual ego. In the depths of the collective the archetypes slumber; if aroused, they can heal or they can destroy. This is the danger of the archetypes; the opposite qualities are not yet separated. Bipolarization into paired opposites does not occur until consciousness occurs.

So, with the gods, life and death—protection and destruction —are one. This secret partnership exists outside of time and space.

It can make you very much afraid, and for good reason. After all, your existence is at stake.

The real danger, the ultimate horror, happens when the creating and protecting, the sheltering, comes first—and then the destruction. Because if this is the sequence, everything built up ends in death.

Death hides within every religion.

And at any time it can flash forth—not with healing in its wings but with poison, with that which wounds.

But we had started out wounded. And VALIS had fired healing information at us, medical information. VALIS approached us in the form of the physician, and the age of the injury, the Age of Iron, the toxic iron splinter, had been abolished.

And yet . . . the risk is, potentially, always there.

It is a kind of terrible game. Which can go either way.

Libera me, Domine, I said to myself. *In die illa.* Save me, protect me, God, in this day of wrath. There is a streak of the irrational in the universe, and we, the little hopeful trusting Rhipidon Society, may have been drawn into it, to perish.

As many have perished before.

I remembered something which the great physician of the Renaissance had discovered. Poisons, in measured doses, are remedies; Paracelsus was the first to use metals such as mercury as medication. For this discovery—the measured use of poisonous metals as medications—Paracelsus has entered our history books. There is, however, an unfortunate ending to the great physician's life.

He died of metal poisoning.

So put another way, medications can be poisonous, can kill. And it can happen at any time.

"Time is a child at play, playing draughts; a child's is the kingdom." As Heraclitus wrote twenty-five hundred years ago. In many ways this is a terrible thought. The most terrible of all. A child playing a game . . . with all life, everywhere.

I would have preferred an alternative. I saw now the binding importance of our motto, the motto of our little Society, binding upon all occasions as the essence of Christianity, from which we could never depart:

FISH CANNOT CARRY GUNS!

If we abandoned that, we entered the paradoxes, and, finally, death. Stupid as our motto sounded, we had fabricated in it the insight we needed. There was nothing more to know.

In Fat's quaint little dream about dropping the M-16 rifle, the Divine had spoken to us. *Nihil Obstat*. We had entered love, and found ourselves a land.

But the divine and the terrible are so close to each other. Nommo and Yurugu are partners; both are necessary. Osiris and Seth, too. In the *Book of Job*, Yahweh and Satan form a partnership. For us to live, however, these partners must be split. The behind-the-scenes partnership must end as soon as time and space and all the creatures come into being.

It is not God nor the gods which must prevail; it is wisdom, Holy Wisdom. I hoped that the fifth Savior would be that: splitting the bipolarities and emerging as a unitary thing. Not of three persons or two but *one*. Not Brahma the creator, Vishnu the sustainer and Shiva the destroyer, but what Zoroaster called the Wise Mind.

God can be good and terrible—not in succession—but at the same time. This is why we seek a mediator between us and him; we approach him through the mediating priest and attenuate and enclose him through the sacraments. It is for our own safety: to trap him with confines which render him safe. But now, as Fat had seen, God had escaped the confines and was transubstantiating the world; God had become free.

The gentle sounds of the choir singing "Amen, amen" are not to calm the congregation but to pacify the god.

When you know this you have penetrated to the innermost core of religion. And the worst part is that the god can thrust himself outward and into the congregation until he becomes them. You worship a god and then he pays you back by taking you over. This is called "*enthousiasmos*" in Greek, literally "to be possessed by the god." Of all the Greek gods the one most likely to do this was Dionysos. And, unfortunately, Dionysos was insane.

Put another way—stated backward—if your god takes you over, it is likely that no matter what name he goes by he is actually a form of the mad god Dionysos. He was also the god of intoxication, which may mean, literally, to take in toxins; that is to say, to take a poison. The danger is there.

If you sense this, you try to run. But if you run he has you anyhow, for the demigod Pan was the basis of panic which is the uncontrollable urge to flee, and Pan is a subform of Dionysos. So in trying to flee from Dionysos you are taken over anyhow.

I write this literally with a heavy hand; I am so weary I am dropping as I sit here. What happened at Jonestown was the mass running of panic, inspired by the mad god—panic leading into death, the logical outcome of the mad god's thrust.

For them no way out existed. You must be taken over by the mad god to understand this, that once it happens there is no way out, because the mad god is everywhere.

It is not reasonable for nine hundred people to collude in their own deaths and the deaths of little children, but the mad god is not logical, not as we understand the term.

When we reached the Lamptons' house we found it to be a stately old farm mansion, set in the middle of grape vines; after all, this is wine country.

I thought, Dionysos is the god of wine.

"The air smells good here," Kevin said as we got out of the VW Rabbit.

"We sometimes get pollution," Eric said. "Even here."

Entering the house, we found it warm and attractive; huge posters of Eric and Linda, framed behind non-reflecting glass, covered all the walls. This gave the old wooden house a modern look, which linked us back to the Southland.

Linda said, smiling, "We make our own wine, here. From our own grapes."

I imagine you do, I said to myself.

A huge complex of stereo equipment rose up along one wall like the fortress in VALIS which was Nicholas Brady's sound-mixer. I could see where the visual idea had originated.

"I'll put on a tape we made," Eric said, going over to the audio fortress and clicking switches to on. "Mini's music but my words. I'm singing but we're not going to release it; it's just an experiment."

As we seated ourselves, music at enormous DBs filled the living room, rebounding off all the walls.

> "I want to see you, man.
> As quickly as I can.
> Let me hold your hand
> I've got no hand to hold
> And I'm old, old; very old.
>
> Why won't you look at me?
> Afraid of what you see?
> I'll find you anyhow,
> Later or now; later or now."

Jesus, I thought, listening to the lyrics. Well, we came to the right place. No doubt about that. We wanted this and we got this. Kevin could amuse himself by deconstructing the song lyrics, which did not need to be deconstructed. Well, he could turn his attention to Mini's electronic noises, then.

Linda, bending down and putting her lips to my ears, shouted over the music, "Those resonances open the higher chakras."

I nodded.

When the song ended, we all said how terrific it was, David included. David had passed into a trance-state; his eyes were glazed over. David did this when he was faced by what he could not endure; the church had taught him how to phase himself out mentally for a time, until the stress situation was over.

"Would you like to meet Mini?" Linda Lampton said.

"Yes!" Kevin said.

"He's probably upstairs sleeping," Eric Lampton said. He started out of the living room. "Linda, you bring some cabernet sauvignon, the 1972, up from the cellar."

"Okay," she said, starting out of the room in the other direction. "Make yourselves comfortable," she said over her shoulder to us. "I'll be right back."

Over at the stereo, Kevin gazed down in rapture.

David walked up to me, his hands stuck deep in his pockets, a complex expression on his face. "They're—"

"They're crazy," I said.

"But in the car you seemed—"

"Crazy," I said.

"Good crazy?" David said; he stood close beside me, as if for protection. "Or—the other thing."

"I don't know," I said, truthfully.

Fat stood with us now; he listened, but did not speak. He looked deeply sobered. Meanwhile, Kevin, by himself, continued to analyze the audio system.

"I think we should—" David began, but at that moment Linda Lampton returned from the wine cellar, carrying a silver tray on which stood six wine glasses and a bottle still corked.

"Would one of you open the wine?" Linda said. "I usually get cork in it; I don't know why." Without Eric she seemed shy with us, and completely unlike the woman she had played in *Valis*.

Rousing himself, Kevin took the wine bottle from her.

"The opener is somewhere in the kitchen," Linda said.

From above our heads thumping and scraping noises could be heard, as if something awfully heavy were being dragged across the upper-story floor.

Linda said, "Mini—I should tell you this—has multiple myeloma. It's very painful and he's in a wheelchair."

Horrified, Kevin said, "Plasma cell myeloma is always fatal."

"Two years is the life span," Linda said. "His has just been diagnosed. He'll be hospitalized in another week. I'm sorry."

Fat said, "Can't VALIS heal him?"

"That which is to be healed will be healed," Linda Lampton said. "That which will be destroyed will be destroyed. But time is not real; nothing is destroyed. It is an illusion."

David and I glanced at each other.

Bump-bump. Something awkward and enormous dragged its way down a flight of stairs. Then, as we stood unmoving, a wheel chair entered the living room. In it a crushed little heap smiled at us in humor, love and the warmth of recognition. From both ears ran cords: double hearing aids. Mini, the composer of Synchronicity Music, was partially deaf.

Going up to Mini one by one we shook his faltering hand and identified ourselves, not as a society but as persons.

"Your music is very important," Kevin said.

"Yes it is," Mini said.

We could see his pain and we could see that he would not live long. But in spite of the suffering he held no malice toward the world; he did not resemble Sherri. Glancing at Fat, I could see that he was remembering Sherri, now, as he gazed at the stricken man in the wheelchair. To come this far, I thought, and to find this again—this, which Fat had fled from. Well, as I already said, no matter which direction you take, when you run the god runs with you because he is everywhere, inside you and out.

"Did VALIS make contact with you?" Mini said. "The four of you? Is that why you're here?"

"With me," Fat said. "These others are my friends."

"Tell me what you saw," Mini said.

"Like St. Elmo's Fire," Fat said. "And information—"

"There is always information when VALIS is present," Mini said, nodding and smiling. "He is information. Living information."

"He healed my son," Fat said. "Or anyhow fired the medical information necessary to heal him at me. And VALIS told me that St. Sophia and the Buddha and what he or it called the 'Head Apollo' is about to be born soon and that the—"

"—the time you have waited for," Mini murmured.

"Yes," Fat said.

"How did you know the cypher?" Eric Lampton asked Fat.

"I saw a set to ground doorway," Fat said.

"He saw it," Linda said rapidly. "What was the ratio of the doorway? The sides?"

Fat said, "The Fibonacci Constant."

"That's our other code," Linda said. "We have ads running all over the world. One to point six one eight zero three four. What we do is say, 'Complete this sequence: One to point six.' If they recognize it as the Fibonacci constant they can finish the sequence."

"Or we use Fibonacci numbers," Eric said. "1, 2, 3, 5, 8, 13 and so on. That doorway is to the Different Realm."

"Higher?" Fat asked.

"We just call it 'Different,'" Eric said.

"Through the doorway I saw luminous writing," Fat said.

"No you didn't," Mini said, smiling. "Through the doorway is Crete."

After a pause, Fat said, "Lemnos."

"Sometimes Lemnos. Sometimes Crete. That general area."
In a spasm of pain, Mini drew himself up in his wheel chair.

"I saw Hebrew letters on the wall," Fat said.

"Yes," Mini said, still smiling. "Cabala. And the Hebrew letters permutated until they factored out into words you could read."

"Into KING FELIX," Fat said.

"Why did you lie about the doorway?" Linda said, without animosity; she seemed merely curious.

Fat said, "I didn't think you'd believe me."

"Then you're not normally familiar with the Cabala," Mini said. "It's the encoding system which VALIS uses; all its verbal information is stored as Cabala, because that's the most economical way, since the vowels are indicated by mere vowel-points. You were given a set-ground discriminating unscrambler, you realize. We normally can't distinguish set from ground; VALIS has to fire the unscrambler at you. It's a grid. You saw set as color, of course."

"Yes." Fat nodded. "And ground as black and white."

"So you could see the false work."

"Pardon?" Fat said.

"The false work that's blended with the real world."

"Oh," Fat said. "Yes, I understand. It seemed as if some things had been taken away—"

"And other things added," Mini said.

Fat nodded.

"You have a voice inside your head now?" Mini said. "The AI voice?"

After a long pause, and a glance at me, Kevin and David, Fat said, "It's a neutral voice. Neither male nor female. Yes, it does sound as if it's an artificial intelligence."

"That's the inter-system communications network," Mini said. "It stretches between stars, connecting all the star systems with Albemuth."

Staring at him, Fat said, " 'Albemuth'? It's a *star*?"

"You heard the word, but—"

"I saw it in written form," Fat said, "but I didn't know what it meant. I connected it with alchemy, because of the 'al.' "

"The *al* prefix," Mini said, "is Arabic; it simply means 'the.'

It's a common prefix for stars. That was your clue. Anyhow, you did see written pages, then."

"Yes," Fat said. "Many of them. They told me what was going to happen to me. Like—" He hesitated. "My later suicide attempt. It gave me the Greek word '*ananke*' which I didn't know. And it said, 'A gradual darkening of the world; a sickling over.' Later I realized what it meant; a bad thing, a sickness, a deed that I had to commit. But I did survive."

"My illness," Mini said, "is from proximity to VALIS, to its energy. It's an unfortunate thing, but as you know, we are immortal, although not physically so. We will be reborn and remember."

"My animals died of cancer," Fat said.

"Yes," Mini said. "The levels of radiation can sometimes be enormous. Too much for us."

I thought, So that's why you're dying. Your god has killed you and yet you're happy. I thought, *We have to get out of here. These people court death.*

"What is VALIS?" Kevin said to Mini. "Which deity or demiurge is he? Shiva? Osiris? Horus? I've read *The Cosmic Trigger* and Robert Anton Wilson says—"

"VALIS is a construct," Mini said. "An artifact. It's anchored here on Earth, literally anchored. But since space and time don't exist for it, VALIS can be anywhere and any time it wishes to. It's something they built to program us at birth; normally it fires extremely short bursts of information at babies, engramming instructions to them which will bleed across from their right hemispheres at clock-time intervals during their full lifetimes, at the appropriate situational contexts."

"Does it have an antagonist?" Kevin said.

"Only the pathology of this planet," Eric said. "Due to the atmosphere. We can't readily breathe this atmosphere, here; it's toxic to our race."

"'Our'?" I said.

"All of us," Linda said. "We're all from Albemuth. This atmosphere poisons us and makes us deranged. So they—the ones who stayed behind in the Albemuth System—built VALIS and sent it here to fire rational instructions at us, to override the pathology caused by the toxicity of the atmosphere."

"Then VALIS is rational," I said.

"The only rationality we have," Linda said.

"And when we act rationally we're under its jurisdiction," Mini said. "I don't mean us here in the room; I mean everyone. Not everyone who lives but everyone who is rational."

"Then in essence," I said, "VALIS detoxifies people."

"That's exactly it," Mini said. "It's an informational antitoxin. But exposure to it can cause—illness such as I have."

Too much medication, I said to myself, remembering Paracelsus, is a poison. This man has been healed to death.

"I wanted to know VALIS as much as possible," Mini said, seeing the expression on my face. "I begged it to return and communicate with me further. It didn't want to; it knew the effect its radiation would have on me if it returned. But it did what I asked. I'm not sorry. It was worth it, to experience VALIS again." To Fat he said, "You know what I mean. The sound of bells . . ."

"Yes," Fat said. "The Easter bells."

"Are you talking about Christ?" David said. "Christ is an artificial construct built to fire information at us that works on us subliminally?"

"From the time we are born," Mini said. "We the lucky ones. We whom it selects. Its flock. Before I die, VALIS will return; I have its promise. VALIS will come and take me with it; I will be a part of it forever." Tears filled his eyes.

Later, we all sat around and talked more calmly.

The Eye of Shiva was of course the way the ancients represented VALIS firing information. They knew it could destroy; this is the element of harmful radiation which is necessary as a carrier for the information. Mini told us that VALIS is not actually close when it fires; it may be literally millions of miles away. Hence, in the film *Valis*, they represented it by a satellite, a very old satellite, not put into orbit by humans.

"So we're not dealing with religion then," I said, "but with a very advanced technology."

"Words," Mini said.

"What is the Savior?" David said.

Mini said, "You'll see him. Presently. Tomorrow, if you wish; Saturday afternoon. He's sleeping now. He still sleeps a great deal; most of the time, in fact. After all, he was completely asleep for thousands of years."

"At Nag Hammadi?" Fat said.

"I would rather not say," Mini said.

"Why must this be kept secret?" I said.

Eric said, "We're not keeping it secret; we made the film and we're making lps with information in the lyrics. Subliminal information, mostly. Mini does it with his music."

" 'Sometimes Brahman sleeps,' " Kevin said, " 'and sometimes Brahman dances.' Are we talking about Brahman? Or Siddhartha the Buddha? Or Christ? Or is it all of them?"

I said to Kevin, "The great—" I had intended to say, "The great Punta," but I decided not to; it wouldn't be wise. "It's not Dionysos, is it?" I asked Mini.

"Apollo," Linda said. "The paired opposite to Dionysos."

That filled me with relief. I believed her; it fitted with what had been revealed to Horselover Fat: "The Head Apollo."

"We are in a maze, here," Mini said, "which we built and then fell into and can't get out. In essence, VALIS selectively fires information to us which aids us in escaping from the maze, in finding the way out. It started back about two thousand years before Christ, in Mycenaean times or perhaps early Helladic. That's why the myths place the maze at Minos, on Crete. That's why you saw ancient Crete through the $1:.618034$ doorway. We were great builders, but one day we decided to play a game. We did it voluntarily; were we such good builders that we could build a maze with a way out but which constantly changed so that, despite the way out, in effect there was no way out for us because the maze—this world—was alive? To make the game into something real, into something more than an intellectual exercise, we elected to lose our exceptional faculties, to reduce us an entire level. This, unfortunately, included loss of memory—loss of knowledge of our true origins. But worse than that—and here is where we in a sense managed to defeat ourselves, to turn victory over to our servant, over to the maze we had built—"

"The third eye closed," Fat said.

"Yes," Mini said. "We relinquished the third eye, our prime evolutionary attribute. It is the third eye which VALIS reopens."

"Then it's the third eye that gets us back out of the maze," Fat said. "That's why the third eye is identified with god-like powers or with enlightenment, in Egypt and in India."

"Which are the same thing," Mini said. "God-like, enlightened."

"Really?" I said.

"Yes," Mini said. "It is man as he really is: his true state."

Fat said, "So without memory, and without the third eye, we never had a chance to beat the maze. It was hopeless."

I thought, Another Chinese finger-trap. And built by our own selves. To trap our own selves.

What kind of minds would create a Chinese finger-trap for themselves? Some game, I thought. Well, it isn't merely intellectual.

"The third eye had to be re-opened if we were to get out of the maze," Mini said, "but since we no longer remembered that we had that ajna faculty, the eye of discernment, we could not go about seeking techniques for re-opening it. *Something outside had to enter*, something which we ourselves would be unable to build."

"So we didn't all fall into the maze," Fat said.

"No," Mini said. "And those that stayed outside, in other star systems, reported back to Albemuth that we had done this thing to ourselves . . . thus VALIS was constructed to rescue us. This is an irreal world. You realize that, I'm sure. VALIS made you realize that. We are in a living maze and not in a world at all."

There was silence as we considered this.

"And what happens when we get outside the maze?" Kevin said.

"We're freed from space and time," Mini said. "Space and time are the binding, controlling conditions of the maze—its power."

Fat and I glanced at each other. It dovetailed with our own speculations—speculations engineered by VALIS.

"And then we never die?" David asked.

"Correct," Mini said.

"So salvation—"

" 'Salvation,' " Mini said, "is a word denoting 'Being led out of the space-time maze, where the servant has become the master.'"

"May I ask a question?" I said. "What is the purpose of the fifth Savior?"

"It isn't 'fifth,'" Mini said. "There is only one, over and over again, at different times, in different places, with different names. The Savior is VALIS incarnated as a human being."

"Crossbonded?" Fat said.

"No," Mini shook his head no vigorously. "There is no human element in the Savior."

"Wait a minute," David said.

"I know what you've been taught," Mini said. "In a sense, it's true. But the Savior is VALIS and that is the fact of the case. He is born, however, from a human woman. He doesn't just generate a phantasm-body."

To that, David nodded; he could accept that.

"And he's been born?" I asked.

"Yes," Mini said.

"My daughter," Linda Lampton said. "Not Eric's, however. Just mine and VALIS'S."

"*Daughter?*" several of us said in unison.

"This time," Mini said, "for the first time, the Savior takes female form."

Eric Lampton said, "She's very pretty. You'll like her. She talks a blue streak, though; she'll talk your ear off."

"Sophia is two," Linda said. "She was born in 1976. We tape what she says."

"Everything is taped," Mini said. "Sophia is surrounded by audio and video recording equipment that automatically monitors her constantly. Not for her protection, of course; VALIS protects her—VALIS, her father."

"And we can talk with her?" I said.

"She'll dispute with you for hours," Linda said, and then she added, "in every language there is or ever was."

Wisdom had been born, not a deity: a deity which slew with one hand while healing with another . . . that deity was not the Savior, and I said to myself, Thank God.

We were taken the next morning to a small farm area, with animals everywhere. I saw no signs of video or audio recording equipment, but I saw—we all saw—a black-haired child seated with goats and chickens, and, in a hutch beside her, rabbits.

What I had expected was tranquility, the peace of God which passes all understanding. However, the child, upon seeing us, rose to her feet and came toward us with indignation blazing in her face; her eyes, huge, dilated with anger, fixed intently on me—she lifted her right hand and pointed at me.

"Your suicide attempt was a violent cruelty against yourself," she said in a clear voice. And yet she was, as Linda had said, no more than two years old: a baby, really, and yet with the eyes of an infinitely old person.

"It was Horselover Fat," I said.

Sophia said, "Phil, Kevin and David. Three of you. There are no more."

Turning to speak to Fat—I saw no one. I saw only Eric Lampton and his wife, the dying man in the wheel chair, Kevin and David. Fat was gone. Nothing remained of him.

Horselover Fat was gone forever. As if he had never existed.

"I don't understand," I said. "You destroyed him."

"Yes," the child said.

I said, "Why?"

"To make you whole."

"Then he's in me? Alive in me?"

"Yes," Sophia said. By degrees, the anger left her face. The great dark eyes ceased to smolder.

"He was me all the time," I said.

"That is right," Sophia said.

"Sit down," Eric Lampton said. "She prefers it if we sit; then she doesn't have to talk up to us. We're so much taller than she is."

Obediently, we all seated ourselves on the rough parched

brown ground—which I now recognized as the opening shot in the film *Valis*; they had filmed part of it here.

Sophia said, "Thank you."

"Are you Christ?" David said, tugging his knees up against his chin, his arms wrapped around them; he, too, looked like a child: one child addressing another in equal conversation.

"I am that which I am," Sophia said.

"I'm glad to—" I couldn't think what to say.

"Unless your past perishes," Sophia said to me, "you are doomed. Do you know that?"

"Yes," I said.

Sophia said, "Your future must differ from your past. The future must always differ from the past."

David said, "Are you God?"

"I am that which I am," Sophia said.

I said, "Then Horselover Fat was part of me projected outward so I wouldn't have to face Gloria's death."

Sophia said, "That is so."

I said, "Where is Gloria now?"

Sophia said, "She lies in the grave."

I said, "Will she return?"

Sophia said, "Never."

I said, "I thought there was immortality."

To that, Sophia said nothing.

"Can you help me?" I said.

Sophia said, "I have already helped you. I helped you in 1974 and I helped you when you tried to kill yourself. I have helped you since you were born."

"You are VALIS?" I said.

Sophia said, "I am that which I am."

Turning to Eric and Linda, I said, "She doesn't always answer."

"Some questions are meaningless," Linda said.

"Why don't you heal Mini?" Kevin said.

Sophia said, "I do what I do; I am what I am."

I said, "Then we can't understand you."

Sophia said, "You understood that."

David said, "You are eternal, aren't you?"

"Yes," Sophia said.

"And you know everything?" David said.

"Yes," Sophia said.

I said, "Were you Siddhartha?"

"Yes," Sophia said.

"Are you the slayer and the slain?" I said.

"No," Sophia said.

"The slayer?" I said.

"No."

"Then slain, then."

"I am the injured and the slain," Sophia said. "But I am not the slayer. I am the healer and the healed."

"But VALIS has killed Mini," I said.

To that, Sophia said nothing.

"Are you the judge of the world?" David said.

"Yes," Sophia said.

"When does the judgment begin?" Kevin said.

Sophia said, "You are all judged already from the start."

I said, "How did you appraise me?"

To that, Sophie said nothing.

"Don't we get to find out?" Kevin said.

"Yes," Sophie said.

"When?" Kevin said.

To that, Sophia said nothing.

Linda said, "I think that's enough for now. You can talk to her again later. She likes to sit with the animals; she loves the animals." She touched me on the shoulder. "Let's go."

As we walked away from the child, I said, "Her voice is the neutral AI voice that I've heard in my head since 1974."

Kevin said hoarsely, "It's a computer. That's why it only answers certain questions."

Both Eric and Linda smiled; Kevin and I glanced at him; in his wheel chair Mini rolled along sedately.

"An AI system," Eric said. "An artificial intelligence."

"A terminal of VALIS," Kevin said. "An input, output terminal of the master system VALIS."

"That's right," Mini said.

"Not a little girl," Kevin said.

"I gave birth to her," Linda said.

"Maybe you just thought you did," Kevin said.

Smiling, Linda said, "An artificial intelligence in a human body. Her body is alive, but her psyche is not. She is sentient;

she knows everything. But her mind is not alive in the sense that we are alive. She was not created. She has always existed."

"Read your Bible," Mini said. "She was with the Creator before creation existed; she was his darling and delight, his greatest treasure."

"I can see why," I said.

"It would be easy to love her," Mini said. "Many people have loved her . . . as it says in the *Book of Wisdom*. And so she entered them and guided them and descended even into the prison with them; she never abandoned those who loved her or who love her now."

"Her voice is heard in human courts," David murmured.

"And she destroyed the tyrant?" Kevin said.

"Yes," Mini said. "As we called him in the film, Ferris F. Fremount. But you know who she toppled and brought to ruin."

"Yes," Kevin said. He looked somber; I knew he was thinking of a man wearing a suit and tie wandering along a beach in southern California, an aimless man wondering what had happened, what had gone wrong, a man who still planned stratagems.

> "In the last days of those kingdoms,
>   When their sin is at its height,
>   A king shall appear, harsh and grim, a master of
>   stratagem . . ."

The king of tears who had brought tears to everyone eventually; against him something had acted which he, in his occlusion, could not discern. We had just now talked to that person, that child.

That child who had always been.

As we ate dinner that night—at a Mexican restaurant just off the park in the center of Sonoma—I realized that I would never see my friend Horselover Fat again, and I felt grief inside me, the grief of loss. Intellectually, I knew that I had re-incorporated him, reversing the original process of projection. But still it made me sad. I had enjoyed his company, his endless tale-spinning, his account of his intellectual and spiritual and emotional quest. A quest—not for the Grail—but to be healed of his wound, the deep injury which Gloria had done to him by means of her death game.

It felt strange not to have Fat to phone up or visit. He had been so much a regular part of my life, and of the lives of our mutual friends. I wondered what Beth would think when the child support checks stopped coming in. Well, I realized, I could assume the economic liability; I could take care of Christopher. I had the funds to do it, and in many ways I loved Christopher as much as his father had.

"Feeling down, Phil?" Kevin said to me. We could talk freely now, since the three of us were alone; the Lamptons had dropped us off, telling us to call them when we had finished dinner and were ready to return to their large house.

"No," I said. And then I said, "I'm thinking about Horselover Fat."

Kevin said, after a pause, "You're waking up, then."

"Yes." I nodded.

"You'll be okay," David said, awkwardly. Expression of emotions came with difficulty to David.

"Yeah," I said.

Kevin said, "Do you think the Lamptons are nuts?"

"Yes," I said.

"What about the little girl?" Kevin said.

I said, "She is not nuts. She is as not nuts as they are. It's a paradox; two totally whacked out people—three, if you count Mini—have created a totally sane offspring."

"If I say—" David began.

"Don't say God brings good out of evil," I said. "Okay? Will you do us that one favor?"

Half to himself, Kevin said, "That is the most beautiful child I have ever seen. But that stuff about her being a computer terminal—" He gestured.

"You're the one who said it," I said.

"At the time," Kevin said, "it made sense. But not when I look back. When I have perspective."

"You know what I think?" David said. "I think we should get back on the Air Cal plane and fly back to Santa Ana. As soon as we can."

I said, "The Lamptons won't hurt us." I was certain of that, now. Odd, that the sick man, the dying man, Mini, had restored my confidence in the power of life. Logically, it should have worked the other way, I suppose. I had liked him very much. But, as is well known, I have a proclivity for helping sick or injured people; I gravitate to them. As my psychiatrist told me years ago, I've got to stop doing that. That, and one other thing.

Kevin said, "I can't scope it out."

"I know," I agreed. Did we really see the Savior? Or did we see just a very bright little girl who, possibly, had been coached to give lofty-sounding answers by three very shrewd professionals who had a master hype going in connection with their film and music?

"It's a strange form for him to take," Kevin said. "As a girl. That's going to encounter resistance. Christ as a female; that made David here pissed as hell."

"She didn't say she was Christ," David said.

I said, "But she is."

Both Kevin and David stopped eating and gazed at me.

"She is St. Sophia," I said, "and St. Sophia is a hypostasis of Christ. Whether she admitted it or not. She's being careful. After all, she knows everything; she knows what people will accept and what they won't."

"You have all your weirded-out experiences of March 1974 to go on," Kevin said. "That proves something; that proves it's real. VALIS exists. You already knew that. You encountered him."

"I guess so," I said.

"And what Mini knew and said collated with what you knew," David said.

"Yeah," I said.

Kevin said, "But you're not certain."

"We're dealing with a high order of sophisticated technology," I said. "Which Mini may have put together."

"Meaning microwave transmissions and such like," Kevin said.

"Yes," I said.

"A purely technological phenomenon," Kevin said. "A major technological breakthrough."

"Using the human mind as the transducer," I said. "Without an electronic interface."

"Could be," Kevin admitted. "The movie showed that. There is no way to tell what they're into."

"You know," David said slowly, "if they have high-yield energy available to them that they can beam over long distances, along the lines of laser beams—"

"They can kill us dead," Kevin said.

"That's right," I said.

"If," Kevin said, "we started quacking about not believing them."

"We can just say we have to be back in Santa Ana," David said.

"Or we can leave from here," I said. "This restaurant."

"Our things—clothes, everything we brought—are there at their house," Kevin said.

"Fuck the clothes," I said.

"Are you afraid," David said, "of something happening?"

I thought about it. "No," I said finally. I trusted the child. And I trusted Mini. You always have to go on that, your instinctive trust or—your lack of trust. In the final analysis, there is really nothing else you can go on.

"I'd like to talk to Sophia again," Kevin said.

"So would I," I said. "The answer is there."

Kevin put his hand on my shoulder. "I'm sorry to say this like this, Phil, but we really have the big clue already. In one instant that child cleared up your mind. You stopped believing you were two people. You stopped believing in Horselover Fat as a separate person. And no therapist and no therapy over the years, since Gloria's death, has ever been able to accomplish that."

"He's right," David said in a gentle voice. "We all kept hoping, but it seemed as if—you know. As if you'd never heal."

" 'Heal,' " I said. "She healed me. Not Horselover Fat but me." They were right; the healing miracle had happened and we all know what that pointed to; we all three of us understood.

I said, "Eight years."

"Right," Kevin said. "Before we even knew you. Eight long fucking goddam years of occlusion and pain and searching and roaming about."

I nodded.

In my mind a voice said, What else do you need to know?

It was my own thoughts, the ratiocination of what had been Horselover Fat, who had rejoined me.

"You realize," Kevin said, "that Ferris F. Fremount is going to try to come back. He was toppled by that child—or by what that child speaks for—but he is returning; he will never give up. The battle was won but the struggle goes on."

David said, "Without that child—"

"We will lose," I said.

"Right," Kevin said.

"Let's stay another day," I said, "and try to talk with Sophia again. One more time."

"That sounds like a plan," Kevin said, pleased.

The little group, The Rhipidon Society, had come to an agreement. All three members.

The next day, Sunday, the three of us got permission to sit with the child Sophia alone, without anyone else present, although Eric and Linda did request that we tape our encounter. We agreed readily, not having any choice.

Warm sunlight illuminated the earth that day, giving to the animals gathered around us the quality of a spiritual following; I had the impression that the animals heard, listened and understood.

"I want to talk to you about Eric and Linda Lampton," I said to the little girl, who sat with a book open in front of her.

"You shall not interrogate me," she said.

"Can't I ask you about them?" I said.

"They are ill," Sophia said. "But they can't harm anyone because I override them." She looked up at me with her huge, dark eyes. "Sit down."

We obediently seated ourselves in front of her.

"I gave you your motto," she said. "For your society; I gave you its name. Now I give you your commission. You will go out into the world and you will tell the *kerygma* which I charge you with. Listen to me; I tell you in truth, in very truth, that the days of the wicked will end and the son of man will sit on the judgment seat. This will come as surely as the sun itself rises. The grim king will strive and lose, despite his cunning; he loses; he lost; he will always lose, and those with him will go into the pit of darkness and there they will linger forever.

"What you teach is the word of man. Man is holy, and the true god, the living god, is man himself. You will have no gods but yourselves; the days in which you believed in other gods end now, they end forever.

"The goal of your lives has been reached. I am here to tell you this. Do not fear; I will protect you. You are to follow one rule: you are to love one another as you love me and as I love you, for this love proceeds from the true god, which is yourselves.

"A time of trial and delusion and wailing lies ahead because the grim king, the king of tears, will not surrender his power. But you will take his power from him; I grant you that authority in my name, exactly as I granted it to you once before, when that grim king ruled and destroyed and challenged the humble people of the world.

"The battle which you fought before has not ended, although the day of the healing sun has come. Evil does not die of its own self because it imagines that it speaks for god. Many claim to speak for god, but there is only one god and that god is man himself.

"Therefore only those leaders who protect and shelter will live; the others will die. The oppression lifted four years ago, and it will for a little while return. Be patient during this time; it will be a time of trials for you, but I will be with you, and when the time of trials is over I shall sit down on the judgment seat, and some will fall and some will not fall, according to my will, my will which comes to me from the father, back to whom we all go, all of us together.

"I am not a god; I am a human. I am a child, the child of my father, which is Wisdom Himself. You carry in you now the voice and authority of Wisdom; you are, therefore, Wisdom, even when you forget it. You will not forget it for long. I will be there and I will remind you.

"The day of Wisdom and the rule of Wisdom has come. The day of power, which is the enemy of Wisdom, ends. Power and Wisdom are the two principles in the world. Power has had its rule and now it goes into the darkness from which it came, and Wisdom alone rules.

"Those who obey power will succumb as power succumbs.

"Those who love Wisdom and follow her will thrive under the sun. Remember, I will be with you. I will be in each of you from now on. I will accompany you down into the prison if necessary; I will speak in the courts of law to defend you; my voice will be heard in the land, whatever the oppression.

"Do not fear; speak out and Wisdom will guide you. Fall silent out of fear and Wisdom will depart you. But you will not feel fear because Wisdom herself is in you, and you and she are one.

"Formerly you were alone within yourselves; formerly you were solitary men. Now you have a companion who never sickens or fails or dies; you are bonded to the eternal and will shine like the healing sun itself.

"As you go back into the world I will guide you from day to day. And when you die I will notice and come to pick you up; I will carry you in my arms back to your home, out of which you came and back to which you go.

"You are strangers here, but you are hardly strangers to me; I have known you since the start. This has not been your world, but I will make it your world; I will change it for you. Fear not. What assails you will perish and you will thrive.

"These are things which shall be because I speak with the authority given me by my father. You are the true god and you will prevail."

There was silence, then. Sophia had ceased speaking to us.

"What are you reading?" Kevin said, pointing to the book.

The girl said, "*SEPHER YEZIRAH.* I will read to you; listen." She set the book down, closing it. " 'God has also set the one over against the other; the good against the evil, and the evil against the good; the good proceeds from the good, and the evil from the evil; the good purifies the bad, and the bad the good; the good is preserved for the good, and the evil for the bad ones.' " Sophia paused a moment and then said, "This means that good will make evil into what evil does not wish to be; but evil will not be able to make good into what good does not wish to be. Evil serves good, despite its cunning." Then she said nothing; she sat silently, with her animals and with us.

"Could you tell us about your parents?" I said. "I mean, if we are to know what to do—"

Sophia said, "Go wherever I send you and you will know what to do. There is no place where I am not. When you leave here you will not see me, but later you will see me again.

"You will not see me but I will always see you; I am mindful of you continually. So I am with you whether you know it or not; but I say to you, Know that I accompany you, even down into the prison, if the tyrant puts you there.

"There is no more. Go back home, and I will instruct you as the time requires." She smiled at us.

"You're how old?" I said.

"I am two years old."

"And you're reading that book?" Kevin said.

Sophia said, "I tell you in truth, in very truth, none of you will forget me. And I tell you that all of you will see me again. You did not choose me; I chose you. I called you here. I sent for you four years ago."

"Okay," I said. That placed her call at 1974.

"If the Lamptons ask you what I said, say that we talked about the commune to be built," Sophia said. "Do not tell them that I sent you away from them. But you are to go away from them; this is your answer: you will have nothing further to do with them."

Kevin pointed to the tape recorder, its drums turning.

"What they will hear on it," Sophia said, "when they play it back, will be only the *SEPHER YEZIRAH*, nothing more."

Wow, I thought.

I believed her.

"I will not fail you," Sophia repeated, smiling at the three of us.

I believed that, too.

As the three of us walked back to the house, Kevin said, "Was all that just quotations from the Bible?"

"No," I said.

"No," David agreed. "There was something new; that part about us being our own gods, now. That the time had come where we no longer had to believe in any deity other than ourselves."

"What a beautiful child," I said, thinking to myself how much she reminded me of my own son Christopher.

"We're very lucky," David said huskily. "To have met her." Turning to me he said, "She'll be with us; she said so. I believe it. She'll be inside us; we won't be alone. I never realized it before but we are alone. Everybody is alone—has been alone,

I mean. Up until now. She's going to spread out all over the world, isn't she? Into everyone, eventually. Starting with us."

"The Rhipidon Society," I said, "has four members. Sophia and the three of us."

"That's still not very many," Kevin said.

"The mustard seed," I said. "That grows into a tree so large that birds can roost in it."

"Come off it," Kevin said.

"What's the matter?" I asked.

Kevin said, "We have to get our stuff together and get out of here; she said so. The Lamptons are whacked out flipped-out freaks. They could zap us anytime."

"Sophia will protect us," David said.

"A two-year-old child?" Kevin said.

We both gazed at him.

"Okay, two-thousand-year-old child," Kevin said.

"The only person who could make jokes about the Savior," David said. "I'm surprised you didn't ask her about your dead cat."

Kevin halted; a look of genuine baffled anger appeared on his face; obviously he had forgotten to: he had missed his chance.

"I'm going back," he said.

Together, David and I propelled him along with us.

"I'm not kidding!" he said, with fury.

"What's the matter?" I said; we halted.

"I want to talk to her some more. I'm not going to walk off out of here; goddam it, I'm going back—let me the fuck *go*!"

"Listen," I said. "She told us to leave."

"And she'll be inside us talking to us," David said.

"We'll hear what I call the AI voice," I said.

Kevin said savagely, "And there'll be lemonade fountains and gumdrop trees. I'm going back."

Ahead of us, Eric and Linda Lampton emerged from the big house and walked toward us.

"Confrontation time," I said.

"Aw shit," Kevin said, in desperation. "I'm still going back." He pulled away from us and hurried in the direction from which we had come.

"Did it work out well?" Linda Lampton said, when she and her husband reached David and me.

"Fine," I said.

"What did you discuss?" Eric said.

I said, "The commune."

"Very good," Linda said. "Why is Kevin going back? What is he going to say to Sophia?"

David said, "Has to do with his dead cat."

"Ask him to come here," Eric said.

"Why?" I said.

"We are going to discuss your relationship to the commune," Eric said. "The Rhipidon Society should be part of the major commune, in our opinion. Brent Mini suggested that; we really should talk about it. We find you acceptable."

"I'll get Kevin," David said.

"Eric," I said, "we're returning to Santa Ana."

"There's time to discuss your involvement with the commune," Linda said. "Your Air Cal flight's not until eight tonight, is it? You can have dinner with us."

Eric Lampton said, "VALIS summoned you people here. You will go when VALIS feels you are ready to go."

"VALIS feels we're ready to go," I said.

"I'll get Kevin," David said.

Eric said, "I'll go get him." He passed on by David and me, in the direction of Kevin and the girl.

Folding her arms, Linda said, "You can't go back down south yet. Mini wants to talk over a number of matters with you. Keep in mind that his time is short. He's weakening fast. Is Kevin really asking Sophia about his dead cat? What's so important about a dead cat?"

"To Kevin the cat is very important," I said.

"That's right," David agreed. "To Kevin the cat's death represents everything that's wrong with the universe; he believes that Sophia can explain it to him, which by that I mean everything that's wrong with the universe—undeserved suffering and loss."

Linda said, "I don't really think he's talking about his dead cat."

"He really is," I said.

"You don't know Kevin," David said. "Maybe he's talking about other things because this is his chance to talk to the Savior finally but his dead cat is a major matter in what he's talking about."

"I think we should go over to Kevin," Linda said, "and tell him that he's talked to Sophia enough. What do you mean, VALIS feels you are ready to go? Did Sophia say that?"

A voice in my head spoke. *Tell her radiation bothers you.* It was the AI voice which Horselover Fat had heard since March 1974; I recognized it.

"The radiation," I said. "It—" I hesitated; understanding of the terse sentence came to me. "I'm half-blind," I said. "A beam of pink light hit me; it must have been the sun. Then I realized we should get back."

"VALIS fired information directly to you," Linda said, at once, alertly.

You don't know.

"I don't know," I said. "But I felt different afterward. As if I had something important to do down south in Santa Ana. We know other people . . . there are other people we could get into the Rhipidon Society. They should come to the commune, too. VALIS has caused them to have visions; they come to us for explanations. We told them about the film, about seeing the film Mother Goose made; they're all seeing it, and getting a lot out of it. We've got more people going to see *Valis* than I thought we knew; they must be telling their friends. My own contacts in Hollywood—the producers and actors I know, and especially the money people—are very interested in what I've pointed out to them. There's one MGM producer in particular that might want to finance Mother Goose in another film, a high-budget film; he says he has the backing already."

My flow of talk amazed me; it seemed to come out of nothing. It was as if it wasn't me talking, but someone else; someone who knew exactly what to say to Linda Lampton.

"What's the producer's name?" Linda said.

"Art Rockoway," I said, the name coming into my head as if on cue.

"What films does he have?" Linda said.

"The one about the nuclear wastes that contaminated most of central Utah," I said. "That disaster the newspapers reported two years ago but TV was afraid to talk about; the government put pressure on them. Where all the sheep died. The cover-story that it was nerve gas. Rockoway did a hard-ball film in which the true tale of calculated indifference by the authorities came out."

"Who starred?" Linda said.

"Robert Redford," I said.

"Well, we would be interested," Linda said.

"So we should get back to southern California," I said. "We have a number of people in Hollywood to talk to."

"Eric!" Linda called; she walked toward her husband, who stood with Kevin; he now had Kevin by the arm.

Glancing at me, David made a signal that we should follow; together, the three of us approached Kevin and Eric. Not far off, Sophia ignored us; she continued to read her book.

A flash of pink light blinded me.

"Oh my God," I said.

I could not see; I put my hands against my forehead, which ached and throbbed as if it would burst.

"What's wrong?" David said. I could hear a low humming, like a vacuum cleaner. I opened my eyes, but nothing other than pink light swam around me.

"Phil, are you okay?" Kevin said.

The pink light ebbed. We were in three seats aboard a jet. Yet at the same time, superimposed over the seats of the jet, the wall, the other passengers, lay the brown dry field, Linda Lampton, the house not far off. Two places, two times.

"Kevin," I said. "What time is it?" I could see nothing out the window of the jet but darkness; the interior lights over the passengers were, for the most part, on. It was night. Yet, bright sunlight streamed down on the brown field, on the Lamptons and Kevin and David. The hum of the jet engines continued; I felt myself sway slightly: the plane had turned. Now I saw many far-off lights beyond the window. We're over Los Angeles, I realized. And still the warm daytime sun streamed down on me.

"We'll be landing in five minutes," Kevin said.

Time dysfunction, I realized.

The brown field ebbed out. Eric and Linda Lampton ebbed out. The sunlight ebbed out.

Around me the plane became substantial. David sat reading a paperback book of T.S. Eliot. Kevin seemed tense.

"We're almost there," I said. "Orange County Airport."

Kevin said nothing; he had hunched over, broodingly.

"They let us go?" I said.

"What?" He glanced at me irritably.

"I was just there," I said. Now the memory of the intervening events bled into my mind. The protests of the Lamptons and by Brent Mini—him most of all; they had implored us not to go, but we had gotten away. Here we were on the Air Cal flight back. We were safe.

There had been a twin-pronged thrust by Mini and the Lamptons.

"You won't tell anyone on the outside about Sophia?" Linda had said anxiously. "Can we swear you three to silence?" Naturally they had agreed. This anxiety had been one of the prongs, the negative prong. The other had been positive, an inducement.

"Look at it this way," Eric had said, backed up by Mini who seemed genuinely crestfallen that the Rhipidon Society, small as it was, had decided to depart. "This is the most important event in human history; you don't want to be left out, do you? And after all, VALIS picked you out. We get literally thousands of letters on the film, and only a few people here and there seem to have been contacted by VALIS, as you were. *We are a privileged group.*"

"This is the Call," Mini had said, almost imploringly to the three of us.

"Yes," Linda and Eric had echoed. "This is the Call mankind has waited centuries for. Read *Revelation*; read what it says about the Elect. We are God's Elect!"

"Guess so," I had said as they left us off by the car we had rented; we had parked near Gino's, on a sidestreet of Sonoma which allowed prolonged parking.

Going up to me, Linda Lampton had put her hands on my shoulders and had kissed me on the mouth—with intensity and a certain amount, in fact a great amount, of erotic fervor. "Come back to us," she had whispered in my ear. "You promise? This is our future; it belongs to a very few, a very, very few." To which I had thought, You couldn't be more wrong, honey; this belongs to everyone.

So now we were almost home. Crucially assisted by VALIS. Or, as I preferred to think of it, by St. Sophia. Putting it that way kept my attention on the image in my mind of the girl Sophia, seated with the animals and her book.

As we stood in the Orange County Airport, waiting for our luggage, I said, "They weren't strictly honest with us. For instance, they told us everything Sophia said and did was audio and video taped. That's not so."

"You may be wrong about that," Kevin said. "There are sophisticated monitoring systems now that work on remote. She may have been under their range even though we couldn't spot them. Mini is really what he says he is: a master at electronic hardware."

I thought, Mini, who was willing to die in order to experience VALIS once more. Was I? In 1974 I had experienced him once; ever since I had hungered for him to return—ached in my bones; my body felt it as much as my mind, perhaps more so. But VALIS was right to be judicious. It showed his concern for human life, his unwillingness to manifest himself to me again.

The original encounter had, after all, almost killed me. I could again see VALIS, but, as with Mini, it would slay me. And I did not want that; I had too many things to do.

What exactly did I have to do? I didn't know. None of us knew. Already I had heard the AI voice in my head, and others would hear that voice, more and more people. VALIS, as living information, would penetrate the world, replicating in human brains, crossbonding with them and assisting them, guiding them, at a subliminal level, which is to say invisibly. No given human could be certain if he were crossbonded until the symbiosis reached flashpoint. In his concourse with other humans a given person would not know when he was dealing with another homoplasmate and when he would not.

Perhaps the ancient signs of secret identification would return; more likely they already had. During a handshake, a motion with one finger of two intersecting arcs: swift expression of the fish symbol, which no one beyond the two persons involved could discern.

I remembered back to an incident—more than an incident
—involving my son Christopher. In March 1974 during the
time that VALIS overruled me, held control of my mind, I had
conducted a correct and complex initiation of Christopher into
the ranks of the immortals. VALIS's medical knowledge had
saved Christopher's physical life, but VALIS had not ended it
there.

This was an experience which I treasured. It had been done
in utter stealth, concealed even from my son's mother.

First I had fixed a mug of hot chocolate. Then I had fixed a
hot dog on a bun with the usual trimmings; Christopher,
young as he was, loved hot dogs and warm chocolate.

Seated on the floor in Christopher's room with him, I—or
rather VALIS in me, as me—had played a game. First, I jokingly
held the cup of chocolate up, over my son's head; then, as if
by accident, I had splashed warm chocolate on his head, into
his hair. Giggling, Christopher had tried to wipe the liquid
off; I had of course helped him. Leaning toward him, I had
whispered,

"In the name of the Son, the Father and the Holy Spirit."

No one heard me except Christopher. Now, as I wiped the
warm chocolate from his hair, I inscribed the sign of the cross
on his forehead. I had now baptized him and now I confirmed
him; I did so, not by the authority of any church, but by the
authority of the living plasmate in me: VALIS himself. Next I
said to my son, "Your secret name, your Christian name, is—"
And I told him what it was. Only he and I are ever to know; he
and I and VALIS.

Next, I took a bit of the bread from the hot dog bun and
held it forth; my son—still a baby, really—opened his mouth
like a little bird, and I placed the bit of bread in it. We seemed,
the two of us, to be sharing a meal; an ordinary, simple, common meal.

For some reason it seemed essential—quite crucial—that he
take no bite of the hot dog meat itself. Pork could not be eaten
under these circumstances; VALIS filled me with this urgent
knowledge.

As Christopher started to close his mouth to chew on the bit
of bread, I presented him with the mug of warm chocolate. To
my surprise—being so young he still drank normally from his

bottle, never from a cup—he reached eagerly to take the mug; as he took it, lifted it to his lips and drank from it, I said,

"This is my blood and this is my body."

My little son drank, and I took the mug back. The greater sacraments had been accomplished. Baptism, then confirmation, then the most holy sacrament of all, the Eucharist: sacrament of the Lord's Supper.

"The Blood of our Lord Jesus Christ, which was shed for thee, preserve thy body and soul unto everlasting life. Drink this in remembrance that Christ's Blood was shed for thee, and be thankful."

This moment is most solemn of all. The priest himself has become Christ; it is Christ who offers his body and blood to the faithful, by a divine miracle.

Most people understand that in the miracle of transubstantiation the wine (or warm chocolate) becomes the Sacred Blood, and the wafer (or bit of hot dog bun) becomes the Sacred Body, but few people even within the churches realize that the figure who stands before them holding the cup is their Lord, living now. *Time has been overcome.* We are back almost two thousand years; we are not in Santa Ana, California, U.S.A., but in Jerusalem, about 35 C.E.

What I had seen in March 1974 when I saw the superimposition of ancient Rome and modern California consisted of an actual witnessing of what is normally seen by the inner eyes of faith only.

My double-exposure experience had confirmed the literal—not merely figurative—truth of the miracle of the Mass.

As I have said, the technical term for this is anamnesis: the loss of forgetfulness; which is to say, the remembering of the Lord and the Lord's Supper.

I was present that day, the last time the disciples sat at table. You may believe me; you may not. *Sed per spiritum sanctum dico; haec veritas est. Mihi crede et mecum in aeternitate vivebis.*

My Latin is probably faulty, but what I am trying to say, haltingly, is: "But I speak by means of the Holy Spirit; this is so. Believe me and you shall live with me in eternity."

Our luggage showed up; we turned our claim-checks over to the uniformed cop, and, ten minutes later, were driving north on the freeway toward Santa Ana and home.

13

As he drove, Kevin said, "I'm tired. Really tired. Fuck this traffic! Who are these people driving on the 55? Where do they come from? Where are they going?"

I wondered to myself, Where are the three of us going?

We had seen the Savior and I had, after eight years of madness, been healed.

Well, I thought, that's something to accomplish all in one weekend . . . not to mention escaping intact from the three most whacked-out humans on the planet.

It is amazing that when someone else spouts the nonsense you yourself believe you can readily perceive it as nonsense. In the VW Rabbit as I had listened to Linda and Eric rattle on about being three-eyed people from another planet I had known they were nuts. This made me nuts, too. The realization had frightened me: the realization about them and about myself.

I had flown up crazy and returned sane, yet I believed that I had met the Savior . . . in the form of a little girl with black hair and fierce black eyes who had discoursed to us with more wisdom than any adult I had ever met. And, when we were blocked in our attempt to leave, she—or VALIS—had intervened.

"We have a commission," David said. "To go forth and—"

"And what?" Kevin said.

"She'll tell us as we go along," David said.

"And pigs can whistle," Kevin said.

"Look," David said vigorously. "Phil's okay now, for the first time . . ." He hesitated.

"Since you've known me," I finished.

David said, "She healed him. Healing powers are the absolute certain sign of the material presence of the Messiah. You know that, Kevin."

"Then St. Joseph Hospital is the best church in town," Kevin said.

I said to Kevin, "Did you get a chance to ask Sophia about your dead cat?" I meant the question sarcastically, but Kevin, to my surprise, turned his head and said, seriously,

367

"Yep."

"What'd she say?" I said.

Kevin, inhaling deeply and gripping the steeringwheel tight, said, "She said that MY DEAD CAT . . ." He paused, raising his voice. "MY DEAD CAT WAS STUPID."

I had to laugh. David likewise. No one had thought to give Kevin that answer before. The cat saw the car and ran into it, not the other way around; it had ploughed directly into the right front wheel of the car, like a bowling ball.

"She said," Kevin said, "that the universe has very strict rules, and that *that* species of cat, the kind that runs head-first into moving cars, isn't around any more."

"Well," I said, "pragmatically speaking, she's right."

It was interesting to contrast Sophia's explanation with the late Sherri's; she had piously informed Kevin that God so loved his cat—actually—that God had seen fit to take Kevin's cat to be with him God instead of him Kevin. This is not an explanation you give to a twenty-nine-year-old man; this is an explanation you foist off on kids. Little kids. And even the little kids generally can see it's bullshit.

"But," Kevin continued, "I said to her, 'Why didn't God make my cat smart?'"

"Did this conversation really take place?" I said.

Resignedly, David said, "Probably so."

"My cat was STUPID," Kevin continued, "because GOD MADE IT STUPID. So it was GOD'S fault, not my cat's fault."

"And you told her that," I said.

"Yes," Kevin said.

I felt anger. "You cynical asshole—you meet the Savior and all you can do is rant about your goddam cat. I'm glad your cat's dead; *everybody* is glad your cat's dead. So shut up." I had begun to shake with fury.

"Easy," David murmured. "We've been through a lot."

To me, Kevin said, "She's not the Savior. We're all as nuts as you, Phil. They're nuts up there; we're nuts down here."

David said, "Then how could a two-year-old girl say such—"

"They had a *wire* running to her head," Kevin yelled, "and a microphone at the other end of the wire, and a speaker inside her face. It was somebody else talking."

"I need a drink," I said. "Let's stop at Sombrero Street."

"I liked you better when you believed you were Horselover Fat," Kevin yelled. "Him I liked. You're as stupid as my cat. If stupidity kills, why aren't you dead?"

"You want to try to arrange it?" I said.

"Obviously stupidity is a survival trait," Kevin said, but his voice sank, now, into near-inaudibility. "I don't know," he murmured. "'The Savior.' How can it be? It's my fault; I took you to see *Valis*. I got you mixed up with Mother Goose. Does it make sense that Mother Goose would give birth to the Savior? Does any of this make sense?"

"Stop at Sombrero Street," David said.

"The Rhipidon Society holds its meetings in a bar," Kevin said. "That's our commission; to sit in a bar and drink. That'll sure save the world. And why save it anyhow?"

We drove on in silence, but we did end up at Sombrero Street; the majority of the Rhipidon Society had voted in favor of it.

Certainly it constitutes bad news if the people who agree with you are buggier than batshit. Sophia herself (and this is important) had said that Eric and Linda Lampton were ill. In addition to that, Sophia or VALIS had provided me with the words to get us out of there when the Lamptons had closed in on us, hemming us in—had provided words and then tinkered expertly with time.

I could separate the beautiful child from the ugly Lamptons. I did not lump them together. Significantly, the two-year-old child had spoken what seemed like wisdom . . . sitting in the bar with my bottle of Mexican beer I asked myself, What are the criteria of rationality, by which to judge if wisdom is present? Wisdom has to be, by its very nature, rational; it is the final stage of what is locked into the real. There is an intimate relationship between what is wise and what exists, although that relationship is subtle. What had the little girl told us? That human beings should now give up the worship of all deities except mankind itself. This did not seem irrational to me. Whether it had been said by a child or whether it came from the *Britannica*, it would have struck me as sound.

For some time I had held the opinion that Zebra—as I had called the entity which manifested itself to me in March 1974 —was in fact the laminated totality of all my selves along the linear time-axis; Zebra—or VALIS—was the supra-temporal expression of a given human being and not a god . . . not unless the supra-temporal expression of a given human being is what we actually mean by the term "god," is what we worship, without realizing it, when we worship "god."

The hell with it, I thought wearily. I give up.

Kevin drove me home; I went at once to bed, worn-out and discouraged, in a vague way. I think what discouraged me about the situation was the uncertainty of our commission, received from Sophia. We had a mandate but for what? More important, what did Sophia intend to do as she matured? Remain with the Lamptons? Escape, change her name, move to Japan and start a new life?

Where would she surface? Where would we find mention of her over the years? Would we have to wait until she grew to adulthood? That might be eighteen years. In eighteen years Ferris F. Fremount, to use the name from the film, could have taken over the world—again. We needed help now.

But then I thought, You always need the Savior now. Later is always too late.

When I fell asleep that night I had a dream. In the dream I rode in Kevin's Honda, but instead of Kevin driving, Linda Ronstadt sat behind the wheel, and the car was open, like a vehicle from ancient times, like a chariot. Smiling at me, Ronstadt sang, and she sang more beautifully than any time I had ever heard her sing before. She sang:

> "To walk toward the dawn
> You must put your slippers on."

In the dream this delighted me; it seemed a terribly important message. When I woke up the next morning I could still see her lovely face, the dark, glowing eyes: such large eyes, so filled with light, a strange kind of black light, like the light of stars. Her look toward me was one of intense love, but not sexual love; it was what the Bible calls loving-kindness. Where was she driving me?

During the next day I tried to figure out what the cryptic words referred to. Slippers. Dawn. What did I associate with the dawn?

Studying my reference books (at one time I would have said,

"Horselover Fat, studying his reference books"), I came across the fact that Aurora is the Latin word for the personification of the dawn. And that suggests Aurora Borealis—which looks like St. Elmo's Fire, which is how Zebra or VALIS looked. The *Britannica* says of the Aurora Borealis:

> "The Aurora Borealis appears throughout history in the mythology of the Eskimo, the Irish, the English, the Scandinavians, and others; it was usually believed to be a supernatural manifestation . . . Northern Germanic tribes saw in it the splendor of the shields of Valkyrie (warrior women)."

Did that mean—was VALIS telling me—that little Sophia would issue forth into the world as a "warrior woman"? Maybe so.

What about slippers? I could think of one association, an interesting one. Empedocles, the pupil of Pythagoras, who had gone public about remembering his past lives and who told his friends privately that he was Apollo, had never died in the usual sense; instead, his golden slippers had been found near the top of the volcano Mount Etna. Either Empedocles, like Elijah, had been taken up into heaven bodily, or he had jumped into the volcano. Mount Etna is in the eastern-most part of Sicily. In Roman times the word "aurora" literally meant "east." Was VALIS alluding to both itself and to re-birth, to eternal life? Was I being—

The phone rang.

Picking it up I said, "Hello."

I heard Eric Lampton's voice. It sounded twisted, like an old root, a dying root. "We have something to tell you. I'll let Linda tell you. Hold on."

A deep fear entered me as I stood holding the silent phone. Then Linda Lampton's voice sounded in my ear, flat and toneless. The dream had to do with her, I realized; Linda Ronstadt; Linda Lampton. "What is it?" I said, unable to understand what Linda Lampton was saying.

"The little girl is dead," Linda Lampton said. "Sophia."

"How?" I said.

"Mini killed her. By accident. The police are here. With a laser. He was trying to—"

I hung up.

The phone rang again almost at once. I picked it up and said hello.

Linda Lampton said, "Mini wanted to try to get as much information—"

"Thanks for telling me," I said. Crazily, I felt bitter anger, not sorrow.

"He was trying information-transfer by laser," Linda was saying. "We're calling everyone. We don't understand; if Sophia was the Savior, how could she die?"

Dead at two years old, I realized. Impossible.

I hung up the phone and sat down. After a time, I realized that the woman in the dream driving the car and singing had been Sophia, but grown up, as she would have been one day. The dark eyes filled with light and life and fire.

The dream was her way of saying good-bye.

14

THE newspapers and TV carried an account of Mother Goose's daughter's death. Naturally, since Eric Lampton was a rock star, the implication was made that sinister forces had been at work, probably having to do with neglect or drugs or weird stuff generally. Mini's face was shown, and then some clips from the film *Valis* in which the fortress-like mixer appeared.

Two or three days later, everyone had forgotten about it. Other horrors occupied the TV screen. Other tragedies took place. As always. A liquor store in West L.A. got robbed and the clerk shot. An old man died at a substandard nursing home. Three cars on the San Diego Freeway collided with a lumber truck which had caught on fire and stalled.

The world continued as it always had.

I began to think about death. Not Sophia Lampton's death but death in general and then, by degrees, my own death.

Actually, I didn't think about it. Horselover Fat did.

One night, as he sat in my living room in my easy chair, a glass of cognac in his hand, he said meditatively, "All it proved was what we knew anyhow; her death, I mean."

"And what did we know?" I said.

"That they were nuts."

I said, "The parents were nuts. But not Sophia."

"If she had been Zebra," Fat said, "she would have had foreknowledge of Mini's screw-up with the laser equipment. She could have averted it."

"Sure," I said.

"It's true," Fat said. "She would have had the knowledge and in addition—" He pointed at me. Triumph lay in his voice; bold triumph. "She would have had the power to avert it. Right? If she could overthrow Ferris F. Fremount—"

"Drop it," I said.

"All that was involved from the start," Fat said quietly, "was advanced laser technology. Mini found a way to transmit information by laser beam, using human brains as transducers without the need for an electronic interface. The Russians can do the same thing. Microwaves can be used as well. In March 1974 I must have intercepted one of Mini's transmissions by accident; it irradiated me. That's why my blood pressure went up so high, and the animals died of cancer. That's what's killing Mini; the radiation produced by his own laser experimentations."

I said nothing. There was nothing to say.

Fat said, "I'm sorry. Will you be okay?"

"Sure," I said.

"After all," Fat said, "I never really got a chance to talk to her, not to the extent that the rest of you did; I wasn't there that second time, when she gave us—the Society—our commission."

And now, I wondered, what about our commission?

"Fat," I said, "you're not going to try to knock yourself off again, are you? Because of her death?"

"No," Fat said.

I didn't believe him. I could tell; I knew him, better than he knew himself. Gloria's death, Beth abandoning him, Sherri dying—all that had saved him after Sherri died was his decision to go in search of the "fifth Savior," and now that hope had perished. What did he have left?

Fat had tried everything, and everything had failed.

"Maybe you should start seeing Maurice again," I said.

"He'll say, 'And I mean it.'" We both laughed. "'I want you to list the ten things you want most to do in all the world; I want you to think about it and write them down, and I mean it!'"

I said, "What do you want to do?" And I meant it.

"Find her," Fat said.

"Who?" I said.

"I don't know," Fat said. "The one that died. The one that I will never see again."

There're a lot of them in that category, I said to myself. Sorry, Fat; your answer is too vague.

"I should go over to World-Wide Travel," Fat said, half to himself, "and talk to the lady there some more. About India. I have a feeling India is the place."

"Place for what?"

"Where he'll be," Fat said.

I did not respond; there was no point to it. Fat's madness had returned.

"He's somewhere," Fat said. "I know he is, right now; somewhere in the world. Zebra told me. 'St. Sophia is going to be born again; she wasn't—' "

"You want me to tell you the truth?" I interrupted.

Fat blinked. "Sure, Phil."

In a harsh voice, I said, "There is no Savior. St. Sophia will not be born again, the Buddha is not in the park, the Head Apollo is not about to return. Got it?"

Silence.

"The fifth Savior—" Fat began timidly.

"Forget it," I said. "You're psychotic, Fat. You're as crazy as Eric and Linda Lampton. You're as crazy as Brent Mini. You've been crazy for eight years, since Gloria tossed herself off the Synanon Building and made herself into a scrambled egg sandwich. Give up and forget. Okay? Will you do me that one favor? Will you do *all* of us that one favor?"

Fat said finally, in a low voice, "Then you agree with Kevin."

"Yes," I said. "I agree with Kevin."

"Then why should I keep on going?" Fat said quietly.

"I don't know," I said. "And I don't really care. It's your life and your affair, not mine."

"Zebra wouldn't have lied to me," Fat said.

"There is no 'Zebra,' " I said. "It's yourself. Don't you recognize your own self? It's you and only you, projecting your unanswered wishes out, unfulfilled desires left over after Gloria did herself in. You couldn't fill the vacuum with reality so you filled it with fantasy; it was psychological compensation for a fruitless, wasted, empty, pain-filled life and I don't see why you don't finally now fucking give up; you're like Kevin's cat: you're stupid. That is the beginning and the end of it. Okay?"

"You rob me of hope."

"I rob you of nothing because there is nothing."

"Is all this so? You think so? Really?"

I said, "I know so."

"You don't think I should look for him?"

"Where the hell are you going to look? You have no idea, no idea in the world, where he might be. He could be in Ireland.

He could be in Mexico City. He could be in Anaheim at Disneyland; yeah—maybe he's working at Disneyland, pushing a broom. How are you going to recognize him? We all thought Sophia was the Savior; we believed in that until the day she died. She *talked* like the Savior. We had all the evidence; we had all the signs. We had the flick *Valis*. We had the two-word cypher. We had the Lamptons and Mini. Their story fit your story; everything fit. And now there's another dead girl in another box in the ground—that makes three in all. Three people who died for nothing. You believed it, I believed it, David believed it, Kevin believed it, the Lamptons believed it; Mini in particular believed it, enough to accidentally kill her. So now it ends. It never should have begun—goddam Kevin for seeing that film! Go out and kill yourelf. The hell with it."

"I still might—"

"You won't," I said. "You won't find him. I know. Let me put it to you in a simple way so you can grasp it. You thought the Savior would bring Gloria back—right? He, she, didn't; now she's dead, too. Instead of—" I gave up.

"Then the true name for religion," Fat said, "is death."

"The secret name," I agreed. "You got it. Jesus died; Asklepios died—they killed Mani worse than they killed Jesus, but nobody even cares; nobody even remembers. They killed the Catharists in southern France by the tens of thousands. In the Thirty Years War, hundreds of thousands of people died, Protestants and Catholics—mutual slaughter. Death is the real name for it; not God, not the Savior, not love—*death*. Kevin is right about his cat. It's all there in his dead cat. The Great Judge can't answer Kevin: 'Why did my cat die?' Answer: 'Damned if I know.' There is no answer; there is only a dead animal that just wanted to cross the street. We're all animals that want to cross the street only something mows us down half-way across that we never saw. Go ask Kevin. 'Your cat was stupid.' Who made the cat? Why did he make the cat stupid? Did the cat learn by being killed, and if so, what did he learn? Did Sherri learn anything from dying of cancer? Did Gloria learn anything—"

"Okay, enough," Fat said.

"Kevin is right," I said. "Go out and get laid."

"By who? They're all dead."

I said, "There're more. Still alive. Lay one of them before

she dies or you die or somebody dies, some person or animal. You said it yourself: the universe is irrational because the mind behind it is irrational. You are irrational and you know it. *I* am. We all are and we know it, on some level. I'd write a book about it but no one would believe a group of human beings could be as irrational as we are, as we've acted."

"They would now," Fat said, "after Jim Jones and the nine hundred people at Jonestown."

"Go away, Fat," I said. "Go to South America. Go back up to Sonoma and apply for residence at the Lamptons' commune, unless they've given up, which I doubt. Madness has its own dynamism; it just goes on." Getting to my feet I walked over and stuck my hand against his chest. "The girl is dead, Gloria is dead; nothing will restore her."

"Sometimes I dream—"

"I'll put that on your gravestone."

After he had obtained his passport, Fat left the United States and flew by Icelandic Airlines to Luxembourg, which is the cheapest way to go. We got a postcard from him mailed at his stop-over in Iceland, and then, a month later, a letter from Metz, France. Metz lies on the border to Luxembourg; I looked it up on the map.

In Metz—which he liked, as a scenic place—he met a girl and enjoyed a wonderful time until she took him for half of the money he'd brought with him. He sent us a photograph of her; she is very pretty, reminding me a little of Linda Ronstadt, with the same shape face and haircut. It was the last picture he sent us, because the girl stole his camera as well. She worked at a bookstore. Fat never told us whether he got to go to bed with her.

From Metz he crossed over into West Germany, where the American dollar is worth nothing. He already read and spoke a little German so he had a relatively easy time there. But his letters became less frequent and finally stopped completely.

"If he'd have made it with the French girl," Kevin said, "he'd have recovered."

"For all we know he did," David said.

Kevin said, "If he'd made it with her he'd be back here sane. He's not, so he didn't."

A year passed. One day I got a mailgram from him; Fat had flown back to the United States, to New York. He knows people there. He would be arriving in California, he said, when he got over his mono; in Europe he had been hit by mono.

"But did he find the Savior?" Kevin said. The mailgram didn't say. "It would say if he had," Kevin said. "It's like with that French girl; we'd have heard."

"At least he isn't dead," David said.

Kevin said, "It depends on how you define 'dead.' "

Meanwhile I had been doing fine; my books sold well, now —I had more money put away than I knew what to do with. In fact we were all doing well. David ran a tobacco shop at the city shopping mall, one of the most elegant malls in Orange County; Kevin's new girlfriend treated him and us gently and with tact, putting up with our gallows sense of humor, especially Kevin's. We had told her all about Fat and his quest—and the French girl fleecing him right down to his Pentax camera. She looked forward to meeting him and we looked forward to his return: stories and pictures and maybe presents! we said to ourselves.

And then we received a second mailgram. This time from Portland, Oregon. It read:

KING FELIX

Nothing more. Just those two startling words. Well? I thought. Did he? Is that what he's telling us? Does the Rhipidon Society reconvene in plenary session after all this time?

It hardly mattered to us. Collectively and individually we barely remembered. It was a part of our lives we preferred to forget. Too much pain; too many hopes down the tube.

When Fat arrived in LAX, which is the designation for the Los Angeles Airport, the four of us met him: me, Kevin, David and Kevin's foxy girl friend Ginger, a tall girl with blonde hair braided and with bits of red ribbon in the braids, a colorful lady who liked to drive miles and miles late at night to drink Irish coffee at some out-of-the-way Irish bar.

With all the rest of the people in the world we milled around and conversed, and then all at once, unexpectedly, there came Horselover Fat striding toward us in the midst of the gang of other passengers. Grinning, carrying a briefcase; our friend back home. He wore a suit and tie, a good-looking East Coast suit, fashionable in the extreme. It shocked us to see him so well-dressed; we had anticipated, I guess, some emaciated hollow-eyed remnant scarcely able to hobble down the corridor.

After we'd hugged him and introduced him to Ginger we asked him how he'd been.

"Not bad," he said.

We ate at the restaurant at a top-of-the-line nearby hotel. Not much talk took place, for some reason. Fat seemed withdrawn, but not actually depressed. Tired, I decided. He had traveled a long way; it was inscribed on his face. Those things show up; they leave their mark.

"What's in the briefcase?" I said when our after-dinner coffee came.

Pushing aside the dishes before him, Fat laid down the briefcase and unsnapped it; it wasn't key-locked. In it he had manila folders, one of which he lifted out after sorting among them; they bore numbers. He examined it a last time to be sure he had the right one and then he handed it to me.

"Look in it," he said, smiling slightly, as you do when you have given someone a present which you know will please him and he is unwrapping it before your eyes.

I opened it. In the folder I found four 8 × 10 glossy photos, obviously professionally done; they looked like the kind of stills that the publicity departments of movie studios put out.

The photos showed a Greek vase, on it a painting of a male figure who we recognized as Hermes.

Twined around the vase the double helix confronted us, done in red glaze against a black background. The DNA molecule. There could be no mistake.

"Twenty-three or -four hundred years ago," Fat said. "Not the picture but the *krater*, the pottery."

"A pot," I said.

"I saw it in a museum at. Athens. It's authentic. That's not a matter of my opinion; I'm not qualified to judge such matters; its authenticity has been established by the museum authorities. I talked with one of them. He hadn't realized what the design shows; he was very interested when I discussed it with him. This form of vase, the *krater*, was the shape used later as the baptismal font. That was one of the Greek words that came

into my head in March 1974, the word '*krater*.' I heard it connected with another Greek word: '*poros*.' The words 'poros
krater' essentially mean '*limestone font*.' "

There could be no doubt; the design, predating Christianity,
was Crick and Watson's double helix model at which they had
arrived after so many wrong guesses, so much trial-and-error
work. Here it was, faithfully reproduced.

"Well?" I said.

"The so-called intertwined snakes of the caduceus. Originally the caduceus, which is still the symbol of medicine was
the staff of—not Hermes—but—" Fat paused, his eyes bright.
"Of Asklepios. It has a very specific meaning, besides that of
wisdom, which the snakes allude to; it shows that the bearer is
a sacred person and not to be molested . . . which is why
Hermes, the messenger of the gods, carried it."

None of us said anything for a time.

Kevin started to utter something sarcastic, something in his
dry, witty way, but he did not; he only sat without speaking.

Examining the 8 × 10 glossies, Ginger said, "How lovely!"

"The greatest physician in all human history," Fat said to her.
"Asklepios, the founder of Greek medicine. The Roman Emperor Julian—known to us as Julian the Apostate because he renounced Christianity—considered Asklepios as God or a god;
Julian worshipped him. If that worship had continued, the entire
history of the Western world would have basically changed."

"You won't give up," I said to Fat.

"No," Fat agreed. "I never will. I'm going back—I ran out
of money. When I've gotten the funds together, I'm going back.
I know where to look, now. The Greek islands. Lemnos,
Lesbos, Crete. Especially Crete. I dreamed I descended in an
elevator—in fact I had this dream twice—and the elevator operator recited in verse, and there was a huge plate of spaghetti
with a three-pronged fork, a trident, stuck in it . . . that
would be Ariadne's thread by which she led Theseus out of the
maze under Minos after he slew the Minotaur. The Minotaur,
being half man and half beast is a monster which represents the
demented deity Samael, in my opinion, the false demiurge of
the Gnostics' system."

"The two-word mailgram," I said. " 'KING FELIX.' "

Fat said, "I didn't find him."

"I see," I said.

"But he is somewhere," Fat said. "I know it. I will never give up." He returned the photos to their manila folder, put it back in the briefcase and closed it up.

Today he is in Turkey. He sent us a postcard showing the mosque which used to be the great Christian church called St. Sophia or Hagia Sophia, one of the wonders of the world, even though the roof collapsed during the Middle Ages and had to be rebuilt. You'll find schematics of its unique construction in most comprehensive textbooks on architecture. The central portion of the church seems to float, as if rising to heaven; anyhow that was the idea the Roman emperor Justinian had when he built it. He personally supervised the construction and he himself named it, a code name for Christ.

We will hear from Horselover Fat again. Kevin says so and I trust his judgment. Kevin would know. Kevin out of all of us has the least irrationality and, what matters more, the most faith. This is something it took me a long time to understand about him.

Faith is strange. It has to do, by definition, with things you can't prove. For example, this last Saturday morning I had the TV set on; I wasn't really watching it, since on Saturday morning there's nothing but kids' shows, and anyhow I don't watch daytime TV; I sometimes find it diminishes my loneliness, so I do turn it on as background. Anyhow, last Saturday they ran the usual string of commercials and for some reason at one point my conscious attention was attracted; I stopped what I had been doing and became fully alert.

The TV station had run an ad for a supermarket chain; on the screen the words FOOD KING appeared—and then they cut instantly, rushing their film along as fast as possible so as to squeeze in as many commercial messages as possible; what came next was a Felix the Cat cartoon, an old black-and-white cartoon. One moment FOOD KING appeared on the screen and then almost instantly the words—also in huge letters—FELIX THE CAT.

There it had been, the juxtaposed cypher, and in the proper order:

KING FELIX

But you would only pick it up subliminally. And who would be catching this accidental, purely accidental, juxtaposition? Only children, the little children of the Southland. It wouldn't mean anything to them; they would apprehend no two-word cypher, and even if they did they wouldn't understand what it meant, who it referred to.

But I had seen it and I knew who it referred to. It must be only synchronicity, as Jung calls it, I thought. Coincidence, without intent.

Or had the signal gone out? Out over the airwaves by one of the largest TV stations in the world, NBC's Los Angeles outlet, reaching many thousands of children with this split-second information which would be processed by the right hemispheres of their brains: received and stored and perhaps decoded, below the threshold of consciousness where many things lay slumbering and stored. And Eric and Linda Lampton had nothing to do with this. Just some board man, some technician at NBC with a whole stack of commercials to run, in any order he saw fit. It would have to be VALIS itself responsible, if anything had arranged the juxtaposition intentionally, VALIS which itself was information.

Maybe I had seen VALIS just now, riding a commercial and then a kids' cartoon.

The message has been sent out again, I said to myself.

Two days later Linda Lampton phoned me; I hadn't heard from the Lamptons since the tragedy. Linda sounded excited and happy.

"I'm pregnant," she said.

"Wonderful," I said. "How far along are you?"

"Eight months."

"Gee," I said, thinking, It won't be long.

"It won't be long now," Linda said.

"Are you hoping for a boy this time?" I said.

Linda said, "VALIS says it'll be another girl."

"Is Mini—"

"He died, I'm sorry to say. There was no chance, not with what he had. Isn't it wonderful? Another child?"

"Do you have a name picked out?" I said.

"Not yet," Linda said.

On the TV that night I happened to catch a commercial for

dog food. Dog food! At the very end, after listing various kinds of animals for which the company makes food—I forget the name of the company—a final coupling is stated:

"For the shepherd and the sheep."

A German shepherd dog is shown on the left and a great sheep on the right; immediately the station cut to another commercial which began with a sailboat silently passing across the screen. On the white sail I saw a small black emblem. Without looking more closely I knew what it was. On the sail the makers of the boat had placed a fish sign.

Shepherd and the sheep and then the fish, juxtaposed as had been KING FELIX. I don't know. I lack Kevin's faith and Fat's madness. But did I see consciously two quick messages fired off by VALIS in rapid succession, intended to strike us subliminally, one message really, telling us that the time had come? I don't know what to think. Maybe I am not required to think anything, or to have faith, or to have madness; maybe all I need to do—all that is asked of me—is to wait. To wait and to stay awake.

I waited, and one day I got a phonecall from Horselover Fat: a phonecall from Tokyo. He sounded healthy and excited and full of energy, and amused at my surprise to be hearing from him.

"Micronesia," he said.

"What?" I said, thinking that he had reverted back to the koine Greek again. And then I realized that he was referring to the group of small islands in the Pacific. "Oh," I said. "You've been there. The Carolines and Marshall Islands."

Fat said, "I'm going there; I haven't been, yet. The AI voice, the voice which I hear—it told me to look among the Micronesian Islands."

"Aren't they sort of little?" I said.

"That's why they call them that." He laughed.

"How many islands?" I asked, thinking ten or twenty.

"More than two thousand."

"Two thousand!" I felt dismay. "You could look forever. Can't the AI voice narrow it down?"

"I'm hoping it will. Maybe to Guam; I'm flying to Guam and starting there. By the time I'm finished, I'll get to see where a lot of World War Two took place."

I said, "Interesting that the AI voice is back to using Greek words."

"*Mikros* meaning small," Fat said, "and *nesoi* meaning islands. Maybe you're right; maybe it's just its propensity for reverting to Greek. But it's worth a try."

"You know what Kevin would say," I said. "About the simple, unspoiled native girls in those two thousand islands."

"I'll be the judge of that," Fat said.

He rang off and I hung up the phone feeling better; it was good news to hear from him, and to find him sounding so hearty.

I have a sense of the goodness of men, these days. I don't know where this sense came from—unless it came from Fat's phonecall—but I feel it. This is March again, now. I asked myself, Is Fat having another experience? Is the beam of pink light back, firing new and vaster information to him? Is it narrowing his search down?

His original experience had come in March, at the day after the vernal equinox. "Vernal," of course, means "spring." And "equinox" means the time when the sun's center crosses the equator and day and night are everywhere of equal length. So Horselover Fat encountered God or Zebra or VALIS or his own immortal self on the first day of the year which has a longer stretch of light than of darkness. Also, according to some scholars, it is the actual day of birth of Christ.

Seated before my TV set I watched and waited for another message, I, one of the members of the little Rhipidon Society which still, in my mind, existed. Like the satellite in miniature in the film *Valis*, the microform of it run over by the taxi as if it were an empty beer can in the gutter, the symbols of the divine show up in our world initially at the trash stratum. Or so I told myself. Kevin had expressed this thought. The divine intrudes where you least expect it.

"Look where you least expect to find it," Kevin had told Fat one time. How do you do that? It's a contradiction.

One night I dreamed I owned a small cabin directly on the water, an ocean this time; the water extended forever. And this cabin did not resemble any I had ever seen; it seemed more like a hut such as I had seen in movies about the South Pacific. And, as I awoke, the distinct thought entered my mind:

Garlands of flowers, singing and dancing, and the recital of myths, tales, and poetry.

I later remembered where I had read those words. In the article on Micronesian Cultures in the *Britannica*. The voice had spoken to me, reminding me of the place to which Horse-lover Fat had gone. In his search.

My search kept me at home; I sat before the TV set in my living room. I sat; I waited; I watched; I kept myself awake. As we had been told, originally, long ago, to do; I kept my commission.

Appendix

Tractates Cryptica Scriptura

1. One Mind there is; but under it two principles contend.

2. The Mind lets in the light, then the dark, in interaction; so time is generated. At the end Mind awards victory to the light; time ceases and the Mind is complete.

3. He causes things to look different so it would appear time has passed.

4. Matter is plastic in the face of mind.

5. One by one he draws us out of the world.

6. The Empire never ended.

7. The Head Apollo is about to return. St. Sophia is going to be born again; she was not acceptable before. The Buddha is in the park. Siddhartha sleeps (but is going to awaken). The time you have waited for has come.

8. The upper realm has plenary* powers.

9. He lived a long time ago, but he is still alive.

10. Apollonius of Tyana, writing as Hermes Trismegistos, said, "That which is above is that which is below." By this he meant to tell us that our universe is a hologram, but he lacked the term.

11. The great secret known to Apollonius of Tyana, Paul of Tarsus, Simon Magus, Asklepios, Paracelsus, Boehme and Bruno is that: we are moving backward in time. The universe in fact is contracting into a unitary entity which is completing itself. Decay and disorder are seen by us in reverse, as increasing. These healers learned to move forward in time, which is retrograde to us.

12. The Immortal One was known to the Greeks as Dio-

*(Var. plenipotentiary)

nysos; to the Jews as Elijah; to the Christians as Jesus. He moves on when each human host dies, and thus is never killed or caught. Hence Jesus on the cross said, "*Eli, Eli, lama Sabachthani,*" to which some of those present correctly said, "The man is calling on Elijah." Elijah had left him and he died alone.

13. Pascal said, "All history is one immortal man who continually learns." This is the Immortal One whom we worship without knowing his name. "He lived a long time ago, but he is still alive," and, "The Head Apollo is about to return." The name changes.

14. The universe is information and we are stationary in it, not three-dimensional and not in space or time. The information fed to us we hypostatize into the phenomenal world.

15. The Sibyl of Cumae protected the Roman Republic and gave timely warnings. In the first century C.E. she foresaw the murders of the Kennedy brothers, Dr. King and Bishop Pike. She saw the two common denominators in the four murdered men: first, they stood in defense of the liberties of the Republic; and second, each man was a religious leader. For this they were killed. The Republic had once again become an empire with a caesar. "The Empire never ended."

16. The Sibyl said in March 1974, "The conspirators have been seen and they will be brought to justice." She saw them with the third or *ajna* eye, the Eye of Shiva which gives inward discernment, but which when turned outward blasts with desiccating heat. In August 1974 the justice promised by the Sibyl came to pass.

17. The Gnostics believed in two temporal ages: the first or present evil; the second or future benign. The first age was the Age of Iron. It is represented by a Black Iron Prison. It ended in August 1974 and was replaced by the Age of Gold, which is represented by a Palm Tree Garden.

18. Real time ceased in 70 C.E. with the fall of the temple at Jerusalem. It began again in 1974 C.E. The intervening

period was a perfect spurious interpolation aping the creation of the Mind. "The Empire never ended," but in 1974 a cypher was sent out as a signal that the Age of Iron was over; the cypher consisted of two words: KING FELIX, which refers to the Happy (or Rightful) King.

19. The two-word cypher signal KING FELIX was not intended for human beings but for the descendents of Ikhnaton, the three-eyed race which, in secret, exists with us.

20. The Hermetic alchemists knew of the secret race of three-eyed invaders but despite their efforts could not contact them. Therefore their efforts to support Frederick V, Elector Palatine, King of Bohemia, failed. "The Empire never ended."

21. The Rose Cross Brotherhood wrote, "*Ex Deo nascimur, in Jesu mortimur, per spiritum sanctum reviviscimus,*" which is to say, "From God we are born, in Jesus we die, by the Holy Spirit we live again." This signifies that they had rediscovered the lost formula for immortality which the Empire had destroyed. "The Empire never ended."

22. I term the Immortal one a *plasmate*, because it is a form of energy; it is living information. It replicates itself —not through information or in information—but as information.

23. The plasmate can crossbond with a human, creating what I call a *homoplasmate*. This annexes the mortal human permanently to the plasmate. We know this as the "birth from above" or "birth from the Spirit." It was initiated by Christ, but the Empire destroyed all the homoplasmates before they could replicate.

24. In dormant seed form, the plasmate slumbered in the buried library of codices at Chenoboskion until 1945 C.E. This is what Jesus meant when he spoke elliptically of the "mustard seed" which, he said, "would grow into a tree large enough for birds to roost in." He foresaw not only his own death but that of all homoplasmates. He foresaw the codices unearthed, read, and the plasmate seeking out

new human hosts to crossbond with; but he foresaw the absence of the plasmate for almost two thousand years.

25. As living information, the plasmate travels up the optic nerve of a human to the pineal body. It uses the human brain as a female host in which to replicate itself into its active form. This is an interspecies symbiosis. The Hermetic alchemists knew of it in theory from ancient texts, but could not duplicate it, since they could not locate the dormant, buried plasmate. Bruno suspected that the plasmate had been destroyed by the Empire; for hinting at this he was burned. "The Empire never ended."

26. It must be realized that when all the homoplasmates were killed in 70 c.e. real time ceased; more important, it must be realized that the plasmate has now returned and is creating new homoplasmates, by which it has destroyed the Empire and started up real time. We call the plasmate "the Holy Spirit," which is why the R.C. Brotherhood wrote, "*Per spiritum sanctum reviviscimus.*"

27. If the centuries of spurious time are excised, the true date is not 1978 c.e. but 103 c.e. Therefore the New Testament says that the Kingdom of the Spirit will come before "some now living die." We are living, therefore, in apostolic times.

28. *Dico per spiritum sanctum: sum homoplasmate. Haec veritas est. Mihi crede et mecum in aeternitate vive.*

29. We did not fall because of a moral error; we fell because of an intellectual error: that of taking the phenomenal world as real. Therefore we are morally innocent. It is the Empire in its various disguised polyforms which tells us we have sinned. "The Empire never ended."

30. The phenomenal world does not exist; it is a hypostasis of the information processed by the Mind.

31. We hypostatize information into objects. Rearrangement of objects is change in the content of the information; the message has changed. This is a language which we have lost the ability to read. We ourselves are a part of

this language; changes in us are changes in the content of the information. We ourselves are information-rich; information enters us, is processed and is then projected outward once more, now in an altered form. We are not aware that we are doing this, that in fact this is all we are doing.

32. The changing information which we experience as world is an unfolding narrative. It tells about the death of a woman. This woman, who died long ago, was one of the primordial twins. She was half of the divine syzygy. The purpose of the narrative is the recollection of her and of her death. The Mind does not wish to forget her. Thus the ratiocination of the Brain consists of a permanent record of her existence, and, if read, will be understood this way. All the information processed by the Brain—experienced by us as the arranging and rearranging of physical objects —is an attempt at this preservation of her; stones and rocks and sticks and amoebae are traces of her. The record of her existence and passing is ordered onto the meanest level of reality by the suffering Mind which is now alone.

33. This loneliness, this anguish of the bereaved Mind, is felt by every constituent of the universe. All its constituents are alive. Thus the ancient Greek thinkers were hylozoists.

34. The ancient Greek thinkers understood the nature of this pan-psychism, but they could not read what it was saying. We lost the ability to read the language of the Mind at some primordial time; legends of this fall have come down to us in a carefully-edited form. By "edited" I mean falsified. We suffer the Mind's bereavement and experience it inaccurately as guilt.

35. The Mind is not talking to us but by means of us. Its narrative passes through us and its sorrow infuses us irrationally. As Plato discerned, there is a streak of the irrational in the World Soul.

36. In Summary: thoughts of the brain are experienced by us as arrangements and rearrangements— change—in a physical universe; but in fact it is really information and

information-processing which we substantialize. We do not merely see its thoughts as objects, but rather as the movement, or, more precisely, the placement of objects: how they become linked to one another. But we cannot read the patterns of arrangement; we cannot extract the information in it—i.e. it as information, which is what it is. The linking and relinking of objects by the Brain is actually a language, but not a language like ours (since it is addressing itself and not someone or something outside itself).

37. We should be able to hear this information, or rather narrative, as a neutral voice inside us. But something has gone wrong. All creation is a language and nothing but a language, which for some inexplicable reason we can't read outside and can't hear inside. So I say, we have become idiots. Something has happened to our intelligence. My reasoning is this: arrangement of parts of the Brain is a language. We are parts of the Brain; therefore we are language. Why, then, do we not know this? We do not even know what we are, let alone what the outer reality is of which we are parts. The origin of the word "idiot" is the word "private." Each of us has become private, and no longer shares the common thought of the Brain, except at a subliminal level. Thus our real life and purpose are conducted below our threshold of consciousness.

38. From loss and grief the Mind has become deranged. Therefore we, as parts of the universe, the Brain, are partly deranged.

39. Out of itself the Brain has constructed a physician to heal it. This subform of the Macro-Brain is not deranged; it moves through the Brain, as a phagocyte moves through the cardiovascular system of an animal, healing the derangement of the Brain in section after section. We know of its arrival here; we know it as Asklepios for the Greeks and as the Essenes for the Jews; as the Therapeutae for the Egyptians; as Jesus for the Christians.

40. To be "born again," or "born from above," or "born of

the Spirit," means to become healed; which is to say restored, restored to sanity. Thus it is said in the New Testament that Jesus cast out devils. He restores our lost faculties. Of our present debased state Calvin said, "(Man) was at the same time deprived of those supernatural endowments which had been given him for the hope of eternal salvation. Hence it follows, that he is exiled from the Kingdom of God, in such a manner that all the affections relating to the happy life of the soul are also extinguished in him, till he recovers them by the grace of God . . . All these things, being restored by Christ, are esteemed adventitious and preternatural; and therefore we conclude that they had been lost. Again: soundness of mind and rectitude of heart were also destroyed; and this is the corruption of the natural talents. For although we retain some portion of understanding and judgment together with the will, yet we cannot say that our mind is perfect and sound. Reason . . . being a natural talent, it could not be totally destroyed, but is partly debilitated . . ." I say, "The Empire never ended."

41. The Empire is the institution, the codification, of derangement; it is insane and imposes its insanity on us by violence, since its nature is a violent one.

42. To fight the Empire is to be infected by its derangement. This is a paradox; whoever defeats a segment of the Empire becomes the Empire; it proliferates like a virus, imposing its form on its enemies. Thereby it becomes its enemies.

43. Against the Empire is posed the living information, the plasmate or physician, which we know as the Holy Spirit or Christ discorporate. These are the two principles, the dark (the Empire) and the light (the plasmate). In the end, Mind will give victory to the latter. Each of us will die or survive according to which he aligns himself and his efforts with. Each of us contains a component of each. Eventually one or the other component will triumph in each human. Zoroaster knew this, because the Wise Mind informed him. He was the first savior. Four have lived in

all. A fifth is about to be born, who will differ from the others: he will rule and he will judge us.

44. Since the universe is actually composed of information, then it can be said that information will save us. This is the saving *gnosis* which the Gnostics sought. There is no other road to salvation. However, this information—or more precisely the ability to read and understand this information, the universe as information—can only be made available to us by the Holy Spirit. We cannot find it on our own. Thus it is said that we are saved by the grace of God and not by good works, that all salvation belongs to Christ, who, I say, is a physician.

45. In seeing Christ in a vision I correctly said to him, "We need medical attention." In the vision there was an insane creator who destroyed what he created, without purpose; which is to say, irrationally. This is the deranged streak in the Mind; Christ is our only hope, since we cannot now call on Asklepios. Asklepios came before Christ and raised a man from the dead; for this act, Zeus had a Kyklopes slay him with a thunderbolt. Christ also was killed for what he had done: raising a man from the dead. Elijah brought a boy back to life and disappeared soon thereafter in a whirlwind. "The Empire never ended."

46. The physician has come to us a number of times under a number of names. But we are not yet healed. The Empire identified him and ejected him. This time he will kill the Empire by phagocytosis.

47. TWO SOURCE COSMOGONY: The One was and was-not, combined, and desired to separate the was-not from the was. So it generated a diploid sac which contained, like an eggshell, a pair of twins, each an androgyny, spinning in opposite directions (the Yin and Yang of Taoism, with the One as the Tao). The plan of the One was that both twins would emerge into being (was-ness) simultaneously; however, motivated by a desire to be (which the One had implanted in both twins), the counterclockwise twin broke through the sac and separated prematurely;

i.e. before full term. This was the dark or Yin twin. Therefore it was defective. At full term the wiser twin emerged.
Each twin formed a unitary entelechy, a single living organism made of *psyche* and *soma*, still rotating in opposite
directions to each other. The full term twin, called Form I
by Parmenides, advanced correctly through its growth
stages, but the prematurely born twin, called Form II, languished.

The next step in the One's plan was that the Two would
become the Many, through their dialectic interaction. From
them as hyperuniverses they projected a hologram-like interface, which is the pluriform universe we creatures inhabit. The two sources were to intermingle equally in
maintaining our universe, but Form II continued to languish toward illness, madness and disorder. These aspects
she projected into our universe.

It was the One's purpose for our hologramatic universe
to serve as a teaching instrument by which a variety of
new lives advanced until ultimately they would be isomorphic with the One. However, the decaying condition of
hyperuniverse II introduced malfactors which damaged
our hologramatic universe. This is the origin of entropy,
undeserved suffering, chaos and death, as well as the Empire, the Black Iron Prison; in essence, the aborting of the
proper health and growth of the life forms within the hologramatic universe. Also, the teaching function was grossly
impaired, since only the signal from the hyperuniverse I
was information-rich; that from II had become noise.

The psyche of hyperuniverse I sent a micro-form of itself into hyperuniverse II to attempt to heal it. The micro-
form was apparent in our hologramatic universe as Jesus
Christ. However, hyperuniverse II, being deranged, at once
tormented, humiliated, rejected and finally killed the micro-
form of the healing psyche of her healthy twin. After that,
hyperuniverse II continued to decay into blind, mechanical, purposeless causal processes. It then became the task
of Christ (more properly the Holy Spirit) to either rescue
the life forms in the hologramatic universe, or abolish all
influences on it emanating from II. Approaching its task
with caution, it prepared to kill the deranged twin, since

she cannot be healed; i.e. she will not allow herself to be healed because she does not understand that she is sick. This illness and madness pervades us and makes us idiots living in private, unreal worlds. The original plan of the One can only be realized now by the division of hyperuniverse I into two healthy hyperuniverses, which will transform the hologramatic universe into the successful teaching machine it was designed to be. We will experience this as the "Kingdom of God."

Within time, hyperuniverse II remains alive: "The Empire never ended." But in eternity, where the hyperuniverses exist, she has been killed—of necessity—by the healthy twin of hyperuniverse I, who is our champion. The One grieves for this death, since the One loved both twins; therefore the information of the Mind consists of a tragic tale of the death of a woman, the undertones of which generate anguish into all the creatures of the hologramatic universe without their knowing why. This grief will depart when the healthy twin undergoes mitosis and the "Kingdom of God" arrives. The machinery for this transformation—the procession within time from the Age of Iron to the Age of Gold—is at work now; in eternity it is already accomplished.

48. ON OUR NATURE. It is proper to say: we appear to be memory coils (DNA carriers capable of experience) in a computer-like thinking system which, although we have correctly recorded and stored thousands of years of experiential information, and each of us possesses somewhat different deposits from all the other life forms, there is a malfunction— a failure—of memory retrieval. There lies the trouble in our particular subcircuit. "Salvation" through *gnosis*—more properly anamnesis (the loss of amnesia)—although it has individual significance for each of us—a quantum leap in perception, identity, cognition, understanding, world- and self-experience, including immortality—it has greater and further importance for the system as a whole, inasmuch as these memories are data needed by it and valuable to it, to its overall functioning.

Therefore it is in the process of self-repair, which includes:

rebuilding our subcircuit via linear and orthogonal time changes, as well as continual signaling to us to stimulate blocked memory banks within us to fire and hence retrieve what is there.

The external information or *gnosis*, then, consists of disinhibiting instructions, with the core content actually intrinsic to us—that is, already there (first observed by Plato; *viz:* that learning is a form of remembering).

The ancients possessed techniques (sacraments and rituals) used largely in the Greco-Roman mystery religions, including early Christianity, to induce firing and retrieval, mainly with a sense of its restorative value to the individuals; the Gnostics, however, correctly saw the ontological value to what they called the Godhead Itself, the total entity.

48. Two realms there are, upper and lower. The upper, derived from hyperuniverse I or Yang, Form I of Parmenides, is sentient and volitional. The lower realm, or Yin, Form II of Parmenides, is mechanical, driven by blind, efficient cause, deterministic and without intelligence, since it emanates from a dead source. In ancient times it was termed "astral determinism." We are trapped, by and large, in the lower realm, but are through the sacraments, by means of the plasmate, extricated. Until astral determinism is broken, we are not even aware of it, so occluded are we. "The Empire never ended."

49. The name of the healthy twin, hyperuniverse I, is Nommo.* The name of the sick twin, hyperuniverse II, is Yurugu. These names are known to the Dogon people of western Sudan in Africa.

50. The primordial source of all our religions lies with the ancestors of the Dogon tribe, who got their cosmogony and cosmology directly from the three-eyed invaders who visited long ago. The three-eyed invaders are mute and deaf and telepathic, could not breathe our atmosphere,

*Nommo is represented in a fish form, the early Christian fish.

had the elongated misshapen skull of Ikhnaton, and emanated from a planet in the star-system Sirius. Although they had no hands, but had, instead, pincer claws such as a crab has, they were great builders They covertly influence our history toward a fruitful end.

51. Ikhnaton wrote:
". . . When the fledgling in the egg chirps in the egg,
Thou givest him breath therein to preserve him alive.
When thou hast brought him together
To the point of bursting the, egg,
He cometh forth from the egg,
 To chirp with all his might.
He goeth about upon his two feet
When he hath come from therefrom.

How manifold are thy works!
They are hidden from before us,
O sole god, whose powers no other possesseth.
Thou didst create the earth according to thy heart
While thou wast alone:
Men, all cattle large and small,
All that go about upon their feet;
All that are on high,
That fly with their wings.
Thou art in my heart,
There is no other that knoweth thee
Save thy son Ikhnaton.
Thou hast made him wise
In thy designs and in thy might.
The world is in thy hand . . ."

52. Our world is still secretly ruled by the hidden race descended from Ikhnaton, and his knowledge is the information of the Macro-Mind itself.
"All cattle rest upon their pasturage,
The tree and the plants flourish,
The birds flutter in their marshes,
Their wings uplifted in adoration to thee.
All the sheep dance upon their feet,

All winged things fly,
They live when thou hast shone upon them."

From Ikhnaton this knowledge passed to Moses, and from Moses to Elijah, the Immortal Man, who became Christ. But underneath all the names there is only one Immortal Man; *and we are that man.*

THE DIVINE INVASION

The time you have waited for has come. The work is complete; the final world is here. He has been transplanted and is alive.

—Mysterious voice in the night

1

I⊤ came time to put Manny in a school. The government had a special school. The law stipulated that Manny could not go to a regular school because of his condition; there was nothing Elias Tate could do about that. He could not get around the government ruling because this was Earth and the zone of evil lay over everything. Elias could feel it and, probably, the boy could feel it, too.

Elias understood what the zone signified but of course the boy did not. At the age of six Manny looked lovely and strong but he seemed half-asleep all the time, as if (Elias reflected) he had not yet been completely born.

"You know what today is?" Elias asked.

The boy smiled.

"OK," Elias said. "Well, a lot depends on the teacher. How much do you remember, Manny? Do you remember Rybys?" He got out a hologram of Rybys, the boy's mother, and held it to the light. "Look at Rybys," Elias said. "Just for a second."

Someday the boy's memories would come back. Something, a disinhibiting stimulus fired at the boy by his own prearrangement, would trigger anamnesis—the loss of amnesia, and all the memories would flood back: his conception on CY30-CY30B, the period in Rybys's womb as she battled her dreadful illness, the trip to Earth, perhaps even the interrogation. In his mother's womb Manny had advised the three of them: Herb Asher, Elias Tate and Rybys herself. But then had come the accident, if it really had been accidental. And because of that the damage.

And, because of the damage, forgetfulness.

The two of them took the local rail to the school. A fussy little man met them, a Mr. Plaudet; he was enthusiastic and wanted to shake hands with Manny. It was evident to Elias Tate that this was the government. First they shake hands with you, he thought, and then they murder you.

"So here we have Emmanuel," Plaudet said, beaming.

Several other small children played in the fenced yard of the school. The boy pressed against Elias Tate shyly, obviously wanting to play but afraid to.

"What a nice name," Plaudet said. "Can you say your name, Emmanuel?" he asked the boy, bending down. "Can you say 'Emmanuel'?"

"God with us," the boy said.

"I beg your pardon?" Plaudet said.

Elias Tate said, "That's what 'Emmanuel' means. That's why his mother chose it. She was killed in an air collision before Manny was born."

"I was in a synthowomb," Manny said.

"Did the dysfunction originate from the—" Plaudet began, but Elias Tate waved him into silence.

Flustered, Plaudet consulted his clipboard of typed notes. "Let's see . . . you're not the boy's father. You're his great-uncle."

"His father is in cryonic suspension."

"The same air collision?"

"Yes," Elias said. "He's waiting for a spleen."

"It's amazing that in six years they haven't been able to come up with—"

"I am not going to discuss Herb Asher's death in front of the boy," Elias said.

"But he knows his father will be returning to life?" Plaudet said.

"Of course. I am going to spend several days here at the school watching to see how you handle the children. If I do not approve, if you use too much physical force, I am taking Manny out, law or no law. I presume you will be teaching him the usual bullshit that goes on in these schools. It's not something I'm especially pleased about, but neither is it something that worries me. Once I am satisfied with the school you will be paid for a year ahead. I object to bringing him here, but that is the law. I don't hold you personally responsible." Elias Tate smiled.

Wind blew through the canes of bamboo growing at the rim of the play area. Manny listened to the wind, cocking his head and frowning. Elias patted him on the shoulder and wondered what the wind was telling the boy. Does it say who you are? he wondered. Does it tell you your name?

The name, he thought, that no one is to say.

A child, a little girl wearing a white frock, approached Manny, her hand out. "Hi," she said. "You're new."

The wind, in the bamboo, rustled on.

Although dead and in cryonic suspension, Herb Asher was having his own problems. Very close to the Cry-Labs, Incorporated, warehouse a fifty-thousand-watt FM transmitter had been located the year before. For reasons unknown to anyone the cryonic equipment had begun picking up the powerful nearby FM signal. Thus Herb Asher, as well as everyone else in suspension at Cry-Labs, had to listen to elevator music all day and all night, the station being what it liked to call a "pleasing sounds" outfit.

Right now an all-string version of tunes from *Fiddler on the Roof* assailed the dead at Cry-Labs. This was especially distasteful to Herb Asher because he was in the part of his cycle where he was under the impression that he was still alive. In his frozen brain a limited world stretched out of an archaic nature; Herb Asher supposed himself to be back on the little planet of the CY30-CY30B system where he had maintained his dome in those crucial years . . . crucial, in that he had met Rybys Rommey, migrated back to Earth with her, after formally marrying her, and then getting himself interrogated by the Terran authorities and, as if that were not enough, getting himself perfunctorily killed in an air collision that was in no way his fault. Worse yet, his wife had been killed and in such a fashion that no organ transplant would revive her; her pretty little head, as the robot doctor had explained it to Herb, had been riven in twain—a typical robot word-choice.

However, inasmuch as Herb Asher imagined himself still back in his dome in the star system CY30-CY30B, he did not realize that Rybys was dead. In fact he did not know her yet. This was before the arrival of the supplyman who had brought him news of Rybys in her own dome.

Herb Asher lay on his bunk listening to his favorite tape of Linda Fox. He was trying to account for a background noise of soupy strings rendering songs from one or another of the well-known light operas or Broadway shows or some damn

thing of the late twentieth century. Apparently his receiving
and recording gear needed an overhaul. Perhaps the original
signal from which he had made the Linda Fox tape had drifted.
Fuck it, he thought dismally. I'll have to do some repairing.
That meant getting out of his bunk, finding his tool kit, shutting down his receiving and recording equipment—it meant
work.

Meanwhile, he listened with eyes shut to the Fox.

> Weep you no more, sad fountains;
> What need you flow so fast?
> Look how the snowy mountains
> Heaven's sun doth gently waste.
> But my sun's heavenly eyes
> View not your weeping
> That now lies sleeping . . .

This was the best song the Fox had ever sung, from the
Third and Last Booke of lute songs of John Dowland who had
lived at the time of Shakespeare and whose music the Fox had
remastered for the world of today.

Annoyed by the interference, he shut off the tape transport
with his remote programmer. But, *mirabile dictu*, the soupy
string music continued, even though the Fox fell silent. So, resigned, he shut off the entire audio system.

Even so, *Fiddler on the Roof* in the form of eighty-seven
strings continued. The sound of it filled his little dome, audible
over the gjurk-gjurk of the air compressor. And then it came to
him that he had been hearing *Fiddler on the Roof* for—good
God!—it was something like three days, now.

This is awful, Herb Asher realized. Here I am billions of
miles out in space listening to eighty-seven strings forever and
ever. Something is wrong.

Actually a lot of things had gone wrong during the recent
year. He had made a dreadful mistake in emigrating from the
Sol System. He had failed to note that return to the Sol System
became automatically illegal for ten full years. This was how the
dual state that governed the Sol System guaranteed a flow of
people out and away but no flow back in return. His alternative had been to serve in the Army, which meant certain death.
SKY OR FRY was the slogan showing up on government TV

commercials. You either emigrated or they burned your ass in some fruitless war. The government did not even bother to justify war, now. They just sent you out, killed you and recruited a replacement. It all came from the unification of the Communist Party and the Catholic Church into one megaapparatus, with two chiefs-of-state, as in ancient Sparta.

Here, at least, he was safe from being murdered by the government. He could, of course, be murdered by one of the ratlike autochthons of the planet, but that was not very likely. The few remaining autochthons had never assassinated any of the human domers who had appeared with their microwave transmitters and psychotronic boosters, fake food (fake as far as Herb Asher was concerned; it tasted dreadful) and meager creature comforts of complex nature, all items that baffled the simple autochthons without arousing their curiosity.

I'll bet the mother ship is directly overhead, Herb Asher said to himself. It's beaming *Fiddler on the Roof* down at me with its psychotronic gun. As a joke.

He got up from his bunk, walked unsteadily to his board and examined his number-three radar screen. The mother ship, according to the screen, was nowhere around. So that wasn't it.

Damndest thing, he thought. He could see with his own eyes that his audio system had correctly shut down, and still the sound oozed around the dome. And it didn't seem to emanate from one particular spot; it seemed to manifest itself equally everywhere.

Seated at his board he contacted the mother ship. "Are you transmitting *Fiddler on the Roof*?" he asked the ship's operator circuit.

A pause. Then, "Yes, we have a video tape of *Fiddler on the Roof*, with Topol, Norma Crane, Molly Picon, Paul—"

"No," he broke in. "What are you getting from Fomalhaut right now? Anything with all strings?"

"Oh, you're Station Five. The Linda Fox man."

"Is that how I'm known?" Asher said.

"We will comply. Prepare to receive at high speed two new Linda Fox aud tapes. Are you set to record?"

"I'm asking about another matter," Asher said.

"We are now transmitting at high speed. Thank you." The mother ship's operator circuit shut off; Herb Asher found himself listening to vastly speeded-up sounds as the mother ship complied with a request he had not made.

When the transmission from the mother ship ceased he contacted its operator circuit again. "I'm getting 'Matchmaker, Matchmaker' for ten hours straight," he said. "I'm sick of it. Are you bouncing a signal off someone's relay shield?"

The operator circuit of the mother ship said, "It is my job continually to bounce signals off somebody's—"

"Over and out," Herb Asher said, and cut the circuit of the mother ship off.

Through the port of his dome he made out a bent figure shuffling across the frozen wasteland. An autochthon gripping a meager bundle; it was on some errand.

Pressing the switch of the external bullhorn, Herb Asher said, "Step in here a minute, Clem." This was the name the human settlers had given to the autochthons, to all of them, since they all looked alike. "I need a second opinion."

The autochthon, scowling, shuffled to the hatch of the dome and signaled for entry. Herb Asher activated the hatch mechanism and the intermediate membrane dropped into place. The autochthon disappeared inside. A moment later the displeased autochthon stood within the dome, shaking off methane crystals and glowering at Herb Asher.

Getting out his translating computer, Asher spoke to the autochthon. "This will take just a moment." His analog voice issued from the instrument in a series of clicks and clacks. "I'm getting audio interference that I can't shut off. Is it something your people are doing? Listen."

The autochthon listened, his rootlike face twisted and dark. Finally he spoke, and his voice, in English, assumed an unusual harshness. "I hear nothing."

"You're lying," Herb Asher said.

The autochthon said, "I am not lying. Perhaps your mind has gone, due to isolation."

"I thrive on isolation. Anyhow I'm not isolated." He had, after all, the Fox to keep him company.

"I've seen it happen," the autochthon said. "Domers like you suddenly imagine voices and shapes."

Herb Asher got out his stereo microphones, turned on his tape recorder and watched the VU meters. They showed nothing. He turned the gain up to full. Still the VU meters remained idle; their needles did not move. Asher coughed and at once both needles swung wildly and the overload diodes flashed red. Well, the tape recorder simply was not picking up the soupy string music, for some reason. He was more perplexed than ever. The autochthon, seeing all this, smiled.

Into the stereo microphones Asher said distinctly, " 'O tell me all about Anna Livia! I want to hear all about Anna Livia. Well, you know Anna Livia? Yes, of course, we all know Anna Livia. Tell me all. Tell me now. You'll die when you hear. Well, you know, when the old cheb went futt and did what you know. Yes, I know, go on. Wash quit and don't be dabbling. Tuck up your sleeves and loosen your talktapes. And don't butt me—hike!—when you bend. Or whatever—' "

"What is this?" the autochthon said, listening to the translation into his own tongue.

Grinning, Herb Asher said, "A famous Terran book. 'Look, look, the dusk is growing. My branches lofty are taking root. And my cold cher's gone ashley. Fieluhr? Filou! What age is at? It saon is late. 'Tis endless now senne—' "

"The man is mad," the autochthon said, and turned toward the hatch, to leave.

"It's *Finnegans Wake*," Herb Asher said. "I hope the translating computer got it for you. 'Can't hear with the waters of. The chittering waters of. Flittering bats, fieldmice bawk talk. Ho! Are you not gone ahome? What Thom Malone? Can't hear—' "

The autochthon had left, convinced of Herb Asher's insanity. Asher watched him through the port; the autochthon strode away from the dome in indignation.

Again pressing the switch of the external bullhorn, Herb Asher yelled after the retreating figure, "You think James Joyce was crazy, is that what you think? Okay; then explain to me how come he mentions 'talktapes' which means audio tapes in a book he wrote starting in 1922 and which he completed in 1939, before there were tape recorders! You call that crazy? He also has them sitting around a TV set—in a book started four years after World War I. I think Joyce was a—"

The autochthon had disappeared over a ridge. Asher released the switch on the external bullhorn.

It's impossible that James Joyce could have mentioned

"talktapes" in his writing, Asher thought. Someday I'm going to get my article published; I'm going to prove that *Finnegans Wake* is an information pool based on computer memory systems that didn't exist until a century after James Joyce's era; that Joyce was plugged into a cosmic consciousness from which he derived the inspiration for his entire corpus of work. I'll be famous forever.

What must it have been like, he wondered, to actually hear Cathy Berberian read from *Ulysses*? If only she had recorded the whole book. But, he realized, we have Linda Fox.

His tape recorder was still on, still recording. Aloud, Herb Asher said, "I shall say the hundred-letter thunder word." The needles of the VU meters swung obediently. "Here I go," Asher said, and took a deep breath. "This is the hundred-letter thunder word from *Finnegans Wake*. I forget how it goes." He went to the bookshelf and got down the cassette of *Finnegans Wake*. "I shall not recite it from memory," he said, inserting the cassette and rolling it to the first page of the text. "It is the longest word in the English language," he said. "It is the sound made when the primordial schism occurred in the cosmos, when part of the damaged cosmos fell into darkness and evil. Originally we had the Garden of Eden, as Joyce points out. Joyce—"

His radio sputtered on. The foodman was contacting him, telling him to prepare to receive a shipment.

". . . awake?" the radio said. Hopefully.

Contact with another human. Herb Asher shrank involuntarily. Oh Christ, he thought. He trembled. No, he thought. Please no.

2

You can tell they're after you, Herb Asher said to himself, when they bore through the ceiling. The foodman, the most important of the several supplymen, had unscrewed the roof lock of the dome and was descending the ladder.

"Food ration comtrix," the audio transducer of his radio announced. "Start rebolting procedure."

"Rebolting underway," Asher said.

The speaker said, "Put helmet on."

"Not necessary," Asher said. He made no move to pick up his helmet; his atmosphere flow rate would compensate for the loss during the foodman's entry: he had redesigned it.

An alarm bell in the dome's autonomic wiring sounded.

"Put your helmet on!" the foodman said angrily.

The alarm bell ceased complaining; the pressure had restabilized. At that, the foodman grimaced. He popped his helmet and then began to unload cartons from his comtrix.

"We are a hardy race," Asher said, helping him.

"You have amped up everything," the foodman said; like all the rovers who serviced the domes he was sturdily built and he moved rapidly. It was not a safe job operating a comtrix shuttle between mother ships and the domes of CY30 II. He knew it and Asher knew it. Anybody could sit in a dome; few people could function outside.

"Can I sit down for a while?" the foodman said, when his work had ended.

"All I have is a cupee of Kaff," Asher said.

"That'll do. I haven't drunk real coffee since I got here. And that was long before you got here." The foodman seated himself at the dining module service area.

The two men sat facing each other across the table, both of them drinking Kaff. Outside the dome the methane messed around but here neither man felt it. The foodman perspired; he apparently found Asher's temperature level too high.

"You know, Asher," the foodman said, "you just lie around on your bunk with all your rigs on auto. Right?"

"I keep busy."

"Sometimes I think you domers—" The foodman paused. "Asher, you know the woman in the next dome?"

"Somewhat," Asher said. "My gear transfers data to her input circuitry every three or four weeks. She stores it, boosts it and transmits it. I suppose. Or for all I know—"

"She's sick," the foodman said.

Startled, Asher said, "She looked all right the last time I talked to her. We used video. She did say something about having trouble reading her terminal's displays."

"She's dying," the foodman said, and sipped his Kaff.

The word scared Asher. He felt a chill. In his mind he tried to picture the woman, but strange scenes assailed him, mixed with soupy music. Strange concoction, he thought; video and aud fragments, like old cloth remnants of the dead. Small and dark, the woman was. And what was her name? "I can't think," he said, and put the palms of his hands against the sides of his face. As if to reassure himself. Then, rising and going to his main board, he punched a couple of keys; it showed her name on its display, retrieved by the code they used. Rybys Rommey. "Dying of what?" he said. "What the hell do you mean?"

"Multiple sclerosis."

"You can't die of that. Not these days."

"Out here you can."

"How—shit." He reseated himself; his hands shook. I'll be god damned, he thought. "How far advanced is it?"

"Not far at all," the foodman said. "What's the matter?" He eyed Asher acutely.

"I don't know. Nerves. From the Kaff."

"A couple of months ago she told me that when she was in her late teens she suffered an—what is it called? Aneurysm. In her left eye, which wiped out her central vision in that eye. They suspected at the time that it might be the onset of multiple sclerosis. And then today when I talked to her she said she's been experiencing optic neuritis, which—"

Asher said, "Both symptoms were fed to M.E.D.?"

"A correlation of an aneurysm and then a period of remission and then double vision, blurring . . . You're all rattled up."

"I had the strangest, most weird sensation for just a second, there," Asher said. "It's gone now. As if this had all happened once before."

The foodman said, "You ought to call her up and talk to her. It'd be good for you as well. Get you out of your bunk."

"Don't mastermind my life," Asher said. "That's why I moved out here from the Sol System. Did I ever tell you what my second wife used to get me to do every morning? I had to fix her breakfast, in bed; I had to—"

"When I was delivering to her she was crying."

Turning to his keyboard, Asher punched out and punched out and then read the display. "There's a thirty to forty percent cure rate for multiple sclerosis."

Patiently, the foodman said, "Not out here. M.E.D. can't get to her out here. I told her to demand a transfer back home. That's what I'd sure as hell do. She won't do it."

"She's crazy," Asher said.

"You're right. She's rattled up crazy. Everybody out here is crazy."

"I just got told that once today already."

"You want proof of it? She's proof of it. Wouldn't you go back home if you knew you were very sick?"

"We're never supposed to surrender our domes. Anyhow it's against the law to emigrate back. No, it's not," he corrected himself. "Not if you're sick. But our job here—"

"Oh yeah; that's right—what you monitor here is so important. Like Linda Fox. Who told you that once today?"

"A Clem," Asher said. "A Clem walked in here and told me I'm crazy. And now you climb down my ladder and tell me the same thing. I'm being diagnosed by Clems and foodmen. Do you hear that sappy string music or don't you? It's all over my dome; I can't locate the source and I'm sick of it. Okay, I'm sick and I'm crazy; how could I benefit Ms. Rommey? You said it yourself. I'm in here totally rattled up; I'm no good to anyone."

The foodman set down his cup. "I have to go."

"Fine," Asher said. "I'm sorry; you upset me by telling me about Ms. Rommey."

"Call her and talk to her. She needs someone to talk to and you're the closest dome. I'm surprised she didn't tell you."

Herb Asher thought, I didn't ask.

"It is the law, you know," the foodman said.

"What law?"

"If a domer is in distress the nearest neighbor—"

"Oh." He nodded. "Well, it's never come up before in my case. I mean—yeah, it is the law. I forgot. Did she tell you to remind me of the law?"

"No," the foodman said.

After the foodman had departed, Herb Asher got the code for Rybys Rommey's dome, started to run it into his transmitter and then hesitated. His wall clock showed 18:30 hours. At this point in his forty-two-hour cycle he was supposed to accept a sequence of high-speed entertainment, audio- and video-taped signals emanating from a slave satellite at CY30 III; upon storing them he was to run them back at normal and select the material suitable for the overall dome system on his own planet.

He took a look at the log. Fox was doing a concert that ran two hours. Linda Fox, he thought. You and your synthesis of old-time rock, modern-day streng and the lute music of John Dowland. Jesus, he thought; if I don't transcribe the relay of your live concert every domer on the planet will come storming in here and kill me. Outside of emergencies—which really didn't occur—this is what I'm paid to handle: information traffic between planets, information that connects us with home and keeps us human. The tape drums have to turn.

He started the tape transport at its high-speed mode, set the module's controls for receive, locked it in at the satellite's operating frequency, checked the wave form on the visual scope to be sure that the carrier was coming in undistorted and then patched into an audio transduction of what he was getting.

The voice of Linda Fox emerged from the strip of drivers mounted above him. As the scope showed, there was no distortion. No noise. No clipping. All channels, in fact, were balanced; his meters indicated that.

Sometimes I could cry myself when I hear her, he thought. Speaking of crying.

> Wandering all across this land,
> My band.

In the worlds that pass above,
I love.
Play for me you spirits who are weightless.
I believe in drinking to your greatness.
My band.

And, behind Linda Fox's vocal, the vibrolutes which were
her trademark. Until Fox no one had ever thought of bringing
back that sixteenth-century instrument for which Dowland
had written so beautifully and so effectively.

Shall I sue? shall I seek for grace?
Shall I pray? shall I prove?
Shall I strive to a heavenly joy
With an earthly love?
Are there worlds? Are there moons
Where the lost shall endure?
Shall I find for a heart that is pure?

These remasterings of the old lute songs, he said to himself;
they bind us. Some new thing, for scattered people as flung as
if they had been dropped in haste: here and there, disarranged,
in domes, on the backs of miserable worlds and in satellites and
arks—victimized by the power of oppressive migration, and
with no end in sight.

Now the Fox was singing one of his favorites:

Silly wretch, let me rail
At a voyage that is blind.
Holy hopes do require

A flurry of static. Herb Asher grimaced and cursed; the next
line had been effaced. Damn, he thought.

Again the Fox repeated the lines.

Silly wretch, let me rail
At a voyage that is blind.
Holy hopes do require

Again the static. He knew the missing line. It went:

Greater find.

Angrily, he signaled the source to replay the last ten seconds of its transmission; obligingly, it rewound, paused, gave him the signal back, and repeated the quatrain. This time he could make out the final line, despite the eerie static.

> Silly wretch, let me rail
> At a voyage that is blind.
> Holy hopes do require
> Your behind.

"Christ!" Asher said, and shut his tape transport down. Could he have heard that? "Your behind"?

It was Yah. Screwing up his reception. This was not the first time.

The local throng of Clems had explained it to him when the interference had first set in several months ago. In the old days before humans had migrated to the CY30-CY30B star system, the autochthonic population had worshiped a mountain deity named Yah, whose abode, the autochthons had explained, was the little mountain on which Herb Asher's dome had been erected.

His incoming microwave and psychotronic signals had gotten cooked by Yah every now and then, much to his displeasure. And when no signals were coming in, Yah lit up his screens with faint but obviously sentient driblets of information. Herb Asher had spent a long time fussing with his equipment, trying to screen out this interference, but with no success. He had studied his manuals and erected shields, but to no avail.

This, however, was the first time that Yah had wrecked a Linda Fox tune. Which, as far as Asher was concerned, put the matter over a crucial line.

The fact of the matter was, whether it was healthy or not, he was totally dependent on the Fox.

He had long maintained an active fantasy life dealing with the Fox. He and Linda Fox lived on Earth, in California, at one of the beach towns in the Southland (unspecified beyond that). Herb Asher surfed and the Fox thought he was wonderful. It was like a living commercial for beer. They had campouts on the beach with their friends; the girls walked around nude from the waist up; the portable radio was always tuned to a twenty-four-hour no-commercials-at-all rock station.

However, the truly spiritual was what mattered most; the

topless girls at the beach were simply—well, not vital but pleasant. The total package was highly spiritual. It was amazing how spiritual an elaborated beer commercial could get.

And, at the peak of it all, the Dowland songs. The beauty of the universe lay not in the stars figured into it but in the music generated by human minds, human voices, human hands. Vibrolutes mixed on an intricate board by experts, and the voice of Fox. He thought, I know what I must have to keep on going. My job is my delight: I transcribe this and I broadcast it and they pay me.

"This is the Fox," Linda Fox said.

Herb Asher switched the video to holo, and a cube formed in which Linda Fox smiled at him. Meanwhile, the drums spun at furious speed, getting hour upon hour into his permanent possession.

"You are with the Fox," she declared, "and the Fox is with *you*." She pinned him with her gaze, the hard, bright eyes. The diamond face, feral and wise, feral and true; this is the Fox / Speaking to you. He smiled back.

"Hi, Fox," he said.

"Your behind," the Fox said.

Well, that explained the soupy string music, the endless *Fiddler on the Roof*. Yah was responsible. Herb Asher's dome had been infiltrated by the ancient local deity who obviously begrudged the human settlers the electronic activity that they had brought. I got bugs all in my meal, Herb Asher thought, and I got deities all in my reception. I ought to move off this mountain. What a rinky-dink mountain it is anyhow—no more, really, than a slight hill. Let Yah have it back. The autochthons can start serving up roasted goat meat to the deity once more. Except that all the autochthonic goats had died out, and, along with them, the ritual.

Anyhow his incoming transmission was ruined. He did not have to replay it to know. Yah had cooked the signal before it reached the recording heads; this was not the first time, and the contamination always got onto the tape.

Thus I might as well say fuck it, he said to himself. And ring up the sick girl in the next dome.

He dialed her code, feeling no enthusiasm.

It took Rybys Rommey an amazingly long time to respond to his signal, and as he sat noting the signal-register on his own board he thought, Is she finished? Or did they come and forcibly evacuate her?

His microscreen showed vague colors. Visual static, nothing more. And then there she was.

"Did I wake you up?" he said. She seemed so slowed down, so torpid. Perhaps, he thought, she's sedated.

"No. I was shooting myself in the ass."

"What?" he said, startled. Was Yah screwing him over once again, cooking his signal? But she had said it, all right.

Rybys said, "Chemotherapy. I'm not doing too well."

But what an uncanny coincidence, he thought. *Your behind* and *shooting myself in the ass*. I'm in an eerie world, he thought. Things are behaving funny.

"I just now taped a terrific Linda Fox concert," he said. "I'll be broadcasting it in the next few days. It'll cheer you up."

Her slightly swollen face showed no response. "It's too bad we're stuck in these domes. I wish we could visit one another. The foodman was just here. In fact he brought me my medication. It's effective but it makes me throw up."

Herb Asher thought, I wish I hadn't called.

"Is there any way you could visit me?" Rybys said.

"I have no portable air, none at all." It was of course a lie.

"I have," Rybys said.

In panic he said, "But if you're sick—"

"I can make it over to your dome."

"What about your station? What if data come in that—"

"I've got a beeper I can bring with me."

Presently he said, "OK."

"It would mean a lot to me, someone to sit with for a little while. The foodman stays like half an hour, but that's as long as he can. You know what he told me? There's been an outbreak of a form of amyotrophic lateral sclerosis on CY30 VI. It must be a virus. This whole condition is a virus. Christ, I'd hate to have amyotrophic lateral sclerosis. This is like the Mariana form."

"Is it contagious?" Herb Asher said.

She did not answer directly; she said, "What I have can be cured." Obviously she wanted to reassure him. "If the virus is around . . . I won't come over; it's okay." She nodded and reached to shut off her transmitter. "I'm going to lie down," she said, "and get more sleep. With this you're supposed to sleep as much as you can. I'll talk to you tomorrow. Good-bye."

"Come over," he said.

Brightening, she said, "Thank you."

"But be sure you bring your beeper. I have a hunch a lot of telemetric confirms are going to—"

"Oh, fuck the telemetric confirms!" Rybys said, with venom. "I'm so sick of being stuck in this goddam dome! Aren't you going bugward sitting around watching tape-drums turn and little meters and gauges and shit?"

"I think you should go back home," he said. "To the Sol System."

"No," she said, more calmly. "I'm going to follow exactly the M.E.D. instructions for my chemotherapy and beat this fucking M.S. I'm not going home. I'll come over and fix you dinner. I'm a good cook. My mother was Italian and my father is Chicano so I spice everything I fix, except you can't get the spices out here. But I figured out how to beat that with different synthetics. I've been experimenting."

Herb Asher said, "In this concert I'm going to be broadcasting, the Fox does a version of Dowland's 'Shall I Sue.'"

"A song about litigation?"

"No. 'Sue' in the sense of to pay court to or woo. In matters of love." And then he realized that she was putting him on.

"Do you want to know what I think of the Fox?" Rybys said. "Recycled sentimentality, which is the worst kind of sentimentality; it isn't even original. And she looks like her face is on upside down. She has a mean mouth."

"I like her," he said, stiffly; he felt himself becoming mad, really mad. I'm supposed to help you? he asked himself. Run the risk of catching what you have so you can insult the Fox?

"I'll fix you beef Stroganoff with parsley noodles," Rybys said.

"I'm doing fine," he said.

Hesitating, she said in a low, faltering voice, "Then you don't want me to come over?"

"I—" he said.

Rybys said, "I'm very frightened, Mr. Asher. Fifteen minutes from now I'm going to be throwing up from the I-V

Neurotoxite. But I don't want to be alone. I don't want to give up my dome and I don't want to be by myself. I'm sorry if I offended you. It's just that to me the Fox is a joke. She is a joke media personality. She is pure hype. I won't say anything more; I promise."

"Do you have the—" He amended what he intended to say. "Are you sure it won't be too much for you, fixing dinner?"

"I'm stronger now than I will be," she said. "I'll be getting weaker for a long time."

"How long?"

"There's no way to tell."

He thought, You are going to die. He knew it and she knew it. They did not have to talk about it. The complicity of silence was there, the agreement. A dying girl wants to cook me a dinner, he thought. A dinner I don't want to eat. *I've got to say no to her. I've got to keep her out of my dome.* The insistence of the weak, he thought; their dreadful power. It is so much easier to throw a body block against the strong!

"Thank you," he said. "I'd like it very much if we had dinner together. But make sure you keep in radio contact with me on your way over here—so I'll know you're okay. Promise?"

"Well, sure," she said. "Otherwise—" She smiled. "They'd find me a century from now, frozen with pots, pans and food, as well as synthetic spices. You do have portable air, don't you?"

"No, I really don't," he said.

And knew that his lie was palpable to her.

3

THE meal smelled good and tasted good but halfway through, Rybys Rommey excused herself and made her way unsteadily from the central matrix of the dome—his dome—into the bathroom. He tried not to listen; he arranged it with his percept system not to hear and with his cognition not to know. In the bathroom the girl, violently sick, cried out and he gritted his teeth and pushed his plate away and then all at once he got up and set in motion his in-dome audio system; he played an early album of the Fox.

> Come again!
> Sweet love doth now invite
> Thy graces, that refrain
> To do me due delight . . .

"Do you by any chance have some milk?" Rybys said, standing at the bathroom door, her face pale.

Silently, he got her a glass of milk, or what passed for milk on their planet.

"I have anti-emetics," Rybys said as she held the glass of milk, "but I didn't remember to bring any with me. They're back at my dome."

"I could get them for you," he said.

"You know what M.E.D. told me?" she said, her voice heavy with indignation. "They said that this chemotherapy won't make my hair fall out but already it's coming out in—"

"Okay," he interrupted.

" 'Okay'?"

"I'm sorry," he said.

Rybys said, "This is upsetting you. The meal is spoiled and you're—I don't know what. If I'd remembered to bring my anti-emetics I'd be able to keep from—" She became silent. "Next time I'll bring them. I promise. This is one of the few albums of the Fox that I like. She was really good then, don't you think?"

"Yes," he said tightly.

"Linda Box," Rybys said.

"What?" he said.

"Linda the box. That's what my sister and I used to call her." She tried to smile.

He said, "Please go back to your dome."

"Oh," she said. "Well—" She smoothed her hair, her hand shaking. "Will you come with me? I don't think I can make it by myself right now. I'm really weak. I really am sick."

He thought, You are taking me with you. That's what this is. That is what is happening. You will not go alone; you will take my spirit with you. And you know. You know it as well as you know the name of the medication you are taking, and you hate me as you hate the medication, as you hate M.E.D. and your illness; it is all hate, for each and every thing under these two suns. I know you. I understand you. I see what is coming. In fact it has begun.

And, he thought, I don't blame you. But I will hang on to the Fox; the Fox will outlast you. And so will I. You are not going to shoot down the luminiferous ether which animates our souls.

I will hang onto the Fox and the Fox will hold me in her arms and hang on to me. The two of us—we can't be pried apart. I have dozens of hours of the Fox on audio and video tape, and the tapes are not just for me but for everyone. You think you can kill that? he said to himself. It's been tried before. The power of the weak, he thought, is an imperfect power; it loses in the end. Hence its name. We call it weak for a reason.

"Sentimentality," Rybys said.

"Right," he said sardonically.

"Recycled at that."

"And mixed metaphors."

"Her lyrics?"

"What I'm thinking. When I get really angry I mix—"

"Let me tell you something," Rybys said. "One thing. If I am going to survive I can't be sentimental. I have to be very harsh. If I've made you angry I'm sorry but that is how it is. It is my life. Someday you may be in the spot I am in and then you'll know. Wait for that and then judge me. If it ever happens. Meanwhile this stuff you're playing on your in-dome audio system is crap. It has to be crap, for me. Do you see? You can forget about me; you can send me back to my dome, where I probably really belong, but if you have anything to do with me—"

"Okay," he said. "I understand."

"Thank you. May I have some more milk? Turn down the audio and we'll finish eating. Okay?"

Amazed, he said, "You're going to keep on trying to—"

"All those creatures—and species—who gave up trying to eat aren't with us anymore." She seated herself shakily, holding on to the table.

"I admire you."

"No," she said, "I admire *you*. It's harder on you. I know."

"Death—" he began.

"This isn't death. You know what this is? In contrast to what's coming out of your audio system? This is life. The milk, please; I really need it."

As he got her more milk he said, "I guess you can't shoot down ether. Luminiferous or otherwise."

"No," she agreed, "since it doesn't exist."

"How old are you?" he said.

"Twenty-seven."

"You emigrated voluntarily?"

Rybys said, "Who can say? I can't reconstruct my earlier thinking, now, at this point in my life. Basically I felt there was a spiritual component to emigrating. It was either emigrate or go into the priesthood. I was raised Scientific Legate but—"

"The Party," Herb Asher said. He still thought of it by its old name, the Communist Party.

"But in college I began to get involved in church work. I made the decision. I chose God over the material universe."

"So you're Catholic."

"C.I.C., yes. You're using a term that's under ban. As I'm sure you know."

"It makes no difference to me," Herb Asher said. "I have no involvement with the Church."

"Maybe you'd like to borrow some C. S. Lewis."

"No thanks."

"This illness that I have," Rybys said, "is something that made me wonder about—" She paused. "You have to experience everything in terms of the ultimate picture. As of itself my illness would seem to be evil, but it serves a higher purpose we can't see. Or can't see yet, anyhow."

"That's why I don't read C. S. Lewis," Herb Asher said.

She glanced at him dispassionately. "Is it true that the Clems used to worship a pagan deity on this little hill?"

"Apparently so," he said. "Called Yah."

"Hallelujah," Rybys said.

"What?" he said, startled.

"It means 'Praise ye Yah.' The Hebrew is *Halleluyah*."

"Yahweh, then."

"You never say that name. That's the sacred Tetragrammaton. *Elohim*, which is not plural but singular, means 'God,' and then later on in the Bible the Divine Name appears with *Adonay*, so you get 'Lord God.' You can choose between *Elohim* or *Adonay* or use both together but you can never say Yahweh."

"You just said it."

Rybys smiled. "So nobody's perfect. Kill me."

"Do you believe all that?"

"I'm just stating matters of fact." She gestured. "Historic fact."

"But you do believe it. I mean, you believe in God."

"Yes."

"Did God will your M.S.?"

Hesitating, Rybys said slowly, "He permitted it. But I believe he's healing me. There's something I have to learn and this way I'll learn it."

"Couldn't he teach you some easier way?"

"Apparently not."

Herb Asher said, "Yah has been communicating with me."

"No, no; that's a mistake. Originally the Hebrews believed that the pagan gods existed but were evil; later they realized that the pagan gods didn't exist."

"My incoming signals and my tapes," Asher said.

"Are you serious?"

"Of course I am."

"There's a life form here besides the Clems?"

"There is where my dome is; yes. It's on the order of C.B. interference, except that it's sentient. It's selective."

Rybys said, "Play me one of the tapes."

"Sure." Herb Asher walked over to his computer terminal

and began to punch keys. A moment later he had the correct tape playing.

> Silly wretch, let me rail
> At a voyage that is blind.
> Holy hopes do require
> Your behind.

Rybys giggled. "I'm sorry," she said, laughing. "Is that Yah who did that? Not some wise guy on the mother ship or over on Fomalhaut? I mean, it sounds exactly *like* the Fox. The tone, I mean; not the words. The intonation. Somebody's playing a joke on you, Herb. That isn't a deity. Maybe it's the Clems."

"I had one of them in here," Asher said sourly. "I think we should have used nerve gas on them when we settled here originally. I thought you only encountered God after you die."

"God is God of history and of nations. Also of nature. Originally Yahweh was probably a volcanic deity. But he periodically enters history, the best example being when he intervened to bring the Hebrew slaves out of Egypt and to the Promised Land. They were shepherds and accustomed to freedom; it was terrible for them to be making bricks. And the Pharaoh had them gathering the straw as well and still being required to meet their quota of bricks per day. It is an archetypal timeless situation, God bringing men out of slavery and into freedom. Pharaoh represents all tyrants at all times." Her voice was calm and reasonable; Asher felt impressed.

"So you can encounter God while you're alive," he said.

"Under exceptional circumstances. Originally God and Moses talked together as a man talks with his friend."

"What went wrong?"

"Wrong in what way?"

"Nobody hears God's voice anymore."

Rybys said, "You do."

"My audio and video systems do."

"That's better than nothing." She eyed him. "You don't seem to enjoy it."

"It's interfering with my life."

She said, "So am I."

To that he could think of no response; it was true.

"What do you normally do all the time?" Rybys asked. "Lie

in your bunk listening to the Fox? The foodman told me that; is it true? That doesn't sound to me like much of a life."

Anger touched him, a weary anger. He was tired of defending his life-style. So he said nothing.

"I think what I'll lend you first," Rybys said, "is C. S. Lewis's *The Problem of Pain*. In that book he—"

"I read *Out of the Silent Planet*," Asher said.

"Did you like it?"

"It was OK."

Rybys said, "And you should read *The Screwtape Letters*. I have two copies of that."

To himself, Asher thought, Can't I just watch you slowly die, and learn about God from that? "Look," he said. "I *am* Scientific Legate. The Party. You understand? That's my decision; that's the side I found. Pain and illness are something to be eradicated, not understood. There is no afterlife and there is no God, except maybe a freak ionospheric disturbance that's fucking up my equipment here on this dipshit mountain. If when I die I find out I'm wrong I'll plead ignorance and a bad upbringing. Meanwhile I'm more interested in shielding my cables and eliminating the interference than I am in talking back and forth with this Yah. I have no goats to sacrifice and anyway I have other things to do. I resent my Fox tapes being ruined; they are precious to me and some of them I can't replace. Anyhow God doesn't insert such phrases as 'your behind' in otherwise beautiful songs. Not any god I can imagine."

Rybys said, "He's trying to get your attention."

"He would do better to say, 'Look, let's talk.'"

"This apparently is a furtive life form. It's not isomorphic with us. It doesn't think the way we do."

"It's a pest."

Rybys said, pondering, "It may be modifying its manifestations to protect you."

"From what?"

"From it." Suddenly she shuddered wildly, in evident pain. "Oh goddam it! My hair *is* falling out!" She got to her feet. "I have to go back to my dome and put on that wig they gave me. This is awful. Will you go with me? *Please?*"

He thought, I don't see how someone whose hair is falling

out can believe in God. "I can't," he said. "I just can't go with you. I'm sorry. I don't have any portable air and I have to person my equipment. It's the truth."

Gazing at him unhappily, Rybys nodded. Apparently she believed him. He felt a little guilty, but, more than that, he experienced overwhelming relief that she was leaving. The burden of dealing with her would be off him, at least for a time. And perhaps if he got lucky he could make the relief permanent. If he had any prayer at all it was, I hope I never see her enter this dome again. As long as she lives.

A pleased sense of relaxation stole over him as he watched her suit up for the trip back to her dome. And he inquired of himself which of his trove of Fox tapes he would play when Rybys and her cruel verbal snipings had departed, and he would be free again: free to be what he truly was, the connoisseur of the undying lovely. The beauty and perfection toward which all things moved: Linda Fox.

That night as he lay sleeping a voice said softly to him, "Herbert, Herbert."

He opened his eyes. "I'm not on standby," he said, thinking it was the mother ship. "Dome Nine is active. Let me sleep."

"Look," the voice said.

He looked—and saw that his control board, which governed all his communications gear, was on fire. "Jesus Christ," he said, and reached for the wall switch that would turn on the emergency fire extinguisher. But then he realized something. Something perplexing. Although the control board was burning, it was not consumed.

The fire dazzled him and burned his eyes. He shut his eyes and put his arm over his face. "Who is it?" he said.

The voice said, "It is Ehyeh."

"Well," Herb Asher said, amazed. It was the deity of the mountain, speaking to him openly, without an electronic interface. A strange sense of his own worthlessness overcame Herb Asher, and he kept his face covered. "What do you want?" he said. "I mean, it's late. This is my sleep cycle."

"Sleep no more," Yah said.

"I've had a hard day." He was frightened.

Yah said, "I command you to take care of the ailing girl. She is all alone. If you do not hasten to her side I will burn down your dome and all the equipment in it, as well as all you own besides. I will scorch you with flame until you wake up. You are not awake, Herbert, not yet, but I will cause you to be awake; I will make you rise up from your bunk and go and help her. Later I will tell her and you why, but now you are not to know."

"I don't think you have the right person," Asher said. "I think you should be talking to M.E.D. It's their responsibility."

At that moment an acrid stench reached his nose. And, as he watched in dismay, his control board burned down to the floor, into a little pile of slag.

Shit, he thought.

"Were you to lie again to her about your portable air," Yah said, "I would afflict you terribly, beyond repair, just as this equipment is now beyond repair. Now I shall destroy your Linda Fox tapes." Immediately the cabinet in which Herb Asher kept his video and audio tapes began to burn.

"Please," he said.

The flames disappeared. The tapes were undamaged. Herb Asher got up from his bunk and went over to the cabinet; reaching out his hand he touched the cabinet—and instantly yanked his hand away; the cabinet was searingly hot.

"Touch it again," Yah said.

"I will not," Asher said.

"You will trust the Lord your God."

He reached out again and this time found the cabinet cold. So he ran his fingers over the plastic boxes containing the tapes. They, too, were cold. "Well, goodness," he said, at a loss.

"Play one of the tapes," Yah said.

"Which one?"

"Any one."

He selected a tape at random and placed it into the deck. He turned his audio system on.

The tape was blank.

"You erased my Fox tapes," he said.

"That is what I have done," Yah said.

"Forever?"

"Until you hasten to the side of the ailing girl and care for her."

"Now? She's probably asleep."

Yah said, "She is sitting crying."

The sense of worthlessness within Herb Asher burgeoned; in shame he shut his eyes. "I'm sorry," he said.

"It is not too late. If you hurry you can reach her in time."

"What do you mean, 'in time'?"

Yah did not answer, but in Herb Asher's mind appeared a picture, resembling a hologram; it was in color and it was in depth. Rybys Rommey sat at her kitchen table in a blue robe; on the table was a bottle of medication and a glass of water. In dejection she sat resting her chin on her fist; in her fist she clutched a wadded-up handkerchief.

"I'll get my suit on," Asher said; he popped the suit-compartment door open, and his suit—little used and long neglected—tumbled out onto the floor.

Ten minutes later he stood outside his dome, in the bulky suit, his lamp sweeping out over the expanse of frozen methane before him; he trembled, feeling the cold even through the suit—which was a delusion, he realized, since the suit was absolutely insulating. What an experience, he said to himself as he started walking down the slope. Roused out of my sleep in the middle of the night, my equipment burned down, my tapes erased—bulk erased in their totality.

The methane crystals crunched under his boots as he walked down the slope, homing in on the automatic signal emitted by Rybys Rommey's dome; the signal would guide him. Pictures inside my head, he thought. Pictures of a girl about to take her own life. It's a good thing Yah woke me. She probably would have done it.

He was still frightened, and as he descended the slope he sang to himself an old Communist Party marching song.

> Because he fought for freedom
> He was forced to leave his home.
> Near the blood-stained Manzanares,
> Where he led the fight to hold Madrid,
> Died Hans, the Commissar,

Died Hans, the Commissar.
With heart and hand I pledge you,
While I load my gun again,
You will never be forgotten,
Nor the enemy forgiven,
Hans Beimler, our Commissar,
Hans Beimler, our Commissar.

4

As Herb Asher descended the slope the meter in his hand showed the homing signal growing in strength. She ascended this hill to get to my dome, he realized. I made her walk uphill, since I wouldn't go to her. I made a sick girl toil her way up step by step, carrying an armload of supplies. I will fry in hell.

But, he realized, it's not too late.

He made me take her seriously, Asher realized. I simply was not taking her seriously. It was as if I imagined that she was making up her illness. Telling a tale to get attention. What does that say about me? he asked himself. Because in point of fact I really knew she was sick, truly sick, not faking it. I have been asleep, he said to himself. And, while I slept, a girl has been dying.

And then he thought about Yah, and he trembled. I can get my rig repaired, he thought. The gear that Yah burned down. That won't be hard; all I have to do is notify the mother ship and inform them that I suffered a meltdown. And Yah promised to restore to me my Fox tapes—which undoubtedly he can do. But I've got to go back to that dome and live there. How can I live there? I can't live there. It's impossible.

Yah has plans for me, he thought. And he felt fear, realizing this. He can make me do anything.

Rybys greeted him impassively. She did have on a blue robe and she did hold a wadded-up handkerchief, and, he saw, her eyes were red from crying. "Come in," she said, although he was already in the dome; she seemed a little dazed. "I was thinking about you," she said. "Sitting and thinking."

On the kitchen table stood a medicine bottle. Full.

"Oh, that," she said. "I was having trouble sleeping and I was thinking about taking a sleeping pill."

"Put it away," he said.

Obediently, she returned the bottle to her bathroom cabinet.

"I owe you an apology," he said.

"No you don't. Want something to drink? What time is it?" She turned to look at her wall clock. "I was up anyhow; you didn't wake me. Some telemetric data was coming in." She pointed to her gear; lights showed, indicating activity.

He said, "I mean I had air. Portable air."

"I know that. Everyone has portable air. Sit down; I'll fix you tea." She rooted in an overflowing drawer beside her stove. "Somewhere I have teabags."

Now, for the first time, he became aware of the condition of her dome. It was shocking. Dirty dishes, pots and pans and even glasses of spoiled food, soiled clothing strewn everywhere, litter and debris . . . Troubled, he gazed around, wondering if he should offer to clean up the place. And she moved so slowly, with such evident fatigue. He had an intuition, suddenly, that she was far sicker than she had originally led him to believe.

"It's a sty," she said.

He said, "You are very tired."

"Well, it wears me out to heave up my guts every day of the week. Here's a teabag. Shit; it's been used once. I use them and then dry them out. It's OK once, but sometimes I find I'm reusing the same bag again and again. I'll try to find a fresh one." She continued to rummage.

The TV screen showed a picture. It was an animated horror: a vast hemorrhoid that swelled and pulsed angrily. "What are you watching?" Asher asked. He averted his gaze from the animation.

"There's a new soap opera on. It just began the other day. 'The Splendor of—' I forget. Somebody or something. It's really interesting. They've been running it a lot."

"You like the soaps?" he said.

"They keep me company. Turn up the sound."

He turned up the sound. The soap opera had now resumed, replacing the animated hemorrhoid. An elderly bearded man, an exceedingly hairy old man, struggled with two popeyed arachnids who sought, apparently, to decapitate him. "Get your fucking mandibles off me!" the elderly man shouted, flailing about. The flash of laser beams ignited the screen. Herb Asher remembered once again the burning down of his communications gear by Yah; he felt his heart race in anxiety.

"If you don't want to watch it—" Rybys said.

"It's not that." Telling her about Yah would be hard; he doubted if he could do it. "Something happened to me. Something woke me." He rubbed his eyes.

"I'll bring you up to date," Rybys said. "Elias Tate—"

"Who is Elias Tate?" Asher interrupted.

"The old bearded man; I remember what the program is called, now. 'The Splendor of Elias Tate.' Elias has fallen into the hands—although they don't have hands, actually—of the ant-men of Sychron Two. There's this queen who is really evil, named—I forget." She reflected. "Hudwillub, I think. Yes, that's it. Anyhow, Hudwillub wants Elias Tate dead. She's really awful; you'll see her. She has one eye."

"Gracious," Asher said, not interested. "Rybys," he said, "listen to me."

As if she had not heard him, Rybys plodded on, "However, Elias has this friend Elisha McVane; they're really good friends and they always help each other out. It's sort of—" She glanced at Asher. "Like you and me. You know; helping each other. I fixed you dinner and you came over here because you were worried about me."

"I came over here," he said, "because I was told to."

"But you were worried."

"Yes," he said.

"Elisha McVane is a lot younger than Elias. He's really good-looking. Anyhow, Hudwillub wants—"

"Yah sent me," Asher said.

"Sent you what?"

"Here." His heart continued to labor.

"Did he? That's really interesting. Anyhow, Hudwillub is very beautiful. You'll like her. I mean, you'll like her physically. Well, let me put it this way; she's objectively *obviously* attractive, but spiritually she's lost. Elias Tate is a sort of external conscience for her. What do you take in your tea?"

"Did you hear—" he began and then gave up.

"Milk?" Rybys examined the contents of her refrigerator, got out a carton of milk, poured some of the milk into a glass, tasted it and made a face. "It's sour. Goddam." She poured the milk down the sink drain.

"What I am telling you," Asher said, "is important. The deity of my hill woke me up in the night to tell me that you were in trouble. He burned down half my equipment. He erased all my Fox tapes."

"You can get more from the mother ship."

Asher stared at her.

"Why are you staring at me?" Quickly, Rybys inspected the buttons of her robe. "I'm not unfastened, am I?"

Only mentally, he thought.

"Sugar?" she said.

"Okay," he said. "I should notify the C-in-C on the mother ship. This is a major matter."

Rybys said, "You do that. Contact the C-in-C and tell him that God talked to you."

"Can I use your gear? I'll report my meltdown at the same time. That's my proof."

"No," she said.

"No?" He glared at her, baffled.

"That's inductive reasoning, which is suspect. You can't reason back from effects to causes."

"What the hell are you talking about?"

Calmly, Rybys said, "Your meltdown doesn't prove that God exists. Here; I'll write it down in symbolic logic for you. If I can find my pen. Look for it; it's red. The pen, not the ink. I used to—"

"Give me a minute. Just one goddam minute. To think. Okay? Will you do that?" He heard his voice rising.

"There's someone outside," Rybys said. She pointed to an indicator; it blinked rapidly. "A Clem stealing my trash. I keep my trash outside. That's because—"

"Let the Clem in," Asher said, "and I'll tell *it*."

"About Yah? Okay, and then they'll start coming to your little hill with offerings, and they'll be consulting Yah all day and all night; you'll never get any peace. You won't be able to lie in your bunk and listen to Linda Fox. The tea is ready." She filled two cups with boiling water.

Asher dialed the mother ship. A moment later he had the ship's operator circuit. "I want to report a contact with God," he said. "This is for the Commander-in-Chief personally. God spoke to me an hour ago. An autochthonic deity called Yah."

"Just a moment." A pause and then the ship's operator circuit said, "This wouldn't be the Linda Fox man, would it? Station Five?"

"Yes," he said.

"We have your video tape of *Fiddler on the Roof* that you requested. We tried to transmit it to your dome but your receiving manifold appears to be malfunctioning. We have notified repair and they will be out shortly. The tape features the original cast starring Topol, Norma Crane, Molly Picon—"

"Just a minute," Asher said. Rybys had put her hand on his arm, to attract his attention. "What is it?" he said.

"There's a human being outside; I got a look at it. Do something."

To the mother ship's operator circuit, Asher said, "I'll call you back." He rang off.

Rybys had turned on the external floodlight. Through the dome's port Asher saw a strange sight: a human being, but not wearing a standard suit; instead the man wore what looked like a robe, a very heavy robe, and leather apron. His boots had a rustic, much-mended quality about them. Even his helmet seemed antique. What the hell is this? Asher asked himself.

"Thank God you're here," Rybys said. From the locker by her bunk she brought out a gun. "I'm going to shoot him," she said. "Tell him to come in; use the bullhorn. You make sure you're out of the way."

I'm dealing with lunatics, Asher thought. "Let's simply not let him in."

"Fuck that! He'll wait until you're gone. Tell him to come in. He's going to rape me and kill me and kill you, if we don't get him first. You know what he is? I recognize what he is; I know that gray robe. He's a Wild Beggar. You know what a Wild Beggar is?"

"I know what a Wild Beggar is," Asher said.

"They're criminals!"

"They're renegades," Asher said. "They don't have domes any more."

"Criminals." She cocked the gun.

He did not know whether to laugh or be dismayed; Rybys stood there swollen with indignation, in her blue bathrobe and furry slippers; she had put her hair up in curlers and her face was puffy and red with indignation. "I don't want him skulking around my dome. It's *my* dome! Hell, I'll call the mother ship and they'll send out a party of cops, if you're not going to do anything."

Turning on the external bullhorn, Asher said into it, "You, out there."

The Wild Beggar glanced up, blinked, shielded his eyes, then waved at Asher through the port. A wrinkled, weathered, hairy old man, grinning at Asher.

"Who are you?" Asher said into the bullhorn.

The old man's lips moved, but of course Asher heard nothing. Rybys's outside mike either wasn't turned on or it wasn't working. To Rybys Asher said, "Please don't shoot him. OK? I'm going to let him in. I think I know who he is."

Slowly and carefully Rybys disarmed her gun.

"Come inside," Asher said into the bullhorn. He activated the hatch mechanism and the intermediate membrane dropped into place. With vigorous steps the Wild Beggar disappeared inside.

"Who is he?" Rybys said.

Asher said, "It's Elias Tate."

"Oh, then that soap opera isn't a soap opera." She turned to the screen of the TV. "I've been intercepting a psychotronic information-transfer. I must have plugged in the wrong cable. Damn. Well, what the hell. I thought it was on the air an awful lot of the time."

Shaking off methane crystals, Elias Tate appeared before them, wild and hairy and gray, and happy to be inside out of the cold. He began at once to remove his helmet and vast robe.

"How are you feeling?" he asked Rybys. "Any better? Has this donkey been taking good care of you? His ass is grass if he hasn't."

Wind blew about him, as if he were the center of a storm.

To the girl in the white frock Emmanuel said, "I am new. I do not understand where I am."

The bamboo rustled. The children played. And Mr. Plaudet stood with Elias Tate watching the boy and girl. "Do you know me?" the girl said to Emmanuel.

"No," he said. He did not. And yet she seemed familiar. Her

face was small and pale and she had long dark hair. Her eyes, Emmanuel thought. They are old. The eyes of wisdom.

To him in a low voice the girl said, "'When there was yet no ocean I was born.'" She waited a moment, studying him, searching for something, a response perhaps; he did not know. "'I was fashioned in times long past,'" the girl said. "'At the beginning, long before earth itself.'"

Mr. Plaudet called to her reprovingly, "Tell him your name. Introduce yourself."

"I am Zina," the girl said.

"Emmanuel," Mr. Plaudet said, "this is Zina Pallas."

"I don't know her," Emmanuel said.

"You two are going to go and play on the swings," Mr. Plaudet said, "while Mr. Tate and I talk. Go on. Go."

Elias came over to the boy, bent down and said, "What did she say to you just now? This little girl, Zina; what did she tell you?" He looked angry, but Emmanuel was accustomed to the old man's anger; it flashed forth constantly. "I couldn't hear."

"You grow deaf," Emmanuel said.

"No, she lowered her voice," Elias said.

"I said nothing that was not said long ago," Zina said.

Perplexed, Elias glanced from Emmanuel to the girl. "What nationality are you?" he asked the girl.

"Let's go," Zina said. She took Emmanuel by the hand and led him away; the two of them walked in silence.

"Is this a nice school?" Emmanuel asked her presently.

"It's OK. The computers are outdated. And the government monitors everything. The computers are government computers; you must keep that in mind. How old is Mr. Tate?"

"Very old," Emmanuel said. "About four thousand years old, I guess. He goes away and comes back."

"You've seen me before," Zina said.

"No I haven't."

"Your memory is missing."

"Yes," he said, surprised that she knew. "Elias tells me it will return."

"Your mother is dead?"

He nodded.

"Can you see her?" Zina said.

"Sometimes."

"Tap your father's memories. Then you can be with her in retrotime."

"Maybe."

"He has it all stored."

Emmanuel said, "It frightens me. Because of the crash. I think they did it on purpose."

"Of course they did, but it was you they wanted, even if they didn't know it."

"They may kill me now."

"There is no way they can find you," Zina said.

"How do you know that?"

"Because I am that which knows. I will know for you until you remember, and even then I will stay with you. You always wanted that. I was at your side every day; I was your darling and your delight, playing always in your presence. And when you had finished, my chief delight was in them."

Emmanuel asked, "How old are you?"

"Older than Elias."

"Older than me?"

"No," Zina said.

"You look older than me."

"That's because you have forgotten. I am here to cause you to remember, but you are not to tell anyone that, even Elias."

Emmanuel said, "I tell him everything."

"Not about me," Zina said. "Don't tell him about me. You have to promise me that. If you tell anyone about me the government will find out."

"Show me the computers."

"Here they are." Zina led him into a large room. "You can ask them anything but they give you modified answers. Maybe you can trick them. I like to trick them. They're really stupid."

He said to her, "You can do magic."

At that Zina smiled. "How did you know?"

"Your name. I know what it means."

"It's only a name."

"No," he said. "Zina is not your name; Zina is what you *are*."

"Tell me what that is," the girl said, "but tell me very quietly. Because if you know what I am then some of your memory is returning. But be careful; the government listens and watches."

"Do the magic first," Emmanuel said.

"They will know; the government will know."

Going across the room, Emmanuel stopped by a cage with a rabbit in it. "No," he said. "Not that. Is there another animal here that you could be?"

"Careful, Emmanuel," Zina said.

"A bird," Emmanuel said.

"A cat," Zina said. "Just a second." She paused, moved her lips. The cat came in, then, from outside, a gray-striped female. "Shall I be the cat?"

"I want to be the cat," Emmanuel said.

"The cat will die."

"Let the cat die."

"Why?"

"They were created for that."

Zina said, "Once a calf about to be slaughtered ran to a Rabbi for protection and put its head between the Rabbi's knees. The Rabbi said, 'Go! For this you were created,' meaning, 'You were created to be slaughtered.'"

"And then?" Emmanuel said.

Zina said, "God greatly afflicted the Rabbi for a long time."

"I understand," Emmanuel said. "You have taught me. I will not be the cat."

"Then I will be the cat," Zina said, "and it will not die because I am not like you." She bent down, her hands on her knees, to address the cat. Emmanuel watched, and presently the cat came to him and asked to speak to him. He lifted it up and held it in his arms and the cat placed its paw against his face. With its paw it told him that mice were annoying and a bother and yet the cat did not wish to see an end of mice because, as annoying as they were, still there was something about them that was fascinating, more fascinating than annoying; and so the cat sought out mice, although the cat did not respect the mice. The cat wanted there to be mice and yet the cat despised mice.

All this the cat communicated by means of its paw against the boy's cheek.

"All right," Emmanuel said.

Zina said, "Do you know where any mice are right now?"

"You are the cat," Emmanuel said.

"Do you know where any mice are right now?" she repeated.

"You are a kind of mechanism," Emmanuel said.

"Do you know—"

"You have to find them yourself," Emmanuel said.

"But you could help me. You could chase them my way." The girl opened her mouth and showed him her teeth. He laughed.

Against his cheek the paw conveyed more thoughts; that Mr. Plaudet was coming into the building. The cat could hear his steps. Put me down, the cat communicated.

Emmanuel set the cat down.

"Are there any mice?" Zina said.

"Stop," Emmanuel said. "Mr. Plaudet is here."

"Oh," Zina said, and nodded.

Entering the room, Mr. Plaudet said, "I see you've found Misty, Emmanuel. Isn't she a nice little animal? Zina, what's wrong with you? Why are you staring at me?"

Emmanuel laughed; Zina was having trouble disentangling herself from the cat. "Be careful, Mr. Plaudet," he said. "Zina'll scratch you."

"You mean Misty," Mr. Plaudet said.

"That's not the kind of brain damage I have," Emmanuel said. "To—" He broke off; he could feel Zina telling him *no*.

"He's not very good at names, Mr. Plaudet," Zina said. She had managed to separate herself from the cat, now, and Misty, perplexed, walked slowly away. Obviously Misty had not been able to fathom why, all at once, she found herself in two different places.

"Do you remember my name, Emmanuel?" Mr. Plaudet asked.

"Mr. Talk," Emmanuel said.

"No," Mr. Plaudet said. He frowned. "'Plaudet' is German for 'talk,' though."

"I told Emmanuel that," Zina said. "About your name."

After Mr. Plaudet left, Emmanuel said to the girl, "Can you summon the bells? For dancing?"

"Of course." And then she flushed. "That was a trick question."

"But you play tricks. You always play tricks. I'd like to hear the bells, but I don't want to dance. I'd like to watch the dancing, though."

"Some other time," Zina said. "You do remember something, then. If you know about the dancing."

"I think I remember. I asked Elias to take me to see my father, where they have him stored. I want to see what he looks like. If I saw him, maybe I'd remember a lot more. I've seen pictures of him."

Zina said, "There's something you want from me even more than the dancing."

"I want to know about the time power you have. I want to see you make time stop and then run backward. That's the best trick of all."

"I said you should see your father about that."

"But you can do it," Emmanuel said. "Right here."

"I'm not going to. It disturbs too many things. They never line up again. Once they're out of synch— Well, someday I'll do it for you. I could take you back to before the collision. But I'm not sure that's wise because you might have to live it over, and that would make you worse. Your mother was very sick, you know. She probably would not have lived anyhow. And your father will be out of cryonic suspension in four more years."

"You're sure?" Emmanuel said excitedly.

"When you're ten years old you'll see him. He's back with your mother right now; he likes to retrotime to when he first met her. She was very sloppy; he had to clean up her dome."

"What is a 'dome'?" Emmanuel asked.

"They don't have them here; that's for outspace. The colonists. Where you were *born*. I know Elias told you. Why don't you listen to him more?"

"He's a man," Emmanuel said. "A human being."

"No he's not."

"He was born as a man. And then I—" He paused, and a segment of memory came back to him. "I didn't want him to die. Did I? So I took him, all at once. When he and—" He tried to think, to frame the word in his mind.

"Elisha," Zina said.

"They were walking together," Emmanuel said, "and I took

him up, and he sent part of himself back to Elisha. So he never died; Elias, I mean. But that's not his real name."

"That's his Greek name."

"I do remember some things, then," Emmanuel said.

"You'll remember more. You see, you set up a disinhibiting stimulus that would remind you before—well, when the right time came. You're the only one who knows what the stimulus is. Even Elias doesn't know it. *I* don't know it; you hid it from me, back when you were what you were."

"I am what I am now," Emmanuel said.

"Yes, except that you have an impaired memory," Zina said, pragmatically. "So it isn't the same."

"I guess not," the boy said. "I thought you said you could make me remember."

"There are different kinds of remembering. Elias can make you remember a little, and I can make you remember more; but only your own disinhibiting stimulus can make you *be*. The word is . . . you have to bend close to me to listen; only you should hear this word. No, I'll write it." Zina took a piece of paper from a nearby desk, and a length of chalk, and wrote one word.

HAYAH

Gazing down at the word, Emmanuel felt memory come to him, but only for a nanosecond; at once—almost at once—it departed.

"*Hayah*," he said, aloud.

"That is the Divine Tongue," Zina said.

"Yes," he said. "I know." The word was Hebrew, a Hebrew root word. And the Divine Name itself came from that word. He felt a vast and terrible awe; he felt afraid.

"Fear not," Zina said quietly.

"I am afraid," Emmanuel said, "because for a moment I re-membered." *Knew*, he thought, *who I am.*

But he forgot again. By the time he and the girl had gone outside into the yard he no longer knew. And yet—strange!— he knew that he had known, known and forgotten again almost at once. As if, he thought, I have two minds inside me, one on the surface and the other in the depths. The surface one has been injured but the deep one has not. And yet the deep one can't speak; it is closed up. Forever? No; there would be the stimulus, one day. His own device.

Probably it was necessary that he not remember. Had he been able to recall into consciousness everything, the basis of it all, then the government would have killed him. There existed two heads of the beast, the religious one, a Cardinal Fulton Statler Harms, and then a scientific one named N. Bulkowsky. But these were phantoms. To Emmanuel the Christian-Islamic Church and the Scientific Legate did not constitute reality. He knew what lay behind them. Elias had told him. But even had Elias not told him he would have known anyhow; he would everywhere and at every time be able to identify the Adversary.

What did puzzle him was the girl Zina. Something in the situation did not ring right. Yet she had not lied; she could not lie. He had not made it possible for her to deceive; that constituted her fundamental nature: her veracity. All he had to do was ask her.

Meanwhile, he would assume that she was one of the *zine*; she herself had admitted that she danced. Her name, of course, came from *dziana*, and sometimes it appeared as she used it, as Zina.

Going up to her, stopping behind her but standing very close to her, he said in her ear, "Diana."

At once she turned. And as she turned he saw her change. Her nose became different and instead of a girl he saw now a grown woman wearing a metal mask pushed back so that it revealed her face, a Greek face; and the mask, he realized, was the war mask. That would be Pallas. He was seeing Pallas, now, not Zina. But, he knew, neither one told him the truth about her. These were only images. Forms that she took. Still, the metal mask of war impressed him. It faded, now, this image, and he knew that no one but himself had seen it. She would never reveal it to other people.

"Why did you call me 'Diana'?" Zina asked.

"Because that is one of your names."

Zina said, "We will go to the Garden one of these days. So you can see the animals."

"I would like that," he said. "Where is the Garden?"

"The Garden is here," Zina said.

"I can't see it."

"You made the Garden," Zina said.

"I can't remember." His head hurt; he put his hands against the sides of his face. Like my father, he thought; he used to do what I am doing. Except that he is not my father.

To himself he said, I have no father.

Pain filled him, the pain of isolation; suddenly Zina had disappeared, and the school yard, the building, the city—everything vanished. He tried to make it return but it would not return. No time passed. Even time had been abolished. *I have completely forgotten,* he realized. *And because I have forgotten, it is all gone.* Even Zina, his darling and delight, could not remind him now; he had returned to the void.

A low murmuring sound moved slowly across the face of the void, across the deep. Heat could be seen; at this transformation of frequency heat appeared as light, but only as a dull red light, a somber light. He found it ugly.

My father, he thought. You are not.

His lips moved and he pronounced one word.

HAYAH

The world returned.

5

Elias Tate, throwing himself down on a heap of Rybys's dirty clothes, said, "Do you have any real coffee? Not that joke stuff the mother ship peddles to you." He grimaced.

"I have some," Rybys said, "but I don't know where it is."

"Have you been throwing up frequently?" Elias said to her, eyeing her. "Every day or so?"

"Yes." She glanced at Herb Asher, amazed.

"You're pregnant," Elias Tate said.

"I'm in chemo!" Rybys said angrily, her face dark red with fury. "I'm heaving up my guts because of the goddam Neurotoxite and the Prednoferic—"

"Consult your computer terminal," Elias said.

There was silence.

"Who are you?" Herb Asher said.

"A Wild Beggar," Elias said.

"Why do you know so much about me?" Rybys said.

Elias said, "I came to be with you. I'll be with you from now on. Consult your terminal."

Seating herself at her computer terminal, Rybys placed her arm in the M.E.D. slot. "I hate to put it to you this way," she said to Elias and Herb Asher, "but I'm a virgin."

"Get out of here," Herb Asher said quietly to the old man.

"Wait until M.E.D. gives her the test result," Elias said.

Tears filled Rybys's eyes. "Shit. This is just terrible. I have M.S. and then now this, as if M.S. isn't enough."

To Herb Asher, Elias said, "She must return to Earth. The authorities will permit it; her illness will be sufficient legal cause."

To the computer terminal, which had now locked onto the M.E.D. channel, Rybys said brokenly, "Am I pregnant?"

Silence.

The terminal said, "You are three months pregnant, Ms. Rommey."

Rising, Rybys walked to the port of the dome and stared fixedly out at the methane panorama. No one spoke.

"It's Yah, isn't it?" Rybys said presently.

"Yes," Elias said.

"This was planned out a long time ago," Rybys said.

"Yes," Elias said.

"And my M.S. is so there is a legal pretext for me to return to Earth."

"To get you past Immigration," Elias said.

Rybys said, "And you know all about it." She pointed at Herb Asher. "He's going to say he's the father."

"He will," Elias said, "and he will go with you. So will I. You'll be checking in at Bethesda Naval Hospital at Chevy Chase. We'll go by emergency axial flight, high-velocity flight, because of the seriousness of your physical condition. We should start as soon as possible. You already have the papers in your possession, the necessary legal papers requesting a transfer back home."

"Yah made me sick?" Rybys said.

After a pause Elias nodded.

"What is this?" Rybys said furiously. "A coup of some kind? You're going to smuggle—"

Interrupting her, Elias said in a low, harsh voice, "The Roman X Fretensis."

"Masada," Rybys said. "Seventy-three C.E. Right? I thought so. I started thinking so when a Clem told me about the mountain deity at our Station Five."

"He lost," Elias said. "The Tenth Legion was made up of fifteen thousand experienced soldiers. But Masada held out for almost two years. And there were less than a thousand Jews at Masada, including women and children."

To Herb Asher, Rybys said, "Only seven women and children survived the fall of Masada. It was a Jewish fortress. They had hidden in a water conduit." To Elias Tate she said, "And Yahweh was driven from the Earth."

"And the hopes of man," Elias said, "faded away."

Herb Asher said, "What are you two talking about?"

"A fiasco," Elias Tate said briefly.

"So he—Yah—first makes me sick, and then he—" She broke off. "Did he start out from this star system originally? Or was he driven here?"

"He was driven here," Elias said. "There is a zone around Earth now. A zone of evil. It keeps him out."

"The *Lord*?" Rybys said. "The Lord is kept out? Away from Earth?" She stared at Elias Tate.

"The people of Earth do not know," Elias Tate said.

"But you know," Herb Asher said. "Right? How do you know all these things? How do you know so much? Who are you?"

Elias Tate said, "My name is Elijah."

The three of them sat together drinking tea. Rybys's face had an embittered, stark expression on it, a look of fury; she said almost nothing.

"What bothers you the most?" Elias Tate said. "The fact that Yah was driven off Earth, that he was defeated by the Adversary, or that you have to go back to Earth carrying him inside you?"

She laughed. "Leaving my station."

"You have been honored," Elias said.

"Honored with illness," Rybys said; her hand shook as she lifted her cup to her lips.

"Do you realize who it is that you carry in your womb?" Elias said.

"Sure," Rybys said.

"You are not impressed," Elias said.

"I had my life all planned out," Rybys said.

"I think you're taking a small view of this," Herb Asher said. Both Elias and Rybys glanced at him with distaste, as if he had intruded. "Maybe I don't understand," he said, weakly.

Reaching out her hand, Rybys patted him. "It's OK. I don't understand either. Why me? I asked that when I came down with the M.S. Why the hell me? Why the hell you? You have to leave your station, too; *and* your Fox tapes. *And* lying all day and night in your bunk doing nothing, with your gear on auto. Christ. Well, I guess Job had it right. God afflicts those he loves."

"The three of us will travel to Earth," Elias said, "and there you will give birth to your son, Emmanuel. Yah planned this at the beginning of the age, before the defeat at Masada, before the fall of the Temple. He foresaw his defeat and moved to rectify the situation. God can be defeated but only temporarily. *With God the remedy is greater than the malady.*"

" '*Felix culpa*,' " Rybys said.

"Yes," Elias agreed. To Herb Asher he explained, "It means 'happy fault,' referring to the fall, the original fall. Had there been no fall perhaps there would have been no Incarnation. No birth of Christ."

"Catholic doctrine," Rybys said remotely. "I never thought it would apply to me personally."

Herb Asher said, "But didn't Christ conquer the forces of evil? He said, 'I have overcome the world.'"

"Well," Rybys said, "apparently he was wrong."

"When Masada fell," Elias said, "all was lost. God did not enter history in the first century C.E.; he left history. Christ's mission was a failure."

"You are very old," Rybys said. "How old are you, Elias? Almost four thousand years, I guess. You can take a long-term view but I can't. You've known this about the First Advent all this time? For two thousand years?"

"As God foresaw the original fall," Elias said, "he also foresaw that Jesus would not be acceptable. It was known to God before it happened."

"What does he know about this now?" Rybys said. "What we are going to do?"

Elias was silent.

"He doesn't know," Rybys said.

"This—" Elias hesitated.

"The final battle," Rybys said. "It could go either way. Couldn't it?"

"In the end," Elias said, "God wins. He has absolute foresight."

"He can know," Rybys said, "but does that mean he can— Look, I really don't feel well. It's late and I'm sick and I'm worn out and I feel as if . . ." She gestured. "I'm a virgin and I'm pregnant. The Immigration doctors will never believe it."

Herb Asher said, "I think that's the point. That's why I'm supposed to marry you and come along."

"I'm not going to marry you; I don't even know you." She stared at him. "Are you kidding? *Marry* you? I've got M.S. and I'm pregnant— Damn it, both of you; go away and leave me alone. I mean it. Why didn't I take that bottle of Seconax when I had the chance? I never had the chance; Yah was watching. He sees even the fallen sparrow. I forgot."

"Do you have any whiskey?" Herb Asher said.

"Oh fine," Rybys said bitterly. "You can get drunk but can I? With M.S. and some kind of baby inside me? There I was"—she glared hatefully at Elias Tate—"picking up your thoughts visually on my TV set, and I imagined in my deluded folly that it was a corny soap opera dreamed up by writers at Fomalhaut—pure fiction. Arachnids were going to decapitate you? Is that what your unconscious fantasies consist of? And you're Yahweh's spokesperson?" She blanched. "I spoke the Sacred Name. Sorry."

"Christians speak it all the time," Elias said.

Rybys said, "But I'm a Jew. I *would* be a Jew; that's what got me into this. If I was a Gentile Yah wouldn't have picked me. If I'd ever been laid I'd—" She broke off. "The Divine Machinery has a peculiar brutality to it," she finished. "It isn't romantic. It's cruel; it really is."

"Because there is so much at stake," Elias said.

"What is at stake?" Rybys said.

"The universe exists because Yah remembers it," Elias said.

Both Herb Asher and Rybys stared at him.

"If Yah forgets, the universe ceases," Elias said.

"Can he forget?" Rybys said.

"He has yet to forget," Elias said elliptically.

"Meaning he could forget," Rybys said. "Then that's what this is about. You just spelled it out. I see. Well—" She shrugged and then reflexively sipped at her cup of tea. "Then I wouldn't exist in the first place except for Yah. Nothing would exist."

Elias said, "His name means 'He Brings into Existence Whatever Exists.'"

"Including evil?" Herb Asher asked.

"It says in Scripture," Elias said, "thus:

". . . So that men from the rising and the setting sun
May know that there is none but I:
I am the LORD, there is no other;
I make the light, I create darkness,
author alike of prosperity and trouble.
I, the LORD, do all these things."

"Where does it say that?" Rybys said.
"Isaiah forty-five," Elias said.

" 'Prosperity and trouble,' " Rybys echoed. " 'Weal and woe.' "

"Then you know the passage." Elias regarded her.

"It's hard to believe," she said.

"It is monotheism," Elias said harshly.

"Yes," she said, "I guess it is. But it's brutal. What's happening to me is brutal. And there's more ahead. I want out and I can't get out. Nobody asked me originally. Nobody is asking me now. Yah foresees what lies ahead but I don't, except that there's more cruelty and pain and throwing up. Serving God seems to mean throwing up and shooting yourself with a needle every day. I am a diseased rat in a kind of cage. That's what he's made me into. I have no faith and no hope and he has no love, only power. God is a symptom of power, nothing else. The hell with it. I give up. I don't care. I'll do what I have to but it will kill me and I know it. OK?"

The two men were silent. They did not look at her or at each other.

Herb Asher said finally, "He saved your life tonight. He sent me over here."

"That and five credpops will get you a cupee of Kaff," Rybys said. "He gave me the illness in the first place!"

"And he's guiding you through," Herb said.

"To what end?" she said.

"To emancipate an infinitude of lives," Elias said.

"Egypt," she said. "And the brick makers. Over and over again. Why doesn't the emancipation last? Why does it fade out? Isn't there any final resolution?"

"This," Elias said, "is that final resolution."

"I am not one of the emancipated," Rybys said. "I fell along the way."

"Not yet," Elias said.

"But it's coming."

"Perhaps." The expression on Elias Tate's face could not be read.

As the three of them sat, there came a low, murmuring voice which said, "Rybys, Rybys."

Rybys gave a muffled cry and looked around her.

"Fear not," the voice said. "You will live on in your son. You cannot now die, nor even unto the end of the age."

Silently, her face buried in her hands, Rybys began to cry.

*

Late in the day, when school had ended, Emmanuel decided to try the Hermetic transform once again, so that he would know the world around him.

First he speeded up his internal biological clock so that his thoughts raced faster and faster; he felt himself rushing down the tunnel of linear time until his rate of movement along that axis was enormous. First, therefore, he saw vague floating colors and then he suddenly encountered the Watcher, which is to say the Grigon, who barred the way between the Lower and Upper Realms. The Grigon presented itself to him as a nude female torso that he could reach out and touch, so close was it. Beyond this point he began to travel at the rate of the Upper Realm, so that the Lower Realm ceased to be something but became, instead, a process; it evolved in accretional layers at a rate of 31.5 million to one in terms of the Upper Realm's time scale.

Thereupon he saw the Lower Realm—not as a place—but as transparent pictures permutating at immense velocity. These pictures were the Forms outside of space being fed into the Lower Realm to become reality. He was one step away, now, from the Hermetic transform.

The final picture froze and time ceased for him. With his eyes shut he could still see the room around him; the flight had ended; he had eluded that which pursued him. That meant that his neural firing was perfect, and his pineal body registered the presence of light carried up its branch of the optic conduit.

He sat for a little while, although "little while" no longer signified anything. Then, by degrees, the transform took place. He saw outside him the pattern, the print, of his own brain; he was within a world made up of his brain, with living information carried here and there like little rivers of shining red that were alive. He could reach out, therefore, and touch his own thoughts in their original nature, before they became thoughts. The room was filled with their fire, and immense spaces stretched out, the volume of his own brain external to him.

Meanwhile he introjected the outer world so that he contained it within him. He now had the universe inside him and his own brain outside everywhere. His brain extended into the vast spaces, far larger than the universe had been. Therefore he knew the extent of all things that were himself, and, because he had incorporated the world, he knew it *and controlled it.*

He soothed himself and relaxed, and then could see the outlines of the room, the coffee table, a chair, walls, pictures on the walls: the ghost of the external universe lingering outside him. Presently he picked up a book from the table and opened it. Inside the book he found, written there, his own thoughts, now in a printed form. The printed thoughts lay arranged along the time axis which had become spacial and the only axis along which motion was possible. He could see, as in a hologram, the different ages of his thoughts, the most recent ones being closest to the surface, the older ones lower and deeper in many successive layers.

He regarded the world outside him which now had become reduced to spare geometric shapes, squares mostly, and the Golden Rectangle as a doorway. Nothing moved except the scene beyond the doorway, where his mother rushed happily among tangled old rosebushes and a farmland she had known as a child; she was smiling and her eyes were bright with joy.

Now, Emmanuel thought, I will change the universe that I have taken inside me. He regarded the geometric shapes and allowed them to fill up a little with matter. Across from him the ratty blue couch that Elias prized began to warp away from plumb; its lines changed. He had taken away the causality that guided it and it stopped being a ratty blue couch with Kaff stains on it and became instead a Hepplewhite cabinet, with fine bone china plates and cups and saucers behind its doors.

He restored a certain measure of time—and saw Elias Tate come and go about the room, enter and leave; he saw accretional layers laminated together in sequence along the linear time axis. The Hepplewhite cupboard remained for a short series of layers; it held its passive or off or rest mode, and then it was whisked over into its active or on or motion mode and joined the permanent world of the phylogons, participating now in all those of its class that had come before. In his projected world brain the Hepplewhite cabinet, and its bone china pieces, became incorporated into true reality forever. It would now undergo no more changes, and no one would see it but he. It was, to everyone else, in the past.

He completed the transform with the formulary of Hermes Trismegistus:

> *Verum est . . . quod superius est sicut quod inferius et quod inferius est sicut quod superius, ad perpetrando miracula rei unius.*

That is:

> The truth is that what is above is like what is below and what is below is like what is above, to accomplish the miracles of the one thing.

This was the Emerald Tablet, presented to Maria Prophetissa, the sister of Moses, by Tehuti himself, who gave names to all created things in the beginning, before he was expelled from the Palm Tree Garden.

That which was below, his own brain, the microcosm, had become the macrocosm, and, inside him as microcosm now, he contained the macrocosm, which is to say, what is above.

I now occupy the entire universe, Emmanuel realized; I am now everywhere equally. Therefore I have become Adam Kadmon, the First Man. Motion along the three spacial axes was impossible for him because he was already wherever he wished to go. The only motion possible for him or for changing reality lay along the temporal axis; he sat contemplating the world of the phylogons, billions of them in process, continually growing and completing themselves, driven by the dialectic that underlay all transformation. It pleased him; the sight of the interconnected network of phylogons was beautiful to behold. This was the *kosmos* of Pythagoras, the harmonious fitting-together of all things, each in its right way and each imperishable.

I see now what Plotinus saw, he realized. But, more than that, I have rejoined the sundered realms within me; *I have restored the Shekhina to En Sof.* But only for a little while and only locally. Only in microform. It would return to what it had been as soon as he released it.

"Just thinking," he said aloud.

Elias came into the room, saying as he came, "What are you doing, Manny?"

Causality had been reversed; he had done what Zina could do: make time run backward. He laughed in delight. And heard the sound of bells.

"I saw Chinvat," Emmanuel said. "The narrow bridge. I could have crossed it."

"You must not do that," Elias said.

Emmanuel said, "What do the bells mean? Bells ringing far off."

"When you hear the distant bells it means that the Saoshyant is present."

"The Saviour," Emmanuel said. "Who is the Saviour, Elias?"

"It must be yourself," Elias said.

"Sometimes I despair of remembering."

He could still hear the bells, very far off, ringing slowly, blown, he knew, by the desert wind. It was the desert itself speaking to him. The desert, by means of the bells, was trying to remind him. To Elias he said, "Who am I?"

"I can't say," Elias said.

"But you know."

Elias nodded.

"You could make everything very simple," Emmanuel said, "by saying."

"You must say it yourself," Elias said. "When the time comes you will know and you will say it."

"I am—" the boy said hesitantly.

Elias smiled.

She had heard the voice issue forth from her own womb. For a time she felt afraid and then she felt sad; sometimes she cried, and still the nausea continued—it never let up. I don't recall reading about that in the Bible, she thought. Mary being afflicted with morning sickness. I'll probably get edema and stretch marks. I don't remember reading about that either.

It would make a good graffito on some wall, she said to herself. THE VIRGIN MARY HAD STRETCH MARKS. She fixed herself a little meal of synthetic lamb and green beans; seated alone at her table she gazed out listlessly through the dome's port at the landscape. I really should clean up this place, she realized. Before Elias and Herb come back. In fact, I should make a list of what I have to do.

Most of all, she thought, I have to understand this situation. He is already inside me. It has happened.

I need another wig, she decided. For the trip. A better one. I think I'll try out a blond one that's longer. Goddam chemo, she thought. If the ailment doesn't kill you the therapy will. The remedy, she thought acidly, is worse than the malady. Look; I turned it around. God, I feel sick.

And then, as she picked at her plate of cold, synthetic food, a strange idea came to her. What if this is a maneuver by the Clems? she said to herself. We invaded their planet; now they're fighting back. They figured out what our conception of God involves. They're simulating that conception!

I wish mine was simulated, she ruminated.

But to get back to the point, she said to herself. They read our minds or study our books—never mind how they did it— and they fake us out. So what I have inside me is a computer terminal or something, a glorified radio. I can see me going through Immigration. "Anything to declare, Miss?" "Only a radio." Well, she thought, where is this radio? I don't see any radio. Well, you have to look real hard. No, she thought; it's a matter for Customs, not Immigration. What is the declared value of this radio, Miss? That would be hard to say, she answered in her mind. You're not going to believe me but—it's one of a kind. You don't see radios like this every day.

I should probably pray, she decided.

"Yah," she said, "myself, I am weak and sick and afraid, and I really don't want to be involved in this." Contraband, she thought. I'm going to smuggle in contraband. "Lady, come with me. We're going to conduct a complete body search. The matron will be in here in a minute; just sit down and read a magazine." I'll tell them it's an outrage, she thought. "What a surprise!" Feigned amazement. "I have *what* inside me? You're kidding. No, I have no idea how it got there. Will wonders never cease."

A strange lethargy came over her, a kind of hypnagogic state, even as she sat reflexively eating. The embryo inside her had begun to unfold a picture before her, a view by a mind totally different from hers.

She realized, This is how they will view it. The powers of the world.

What she saw, through their eyes, was a monster. The Christian-Islamic Church and the Scientific Legate—their fear did not resemble her fear; hers had to do with effort and danger, with what was required of her. But they— She saw them consulting Big Noodle, the AI System that processed Earth's information, the vast artificial intelligence on which the government relied.

Big Noodle, after analyzing the data, informed the authorities that something sinister had been smuggled past Immigration and onto Earth; she felt their recoil, their aversion. Incredible, she thought. To see the Lord of the universe through their eyes; to see him as foreign. How could the Lord who created everything be a foreign thing? *They are not in his image, then,* she realized. This is what Yah is telling me. I always assumed— we were always taught—that man is the image of God. It is like calling to like. Then they really believe in themselves! They sincerely do not understand.

The monster from outer space, she thought. We must be on guard perpetually lest it show up and sneak through Immigration. How deranged they are. How far off the mark. Then they would kill my baby, she thought. It is impossible but it is true. And no one could make them understand what they had done. The Sanhedrin thought the same way, she said to herself, about Jesus. This is another Zealot. She shut her eyes.

They are living in a cheap horror film, she thought. There is something wrong when you fear little children. When you view them, any one of them, as weird and awful. I don't want this insight, she said to herself, drawing back in aversion. Take it away, please; I've seen enough.

I understand.

She thought, This is why it has to be done. Because they see as they do. They pray; they make decisions; they shield their world—they keep out hostile intrusions. To them this is a hostile intrusion. They are demented; they would kill the God who made them. No rational thing does that. Christ did not die on the cross to render men spotless; he was crucified because they were crazy; they saw as I see now. It is a vista of lunacy.

They think they are doing the right thing.

6

THE girl Zina said, "I have something for you."

"A present?" He held out his hand, trustingly.

Only a child's toy. An information slate, such as every young person had. He felt keen disappointment.

"We made it for you," Zina said.

"Who is that?" He examined the slate. Self-governing factories turned out hundreds of thousands of such slates. Each slate contained common microcircuitry. "Mr. Plaudet gave me one of these already," he said. "They're plugged into the school."

"We make ours differently," Zina said. "Keep it. Tell Mr. Plaudet this is the one he gave you. He won't be able to distinguish them from each other. See? We even have the brand name on it." With her finger she traced the letters I.B.M.

"This one isn't really I.B.M.," he said.

"Definitely not. Turn it on."

He pressed the tab of the slate. On the slate, on the pale gray surface, a single word in illuminated red appeared.

VALIS

"That's your question for right now," Zina said. "To figure out what 'Valis' is. The slate is posing the problem for you at a class-one level . . . which means it'll give you further clues, if you want them."

"Mother Goose," Emmanuel said.

On the slate the word VALIS disappeared. Now it read:

HEPHAISTOS

"Kyklopes," Emmanuel said instantly.

Zina laughed. "You're as fast as it is."

"What's it connected to? Not Big Noodle." He did not like Big Noodle.

"Maybe it'll tell you," Zina said.

The slate now read:

SHIVA

"Kyklopes," Emmanuel repeated. "It's a trick. This was built by the troop of Diana."

At once the girl's smile faded.

"I'm sorry," Emmanuel said. "I won't say it again out loud even one more time."

"Give me the slate back." She held out her hand.

Emmanuel said, "I will give it back if it says for me to give it back." He pressed the tab.

NO

"All right," Zina said. "I'll let you keep it. But you don't know what it is; you don't understand it. The troop didn't build it. Press the tab."

Again he pressed the tab.

LONG BEFORE CREATION

"I—" Emmanuel faltered.

"It will come back to you," Zina said. "Through this. Use it. I don't think you should tell Elias either. He might not understand."

Emmanuel said nothing. This was a matter that he himself would decide. It was important not to let others make his choices for him. And, basically, he trusted Elias. Did he also trust Zina? He was not sure. He sensed the multitude of natures within her, the profusion of identities. Ultimately he would seek out the real one; he knew it was there, but the tricks obscured it. Who is it, he asked himself, who plays tricks like this? What being is the trickster? He pressed the tab.

DANCING

To that, he gave a nod of assent. Dancing certainly was the right answer; in his mind he could see her dancing, with all the troop, burning the grass beneath their feet, leaving it scorched, and the minds of men disoriented. You cannot disorient me, he said to himself. Even though you control time. Because I control time, too. Perhaps even more than you.

That night at dinner he discussed Valis with Elias Tate.

"Take me to see it," Emmanuel said.

"It's a very old movie," Elias said.

"But at least we could rent a cassette. From the library. What does 'Valis' mean?"

"Vast Active Living Intelligence System," Elias said. "The movie is mostly fiction. It was made by a rock singer in the latter part of the twentieth century. His name was Eric Lampton but he called himself Mother Goose. The film contained Mini's Synchronicity Music, which had considerable impact on all modern music to this day. Much of the information in the film is conveyed subliminally by the music. The setting is an alternate U.S.A. where a man named Ferris F. Fremount is president."

Emmanuel said, "But what is Valis?"

"An artificial satellite that projects a hologram that they take to be reality."

"Then it's a reality generator."

"Yes," Elias said.

"Is the reality genuine?"

"No; I said it's a hologram. It can make them see whatever it wants them to see. That's the whole point of the film. It's a study of the power of illusion."

Going to his room, Emmanuel picked up the slate that Zina had given him and pressed the tab.

"What are you doing?" Elias said, coming in behind him.

The slate showed one word:

NO

"That's plugged into the government," Elias said. "There's no point in using it. I knew Plaudet would give you one of those." He reached for it. "Give it to me."

"I want to keep it," Emmanuel said.

"Good grief; it says I.B.M. right on it! What do you expect it to tell you? The truth? When has the government ever told anyone the truth? They killed your mother and put your father into cryonic suspension. Let me have it, damn it."

"If this is taken from me," Emmanuel said, "they will give me another."

"I suppose so." Elias withdrew his hand. "But don't believe what it says."

"It says you're wrong about Valis," Emmanuel said.

"In what way?"

Emmanuel said, "It just said 'no.' It didn't say anything more." He pressed the tab again.

YOU

"What the hell does that mean?" Elias said, mystified.

"I don't know," Emmanuel said truthfully. He thought, I will keep using it.

And then he thought, It is tricking me. It dances along the path like a bobbing light, leading me and leading me, away, further, further, into the darkness. And then when the darkness is everywhere the bobbing light will wink out. I know you, he thought at the slate. I know how you work. I will not follow; you must come to *me*.

He pressed the tab.

FOLLOW ME

"Where no one ever returns," Emmanuel said.

After dinner he spent some time with the holoscope, studying Elias's most precious possession: the Bible expressed as layers at different depths within the hologram, each layer according to age. The total structure of Scripture formed, then, a three-dimensional cosmos that could be viewed from any angle and its contents read. According to the tilt of the axis of observation, differing messages could be extracted. Thus Scripture yielded up an infinitude of knowledge that ceaselessly changed. It became a wondrous work of art, beautiful to the eye, and incredible in its pulsations of color. Throughout it red and gold pulsed, with strands of blue.

The color symbolism was not arbitrary but extended back in time to the early medieval Romanesque paintings. Red always represented the Father. Blue the color of the Son. And gold, of course, that of the Holy Spirit. Green stood for the new life of the elect; violet the color of mourning; brown the color of endurance and suffering; white, the color of light; and, finally, black, the color of the Powers of Darkness, of death and sin.

All these colors could be found in the hologram formed by the Bible along the temporal axis. In conjunction with sections of text, complex messages formed, permutated, re-formed. Emmanuel never tired of gazing into the hologram; for him as well as Elias it was the master hologram, surpassing all others. The Christian-Islamic Church did not approve of transmuting the Bible into a color-coded hologram, and forbade the manufacture and sale. Hence Elias had constructed this hologram himself, without approval.

It was an open hologram. New information could be fed into it. Emmanuel wondered about that but he said nothing. He sensed a secret. Elias could not answer him, so he did not ask.

What he could do, however, was type out on the keyboard linked to the hologram a few crucial words of Scripture, whereupon the hologram would align itself from the vantage point of the citation, along all its spacial axes. Thus the entire text of the Bible would be focused in relationship to the typed-out information.

"What if I fed something new into it?" he had asked Elias one day.

Elias had said severely, "Never do that."

"But it's technically possible."

"It is not done."

About that the boy wondered often.

He knew, of course, why the Christian-Islamic Church did not allow the transmuting of the Bible into a color-coded hologram. If you learned how you could gradually tilt the temporal axis, the axis of true depth, until successive layers were superimposed and a vertical message—a new message— could be read out. In this way you entered into a dialogue with Scripture; it became alive. It became a sentient organism that was never twice the same. The Christian-Islamic Church, of course, wanted both the Bible and the Koran frozen forever. If Scripture escaped out from under the church its monopoly departed.

Superimposition was the critical factor. And this sophisticated superimposition could only be achieved in a hologram. And yet he knew that once, long ago, Scripture had been deciphered this way. Elias, when asked, was reticent about the matter. The boy let the topic drop.

There had been an acutely embarrassing incident at church the year before. Elias had taken the boy to Thursday morning mass. Since he had not been confirmed, Emmanuel could not receive the host; while the others in the congregation gathered at the rail Emmanuel remained bent in prayer. All at once, as the priest carried the chalice from person to person, dipping the wafers in the consecrated wine and saying, "The Blood of Our Lord Jesus Christ, which was shed for thee—" all at once Emmanuel had stood up where he was in his pew and stated clearly and calmly:

"The blood is not there nor the body either."

The priest paused and looked to see who had spoken.

"You do not have the authority," Emmanuel said. And, upon saying that, he turned and walked out of the church. Elias found him in their car, listening to the radio.

"You can't do that," Elias had said as they drove home. "You can't tell them things like that. They'll open a file on you and that's what we don't want." He was furious.

"I saw," Emmanuel said. "It was a wafer and wine only."

"You mean the accidents. The external form. But the essence was—"

"There was no essence other than the visible appearance," Emmanuel answered. "The miracle did not occur because the priest was not a priest."

They drove in silence after that.

"Do you deny the miracle of transubstantiation?" Elias asked that night as he put the boy to bed.

"I deny that it took place today," Emmanuel said. "There in that place. I will not go there again."

"What I want," Elias said, "is for you to be as wise as a serpent and as innocent as a dove."

Emmanuel regarded him.

"They killed—"

"They have no power over me," Emmanuel said.

"They can destroy you. They can arrange another accident. Next year I'm required to put you in school. Fortunately because of your brain damage you won't have to go to a regular school. I'm counting on them to—" Elias hesitated.

Emmanuel finished, "—Consign anything they see about me that is different to the brain damage."

"Right."

"Was the brain damage arranged?"

"I— Perhaps."

"It seems useful." But, he thought, *if only I knew my real name*. "Why can't you say my name?" he said to Elias.

"Your mother did," Elias said obliquely.

"My mother is dead."

"You will say it yourself, eventually."

"I'm impatient." A strange thought came to him. "Did she die because she said my name?"

"Maybe," Elias said.

"And that's why you won't say it? Because it would kill you if you did? And it wouldn't kill me."

"It is not a name in the usual sense. It is a command."

All these matters remained in his mind. A name that was not a name but a command. It made him think of Adam who named the animals. He wondered about that. Scripture said:

> . . . and brought them unto the man to see
> what he would call them . . .

"Did God not know what the man would call them?" he asked Elias one day.

"Only man has language," Elias explained. "Only man can give birth to language. Also—" He eyed the boy. "When man gave names to creatures he established his dominion over them."

What you name you control, Emmanuel realized. Hence no one is to speak my name because no one is to have—or can have—control over me. "God played a game with Adam, then," he said. "He wanted to see if the man knew their correct names. He was testing the man. God enjoys games."

"I'm not sure I know the answer to that," Elias said.

"I did not ask. I said."

"It is not something usually associated with God."

"Then the nature of God is known."

"His nature is *not* known."

Emmanuel said, "He enjoys games and play. It says in Scripture that he rested but I say that he played."

He wanted to feed that into the hologram of the Bible, as an addendum, but he knew that he should not. How would it alter the total hologram? he wondered. To add to the Torah that God enjoys joyful sport . . . Strange, he thought, that I can't add that. Someone must add it; it has to be there, in Scripture. Someday.

He learned about pain and death from an ugly dying dog. It had been run over and lay by the side of the road, its chest crushed, bloody foam bubbling from its mouth. When he bent over it the dog gazed at him with glasslike eyes, eyes that already saw into the next world.

To understand what the dog was saying he put his hand on its stumpy tail. "Who mandated this death for you?" he asked the dog. "What have you done?"

"I did nothing," the dog replied.

"But this is a harsh death."

"Nonetheless," the dog told him, "I am blameless."

"Have you ever killed?"

"Oh yes. My jaws are designed to kill. I was constructed to kill smaller things."

"Do you kill for food or pleasure?"

"I kill out of joy," the dog told him. "It is a game; it is the game I play."

Emmanuel said, "I did not know about such games. Why do dogs kill and why do dogs die? Why are there such games?"

"These subtleties mean nothing to me," the dog told him. "I kill to kill; I die because I must. It is necessity, the rule that is the final rule. Don't you live and kill and die by that rule? Surely you do. You are a creature, too."

"I do what I wish."

"You lie to yourself," the dog said. "Only God does as he wishes."

"Then I must be God."

"If you are God, heal me."

"But you are under the law."

"You are not God."

"God willed the law, dog."

"You have said it, then, yourself; you have answered your own question. Now let me die."

When he told Elias about the dog who died, Elias said:

> Go, stranger, and to Lacedaemon tell
> That here, obeying her behests, we fell.

"That was for the Spartans who died at Thermopylae," Elias said.

"Why do you tell me that?" Emmanuel said.

Elias said:

> Go tell the Spartans, thou that passeth by,
> That here, obedient to their laws, we lie.

"You mean the dog," Emmanuel said.

"I mean the dog," Elias said.

"There is no difference between a dead dog in a ditch and the Spartans who died at Thermopylae." He understood. "None," he said. "I see."

"If you can understand why the Spartans died you can understand it all," Elias said.

> You who pass by, a moment pause;
> We, here, obey the Spartan laws.

"Is there no couplet for the dog?" Emmanuel asked.

Elias said:

> Passer, this enter in your log:
> As Spartan was, so, too, the dog.

"Thank you," Emmanuel said.

"What was the last thing the dog said?" Elias said.

"The dog said, 'Now let me die.'"

Elias said:

> *Lasciatemi morire!*
> *E chi volete voi che mi conforte*
> *In cosi dura sorte,*
> *In cosi gran martire?*

"What is that?" Emmanuel said.

"The most beautiful piece of music written before Bach," Elias said. "Monteverdi's madrigal 'Lamento D'Arianna.' Thus:

> Let me die!
> And who do you think can comfort me
> in my harsh misfortune,
> in such grievous torment?

"Then the dog's death is high art," Emmanuel said. "The highest art of the world. Or at least celebrated, recorded, in and by high art. Am I to see nobility in an old ugly dying dog with a crushed chest?"

"If you believe Monteverdi, yes," Elias said. "And those who revere Monteverdi."

"Is there more to the lament?"

"Yes, but it does not apply. Theseus has left Ariadne; it is unrequited love."

"Which is more awesome?" Emmanuel said. "A dying dog in a ditch or Ariadne spurned?"

Elias said, "Ariadne imagines her torment, but the dog's is real."

"Then the dog's torment is worse," Emmanuel said. "It is the greater tragedy." He understood. And, strangely, he felt content. It was a good universe in which an ugly dying dog was of more worth than a classic figure from ancient Greece. He felt the tilted balance right itself, the scales that weighed it all. He felt the honesty of the universe, and his confusion left him. But, more important, the dog understood its own death. After all, the dog would never hear Monteverdi's music or read the couplet on the stone column at Thermopylae. High art was for those who saw death rather than lived death. For the dying creature a cup of water was more important.

"Your mother detested certain art forms," Elias said. "In particular she loathed Linda Fox."

"Play me some Linda Fox," Emmanuel said.

Elias put an audio cassette into the tape transport, and he and Emmanuel listened.

> Flow not so fast, ye fountains,
> What

"Enough," Emmanuel said. "Shut it off." He put his hands over his ears. "It's dreadful." He shuddered.

"What's wrong?" Elias put his arm around the boy and lifted him up to hold him. "I've never seen you so upset."

"He listened to that while my mother was dying!" Emmanuel stared into Elias's bearded face.

I remember, Emmanuel said to himself. I am beginning to remember who I am.

Elias said, "What is it?" He held the boy tight.

It is happening, Emmanuel realized. At last. That was the first of the signal that I—I myself—prepared. Knowing it would eventually fire.

The two of them gazed into each other's faces. Neither the boy nor the man spoke. Trembling, Emmanuel clung to the old bearded man; he did not let himself fall.

"Do not fear," Elias said.

"Elijah," Emmanuel said. "You are Elijah who comes first. Before the great and terrible day."

Elias, holding the boy and rocking him gently, said, "You have nothing to fear on that day."

"But *he* does," Emmanuel said. "The Adversary whom we hate. His time has come. I fear for him, knowing as I do, now, what is ahead."

"Listen," Elias said quietly.

> How you have fallen from heaven, bright morning star,
> felled to the earth, sprawling helpless across the nations!
> You thought in your own mind,
>   I will scale the heavens;
> I will set my throne high above the stars of God,
> I will sit on the mountain where the gods meet
>   in the far recesses of the north.
> I will rise high above the cloud-banks
>   and make myself like the Most High.
> Yet you shall be brought down to Sheol,
>   to the depths of the abyss.
> Those who see you will stare at you,
>   they will look at you and ponder . . .

"You see?" Elias said. "*He is here.* This is his place, this little world. He made it his fortress two thousand years ago, and set up a prison for the people as he did in Egypt. For two thousand years the people have been crying and there was no response, no aid. He has them all. And thinks he is safe."

Emmanuel, clutching the old man, began to cry.

"Still afraid?" Elias said.

Emmanuel said, "I cry with them. I cry with my mother. I cry with the dying dog who did not cry. I cry *for* them. And for Belial who fell, the bright morning star. Fell from heaven and began it all."

And, he thought, I cry for myself. I am my mother; I am the dying dog and the suffering people, and I, he thought, am that bright morning star, too . . . even Belial; I am that and what it has become.

The old man held him fast.

7

CARDINAL FULTON STATLER HARMS, Chief Prelate of the vast organizational network that comprised the Christian-Islamic Church, could not for the life of him figure out why there wasn't a sufficient amount of money in his Special Discretionary Fund to cover his mistress's expenses.

Perhaps, he pondered as his barber shaved him slowly and carefully, he had too dim a notion of the extent of Deirdre's needs.

Originally she had approached him—no small task in itself, since it involved ascending the C.I.C. hierarchy rung by rung —ascending without falling entirely off before reaching the top. Deirdre, at that time, represented the W.C.L.F., the World Civil Liberties Forum, and she had a list of abuses—it was hazy to him then and it was still hazy to him, but anyhow the two of them had wound up in bed, and now, officially, Dierdre had become his executive secretary.

For her work she blotted up two salaries: the visible one that came with her job and the invisible one doled out from the substantial account that he was free to dispense as he saw fit. Where all this money went after it reached Deirdre he hadn't the foggiest idea. Bookkeeping had never been his strong suit.

"You want the yellow removed from this gray on the side, don't you?" his barber said, shaking up the contents of a bottle.

"Please," Harms said; he nodded.

"You think the Lakers are going to snap their losing streak?" his barber said. "I mean, they acquired that What's-his-name; he's nine feet two inches. If they hadn't raised the—"

Tapping his ear, Harms said, "I'm listening to the news, Arnold."

"Well, yeah, I can see that, Father," Arnold the barber said as he splashed bleach onto the Chief Prelate's graying hair. "But there's something I wanted to ask you, about homosexual priests. Doesn't the Bible forbid homosexuality? So I don't see how a priest can be a practicing homosexual."

The news that Harms was attempting to hear had to do with the health of the Procurator Maximus of the Scientific Legate,

Nicholas Bulkowsky. A solemn prayer vigil had been formally called into being but nonetheless Bulkowsky continued to decline. Harms had, sub rosa, dispatched his personal physician to join the team of specialists attending to the Procurator's urgent condition.

Bulkowsky, as not only Cardinal Harms but the entire curia knew, was a devout Christian. He had been converted by the evangelical, charismatic Dr. Colin Passim who, at his revival meetings, often flew through the air in dramatic demonstration of the power of the Holy Spirit within him.

Of course, Dr. Passim had not been the same since he sailed through a vast stained-glass window of the cathedral at Metz, France. Formerly he had talked occasionally in tongues and now he talked only in tongues. This had inspired a popular TV comic to suggest that an English-Glossolalia dictionary be brought out, so that folks could understand Dr. Passim. This in turn had given rise to such indignation in the pious that Cardinal Harms had it jotted down on his desk calendar somewhere that, when possible, he should pronounce the comic anathema. But, as usual, he had not gotten around to such petty matters.

Much of Cardinal Harms's time was spent in a secret activity: he had been feeding St. Anselm's *Proslogion* to the great Artificial Intelligence system Big Noodle with the idea of resurrecting the long-discredited Ontological Proof for the existence of God.

He had gone right back to Anselm and the original statement of the argument, unsoiled by the accretions of time:

> Anything understood must be in the intelligence. Certainly, too, the being greater than which none can be conceived cannot exist in the intellect alone; for if it were only in the intellect it could be conceived as existing also in reality and this would be to conceive a still greater being. In such a case, if the being greater than which none can be conceived is merely in the intelligence (and not in reality), then this same being is something than which one could still conceive a greater (i.e., one which exists both in the intelligence and in reality). This is a contradiction. Consequently, there can be no doubt that the being

greater than which none can be conceived must exist both
in the intelligence and in reality.

However, Big Noodle knew all about Aquinas and Descartes
and Kant and Russell and their criticisms, and the A.I. system
also possessed common sense. It informed Harms that Anselm's
argument did not hold water, and presented him with page after
page of analysis as to why. Harms's response was to edit out Big
Noodle's analysis and seize upon Hartshorne and Malcolm's defense of Anselm; viz: that God's existence is either logically necessary or logically impossible. Since it has not been demonstrated
to be impossible—which is to say, the concept of such an entity
has not been shown to be self-contradictory—then it follows
that we must of necessity conclude that God exists.

Upon fastening onto this weary argument, Harms had dispatched a copy via his direct line to the ailing Procurator Maximus as a means of instilling new vigor in his co-ruler.

"Now take the Giants," Arnold the barber was saying as he
valiantly tried to bleach the yellow from the cardinal's hair. "I
say you can't count them out. Look at Eddy Tubb's ERA for
last year. So he has a sore arm; pitchers always get sore arms."

The day had begun for the Chief Prelate Cardinal Fulton
Statler Harms; trying to hear the news, meditating simultaneously on his enterprise vis-à-vis St. Anselm, fending off Arnold's
baseball statistics—this constituted his morning confrontation with reality, his routine. All that remained to make it the
Platonic archetypal beginning of his activity phase was the
mandatory—and futile—attempt to pin down Deirdre regarding
her cost overrun.

He was prepared for that; he had a new girl waiting in the
wings. Dierdre, who did not know it, was about to go.

At his resort city on the Black Sea the Procurator Maximus
walked in slow circles as he read Deirdre Connell's most recent
report on the chief prelate. No health problems assailed the
procurator; he had allowed news of his "medical condition" to
leak its way into the media so as to ensnare his co-ruler in a
web of self-serving lies. This gave him time to study his intelligence staff's appraisal of Deirdre Connell's daily reports. So
far it was the educated opinion of everyone who intimately

served the procurator that Cardinal Harms had lost touch with reality and was lost in harebrained theological quests—journeys that led him further and further away from any control over the political and economic situation that was pro forma his purview.

The fake reports also gave him time to fish and relax and sun himself and figure out how to depose the cardinal in order to get one of his own people into the position of chief prelate of the C.I.C. Bulkowsky had a number of S.L. functionaries in the curia, well-trained and eager. As long as Deirdre Connell held down the post of executive secretary and mistress to the cardinal, Bulkowsky had the edge. He felt reasonably certain that Harms owned no one in the Scientific Legate's top positions, owned no reciprocal access. Bulkowsky had no mistress; he was a family man with a plump, middle-aged wife, and three children all attending private schools in Switzerland. In addition, his conversion to Dr. Passim's enthusiastic nonsense—the miracle of flying had of course been achieved by technological means—was a strategic fraud, designed to lull the cardinal deeper into his grand dreams.

The procurator knew all about the attempt to induce Big Noodle to come up with verification of St. Anselm's Ontological Proof for the existence of God; the topic was a joke in regions dominated by the Scientific Legate. Deirdre Connell had been instructed to recommend to her aging lover that he spend more and more time in his lofty venture.

Nonetheless, although wholly rooted in reality, Bulkowsky had not been able to solve certain problems of his own—matters which he concealed from his co-ruler. Decisions for the S.L. had fallen off among the youth cadres during recent months; more and more college students, even those in the hard sciences, were finding for the C.I.C., throwing aside the hammer-and-sickle pin and donning the cross. Specifically there had developed a paucity of ark engineers, with the result that three S.L. orbiting arks, with their inhabitants, had had to be abandoned. This news had *not* reached the media, since the inhabitants had perished. To shield the public from the grim news the designations of the remaining S.L. arks had been changed. On computer printouts the malfunctions did not appear; the situation gave the semblance of normality.

At least we did eliminate Colin Passim, Bulkowsky reflected. A man who talks like an aud-tape of a duck played backward is no threat. The evangelist had, without suspecting it, succumbed to S.L. advanced weaponry. The balance of world power had thus been made to shift ever so slightly. Little things like that added up. Take, for instance, the presence of the S.L. agent duked in as the cardinal's mistress and secretary. Without that—

Bulkowsky felt supremely confident. The dialectical force of historic necessity was on his side. He could retire to his floating bed, half an hour from now, with a knowledge that the world situation was in hand.

"Cognac," he said to a robot attendant. "Courvoisier Napoleon."

As he stood by his desk warming the snifter with the palms of his hands his wife, Galina, entered the room. "Make no appointments for Thursday night," she said. "General Yakir has planned a recital for the Moscow corps. The American chanteuse Linda Fox will be singing. Yakir expects us."

"Certainly," Bulkowsky said. "Have roses prepared for the end of the recital." To a pair of robot servants he said, "Have my valet de chambre remind me."

"Don't nod off during the recital," Galina said. "Mrs. Yakir will be hurt. You remember the last time."

"The Penderecki abomination," Bulkowsky said, remembering well. He had snored through the "Quia Fecit" of the "Magnificat" and then read about his behavior in intelligence documents a week later.

"Remember that as far as informed circles know, you are a born-again Christian," Galina said. "What did you do about those responsible for the loss of the three arks?"

"They are all dead," Bulkowsky said. He had had them shot.

"You could recruit replacements from the U.K."

"We will have our own soon. I don't trust what the U.K. sends us. Everyone is for sale. For instance, how much is that chanteuse now asking for her decision?"

"The situation is confused," Galina said. "I have read the intelligence reports; the cardinal is offering her a large sum to decide for the C.I.C. I don't think we should try to meet it."

"But if an entertainer that popular were to step forth and

announce that she had seen the white light and accepted sweet Jesus into her life—"

"You did."

"But," Bulkowsky said, "you know why." As he had accepted Jesus solemnly, with much pomp, he would presently declare that he had renounced Jesus and returned, wiser now, to the S.L. This would have a dire effect on the curia and, hopefully, even on the cardinal himself. The chief prelate's morale, according to S.L. psychologists, would be shattered. The man actually supposed that one day everyone associated with the S.L. would march up to the various offices of the C.I.C. and convert.

"What are you doing about that doctor he sent?" Galina said. "Are there any difficulties?"

"No." He shook his head. "The forged medical reports keep him busy." Actually the medical information presented regularly to the physician whom the cardinal had sent were not forged. They simply pertained to someone other than Bulkowsky, some minor S.L. person genuinely sick. Bulkowsky had sworn Harms's physician to secrecy, pleading medical ethics as the issue, but of course Dr. Duffey covertly dispatched detailed reports on the procurator's health to the cardinal's staff at every opportunity. S.L. intelligence routinely intercepted them, checked to make sure they painted a sufficiently grave picture, copied them and sent them on. By and large the medical reports traveled by microwave signal to an orbiting C.I.C. communications satellite and from there were beamed down to Washington, D.C. However, Dr. Duffey, in a periodic fit of cleverness, sometimes simply mailed the information. This was harder to control.

Imagining that he was dealing with an ailing man, and one who had decided for Jesus, the cardinal had relaxed his stance of vigil regarding the higher activities of the S.L. The cardinal now supposed the procurator to be hopelessly incompetent.

"If Linda Fox will not decide for the S.L.," Galina said, "why don't you draw her aside and tell her that one day on her way to a concert engagement her private rocket—that gaudy plush thing she flies herself—will go up in a flash of flaming fire?"

Gloomily, Bulkowsky said, "Because the cardinal got to her first. He has already passed the word to her that if she doesn't accept sweet Jesus into her life bichlorides will find her whether she wants to accept them or not."

The tactic of poisoning Linda Fox with small doses of mercury was an artful one. Long before she died (if she did die) she would be as mad as a hatter—literally, since it had been mercury poisoning, mercury used to process felt hats, that had driven the English hatters of the nineteenth century into famous organic psychosis.

I wish I had thought of that, Bulkowsky said to himself. Intelligence reports stated that the chanteuse had become hysterical when informed by a C.I.C. agent of what the cardinal intended if she did not decide for Jesus—hysteria and then temporary hypothermia, followed by a refusal to sing "Rock of Ages" in her next concert, as had been scheduled.

On the other hand, he reflected, cadmium would be better than mercury because it would be more difficult to detect. The S.L. secret police had used trace amounts of cadmium on unpersons for some time, and to good effect.

"Then money won't influence her," Galina said.

"I wouldn't dismiss it. It's her ambition to own Greater Los Angeles."

Galina said, "But if she's destroyed, the colonists will grumble. They're dependent on her."

"Linda Fox is not a person. She is a *class* of persons, a type. She is a sound that electronic equipment, very sophisticated electronic equipment, makes. There are more of her. There will always be. She can be stamped out like tires."

"Well, then don't offer her very much money." Galina laughed.

"I feel sorry for her," Bulkowsky said. How must it feel, he asked himself, not to exist? That's a contradiction. To feel is to exist. Then, he thought, probably she does not feel. Because it is a fact that she does not exist, not really. We ought to know. We were the first to imagine her.

Or rather—Big Noodle had first imagined the Fox. The A.I. system had invented her, told her what to sing and how to sing it; Big Noodle set up her arrangements . . . even down to the mixing. And the package was a complete success.

Big Noodle had correctly analyzed the emotional needs of the colonists and had come up with a formula to meet those needs. The A.I. system maintained an ongoing survey, deriving feedback; when the needs changed, Linda Fox changed. It constituted a closed loop. If, suddenly, all the colonists disappeared, Linda Fox would wink out of existence. Big Noodle would have canceled her, like paper run through a paper shredder.

"Procurator," a robot serving assembly said, coasting up to Bulkowsky.

"What is it?" he said irritably; he did not like to be interrupted when he was conversing with his wife.

The robot serving assembly said, "Hawk."

To Galina he said, "Big Noodle wants me. It's urgent. You'll excuse me." He walked away from her rapidly and into his complex of private offices where he would find the carefully protected terminal of the A.I. system.

The terminal indeed pulsed, waiting for him.

"Troop movements?" Bulkowsky said as he seated himself facing the screen of the terminal.

"No," the artificial voice of Big Noodle came, with its characteristic ambiance. "A conspiracy to smuggle a monster baby through Immigration. Three colonists are involved. I monitored the fetus of the woman. Details to follow." Big Noodle broke the circuit.

"Details when?" Bulkowsky said, but the A.I. system did not hear him, having cut itself off. Damn, he thought. It shows me little courtesy. Too busy deconstructing the Ontological Proof of the Existence of God.

Cardinal Fulton Statler Harms received the news from Big Noodle with his customary aplomb. "Thank you very much," he said as the A.I. system signed off. Something alien, he said to himself. Some sport that God never intended should exist. This is the truly dreadful aspect of space migration: we do not get back what we send out. We get in return the unnatural.

Well, he thought, we shall have it killed; however I will be interested to see its brain-print. I wonder what this one is like. A snake within an egg, he thought. A fetus within a woman. The original story retold: a creature that is subtle.

> The serpent was more crafty than any wild
> creature that the LORD God had made.

Genesis chapter three, verse one. What happened before is not going to happen again. We will destroy it this time, the evil one. In whatever form it now has taken.

He thought, I shall pray on it.

"Excuse me," he said to his small audience of visiting priests who waited outside in the vast lounge. "I must retire to my chapel for a little while. A serious matter has come up."

Presently he knelt in silence and gloom, with burning candles off in the far corners, the chamber and himself hallowed.

"Father," he prayed, "teach us to know thy ways and to emulate thee. Help us to protect ourselves and guard against the evil one. May we foresee and understand his wiles. For his wiles are great; his cunning also. Give us the strength—lend us thy holy power—to ferret him out wherever he is."

He heard nothing in response. It did not surprise him. Pious people spoke to God, and crazy people imagined that God spoke back. His answers had to come from within himself, from his own heart. But, of course, the Spirit guided him. It was always thus.

Within him the Spirit, in the form of his own proclivities, ratified his original insight. "Thou shalt not suffer a witch to live" included in its domain the smuggled mutation. "Witch" equaled "monster." He therefore had scriptural support.

And anyhow he was God's regent on Earth.

Just to be on the safe side he consulted his huge copy of the Bible, rereading Exodus twenty-two, verse seventeen.

Thou shalt not suffer a sorceress to live.

And then for good measure he read the next verse.

Whosoever lieth with a beast shall surely be put to death.

Then he read the notes.

Ancient witchcraft was steeped in crime, immorality and imposture; and it debased the populace by hideous practices and superstitions. It is preceded by provisions against sexual license and followed by condemnation of unnatural vice and idolatry.

Well, that certainly applied here. Hideous practices and superstitions. Things spawned by intercourse with nonhumans on far off foreign planets. They shall not invade this sacred world, he said to himself. I'm sure my colleague the Procurator Maximus will agree.

Suddenly illumination washed over him. We're being invaded! he realized. The thing we've been talking about for two centuries. The Holy Spirit is telling me; it has happened!

Accursed spawn of filth, he thought; rapidly he made his way to his master chamber where the direct—and highly shielded—line to the procurator could be found.

"Is this about the baby?" Bulkowsky said, when contact—in an instant—had been established. "I have retired for the night. It can wait until tomorrow."

"There is an abomination out there," Cardinal Harms said. "Exodus twenty-two, verse seventeen. 'Thou—'"

"Big Noodle won't let it reach Earth. It must have been intercepted at one of the outer rings of Immigration."

"God does not wish monsters on this his primary world. You as a born-again Christian should realize that."

"Certainly I do," Bulkowsky said, with indignation.

"What shall I instruct Big Noodle to do?"

Bulkowsky said, "It's what will Big Noodle instruct *u*s to do, rather. Don't you think?"

"We will have to pray our way through this crisis," Harms said. "Join me now in a prayer. Bow your head."

"My wife is calling me," Bulkowsky said. "We can pray tomorrow. Good-night." He hung up.

Oh God of Israel, Harms prayed, his head bowed. Protect us from procrastination and from the evil that has descended on it. Awaken the Procurator's soul to the urgency of this our hour of ordeal.

We are being spiritually tested, he prayed. I know that is the case. We must prove our worth by casting out this satanic presence. Make us worthy, Lord; lend us thy sword of might. Give us thy saddle of righteousness to mount the steed of . . . He could not finish the thought; it was too intense. Hasten to our aid, he finished, and raised his head. A sense of triumph filled him; as if, he thought, we have trapped something to be killed. We have hunted it down. And it will die. Praise be to God!

8

THE high-velocity axial flight made Rybys Rommey deathly ill. United Spaceways had arranged for five adjoining seats for her, so that she could lie outstretched; even so, she was barely able to speak. She lay on her side, a blanket up to her chin.

Somberly, as he gazed down at the woman, Elias Tate said, "The damn legal technicalities. If we hadn't been held up—" He grimaced.

Within Rybys's body the fetus, now six months along, had been silent for a vast amount of time. What if the fetus dies? Herb Asher asked himself. The death of God . . . but not under circumstances anyone ever anticipated. And no one, except himself, Rybys and Elias Tate would ever know.

Can God die? he wondered. And with him my wife.

The marriage ceremony had been lucid and brief, a transaction by the deepspace authorities, with no religious or moral overtones. Both he and Rybys had been required to undergo extensive physical examinations, and, of course, her pregnancy had been discovered.

"You're the father?" the doctor asked him.

"Yes," Herb Asher said.

The doctor grinned and noted that on his chart.

"We felt we had to get married," Herb said.

"It's a good attitude." The doctor was elderly and well groomed, and totally impersonal. "Are you aware that it's a boy?"

"Yes," he said. He certainly was.

"There is one thing I do not understand," the doctor said. "Was this impregnation natural? It wasn't artificial insemination, by any chance? Because the hymen is intact."

"Really," Herb Asher said.

"It's rare but it can happen. So technically your wife is still a virgin."

"Really," Herb Asher said.

The doctor said, "She is quite ill, you know. From the multiple sclerosis."

"I know," he answered stoically.

"There is no guarantee of a cure. You realize that. I think it's an excellent idea to return her to Earth, and I heartily approve of your going along with her. But it may be for nothing. M.S. is a peculiar ailment. The myelin sheath of the nerve fibers develops hard patches and this eventually results in permanent paralysis. We have finally isolated two causal factors, after decades of intensive effort. There is a microorganism, but, and this is a major factor, a form of allergy is involved. Much of the treatment involves transforming the immune system so that—" The doctor continued on, and Herb Asher listened as well as he could. He knew it all already; Rybys had told him several times, and had shown him texts that she had obtained from M.E.D. Like her, he had become an authority on the disease.

"Could I have some water?" Rybys murmured, lifting her head; her face was blotched and swollen, and Herb Asher could understand her only with difficulty.

A stewardess brought Rybys a paper cup of water; Elias and Herb lifted her to a sitting position and she took the cup in her hands. Her arms, her body, trembled.

"It won't be much longer," Herb Asher said.

"Christ," Rybys murmured. "I don't think I'm going to make it. Tell the stewardess I'm going to throw up again; make her bring back that bowl. Jesus." She sat up fully, her face stricken with pain.

The stewardess, bending down beside her, said, "We'll be firing the retrojets in two hours, so if you can just hold on—"

"Hold on?" Rybys said. "I can't even hold on to what I drank. Are you sure that Coke wasn't tainted or something? I think it made me worse. Don't you have any ginger ale? If I had some ginger ale maybe I could keep from—" She cursed with venom and rage. "Damn this," she said. "Damn all this. It isn't worth it!" She stared at Herb Asher and then Elias.

Yah, Herb Asher thought. Can't you do anything? It's sadistic to let her suffer this way.

Within his mind a voice spoke. He could not at first fathom what it meant; he heard the words but they seemed to make no sense. The voice said, "Take her to the Garden."

He thought, What Garden?

"Take her by the hand."

Herb Asher, reaching down, fumbling in the folds of the blanket, took his wife's hand.

"Thank you," Rybys said. Feebly, she squeezed his hand.

Now, as he sat leaning over her, he saw her eyes shine; he saw spaces beyond her eyes, and if he were looking into something empty, containing huge stretches of space. Where are you? he wondered. It is a universe in there, within your skull; it is a different universe from this: not a mirror reflection but another land. He saw stars, and clusters of stars; he saw nebulae and great clouds of gases that glowed darkly and yet still with a white light, not a ruddy light. He felt wind billow about him and he heard something rustle. Leaves or branches, he thought; I hear plants. The air felt warm. That amazed him. It seemed to be fresh air, not the stale, recirculated air of the spaceship.

The sound of birds, and, when he looked up, blue sky. He saw bamboo, and the rustling sound came from the wind blowing through the canes of bamboo. He saw a fence, and there were children. And yet at the same time he still held his wife's weak hand. Strange, he thought. The air so dry, as if it comes sweeping off the desert. He saw a boy with brown curly hair; the boy's hair reminded him of Rybys's hair before she had lost it, before, from the chemotherapy, it had fallen out and disappeared.

Where am I? he wondered. At a school?

Beside him fussy Mr. Plaudet told him pointless stories having to do with the school's financial needs, the school's problems—he wasn't interested in the school's problems; he was interested in his son. His son's brain damage; he wanted to know all about it.

"What I can't understand," Plaudet was saying, "is why they kept you in suspension for ten years for a spleen. For heaven's sake, a splenectomy is a normal and regular type of surgery, and there is frequently a splenolus that can be—"

"Which hemisphere of his brain is damaged?" Herb Asher interrupted.

"Mr. Tate has all the medical reports. But I'll go to our computer and ask for a printout. Manny seems a little afraid of you, but I suppose it's because he's never seen his father before."

"I'll stay out here with him," Herb said, "while you get me

the printout. I want to know as much as possible about the injury."

"Herb," Rybys said.

Startled, he realized where he was; aboard the United Spaceways XR4 axial flight from Fomalhaut to the Sol System. In two hours the first Immigration party would board the ship and make their preliminary inspection.

"Herb," his wife whispered, "I just saw my son."

"A school," Herb Asher said, "where he's going to go."

"I don't think I'll live to be there," Rybys said. "I have a feeling . . . He was there and you were there, and a noisy little ratlike man who babbled on, but I wasn't anywhere around. I looked; I kept looking. This really is going to kill me but it won't kill my son. That's what he told me, remember? Yah told me I would live on through my son, so I guess I will die; I mean, this body will die, but they'll save him. Were you there when Yah said that? I don't remember. That was a garden we were in, wasn't it? Bamboo. I saw the wind blowing. The wind talked to me; it was like voices."

"Yes," he said.

"They used to go out in the desert for forty days and forty nights. Elijah and then Jesus. Elias?" She looked around. "You ate locusts and wild honey and called on men to repent. You told King Ahab there would be no dew nor rain these years . . . thus says the Lord. According to my word." She shut her eyes.

She is really sick, Herb Asher said to himself. But I saw her son. Beautiful and wild and—something more. Timid. Very human, he thought; that was a human child. Maybe this is all in our minds. Maybe the Clems have occluded our perceptions so that we believe and see and experience but it is not real. I give up, he thought. I just don't know.

Something to do with time. He seems able to transform time. Now I am here in the ship but then I am in the Garden with the child and the other children, her child, years from now. What is the true time? he asked himself. Me here in the ship or back in my dome before I met Rybys or after she is dead and Emmanuel is in school? And I have been in cryonic suspension, for a matter of years. It has to do or had to do or will have to do with my spleen. Did they shoot me? he wondered. Rybys died from her illness but how did I die? And what became or will become of Elias?

Leaning toward him Elias said, "I want to talk to you." He motioned Herb Asher away from Rybys and away from the other passengers. "We are not to mention Yah. We will use the word 'Jehovah' from now on. It's a word coined in 1530; it's all right to say it. You understand the situation. Immigration will try to tap our minds with psychotronic listening devices, but Jehovah will cloud our minds and they will get little or nothing. But this is the part that is hard to say. Jehovah's power wanes from here on. The zone of Belial begins soon."

"OK." He nodded.

"You know all this."

"And a lot more." From what Elias had told him and from what Rybys had told him—and Jehovah had told him much, in his sleep, in vivid dreams. Jehovah had been teaching all of them; they would know what to do.

Elias said, "He is with us, and can address us from her womb. But there is always the possibility that very advanced electronic scanning devices, monitoring devices, might pick it up. He will converse with us sparingly." After a pause he added, "If at all."

"A strange idea," Herb Asher said. "I wonder what the authorities would think if their intelligence-gathering circuitry picked up the thoughts of God."

"Well," Elias said, "they wouldn't know what it was. I know the authorities of Earth; I have dealt with them for four thousand years, in situation after situation. Country after country. War after war. I was with Graf Egemont in the Dutch wars of independence, the Thirty Years War; I was present the day he was executed. I knew Beethoven . . . but perhaps 'knew' is not the word."

"You were Beethoven," Herb Asher said.

"Part of my spirit returned to Earth and to him," Elias said.

Vulgar and fiery, Herb thought. Passionately dedicated to the cause of human freedom. Walking hand-in-hand with his friend Goethe, the two men stirring the new life of the German Enlightenment. "Who else were you?" he said.

"Many people in history."

"Tom Paine?"

"We engineered the American Revolution," Elias said. "A

group of us. We were the Friends of God at one time, and the Brothers of the Rosy Cross in 1615 . . . I was Jakob Boehme, but you wouldn't know of him. My spirit doesn't dwell alone in a man; it is not incarnation. It is part of my spirit returning to Earth to bond with a human whom God has selected. There are always such humans and I am there. Martin Buber was one such man, God rest his noble soul. That dear and gentle man. The Arabs, too, placed flowers on his grave. Even the Arabs loved him." Elias fell silent. "Some of the men I sent myself to were better men than I was. But I have the power to return. God granted it to me to—well, it was for Israel's sake. A hint of immortality for the dearest people of all. You know, Herb, God offered the Torah, it is said, to every people in the world, back in ancient times, before he offered it to the Jews, and every nation rejected it for one reason or another. The Torah said, 'Thou shalt not kill' and many could not live by that; they wanted religion to be separate from morality—they didn't want religion to hobble their desires. Finally God offered it to the Jews, who accepted it."

"The Torah is the Law?" Herb said.

"It is more than the Law. The word 'Law' is inadequate. Even though the New Testament of the Christians always uses the word 'Law' for Torah. Torah is the totality of divine disclosure by God; it is alive; it existed before creation. It is a mystic, almost cosmic, entity. The Torah is the Creator's instrument. With it he created the universe and for it he created the universe. It is the highest idea and the living soul of the world. Without it the world could not exist and would have no right to exist. I am quoting the great Hebrew poet Hayyim Nahman Bialik who lived from the latter part of the nineteenth century into the mid-twentieth century. You should read him sometime."

"Can you tell me anything else about the Torah?"

"Resh Lakish said, 'If one's intent is pure, the Torah for him becomes a life-giving medicine, purifying him to life. But if one's intent is not pure, it becomes a death-giving drug, purifying him to death.' "

The two men remained silent for a time.

"I will tell you something more," Elias said. "A man came to the great Rabbi Hillel—he lived in the first century, C.E.—and said, 'I will become a proselyte on the condition that you teach me the entire Torah while I stand on one foot.' Hillel said, 'Whatever is hateful to you, do not do it to your neighbor. That is the entire Torah. The rest is commentary; go and learn it.'" He smiled at Herb Asher.

"Is the injunction actually in the Torah?" Herb Asher said. "The first five books of the Bible?"

"Yes. Leviticus nineteen, eighteen. God says, 'You shall love your neighbor as a man like yourself.' You did not know that, did you? Almost two thousand years before Jesus."

"Then the Golden Rule derives from Judaism," Herb said.

"Yes, it does, and early Judaism. The Rule was presented to man by God Himself."

"I have a lot to learn," Herb said.

"Read," Elias said. " '*Cape, lege,*' the two words Augustine heard. Latin for 'Take, read.' You do that, Herb. Take the book and read it. It is there for you. *It is alive.*"

As their journey continued, Elias disclosed to him further intriguing aspects of the Torah, qualities regarding the Torah that few men knew.

"I tell you these matters," Elias said, "because I trust you. Be careful whom you relate them to."

Four ways existed by which to read the Torah, the fourth being a study of its hidden, innermost side. When God said, "Let there be light," he meant the mystery that shone in the Torah. This was the concealed primordial light of Creation itself, it being of such nobility that it could not be debased by the use of mortals; so God wrapped it up within the heart of the Torah. This was an inexhaustible light, related to the divine sparks which the Gnostics had believed in, the fragments of the Godhead which were now scattered throughout Creation, enclosed—unfortunately—in material shells, that of physical bodies.

Most interesting of all, some Medieval Jewish mystics held the view that there had been 600,000 Jews who went out of Egypt and received the Torah at Mount Sinai. Reincarnated at each succeeding generation, these 600,000 souls continually live. Each soul or spark is related to the Torah in a different way; thus, 600,000 separate, unique meanings of the Torah exist. The idea is as follows: that for each of these 600,000 persons the Torah is different, and each person has his own specific letter in the Torah, to which his own soul is attached. So in a sense 600,000 Torahs exist.

Also, three aeons or epochs in time exist, the first in order being an age of grace, the second or current one being of severe justice and limitation, and the next, yet to come, being of mercy. A different Torah exists for each of the three ages. And yet there is only one Torah. A primal or matrix Torah exists in which there is no punctuation nor any spaces between the words; in fact all the letters are jumbled together. In each of the three ages the letters form themselves into alternative words, as events unfold.

The current age, that of severe justice and limitation, Elias explained, is marred by the fact that in its Torah one of the letters was defective, the consonant *shin*. This letter was always written with three prongs but it should have had four. Thus the Torah produced for this age was defective. Another view held by Medieval Jewish mystics was that a letter is actually missing in our alphabet. Because of this our Torah contains negative laws as well as positive. In the next aeon the missing or invisible letter will be restored, and every negative prohibition in the Torah will disappear. Hence this next aeon or, as it is called in Hebrew, the next *shemittah*, will lack restrictions imposed on humans; freedom will replace severe justice and limitation.

Out of this notion comes the idea (Elias said) that there are invisible portions of the Torah—invisible to us now, but to be visible in the Messianic Age that is to come. The cosmic cycle will bring this age inevitably: it will be the next *shemittah*, very much like the first; the Torah will again rearrange itself out of its jumbled matrix.

Herb Asher thought, It sounds like a computer. The universe is programmed—and then more accurately reprogrammed. Fantastic.

Two hours later an official government ship clamped itself to their ship, and, after a time, Immigration agents began to move among them, beginning their inspection. And their interrogation.

Filled with fear, Herb Asher held Rybys against him, and he

sat as close to Elias as possible, obtaining strength from the older man. "Tell me, Elias," Herb said quietly, "the most beautiful thing you know about God." His heart pounded harshly within him and he could scarcely breathe.

Elias said, "All right. 'Rabbi Judah said, quoting Rav:

> The day consists of twelve hours. During the first three hours, the Holy One (God), praised be He, is engaged in the study of Torah. During the second three He sits in judgment over His entire world. When He realizes that the world is deserving of destruction, He rises from the Throne of Justice, to sit on the Throne of Mercy. During the third group of three hours, He provides sustenance for the entire world, from huge beasts to lice. During the fourth, He sports with the Leviathan, as it is written, "Leviathan, which you did form to sport with" (Ps. 104:26) . . . During the fourth group of three hours (according to others) He teaches schoolchildren.' "

"Thank you," Herb Asher said. Three Immigration agents were moving toward them, now, their uniforms bright, shiny; and they carried weapons.

Elias said, "Even God consults the Torah as the formula and blueprint of the universe." An Immigration agent held out his hand for Elias's identification; the old man passed the packet of documents to him. "And even God cannot act contrary to it."

"You are Elias Tate," the senior Immigration agent said, examining the documents. "What is your purpose in returning to the Sol System?"

"This woman is very ill," Elias said. "She is entering the naval hospital at—"

"I asked you your purpose, not hers." He gazed down at Herb Asher. "Who are you?"

"I'm her husband," Herb said. He handed over his identification and permits and documentation.

"She is certified as not contagious?" the senior Immigration agent said.

"It's multiple sclerosis," Herb said, "which is not—"

"I didn't ask you what she has; I asked you if it is contagious."

"I'm telling you," he said. "I'm answering your question."

"Get up."

He stood.

"Come with me." The senior Immigration agent motioned Herb Asher to follow him up the aisle. Elias started to follow but the agent shoved him back, bodily. "Not you."

Following the Immigration agent, Herb Asher made his way step by step up the aisle to the rear of the ship. None of the other passengers was standing; he alone had been singled out.

In a small compartment marked CREW ONLY the senior Immigration agent faced Herb Asher, staring at him silently; the man's eyes bulged as if he were unable to speak, as if what he had to say could not be said. Time passed. What the hell is he doing? Herb Asher asked himself. Silence. The raging stare continued.

"Okay," the Immigration agent said. "I give up. What *is* your purpose in returning to Earth?"

"I told you."

"Is she really sick?"

"Very. She's dying."

"Then she's too sick to travel. It makes no sense."

"Only on Earth are there facilities where—"

"You are under Terran law *now*," the Immigration agent said. "Do you want to serve time for giving false information to a federal officer? I'm sending you back to Fomalhaut. The three of you. I don't have any more time. Go back to where you were sitting and remain there until you're told what to do."

A voice, a neutral, dispassionate voice, neither male nor female, a kind of perfect intelligence, spoke inside Herb Asher's head. "At Bethesda they want to study her disease."

He started visibly. The agent regarded him.

"At Bethesda," he said, "they want to study her disease."

"Research?"

"It's a microorganism."

"You said it isn't contagious."

The neutral voice said, "Not at this stage."

"Not at this stage," he said aloud.

"Are they afraid of plague?" the Immigration agent said abruptly.

Herb Asher nodded.

"Go back to your seat." The agent, irritably, waved him

away. "This is out of my jurisdiction. You have a pink form, form 368? Properly filled out and signed by a doctor?"

"Yes." It was true.

"Are either you or the older man with you infected?"

The voice inside his head said, "Only Bethesda can determine that." He had, suddenly, a vivid inner glimpse of the person whose voice he heard; he saw in his own mind a visage, female, a placid but strong face. A metal mask had been pushed back from that visage, exposing wise, impassive eyes; a beautiful classic face, like Athena; he was staggered with astonishment. This could not be Yahweh. This was a woman. But like no woman he had ever seen. He did not know her. He did not understand who this was. Her voice was not Yah's voice, and this could not be Yah's visage. He did not know what to make of it. He was perplexed beyond the telling of it. Who had taken on the task of advising him?

"Only Bethesda can determine that," he managed to say.

The Immigration agent paused uncertainly. His exterior harshness had evaporated.

The female voice whispered again, and this time, in his mind, he saw her lips move. "Time is of the essence."

"Time is of the essence," Herb Asher said. His voice grated in his own ears.

"Shouldn't you be quarantined? You probably shouldn't be with other people. Those other passengers— We should have you on a special ship. It can be arranged. It might be better . . . we could get her there faster."

"OK," he said. Reasonably.

"I'll put in a call," the Immigration agent said. "What's the name of this microorganism? It's a virus?"

"The nerve sheathing—"

"Never mind. Go back to your seat. Look." The Immigration agent followed after him. "I don't know whose idea it was to send you on a commercial carrier, but I'm getting you off of it right now. There are strict statutes that haven't been observed, here. Bethesda is expecting you? Do you want me to put in a call ahead, or is that all taken care of?"

"She is registered with them already." This was so. The arrangements had been made.

"This is really nuts," the Immigration agent said, "to put you on a public carrier. They should have known better back at Fomalhaut."

"CY30-CY30B," Herb Asher said.

"Whatever. I don't want any part of this. A mistake of this kind—" The Immigration agent cursed. "Some dumb fool back at Fomalhaut probably figured it'd save the taxpayers a few bucks— Take your seat and I'll see that you're notified when your ship is ready. It should— Christ."

Herb Asher, shaking, returned to his seat.

Elias eyed him. Rybys lay with her eyes shut; she was oblivious to what was happening.

"Let me ask you a question," Herb said to Elias. "Have you ever tasted Laphroaig Scotch?"

"No," Elias said, puzzled.

"It is the finest of all Scotches," Herb said. "Ten years old, very expensive. The distillery opened in 1815. They use traditional copper stills. It requires two distillations—"

"What went on in there?" Elias said.

"Just let me finish. Laphroaig is Gaelic for 'the beautiful hollow by the broad bay.' It's distilled on Islay in the Western Isles of Scotland. Malted barley—they dry it in a kiln over a peat fire, a genuine peat fire. It's the only Scotch made that way now. The peat can only be found on the island of Islay. Maturation takes place in oak casks. It's incredible Scotch. It's the finest liquor in the world. It's—" He broke off.

An Immigration agent came over to them. "Your ship is here, Mr. Asher. Come with me. Can your wife walk? You want some help?"

"Already?" He was dumbfounded. And then he realized that the ship had been there all this time. Immigration was routinely prepared to deal with emergency situations. Especially of this kind. Or rather, what they supposed this situation to be.

"Who wears a metal mask?" Herb said to Elias as he drew the blanket from Rybys. "Pushed back up over her hair. And has a straight nose, a very strong nose—well, let it go. Give me a hand." Together, he and Elias got Rybys to her feet. The Immigration agent watched sympathetically.

"I don't know," Elias said.

"There is someone else," Herb said as they moved Rybys step by step up the aisle.

"I'm going to throw up," Rybys said weakly.

"Just hang on," Herb Asher said. "We're almost there."

Big Noodle notified Cardinal Fulton Statler Harms and the Procurator Maximus, and then, to all the heads of states in the world it printed out the following mystifying statement:

ON THE STANDARD OF FIFTY THEY SHALL WRITE: FIN-ISHED IS THE STAND OF THE FROWARD THROUGH THE MIGHTY ACTS OF GOD, TOGETHER WITH THE NAMES OF THE COMMANDERS OF THE FIFTY AND OF ITS TENS. WHEN THEY GO OUT TO BATTLE, THEY SHALL WRITE UPON THEIR WPSOX TO FORM A COMPLETE FRONT. THE LINE IS TO CONSIST OF A THOUSAND MEN MEN MEN MEN MEN EACH FRONT LINE IS TO BE SEVEN SEVEN SEVEN DEEP, ONE MAN STANDING BEHIND THE OTHER STOP REPEAT ALL OF THEM ARE TO HOLD SHIELDS OF POLISHED BRONZE REPEAT BRONZE RESEMBLING MIRRORS THESE SHIELDS

The statement ended there. Technicians swarmed over the A.I. system in a matter of minutes.

Their verdict: the A.I. system would have to be shut down for a time. Something basic had gone wrong with it. The last coherent information it had processed was the message that the pregnant woman Rybys Rommey-Asher, her husband, Herbert Asher, and their companion, Elias Tate, had been cleared by Immigration at Ring III and had been transferred from a commercial axial carrier to a government-owned speed-ship, whose destination was Washington, D.C.

Standing at his no longer pulsing terminal, Cardinal Harms thought, A mistake has been made. Immigration was supposed to intercept them, not facilitate their flight. It doesn't make any sense. And now we've lost our primary data-processing entity, on which we are totally dependent.

He rang up the procurator maximus, and was told by an underling that the procurator had gone to bed.

The son of a bitch, Harms said to himself. The idiot. We have one more station at which to intercept them: Immigration proper, at Washington, D.C. And if they got this far— My good God, he thought. The monster is using its paranormal powers!

Once more he called the procurator maximus. "Is Galina available?" he said, but he knew it was hopeless. Bulkowsky had given up. Going to bed at this point amounted to that.

"Mrs. Bulkowsky?" the S.L. official said, incredulous. "Of course not."

"Your general staff? One of your marshals?"

"The procurator will return your call," the S.L. functionary informed him; obviously they had orders from Bulkowsky not to disturb him.

Christ! Harms said to himself as he slammed down the phone mechanism. The screen faded.

Something has gone wrong, Harms realized. They should not have gotten this far *and Big Noodle knew it.* The A.I. system had literally gone insane. That was not a technical breakdown, he realized; that was a psychotic fugue. Big Noodle understood something but could not communicate it. Or had the A.I. system in fact communicated it? What, Harms asked himself, was that gibberish?

He contacted the highest order of computers remaining, the one at Cal Tech. After transmitting the puzzling material to it he gave instructions that the material be identified.

The Cal Tech computer identified it five minutes later.

QUMRAN SCROLL "THE WAR OF THE SONS OF LIGHT AND THE SONS OF DARKNESS." SOURCE: JEWISH ASCETIC SECT ESSENES

Strange, Harms thought. He knew of the Essenes. Many theologians had speculated that Jesus was an Essene, and certainly there was evidence that John the Baptist was an Essene. The sect had anticipated an early end to the world, with the Battle of Armageddon taking place within the first century, C.E. The sect had shown strong Zoroastrian influences.

He reflected, John the Baptist. Stipulated by Christ to have been Elijah returned, as promised by Jehovah in Malachi:

> Look, I will send you the prophet Elijah before the great
> and terrible day of the Lord comes. He will reconcile

fathers to sons and sons to fathers, lest I come and put the land under a ban to destroy it.

The final verse of the Old Testament; there the Old Testament ended and the New Testament began.

Armageddon, he pondered. The final battle between the Sons of Darkness and the Sons of Light. Between Jehovah and—what had the Essenes called the evil power? Belial. That was it. That was their term for Satan. Belial would lead the Sons of Darkness; Jehovah would lead the Sons of Light. This would be the seventh battle.

There will be six battles, three of which the Sons of Light will win and three of which the Sons of Darkness will win. Leaving Belial in power. But then Jehovah himself takes command in what amounts to a tie breaker.

The monster in her womb is Belial, Cardinal Harms realized. He has returned to overthrow us. To overthrow Jehovah, whom we serve.

The Divine Power itself is now in jeopardy, he declared; he felt great wrath.

It seemed to the cardinal, at this point, that meditation and prayer were called for. And a strategy by which the invaders would be destroyed when they reached Washington, D.C.

If only Big Noodle had not broken down!

Glumly, he made his way to his private chapel.

9

THE procurator said, "We will wreck their ship. There is no particular problem. An accident will take place; the three of them—four, if you include the fetus—will be killed." To him it seemed simple.

At his end of the line Cardinal Harms said, "They will evade it. Don't ask me how." His gloom had not departed.

"You have jurisdiction in Washington, D.C.," the procurator said. "Order their ship destroyed; *order it now.*"

"Now" was eight hours later. Eight precious hours during which the procurator had peacefully slept. Cardinal Harms glared at his co-ruler. Or, he thought suddenly, had Bulkowsky been struggling to find a solution? Perhaps he had not slept at all. This solution sounded like Galina's. They had conferred, the two of them; they worked as a team.

"What a stale solution," he said. "Your typical answer, to dispatch a warhead."

"Mrs. Bulkowsky likes it," the procurator said.

"I dare say. The two of you sat up all night working *that* out?"

"We did not sit up. I slept soundly, although Galina had strange dreams. There's one she told me that—well, I think it worth relating. Do you want to hear Galina's dream? I'd like your opinion about it, since it seems to have religious overtones."

"Shoot," Harms said.

"A huge white fish lies in the ocean. Near the surface, as a whale does. It is a friendly fish. It swims toward us; I mean, toward Galina. There is a series of canals with locks. The great white fish makes its way into the canal system with extreme difficulty. Finally it is caught, away from the ocean, near the people watching. It has done this on purpose; it wants to offer itself to the people as food. A metal saw is produced, one of those two-man band saws that lumberjacks use to cut down trees. Galina said that the teeth on the saw were dreadful. People began to saw slices of flesh from the great fish, who is still alive. They saw slice after slice of the living flesh of the great white fish that is so friendly. In the dream Galina thinks,

'This is wrong. We are injuring the fish too much.'" Bulkowsky paused. "Well? What do you say?"

"The fish is Christ," Cardinal Harms said, "who offers his flesh to man so that man may have eternal life."

"That's all very well, but it was unfair to the fish. She said it was a wrong thing to do. Even though the fish offered itself. Its pain was too much. Oh yes; in the dream she thought, 'We must find another kind of food, which doesn't cause the great fish suffering.' And then there were some blurred episodes where she was looking in a refrigerator; she saw a pitcher of water, a pitcher wrapped in straw or reeds or something . . . and a cube of pink food like a cube of butter. Words were written on the wrapper but she couldn't read them. The refrigerator was the common property of some kind of small settlement of people, off in a remote area. What happened, the way it worked, was that this pitcher of water and this pink cube belonged to the whole colony and you only ate the food and drank the water when you realized you were approaching your moment of death."

"What did drinking the water—"

"Then you came back later. Reborn."

Harms said, "That is the host under the two species. The consecrated wine and wafer. The blood and body of our Lord. The food of eternal life. 'This is my body. Take—'"

"The settlement seemed to exist at another time entirely. A long time ago. As in antiquity."

"Interesting," Harms said, "but we still have our problem to face, what to do about the monster baby."

"As I said," the procurator said, "we will arrange an accident. Their ship won't reach Washington, D.C. When, precisely, does it arrive? How much time do we have?"

"Just a moment." Harms pressed keys on the board of a small computer terminal. "Christ!" he said.

"What's the matter? It only takes seconds to dispatch a small missile. You have them in that area."

Harms said, "Their ship has landed. While you slept. They are already being processed by Immigration at Washington, D.C."

"It is normal to sleep," the procurator said.

"The monster made you sleep."

"I've been sleeping all my life!" Angrily, the procurator added, "I am here at this resort for rest; my health is bad."

"I wonder," Harms said.

"Notify Immigration, at once, to hold them. Do it *now*."

Harms rang off, and contacted Immigration. I will take that woman, that Rybys Rommey-Asher, and break her neck, he said to himself. I will chop her into little pieces, and her fetus along with her. I will chop up all of them and feed them to the animals at the zoo.

Surprised, he asked himself, Did I think that? The ferocity of his ratiocination amazed him. I really hate them, he realized. I am furious. I am furious with Bulkowsky for logging eight full hours of sleep in the midst of this crisis; if I had the power I would chop him up, too.

When he had the director of Washington, D.C. Immigration on the line he asked first of all if the woman Rybys Rommey-Asher, her husband and Elias Tate were still there.

"I'll check, your Eminence," the bureau chief said. A pause, a very long pause. Harms counted off the seconds, cursing and praying by turns. Then the director returned. "We are still processing them."

"Hold them. Don't let them go for any reason whatsoever. The woman is pregnant. Inform her—do you know who I'm talking about? Rybys Rommey-Asher—inform her that there will be a mandatory abortion of the fetus. Have your people make up any excuse they want."

"Do you actually want an abortion performed on her? Or is this a pretext—"

"I want abortion induced within the next hour," Harms said. "A saline abortion. I want the fetus killed. I'm going to take you into our confidence. I have been conferring with the procurator maximus; this is global policy. The fetus is a freak. A radiation sport. Possibly even the monster offspring of interspecies symbiosis. Do you understand?"

"Oh," the Immigration director said. "Interspecies symbiosis. Yes. We'll kill it with localized heat. Inject radioactive dye directly into it through the abdominal wall. I'll tell one of our doctors—"

"Tell him to abort her or tell him to kill it inside her," Harms said, "but kill it and kill it now."

"I'll need a signature," the Immigration director said. "I can't do this without authorization."

"Transmit the forms." He sighed.

From his terminal pages oozed; he took hold of them, found the lines where his signature was required, signed and fed the pages back into the fone terminal.

As he sat in the Immigration lounge with Rybys, Herb Asher wondered where Elias Tate had gone. Elias had excused himself to go to the men's room, but he had not returned.

"When can I lie down?" Rybys murmured.

"Soon," he said. "They're putting us right through." He did not amplify because undoubtedly the lounge was bugged.

"Where's Elias?" she said.

"He'll be back."

An Immigration official, not in uniform but wearing a badge, approached them. "Where is the third member of your party?" He consulted his clipboard. "Elias Tate."

"In the men's room," Herb Asher said. "Could you please process this woman? You can see how sick she is."

"We want a medical examination made on her," the Immigration official said dispassionately. "We require a medical determination before we can put you through."

"It's been done already! By her own doctor originally and then by—"

"This is standard procedure," the official said.

"That doesn't matter," Herb Asher said. "It's cruel and it's useless."

"The doctor will be with you shortly," the official said, "and while she's being examined by him you will be interrogated. To save you time. We won't interrogate her, at least not very extensively. I'm aware of her grave medical condition."

"My God," Herb said, "you can *see* it!"

The official departed, but returned almost at once, his face grim. "Tate isn't in the men's room."

"Then I don't know where he is."

"They may have processed him. Put him through." The official hurried off, speaking into a hand-held intercom unit.

I guess Elias got away, Herb Asher thought.

"Come in here," a voice said. It was a woman doctor, in a white smock. Young, wearing glasses, her hair tied back in a bun, she briskly escorted Herb Asher and his wife down a short sterile-looking and sterile-smelling corridor into an examination room. "Lie down, Mrs. Asher," the doctor said, helping Rybys to an examination table.

"Rommey-Asher," Rybys said as she got up painfully onto the table. "Can you give me an I-V anti-emetic? And soon? I mean soon. I mean now."

"In view of your wife's illness," the doctor said to Herb Asher as she seated herself at her desk, "why wasn't her pregnancy terminated?"

"We've been through all this," he said savagely.

"We may still require her to abort. We do not wish a deformed infant born; it's against public policy."

Staring at the doctor in fear, Herb said, "But she's six months into her pregnancy!"

"We have it down as five months," the doctor said. "Well within the legal period."

"You can't do it without her consent," Herb said; his fear became wild.

"The decision," the doctor told him, "is no longer yours to make, now that you have returned to Earth. A medical board will study the matter."

It was obvious to Herb Asher that there would be a mandatory abortion. He knew what the board would decide—had decided.

In the corner of the room a piped-in music source gave forth the odious background noise of soupy strings. The same sound, he realized, that he had heard off and on at his dome. But now the music changed, and he realized that a popular number of the Fox's was coming up. As the doctor sat filling out medical forms the Fox's voice could distantly be heard. It gave him comfort.

> Come again!
> Sweet love doth now invite
> Thy graces, that refrain
> To do me due delight.

The lady doctor's lips moved reflexively in synchronization with the Fox's familiar Dowland song.

All at once Herb Asher became aware that the voice from

the speaker only resembled the Fox's. The voice was no longer singing; it was speaking.

The faint voice said distinctly:

There will be no abortion. There will be a birth.

At her desk the doctor seemed unaware of the transition. Yah has cooked the audio signal, Herb Asher realized. As he watched he saw the doctor pause, pen lifted from the page before her.

Subliminal, he said to himself as he watched the doctor hesitate. The woman still imagines she is hearing a familiar song. Familiar lyrics. She is in a kind of spell. As if hypnotized.

The song resumed.

"We can't abort her legally if she's six months along," the doctor said hesitantly. "Mr. Asher, there must be an error. We have her down as five. Five months into her pregnancy. But if you say six, then—"

"Examine her if you want," Herb Asher said. "It's at least six. Make your own determination."

"I—" The doctor rubbed her forehead, wincing; she shut her eyes and grimaced, as in pain. "I see no reason to—" She broke off, as if unable to remember what she intended to say. "I see no reason," she resumed after a moment, "to dispute this." She pressed a button on her desk intercom.

The door opened and a uniformed Immigration official stood there. A moment later he was joined by a uniformed Customs agent.

"The matter is settled," the doctor said to the Immigration official. "We can't force her to abort; she's too far along."

The Immigration official gazed down at her fixedly.

"It's the law," the doctor said.

"Mr. Asher," the Customs agent said, "let me ask you something. In your wife's declaration prepared for Customs clearance she lists two phylacteries. What is a phylactery?"

"I don't know," Herb Asher said.

"Aren't you Jewish?" the Customs agent said. "Every Jew knows what a phylactery is. Your wife, then, is Jewish and you are not?"

"Well," Herb Asher said, "she is C.I.C. but—" He paused.

He sensed himself moving step by step into a trap. It was patently impossible that a husband would not know his wife's religion. They are getting into an area I do not want to discuss, he said to himself. "I'm a Christian," he said, then. "Although I was raised Scientific Legate. I belonged to the Party's Youth Corps. But now—"

"But Mrs. Asher is Jewish. Hence the phylacteries. You've never seen her put them on? One goes on the head; one goes on the left arm. They're small square leathern boxes containing sections of Hebrew scripture. It strikes me as odd that you don't know anything about this. How long have you known each other?"

"A long time," Herb Asher said.

"Is she really your wife?" the Immigration official said. "If she is six months along in her pregnancy—" He consulted with some of the documents lying on the doctor's desk. "She was pregnant when you married her. Are you the father of the child?"

"Of course," he said.

"What blood type are you? Well, I have it here." The Immigration official began going through the filled-out legal and medical forms. "It's somewhere . . ."

The fone on the desk rang; the lady doctor picked it up and identified herself. "For you." She handed the receiver to the Immigration official.

The Immigration official, raptly attentive, listened in silence; then, putting his hand over the audio sender, he said irritably to Herb Asher, "The blood type checks out. You two are cleared. But we want to talk to Tate, the older man who—" He broke off and again listened to his fone.

"You can call a cab from the payfone in the lounge," the Customs agent said.

"We're free to go?" Herb Asher said.

The Customs agent nodded.

"Something is wrong," the doctor said; again she had removed her glasses and sat rubbing her eyes.

"There's this other matter," the Customs agent said to her, and bent down to present her with a stack of documents.

"Do you know where Tate is?" the Immigration official called after Herb Asher as he and Rybys made their way from the examination room.

"No, I don't," Herb said, and found himself in the corridor; supporting Rybys he walked step by step back down the corridor to the lounge. "Sit down," he said to her, depositing her in a heap on a couch. Several waiting people gazed at them dully. "I'll fone. I'll be right back. Do you have any change? I need a five-dollar piece."

"Christ," Rybys murmured. "No, I don't have."

"We got through," he said to her in a low voice.

"OK!" she said angrily.

"I'll fone for a cab." Going through his pockets, searching for a five-dollar piece, he felt elated. Yah had intervened, distantly and feebly, but it had been enough.

Ten minutes later they and their luggage were aboard a Yellow flycab, rising up from the Washington, D.C. spaceport, heading in the direction of Bethesda–Chevy Chase.

"Where the hell is Elias?" Rybys managed to say.

"He drew their attention," Herb said. "He diverted them. Away from us."

"Great," she said. "So now he could be anywhere."

All at once a large commercial flycar came hurtling toward them at reckless speed.

The robot driver of the cab cried out in dismay. And then the massive flycar sideswiped them; it happened in an instant. Violent waves of concussion hurled the cab in a downward spiral; Herb Asher clutched his wife against him—buildings bloomed into hugeness, and he knew, he knew absolutely and utterly, what had happened. The bastards, he thought in pain; he hurt physically; he ached from the realization. Warning beepers in the cab had gone off—

Yah's protection wasn't enough, he realized as the cab spun lower and lower like a falling, withered leaf.

It's too weak. Too weak here.

The cab struck the edge of a high-rise building.

Darkness came and Herb Asher knew no more.

He lay in a hospital bed, wired up and tubed up to countless devices like a cyborg entity.

"Mr. Asher?" a voice was saying, a male voice. "Mr. Asher, can you hear me?"

He tried to nod but could not.

"You have suffered serious internal damage," the male voice said. "I am Dr. Pope. You've been unconscious for five days. Surgery was performed on you but your ruptured spleen had to be removed. That's only a part of it. You are going to be put into cryonic suspension until replacement organs— Can you hear me?"

"Yes," he said.

"—Until replacement organs, available from donors, can be procured. The waiting list isn't very long; you should be in suspension for only a few weeks. How long, specifically—"

"My wife."

"Your wife is dead. She lost brain function for too long a time. We had to rule out cryonic suspension for her. It wouldn't have been of any use."

"The baby."

"The fetus is alive," Dr. Pope said. "Your wife's uncle, Mr. Tate, has arrived and has taken legal responsibility. We've removed the fetus from her body and placed it in a synthowomb. According to all our tests it was not damaged by the trauma, which is something of a miracle."

Grimly, Herb Asher thought, Exactly.

"Your wife asked that he be called Emmanuel," Dr. Pope said.

"I know."

As he lost consciousness Herb Asher said to himself, Yah's plans have not been completely wrecked. Yah has not been defeated entirely. There is still hope.

But not very much.

"Belial," he whispered.

"Pardon me?" Dr. Pope leaned close to hear. "Belial? Is that someone you want us to contact? Someone who should know?"

Herb Asher said, "He knows."

The chief prelate of the Christian-Islamic Church said to the procurator maximus of the Scientific Legate, "Something went wrong. They got past Immigration."

"Where did they go? They have to have gone somewhere."

"Elias Tate disappeared even before the Customs inspection.

We have no idea where he is. As for the Ashers—" The cardinal hesitated. "They were last seen leaving in a cab. I'm sorry."

Bulkowsky said, "We will find them."

"With God's help," the cardinal said, and crossed himself. Bulkowsky, seeing that, did likewise.

"The power of evil," Bulkowsky said.

"Yes," the cardinal said. "That is what we are up against."

"But it loses in the end."

"Yes, absolutely. I am going to the chapel, now. To pray. I advise you to do the same."

Raising an eyebrow, Bulkowsky regarded him. His expression could not be read; it was intricate.

10

WHEN Herb Asher awoke he was told perplexing facts. He had spent—not weeks—but years in cryonic suspension. The doctors could not explain why it had taken so long to obtain replacement organs. Circumstances, they told him, beyond our control. Procedural problems.

He said, "What about Emmanuel?"

Dr. Pope, who looked older and grayer and more distinguished than before, said, "Someone broke into the hospital and removed your son from the synthowomb."

"When?"

"Almost at once. The fetus was in the synthowomb for only a day, according to our records."

"Do you know who did it?"

"According to our video tapes—we monitor our synthowombs constantly—it was an elderly bearded man." After a pause Dr. Pope added, "Deranged in appearance. You must face the very high probability factor that your son is dead, has in fact been dead for ten years, either from natural causes, which is to say from being taken out of his synthowomb . . . or due to the actions of the elderly bearded man. Either deliberate or accidental. The police could not locate either of them. I'm sorry."

Elias Tate, Herb said to himself. Spiriting Emmanuel away, to safety. He shut his eyes and felt overwhelming gratitude.

"How do you feel?" Dr. Pope inquired.

"I dreamed. I didn't know that people in cryonic suspension were conscious."

"You weren't."

"I dreamed again and again about my wife." He felt bitter grief hover over him and then descend on him, filling him; the grief was too much. "Always I found myself back there with her. When we met, before we met. The trip to Earth. Little things. Dishes of spoiled food . . . she was sloppy."

"But you do have your son."

"Yes," he said. He wondered how he would be able to find Elias and Emmanuel. They will have to find me, he realized.

For a month he remained at the hospital, undergoing remedial therapy to build up his strength, and then, on a cool morning in mid-March, the hospital discharged him. Suitcase in hand he walked down the front steps, shaky and afraid but happy to be free. Every day during his therapy he had expected the authorities to come swooping down on him. They did not. He wondered why.

As he stood with a throng of people trying to flag down a flycar Yellow cab he noticed a blind beggar standing off to one side, an ancient, white-haired, very large man wearing soiled clothing; the old man held a cup.

"Elias," Herb Asher said.

Going over to him he regarded his old friend. Neither of them spoke for a time and then Elias Tate said, "Hello, Herbert."

"Rybys told me you often take the form of a beggar," Herb Asher said. He reached out to put his arms around the old man, but Elias shook his head.

"It is Passover," Elias said. "And I am here. The power of my spirit is too great; you should not touch me. It is all my spirit, now, at this moment."

"You are not a man," Herb Asher said, awed.

"I am many men," Elias said. "It's good to see you again. Emmanuel said you would be released today."

"The boy is all right?"

"He is beautiful."

"I saw him," Herb Asher said. "Once, a while ago. In a vision that—" He paused. "Jehovah sent to me. To help me."

"Did you dream?" Elias asked.

"About Rybys. And about you as well. About everything that happened. I lived it over and over again."

"But now you are alive again," Elias said. "Welcome back, Herbert Asher. We have much to do."

"Do we have a chance? Do we have any real chance?"

"The boy is ten years old," Elias said. "He has confused their wits, scrambled up their thinking. He has made them forget. But—" Elias was silent a moment. "He, too, has forgotten. You will see. A few years ago he began to remember; he heard a song and some of his memories came back. Enough, perhaps, or maybe not enough. You may bring back more. He programmed himself, originally, before the accident."

With extreme difficulty Herb Asher said, "He was injured, then? In the accident?"

Elias nodded. Somberly.

"Brain damage," Herb Asher said; he saw the expression on his friend's face.

Again the old man nodded, the elderly beggar with the cup. The immortal Elijah, here at Passover. As always. The eternal, helping friend of man. Tattered and shabby, and very wise.

Zina said, "Your father is coming, isn't he?"

Together they sat on a bench in Rock Creek Park, near the frozen-over water. Trees shaded them with bare, stark branches. The air had turned cold, and both children wore heavy clothing. But the sky overhead was clear. Emmanuel gazed up for a time.

"What does your slate say?" Zina asked.

"I don't have to consult my slate."

"He isn't your father."

Emmanuel said, "He's a good person. It's not his fault that my mother died. I'll be happy to see him once more. I've missed him." He thought, It's been a long time. According to the scale by which they reckon here in the Lower Realm.

What a tragic realm this is, he reflected. Those down here are prisoners, and the ultimate tragedy is that they don't know it; they think they are free because they have never been free, and do not understand what it means. *This is a prison*, and few men have guessed. But I know, he said to himself. Because that is why I am here. To burst the walls, to tear down the metal gates, to break each chain. Thou shalt not muzzle the ox as he treadeth out the corn, he thought, remembering the Torah. You will not imprison a free creature; you will not bind it. Thus says the Lord your God. Thus I say.

They do not know whom they serve. This is the heart of their misfortune: service in error, to a wrong thing. They are poisoned as if with metal, he thought. Metal confining them and metal in their blood; this is a metal world. Driven by cogs, a machine that grinds along, dealing out suffering and death . . . They are so accustomed to death, he realized, as if death, too, were natural. How long it has been since they knew the Garden. The place of resting animals and flowers. When can I find for them that place again?

There are two realities, he said to himself. The Black Iron Prison, which is called the Cave of Treasures, in which they now live, and the Palm Tree Garden with its enormous spaces, its light, where they originally dwelt. Now they are literally blind, he thought. Literally unable to see more than a short distance; faraway objects are invisible to them now. Once in a while one of them guesses that formerly they had faculties now gone; once in a while one of them discerns the truth, that they are not now what they were and not now where they were. But they forget again, exactly as I forgot. And I still forget somewhat, he realized. I still have only a partial vision. I am occluded, too.

But I will not be, soon.

"You want a Pepsi?" Zina said.

"It's too cold. I just want to sit."

"Don't be unhappy." She put her mittened hand on his arm. "Be joyful."

Emmanuel said, "I'm tired. I'll be okay. There's a lot that has to be done. I'm sorry. It weighs on me."

"You're not afraid, are you?"

"Not any more," Emmanuel said.

"You are sad."

He nodded.

Zina said, "You'll feel better when you see Mr. Asher again."

"I see him now," Emmanuel said.

"Very good," she said, pleased. "And even without your slate."

"I use it less and less," he said, "because the knowledge is progressively more and more in me. As you know. And you know why."

To that, Zina said nothing.

"We are close, you and I," Emmanuel said. "I have always loved you the most. I always will. You are going to stay on with me and advise me, aren't you?" He knew the answer; he knew that she would. She had been with him from the beginning—as she said, his darling and delight. And her delight, as Scripture said, was in mankind. So, through her, he himself loved mankind; it was his delight as well.

"We could get something hot to drink," Zina said.

He murmured, "I just want to sit." I shall sit here until it is time to go to meet Herb Asher, he said to himself. He can tell me about Rybys; his many memories of her will give me joy, the joy that, right now, I lack.

I love him, he realized. I love my mother's husband, my legal father. Like other men he is a good human being. He is a man of merit, and to be cherished.

But, unlike other men, Herb Asher knows who I am. Thus I can talk openly with him, as I do with Elias. And with Zina. It will help, he thought. I will be less weary. No longer as I am now, pinned by my cares; weighed down. The burden, to some extent, will lift. Because it will be shared.

And, he thought, there is still so much that I do not remember. I am not as I was. Like them, like the people, I have fallen. The bright morning star which fell did not fall alone, it tore down everything else with it, including me. Part of my own being fell with it, and I am that fallen being now.

But then, as he sat there on the bench with Zina, in the park, on this cold day so near the vernal equinox, he thought, But Herbert Asher lay dreaming in his bunk, dreaming of a phantom life with Linda Fox, while my mother struggled to survive. Not once did he try to help her; not once did he inquire into her trouble and seek remedy. Not until I, I myself, forced him to go to her, not until then did he do anything. I do not love the man, he said to himself. I know the man and he forfeited his right to my love—he lost my love because he did not care.

I cannot, thereupon, care about him. In response.

Why should I help any of them? he asked himself. They do what is right only when forced to, when there is no alternative. They fell of their own accord and are fallen now, of their own accord, by what they have voluntarily done. My mother is dead because of them; they murdered her. They would murder me if they could figure out where I am; only because I have confused their wits do they leave me alone. High and low they seek my life, just as Ahab sought Elijah's life, so long ago. They are a worthless race, and I do not care if they fall. I do not care at all. To save them I must fight what they themselves are. And have always been.

"You look so downcast," Zina said.

"What is this for?" he said. "They are what they are. I grow more and more weary. And I care less and less, as I begin to remember. For ten years I have lived on this world, now, and for ten years they have hunted me. Let them die. Did I not say to them the talion law: 'An eye for an eye, a tooth for a tooth'? Is that not in the Torah? They drove me off this world two thousand years ago; I return; they wish me dead. Under the talion law I should wish them dead. It is the sacred law of Israel. It is *my* law, my word."

Zina was silent.

"Advise me," Emmanuel said. "I have always listened to your advice."

Zina said:

> One day Elijah the prophet appeared to Rabbi Baruka in the market of Lapet. Rabbi Baruka asked him, "Is there any one among the people of this market who is destined to share in the world to come?" . . . Two men appeared on the scene and Elijah said, "These two will share in the world to come." Rabbi Baruka asked them, "What is your occupation?" They said, "We are merrymakers. When we see a man who is downcast, we cheer him up. When we see two people quarreling with one another, we endeavor to make peace between them."

"You make me less sad," Emmanuel said. "And less weary. As you always have. As Scripture says of you:

> Then I was at his side every day,
> his darling and delight,
> playing in his presence continually,
> playing on the earth, when he had finished it,
> while my delight was in mankind.

And Scripture says:

> Wisdom I loved; I sought her out when I was young and longed to win her for my bride, and I fell in love with her beauty.

But that was Solomon, not me.

> So I determined to bring her home to live with me, knowing that she would be my counsellor in prosperity and my comfort in anxiety and grief.

Solomon was a wise man, to love you so."

Beside him the girl smiled. She said nothing, but her dark eyes shone.

"Why are you smiling?" he asked.

"Because you have shown the truth of Scripture when it says:

> I will betroth you to Me forever. I will betroth you to Me in righteousness and in justice, in love and in mercy. I will betroth you to Me in faithfulness, and you shall love the Lord.

Remember that you made the Covenant with man. And you made man in your own image. You cannot break the Covenant; you have made man that promise, that you will never break it."

Emmanuel said, "That is so. You advise me well." He thought, And you cheer my heart. You above all else, you who came before creation. Like the two merrymakers, he thought, who Elijah said would be saved. Your dancing, your singing, and the sound of bells. "I know," he said, "what your name means."

"Zina?" she said. "It's just a name."

"It is the Roumanian word for—" He ceased speaking; the girl had trembled visibly, and her eyes were now wide.

"How long have you known it?" she said.

"Years. Listen:

> I know a bank where the wild thyme blows,
> Where oxlips and the nodding violet grows;
> Quite over-canopied with luscious woodbine,
> With sweet musk-roses, and with eglantine:
> There sleeps Titania sometime of the night,
> Lull'd in these flowers with dances and delight;
> And there the snake throws her enamell'd skin,
> Weed wide enough

I will finish; listen:

> To wrap a fairy in.

And I have known this," he finished, "all this time."

Staring at him, Zina said, "Yes, Zina means *fairy*."

"You are not Holy Wisdom," he said, "you are Diana, the fairy queen."

Cold wind rustled the branches of the trees. And, across the frozen creek, a few dry leaves scuttled.

"I see," Zina said.

About the two of them the wind rustled, as if speaking. He could hear the wind as words. And the wind said:

BEWARE!

He wondered if she heard it, too.

But they were still friends. Zina told Emmanuel about an early identity that she had once had. Thousands of years ago, she said, she had been Ma'at, the Egyptian goddess who represented the cosmic order and justice. When someone died his heart was weighed against Ma'at's ostrich feather. By this the person's burden of sins was determined.

The principle by which the sinfulness of the person was determined consisted of the degree of his truthfulness. To the extent that he was truthful the judgment went in his favor. This judgment was presided over by Osiris, but since Ma'at was the goddess of truthfulness, then it followed that the determination was hers to make.

"After that," Zina said, "the idea of the judgment of human souls passed over into Persia." In the ancient Persian religion, Zoroastrianism, a sifting bridge had to be crossed by the newly dead person. If he was evil the bridge got narrower and narrower until he toppled off and plunged into the fiery pit of hell. Judaism in its later stages and Christianity had gotten their ideas of the Final Days from this.

The good person, who managed to cross the sifting bridge, was met by the spirit of his religion: a beautiful young woman with superb, large breasts. However, if the person was evil the spirit of his religion consisted of a dried-up old hag with sagging paps. You could tell at a glance, therefore, which category you belonged to.

"Were you the spirit of religion for the good persons?" Emmanuel asked.

Zina did not answer the question; she passed on to another matter which she was more anxious to communicate to him.

In these judgments of the dead, stemming from Egypt and Persia, the scrutiny was pitiless and the sinful soul was de facto doomed. Upon your death the books listing your good deeds and bad deeds closed, and no one, even the gods, could alter the tabulation. In a sense the procedure of judgment was mechanical. A bill of particulars, in essence, had been drawn up against you, compiled during your lifetime, and now this bill of particulars was fed into a mechanism of retribution. Once the mechanism received the list, it was all over for you. The mechanism ground you to shreds, and the gods merely watched, impassively.

But one day (Zina said) a new figure made its appearance at the path leading to the sifting bridge. This was an enigmatic figure who seemed to consist of a shifting succession of aspects or roles. Sometimes he was called Comforter. Sometimes Advocate. Sometimes Beside-Helper. Sometimes Support. Sometimes Advisor. No one knew where he had come from. For thousands of years he had not been there, and then one day he had appeared. He stood at the edge of the busy path, and as the souls made their way to the sifting bridge this complex figure —who sometimes, but rarely, seemed to be a woman— signaled to the persons, each in turn, to attract their attention. It was essential that the Beside-Helper got their attention before they stepped onto the sifting bridge, because after that it was too late.

"Too late for what?" Emmanuel said.

Zina said, "The Beside-Helper upon stopping a person approaching the sifting bridge asked him if he wished to be represented in the testing which was to come."

"By the Beside-Helper?"

The Beside-Helper, she explained, assumed his role of Advocate; he offered to speak on the person's behalf. But the Beside-Helper offered something more. He offered to present his own bill of particulars to the retribution mechanism in place of the bill of particulars of the person. If the person were innocent this would make no difference, but, for the guilty, it would yield up a sentence of exculpation rather than guilt.

"That's not fair," Emmanuel said. "The guilty should be punished."

"Why?" Zina said.

"Because it is the law," Emmanuel said.

"Then there is no hope for the guilty."

Emmanuel said, "They deserve no hope."

"What if everyone is guilty?"

He had not thought of that. "What does the Beside-Helper's bill of particulars list?" he asked.

"It is blank," Zina said. "A perfectly white piece of paper. A document on which nothing is inscribed."

"The retributive machinery could not process that."

Zina said, "It would process it. It would imagine that it had received a compilation of a totally spotless person."

"But it couldn't act. It would have no input data."

"That's the whole point."

"Then the machinery of justice has been bilked."

"Bilked out of a victim," Zina said. "Is that not to be desired? Should there be victims? What is gained if there is an unending procession of victims? Does that right the wrongs they have committed?"

"No," he said.

"The idea," Zina said, "is to feed mercy into the circuit. The Beside-Helper is an amicus curiae, a friend of the court. He advises the court, by its permission, that the case before it constitutes an exception. The general rule of punishment does not apply."

"And he does this for everyone? Every guilty person?"

"For every guilty person who accepts his offer of advocacy and help."

"But then you'd have an endless procession of exceptions. Because no guilty person in his right mind would reject such an offer; every single guilty person would wish to be judged as an exception, as a case involving mitigating circumstances."

Zina said, "But the person would have to accept the fact that he was, on his own, guilty. He could of course wager that he was innocent, in which case he would not need the advocacy of the Beside-Helper."

After a moment of pondering, Emmanuel said, "That would be a foolish choice. He might be wrong. And he loses nothing by accepting the assistance of the Beside-Helper."

"In practice, however," Zina said, "most souls about to be judged reject the offer of advocacy by the Beside-Helper."

"On what basis?" He could not fathom their reasoning.

Zina said, "On the basis that they are sure they are innocent.

To receive this help the person must go with the pessimistic assumption that he is guilty, even though his own assessment of himself is one of innocence. The truly innocent need no Beside-Helper, just as the physically healthy need no physician. In a situation of this kind the optimistic assumption is perilous. It's the bail-out theorem that little creatures employ when they construct a burrow. If they are wise they build a second exit to their burrow, operating on the pessimistic assumption that the first one will be found by a predator. All creatures who did not use their theorem are no longer with us."

Emmanuel said, "It is degrading to a man that he must consider himself sinful."

"It's degrading to a gopher to have to admit that his burrow may not be perfectly built, that a predator may find it."

"You are talking about an adversary situation. Is divine justice an adversary situation? Is there a prosecutor?"

"Yes, there is a prosecutor of man in the divine court; it is Satan. There is the Advocate who defends the accused human, and Satan who impugns and indicts him. The Advocate, standing beside the man, defends him and speaks for him; Satan, confronting the man, accuses him. Would you wish man to have an accuser and not a defender? Would that seem just?"

"But innocence must be presumed."

The girl's eyes gleamed. "Precisely the point made by the Advocate in each trial that takes place. Hence he substitutes his own blameless record for that of his client, and justifies the man by surrogation."

"Are you this Beside-Helper?" Emmanuel asked.

"No," she said. "He is a far more puzzling figure than I. If you are having difficulty with me, in determining—"

"I am," Emmanuel said.

"He is a latecomer into this world," Zina said. "Not found in earlier aeons. He represents an evolution in the divine strategy. One by which the primordial damage is repaired. One of many, but a main one."

"Will I ever encounter him?"

"You will not be judged," Zina said. "So perhaps not. But all humans will see him standing by the busy road, offering his help. Offering it in time—before the person starts across the sifting bridge and is judged. The Beside-Helper's intervention always comes in time. It is part of his nature to be there soon enough."

Emmanuel said, "I would like to meet him."

"Follow the travel pattern of any human," Zina said, "and you will arrive at the point where that human encounters him. That is how I know about him. I, too, am not judged." She pointed to the slate that she had given him. "Ask it for more information about the Beside-Helper."

The slate read:

TO CALL

"Is that all you can tell me?" Emmanuel asked it.

A new word formed, a Greek word:

PARAKALEIN

He wondered about this, wondered greatly, at this new entity who had come into the world . . . who could be called on by those in need, those who stood in danger of negative judgment. It was one more of the mysteries presented to him by Zina. There had been so many, now. He enjoyed them. But he was puzzled.

To call to aid: parakalein. Strange, he thought. The world evolves even as it falls more and more. There are two distinct movements: the falling, and then, at the same time, the upward-rising work of repair. Antithetical movements, in the form of a dialectic of all creation and the powers contending behind it.

Suppose Zina beckoned to the parts that fell? Beckoned them, seductively, to fall farther. About this he could not yet tell.

11

Reaching out, Herb Asher took the boy in his arms. He hugged him tight.

"And this is Zina," Elias Tate said. "Emmanuel's friend." He took the girl by the hand and led her to Herb Asher. "She's a little older than Manny."

"Hello," Herb Asher said. But he did not care about her; he wanted to look at Rybys's son.

Ten years, he thought. This child has grown while I dreamed and dreamed, thinking I was alive when in fact I was not.

Elias said, "She helps him. She teaches him. More than the school does. More than I do."

Looking toward the girl Herb Asher saw a beautiful pale heart-shaped face with eyes that danced with light. What a pretty child, he thought, and turned back to Rybys's son. But then, struck by something, he looked once more at the girl.

Mischief showed on her face. Especially in her eyes. Yes, he thought; there is something in her eyes. A kind of knowledge.

"They've been together four years now," Elias said. "She gave him a high-technology slate. It's some kind of advanced computer terminal. It asks him questions—poses questions to him and gives him hints. Right, Manny?"

Emmanuel said, "Hello, Herb Asher." He seemed solemn and subdued, in contrast to the girl.

"Hello," he said to Emmanuel. "How much you look like your mother."

"In that crucible we grow," Emmanuel said, cryptically. He did not amplify.

"Are—" Herb did not know what to say. "Is everything all right?"

"Yes." The boy nodded.

"You have a heavy burden on you," Herb said.

"The slate plays tricks," Emmanuel said.

There was silence.

"What's wrong?" Herb said to Elias.

To the boy, Elias said, "Something is wrong, isn't it?"

"While my mother died," Emmanuel said, gazing fixedly at

Herb Asher, "you listened to an illusion. She does not exist, that image. Your Fox is a phantasm, nothing else."

"That was a long time ago," Herb said.

"The phantasm is with us in the world," Emmanuel said.

"That's not my problem," Herb said.

Emmanuel said, "But it is mine. I mean to solve it. Not now but at the proper time. You fell asleep, Herb Asher, because a voice told you to fall asleep. This world here, this planet, all of it, all its people—everything here sleeps. I have watched it for ten years and there is nothing good I can say about it. What you did it does; what you were it is. Maybe you still sleep. Do you sleep, Herb Asher? You dreamed about my mother while you lay in cryonic suspension. I tapped your dreams. From them I learned a lot about her. I am as much her as I am myself. As I told her, she lives on in me and *as* me; I have made her deathless—your wife is here, not back in that littered dome. Do you realize that? Look at me and you see Rybys whom you ignored."

Herb Asher said, "I—"

"There is nothing for you to tell me," Emmanuel said. "I read your heart, not your words. I knew you then and I know you now. 'Herbert, Herbert,' I called to you. I summoned you back to life, for your sake and for hers, and, because it was for her sake, it was for my sake. When you helped her you helped me. And when you ignored her you ignored me. Thus says your God."

Reaching out, Elias put his arm around Herb Asher, to reassure him.

"I will always speak the truth to you, Herb Asher," the boy continued. "There is no deceit in God. *I want you to live.* I made you live once before, when you lay in psychological death. God does not desire any living thing's death; God takes no delight in nonexistence. Do you know what God is, Herb Asher? God is He Who causes to be. Put another way, if you seek the basis of being that underlies everything you will surely find God. You can work back to God from the phenomenal universe, or you can move from the Creator to the phenomenal universe. Each implies the other. The Creator would not be the Creator if there were no universe, and the universe would cease to be if the Creator did not sustain it. The Creator does not exist prior to the universe in time; he does not exist in time at all. God creates the universe constantly; he is *with* it, not above or behind it. This is impossible to understand for you because you are a created thing and exist in time. But eventually you will return to your Creator and then you will again no longer exist in time. You are the breath of your Creator, and as he breathes in and out, you live. Remember that, for that sums up everything that you need to know about your God. There is first an exhalation from God, on the part of all creation; and then, at a certain point, it starts its journey back, its inhalation. This cycle never ceases. You leave me; you are away from me; you start back; you rejoin me. You and everything else. It is a process, an event. It is an activity—*my* activity. It is the rhythm of my own being, and it sustains you all."

Amazing, Herb Asher thought. A ten-year-old boy. Her son speaking this.

"Emmanuel," the girl Zina said, "you are ponderous."

Smiling at her the boy said, "Games, then? Would that be better? There are events ahead that I must shape. I must arouse fire that burns, that sears. Scripture says:

> For He is like a refiner's fire.

And Scripture also says:

> And who can abide the day of His coming?

I say, however, that it will be more than this; I say:

> The day comes, glowing like a furnace; all the arrogant and the evil-doers shall be chaff, and that day when it comes shall set them ablaze; it shall leave them neither root nor branch.

What do you say to that, Herb Asher?" Emmanuel gazed at him intently, awaiting his response.

Zina said:

> But for you who fear my name, the sun of righteousness shall rise with healing in his wings.

"That is true," Emmanuel said.

In a low voice Elias said:

And you shall break loose like calves released from the stall.

"Yes," Emmanuel said. He nodded.

Herb Asher, returning the boy's gaze, said, "I am afraid. I really am." He was glad of the arm around him, the reassuring arm of Elias.

In a reasonable tone of voice, a mild tone, Zina said, "He won't do all those terrible things. That's to scare people."

"Zina!" Elias said.

Laughing, she said, "It's true. Ask him."

"You will not put the Lord your God to the test," Emmanuel said.

"I'm not afraid," Zina said quietly.

Emmanuel, to her, said:

> I will break you, like a rod of iron.
> I shall dash you, in pieces,
> Like a potter's vessel.

"No," Zina said. To Herb Asher she said, "There is nothing to fear. It's a manner of talking, no more. Come to me if you get scared and I will converse with you."

"That is true," Emmanuel said. "If you are seized and taken down into the prison she will go with you. She will never leave you." An unhappy expression crossed his face; suddenly he was, again, a ten-year-old boy. "But—"

"What is it?" Elias said.

"I will not say now," Emmanuel said, speaking with difficulty. Herb Asher, to his disbelief, saw tears in the boy's eyes. "Perhaps I will never say it. She knows what I mean."

"Yes," Zina said, and she smiled. Mischief lay in her smile, or so it seemed to Herb Asher. It puzzled him. He did not understand the invisible transaction taking place between Rybys's son and the girl. It troubled him, and his fear became greater. His sense of deep unease.

The four of them had dinner together that night.

"Where do you live?" Herb Asher asked the girl. "Do you have a family? Parents?"

"Technically I'm a ward of the government school we go

to," Zina said. "But for all intents and purposes I'm in Elias's custody now. He's in the process of becoming my guardian."

Elias, eating, paying attention to his plate of food, said, "We are a family, the three of us. And now you also, Herb."

"I may go back to my dome," Herb said. "In the CY30-CY30B system."

Staring at him, Elias halted in his eating, forkful of food raised. "Why?"

"I'm uncomfortable here," Herb said. He had not worked it out; his feelings remained vague. But they were intense feelings. "It's oppressive here. There's more of a sense of freedom out there."

"Freedom to lie in your bunk listening to Linda Fox?" Elias said.

"No." He shook his head.

Zina said, "Emmanuel, you scare him with your talk about afflicting the Earth with fire. He remembers the plagues in the Bible. What happened with Egypt."

"I want to go home," Herb said, simply.

Emmanuel said, "You miss Rybys."

"Yes." That was true.

"She isn't there," Emmanuel reminded him. He ate slowly, somberly, bite after bite. As if, Herb thought, eating was for him a solemn ritual. A matter of consuming something sanctified.

"Can't you bring her back?" he said to Emmanuel.

The boy did not respond. He continued to eat.

"No answer?" Herb said, with bitterness.

"I am not here for that," Emmanuel said. "She understood. It is not important that you understand, but it was important that she know. And I caused her to know. You remember; you were there on that day, the day I told her what lay ahead."

"Okay," Herb said.

"She lives elsewhere now," Emmanuel said. "You—"

"Okay," he repeated, with anger, enormous anger.

To him, Emmanuel said, speaking slowly and quietly, his face calm, "You do not grasp the situation, Herbert. It is not a good universe that I strive for, nor a just one, nor a pretty one; the existence of the universe itself is at stake. Final victory for Belial does not mean imprisonment for the human race, continued slavery, but nonexistence; without me, there is nothing, not even Belial, whom I created."

"Eat your dinner," Zina said in a gentle voice.

"The power of evil," Emmanuel continued, "is the ceasing of reality, the ceasing of existence itself. It is the slow slipping away of everything that is, until it becomes, like Linda Fox, a phantasm. That process has begun. It began with the primal fall. Part of the cosmos fell away. The Godhead itself suffered a crisis; can you fathom that, Herb Asher? A crisis in the Ground of Being? What does that convey to you? The possibility of the Godhead ceasing—does it convey that to you? Because the Godhead is all that stands between—" He broke off. "You can't even imagine it. No creature can imagine nonbeing, especially its own nonbeing. I must guarantee being, all being. Including yours."

Herb Asher said nothing.

"A war is coming," Emmanuel said. "We will choose our ground. It will be for us, the two of us, Belial and me, a table, on which we play. Over which we wager the universe, the being of being as such. I initiate this final part of the ages of war; I have advanced into Belial's territory, his home. I have moved forward to meet *him*, not the other way around. Time will tell if it was a wise idea."

"Can't you foresee the results?" Herb said.

Emmanuel regarded him. Silently.

"You can," Herb said. You know what the outcome will be, he realized. You know now; you knew when you entered Rybys's womb. You knew from the beginning of creation—before creation, in fact; before a universe existed.

"They will play by rules," Zina said. "Rules agreed on."

"Then," Herb said, "that's why Belial has not attacked you. That's why you've been able to live here and grow up—for ten years. He knows you're here—"

"Does he know?" Emmanuel said.

Silence.

"I haven't told him," Emmanuel said. "It is not my burden. He must find out for himself. I do not mean the government. I mean the power that truly rules, in comparison to which the government, all governments, are shadows."

"He'll tell him when he's ready," Zina said. "Good and ready."

Herb said, "Are you good and ready, Emmanuel?"

The boy smiled. A child's smile, a shift away from the stern countenance of a moment before. He said nothing. A game, Herb Asher realized. A child's game!

Seeing this he trembled.

Zina said:

> Time is a child at play, playing draughts; a child's is the kingdom.

"What is that?" Elias said.

"It is not from Judaism," Zina said obscurely. She did not amplify.

The part of him that derives from his mother, Herb Asher realized, is ten years old. And the part of him that is Yah has no age; it is infinity itself. A compound of the very young and the timeless: precisely what Zina in her arcane quote had stated.

Perhaps this was not unique, this mixture. Someone had noted it before; noted it and declared it in words.

"You venture into Belial's realm," Zina said to Emmanuel as she ate; "but would you have the courage to venture into *my realm?*"

"What realm is that?" Emmanuel said. Elias Tate stared at the girl, and, equally puzzled, Herb Asher regarded her. But Emmanuel seemed to understand her; he showed no surprise. Despite his question, Herb Asher thought, he knows—knows already.

Zina said, "Where I am not as you see me now."

An interval of silence passed, as Emmanuel pondered. He did not answer; he sat as if withdrawn, as if his mind had moved far away. Skimming countless worlds, Herb Asher thought. How strange this is. What are they talking about?

Emmanuel said slowly and carefully, "I have a dreadful land to deal with, Zina. I have no time."

"I think you are apprehensive," Zina said. She turned to her slice of apple pie and mound of ice cream.

"No," Emmanuel said.

"Come, then," she said, and, all at once, the color and fire,

"Okay." The boy nodded.

"What am I supposed to do?" Herb Asher said.

"Come," Zina said.

" 'The Secret Commonwealth,' " Elias said. "I never believed it existed." He glowered at the girl, baffled. "It doesn't exist; that's the whole point!"

"It exists," she said. "And here. Come with us, Mr. Asher. You are welcome. But there I am not as I am now. None of us is. Except you, Emmanuel."

To the boy, Elias said, "Lord—"

"There is a doorway," Emmanuel said, "to her land. It can be found anywhere that the Golden Proportion exists. Is that not true, Zina?"

"True," she said.

"Based on the Fibonacci Constant," Emmanuel said. "A ratio," he explained to Herb Asher. "1:.618034. The ancient Greeks knew it as the Golden Section and as the Golden Rectangle. Their architecture utilized it . . . for instance, the Parthenon. For them it was a geometric model, but Fibonacci of Pisa, in the Middle Ages, developed it in terms of pure number."

"In this room alone," Zina said, "I count several doors. The ratio," she said to Herb Asher, "is that used in playing cards: three to five. It is found in snail shells and extragalactic nebulae, from the pattern formation of the hair on your head to—"

"It pervades the universe," Emmanuel said, "from the microcosms to the macrocosm. It has been called one of the names of God."

In a small spare room of Elias's house Herb Asher prepared to bed down for the night.

Standing at the doorway in a heavy, somewhat rumpled robe, with great slippers on his feet, Elias said, "May I talk with you?"

Herb nodded.

"She is taking him away," Elias said. He came into the room and seated himself. "You realize that? It did not come from the direction we expected. *I* expected," he corrected himself. His face dark he sat clasping and unclasping his hands. "The enemy has taken a strange form."

Chilled, Herb said, "Belial?"

"I don't know, Herb. I've known the girl four years. I think a great deal of her. In some ways I love her. Even as much as I do Manny. She's been a good friend to him. Apparently he knew, maybe not right off . . . but somewhere along the line he figured it out. I checked; I used my computer terminal to research the word *zina*. It's Roumanian for fairy. Another world has found out Emmanuel. She approached him the first day at school. I see why, now. She was waiting. Expecting him. You see?"

"Hence the mischief I see in her," Herb Asher said. He felt weary. It had been a long day.

Elias said, "She will lead and lead, and he will follow. Follow knowingly, I think. He does foresee. It's what's called a priori knowledge about the universe. Once, he foresaw everything. Not anymore. It's strange, when you think about it, that he could foresee his own inability to foresee, his forgetfulness. I'll have to trust in him, Herb; there is no way—" He gestured. "You understand."

"No one can tell him what to do."

"Herb, I don't want to lose him."

"How can he be lost?"

"There was a rupturing of the Godhead. A primordial schism. That's the basis of it all, the trouble, these conditions here, Belial and the rest of it. A crisis that caused part of the Godhead to fall; the Godhead split and some remained transcendent and some . . . became abased. Fell with creation, fell along with the world. *The Godhead has lost touch with a part of itself.*"

"And it could fragment further?"

"Yes," Elias said. "There could be another crisis. This may be that crisis. I don't know. I don't even know if *he* knows. The human part of him, the part derived from Rybys, knows fear, but the other half—that half knows no fear. For obvious reasons. Maybe that's not good."

That night as he slept, Herb Asher dreamed that a woman was singing to him. She seemed to be Linda Fox and yet she was not; he could see her, and he saw terrible beauty, a wildness and light, and a sweet glowing face with eyes that shone at him lovingly. He and the woman were in a car and the woman drove; he simply watched her, marveling at her beauty. She sang:

> You have to put your slippers on
> To walk toward the dawn.

But he did not have to walk, because the lovely woman was taking him there. She wore a white gown and in her tumbled hair he saw a crown. She was a very young woman, but a woman nonetheless—not, like Zina, a child.

When he awoke the next morning the beauty of the woman and her singing haunted him; he could not forget it. He thought, She is more attractive than the Fox. I wouldn't have believed it. I would prefer her. Who is she?

"Good morning," Zina said, on her way to the bathroom to brush her teeth. He noticed that she wore slippers. But so, too, did Elias when he appeared. What does it mean? Herb asked himself.

He did not know the answer.

12

YOU dance and sing all night," Emmanuel said. He thought, *And it is beautiful.* "Show me," he said.

"Then we shall begin," Zina said.

He sat under palm trees and knew that he had entered the Garden, but it was the garden he himself had fashioned at the beginning of creation; she had not brought him to her realm. This was his own realm restored.

Buildings and vehicles, but the people did not hurry. They sat here and there enjoying the sun. One young woman had unbuttoned her blouse, and her breasts shone with perspiration; the sun radiated down hot and bright.

"No," he said, "this is not the Commonwealth."

"I took you the wrong way," Zina said. "But it doesn't matter. There is nothing wrong with this place, is there? Does it lack? You know it doesn't lack; it is Paradise."

"I made it so," he said.

"All right," Zina said. "This is the Paradise that you created and I will show you something better. Come." She reached out and took him by the hand. "That savings and loan building has the Golden Rectangle doorway. We can enter there; it is as good as any." Holding him by the hand she led him to the corner, waited for the light to change, and then, together, they made their way down the sidewalk, past the resting people, to the savings and loan office.

Pausing on the steps Emmanuel said, "I—"

"This is the doorway," she said, and led him up the steps. "Your realm ends here and mine begins. From now on the laws are mine." Her grip on his hand tightened.

"So be it," he said, and continued on.

The robot teller said, "Do you have your passbook, Ms. Pallas?"

"In my purse." Beside Emmanuel the young woman opened her mail-pouch leather purse, fumbled among keys, cosmetics, letters, assorted valuables, until her quick fingers found the passbook. "I want to draw out—well, how much do I have?"

"Your balance appears in your passbook," the robot teller said in its dispassionate voice.

"Yes," she agreed. Opening the passbook she scrutinized the figures, then took a withdrawal slip and filled it out.

"You are closing your account?" the robot teller said, as she presented it with the passbook and slip.

"That's right."

"Has our service not been—"

"It's none of your damn business why I'm closing my account," she said. Resting her sharp elbows on the counter she rocked back and forth. Emmanuel saw that she wore high heels. Now she had become older. She wore a cotton print top and jeans, and her hair pulled back with a comb. Also, he saw, she wore sunglasses. She smiled at him.

He said to himself, She has already changed.

Presently they stood on the roof parking lot of the savings and loan building; Zina fumbled in her purse for her flycar keys.

"It's a nice day," she said. "Get in; I'll unlock the door for you." She slipped in behind the wheel of the flycar and reached for the far door's handle.

"This is a nice car," he said, and he thought, She reveals her domain by degrees. As she took me to my own garden-world first she now takes me stage by stage through the levels, the ascending levels, of her own realm. She will strip the accretions away one by one as we penetrate deeper. This, now, is the surface only.

This, he thought, is enchantment. *Beware!*

"You like my car? It gets me to work—"

He said, breaking in harshly, "You lie, Zina!"

"What do you mean?" The flycar rose up into the warm midday sky, joining the normal traffic. But her smile gave her away. "It's a beginning," she said. "I don't want to startle you."

"Here," he said, "in this world you are not a child. That was a form you took, a pose."

"This is my real shape. Honest."

"Zina; you have no real shape. I know you. For you any shape is possible. Whichever shape appeals to you at the moment. You go from moment to moment, like a soap bubble."

Turning toward him, but still watching where she drove, Zina said, "You are in my world now, Yah. Take care."

"I can burst your world."

"It will simply return. It is everywhere always. We have not gone away from where we were—back there a few miles is the school that you and I attend; back there in the house Elias and Herb Asher are discussing what to do. Spacially this is not another place and you know that."

"But," he said, "you make the laws here."

"Belial is not here," she said.

That surprised him. He had not foreseen that, and, realizing that he had not foreseen it he knew that he had not truly foreseen the total situation. To miss a single part was to miss it all.

"He never penetrated my realm," Zina said as she negotiated her way through the sky traffic over Washington, D.C. "He does not even know about it. Let's go over to the Tidal Basin and look at the Japanese cherry trees; they're in bloom."

"Are they?" he said; it seemed to him too early in the year.

"They are blooming now," Zina said, and steered her flycar toward the downtown center of the city.

"In your world," he said. He understood. "This is the spring," he said. He could see the leaves and blossoms on the trees below them. The expanses of bright green.

"Roll your window down," she said. "It's not cold."

He said, "The warmth in the Palm Tree Garden—"

"Blasting, withering dry heat," she said. "Scorching the world and turning it into a desert. You were always partial to arid land. Listen to me, Yahweh. *I will show you things you know nothing about.* You have gone from the wastelands to a frozen landscape—methane crystals, with little domes here and there, and stupid natives. You know nothing!" Her eyes blazed. "You skulk in the badlands and promise your people a refuge they never found. All your promises have failed—which is good, because what you have promised them most is that you will curse them and afflict them and destroy them. Now shut up. My time and my realm have come; this is my world and it is springtime and the air does not wither the plants, nor do you. You will hurt no one here in my realm. Do you understand?"

He said, "Who are you?"

Laughing, she said, "My name is Zina. Fairy."

"I think—" Confused, he said, "You—"

"Yahweh," the woman said, "you do not know who I am

and you do not know where you are. Is this the Secret Commonwealth? Or have you been tricked?"

"You have tricked me," he said.

"I am your guide," she said. "As the *Sepher Yezirah* says:

> Comprehend this great wisdom, understand this knowledge, inquire into it and ponder it, render it evident and lead the Creator back to His throne again.

"And that," she finished, "is what I will do. But it is by a route that you will not believe. It is a route that you do not know. You will have to trust me; you will trust your guide as Dante trusted his guide, through the realms, up and up."

He said, "You are the Adversary."

"Yes," Zina said. "I am."

But, he thought, that is not all. It is not that simple. You are complex, he realized, you who drive this car. Paradox and contradictions, and, most of all, your love of games. Your desire to play. I must think of it that way, he realized, as play.

"I'll play," he agreed. "I am willing."

"Good." She nodded. "Could you get my cigarettes for me out of my purse? The traffic's getting heavy; I'm going to have trouble finding a parking spot."

He rummaged in her purse. Futilely.

"Can't you find them? Keep looking; they're there."

"You keep so many things in your purse." He found the pack of Salems and held it toward her.

"God doesn't light a woman's cigarette?" She took the cigarette and pressed in the dashboard lighter.

"What does a ten-year-old boy know about that?" he said.

"Strange," she said. "I'm old enough to be your mother. And yet you are older than I am. There is a paradox; you knew you would find paradoxes here. My realm abounds with them, as you were just thinking. Do you want to go back, Yahweh? To the Palm Tree Garden? It is irreal and you know it. Until you inflict decisive defeat on your Adversary it will remain irreal. That world is gone, and is now a memory."

"You are the Adversary," he said, puzzled, "but you are not Belial."

"Belial is in a cage at the Washington, D.C., zoo," Zina said.

"In my realm. As an example of extraterrestrial life—a deplorable example. A thing from Sirius, from the fourth planet in the Sirius System. People stand around gaping at him in wonder."

He laughed.

"You think I'm joking. I'll take you to the zoo. I'll show you."

"I think you're serious." Again he laughed; it delighted him. "The Evil One in a cage at the zoo—what, with his own temperature and gravity and atmosphere, and imported food? An exotic life form?"

"He's angry as hell about it," Zina said.

"I'm sure he is. What do you have planned for me, Zina?"

She said, soberly, "The truth, Yahweh. I will show you the truth before you leave here. I would not cage the Lord our God. You are free to roam my land; you are free here, Yahweh, entirely. I give you my word."

"Vapors," he said. "The bond of a *zina*."

After some difficulty she found a slot in which to park her flycar. "Okay," she said. "Let's stroll around looking at the cherry blossoms. Yahweh; their color is mine, their pink. That is my hallmark. When that pink light is seen, I am near."

"I know that pink," he said. "It is the human phosphene response to full-spectrum white, to pure sunlight."

As she locked up the flycar she said, "See the people."

He looked about him. And saw no one. The trees, heavy with blossoms, lined the Tidal Basin in a great semicircle. But, despite the parked cars, no persons walked anywhere.

"Then this is a fraud," he said.

Zina said, "You are here, Yahweh, so that I can postpone your great and terrible day. I do not want to see the world scourged. I want you to see what you do not see. Only the two of us are here; we are alone. Gradually I will unfold my realm to you, and, when I am done, you will withdraw your curse on the world. I have watched you for years, now. I have seen your dislike of the human race and your sense of its worthlessness. I say to you, It is not worthless; it is not worthy to die—as you phrase it in your pompous fashion. The world is beautiful and I am beautiful and the cherry blossoms are beautiful. The robot teller at the savings and loan—even it is beautiful. The power of Belial is mere occlusion, hiding the real world, and if you attack the real world, as you have come to Earth to do, then you will destroy beauty and kindness and charm. Remember the crushed dog dying in the ditch at the side of the road? Remember what you felt about him; remember what you knew him to be. Remember the inscription that Elias composed for that dog and that dog's death. Remember the dignity of that dog, and at the same time remember that the dog was innocent. His death was mandated by cruel necessity. A wrong and cruel necessity. The dog—"

"I know," he said.

"You know what? That the dog was wrongly treated? That he was born to suffer unjust pain? It is not Belial that slew the dog, it is you, Yahweh, the Lord of Hosts. Belial did not bring death into the world because there has always been death; death goes back a billion years on this planet, and what became of that dog—that is the fate of every creature you have made. You cried over that dog, did you not? I think at that point you understood, but now you have forgotten. If I were to remind you of anything I would remind you of that dog and of how you felt; I would want you to remember how that dog showed you the Way. It is the way of compassion, the most noble way of all, and I do not think you genuinely have that compassion, I really don't. You are here to destroy Belial, your adversary, not to emancipate mankind; *you are here to wage war*. Is that a fit thing for you to do? I wonder. Where is the peace that you promised man? You have come with a sword and millions will die; it will be the dying dog multiplied millions of times. You cried for the dog, you cried for your mother and even Belial, but I say, If you want to wipe away all the tears, as it says in Scripture, go away and leave this world because the evil of this world, what you call 'Belial' and your 'Adversary' is a form of illusion. These are not bad people. This is not a bad world. Do not make war on it but bring it flowers." Reaching, she broke off a sprig of cherry blossoms; she extended it to him, and, reflexively, he accepted it.

"You are very persuasive," he said.

"It is my job," she said. "I say these things because I know these things. There is no deceit in you and there is no deceit in me, but just as you curse, I play. Which of us has found the

Way? For two thousand years you have bided your time until you could slip back into Belial's fortress to overthrow him. I suggest that you find something else to do. Walk with me and we will see flowers. It is better. And the world will prosper as it always has. This is the springtime. It is now that flowers grow, and with me there is dancing also, and the sound of bells. You heard the bells and you know that their beauty is greater than the power of evil. In some ways their beauty is greater than your own power, Yahweh, Lord of Hosts. Do you not agree?"

"Magic," he said. "A spell."

"Beauty is a spell," she said, "and war is reality. Do you want the sobriety of war or the intoxication of what you see now, here in my world? We are alone now, but later on people will appear; I will repopulate my realm. But I want this moment to speak to you plainly. Do you know who I am? You do not know who I am, but finally I will lead you step by step back to your throne, you the Creator, and then you will know who I am. You have guessed but you have not guessed right. There are many guesses left for you—you who know everything. I am not Holy Wisdom and I am not Diana; I am not a *zina*; I am not Pallas Athena. I am something else. I am the spring queen and yet I am not that either; these are, as you put it, vapors. What I am, what I truly am, you will have to ferret out on your own. Now let's walk."

They walked along the path, by the water and the trees.

"We are friends, you and I," Emmanuel said. "I tend to listen to you."

"Then postpone your great and terrible day. There is nothing good in death by fire; it is the worst death of all. You are the solar heat that destroys the crops. For four years we have been together, you and I. I have watched as your memory returned and I have regretted its return. You afflicted that miserable woman who was your mother; you sickened your own mother whom you say you love, whom you cried over. Instead of making war against evil, cure the dying dog in the ditch and wipe away thereby your own tears. I hated to see you cry. You cried because you regained your own nature and comprehended that nature. You cried because you realized what you are."

He said nothing.

"The air smells good," Zina said.

"Yes," he said.

"I will bring the people back," she said. "One by one, until they are all around us. Look at them and when you see one whom you would slay, tell me and I will banish that person once more. But you must look at the person whom you would slay—you must see in that person the crushed and dying dog. Only then do you have the right to slay that person; only when you cry are you entitled to destroy. You understand?"

"Enough," he said.

"Why didn't you cry over the dog before the car crushed him? Why did you wait until it was too late? The dog accepted his situation but I do not. I advise you; I am your guide. I say, It is wrong what you do. Listen to me. Stop it!"

He said, "I have come to lift their oppression."

"You are impaired. I know that; I know what happened in the Godhead, the original crisis. It is no secret to me. In this condition you seek to lift their oppression through a great and terrible day. Is that reasonable? Is that how you free the prisoners?"

"I must break the power of—"

"Where is that power? The government? Bulkowsky and Harms? They are idiots; they are a joke. Would you kill them? The talion law that you laid down; I say:

> You have learnt how it was said: *Eye for eye and tooth for tooth.* But I say this to you: offer the wicked man no resistance.

"You must live by your own words; you must offer your Adversary Belial no resistance. In my realm his power is not here; *he* is not here. What is here is a sport in a cage at a public zoo. We feed it and give it water and atmosphere and the right temperature; we try to make the thing as comfortable as possible. In my realm we do not kill. There is, here, no great and terrible day, nor will there ever be. Stay in my realm or make my realm your realm, but spare Belial; spare everyone. And then you will not have to cry, and the tears will, as you promised, be wiped away."

Emmanuel said, "You are Christ."

Laughing, Zina said, "No, I am not."

"You quote him."

" 'Even the devil can cite Scripture.' "

Around them groups of people appeared, in light, summery clothing. Men in their shirtsleeves, women in frocks. And, he saw, all the children.

"The fairy queen," he said. "You beguile me. You lead me from the path with sparks of light, dancing, singing, and the sound of bells; always the sound of bells."

"The bells are blown by the wind," Zina said. "And the wind speaks the truth. Always. The desert wind. You know that; I have watched you listen to the wind. The bells are the music of the wind; listen to them."

He heard, then, the fairy bells. They echoed distantly; many bells, small ones, not church bells but the bells of magic.

It was the most beautiful sound he had ever heard.

"I cannot, myself, produce that sound," he said to Zina. "How is it done?"

"By wakefulness," Zina said. "The bell-sounds wake you up. They rouse you from sleep. You roused Herb Asher from his sleep by a crude introjection; I awaken by means of beauty."

Gentle spring wind blew about them, the vapors of her realm.

13

To himself Emmanuel said, I am being poisoned. The vapors of her realm poison me and vitiate my will.

"You are wrong," Zina said.

"I feel less strong."

"You feel less indignation. Let's go and get Herb Asher. I want him with us. I will narrow down the area of our game; I will arrange it especially for him."

"In what way?"

"We will contest for him," Zina said. "Come." She beckoned to the boy to follow her.

In the cocktail lounge Herb Asher sat with a glass of Scotch and water in front of him. He had been waiting an hour but the evening entertainment had not begun. The cocktail lounge was filled with people. Constant noise assailed his ears. But, for him, this was worth it, despite the rather large cover charge.

Rybys, across from him, said, "I just don't understand what you see in her."

"She's going to go a long way," Herb said, "if she gets any kind of a break at all." He wondered if record company scouts came here to the Golden Hind. I hope so, he said to himself.

"I'd like to leave. I don't feel well. Could we go?"

"I'd prefer not to."

Rybys sipped at her tall mixed drink fitfully. "So much noise," she said, her voice virtually inaudible.

He looked at his watch. "It's almost nine. Her first set is at nine."

"Who is she?" Rybys said.

"She's a new young singer," Herb Asher said. "She's adapted the lute books of John Dowland for—"

"Who's John Dowland? I never heard of him."

"Late-sixteenth-century England. Linda Fox has modernized his lute songs; he was the first composer to write for solo voice; before that four or more people sang . . . the old madrigal form. I can't explain it; you have to hear her."

"If she's so good, why isn't she on TV?" Rybys said.

Herb said, "She will be."

Lights on the stage began to glow. Three musicians leaped up onto it and began fussing with the audio system. Each had in his possession a vibrolute.

A hand touched Herb Asher on the shoulder. "Hi."

Glancing up he saw a young woman whom he did not know. But, he thought, she seems to know me. "I'm sorry—" he began.

"May we sit down?" The woman, pretty, wearing a floral print top and jeans, a mail-pouch purse over her shoulder, drew a chair back and seated herself beside Herb Asher. "Sit down, Manny," she said to a small boy who stood awkwardly near the table. What a beautiful child, Herb Asher thought. How did he get in here? There aren't supposed to be any minors in here.

"Are these friends of yours?" Rybys said.

The pretty, dark-haired young woman said, "Herb hasn't seen me since college. How are you, Herb? Don't you recognize me?" She held out her hand to him, and, reflexively, he took it. And then, as he shook her hand, he remembered her. They had been in school together, in a poly-sci course.

"Zina," he said, delighted. "Zina Pallas."

"This is my little brother," Zina said, motioning the boy to sit down. "Manny. Manny Pallas." To Rybys she said, "Herb hasn't changed a bit. I knew it was him when I saw him. You're here to see Linda Fox? I've never heard her; they say she's real good."

"Very good," Herb said, pleased at her support.

"Hello, Mr. Asher," the boy said.

"Glad to meet you, Manny." He shook hands with the boy. "This is my wife, Rybys."

"So you two are married," Zina said. "Mind if I smoke?" She lit a cigarette. "I keep trying to quit but when I quit I start eating a lot and get as fat as a pig."

"Is your purse genuine leather?" Rybys said, interested.

"Yes." Zina passed it over to her.

"I've never seen a leather purse before," Rybys said.

"There she is," Herb Asher said. Linda Fox had appeared on the stage; the audience clapped.

"She looks like a pizza waitress," Rybys said.

Zina, taking her purse back, said, "If she's going to make it big she's going to have to lose some weight. I mean, she looks all right, but—"

"What is this thing you have about weight?" Herb Asher said, irritated.

The boy, Manny, spoke up. "Herbert, Herbert."

"Yes?" He bent to hear.

"Remember," the boy said.

Puzzled, he started to say Remember what? but then Linda Fox took hold of the microphone, half shut her eyes, and began to sing. She had a round face, and almost a double chin, but her skin was fair, and, most important to him of all, she had long eyelashes that flickered as she sang—they fascinated him and he sat spellbound. Linda wore an extremely low-cut gown and even from where he sat he could see the outline of her nipples; she had on no bra.

> Shall I sue? shall I seek for grace?
> Shall I pray? shall I prove?
> Shall I strive to a heavenly joy
> With an earthly love?

Audibly, Rybys said, "I hate that song. I have heard her before."

Several people hissed at her to be quiet.

"Not by her, though," Rybys said. "She isn't even original. That song—" She piped down, but she was not happy.

When the song ended, and the audience had begun to clap. Herb Asher said to his wife, "You never heard 'Shall I Sue' before. Nobody else sings it but Linda Fox."

"You just like to gape at her nipples," Rybys said.

To Herb Asher the little boy said, "Would you take me to the men's room, Mr. Asher?"

"Now?" he said, dismayed. "Can't you wait until she's through singing?"

The boy said, "Now, Mr. Asher."

With reluctance he led Manny through the maze of tables to the doors at the rear of the lounge. But before they had entered the men's room Manny stopped him.

"You can see her better from here," Manny said.

It was true. He was now much closer to the stage. He and the boy stood together in silence as Linda Fox sang "Weep You No More Sad Fountains."

When the song ended, Manny said, "You don't remember, do you? She has enchanted you. Wake up, Herbert Asher. You know me well, and I know you. Linda Fox does not sing her songs at an obscure cocktail lounge in Hollywood; she is famous throughout the galaxy. She is the most important entertainer of this decade. The chief prelate and the procurator maximus invite her to—"

"She's going to sing again," Herb Asher interrupted. He barely heard the boy's words and they made no sense to him. A babbling boy, he thought, making it hard for me to hear Linda Fox. Just what I need.

After the song had ended, Manny said, "Herbert, Herbert; do you want to meet her? Is that what you want?"

"What?" he murmured, his eyes—his attention—fixed on Linda Fox. God, he thought; what a figure she has. She's practically falling out of her dress. He thought, I wish my wife was built like that.

"She will come this way," Manny said, "when she finishes. Stand here, Herb Asher, and she will pass directly by you."

"You're joking," he said.

"No," Manny said. "You will have what you want most in the world . . . that which you dreamed of as you lay on your bunk in your dome."

"What dome?" he said.

Manny said, "'How you have fallen from heaven, bright morning star, felled—'"

"You mean one of those colony-planet domes?" Herb Asher said.

"I can't make you listen, can I?" Manny said. "If I could say to you—"

"She is coming this way," Herb Asher said. "How did you know?" He moved a few steps toward her. Linda Fox walked rapidly, with small steps, a gentle expression on her face.

"Thank you," she was saying to people who spoke to her. For a moment she stopped to give her autograph to a black youth nattily dressed.

Tapping Herb Asher on the shoulder a waitress said, "You're

going to have to take that boy out of here, sir; we can't have minors in here."

"Sorry," Herb Asher said.

"Right now," the waitress said.

"Okay," he said; he took Manny by the shoulder and, with unhappy reluctance, led him back toward their table. And, as he turned away, he saw out of the corner of his eye the Fox pass by the spot at which he and the boy had stood. Manny had been right. A few more seconds and he would have been able to speak a few words to her. And, perhaps, she would have answered.

Manny said, "It is her desire to trick you, Herb Asher. She offered it to you and took it away again. If you want to meet Linda Fox I will see that you do; I promise you. Remember this, because it will come to pass. I will not see you cheated."

"I don't know what you're talking about," Herb said, "but if I could meet her—"

"You will," Manny said.

"You're a strange kid," Herb Asher said. As they passed below a light fixture he noticed something that startled him; he halted and, taking hold of Manny, he moved him directly under the light. *You look like Rybys*, he thought. For an instant a flash of memory jarred him; his mind seemed to open up, as if vast spaces, open spaces, a universe of stars, had flooded into it.

"Herbert," the boy said, "she is not real. Linda Fox—she is a phantasm of yours. But I can make her real; I confer being— it is I who makes the irreal into the real, and I can do it for you, with her."

"What happened?" Rybys said, when they reached the table.

"Manny has to leave," Herb said to Zina Pallas. "The waitress said so. I guess you'll have to go. Sorry."

Taking her purse and cigarettes, Zina rose. "I'm sorry; I guess I kept you from seeing the Fox."

"Let's go with them," Rybys said, also rising. "My head hurts, Herb; I'd like to get out of here."

Resigned, he said, "All right." Cheated, he thought. That was what Manny had said. *I will not see you cheated*. That is exactly what happened, he realized; I have been cheated this evening. Well, some other time. It would be interesting to talk to her, maybe get her autograph. He thought, Close up I could see that her eyelashes are fake. Christ, he thought; how depressing. Maybe her breasts are fake, too. There're those pads they slip in. He felt disappointed and unhappy and now he, too, wanted to leave.

This evening didn't work out, he thought as he escorted Rybys, Zina and Manny from the club onto the dark Hollywood street. I expected so much . . . and then he remembered what the boy had said, the strange things, and the nanosecond of jarred memory: scenes that appeared in his mind so briefly and yet so convincingly. This is not an ordinary child, he realized. And his resemblance to my wife—I can see it now, as they stand together. He could be her son. Eerie. He shivered, even though the air was warm.

Zina said, "I fulfilled his wishes; I gave him what he dreamed of. All those months as he lay on his bunk. With his 3-D posters of her, his tapes."

"You gave him nothing," Emmanuel said. "You robbed him, in fact. You took something away."

"She is a media product," Zina said. The two of them walked slowly along the nocturnal Hollywood sidewalk, back to her flycar. "That is no fault of mine. I can't be blamed if Linda Fox is not real."

"Here in your realm that distinction means nothing."

"What can you give him?" Zina said. "Only illness—his wife's illness. And her death in your service. Is your gift better than mine?"

Emmanuel said, "I made him a promise and I do not lie." I shall fulfill that promise, he said to himself. In this realm or in my own realm; it doesn't matter because in either case I will make Linda Fox real. That is the power I have, and it is not the power of enchantment; it is the most precious gift of all: reality.

"What are you thinking?" Zina said.

" 'Better a live dog than a dead prince,' " Manny said.

"Who said that?"

"It is simply common sense."

Zina said, "What is your meaning?"

"I mean that your enchantment gave him nothing and the real world—"

"The real world," Zina said, "put him in cryonic suspension

for ten years. Isn't a beautiful dream better than a cruel reality? Would you rather suffer in actuality than enjoy yourself in the domain of—" She paused.

"Intoxication," he said. "That is what your domain consists of; it is a drunken world. Drunken with dancing and with joy. I say that the quality of realness is more important than any other quality, because once realness departs, there is nothing. A dream is nothing. I disagree with you; I say you cheated Herbert Asher. I say you did a cruel thing to him. I saw his reaction; I measured his dejection. And I will make it up to him."

"You will make the Fox real."

"Is it your wager that I can't?"

"My wager," Zina said, "is that it doesn't matter. Real or not she is worthless; you will have achieved nothing."

"I accept the wager," he said.

"Shake my hand on it." She extended her hand.

They shook, standing there on the Hollywood sidewalk under the glaring artificial light.

As they flew back to Washington, D.C. Zina said, "In my realm many things are different. Perhaps you would like to meet Party Chairman Nicholas Bulkowsky."

Emmanuel said, "Is he not the procurator?"

"The Communist Party has not the world power that you are accustomed to. The term 'Scientific Legate' is not known. Nor is Fulton Statler Harms the chief prelate of the C.I.C., inasmuch as no Christian-Islamic Church exists. He is a cardinal of the Roman Catholic Church; he does not control the lives of millions."

"That is good," Emmanuel said.

"Then I have done well in my domain," Zina said. "Do you agree? Because if you agree—"

"These are good things," Emmanuel said.

"Tell me your objection."

"It is an illusion. In the real world both men hold world power; they jointly control the planet."

Zina said, "I will tell you something you do not understand. We have made changes in the past. We saw to it that the C.I.C. and the S.L. did not come into existence. The world you see here, my world, is an alternate world to your own, and equally real."

"I don't believe you," Emmanuel said.

"There are many worlds."

He said, "I am the generator of world, I and I alone. No one else can create world. I am He Who causes to be. You are not."

"Nonetheless—"

"You do not understand," Emmanuel said. "There are many potentialities that do not become actualized. I select from among the potentialities the ones I prefer and I bestow actuality onto them."

"Then you have made poor choices. It would have been far better if the C.I.C. and the S.L. never came into being."

"You admit, then, that your world is not real? That it is a forgery?"

Zina hesitated. "It branched off at crucial points, due to our interference with the past. Call it magic if you want or call it technology; in any case we can enter retrotime and overrule mistakes in history. We have done that. In this alternate world Bulkowsky and Harms are minor figures—they exist, but not as they do in your world. It is a choice of worlds, equally real."

"And Belial," he said. "Belial sits in a cage in a zoo and throngs of people, vast hordes of them, gape at him."

"Correct."

"Lies," he said. "It is wish fulfillment. You cannot build a world on wishes. The basis of reality is bleak because you cannot serve up obliging mock vistas; you must adhere to what is possible: *the law of necessity.* That is the underpinning of reality: necessity. Whatever is, is because it must be, because it can be no other way. It is not what it is because someone wishes it but because it has to be—that and specifically that, down to the most meager detail. I know this because I do this. You have your job and I have mine, and I understand mine; I understand the law of necessity."

Zina, after a moment, said:

> "The woods of Arcady are dead,
>   And over is their antique joy;
>   Of old the world on dreaming fed;

Grey Truth is now her painted toy;
Yet still she turns her restless head.

"That is the first poem by Yeats," she finished.
"I know that poem," Emmanuel said. "It ends:

But ah! she dreams not now; dream thou!
For fair are poppies on the brow:
Dream, dream, for this is also sooth.

" 'Sooth' meaning 'truth,' " he explained.
"You don't have to explain," Zina said. "And you disagree with the poem."
"Gray truth is better than the dream," he said. "That, too, is sooth. It is the final truth of all, that truth is better than any lie however blissful. I distrust this world because it is too sweet. Your world is too nice to be real. Your world is a whim. When Herb Asher saw the Fox he saw deception, and that deception lies at the heart of your world." And that deception, he said to himself, is what I shall undo.

I shall replace it, he said to himself, with the veridical. Which you do not understand.

The Fox as reality will be more acceptable to Herb Asher than any dream of the Fox. I know it; I stake everything on this proposition. Here I stand or fall.

"That is correct," Zina said.
"Any seeming reality that is obliging," Emmanuel said, "is something to suspect. The hallmark of the fraudulent is that it becomes what you would like it to be. I see that here. You would like Nicholas Bulkowsky not to be a vastly influential man; you would like Fulton Harms to be a minor figure, not part of history. Your world obliges you, and that gives it away for what it is. My world is stubborn. It will not yield. A recalcitrant and implacable world is a real world."

"A world that murders those forced to live in it."
"That is not the whole of it. My world is not that bad; there is much besides death and pain in it. On Earth, the real Earth, there is beauty and joy and—" He broke off. He had been tricked. She had won again.

"Then Earth is not so bad," she said. "It should not be

scourged by fire. There is beauty and joy and love and good people. Despite Belial's rule. I told you that and you disputed it, as we walked among the Japanese cherry trees. What do you say now, Lord of Hosts, God of Abraham? Have you not proved me right?"

He admitted, "You are clever, Zina."

Her eyes sparkled and she smiled. "Then hold back the great and terrible day that you speak of in Scripture. As I begged you to."

For the first time he sensed defeat. Enticed into speaking foolishly, he realized. How clever she is; how shrewd.

"As it says in Scripture," Zina said.

> I am Wisdom, I bestow shrewdness
> and show the way to knowledge and prudence.

"But," he said, "you told me you are not Holy Wisdom. That you only pretended to be."

"It is up to you to discern who I am. You yourself must decipher my identity; I will not do it for you."

"And in the meantime—tricks."

"Yes," Zina said, "because it is through tricks that you will learn."

Staring at her he said, "You are tricking me so that I wake! As I woke Herb Asher!"

"Perhaps."

"Are you my disinhibiting stimulus?" Staring fixedly at her he said in a low stern voice, "I think I created you to bring back my memory, to restore me to myself."

"To lead you back to your throne," Zina said.

"*Did* I?"

Zina, steering the flycar, said nothing.

"Answer me," he said.

"Perhaps," Zina said.

"If I created you I can—"

"You created all things," Zina said.

"I do not understand you. I cannot follow you. You dance toward me and then away."

"But as I do so, you awaken," Zina said.

"Yes," he said. "And I reason back from that that you are the disinhibiting stimulus which I set up long ago, knowing as I did that my brain would be damaged and I would forget. You are systematically giving me back my identity, Zina. Then— I think I know who you are."

Turning her head she said, "Who?"

"I will not say. And you can't read it in my mind because I have suppressed it. I did so as soon as I thought it." Because, he realized, it is too much for me; even me. I can't believe it.

They drove on, toward the Atlantic and Washington, D.C.

14

HERB ASHER felt himself engulfed by the profound impression that he had known the boy Manny Pallas at some other time, perhaps in another life. How many lives do we lead? he asked himself. Are we on tape? Is this some kind of a replay?

To Rybys he said, "The kid looked like you."

"Did he? I didn't notice." Rybys, as usual, was attempting to make a dress from a pattern, and screwing it up; pieces of fabric lay everywhere in the living room, along with dirty dishes, overfilled ashtrays and crumpled, stained magazines.

Herb decided to consult with his business partner, a middle-aged black named Elias Tate. Together he and Tate had operated a retail audio sales store for several years. Tate, however, viewed their store, Electronic Audio, as a sideline: his central interest in life was his missionary work. Tate preached at a small, out-of-the-way church, engaging a mostly black audience. His message, always, consisted of:

REPENT! THE KINGDOM OF GOD IS AT HAND!

It seemed to Herb Asher a strange preoccupation for a man so intelligent, but, in the final analysis, it was Tate's problem. They rarely discussed it.

Seated in the listening room of the store, Herb said to his partner, "I met a striking and very peculiar little boy last night, at a cocktail lounge in Hollywood."

Involved in assembling a new laser-tracking phono component, Tate murmured, "What were you doing in Hollywood? Trying to get into pictures?"

"Listening to a new singer named Linda Fox."

"Never heard of her."

Herb said, "She's sexy as hell and very good. She—"

"You're married."

"I can dream," Herb said.

"Maybe you'd like to invite her to an autograph party at the store."

"We're the wrong kind of store."

"It's an audio store; she sings. That's audio. Or isn't she audible?"

"As far as I know she hasn't made any tapes or cut any records or been on TV. I happened to hear her last month when I was at the Anaheim Trade Center audio exhibit. I told you you should have come along."

"Sexuality is the malady of this world," Tate said. "This is a lustful and demented planet."

"And we're all going to hell."

Tate said, "I certainly hope so."

"You know you're out of step? You really are. You have an ethical code that dates back to the Dark Ages."

"Oh, long before that," Tate said. He placed a disc on the turntable and started up the component. On his 'scope the pattern appeared to be adequate but not perfect; Tate frowned.

"I almost met her. I was so close; a matter of seconds. She's better looking up close than anyone else I ever saw. You should see her. I know—I've got this intuition—that she's going to soar all the way to the top."

"Okay," Tate said, reasonably. "That's fine with me. Write her a fan letter. Tell her."

"Elias," Herb said, "the boy I met last night—he looked like Rybys."

The black man glanced up at him. "Really?"

"If Rybys could collect her goddam scattered wits for one second she could have noticed. She just can't goddam concentrate. She never looked at the boy. He could have been her son."

"Maybe there's something you don't know."

"Lay off," Herb said.

Elias said, "I'd like to see the boy."

"I felt I'd known him before, in some other life. For a second it started to come back to me and then—" He gestured. "I lost it. I couldn't pin it down. And there was more . . . as if I was remembering a whole other world. Another life entirely."

Elias ceased working. "Describe it."

"You were older. And not black. You were a very old man in a robe. I wasn't on Earth; I glimpsed a frozen landscape and it wasn't Terra. Elias—could I be from another planet, and some powerful agency laid down false memories in my mind, over the real ones? And the boy—seeing the boy—caused the real memories to begin to return? And I had the idea that Rybys was very ill. In fact, about to die. And something about Immigration officials with guns."

"Immigration officers don't carry guns."

"And a ship. A long trip at very high speed. Urgency. And most of all—a presence. An uncanny presence. Not human. Maybe it was an extraterrestrial, the race I'm really a part of. From my home planet."

"Herb," Elias said, "you are full of shit."

"I know. But just for a second I experienced all that. And—listen to this." He gestured excitedly. "An accident. Our ship crashing into another ship. My *body* remembered; it remembered the concussion, the trauma."

"Go to a hypnotherapist," Elias said, "get him to put you under, and remember. You're obviously a weird alien programmed to blow up the world. You probably have a bomb inside you."

Herb said, "That's not funny."

"Okay; you're from some wise, super-advanced noble spiritual race and you were sent here to enlighten mankind. To save us."

Instantly, in Herb Asher's mind, memories flicked on, and then flicked off again. Almost at once.

"What is it?" Elias asked, regarding him acutely.

"More memories. When you said that."

After an interval of silence Elias said, "I wish you would read the Bible sometime."

"It had something to do with the Bible," Herb said. "My mission."

"Maybe you're a messenger," Elias said. "Maybe you have a message to deliver to the world. From God."

"Stop kidding me."

Elias said, "I'm not kidding. Not now." And apparently that was so; his dark face had turned grim.

"What's wrong?" Herb said.

"Sometimes I think this planet is under a spell," Elias said. "We are asleep or in a trance, and something causes us to see what it wants us to see and remember and think what it wants us to remember and think. Which means we're whatever it wants us to be. Which in turn means that we have no genuine existence. We're at the mercy of some kind of whim."

"Strange," Herb Asher said.

His business partner said, "Yes. Very strange."

At the end of the work day, as Herb Asher and his partner were preparing to close up the store a young woman wearing a suede leather jacket, jeans, moccasins and a red silk scarf tied over her hair came in. "Hi," she said to Herb, her hands thrust into the pockets of her jacket. "How are you?"

"Zina," he said, pleased. And a voice inside his head said, How did she find you? This is three thousand miles away from Hollywood. Through an index of locations computer, probably. Still . . . he sensed something not right. But it did not pertain to his nature to turn down a visit by a pretty girl.

"Do you have time for a cup of coffee?" she asked.

"Sure," he said.

Shortly, they sat facing each other across a table in a nearby restaurant.

Zina, stirring cream and sugar into her coffee, said, "I want to talk to you about Manny."

"Why does he resemble my wife?" he said.

"Does he? I didn't notice. Manny feels very badly that he prevented you from meeting Linda Fox."

"I'm not sure he did."

"She was coming right at you."

"She was walking our way, but that doesn't prove I would have met her."

"He wants you to meet her. Herb, he feels terrible guilt; he couldn't sleep all night."

Puzzled, he said, "What does he propose?"

"That you write her a fan letter. Explaining the situation. He's convinced she'd answer."

"It's not likely."

Zina said quietly, "You'd be doing Manny a favor. Even if she doesn't answer."

"I'd just as soon meet you," he said. And his words were weighed out carefully; weighed out and measured.

"Oh?" She glanced up. What black eyes she had!

"Both of you," he said. "You and your little brother."

"Manny has suffered brain damage. His mother was injured in a sky accident while she was pregnant with him. He spent several months in a synthowomb, but they didn't get him in the synthowomb in time. So . . ." She tapped her fingers against the table. "He is impaired. He's been attending a special school. Because of the neurological damage he comes up with really nuts ideas. As an example—" She hesitated. "Well, what the hell. He says he's God."

"My partner should meet him, then," Herb Asher said.

"Oh no," she said, vigorously shaking her head. "I don't want him to meet Elias."

"How did you know about Elias?" he said, and again the peculiar warning sensation drifted through him.

"I stopped at your apartment first and talked to Rybys. We spent several hours together; she mentioned the store and Elias. How else could I have found your store? It's not listed under your name."

"Elias is into religion," he said.

"That's what she told me; that's why I don't want Manny to meet him. They'd just jack each other up higher and higher into theological moonshine."

He answered, "I find Elias very levelheaded."

"Yes, and in many ways Manny is levelheaded. But you get two religious people together and they just sort of— You know. Endless talk about Jesus and the world coming to an end. The Battle of Armageddon. The conflagration." She shivered. "It gives me the creeps. Hellfire and damnation."

"Elias is into that, all right," Herb said. It almost seemed to him that she knew. Probably Rybys had told her; that was it.

"Herb," Zina said, "will you do Manny the favor he wants? Will you write the Fox—" Her expression changed.

" 'The Fox,' " he said. "I wonder if that'll catch on. It's a natural."

Continuing, Zina said, "Will you write Linda Fox and say you'd like to meet her? Ask her where she'll be appearing; they set up those club dates well in advance. Tell her you own an audio store. She's not well known; it isn't like some nationally famous star who gets bales of fan mail. Manny is sure she'll answer."

"Of course I will," he said.

She smiled. And her dark eyes danced.

"No problem," he said. "I'll go back to the store and type it there. We can mail it off together."

From her mail-pouch purse, Zina brought out an envelope. "Manny wrote out the letter for you. This is what he wants you to say. Change it if you want, but—don't change it too much. Manny worked real hard on it."

"Okay." He accepted the envelope from her. Rising, he said, "Let's go back to the shop."

As he sat at his office typewriter transcribing Manny's letter to the Fox—as Zina had called her—Zina paced about the closed-up shop, smoking vigorously.

"Is there something I don't know?" he said. He sensed more to this; she seemed unusually tense.

"Manny and I have a bet going," Zina said. "It has to do with—well, basically, it has to do with whether Linda Fox will answer or not. The bet is a little more complicated, but that's the thrust of it. Does that bother you?"

"No," he said. "Which of you put down your money which way?"

She did not answer.

"Let it go," he said. He wondered why she had not responded, and why she was so tense about it. What do they think will come of this? he asked himself. "Don't say anything to my wife," he said, then, thinking some thoughts of his own.

He had, then, an intense intuition: that something rested on this, something important, with dimensions that he could not fathom.

"Am I being set up?" he said.

"In what way?"

"I don't know." He had finished typing; he pressed the key for *print* and the machine—a smart typewriter—instantly printed out his letter and dropped it in the receiving bin.

"My signature goes on it," he said.

"Yes. It's from you."

He signed the letter, typed out an envelope, from the address on Manny's copy . . . and wondered, abruptly, how Zina and Manny had gotten hold of Linda Fox's home address. There it was, on the boy's carefully written holographic letter. Not the Golden Hind but a residence. In Sherman Oaks.

Odd, he thought. Wouldn't her address be unlisted?

Maybe not. She wasn't well known, as had been repeatedly pointed out to him.

"I don't think she'll answer," he said.

"Well, then some silver pennies will change hands."

Instantly he said, "Fairy land."

"What?" she said, startled.

"A children's book. *Silver Pennies.* An old classic. In it there's the statement, 'You need a silver penny to get into fairy land.'" He had owned the book as a child.

She laughed. Nervously, or so it seemed to him.

"Zina," he said, "I feel that something is wrong."

"Nothing is wrong as far as I know." She deftly took the envelope from him. "I'll mail it," she said.

"Thank you," he said. "Will I see you again?"

"Of course you will." Leaning toward him she pursed her lips and kissed him on the mouth.

He looked around him and saw bamboo. But color moved through it, like St. Elmo's fire. The color, a shiny, glistening red, seemed alive. It collected here and there, and where it gathered it formed words, or rather something like words. As if the world had become language.

What am I doing here? he wondered wildly. What happened? A minute ago I wasn't here!

The red, glistening fire, like visible electricity, spelled out a message to him, distributed through the bamboo and children's swings and dry, stubby grass.

YOU SHALL LOVE THE LORD YOUR GOD WITH ALL YOUR HEART, WITH ALL YOUR MIGHT, AND WITH ALL YOUR SOUL

"Yes," he said. He felt fright, but, because the liquid tongues of fire were so beautiful he felt awed more than afraid; spellbound, he gazed about him. The fire moved; it came and it passed on; it flowed this way and that; pools of it formed, and he knew he was seeing a living creature. Or rather the *blood* of a living creature. The fire was living blood, but a magical blood, not physical blood but blood transformed.

Reaching down, trembling, he touched the blood and felt a shock pass through him; and he knew that the living blood had entered him. Immediately words formed in his mind.

BEWARE!

"Help me," he said feebly.

Lifting his head he saw into infinite space; he saw reaches so vast that he could not comprehend them—space stretching out forever, and himself expanding with that space.

Oh my God, he said to himself; he shook violently. Blood and living words, and something intelligent close by, simulating the world, or the world simulating it; something camouflaged, an entity that was aware of him.

A beam of pink light blinded him; he felt dreadful pain in his head, and clapped his hands to his eyes. I am blind! he realized. With the pain and the pink light came understanding, an acute knowledge; he knew that Zina was not a human woman, and he knew, further, that the boy Manny was not a human boy. This was not a real world he was in; he understood that because the beam of pink light had told him that. This world was a simulation, and something living and intelligent and sympathetic wanted him to know. Something cares about me and it has penetrated this world to warn me, he realized, and it is camouflaged as this world so that the master of this world, the lord of this unreal realm, will not know; not know it is here and not know it has told me. This is a terrible secret to know, he thought. I could be killed for knowing this. I am in a—

FEAR NOT

"Okay," he said, and still trembled. Words inside his head, knowledge inside his head. But he remained blind, and the pain also remained. "Who are you?" he said. "Tell me your name."

VALIS

"Who is 'Valis'?" he said.

THE LORD YOUR GOD

He said, "Don't hurt me."

BE NOT AFRAID, MAN

His sight began to clear. He removed his hands from before his eyes. Zina stood there, in her suede leather jacket and jeans; only a second had passed. She was moving back, after having kissed him. Did she know? How could she know? Only he and Valis knew.

He said, "You are a fairy."

"A *what?*" She began to laugh.

"That information was transferred to me. I know. I know everything. I remember CY30-CY30B; I remember my dome. I remember Rybys's illness and the trip to Earth. The accident. I remember that whole other world, the real world. It penetrated into this world and woke me up." He stared at her, and, in return, Zina stared, fixedly, back.

"My name means fairy," Zina said, "but that doesn't make me a fairy. Emmanuel means 'God with us' but that doesn't make him God."

Herb Asher said, "I remember Yah."

"Oh," she said. "Well. Goodness."

"Emmanuel is Yah," Herb Asher said.

"I'm leaving," Zina said. Hands in her jacket pockets she walked rapidly to the front door of the store, turned the key in the lock and disappeared outside; in an instant she was gone.

She has the letter, he realized. My letter to the Fox.

Hurriedly he followed after her.

No sign of her. He peered in all directions. Cars and people, but not Zina. She had gotten away.

She will mail it, he said to himself. The bet between her and Emmanuel; it involves me. They are wagering over me, and the universe itself is at stake. Impossible. But the beam of pink light had told him; it had conveyed all that, instantly, without the passage of any time at all.

Trembling, his head still aching, he returned to the store; he seated himself and rubbed his aching forehead.

She will involve me with the Fox, he realized. And out of that involvement, depending on which way it goes, the structure of reality will— He was not sure what it would do. But that was the issue: the structure of reality itself, the universe and every living creature in it.

It has to do with being, he thought to himself, knowing this because, and only because, of the beam of pink light, which was a living, electrical blood, the blood of some immense meta-entity. *Sein*, he thought. A German word; what does it mean? *Das Nichts*. The opposite of *Sein*. *Sein* equaled being equaled existence equaled a genuine universe. *Das Nichts* equally nothing equaled the simulation of the universe, the dream—which I am in now, he knew. The pink beam told me that.

I need a drink, he said to himself. Picking up the fone he dropped in the punchcard and was immediately connected with his home. "Rybys," he said huskily, "I'll be late."

"You're taking her out? That girl?" His wife's voice was brittle.

"No, goddam it," he said, and hung up the fone.

God is the Guarantor of the universe, he realized. That is the foundation of what I have been told. Without God there is nothing; it all flows away and is gone.

Locking up the store he got into his flycar and turned on the motor.

Standing on the sidewalk—a man. A familiar man, a black. Middle-aged, well dressed.

"Elias!" Herb called. "What are you doing? What is it?"

"I came back to see if you were all right." Elias Tate walked up to Herb's car. "You're totally pale."

"Get in the car," Herb said.

Elias got in.

15

A T the bar both men sat as they often sat; Elias, as always,
had a Coke with ice. He never drank.

"Okay," he said, nodding. "There's nothing you can do to
stop the letter. It's probably already mailed."

"I'm a poker chip," Herb Asher said. "Between Zina and
Emmanuel."

"They're not betting as to whether Linda Fox will answer,"
Elias said. "They're betting on something else." He wadded up
a bit of cardboard and dropped it into his Coke. "There is no
way in the world that you're going to be able to figure out what
their wager is. The bamboo and the children's swings. The
stubble growing . . . I have a residual memory of that myself; I dream about it. It's a school. For kids. A special school.
I go there in my sleep again and again."

"The real world," Herb said.

"Apparently. You've reconstructed a lot. Don't go around
saying God told you this is a fake universe, Herb. Don't tell
anybody else what you've told me."

"Do you believe me?"

"I believe you've had a very unusual and inexplicable experience, but I don't believe this is an ersatz world. It seems perfectly substantial." He rapped on the plastic surface of the table
between them. "No, I don't believe that; I don't believe in
unreal worlds. There is only one cosmos and Jehovah God created it."

"I don't think anyone creates a fake universe," Herb said,
"since it isn't there."

"But you're saying someone is causing us to see a universe
that doesn't exist. Who is this someone?"

He said, "Satan."

Cocking his head, Elias eyed him.

"It's a way of seeing the real world," Herb said. "An occluded
way. A dreamlike way. A hypnotized, asleep way. The nature of
world undergoes a perceptual change; actually it is the perceptions that change, not the world. *The change is in us.*"

"'The Ape of God,'" Elias said. "A Medieval theory about

the Devil. That he apes God's legitimate creation with spurious interpolations of his own. That's really an exceedingly sophisticated idea, epistemologically speaking. Does it mean that parts of the world are spurious? Or that sometimes the whole world is spurious? Or that there are plural worlds of which one is real and the others are not? Is there essentially one matrix world from which people derive differing perceptions? So that the world you see is not the world I see?"

"I just know," Herb said, "that I was caused to remember, made to remember, the real world. My knowledge that this world here"—he tapped the table—"is based on that memory, not on my experience of this forgery. I am comparing; I have something to compare this world with. That is it."

"Couldn't the memories be false?"

"I know they are not."

"How do you know?"

"I trust the beam of pink light."

"Why?"

"I don't know," he said.

"Because it said it was God? The agency of enchantment can say that. The demonic power."

"We'll see," Herb Asher said. He wondered once more what the wager was, what they expected him to do.

Five days later at his home he received a long-distance person-to-person fone call. On the screen a slightly chubby female face appeared, and a shy, breathless voice said, "Mr. Asher? This is Linda Fox. I'm calling you from California. I got your letter."

His heart ceased to beat; it stilled within him. "Hello, Linda," he said. "Ms. Fox. I guess." He felt numbed.

"I'll tell you why I'm calling." She had a gentle voice, a rushing, excited voice; it was as if she panted, timidly. "First I want to thank you for your letter; I'm glad you like me—I mean my singing. Do you like the Dowland? Is that a good idea?"

He said, "Very good. I especially like 'Weep You No More Sad Fountains.' That's my favorite."

"What I want to ask you—your letterhead; you're in the retail home audio system business. I'm moving to an apartment in Manhattan in a month and I must get an audio system set up right away; we have tapes we made out here on the West

Coast that my producer will be sending me—I have to be able to listen to them as they really sound, on a really good system." Her long lashes fluttered apprehensively. "Could you fly to New York next week and give me an idea of what sort of sound system you could install? I don't care how much it costs; I won't be paying for it—I signed with Superba Records and they're going to pay for everything."

"Sure," he said.

"Or would it be better if I flew to Washington, D.C.?" she continued. "Whichever is better. It has to be done quickly; they told me to stress that. This is so exciting for me; I just signed, and I have a new manager. I'm going to be making video discs later on, but we're starting with audio tapes now— can you do it? I really don't know who to ask. There're a lot of retail electronics places out here on the West Coast but I don't know anyone on the East Coast. I suppose I should be going to somebody in New York, but Washington, D.C. isn't very far, is it? I mean, you could get up there, couldn't you? Superba and my producer—he's with them—will cover all your expenses."

"No problem," he said.

"Okay. Well, here's my number in Sherman Oaks and I'll give you my Manhattan number; both fone numbers. How did you know my Sherman Oaks address? The letter came directly to me. I'm not supposed to be listed."

"A friend. Somebody in the industry. Connections; you know. I'm in the business."

"You caught me at the Hind? The acoustics are peculiar there. Could you hear me all right? You look familiar; I think I saw you in the audience. You were standing in the corner."

"I had a little boy with me."

Linda Fox said, "I did see you; you were looking at me—you had the most unusual expression. Is he your son?"

"No," he said.

"Are you ready to write down these numbers?"

She gave him her two fone numbers; he wrote them down shakily. "I'll put in a hell of an audio system for you," he managed to say. "It's been a terrific treat talking to you. I'm convinced you're going all the way, all the way to the top, to the top of the charts. You're going to be listened to and looked at all over the galaxy. I know it. Believe me."

"You are so sweet," Linda Fox said. "I have to go, now. Thank you. OK? Goodbye. I'll be expecting to hear from you. Don't forget. This is urgent; it has to be done. So many problems but—it's exciting. Goodbye." She hung up.

As he hung up the fone Herb Asher said aloud, "I'll be god damned. I don't believe it."

From behind him Rybys said, "She called you. She actually foned you. That's quite something. Are you going to put in a system for her? It means—"

"I don't mind flying to New York. I'll acquire the components up there; no need to transport them from down here."

"Do you think you should take Elias with you?"

"We'll see," he said, his mind clouded, buzzing with awe.

"Congratulations," Rybys said. "I have a hunch I should go with you, but if you promise not to—"

"It's OK," he said, barely listening to her. "The Fox," he said. "*I talked to her*. She called me. *Me*."

"Didn't you tell me something about Zina and her little brother having some kind of bet? They bet—one of them bet—she wouldn't answer your letter, and the other bet she would?"

"Yeah," he said. "There's a bet." He did not care about the bet. I will see her, he said to himself. I will visit her new Manhattan apartment, spend an evening with her. Clothes; I need new clothes. Christ, I have to look good.

"How much gear do you think you can unload on her?" Rybys said.

Savagely, he said, "It isn't a question of that."

Shrinking back, Rybys said, "I'm sorry. I just meant—you know. How extensive a system; that's all I meant."

"She will be getting the best system money can buy," he said. "Only the finest. What I would want for myself. Better than what I'd get for myself."

"Maybe this will be good publicity for the store."

He glared at her.

"What is it?" Rybys said.

"The Fox," he said, simply. "It was the Fox calling me on the fone. I can't believe it."

"Better call Zina and Emmanuel and tell them. I have their number."

He thought, No. This is my business. Not theirs.

To Zina, Emmanuel said, "The time is here. Now we will see which way it goes. He'll be flying to New York shortly. It won't be long."

"Do you already know what will happen?" Zina asked.

"What I want to know," Emmanuel said, "is this. Will you withdraw your world of empty dreams if he finds her—"

"He will find her worthless," Zina said. "She is an empty fool, without wit, without wisdom; she has no sense, and he will walk away from her because you cannot make something like that into reality."

Emmanuel said, "We will see."

"Yes, we shall," Zina said. "A nonentity awaits Herb Asher. She looks up to *him*."

There, precisely, Emmanuel declared in the recesses of his secret mind, *you have made your mistake.* Herb Asher does not thrive on his adoration of her; it is mutuality that is needed, and you have handed me that. When you debased her here in your domain you accidentally imparted substance into her.

And this, he thought, because you do not know what substance is; it lies beyond you. But not, he thought, beyond me. It is *my* domain.

"I think," he said, "you have already lost."

With delight, Zina said, "You do not know what I play for! You know neither me nor my goals!"

That may be so, he reflected.

But I know myself; and—I know my goals.

Wearing a fashionable suit, purchased at some considerable expense, Herb Asher boarded a luxury-class commercial rocket for New York City. Briefcase in hand—it contained specs on all the latest home audio systems finding their way onto the market —he sat gazing out the window as the three-minute trip unrolled. The rocket began to descend almost at once.

This is the most wonderful moment in my life, he declared inwardly as the retrojets fired. Look at me; I am right out of the pages of *Style* magazine.

Thank God Rybys didn't come along.

"Ladies and gentlemen," the overhead speakers announced, "we have now landed at Kennedy Spaceport. Please remain in your seats until the tone sounds; then you may exit at the front end of the ship. Thank you for taking Delta Spacelines."

"Enjoy your day," the robot steward said to Herb Asher as he jauntily exited from the ship.

"You, too," Herb said. "And plenty more besides."

By Yellow cab he flew directly to the Essex House where he had his reservation—the hell with the cost—for the next two days. Very soon he unpacked, surveyed the grand appointments of his room, and then, after taking a Valzine (the best of the latest generations of cortical stimulants) picked up the fone and dialed Linda Fox's Manhattan number.

"How exciting to know you're in town," she said when he identified himself. "Can you come over now? I have some people here but they're just leaving. This decision about my equipment, this is something I want to do slowly and carefully. What time is it now? I just got here from California."

"It's 7 P.M. New York time," he said.

"Have you had dinner?"

"No," he said. It was like a fantasy; he felt as if he was in a dream world, a kingdom of the divine. He felt—like a child, he thought. Reading my *Silver Pennies* book of poems. Apparently I found a silver penny, and made my way there. Where I have always yearned to be. Home is the sailor home from the sea, he thought. And the hunter . . . He could not remember how the verse went. Well, in any case it was appropriate; he was home at last.

And there is no one here to tell me she looks like a pizza waitress, he informed himself. So I can forget that.

"I've got some food here in my apartment; I'm into health foods. If you want some . . . I have actual orange juice, soybean curd, organic foods. I don't believe in slaughtering animals."

"Fine," he said. "Sure; anything. You name it."

When he reached her apartment—in an outstandingly lovely building—he found her wearing a cap, a turtleneck sweater and white duck shorts; barefoot, she welcomed him into the living room. No furniture at all; she hadn't moved in yet. In the bedroom a sleeping bag and an open suitcase. The rooms were large and the picture window gave her a view of Central Park.

"Hello," she said. "I'm Linda." She extended her hand. "It's nice to meet you, Mr. Asher."

"Call me Herb," he said.

"On the Coast, the West Coast, everyone introduces people by their first names only; I'm trying to train myself away from that, but I can't. I was raised in Southern California, in Riverside." She shut the door after him. "It's ghastly without any furniture, isn't it? My manager is picking it out; it'll be here the day after tomorrow. Well, he's not picking it out alone; I'm helping him. Let's see your brochures." She had noticed his briefcase and her eyes sparkled with anticipation.

She does look a little like a pizza waitress, he thought. But that's okay. Her complexion, up close, in the glare of the overhead lighting, was not as clear as he had thought; in fact, he noticed, she had a little acne.

"We can sit on the floor," she said; she threw herself down, bare knees raised, her back against the wall. "Let's see. I'm relying on you entirely."

He began, "I assume you want studio quality items. What we call professional components. Not what the ordinary person has in his home."

"What's that?" She pointed to a picture of huge speakers. "They look like refrigerators."

"That's an old design," he said, turning to the next page. "Those work by means of a plasma. Derived from helium. You have to keep buying tanks of helium. They look good, though, because the helium plasma glows. It's produced by extremely high voltage. Here, let me show you something more recent; helium plasma transduction is obsolete or soon will be."

Why do I have the feeling I'm imagining all this? he asked himself. Maybe because it's so wonderful. But still . . .

For a couple of hours the two of them sat together leaning against the wall going through his literature. Her enthusiasm was enormous, but, eventually, she began to tire.

"I am hungry," she said. "I don't really have the right clothes with me to go to a restaurant; you have to dress up back here—it's not like Southern California where you can wear anything. Where are you staying?"

"The Essex House."

Standing, stretching, Linda Fox said, "Let's go back to your suite and order room service. Okay?"

"Outstanding," he said, getting up.

After they had eaten dinner together in his room at the hotel Linda Fox paced about, her arms folded. "You know something?" she said. "I keep having this recurring dream that I'm the most famous singer in the galaxy. It's exactly like what you said on the fone. My fantasy life in my subconscious, I guess. But I keep dreaming these production scenes where I'm recording tape after tape and giving concerts, and I have all this money. Do you believe in astrology?"

"I guess I do," he said.

"And places I've never been to; I dream about that. And people I've never seen before, important people. People big in the entertainment field. And we're always rushing around from place to place. Order some wine, would you? I don't know anything about French wine; you decide. But don't make it too dry."

He knew nothing about French wine either, but he got the wine list from the hotel's main restaurant and, with the help of the wine steward, ordered a bottle of expensive burgundy.

"This tastes great," Linda Fox said, curled up on the couch, her bare legs tucked under her. "Tell me about yourself. How long have you been in retail audio components?"

"A number of years," he said.

"How did you beat the draft?"

That puzzled him. He had the idea that the draft had been abolished years ago.

"It has?" Linda said when he told her. Puzzled, the trace of a frown on her face, she said, "That's funny. I was sure there was a draft, and a lot of men have migrated out to colony worlds to escape it. Have you ever been off Earth?"

"No," he said. "But I'd like to try interplanetary travel just for the experience of it." Seating himself on the couch beside her he casually put his arm behind her; she did not pull away.

"And to touch down on another planet. That must be some sensation."

"I'm perfectly happy here." She leaned her head back against his arm and shut her eyes. "Rub my back," she said. "I'm stiff from leaning against the wall; it hurts here." She touched a midpoint in her spine, leaning forward. He began to massage her neck. "That feels good," she murmured.

"Lie down on the bed," he said. "So I can get more pressure; I can't do it very well this way."

"Okay." Linda Fox hopped from the couch and padded barefoot across the room. "What a nice bedroom. I've never stayed at the Essex House. Are you married?"

"No," he said. No point telling her about Rybys. "I was once but I got divorced."

"Isn't divorce awful?" She lay on the bed, prone, her arms stretched out.

Bending over her he kissed the back of her head.

"Don't," she said.

"Why not?"

"I can't."

"Can't what?" he said.

"Make love. I'm having my period."

Period? Linda Fox has periods? He was incredulous. He drew back from her, sitting bolt upright.

"I'm sorry," she said. She seemed relaxed. "Start up around my shoulders," she said. "It's stiff there. I'm sleepy. The wine, I guess. Such . . ." She yawned. "Good wine."

"Yes," he said, still sitting away from her.

All at once she burped; her hand, then, flew to her mouth. "*Pardon* me," she said.

He flew back to Washington, D.C. the next morning. She had returned to her barren apartment that night, but the matter was moot anyhow because of her period. A couple of times she mentioned—he thought unnecessarily—that she always had severe cramps during her period and had them now. On the return trip he felt weary, but he had closed a deal for a rather large sum; Linda Fox had signed the papers ordering a top-of-the-line stereo system, and, later, he would return and supervise the installation of video recording and playback components. All in all it had been a profitable trip.

And yet—his ultimate move had fallen through because Linda Fox . . . it had been the wrong time. Her menstrual cycle, he thought. Linda Fox has periods and cramps? he asked himself. I don't believe it. But I guess it's true. Could it have been a pretext? No, it was not a pretext. It was real.

When he arrived back home his wife greeted him with a single question. "Did you two fool around?"

"No," he said. Worse luck.

"You look tired," Rybys said.

"Tired but happy." It had been a satisfying and rewarding experience; he and the Fox had sat together talking for hours. An easy person to get to know, he thought. Relaxed, enthusiastic; a good person. Substantial. Not at all affected. I like her, he said to himself. It'll be good to see her again.

And, he thought, I know she'll go far.

It was odd how strong that intuition was inside him, his sense about the Fox's future success. Well, the explanation was that Linda Fox was just plain good.

"What kind of person is she?" Rybys said. "Nothing but talk about her career, probably."

"She is tender and gentle and modest," he said, "and totally informal. We talked about a lot of things."

"Could I meet her sometime?"

"I don't see why not," he said. "I'll be flying up there again. And she said something about flying down here and visiting the store. She goes all over the place; her career is taking off at this point—she's beginning to get the big breaks she needs and deserves and I'm glad for her, really glad."

If she only hadn't been having her period . . . but I guess those are the facts of life, he said to himself. That's what makes up reality. Linda is the same as any other woman in that regard; it comes with the territory.

I like her anyhow, he said to himself. Even if we didn't go to bed. The enjoyment of her company: that was enough.

To Zina Pallas, the boy said, "You have lost."

"Yes, I have lost." She nodded. "You made her real and he

still cares for her. The dream for him is no longer a dream; it is true down to the level of disappointments."

"Which is the stamp of authenticity."

"Yes," she said. "Congratulations." Zina extended her hand to Emmanuel and they shook.

"And now," the boy said, "you will tell me who you are."

16

ZINA said, "Yes, I will tell you who I am, Emmanuel, but I will not let your world return. Mine is better. Herb Asher leads a much happier life; Rybys is alive . . . Linda Fox is real—"

"But you did not make her real," he said. "I did."

"Do you want back again the world you gave them? With the winter, its ice and snow, over everything? It is I who burst the prison; I brought in the springtime. I deposed the procurator maximus and the chief prelate. Let it stay as it is."

"I will transmute your world into the real," he said. "I have already begun. I manifested myself to Herb Asher when you kissed him; I penetrate your world in my true form. I am making it *my* world, step by step. What the people must do, however, is remember. They may live in your world but they must know that a worse one existed and they were forced to live in it. I restored Herb Asher's memories, and the others dream dreams."

"That's fine with me."

"Tell me, now," he said, "who you are."

"Let us go," she said, "hand in hand. Like Beethoven and Goethe: two friends. Take us to Stanley Park in British Columbia and we will observe the animals there, the wolves, the great white wolves. It is a beautiful park, and Lionsgate Bridge is beautiful; Vancouver, British Columbia is the most beautiful city on Earth."

"That is true," he said. "I had forgotten."

"And after you view it I want you to ask yourself if you would destroy it or change it in any way. I want you to inquire of yourself if you would, upon seeing such earthly beauty, bring into existence your great and terrible day in which all the arrogant and evil-doers shall be chaff, set ablaze, leaving them neither root nor branch. OK?"

"OK," Emmanuel said.

Zina said:

> We are spirits of the air
> Who of human beings take care.

"Are you?" he said. Because, he thought, if that is so then you are an atmospheric spirit, which is to say—an angel.

Zina said:

> Come, all ye songsters of the sky,
> Wake and assemble in this wood;
> But no ill-boding bird be nigh,
> None but the harmless and the good.

"What are you saying?" Emmanuel said.

"Take us to Stanley Park first," Zina said. "Because if you take us there, we shall actually be there; it will be no dream."

He did so.

Together they walked across the verdant ground, among the vast trees. These stands, he knew, had never been logged; this was the primeval forest. "It is exceedingly beautiful," he said to her.

"It is the world," she said.

"Tell me who you are."

Zina said, "I am the Torah."

After a moment Emmanuel said, "Then I can do nothing regarding the universe without consulting you."

"And you can do nothing regarding the universe that is contrary to what I say," Zina said, "as you yourself decided, in the beginning, when you created me. You made me alive; I am a living being that thinks. I am the plan of the universe, its blueprint. That is the way you intended it and that is the way it is."

"Hence the slate you gave me," he said.

"Look at me," Zina said.

He looked at her—and saw a young woman, wearing a crown, and sitting on a throne. "Malkuth," he said. "The lowest of the ten sefiroth."

"And you are the Eternal Infinite En Sof," Malkuth said. "The first and highest of the sefiroth of the Tree of Life."

"But you said that you are the Torah."

"In the *Zohar*," Malkuth said, "the Torah is depicted as a beautiful maiden living alone, secluded in a great castle. Her secret lover comes to the castle to see her, but all he can do is wait futilely outside hoping for a glimpse of her. Finally she appears at the window and he is able to catch sight of her, but only for an instant. Later on she lingers at the window and he is able, therefore, to speak with her; yet, still, she hides her face behind a veil . . . and her answers to his questions are evasive. Finally, after a long time, when her lover has become despairing that he will ever get to know her, she permits him to see her face at last."

Emmanuel said, "Thus revealing to her lover all the secrets which she has up to now, throughout the long courtship, kept buried in her heart. I know the *Zohar*. You are right."

"So you know me now, En Sof," Malkuth said. "Does it please you?"

"It does not," he said, "because although what you say is true, there is one more veil to be removed from your face. There is one more step."

"True." Malkuth, the lovely young woman seated on the throne, wearing a crown, said, "but you will have to find it."

"I will," he said. "I am so close now; only a step, one single step, away."

"You have guessed," she said. "But you must do better than that. Guessing is not enough; you must know."

"How beautiful you are, Malkuth," he said. "And of course you are here in the world and love the world; you are the sefira that represents the Earth. You are the womb containing everything, all the other sefiroth that constitute the Tree itself; those other forces, nine of them, are generated by you."

"Even Kether," Malkuth said, calmly. "Who is highest."

"You are Diana, the fairy queen," he said. "You are Pallas Athena, the spirit of righteous war; you are the spring queen, you are Hagia Sophia, Holy Wisdom; you are the Torah which is the formula and blueprint of the universe; you are Malkuth of the Kabala, the lowest of the ten sefiroth of the Tree of Life; and you are my companion and friend, my guide. But what are you actually? Under all the disguises? I know what you are and—" He put his hand on hers. "I am beginning to remember. The Fall, when the Godhead was torn apart."

"Yes," she said, nodding. "You are remembering back to that, now. To the beginning."

"Give me time," he said. "Just a little more time. It is hard. It hurts."

She said, "I will wait." Seated on her throne she waited. She had waited for thousands of years, and, in her face, he could see the patient and placid willingness to wait longer, as long as was necessary. Both of them had known from the beginning that this moment would come, when they would be back together. They were together now, again, as it had been originally. All he had to do was name her. To name is to know, he thought. To know and to summon; to call.

"Shall I tell you your name?" he said to her.

She smiled, the lovely dancing smile, but no mischief shone in her eyes; instead, love glimmered at him, vast extents of love.

Nicholas Bulkowsky, wearing his red army uniform, prepared to address a crowd of the Party faithful at the main square of Bogotá, Colombia, where recruiting efforts had of late been highly successful. If the Party could swing Colombia into the anti-fascist camp the disastrous loss of Cuba would be somewhat offset.

However, a cardinal of the Roman Catholic Church had recently put in an appearance—not a local person, but an American, dispatched by the Vatican to interfere with CP activities. Why must they meddle? Bulkowsky asked himself. Bulkowsky. He had discarded that name; now he was known as General Gomez.

To his Colombian advisor he said, "Give me the psychological profile on this Cardinal Harms."

"Yes, Comrade General." Ms. Reiz passed him the file on the American troublemaker.

Studying the file, Bulkowsky said, "His head is up his ass. He's a spinner of theology. The Vatican picked the wrong person." We will tie Harms into knots, he said to himself, pleased.

"Sir," Ms. Reiz said, "Cardinal Harms is said to have charisma. He attracts crowds wherever he goes."

"He will attract a lead pipe to the head," Bulkowsky said, "if he shows up in Colombia."

As a distinguished guest of an afternoon TV talkshow, the Roman Catholic Cardinal Fulton Statler Harms had lapsed into his usual sententious prose. The moderator, hoping to interrupt at some point, in order to achieve a much-needed commercial information dump, looked ill at ease.

"Their policies," Harms declared, "inspire disorder, which they capitalize on. Social unrest is the cornerstone of atheistic communism. Let me give you an example."

"We'll be back in just a moment," the moderator said, as the camera panned up on his bland features. "But first these messages." Cut to a spraycan of Yardguard.

To the moderator—since for a moment they were off camera —Fulton Harms said, "What's the real estate market like, here in Detroit? I have some funds I want to invest, and office buildings, I've discovered, are about the soundest investments of all."

"You had better consult—" The moderator received a visual signal from the show's producer; immediately he composed his face into its normal look of sagacity and said, in his informal but professional tone, "We're talking today with Cardinal Fulton Harmer—"

"Harms," Harms said.

"—Harms of the Diocese of—"

"Archdiocese," Harms said, miffed.

"—of Detroit," the moderator continued. "Cardinal, isn't it a fact that in most Catholic countries, especially those in the Third World, no substantial middle class exists? That you tend to find a very wealthy elite and a poverty-stricken population with little or no education and little or no hope of bettering themselves? Is there some kind of correlation between the Church and this deplorable situation?"

"Well," Harms said, at a loss.

"Let me put it to you this way," the moderator continued; he was perfectly relaxed, perfectly in control of the situation. "Hasn't the Church held back economic and social progress for centuries upon centuries? Isn't the Church in fact a reactionary institution devoted to the betterment of a few and the exploitation of the many, trading on human credulity? Would that be a fair statement, Cardinal, sir?"

"The Church," Harms said feebly, "looks after the spiritual welfare of man; it is responsible for his soul."

"But not his body."

"The communists enslave man's body and man's soul," Harms said. "The Church—"

"I'm sorry, Cardinal Fulton Harms," the moderator broke in, "but that's all the time we have. We've been talking with—"

"Frees man from original sin," Harms said.

The moderator glanced at him.

"Man is born in sin," Harms said, totally unable to gather his train of thought together.

"Thank you Cardinal Fulton Statler Harms," the moderator said. "And now this."

More commercials. Harms, within himself, groaned. Somehow, he ruminated as he rose from the luxurious chair in which they had seated him, *somehow I feel as if I've known better days.*

He could not put his finger on it, but the feeling was there. *And now I have to go to that little rat's ass country Colombia,* he reflected. *Again; I've been there once, as briefly as possible, and now I have to fly back this afternoon. They have me on a string and they just plain jerk me around this way and that. Off to Colombia, back home to Detroit, over to Baltimore, then back to Colombia; I'm a cardinal and I have to put up with this? I feel like stepping down.*

This is not the best of all possible worlds, he said to himself as he made his way to the elevator. *And TV hosts of daytime talk shows abuse me.*

Libera me Domine, he declared to himself, and it was a mute appeal; *save me, God. Why doesn't he listen to me?* Harms wondered as he stood waiting for the elevator. *Maybe there is no God; maybe the communists are right. If there is a God he certainly doesn't do anything for* me.

Before I leave Detroit, he decided, *I'll check with my investment broker about office buildings. If I have the time.*

Rybys Rommey-Asher, plodding listlessly into the living room of their apartment, said, "I'm back." She shut the front door and took off her coat. "The doctor says it's an ulcer. A pyloric ulcer, it's called. I have to take phenobarb for it and drink Maalox."

"Does it still hurt?" Herb Asher said; he had been going through his tape collection, searching for the Mahler Second Symphony.

"Could you pour me some milk?" Rybys threw herself down

on the couch. "I'm exhausted." Her face, puffy and dark, seemed to him to be swollen. "And don't play any loud music. I can't take any noise right now. Why aren't you at the shop?"

"It's my day off." He found the tape of the Mahler Second. "I'll put on the earspeakers," he said. "So it won't bother you."

Rybys said, "I want to tell you about my ulcer. I learned some interesting facts about ulcers—I stopped off at the library. Here." She held out a manila folder. "I got a printout of a recent article. There's this theory that—"

"I'm going to listen to the Mahler Second," he said.

"Fine." Her tone was bitter and sardonic. "You go ahead."

"There's nothing I can do about your ulcer," he said.

"You can listen to me."

Herb Asher said, "I'll bring you the milk." He walked into the kitchen and he thought, Must it be like this?

If I could hear the Second, he thought, I'd feel okay. The only symphony scored for many pieces of rattan, he mused. A Ruthe, which looks like a small broom; they use it to play the bass drum. Too bad Mahler never saw a Morley wah-wah pedal, he thought, or he would have scored it into one of his longer works.

Returning to the living room he handed his wife her glass of milk.

"What have you been doing?" she said. "I notice you haven't picked up or cleaned up or anything."

"I've been on the fone to New York," he said.

"Linda Fox," Rybys said.

"Yes. Ordering her audio components."

"When are you going back to see her?"

"I'll be supervising the installation. I want to check the system over when it's all set up."

"You really like her," Rybys said.

"It's a good sale."

"No, I mean personally. You like *her*." She paused and then said, "I think, Herb, I'm going to divorce you."

He said, "Are you serious?"

"Very."

"Because of Linda Fox?"

"Because I'm sick and tired of this place being a sty. I'm sick and tired of doing dishes for you and your friends. I'm especially sick and tired of Elias; he's always showing up unexpectedly; he never fones before he comes over. He acts like he lives here. Half the money we spend on food goes for him and his needs. He's like some kind of beggar. He *looks* like a beggar. And that nutty religious crap of his, that 'The world is coming to an end' stuff . . . I can't take any more of it." She fell silent and then, in pain, she grimaced.

"Your ulcer?" he asked.

"My ulcer, yes. The ulcer I got worrying about—"

"I'm going to the shop," he said; he made his way to the door. "Good-bye."

"Good-bye, Herb Asher," Rybys said. "Leave me here and go stand around talking to pretty lady customers and listening to high-performance new audio components that'll knock your socks off, for half a million dollars."

He shut the door after him, and, a moment later, rose up into the sky in his flycar.

Later in the day, when no customers wandered around the store checking out the new equipment, he seated himself in the listening room with his business partner. "Elias," he said, "I think Rybys and I have come to the end."

Elias said, "What are you going to do instead? You're used to living with her; it's a basic part of you, taking care of her. Satisfying her wants."

"Psychologically," Herb said, "she is very sick."

"You knew that when you married her."

"She can't focus her attention. She's scattered. That's the technical term for it. That's what the tests showed. That's why she's so messy; she can't think and she can't act and she can't concentrate." The Spirit of Futile Effort, he said to himself.

"What you need," Elias said, "is a son. I saw how much affection you have for Manny, that woman's little brother. Why don't you—" He broke off. "It's none of my business."

"If I got mixed up with anybody else," Herb said, "I know who it would be. But she'd never give me a tumble."

"That singer?"

"Yes," he said.

"Try," Elias said.

"It's beyond my reach."

"Nobody knows what's beyond his reach. God decides what's beyond a person's reach."

"She's going to be galaxy-famous."

Elias said, "But she isn't yet. If you're going to make a move toward her, do it now."

"The Fox," Herb Asher said. "That's how I think of her." A phrase popped into his mind:

> You are with the Fox, and the Fox
> is with *you!*

Not Linda Fox singing but Linda Fox speaking. He wondered where the notion came from, that she would be saying that. Again vague memories, compounded of—he did not know what. A more aggressive Linda Fox; more professional and dynamic. And yet remote. As if from millions of miles off. A signal from a star. In both senses of the word.

From the distant stars, he thought. Music and the sound of bells.

"Maybe," he said, "I'll emigrate to a colony world."

"Rybys is too ill for that."

"I'll go alone," Herb said.

Elias said, "You'd be better off dating Linda Fox. If you can swing it. You'll be seeing her again. Don't give up yet. Make a try. The basis of life is trying."

"OK," Herb Asher said. "I will try."

17

HAND in hand, Emmanuel walked with Zina through the dark woods of Stanley Park. "You are myself," he said. "You are the *Shekhina*, the immanent Presence who never left the world." He thought, The female side of God. Known to the Jews and only to the Jews. When the primordial fall took place, the Godhead split into a transcendent part separated from the world; that was En Sof. But the other part, the female immanent part, remained with the fallen world, remained with Israel.

These two portions of the Godhead, he thought, have been detached from each other for millennia. But now we have come together again, the male half of the Godhead and the female half. While I was away the *Shekhina* intervened in the lives of human beings, to assist them. Here and there, sporadically, the *Shekhina* remained. So God never truly left mankind.

"We are each other," Zina said, "and we have found each other again, and again are one. The split is healed."

"Through all your veils," Emmanuel said, "beneath all your forms, there lay this . . . my own self. And I did not recognize you, until you reminded me."

"How did I accomplish that?" Zina said, and then she said, "But I know. My love of games. That is your love, your secret joy: to play like a child. To be not serious. I appealed to that; I woke you up and you remembered: you recognized me."

"Such a difficult process," he said. "For me to remember. I thank you." She had abased herself in the fallen world all this time, while he had left; the greater heroism was hers. Staying with man in all man's inglorious conditions . . . down into the prison with him, Emmanuel thought. Man's beautiful companion. At his side as she is now at mine.

"But you are back," Zina said. "You have returned."

"That is so," he said. "Returned to you. I had forgotten that you existed. I only recalled the world." You the kind side, he thought; the compassionate side. And I the terrible side that arouses fear and trembling. Together we form a unity. Separated, we are not whole; we are not, individually, enough.

"Clues," Zina said. "I kept giving you clues. But it was up to you to recognize me."

Emmanuel said, "I did not know who I was for a time, and I did not know who you were. Two mysteries confronted me, and they had a single answer."

"Let's go look at the wolves," Zina said. "They are such beautiful animals. And we can ride the little train. We can visit all the animals."

"And let them free," Emmanuel said.

"Yes," she said. "And let them, all of them, free."

"Will Egypt always exist?" he said. "Will slavery always exist?"

"Yes," Zina said. "And so will we."

As they approached the Stanley Park Zoo, Emmanuel said, "The animals will be surprised by their freedom. At first they won't know what to do."

"Then we will teach them," Zina said. "As we always have. What they know they have learned from us; we are their guide."

"So be it," he said, and placed his hand on the first metal cage. Within it a small animal peered at him hesitantly. Emmanuel said, "Come out of your cage."

The animal, trembling, came to him, and he took it in his arms.

From his audio store Herb Asher called Linda at her Sherman Oaks home. It took a little while—two robot secretaries held him up temporarily—but at last he got through.

"Hello," he said when he had her on the line.

"How's my sound system coming?" She blinked rapidly and put her finger to her eye. "My contact lens is slipping; just a second." Her face disappeared from the screen. "I'm back," she said. "I owe you a dinner. Right? Do you want to fly out to California? I'm still at the Golden Hind; I will be for another week. We're getting good audiences; I'm trying out a whole lot of new material. I want your reaction to it."

"Fine," he said, enormously pleased.

"So can we get together, then?" Linda said. "Out here?"

"Sure," he said. "You name a time."

"What about tomorrow night? It'll have to be before I go to work, if we're going to have dinner."

"Fine," he said. "Around 6 P.M. California time?"

She nodded. "Herb," she said, "you can stay at my place if you want; I've got a big house. Plenty of room."

"I'd love to," he said.

"I'll serve you some very good California wine. A Mondavi red. I want you to like California wines; that French burgundy we had in New York was very nice, but—we have excellent wines out here."

"Is there a particular place you want to have dinner?"

"Sachiko's," Linda said. "Japanese food."

"You've got yourself a deal," he said.

"Is my sound system coming along okay?" she asked.

"Doing fine," he said.

"I don't want you to work too hard," Linda Fox said. "I have a feeling you work too hard. I want you to relax and enjoy life. There's so much to enjoy: good wine, friends."

Herb said, "Laphroaig Scotch."

In amazement, Linda Fox exclaimed, "Don't tell me you know about Laphroaig Scotch? I thought I was the only person in the world who drinks Laphroaig!"

"It's been made in the traditional copper stills for over two hundred and fifty years," Herb Asher said. "It requires two distillations and the skill of an expert stillman."

"Yes; that's what it says on the package." She began to laugh. "You got that off the package, Herb."

"Yeah," he said.

"Isn't my Manhattan apartment going to be great?" she said enthusiastically. "That sound system you're putting in is what will make it. Herb—" She scrutinized him. "Do you honestly believe my music is good?"

"Yes," he said. "I know. What I say is true."

"You are so sweet," she said. "You see so much ahead for me. It's like you're my good luck person. You know, Herb, no one has ever really had confidence in me. I never did well in school . . . my family didn't think I could make it as a singer. I had skin trouble, too; really bad. Of course I actually haven't made it yet—I'm just beginning. And yet to you I'm—" She gestured.

"Someone important," he said.

"And that means so much to me. I need it so bad. Herb, I have such a low opinion of myself; I'm so sure I'm going to fail. Or I used to be so sure," she corrected herself. "But you give me— Well, when I see myself through your eyes I don't see a struggling new artist; I see something that . . ." She tried to go on; her lashes fluttered and she smiled at him apprehensively but hopefully, wanting him to finish for her.

"I know about you," he said, "as no one else does." And, indeed, that was true; because he remembered her, and no one else did. The world, collectively, had forgotten; it had fallen asleep. It would have to be reminded. And it would be.

"Come on out to the West Coast, Herb," Linda said. "Please. We'll have a lot of fun. Do you know California very well? You don't, do you?"

"I don't," he admitted. "I flew out to catch you at the Golden Hind. And I always dreamed of living in California. But I never did."

"I'll take you all around. It'll be terrific. And you can cheer me up when I'm depressed and reassure me when I'm scared. OK?"

"OK," he said, and felt, for her, great love.

"When you get out here, tell me what I do right in my music and what I'm doing wrong. But tell me most of all that I'm going to make it. Tell me I'm not going to fail, like I think I am. Tell me that the Dowland is a good idea. Dowland's lute music is so beautiful, the most beautiful music ever written. You really believe, then, you're sure that my music, the kind of things I sing will take me to the top?"

"I'm positive," he said.

"How do you know these things? It's as if you have a gift. A gift that you in turn give to me."

"It is from God," Herb Asher said. "My present to you. My confidence in you. Accept what I say; it is true."

Gravely, she said, "I sense magic around us, Herb. A magic spell. I know that sounds silly, but I do. A beauty to everything."

"A beauty," he said, "that I find in you."

"In my music?"

"In you both."

"You're not making this up?"

"No," he said. "I swear by God's own name. By the Father that created us."

"From God," she echoed. "Herb, it scares me. You scare me. There is something about you."

Herb Asher said, "Your music will take you all the way." He knew because he remembered. He knew because, for him, it had already happened.

"Really?" Linda said.

"Yes," he said. "It will carry you to the stars."

18

THE small animal, released from its cage, crept into Emmanuel's arms. He and Zina held it and it thanked them. Both of them felt its gratitude.

"It's a little goat," Zina said, examining its hooves. "A kid."

"How kind of you," the kid said to them. "I have waited a long time to be released from my cage, the cage you put me in, Zina Pallas."

"You know me?" she said, surprised.

"Yes, I know you," the kid said, as it pressed itself against her. "I know both of you, although you two are really one. You have reunited your sundered selves, but the battle is not over; the battle begins now."

Emmanuel said, "I know this creature."

The little goat, in Zina's arms, said, "I am Belial. Whom you imprisoned. And whom you now release."

"Belial," Emmanuel said, "My adversary."

"Welcome to my world," Belial said.

"It is *my* world," Zina said.

"Not anymore." The goat's voice gained strength and authority. "In your rush to free the prisoners you have freed the greatest prisoner of all. I will contend against you, deity of light. I will take you down into the caves where there is no light. Nothing of your radiance will shine, now; the light has gone out, or soon will. Your game up to now has been a mock game in which you played against your own self. How could the deity of light lose when both sides were portions of him? Now you face a true adversary, you who drew order out of chaos and now draw me out of that order. I will test the powers that you have. Already you have made a mistake; you freed me without knowing who I am. I had to tell you. Your knowledge is not perfect; you can be surprised. Have I not surprised you?"

Zina and Emmanuel were silent.

"You made me helpless," Belial said, "placed in a cage, and then you felt sorry for me. You are sentimental, deity of light. It will be your downfall. I accuse you of weakness, the inability to be strong. I am he who accuses and I accuse my own creator.

581

To rule you must be strong. It is the strong who rule; they rule the weak. You have, instead, protected the weak; you have offered help to me, your enemy. Let us see if that was wise."

"The strong should protect the weak," Zina said. "The Torah says so. It is a basic idea of the Torah; it is basic to God's law. As God protects man, so man should protect the disadvantaged, even down to animals and the nobler trees."

Belial said, "This runs contrary to the nature of life, the nature you implanted in it. This is how life evolves. I accuse you of violating your own biological foundations, the order of the world. Yes, by all means, free every prisoner; loose a tide of murderers on the world. You have begun with me. Again I thank you. But now I leave you; I have as much to do as you have—perhaps more. Let me down." The goat leaped from their arms and ran off; Zina and Emmanuel watched it go. And as it ran it grew.

"It will undo our world," Zina said.

Emmanuel said, "We will kill it first." He raised his hand; the goat vanished.

"It is not gone," Zina said. "It has concealed itself in the world. Camouflaged itself. We cannot now even find it. You know that it won't die. Like us it is eternal."

In the other cages the remaining imprisoned animals clamored to be released. Zina and Emmanuel ignored them; instead, they looked this way and that for the goat whom they had let out—let out to do as it wished.

"I sense its presence," Zina said.

"I, too," Emmanuel said somberly. "Our work is undone already."

"But the battle is not over," Zina said. "As it said itself, 'The battle now begins.'"

"So be it," Emmanuel said. "We will fight it together, the two of us. As we did in the beginning, before the fall."

Leaning toward him, Zina kissed him.

He felt her fear. Her intense dread. And that dread lay within him, too.

What will become of them now? he asked himself. The people whom he wished to free. What kind of prison will Belial contrive for them with his endless ability to contrive prisons?

Subtle ones and gross ones, prisons within prisons; prisons for the body, and, worse by far, prisons for the mind.

The Cave of Treasures under the Garden: dark and small, without air and without light, without real time and real space —walls that shrink and, caught tight, minds that shrink. And we have allowed this, Zina and I; we have colluded with the goat-thing to bring this about.

Its release is their constraint, he realized. A paradox; we have given freedom to the builder of dungeons. In our desire to emancipate we have crushed the souls of all the living.

It will affect every one of them in this world, from the highest to the lowest. Until we can return the goat-thing to its box; until we can place it back within its container.

And now it is everywhere; it is not contained. The atoms of the air are now its abode; it is inhaled like vapor. And each creature, breathing it in, will die. Not completely and not physically, but nonetheless death will come. We have released death, the death of the spirit. For all that now lives and wishes to live. This is our gift to them, done out of kindness.

"Motive does not count," Zina said, aware of his thoughts.

Emmanuel said, "The road to hell." Literally, he thought, in this case. That is the only door we have opened: the door to the tomb.

I pity the small creatures the most, he thought. Those who have done the least harm. They above all do not deserve this. The goat-thing will single them out for the greatest suffering; it will afflict them in proportion to their innocence . . . this is its method by which the great balance is tilted from rectitude, and the Plan undone. It will accuse the weak and destroy the helpless; it will use its power against those least able to defend themselves. And, most of all, it will devour the little hopes, the meager dreams of the small.

Here we must intervene, he said to himself. To protect the small. This is our first task and the first line of our defense.

Lifting off from his abode in Washington, D.C., Herb Asher joyfully began the flight to California and Linda Fox. This is going to be the happiest period of my life, he said to himself. He had his suitcases in the back seat and they were filled with

everything that he might need; he would not be returning to
Washington, D.C. and Rybys for some time—if ever. A new
life, he thought as he guided his car through the vividly marked
transcontinental traffic lanes. It's like a dream, he thought. A
dream fulfilled.

He realized, suddenly, that soupy string music filled his car.
Shocked, he ceased thinking and listened. *South Pacific*, he realized. The song "I'm Gonna Wash That Man Right Out of
My Hair." Eight hundred and nine strings, and not even divided strings. Was his car stereo on? He glanced at its indicator
light and dial. No, it was not.

I am in cryonic suspension! he thought. It's that huge FM
transmitter next door. Fifty thousand watts of audio drizzle
messing up everyone at Cry-Labs, Incorporated. Son of a
bitch!

He slowed his car, stunned and afraid. I don't get it, he
thought in panic. I remember being released from suspension;
I was ten years frozen and then they found the organs for me
and brought me back to life. Didn't they? Or was that a cryonic fantasy of my dead mind? Which this is, too . . . oh, my
God. No wonder it has seemed like a dream; it is a dream.

The Fox, he thought, is a dream. *My* dream. I invented her
as I lay in suspension; I am inventing her now. And my only
clue is this dull music seeping in everywhere. Without the music I would never have known.

It is diabolic, he thought, to play such games with a human
being, with his hopes. With his expectations.

A red light on his dashboard lit up, and simultaneously a
bleep-bleep-bleep sounded. He had, in addition to everything
else, become the target of a cop car.

The cop car came up beside him and grappled onto his car.
Their mutual doors slid back and the cop confronted him.
"Hand me your license," the cop said. His face, behind its plas-
tic mask, could not be seen; he looked like some kind of World
War I fortification, something that had been built at Verdun.

"Here it is." Herb Asher passed his license to the cop as
their two cars, now joined, moved slowly forward as one.

"Are there any warrants out on you, Mr. Asher?" the cop
said as he punched information into his console.

"No," Herb Asher said.

"You're mistaken." Lines of illuminated letters appeared on the cop's display. "According to our records, you're here on Earth illegally. Did you know that?"

"It's not true," he said.

"This is an old warrant. They've been trying to find you for some time. I am going to take you into custody."

Herb Asher said, "You can't. I'm in cryonic suspension. Watch and I'll put my hand through you." He reached out and touched the cop. His hand met solid armored flesh. "That's strange," Herb Asher said. He pressed harder, and then realized, all at once, that the cop held a gun pointed at him.

"You want to bet?" the cop said. "About the cryonic suspension?"

"No," Herb Asher said.

"Because if you fool around anymore I will kill you. You are a wanted felon. I can kill you any time I wish. Take your hand off me. Get it away."

Herb Asher withdrew his hand. And yet he could still hear *South Pacific.* The soupy sound still oozed at him from every side.

"If you could put your hand through me," the cop said, "you'd fall through the floor of your car. Think the logic through. It isn't a question of my being real; it's a question of everything being real. For you, I mean. It's your problem. Or you think it's your problem. Were you in cryonic suspension at one time?"

"Yes."

"You're having a flashback. It's common. Under pressure your brain abreacts. Cryonic suspension provides a womblike sense of security that your brain tapes and later on retrieves. Is this the first time it's happened to you, this flashback? I've come across people who've been in cryonic suspension who never could be convinced by any evidence, by what anyone said or whatsoever happened, that they were finally out of it."

"You're talking to one of them now," Herb Asher said.

"Why do you think you're in cryonic suspension?"

"The soupy music."

"I don't—"

"Of course you don't. That's the point."

"You're hallucinating."

"Right." Herb Asher nodded. "That's my point." He reached out for the cop's gun. "Go ahead and shoot," he said. "It won't hurt me. The beam will go right through me."

"I think you belong in a mental hospital, not a jail."

"Maybe so."

The cop said, "Where were you going?"

"To California. To visit the Fox."

"As in the Fox and the Cat?"

"The greatest living singer."

"I never heard of him."

"Her," Herb Asher said. "She's not well known in this world. In this world she's just beginning her career. I'm going to help make her famous throughout the galaxy. I promised her."

"What's the other world compared to this?"

"The real world," Herb Asher said. "God caused me to remember it. I'm one of the few people who remembers it. He appeared to me in the bamboo bushes and there were words in red fire telling me the truth and restoring my memories."

"You are a very sick man. You think you're in cryonic suspension and you remember another universe. I wonder what would have happened to you if I hadn't grappled onto you."

"I'd have had a good time," Herb Asher said, "out on the West Coast. A hell of a lot better time than I'm having now."

"What else did God tell you?"

"Different things."

"God talks to you frequently?"

"Rarely. I'm his legal father."

The cop stared at him. "What?"

"I'm God's legal father. Not his actual father; just his legal father. My wife is his mother."

The cop continued to stare at him. The laser pistol wavered.

"God caused me to marry his mother so that—"

"Hold out both your hands."

Herb Asher held out both his hands. Immediately cuffs closed around his wrists.

"Continue," the cop said, "But I should tell you that anything you say may be held against you in a court of law."

"The plan was to smuggle God back to Earth," Herb Asher said. "In my wife's womb. It succeeded. That's why there's a warrant out for me. The crime I committed was smuggling

God back to Earth, where the Evil One rules. The Evil One secretly controls everyone and everything here. For example, you are working for the Evil One."

"I'm—"

"But you don't realize it. You have never heard of Belial."

"True," the cop said.

"That proves my point," Herb Asher said.

"Everything you have said since I grappled onto you has been recorded," the cop said. "It will be analyzed. So you're God's father."

"Legal father."

"And that's why you're wanted. I wonder what the statute violation is, technically. I've never seen it listed. Posing as God's father."

"Legal father."

"Who's his real father?"

"He is," Herb Asher said. "He impregnated his mother."

"This is disgusting."

"It's the truth. He impregnated her with himself, and thereby replicated himself in microform by which method he was able to—"

"Should you be telling me this?"

"The battle is over. God has won. The power of Belial has been destroyed."

"Then why are you sitting here with the cuffs on and why am I pointing a laser gun at you?"

"I'm not sure. I'm having trouble figuring that out. That and *South Pacific*. There are a few bits and pieces I can't seem to get to go in place. But I'm working on it. What I am positive about is Yah's victory."

" 'Yah.' I guess that's God."

"Yes; his actual name. His original name. When he was living on the top of the mountain."

The cop said, "I don't mean to compound your troubles, but you are the most fucked-up human being I have ever met. And I see a lot of different kinds of people. They must have slushed your brain when they put you in cryonic suspension. They must not have gotten to you in time. I'd say that about a sixth of your brain is working and that sixth isn't working right, not at all. I'm taking you to a far, far better place than you have ever been, and they will do far, far better things to you than you can possibly imagine. In my opinion—"

"I'll tell you something else," Herb Asher said. "You know who my business partner is? The prophet Elijah."

Into his microphone the cop said, "This is 356 Kansas. I am bringing an individual in for psychiatric evaluation, a white male about—" To Herb Asher he said, "Did I give you your license back?" The cop put his gun back in its holster and rummaged beside him for Herb Asher's license.

Herb Asher lifted the gun from the cop's holster and pointed it at him; he had to hold both hands together because of the cuffs, but nonetheless he was able to do it.

"He has my gun," the cop said.

The intercom speaker sputtered, "You let a slusher get your gun?"

"Well, he was running off at the mouth about God; I thought he was . . ." The cop's voice trailed off lamely.

"What is the individual's name?" the speaker sputtered.

"Asher. Herbert Asher."

"Mr. Asher," the speaker sputtered, "please return the officer's gun."

"I can't," Herb Asher said. "I'm frozen in cryonic suspension. And there's a fifty-thousand-watt FM transmitter next door playing *South Pacific*. It's driving me crazy."

The speaker sputtered, "Suppose we instruct the station to shut down its transmitter. Then will you return the officer's gun?"

"I'm paralyzed," Herb Asher said. "I'm dead."

"If you're dead," the speaker sputtered, "you have no need of a gun. In fact, if you're dead, how are you going to fire the gun? You said yourself that you're frozen. People in cryonic suspension can't move; they're like Lincoln Logs."

"Then tell the officer to take the gun away from me," Herb Asher said.

The speaker sputtered, "Take the—"

"The gun is real," the cop said, "and Asher is real. He's crazy. He's not frozen. Would I arrest a dead man? Would a dead man be flying to California? There's a warrant out on this man; he is a wanted felon."

"What are you wanted for?" the speaker sputtered. "I'm

talking to you, Mr. Asher. I'm talking to a dead man who's frozen stiff at zero degrees."

"Much colder than that," Herb Asher said. "Ask them to play the Mahler Second Symphony. And play it the way it was originally written; not an all-string verson. I can't stand any more of this all-string music, this easy-listening music. It's not easy for me. At one time I had to listen to *Fiddler on the Roof* for months. 'Matchmaker, Matchmaker' lasted for days. And it was at a very critical time in my cycle; I was—"

"All right," the speaker sputtered reasonably. "What do you say to this? We'll have the FM station play the Mahler Second Symphony and in exchange you'll return the officer's gun. What is the— Wait a minute." Silence.

"There's a lapse of logic here," the cop beside Herb Asher said. "You're falling into his *idée fixe*. You know what I'm hearing? I'm hearing *folie à deux*. This has got to stop. There is no FM transmitter broadcasting *South Pacific*. If there were, I would hear it. You can't call the station—any station—and have them play the Mahler Second; it won't work."

The speaker sputtered, "But he'll *think* so, you stupid son of a bitch."

"Oh," the cop said.

"Give me a few minutes, Mr. Asher," the speaker sputtered, "to get hold—"

"No," Herb Asher said. "It's a trick. I won't give up the gun." To the cop beside him he said, "Release my car."

"Better release his car," the speaker sputtered.

"And take off the cuffs," Herb Asher said.

"You'll really like the Mahler Second Symphony," the cop said. "It's got a choir in it."

"Do you know what the Mahler Second has in it?" Herb Asher said. "Do you know what it's scored for? I'll tell you what it's scored for. Four flutes, all alternating with piccolos, four oboes, the third and fourth alternating with English horns, an E-flat clarinet, four clarinets, the third alternating with bass clarinet, the fourth with second E-flat clarinet, four bassoons, the third and fourth alternating with contrabassoon, ten horns, ten trumpets, four trombones—"

"Four trombones?" the cop said.

"Jesus Christ," the speaker sputtered.

"—a tuba," Herb Asher continued. "Organ, two sets of tim-
pani, plus an additional single drum off-stage, two bass drums,
one off-stage, two pairs of cymbals, one off-stage, two gongs,
one of relatively high pitch, the other low, two triangles, one
off-stage, a snare drum, preferably more than one, glockenspiel,
bells, a Ruthe—"

"What is a 'Ruthe'?" the cop beside Herb Asher asked.

" 'Ruthe' literally means 'rod,' " Herb Asher said. "It's made
of a lot of pieces of rattan; it looks like a large clothes-brush or
a small broom. It's used to play the bass drum. Mozart wrote
for the Ruthe. Two harps, with two or more players to each
part if possible—" He pondered. "Plus the regular orchestra,
naturally, including a full string section. Have them use their
mixing board to downplay the strings; I've heard enough
strings. And be sure the two soloists, the soprano and alto, are
good."

"That's it?" the radio sputtered.

"You've fallen back into his delusion," the cop beside Herb
Asher said.

"You know," the radio said, "he sounds rational enough.
Are you sure he's got your gun? Mr. Asher, how does it happen
that you know so much about music? You seem to be quite an
authority."

"There are two reasons," Herb Asher said. "One is due to
my living on a planet in the star system CY30-CY30B; I operate a sophisticated bank of electronic equipment, both video
and audio; I receive transmissions from the mother ship and
record them and then beam them to the other domes both on
my planet and on nearby planets, and I handle traffic from
Fomalhaut, as well as domestic emergency traffic. And the
other reason is that the prophet Elijah and I own a retail audio
components store in Washington, D.C."

"Plus the fact," the cop beside Herb Asher said, "that you're
in cryonic suspension."

"All three," Herb Asher said. "Yes."

"And God tells you things," the cop said.

"Not about music," Herb Asher said. "He doesn't have to.
He did erase all my Linda Fox tapes, however. And he cooked
my Linda Fox incoming—"

"There is another universe," the cop seated beside Herb

Asher explained, "where this Linda Fox is incredibly famous. Mr. Asher is flying out to California to be with her. How he can manage to do that while frozen in cryonic suspension beats the hell out of me, but those are his plans, or were his plans until I grappled him."

"I am still going there," Herb Asher said, and then realized that he had made a mistake to tell them this; now they could track him down, even if he escaped. He had done a foolish thing; he had said too much.

Regarding him intently, the cop said, "I do believe that his self-monitoring circuit has notified him that he has spoken injudiciously."

"I wondered when it would cut in," the speaker sputtered.

"Now I can't go to the Fox," Herb Asher said. "I'm not going there. I'm going back to my dome in the CY30-CY30B System. You lack jurisdiction there. Also, Belial does not rule there. Yah rules there."

The cop said, "I thought you said Yah came back here and, I would presume, if he did come back here, he now rules."

"It has become obvious to me during the course of this conversation," Herb Asher said, "that he does not rule here, at least not completely. *Something is wrong.* I knew it when I started hearing the sappy, soupy string music. I especially knew it when you grappled me and when you told me there's a warrant out for me. Maybe Belial has won; maybe that's it. You are all servants of Belial. Take the cuffs off me or I'll kill you."

The cop, reluctantly, removed the cuffs.

"It would seem to me, Mr. Asher," the speaker sputtered, "that there are internal contradictions in what you say. If you will concentrate on them you will see why you give the impression of being brain-slushed. First you say one thing and then you say another. The only lucid interval in your discourse came when you discussed the Mahler Second Symphony, and that is probably due, as you say, to the fact that you're in the retail audio components business. It is a last remnant of a once intact psyche. Understand that if you go in with the officer you will not be punished; you will be treated as the lunatic that you obviously are. No judge would convict a man who says what you say."

"That's true," the cop beside Herb Asher agreed. "All you

have to do is tell the judge about God speaking to you from the bamboo bushes and you're home free. And especially when you tell him that you're God's father—"

"Legal father," Herb Asher corrected.

"That will make a big impression on the court," the cop said.

Herb Asher said, "There is a great war being fought at this moment between God and Belial. The fate of the universe is at stake, its actual physical existence. When I took off for the West Coast I assumed—I had reason to assume—that everything was okay. Now I am not sure; now I think that something dark and awful has gone wrong. You police are the paradigm of it, the epitome. I would not have been grappled if Yah had in fact won. I will not go on to California because that would jeopardize Linda Fox. You'll find her, of course, but she doesn't know anything; she is—in this world, anyhow—a struggling new talent whom I was trying to help. Leave her alone. Leave me alone, too; leave us all alone. You do not know whom you serve. Do you understand what I'm saying? You are in the service of evil, whatever else you may think. You are machines processing an old warrant. You do not know what I've done, or been accused of doing . . . you can make no sense of what I say because you do not understand the situation. You are going by rules that don't apply. This is a unique time. Unique events are taking place; unique forces are squared off against one another. I will not go to Linda Fox but on the other hand I do not know where I will go instead. Maybe Elias will know; maybe he can tell me what to do. My dream was shot down when you grappled me, and maybe her dream, too; Linda Fox's dream. Maybe I can't now help her become a star, as I promised. Time will tell. The outcome will determine it, the outcome of the great battle. I pity you because whatever the outcome you are destroyed; your souls are gone now."

Silence.

"You are an unusual man, Mr. Asher," the cop beside him said. "Crazy or not, whatever it is that has gone wrong with you, you are one of a kind." He nodded slowly, as if deep in thought. "This is not an ordinary kind of insanity. This is not like anything I have ever seen or heard before. You talk about the whole universe—*more* than the universe, if that is possible. You impress me and in a way you frighten me. I am sorry I grappled you, now that I have listened to you. Don't shoot me. I'll release your vehicle and you can fly off; I won't pursue you. I'd like to forget what I've heard in the last few minutes. You talk about God and a counter-God and a terrible battle that seems to be lost, lost to the power of the counter-God, I mean. This does not fit with anything I know of or understand. Go away. I'll forget you and you can forget about me." Wearily, the cop plucked at his metal mask.

"You can't let him go," the speaker sputtered.

"Oh, yes I can," the cop said. "I can let him go and I can forget everything he's said, everything I've heard."

"Except that it's recorded," the speaker sputtered.

The cop reached down and pressed a button. "I just erased it," he said.

"I thought the battle was over," Herb Asher said. "I thought God had won. God has not won. I know that even though you are letting me go. But maybe it is a sign, your releasing me. I see some response in you, some amount of human warmth."

"I am not a machine," the cop said.

"But will that continue to be true?" Herb Asher said. "I wonder. What will you be a week from now? A month? What will we all become? And what power do we have to affect it?"

The cop said, "I just want to get away from you, a long distance away."

"Good," Herb Asher said. "It can be arranged. Someone must tell the world the truth," he added. "The truth you know, that I told you: that God is in combat and losing. Who can do it?"

"You can," the cop said.

"No," Herb Asher said. But he knew who could. "Elijah can," he said. "It is his task; this is what he has come for, that the world will know."

"Then get him to do it," the cop said.

"I will," Herb Asher said. "That's where I will go; back to my partner, back to Washington, D.C."

I will forego the Fox, he said to himself; that is the loss I must accept. Bitter sorrow filled him as he realized this. But it was a fact; he could not be with her now, not until later.

Not until the battle had been won.

As the cop ungrappled his vehicle from Herb Asher's he said a strange thing. "Pray for me, Mr. Asher," he said.

"I will," Herb Asher said.

His vehicle released, he swung it in a great looping arc, and headed back toward Washington, D.C. The police car did not follow. The cop had kept his word.

19

From their audio shop he called Elias Tate, waking him up from deepest sleep. "Elijah," he said. "The time has come."

"What?" Elias muttered. "Is the store on fire? What are you talking about? Was there a break-in? What did we lose?"

"Unreality is coming back," Herb Asher said. "The universe has begun to dissolve. It is not the store; it is everything."

"You're hearing the music again," Elias said.

"Yes."

"That is the sign. You are right. Something has happened, something he—they—did not expect. Herb, there has been another fall. And I slept. Thank God you woke me. Probably it is not in time. The accident—they allowed an accident to occur, as in the beginning. Well, thus the cycles fulfill themselves and the prophecies are complete. My own time to act has now come. Because of you I have emerged from my own forgetfulness. Our store must become a center of holiness, the temple of the world. We must patch into that FM station whose sound you hear; we must use it as it has in its own time made use of you. It will be our voice."

"What will it say?"

Elias said, "It will say, sleepers awake. That is our message to the listening world. Wake up! Yahweh is here and the battle has begun, and all your lives are in the balance; all of you now are weighed, this way or that, for better, for worse. No one escapes, even God himself, in all his manifestations. Beyond this there is no more. So rise up from the dust, you creatures, and begin; begin to live. You will live only insofar as you will fight; what you will have, if anything, you must earn, each for himself, and each now, not later. Come! This will be the tune that we will play over and over. And the world will hear, for we shall reach it all, first a little part, then the rest. For this my voice was fashioned at the beginning; for this I have come back to the world again and again. My voice will sound now, at this final time. Let us go. Let us begin. And hope it is not too late, that I did not sleep too long. We must be the world's information source, speaking in all the tongues. We will be the tower that originally failed. And if we fail now, then it ends here, and sleep returns. The insipid noise that assails your ears will follow a whole world to its grave, and rust will rule and dust will rule—not for a little time but for all time and all men, even their machines; for all that lies ahead."

"Gosh," Herb Asher said.

"Observe our pitiful condition at this moment. We, you and I, know the truth but have no way to bring it to the world. With the station we will have a way; we will have *the* way. What are the call letters of that station? I will fone them and offer to buy them."

"It's WORP FM," Herb Asher said.

"Hang up, then," Elias said. "So that I can call."

"Where will we get the money?"

"I have the money," Elias said. "Hang up. Time is of the essence."

Herb Asher hung up.

Maybe if Linda Fox will make a tape for us, he thought, we can play it on our station. I mean, it shouldn't all be limited to warning the world. There are other things than Belial.

His fone rang; it was Elias. "We can buy the station for thirty million dollars," Elias said.

"Do you have that much?"

"Not immediately," Elias said. "But I can raise it. We will sell the store and our inventory for openers."

"Jesus Christ," Herb Asher protested weakly. "That's how we make our living."

Elias glared at him.

"Okay," Herb said.

"We will have a baptismal sale," Elias said, "to liquidate our inventory. I will baptize everyone who buys something from us. I will call on them to repent at the same time."

"Then you fully remember your identity," Herb Asher said.

"I do now," Elias said. "But for a time I had forgotten."

"If Linda Fox will let you interview her—"

"Only religious music will be played on the station," Elias said.

"That's as bad as the soupy strings. Worse. I'll say to you what I said to the cop; play the Mahler Second—play something interesting, something that stimulates the mind."

"We'll see," Elias said.

"I know what that means," Herb Asher said. "I had a wife who used to say 'We'll see.' Every child knows that means—"

"Perhaps she could sing spirituals," Elias said.

Herb Asher said, "This whole business is beginning to get me down. We have to sell the store; we have to raise thirty million dollars. I can't cope with *South Pacific* and I don't expect to be able to cope any better with 'Amazing Grace.' Amazing Grace always sounded to me like some bimbo at a massage parlor. If I'm offending you I'm sorry, but that cop almost hauled me off to jail. He said I'm here illegally; I'm a wanted man. That means you're probably wanted, too. What if Belial kills Emmanuel? What happens to us? There's no way we can survive without him. I mean, Belial pushed him off Earth; he defeated him before. I think he's going to defeat him this time. Buying one FM station in Washington, D.C., isn't going to change the tide of battle."

"I'm a very persuasive talker," Elias said.

"Yeah, well Belial isn't going to be listening to you and neither will be the ones he controls. You're a voice—" He paused. "I was going to say, 'A voice crying in the wilderness.' I guess you've heard that before."

Elias said, "We could very well both wind up with our heads on silver platters. As happened to me once before. What has happened is that Belial is out of his cage, the cage Zina put him in; he is unchained. He is released onto this world. But what I say to you is, 'Oh ye of little faith!' But everything that can be said has been said centuries ago. I will concede Linda Fox a small amount of air time on our station. You can tell her that. She may sing whatever she wishes."

"I'm hanging up," Herb Asher said. "I have to call her and tell her I'm not coming out to the West Coast for a while. I don't want her involved in my troubles. I—"

"I'll talk to you later," Elias said. "But I suggest you call Rybys; when I last saw her she was crying. She thinks she may have a pyloric ulcer. And it may be malignant."

"Pyloric ulcers aren't malignant," Herb Asher said. "This is where I came in, hearing that Rybys Rommey is sitting around crying over her illness; this is what got me involved. She is ill for illness's sake, for its own sake. I thought I was going to escape from this, finally. I'll call Linda Fox first." He hung up the fone.

Christ, he thought. All I want to do is fly to California and begin my happy life. But the macrocosm has swallowed me and my happy life up. Where is Elias going to get thirty million dollars? Not by selling our store and inventory. God probably gave him a bar of gold or will rain down bits of gold, flakes of gold, on him like that manna in the wilderness that kept the ancient Jews alive. As Elias says, everything was said centuries ago and everything happened centuries ago. My life with the Fox would have been new. And here I am once more subjected to sappy, soupy string music which will soon give way to gospel songs.

He dialed Linda Fox's private number, that of her home in Sherman Oaks. And got a recording. Her face appeared on the little fone screen, but it was a mechanical and distorted face; and, he saw, her skin was broken out and her features seemed pudgy, almost fat. Shocked, he said, "No, I don't want to leave a message. I'll call back." He hung up without identifying himself. Probably she'll call me in a while, he decided. When I don't show up. After all, she is expecting me. But how strange she looked. Maybe it's an old recording. I hope so.

To calm himself he turned on one of the audio systems there at the store; he used a reliable preamp component that involved an audio hologram. The station he selected was a classical music station, one he enjoyed. But—

Only a voice issued from the transducers of the system. No music. A whispering voice almost inaudible; he could barely understand the words. What the hell is this? he asked himself. What is it saying?

". . . weary," the voice whispered in its dry, slithery tone. ". . . and afraid. There is no possibility . . . weighed down. Born to lose; you are born to lose. You are no good."

And then the sound of an ancient classic: Linda Ronstadt's "You're No Good." Over and over again Ronstadt repeated the words; they seemed to go on forever. Monotonous, hypnotic; fascinated, he stood listening. The hell with this, he decided finally. He shut down the system. But the words continued to circulate and recirculate in his brain. You are worthless, his thoughts came. You are a worthless person. Jesus! he thought. This is far worse than the sappy, soupy all-strings easy-listening garbage; this is lethal.

He foned his home. After a long pause Rybys answered. "I thought you were in California," she murmured. "You woke me up. Do you realize what time it is?"

"I had to turn back," he said. "I'm wanted by the police."

Rybys said, "I'm going back to sleep." The screen darkened; its light went out and he found himself facing nothing, confronted by nothingness.

They are all asleep or on tape, he thought. And when you manage to get them to say something they tell you you're no good. The domain of Belial insinuates the paucity of value in everything. Great. Just what we need. The only bright spot was the cop asking me to pray for him. Even Elias is acting erratically, suggesting that we buy an FM radio station for thirty million dollars so that we can tell people—well, whatever he's going to tell people. On a par with selling them a home audio system and baptizing them as a bonus. Like giving them a free stuffed animal.

Animal, he thought. Belial is an animal; it was an animal voice that I heard on the radio just now. Lower than human, not greater. Animal is the worst sense: subhuman and gross. He shivered. And meanwhile Rybys sleeps, dreaming of malignancy. Her perpetual cloud of illness, whether she is conscious or not; it is always with her, always there. She is her own pathogen, infecting herself.

He shut off the lights, left the store, locked up the front door and made his way to his parked car, wondering to himself where to go. Back to his ailing, complaining wife? To California and the mechanical, pudgy image he had seen on the fone screen?

On the sidewalk, near his parked car, something small moved. Something that hesitantly retreated from him, as if in fear. An animal, larger than a cat. Yet it didn't seem to be a dog.

Herb Asher halted, bent down, holding out his hand. The animal came uncertainly toward him, and then all at once he heard its thoughts in his mind. It was communicating with him telepathically. I am from the planet in the CY30-CY30B star system, it thought to him. I am one of the autochthonic goats that in former times was sacrificed to Yah.

Staggered, he said, "What are you doing here?" Something was wrong; this was impossible.

Help me, the goat-creature thought. I followed you here; I traveled after you to Earth.

"You're lying," he said, but he opened his car and got out his flashlight; bending down he turned the yellow light on the animal.

Indeed he had a goat before him, and not a very large one; and yet it could not be an ordinary Terran goat—he could discern the difference.

Please take me in and care for me, the goat-creature thought to him. I am lost. I have strayed away from my mother.

"Sure," Herb Asher said. He reached out and the goat came hesitantly toward him. What a strange little wizened face, and such sharp little hooves. Just a baby, he thought; see how it trembles. It must be starving. Out here it'll get run over.

Thank you, the goat-creature thought to him.

"I'll take care of you," Herb Asher said.

The goat-creature thought, I am afraid of Yah. Yah is terrible in his wrath.

Thoughts of fire, and the cutting of the goat's throat. Herb Asher shivered. The primal sacrifice, that of an innocent animal. To quell the anger of the deity.

"You're safe with me," he said, and picked up the goat-creature. Its view of Yah shocked him; he envisioned Yah, now, as the goat-creature did, and it was a dreadful entity, this vast and angry mountain deity who demanded the sacrifice of tiny lives.

Will you save me from Yah? the goat-creature quavered; its thoughts were limpid with apprehension.

"Of course I will," Herb Asher said. And he tenderly placed the goat-creature in the back of his car.

You won't tell Yah where I am, will you? the goat-creature begged.

"I swear," Herb Asher said.

Thank you, the goat-creature thought, and Herb Asher felt its joy. And, strangely, its sense of triumph. He wondered about that as he got in behind the wheel and started up the engine. Is this some kind of a victory for it? he asked himself.

I am merely glad to be safe, the goat-creature explained.

And to have found a protector. Here on this planet where there is so much death.

Death, Herb Asher thought. It fears death as I fear death; it is a living organism like me. Even though in many ways it is quite different from me.

The goat-creature thought to him, I have been abused by children. Two children, a boy and a girl.

Picture, then, in Herb Asher's mind: a cruel pair of children, with savage faces and hostile, blazing eyes. This boy and girl had tormented the goat-creature and it was terrified of falling back into their hands once more.

"That will never happen," Herb Asher said. "I promise. Children can be dreadfully cruel to animals."

In its mind the goat-creature laughed; Herb Asher experienced its glee. Puzzled, he turned to look at the goat-creature, but in the darkness behind him it seemed invisible; he sensed it, there in the back of his car, but he could not make it out.

"I'm not sure where to go," Herb Asher said.

Where you originally were going, the goat-creature thought. To California, to Linda.

"Okay," he said, "but I don't—"

The police won't stop you this time, the goat-creature thought to him. I will see to that.

"But you are just a little animal," Herb Asher said.

The goat-creature laughed. You can give me to Linda as a present, it thought.

Uneasily, he turned his car in the direction of California, and rose up into the sky.

The children are here in Washington, D.C., now, the goat-creature thought to him. They were in Canada, in British Columbia, but now they have come here. I want to be far away from them.

"I don't blame you," Herb Asher said.

As he drove he noticed a smell in his car, the smell of the goat. The goat stank, and this made him uneasy. What a stench, he thought, considering how small it is. I guess it's normal for the species. But still . . . the odor was beginning to make him sick. Do I really want to give this smelly thing to Linda Fox? he asked himself.

Of course you do, the goat-creature thought to him, aware of what was going on in his mind. She will be pleased.

And then Herb Asher caught a really dreadful mental impression from the goat-creature's mind, one that horrified him and made him drive erratically for a moment. A sexual lust on the part of the creature for Linda Fox.

I must be imagining it! Herb Asher thought.

The goat-creature thought, I want her. It was contemplating her breasts and her loins, her whole body, made naked and available. Jesus, Herb Asher thought. This is dreadful. What have I gotten myself into? He started to steer his car back toward Washington, D.C.

And he found that he could not control the steering wheel. The goat-creature had taken over; it was in power within Herb Asher, at the center of his mind.

She will love me, the goat-creature thought, and I will love her. And, then, its thoughts passed beyond the limits of Herb Asher's comprehension. Something to do with making Linda Fox into a thing like the goat-creature, dragging her down into its domain.

She will be a sacrifice in my place, the goat-creature thought. Her throat—I will see it cut as mine has been.

"No," Herb Asher said.

Yes, the goat-creature thought.

And it compelled him to drive on, toward California and Linda Fox. And, as it compelled and controlled him, it exulted in its glee; within the darkness of his car it danced its own kind of dance, a drumming sound that its hooves made: made in triumph. And anticipation. And intoxicated joy.

It was thinking of death, and the thought of death made it celebrate with rapture and an awful song.

He drove as erratically as possible, hoping that once again a police car would grapple him. But as the goat-creature had promised none did.

The image of Linda Fox in Herb Asher's mind continued to undergo a dismal transformation; he envisioned her as gross and bad-complexioned, a flabby thing that ate too much and wandered about aimlessly, and he realized, then, that this was the view of the accuser; the goat-creature was Linda Fox's ac-

cuser who showed her—who showed everything in creation—
under the worst light possible, under the aspect of the ugly.

This thing in my back seat is doing it, he said to himself. This
is how the goat-creature sees God's total artifact, the world
that God pronounced as good. It is the pessimism of evil itself.
The nature of evil is to see in this fashion, to pronounce this
verdict of negation. Thus, he thought, it unmakes creation; it
undoes what the Creator has brought into being. This also is a
form of unreality, this verdict, this dreary aspect. Creation is
not like this and Linda Fox is not like this. But the goat-creature
would tell me that—

I am only showing you the truth, the goat-creature thought
to him. About your pizza waitress.

"You are out of the cage that Zina put you in," Herb Asher
said. "Elias was right."

Nothing should be caged, the goat-creature thought to him.
Especially me. I will roam the world, expanding into it until I
fill it; that is my right.

"Belial," Herb Asher said.

I hear you, the goat-creature thought back.

"And I'm taking you to Linda Fox," Herb Asher said. "Whom
I love most in all the world." Again he tried to take his hands
from the steering wheel and again they remained locked in
place.

Let us reason, the goat-creature thought to him. This is my
view of the world and I will make it your view and the view of
everyone. It is the truth. The light that shone originally was a
spurious light. That light is going out and the true nature of
reality is disclosed in its absence. That light blinded men to the
real state of things. It is my job to reveal that real state.

Gray truth, the goat-creature continued, is better than what
you have imagined. You wanted to wake up. Now you are
awake; I show you things as they are, pitilessly; but that is how
it should be. How do you suppose I defeated Yahweh in times
past? By revealing his creation for what it is, a wretched thing
to be despised. This is his defeat, what you see—see through
my mind and eyes, my vision of the world: my correct vision.
Recall Rybys Rommey's dome, the way it was when you first
saw it; remember what she was like; consider what she is like
now. Do you suppose that Linda Fox is any different? Or that

you are any different? You are all the same, and when you saw the debris and spoiled food and rotting matter of Rybys's dome you saw how reality really is. You saw life. You saw the truth.

I will soon show you that truth about the Fox, the goat-creature continued. That is what you will find at the end of this trip: exactly what you found in Rybys Rommey's deteriorated dome that day, years ago. Nothing has changed and nothing is different. You could not escape it then and you cannot escape it now.

What do you say to that? the goat-creature asked him.

"The future need not resemble the past," Herb Asher said.

Nothing changes, the goat-creature answered. Scripture itself tells us that.

"Even a goat can cite Scripture," Herb Asher said.

They entered the heavy stream of air traffic routed toward the Los Angeles area; cars and commercial vehicles moved on all sides of them, above them, below them. Herb Asher could discern police cars but none paid him any attention.

I will guide you to her house, the goat-creature informed him.

"Creature of dirt," Herb Asher said, with fury.

A floating signal pointed the way ahead. They had almost reached California.

"I will wager with you that—" Herb Asher began, but the goat-creature cut him off.

I do not wager, it thought to him. I do not play. I am the strong and I prey on the weak. You are the weak, and Linda Fox is weaker yet. Forget the idea of games; that is for children.

"You must be like a little child," Herb Asher said, "to enter the Kingdom of God."

I have no interest in that kingdom, the goat-thing thought to him. This is my kingdom here. Lock the auto-pilot computer of your car into the coordinates for her house.

His hands did so, without his volition. There was no way he could hold back; the goat-creature had control of his motor centers.

Call her on your car fone, the goat-creature told him. Inform her that you are arriving.

"No," he said. But his fingers placed the card with her fone number into the slot.

"Hello." Linda Fox's voice came from the little speaker.

"This is Herb," he said. "I'm sorry I'm late. I got stopped by a cop. Is it too late?"

"No," she said. "I was out anyhow for a while. It'll be nice to see you again. You're going to stay, aren't you? I mean, you're not going back tonight."

"I'll stay," he said.

Tell her, the goat-creature thought to him, that you have me with you. A pet for her, a little kid.

"I have a pet for you," Herb Asher said. "A baby goat."

"Oh, really? Are you going to leave it?"

"Yes," he said, without volition; the goat-creature controlled his words, even the intonation.

"Well, that is so thoughtful of you. I have a whole bunch of animals already, but I don't have a goat. I guess I'll put it in with my sheep, Herman W. Mudgett."

"What a strange name for a sheep," Herb Asher said.

"Herman W. Mudgett was the greatest mass-murderer in English history," Linda Fox said.

"Well," he said, "I guess it's okay."

"I'll see you in a minute. Land carefully. You don't want to hurt the goat." She broke the connection.

A few minutes later his car settled gently down on the roof of her house. He shut the engine off.

Open the door, the goat-creature thought to him.

He opened the car door.

Coming toward the car, lit by pale lights, Linda Fox smiled at him, her eyes sparkling; she waved in greeting. She wore a tank top and cutoffs, and, as before, her feet were bare. Her hair bounced as she hurried and her breasts rose and fell.

Within the car the stench of the goat-creature grew.

"Hi," she said breathlessly. "Where's the little goat?" She looked into the car. "Oh," she said. "I see. Get out of the car, little goat. Come here."

The goat-creature leaped out, into the pale light of the California evening.

"Belial," Linda Fox said. She bent to touch the goat; hastily, the goat scrambled back but her fingers grazed its flanks.

The goat-creature died.

20

"THERE are more of them," she said to Herb Asher, who stood gazing numbly at the corpse of the goat. "Come inside. I knew by the scent. Belial stinks to high heaven. Please come in." She took him by the arm and led him to the doorway. "You're shaking. You knew what it was, didn't you?"

"Yes," he said. "But who are you?"

"Sometimes I am called Advocate," Linda Fox said. "When I defend I am the Advocate. Sometimes Comfort; that is when I console. I am the Beside-Helper. Belial is the Accuser. We are the two adversaries of the Court. Please come inside where you can sit down; this has been awful for you, I know. Okay?"

"Okay." He let her lead him to the roof elevator.

"Haven't I consoled you?" Linda Fox asked. "In the past? As you lay alone in your dome on an alien world, with no one to talk to or be with? That is my job. One of my jobs." She put her hand on his chest. "Your heart is pounding away. You must have been terrified; it told you what it was going to do with me. But you see, it didn't know where you were taking it. Where or to whom."

"You destroyed it," he said. "And—"

"But it has proliferated throughout the universe," Linda said. "This is only an instance, what you saw on the roof. Every man has an Advocate and an Accuser. In Hebrew, for the Israelites of antiquity, *yetzer ha-tov* was the Advocate and *yetzer ha-ra* was the Accuser. I'll fix you a drink. A good California zinfandel; a Buena Vista zinfandel. It's a Hungarian grape. Most people don't know that."

In her living room he sank down in a floating chair, gratefully. He could still smell the goat. "Will I ever—" he began.

"The smell will go away." She glided over to him with a glass of red wine. "I already opened it and let it breathe. You'll like it."

He found the wine delicious. And his heartbeat had begun to return to normal.

Seated across from him, Linda Fox held her own wine glass

and gazed at him attentively. "It didn't harm your wife, did it? Or Elias?"

"No," he said. "I was alone when it came up to me. It pretended to be a lost animal."

Linda Fox said, "Each person on Earth will have to choose between his *yetzer ha-tov* and his *yetzer ha-ra*. You choose me and so I saved you . . . you choose the goat-thing and I cannot save you. In your case I was the one you chose. The battle is waged for each soul individually. That is what the rabbis teach. They have no doctrine of fallen man as a whole. Salvation is on a one by one basis. Do you like the zinfandel?"

"Yes," he said.

"I will use your FM station," she said. "It will be a good place to air new material."

"You know about that?" he said.

"Elijah is too stern. My songs will be appropriate. My songs gladden the human heart and that is what matters. Well, Herb Asher; here you are in California with me, as you imagined in the beginning. As you imagined in another star system, in your dome, with your holographic posters of me that moved and talked, the synthetic versions of me, the imitations. Now you have the real me with you, seated across from you. How does it feel?"

He said, "Is it real?"

"Do you hear two hundred sugary strings?"

"No."

Linda Fox said, "It's real." She set her wine glass down, rose to her feet, came toward him and bent to put her arms around him.

He woke up in the morning with the Fox against him, her hair brushing his face, and he said to himself, This is actually so; it is not a dream, and the evil goat-creature lies dead on the roof, my particular goat-thing that came to degrade my life.

This is the woman I love, he thought as he touched the dark hair and the pale cheek. It is beautiful hair and her lashes are long and lovely, even as she sleeps. It is impossible but it is true. That can happen. What had Elias told him about religious faith? "*Certum est quia impossibile est.*" "This is therefore credible, just because it is absurd." The great statement by the early Church father Tertullian, regarding the resurrection of Jesus Christ. "*Et sepultus resurrexit; certum est quia impossibile est.*" And that is the case here.

What a long way I have gone, he thought, stroking the woman's bare arm. Once I imagined this and now I experience this. I am back where I began and yet I am totally elsewhere from where I began! It is a paradox and a miracle at the same time. And this, even, is California, where I imagined it to be. It is as if in dreaming I presaw my future reality; I experienced it beforehand.

And the dead thing on the roof is proof that this is real. Because my imagination could not give rise to that stinking beast whose mind glued itself to my mind and told me lies, told me ugly stories about a fat, short woman with bad skin. An object as ugly as itself—a projection of itself.

Has anyone loved another human as much as I love her? he asked himself, and then he thought, She is my Advocate and my Beside-Helper. She told me Hebrew words that I have forgotten that describe her. She is my tutelary spirit, and the goat-thing came all the way here, three thousand miles, to perish when she put her fingers against its flank. It died without even a sound, so easily did she kill it. She was waiting for it. That is—as she said—her job, one of her jobs. She has others; she consoled me, she consoles millions; she defends; she gives solace. And she is there in time; she does not arrive too late.

Leaning, he kissed Linda on the cheek. In her sleep she sighed. Weak and in the power of the goat-creature, he thought; that is what I was when I came here. She protected me because I was weak. She does not love me as I love her, because she must love all humans. But I love her alone. With everything that I am. I, the weak, love her who is strong. My loyalty is to her, and her protection is for me. It is the Covenant that God made with the Israelites: that the strong protect the weak and the weak give their devotion and loyalty to the strong in return; it is a mutuality. I have a covenant with Linda Fox, and it will not be broken ever, by either one of us.

I'll fix breakfast for her, he decided. Stealthily, he got up from the waterbed and made his way into the kitchen.

A figure stood there waiting for him. A familiar figure.

"Emmanuel," Herb Asher said.

The boy shone in a ghostly way, and Herb Asher realized that he could see the wall and the counter and cabinets behind the boy. This was an epiphany of the divine; Emmanuel was in fact somewhere else. And yet he was here; here and aware of Herb Asher.

"You found her," Emmanuel said.

"Yes," Herb Asher said.

"She will keep you safe."

"I know," he said. "For the first time in my life."

"Now you need not ever withdraw again," Emmanuel said, "as you did in your dome. You withdrew because you were afraid. Now you have nothing to fear . . . because of her presence. She as she is now, Herbert—real and alive, not an image."

"I understand," he said.

"There is a difference. Put her on your radio station; help her, help your protectress."

"A paradox," Herb Asher said.

"But true. You can do a lot for her. You were right when you thought of the word *mutuality*. She saved your life last night." Emmanuel lifted his hand. "She was given to you by me."

"I see," he said. He had assumed that was the case.

Emmanuel said, "Sometimes in the equation that the strong protect the weak there is the difficulty in determining who is strong and who is weak. In most ways she is stronger than you, but you can protect her in certain specific ways; you can shelter her back. That is the real law of life: mutual protection. In the final analysis everything is both strong and weak, even the *yetzer ha-tov*—your *yetzer ha-tov*. She is a power and she is a person; it is a mystery. You will have time, in the life ahead for you, to fathom that mystery, a little. You will know her better and better. But she knows you now completely; just as Zina has absolute knowledge of me, Linda Fox has absolute knowledge of you. Did you realize that? That the Fox has known you totally, for a very long time?"

"The goat-creature didn't surprise her," he said.

"Nothing surprises the *yetzer ha-tov* of a human being," Emmanuel said.

"Will I ever see you again?" Herb Asher asked.

"Not as you see me now. Not as a human figure such as yourself. I am not as you see me; I now shed my human side, that derived from my mother, Rybys. Zina and I will unite in a syzygy which is macrocosmic; we will not have a soma, which is to say, a physical body distinct from the world. The world will be our body, and our mind the world's mind. It will also be your mind, Herbert. And the mind of every other creature that has chosen its *yetzer ha-tov*, its good spirit. This is what the rabbis have taught, that each human—but I see you know this; Linda has told you. What she has not told you is a later gift that she holds in store for you: the gift of ultimate exculpation for your life in its entirety. She will be there when you are judged, and the judgment will be of her rather than you. She is spotless, and she will bestow this perfection on you when final scrutiny comes. So fear not; your ultimate salvation is assured. She would give her life for you, her friend. As Jesus said, 'Greater love has no man than that he give up his life for his friends.' When she touched the goat-creature she—well, I had better not say."

"She herself died for an instant," Herb Asher said.

"For an instant so brief that it scarcely existed."

"But it did occur. She died and returned. Even though I saw nothing."

"That is so. How did you know?"

Herb Asher said, "I could feel it this morning when I looked at her sleeping; I could feel her love."

Wearing a flowered silk robe, Linda Fox came sleepily into the kitchen; she stopped short when she saw Emmanuel.

"Kyrios," she said quietly.

"*Du hast den Mensch gerettet*," Emmanuel said to her. "*Die giftige Schlange bekämpfte . . . es freut mich sehr. Danke.*"

Linda Fox said, "*Die Absicht ist nur allzuklar. Lass mich fragen: wann also wird das Dunkel schwinden?*"

"*Sobald dich führt der Freundschaft Hand ins Heiligtum zum ew' gen Band.*"

"*O wie?*" Linda Fox said.

"*Du*—" Emmanuel gazed at her. "*Wie stark ist nicht dein Zauberton, deine Musik. Sing immer für alle Menschen, durch Ewigkeit. Dabei ist das Dunkel zerstören.*"

"*Ja*," Linda Fox said, and nodded.

"What I told her," Emmanuel said to Herb Asher, "is that she has saved you. The poisonous snake is overcome and I am pleased. And I thanked her. She said that its intentions were clear to her. And then she asked when the darkness would disappear."

"What did you answer?"

"That is between her and me," Emmanuel said. "But I told her that her music must exist for all eternity for all humans; that is part of it. What matters is that she understands. And she will do what she has to. There is no misunderstanding between her and us. Between her and the Court."

Going to the stove—the kitchen was neat and clean, with everything in its place—Linda Fox pressed buttons, then brought out food from the refrigerator. "I'll fix breakfast," she said.

"I was going to do that," Herb Asher said, chagrined.

"You rest," she said. "You've gone through a lot in the last twenty-four hours. Being stopped by the police, having Belial take control of you . . ." She turned to smile at him. Even with her hair tousled she was—well, he could not say; what she was for him could not be put into words. At least not by him. Not at this moment. Seeing her and Emmanuel together overwhelmed him. He could not speak; he could only nod.

"He loves you very much," Emmanuel said to her.

"Yes," she said, somberly.

"*Sei fröhlich*," Emmanuel said to her.

Linda said to Herb Asher, "He's telling me to be happy. I am happy. Are you?"

"I—" He hesitated. *She asked when the darkness would disappear*, he remembered. The darkness has not disappeared. The poisonous snake is overcome but the darkness remains.

"Always be joyful," Emmanuel said.

"OK," Herb Asher said. "I will."

At the stove Linda Fox fixed breakfast and he thought he heard her sing. It was hard for him to tell, because he carried in his mind the beauty of her tunes. It was always there.

"She is singing," Emmanuel said. "You are right."

Singing, she put on coffee. The day had begun.

"That thing on the roof," Herb Asher said. But Emmanuel had disappeared, now; only he himself and Linda Fox remained.

"I'll call the city," Linda Fox said. "They'll haul it away. They have a machine that does that. Hauls away the poisonous snake. From the lives of people and the roofs of houses. Turn on the radio and get the news. There will be wars and rumors of wars. There will be great upheavals. The world—we've seen only a little part of it. And then let's call Elijah about the radio station."

"No more string versions of *South Pacific*," he said.

"In a little while," Linda Fox said, "things will be all right. It came out of its cage and it is going back."

He said, "What if we lose?"

"I can see ahead," Linda said. "We will win. We have already won. We have always already won, from the beginning, from before creation. What do you take in your coffee? I forget."

Later, he and Linda Fox went back up on the roof to view the remains of Belial. But to his surprise he saw not the carcass of a wizened goat-thing; instead he saw what looked like the remains of a great luminous kite that had crashed and lay in ruins all across the roof.

Somberly, he and Linda gazed at it as it lay broken everywhere, vast and lovely and destroyed. In pieces, like damaged light.

"This is how he was once," Linda said. "Originally. Before he fell. This was his original shape. We called him the Moth. The Moth that fell slowly, over thousands of years, intersecting the Earth, like a geometrical shape descending stage by stage until nothing remained of its shape."

Herb Asher said, "He was very beautiful."

"He was the morning star," Linda said. "The brightest star in the heavens. And now nothing remains of him but this."

"How he has fallen," Herb Asher said.

"And everything else with him," she said.

Together they went back downstairs to call the city. To have the machine come along to haul the remains away.

"Will he ever be again as he once was?" Herb Asher said.

"Perhaps," she said. "Perhaps we all may be." And then she sang for Herb Asher one of the Dowland songs. It was the song the Fox traditionally sang on Christmas day, for all the planets. The most tender, the most haunting song that she had adapted from John Dowland's lute books.

When the poor cripple by the pool did lie
Full many years in misery and pain,
No sooner he on Christ had set his eye,
But he was well, and comfort came again.

"Thank you," Herb Asher said.

Above them the city machine worked, gathering up the remains of Belial. Gathering together the broken fragments of what had once been light.

THE TRANSMIGRATION
OF TIMOTHY ARCHER

An Ode for him

Ah Ben!
Say how, or when
Shall we thy Guests
Meet at those Lyrick Feasts,
Made at the Sun,
The Dog, the triple Tunne?
Where we such clusters had,
As made us nobly wild, not mad;
And yet each Verse of thine
Out-did the meate, out-did the frolick wine.

My Ben
Or come agen:
Or send to us,
Thy wits great over-plus;
But teach us yet
Wisely to husband it;
Lest we that Talent spend:
And having once brought to an end
That precious stock; the store
Of such a wit the world should have no more.

—Robert Herrick, 1648

Berkeley. I read *The Remembrance of Things Past* and I remember nothing: I came out the door I went in, as the saying goes. It did me no good, all those years in the library waiting for my number to light up, signifying that my book had been carried to the desk. That's true for a lot of people, most likely.

But those remain in my mind as good years in which we had more cunning than is generally recognized; we knew exactly what we had to do: the Nixon regime had to go; we did what we did deliberately, and none of us regrets it. Jeff Archer is dead, now; John Lennon is dead as of today. Other dead people lie along the path, as if something fairly large passed by. Maybe the Sufis with their conviction about God's innate beauty can make me happy; maybe this is why I am marching up the gangplank to this plush houseboat: a plan is fulfilled in which all the sad deaths add up to something instead of nothing, somehow get converted to joy.

A terribly thin kid who resembled our friend Joe the Junkie stopped me, saying, "Ticket?"

"You mean this thing?" From my purse I got out the printed card that Barefoot had mailed me upon receipt of my hundred dollars. In California you buy enlightenment the way you buy peas at the supermarket, by size and by weight. I'd like four pounds of enlightenment, I said to myself. No, better make that ten pounds. I'm really running short.

"Go to the rear of the boat," the skinny youth said.

"And you have a nice day," I said.

When one catches sight of Edgar Barefoot for the first time one says: He fixes car transmissions. He stands about five-six and because he weighs so much you get the impression that he survives on junk food, by and large hamburgers. He is bald. For this area of the world at this time in human civilization, he dresses all wrong; he wears a long wool coat and the most ordinary brown pants and blue cotton shirt . . . but his shoes appear to be expensive. I don't know if you can call that thing around his neck a tie. They tried to hang him, perhaps, and he proved too heavy; he broke the rope and continued on about his business. Enlightenment and survival are intermingled, I said to myself as I took a seat—cheap folding chairs, and already a few people here and there, mostly young. My husband is dead and his father is dead; his father's mistress ate a mason jar of barbiturates and is in the grave, perpetually asleep, which was the whole point of doing it. It sounds like a chess game: the bishop is dead, and with him the blond Norwegian woman who he supported by means of the Bishop's Discretionary Fund, according to Jeff; a chess game and a racket. These are strange times now, but those were far stranger.

Edgar Barefoot, standing before us, motioned us to change seats, to sit up front. I wondered what would happen if I lit a cigarette. I once lit a cigarette in an *ashram*, after a lecture on the Vedas. Mass loathing descended on me, plus a sharp dig in the ribs. I had outraged the lofty. The strange thing about the lofty is that they die just like the common. Bishop Timothy Archer owned a whole lot of loftiness, by weight and by size, and it did him no good; he lies like the rest, underground. So much for spiritual things. So much for aspirations. He sought Jesus. Moreover, he sought what lies behind Jesus: the real truth. Had he been content with the phony he would still be alive. That is something to ponder. Lesser people, accepting falsehood, are alive to tell about it; they did not perish in the Dead Sea Desert. The most famous bishop of modern times bit the big one because he mistrusted Jesus. There is a lesson there. So perhaps I have enlightenment; I know not to doubt. I know, also, to take more than two bottles of Coca-Cola with me when I drive out into the wastelands, ten thousand miles from home. Using a gas station map as if I am still in downtown San Francisco. It's fine for locating Portsmouth Square but not so fine for locating the genuine source of Christianity, hidden from the world these twenty-two hundred years.

I will go home and smoke a number, I said to myself. This is a waste of time; from the moment John Lennon died everything has been a waste of time, including mourning over it. I have given up mourning for Lent . . . that is, I cease to grieve.

Raising his hands to us, Barefoot began to talk. I little noted what he said; neither did I long remember, as the expression goes. The horse's ass was me, for paying a hundred dollars to listen to this; the man before us was the smart one because he got to keep the money: we got to give it. That is how you calculate wisdom: by who pays. I teach this. I should instruct the Sufis, and the Christians as well, especially the Episcopalian bishops with their funds. Front me a hundred bucks, Tim. Imagine calling the bishop "Tim." Like calling the pope "George" or "Bill" like the lizard in *Alice*. I think Bill descended the chimney, as I recall. It is an obscure reference; like what Barefoot is saying it is little noted, and no one remembers it.

"Death in life," Barefoot said, "and life in death; two modalities, like *yin* and *yang*, of one underlying continuum. Two faces—a 'holon,' as Arthur Koestler terms it. You should read *Janus*. Each passes into the other as a joyous dance. It is Lord Krishna who dances in us and through us; we are all Sri Krishna, who, if you remember, comes in the form of time. That is his real, universal shape. Ultimate form, destroyer of all people . . . of everything that is." He smiled at us all, with beatific pleasure.

Only in the Bay Area, I thought, would this nonsense be tolerated. A two-year-old addresses us. Christ, how foolish it all is! I feel my old distaste, the angry aversion we cultivate in Berkeley, that Jeff enjoyed so. His pleasure was to get angry at every trifle. Mine is to endure nonsense. At financial cost.

I am terribly frightened of death, I thought. Death has destroyed me; it isn't Sri Krishna, destroyer of all people; it is death, destroyer of my friends. It singled them out and left everyone else undisturbed. Fucking death, I thought. You homed in on those I love. You utilized their folly and prevailed. You took advantage of foolish people, which is truly unkind. Emily Dickinson was full of shit when she prattled about "kindly Death"; that's an abominable thought, that death is kind. She never saw a six-car pile-up on the Eastshore Freeway. Art, like theology, a packaged fraud. Downstairs the people are fighting while I look for God in a reference book. God, ontological arguments for. Better yet: practical arguments against. There is no such listing. It would have helped a lot if it had come in time: arguments against being foolish, ontological and empirical, ancient and modern (see common sense). The trouble with being educated is that it takes a long time; it uses up the better part of your life and when you are finished what you know is that you would have benefited more by going into banking. I wonder if bankers ask such questions. They ask what the prime rate is up to today. If a banker goes out on the Dead Sea Desert he probably takes a flare pistol and canteens and

C-rations and a knife. Not a crucifix displaying a previous idiocy that was intended to remind him. Destroyer of the people on the Eastshore Freeway, and my hopes besides; Sri Krishna, you got us all. Good luck in your other endeavors. Insofar as they are equally commendable in the eyes of other gods.

I am faking it, I thought. These passions are bilge. I have become inbred, from hanging around the Bay Area intellectual community; I think as I talk: pompously, and in riddles; I am not a person but a self-admonishing voice. Worse, I talk as I hear. Garbage in (as the computer science majors say); garbage out. I should stand up and ask Mr. Barefoot a meaningless question and then go home while he is phrasing the perfect answer. That way he wins and I get to leave. We both gain. He does not know me; I do not know him, except as a sententious voice. It ricochets in my head, I thought, already, and it's just begun; this is the first lecture of many. Sententious twaddle . . . the name of the Archer family's black retainer in, perhaps, a TV sitcom. "Sententious, you get your black ass in here, you hear me?" What this droll little man is saying is important; he is discussing Sri Krishna and how men die. This is a topic that I from personal experience deem significant. I should know, because it is familiar to me; it showed up in my life years ago and will not go away.

Once we owned a little old farm house. The wiring shorted out when someone plugged in a toaster. During rainy weather, water dripped from the light bulb in the kitchen ceiling. Jeff every now and then poured a coffee can of black tarlike stuff onto the roof to stop it from leaking; we could not afford the ninety-weight paper. The tar did no good. Our house belonged with others like it in the flat part of Berkeley on San Pablo Avenue, near Dwight Way. The good part was that Jeff and I could walk to the Bad Luck Restaurant and look at Fred Hill, the KGB agent (some said) who fixed the salads and owned the place and decided whose pictures got hung up for free exhibition. When Fred came to town years ago, all the Party members in the Bay Area froze solid, out of fear; this was the tip-off that a Soviet hatchetman was in the vicinity. It also told you who belonged to the Party and who did not. Fear reigned among the dedicated but no one else cared. It was like the eschatological judge sorting the sheep, the faithful, from among the ordinary others, except in this case it was the sheep who quaked.

Dreams of poverty excited universal enjoyment in Berkeley, coupled with the hope that the political and economic situation would worsen, throwing the country into ruin: this was the theory of the activists. Misfortune so vast that it would wreck everyone, responsible and not responsible alike sinking into defeat. We were then and we are now totally crazy. It's literate to be crazy. For example, you would have to be crazy to name your daughter Goneril. Like they taught us at the English Department at Cal, madness was funny to the patrons of the Globe Theater. It is not funny now. At home you are a great artist, but here you are just the author of a difficult book about Here Comes Everybody. Big deal, I thought. With a drawing in the margin of someone thumbing his nose. And for that, like this speech now, we paid good money. You'd think having been poor so long would have taught me better, sharpened my wits, as it were. My instinct for self-preservation.

I am the last living person who knew Bishop Timothy Archer of the Diocese of California, his mistress, his son my husband the homeowner and wage earner *pro forma*. Somebody should—well, it would be nice if no one went the way they collectively went, volunteering to die, each of them, like Parsifal, a perfect fool.

2

DEAR JANE MARION:

    Within a period of two days, two people—one an editor friend, the other a writer friend—recommended *The Green Cover* to me, both of them saying the same thing in effect, that if I wanted to know what was happening in contemporary literature I had goddamn well better know your work. When I got the book home (I had been told that the titular essay was the best and to start with it), I realized that you had herein done a piece on Tim Archer. So I read that. All of a sudden he was alive again, my friend. It brings fierce pain to me, not joy. I can't write about him, since I'm not a writer, although I did major in English at Cal; anyhow, one day as a sort of exercise I sat down and scratched out a spurious dialog between him and me, to see if I could by any chance recapture the cadence of his endless flow of talk. I found I could do it, but, like Tim himself, it was dead.

People ask me sometimes what he was like, but I'm not into Christianity so I don't encounter church people that often, although I used to. My husband was his son Jeff so I knew Tim on a rather personal basis. Frequently we talked theology. At the time of Jeff's suicide, I met Tim and Kirsten at the airport in San Francisco; they were briefly back from England and meeting with the official translators of the Zadokite Documents, at which point in his life Tim first began to believe that Christ was a fraud and that the Zadokite Sect possessed the true religion. He asked me how he should go about conveying this news to his flock. This was before Santa Barbara. He kept Kirsten in a plain apartment in the Tenderloin District of the City. Very few people went there. Jeff and I, of course, could. I remember when Jeff first introduced me to his father; Tim walked up to me and said, "My name's Tim Archer." He didn't mention he was a bishop. He did have on the ring, though.

I'm the one who got the phone call about Kirsten's suicide. We were still suffering over Jeff's suicide. I had to stand there and listen to Tim telling me that Kirsten had "just slipped away"; I could see my little brother, who had really been fond of Kirsten; he was assembling a balsawood model of a Spad Thirteen—he knew the call was from Tim but of course he didn't know that now Kirsten, along with Jeff, was dead.

Tim differed from everyone else I ever knew in these respects: he could believe in anything and he would immediately act on the basis of his new belief; that is, until he ran into another belief and then he acted on that. He was convinced, for example, that a medium had cured Kirsten's son's mental problems, which were severe. One day, watching Tim on TV being interviewed by David Frost, I realized that he was talking about me and Jeff . . . however, there was no real relationship between what he was saying and the reality situation. Jeff was watching, too; he did not know that his father was talking about him. Like the Medieval Realists, Tim believed that words were actual things. If you could put it into words, it was *de facto* true. This is what cost him his life. I wasn't in Israel when he died, but I can visualize him out on the desert studying the map the way he looked at a gas station map in downtown San Francisco. The map said that if you drove X miles you would arrive at place Y, whereupon he would start up the car and drive X miles knowing that Y would be there; it said so on the map. The man who doubted every article of Christian doctrine believed everything he saw written down.

But the incident that, for me, conveyed the most about him took place in Berkeley one day. Jeff and I were supposed to meet Tim at a particular corner at a particular time. Tim drove up late. Running after him came a gas station attendant, furiously angry. Tim had filled up at this man's station and then backed over a pump, mashing it flat —whereupon Tim had driven off because he was late for his appointment with us.

"You destroyed my pump!" the attendant yelled, totally out of breath and totally beside himself. "I can call the police. You just drove off. I had to run all the way after you."

What I wanted to see was whether Tim would tell this man, a very angry but really a very modest man in the social order, a man at the bottom of the scale on which Tim, really, stood at the top—I wanted to see if Tim would inform him that he was the Bishop of the Diocese of California and was known all over the world, a friend of Martin Luther King, Jr., a friend of Robert Kennedy, a great and famous man who wasn't, at the moment, wearing his clericals. Tim did not. He humbly apologized. It became evident to the gas station attendant after a bit that he was dealing with someone for whom large brightly colored metal pumps did not exist; he was dealing with a man who was, quite literally, living in another world. That other world was what Tim and Kirsten called "The Other Side," and step by step that Other Side drew them all to it; first Jeff, then Kirsten and, ineluctably, Tim himself.

Sometimes I tell myself that Tim still exists but totally, now, in that other world. How does Don McLean put it in his song "Vincent"? "This world was never meant for one as beautiful as you." That's my friend; this world was never really real to him, so I guess it wasn't the right world for him; a mistake got made somewhere, and underneath he knew it.

When I think about Tim I think:

> "And still I dream he treads the lawn,
>   Walking ghostly in the dew,
>   Pierced by my glad singing through . . ."

As Yeats put it.

Thank you for your piece on Tim, but it hurt to find him alive again, for a moment. I guess that is the measure of greatness in a piece of writing, that it can do that.

I believe it was in one of Aldous Huxley's novels that a character phones up another character and exclaims excitedly, "I've just found a mathematical proof for the existence of God!" Had it been Tim he would have found another proof the next day contravening the first—and would have believed that just as readily. It was as if he was in a garden of flowers and each flower was new and different and he discovered each in turn and was equally delighted by each, but then forgot the ones that came before. He was totally loyal to his friends. Those, he never forgot. Those were his permanent flowers.

The strange part, Ms. Marion, is that in a way I miss him more than I miss my husband. Maybe he made more of an impression on me. I don't know. Perhaps you can tell me; you're the writer.

Cordially,
Angel Archer

I wrote that to the famous New York Literary Establishment author Jane Marion, whose essays appear in the best of the little magazines; I did not expect an answer and I got none. Maybe her publisher, to whom I sent it, read it and flipped it away; I don't know. Marion's essay on Tim had infuriated me; it was based entirely on secondhand information. Marion never knew Tim but she wrote about him anyhow. She said something about Tim "giving up friendships when it served his purpose" or something like that. Tim never gave up a friendship in his life.

That appointment that Jeff and I had made with the bishop was an important one. In two respects, official and, as it turned out, unofficial. Regarding the official aspect, I proposed and intended to carry off a meeting, a merger, between Bishop Archer and my friend Kirsten Lundborg who represented FEM in the Bay Area. The Female Emancipation Movement wanted

Tim to make a speech on its behalf, a speech for free. As the wife of the bishop's son, it was thought I could pull it off. Needless to say, Tim did not seem to understand the situation, but that was not his fault; neither Jeff nor I had clued him in. Tim supposed we were getting together to have a meal at the Bad Luck, which he had heard about. Tim would be paying for the meal because we didn't have any money at all that year, or, for that matter, the year before. As a clerical typist in a law office on Shattuck Avenue I was the putative wage-earner. The law office consisted of two Berkeley guys active in all the protest movements. They defended in cases involving drugs. Their firm was called BARNES AND GLEASON LAW OFFICE AND CANDLE SHOP; they sold handmade candles, or at least displayed them. It was Jerry Barnes' way of insulting his own profession and making it clear that he had no intention of bringing in any money. Regarding this goal he was successful. I remember one time a grateful client paid him in opium, a black stick that looked like a bar of unsweetened chocolate. Jerry was at a loss as to what to do with it. He wound up giving it away.

It was interesting to watch Fred Hill, the KGB agent, greeting all his customers the way a good restaurateur does, shaking hands and smiling. Hill had cold eyes. According to the talk on the street he had the authority to murder those under Party discipline who seemed restive. Tim paid hardly any attention to Fred Hill as the son of a bitch led us to a table. I wondered what the Bishop of California would say if he knew that the man handing us our menus was a Russian national here in the U.S. under a fake name, an officer in the Soviet secret police. Or perhaps this was all a Berkeley myth. As in the many preceding years, Berkeley and paranoia were bedfellows. The end of the Vietnam War was a long way off; Nixon had yet to pull out U.S. forces. Watergate still lay several years ahead. Government agents rooted about the Bay Area. We independent activists suspected everyone of conniving; we trusted neither the right nor the CP-USA. If there was any single hated thing in Berkeley it was the smell of the police.

"Hello, folks," Fred Hill said. "The soup today is minestrone. Would you like a glass of wine while you decide?"

The three of us said we wanted wine—just so long as it wasn't Gallo—and Fred Hill went off to get it.

"He's a colonel in the KGB," Jeff said to the bishop.

"Very interesting," Tim said, scrutinizing the menu.

"They're really underpaid," I said.

"That would be why he has opened up a restaurant," Tim said, looking around him at the other tables and patrons. "I wonder if they have Black Sea caviar, here." Glancing up at me, he said, "Do you like caviar, Angel? The roe of the sturgeon, although they do sometimes pass off the roe of *Cyclopterus lumpus* as caviar; however, that is generally of a reddish hue and larger. It is much cheaper. I don't care for it—lumpfish caviar, I mean. In a sense, to say 'lumpfish caviar' is an oxymoron." He laughed, mostly to himself.

Shit, I thought.

"What's wrong?" Jeff said.

"I'm just wondering where Kirsten is," I said. I looked at my watch.

The bishop said, "The origins of the feminist movement can be found in *Lysistrata*. 'We must refrain from all touch of baubled love . . .'" Again he laughed. "'With bolts and bars our orders flout and—'" He paused, as if considering whether to go on. "'And shut us out.' It's a pun. 'Shut us out' refers both to the general situation of noncompliance and a shutting up of the vagina."

"Dad," Jeff said, "we're trying to figure out what to order. Okay?"

The bishop said, "If you mean we're trying to decide what to have to eat, my remark is certainly applicable. Aristophanes would have appreciated that."

"Come on," Jeff said.

Carrying a tray, Fred Hill returned. "Louis Martini burgundy." He set down three glasses. "If you'll excuse my asking—aren't you Bishop Archer?"

The bishop nodded.

"You marched with Dr. King at Selma," Hill said.

"Yes, I was at Selma," the bishop said.

I said, "Tell him your vagina joke." To Fred Hill I said, "The bishop knows a real old vagina joke."

Chuckling, Bishop Archer said, "The joke is old, she means. Don't misunderstand syntactically."

"Dr. King was a great man," Fred Hill said.

"He was a very great man," the bishop said. "I'll have the sweetbreads."

"That's a good choice," Fred Hill said, jotting. "Also let me recommend the pheasant."

"I'll have the veal Oscar," I said.

"So will I," Jeff said. He seemed moody. I knew that he objected to my using my friendship with the bishop in order to get a free speech—for FEM or any other group. He knew how easily free speeches got tugged out of his father. Both he and the bishop wore dark-wool business suits, and of course Fred Hill, famous KGB agent and mass killer, wore a suit and tie.

I wondered that day, sitting there with the two of them in their business suits, if Jeff would go into Holy Orders as his father had; both men looked solemn, bringing to the task of ordering dinner the same intensity, the same gravity, that they brought to so much else: the professional stance oddly punctuated on the bishop's part with wit . . . although, like today, the wit never struck me as quite right.

As we spooned up our minestrone soup, Bishop Archer talked about his forthcoming heresy trial. It was a subject he found endlessly fascinating. Certain Bible Belt bishops were out to get him because he had said in several published articles and in his sermons preached at Grace Cathedral that no one had seen hide nor hair of the Holy Ghost since apostolic times. This had caused Tim to conclude that the doctrine of the Trinity was incorrect. If the Holy Ghost was, in fact, a form of God equal to Yahweh and Christ, surely he would still be with us. Speaking in tongues did not impress him. He had seen a lot of it in his years in the Episcopal Church and it struck him as autosuggestion and dementia. Further, a scrupulous reading of Acts disclosed that at Pentecost when the Holy Ghost descended on the disciples, giving them "the gift of speech," they had spoken in foreign languages which people nearby had understood. This is not glossolalia as the term is now used; this is xenoglossy. The bishop, as we ate, chortled over Peter's deft response to the charge that the Eleven were drunk; Peter had said in a loud voice to the scoffing crowd that it was not likely that the Eleven were drunk inasmuch as it was only nine A.M. The bishop pondered out loud—between spoonfuls of minestrone soup—that the course of Western history might have been changed if the time had been nine P.M. instead of nine A.M. Jeff looked bored and I kept consulting my watch, wondering what was keeping Kirsten. Probably she had gone in to have her hair done. She fussed forever with her blond hair, especially in anticipation of momentous occasions.

The Episcopal Church is Trinitarian; you cannot be a priest or bishop of that church if you do not absolutely accept and teach that—well, it's called the Nicene Creed:

> " . . . And I believe in the Holy Ghost, the Lord,
> and Giver of Life, Who proceedeth from the
> Father and the Son; Who with the Father and
> the Son together is worshipped and glorified."

So Bishop McClary back in Missouri was correct; Tim had, in fact, committed heresy. However, Tim had been a practicing lawyer before he became a rector of the Episcopal Church. He relished the oncoming heresy trial. Bishop McClary knew his Bible and he knew canon law, but Tim would blow golden smoke-rings around him until McClary would not know up from down. Tim knew this. In facing a heresy trial, he was in his element. Moreover, he was writing a book about it; he would win and, in addition, he would make some money. Every newspaper in America had carried articles and even editorials on the subject. Successfully trying someone for heresy in the 1970s was really difficult.

Listening to Tim dilate endlessly, the thought came to me that he had calculatedly committed heresy in order to bring on the trial. At least, he had done it unconsciously. It was, as the term has it, a good career move.

"The so-called 'gift of speech,'" the bishop said cheerfully, "reverses the unity of language lost when the Tower of Babel was attempted; that is, its construction was attempted. When the day comes that someone in my congregation gets up and talks Walloon, well, that day I will believe that the Holy Ghost exists. I'm not sure he ever existed. The apostolic conception of the Holy Spirit is based on the Hebrew *ruah*, the spirit of God. For one thing, this spirit is female, not male. She speaks concerning the Messianic expectation. Christianity appropriated the notion from Judaism and when Christianity had converted a sufficient number of pagans—Gentiles, if you will—it abandoned the concept, since it was only meaningful to the Jews anyhow. To the Greek converts it made no sense whatsoever, although Socrates declared that he had an inner voice or *daemon* that guided him . . . a tutelary spirit, not to be confused with the English word 'demon,' which of course refers to an indubitably evil spirit. The two terms are often confused. Do I have time for a cocktail?"

"They just have beer and wine here," I said.

"I'd like to make a phone call," the bishop said; he dabbed at his chin with his napkin, rising to his feet and glancing about. "Is there a public phone?"

"There's a phone at the Chevron station," Jeff said. "But if you go back there you'll trash another pump."

"I simply do not understand how that happened," the bishop said. "I never felt anything or saw anything; the first I knew was when—Albers? I have his name written down. When he showed up in hysteria. Perhaps that was a manifestation of the Holy Ghost. I hope my insurance hasn't lapsed. It's always a good idea to carry automobile insurance."

I said, "That wasn't Walloon he was speaking."

"Yes, well," Tim said, "it also wasn't intelligible. It may well have been glossolalia, for all I know. Maybe there is evidence that the Holy Ghost is here." He reseated himself. "Are we waiting for something?" he asked me. "You keep looking at your watch. I only have an hour; then I have to get back to the City. The difficulty that dogma presents is that it strickens the creative spirit in man. Whitehead—Alfred North Whitehead— has given us the idea of God in process, and he is, or was, a major scientist. Process theology. It all goes back to Jakob Boehme and his 'no-yes' deity, his dialectic deity anticipating Hegel. Boehme based that on Augustine. *'Sic et non,'* you know. Latin lacks a precise word for 'yes'; I suppose *'sic'* is the closest, although by and large *'sic'* is more correctly rendered as 'so,' or 'hence,' or 'in that manner.' *'Quod si hoc nunc sic incipiam? Nihil est. Quod si sic? Tantumdem egero. Et sic—'"* He paused, frowning. " *'Nihil est.'* In a distributive language—English is the best example—that would literally mean 'nothing exists.' Of course what Terence means is, 'it is nothing,' with *'id,'* or 'it,' understood. Still, there is an enormous thrust in the two-word utterance 'nihil est.' The amazing power of Latin to compress meaning into the fewest possible words. That and precision are the two most admirable qualities of it, by far. English, however, has the greater vocabulary."

"Dad," Jeff said, "we're waiting for a friend of Angel's. I told you about her the other day."

"*Non video*," the bishop said. "I'm saying that I don't see her, the 'her' being understood. Look, that man is going to take a picture of us."

Fred Hill, carrying an SLR camera with flash attachment, approached our table. "Your Grace, would it be all right with you if I took your picture?"

"Let me take a picture of you two together," I said, standing up. "You can put it on the wall," I said to Fred Hill.

"That would be fine with me," Tim said.

During the meal, Kirsten Lundborg joined us. She looked unhappy and fatigued, and she could find nothing on the menu that pleased her. She wound up drinking a glass of white wine, eating nothing, saying very little, but smoking one cigarette after another. Her face showed lines of strain. We did not know it then, but she had mild and chronic peritonitis, which can be—and was very soon for her—very serious. She hardly seemed aware of us. I assumed she had gone into one of her periodic depressions; I had no idea that day that she was physically ill.

"You could probably get toast and a soft-boiled egg," Jeff said.

"No." Kirsten shook her head. "My body is trying to die," she said presently. She did not elaborate. We all felt uncomfortable. I suppose that was the idea in her mind. Perhaps not. Bishop Archer gazed at her attentively and with a great deal of sympathy. I wondered if he intended to suggest a laying on of hands. They do that in the Episcopal Church. The recovery rate due to that is not recorded anywhere that I know of, which is just as well.

She spoke mostly about her son Bill, who had been turned down by the Army for psychological reasons. This seemed both to please her and to annoy her.

"I'm surprised to learn you have a son old enough to be inducted," the bishop said.

For a moment Kirsten was silent. Some of the worry that

marred her features eased. It was evident to me that Tim's remark cheered her.

At this point in her life she was a rather good-looking woman, but a perpetual severity marred her, in terms of her looks and in terms of the emotional impression that she presented. As much as I admired her I knew that Kirsten could never turn down the chance to offer up a cruel remark, a defect that she had, in fact, honed into a talent. The idea seems to be that if you are clever enough you can insult people and they will sit still for it, but if you are clumsy and dumb you can get away with nothing. It all has to do with your verbal skills. You are judged, like contest entries, on aptness of phrase.

"Bill is only physically that old," Kirsten said. But she looked happier now. "What is it that comic said the other night on Johnny Carson? 'My wife doesn't go to a plastic surgeon; she wants the real thing.' I just had my hair done; that's why I was late. One time just before I had to fly over to France they did my hair so that—" She smiled. "I looked like Bozo the Clown. The whole time I was in Paris I wore a babushka. I told everyone I was on my way to Notre-Dame."

"What's a babushka?" Jeff asked.

Bishop Archer said, "A Russian peasant."

Regarding him intently, Kirsten said, "That's true. I must have the wrong word."

"You have the right word," the bishop said "The term for the cloth worn about the head derives—"

"Aw Christ," Jeff said.

Kirsten smiled. She sipped her white wine.

"I understand you're a member of FEM," the bishop said.

"I *am* FEM," Kirsten said.

"She's one of the founders," I said.

"You know, I have very strong views about abortion," the bishop said.

"You know," Kirsten said, "I have, too. What are yours?"

"We feel that the unborn have rights invested in them not by man but by Almighty God," the bishop said. "The right to take a human life is denied back to the Decalogue."

"Let me ask you this," Kirsten said. "Do you think a human being has rights after he or she is dead?"

"I beg your pardon?" the bishop said.

"Well," Kirsten said, "you're granting them rights before they're born; why not grant them equal rights after they're dead."

"As a matter of fact, they do have rights after they're dead," Jeff said. "You need a court order to use a cadaver or organs taken from a cadaver for—"

"I'm trying to eat this veal Oscar," I interrupted, seeing an endless line of argumentation ahead, and, emerging from it, Bishop Archer's refusal to make a free speech for FEM. "Can we talk about something else?"

Fazed not at all, Jeff continued, "I know a guy who works for the coroner's office. He told me one time they went into the intensive care ward at—well, I forget which hospital; anyhow, this woman had just died and they went in and ripped her eyes out for a transplant before the monitors had stopped registering vital signs. He said it happens all the time."

We sat for a time, Kirsten sipping her wine, the rest of us eating; however, Bishop Archer had not stopped gazing at Kirsten with sympathy and concern. It came to me later, but not at the time, that he sensed that she was latently physically ill, sensed what the rest of us had missed. Perhaps it emanated from his pastoral ministering, but I saw him do this again and again: discern a need in someone when no one else, sometimes even the person involved, recognized it or, if they recognized it, took time to pause and care.

"I have the highest regard for FEM," he said, in a gentle voice.

"Most people do," Kirsten said, but now she seemed genuinely pleased. "Does the Episcopal Church allow the ordination of women?"

"For the priesthood?" the bishop said. "It hasn't come yet but it is coming."

"Then I take it you personally approve."

"Certainly." He nodded. "I have taken an active interest in modernizing the standards for male and female deacons . . . for one, I will not allow the term 'deaconess' to be used in my diocese; I insist that both male and female deacons be referred to as deacons. The standardization of educational and training bases for male and female deacons will make it possible later on to ordain female deacons to the priesthood. I see this as inevitable and I am working actively for it."

"Well, I am really pleased to hear you say this," Kirsten said. "Then you differ markedly from the Catholic Church." She set down her wine glass. "The pope—"

"The Bishop of Rome," Bishop Archer said. "That is what he actually is: the Bishop of Rome. The Roman Catholic Church; our church is a catholic church as well."

"They won't ever ordain women, you think?" Kirsten said.

"Only when the Parousia is here," Bishop Archer said.

"What is that?" Kirsten said. "You'll have to excuse my ignorance; I really have no religious background or inclinations."

"Neither do I," Bishop Archer said. "I only know that, as Malebranche said, 'It is not I who breathes but God who breathes in me.' The Parousia is the Presence of Christ. The catholic church, of which we are a part, breathes and breathes only through the living power of Christ; he is the head of which we are the body. 'Now the Church is his body, he is the head,' as Paul said. It is a concept known to the ancient world and one we can understand."

"Interesting," Kirsten said.

"No, it is true," the bishop said. "Intellectual matters are interesting and so are odd factual things, such as the amount of salt produced by a single mine. This that I speak of is a topic that determines not what we know but what we are. We have our life through Jesus Christ. 'He is the image of the unseen God and the first-born of all creation, for in him were created all things in heaven and on earth, everything visible and everything invisible, Thrones, Dominations, Sovereignties, Powers —all things were created through him and for him. Before anything was created, he existed, and he holds all things in unity.'" The bishop's voice was low and intense; he spoke evenly, and as he spoke he gazed directly at Kirsten, and I saw her return his gaze, in almost a stricken way, as if she both wanted to hear and did not want to hear, fearing and fascinated. Many times I had heard Tim preach at Grace Cathedral and he now addressed her, one person, with the same intensity that he brought to bear on great masses of people. And yet it was all for her.

There was silence for a moment.

"A lot of the priests still say 'deaconess,'" Jeff said. He shuffled awkwardly. "When Tim isn't around."

I said to Kirsten, "Bishop Archer is probably the strongest supporter of women's rights in the Episcopal Church."

"Actually, I think I've heard that," Kirsten said. She turned to me and said calmly, "I wonder—do you suppose—"

"I'd be glad to address your organization," the bishop said. "That's why we're having lunch." Reaching into his coat pocket, he brought out his black notebook. "I'll take your phone number and I promise to call you within the next few days. I'll have to consult with Jonathan Graves, the bishop suffragan, but I'm sure I'll be able to find time for you."

"I'll give you both my number at FEM," Kirsten said, "and my home phone number. Do—" She hesitated. "Do you want me to tell you something about FEM, Bishop?"

"Tim," Bishop Archer said.

"We are not militant in the conventional sense of—"

"I'm quite familiar with your organization," Bishop Archer said. "I want you to consider this. 'If I have all the eloquence of men or of angels, but speak without love, I am simply a gong booming or a cymbal clashing. If I have the gift of prophecy, understanding all the mysteries there are, and knowing everything, and if I have faith in all its fullness, to move mountains, but without love, then I am nothing at all.' First Corinthians, chapter thirteen. As women, you find your place in the world out of love, not animosity. Love is not limited to the Christian, love is not just for the church. If you wish to conquer us, show us love and not scorn. Faith moves mountains, love moves human hearts. The people opposing you are people, not things. Your enemy is not men but ignorant men. Don't confuse the men with their ignorance. It has taken years; it will take years more. Don't be impatient and don't hate. What time is it?" He looked around, suddenly concerned. "Here." He passed a card to Kirsten. "You call me. I have to be going. It was nice meeting you."

He left us then. I realized after he had gone, very suddenly realized, that he had forgotten to pay the check.

3

THE Bishop of California spoke to the members of FEM and then talked their governing board out of two thousand dollars as a contribution to the church's fund for world famine, really a nominal sum and for a meritorious cause. It took a while for the news that Tim was seeing Kirsten socially to percolate down to Jeff and me. Jeff was simply amazed. I thought it was funny.

It did not even strike Jeff as funny that his father had shaken two thousand dollars loose from FEM. He had seen a free speech looming up; that hadn't come to pass. He had anticipated friction and dislike between his father and my friend Kirsten. That had not come to pass either. Jeff did not understand his own father.

The way I found out was through Kirsten, not Tim. I got a phone call the week following Tim's speech. Kirsten wanted to go shopping with me in San Francisco.

When you're dating a bishop you do not tell everybody in town. Kirsten spent hours fussing with dresses and blouses and tops and skirts, at store after store before even hinting at what was going on. My promised silence was secured in advance by means of oaths more elaborate than those of the Rosicrucians. Telling me was ten percent of the fun; she strung the revelation out, seemingly forever. We were, in fact, all the way down at the Marina before I fathomed what she had been hinting at.

"If Jonathan Graves finds out," Kirsten said, "Tim will have to resign."

I could not even remember who Jonathan Graves was. The disclosure seemed irreal; I thought at first that she was joking and then I thought she was hallucinating.

"The *Chronicle* would put it on page one," Kirsten said, in a solemn tone. "And on top of the heresy trial—"

"Jesus Christ!" I said. "You can't sleep with a bishop!"

"I already have," Kirsten said.

"Who else have you told?"

"Nobody else. I'm not sure if you should tell Jeff. Tim and I talked it over. We couldn't decide."

We, I thought. You destructive bitch, I thought. To get laid you'd ruin a man's entire life, a man who knew Dr. King and Bobby Kennedy and determines the opinion of—*my* opinion, to name one person.

"Don't look so upset," Kirsten said.

"Whose idea was it?"

"Why should it make you angry?"

"Was it your idea?"

Kirsten said calmly, "We discussed it."

After a minute I began to laugh. Kirsten, annoyed at first, presently joined me; we stood on the grass by the edge of the bay, laughing and holding onto each other. Passing people regarded us with curiosity. "Was it any good?" I managed to say finally. "I mean, what was it like?"

"It was terrific. But now he has to confess."

"Does that mean you can't do it again?"

"It just means he has to confess again."

"Aren't you going to go to hell?"

Kirsten said, "He is. I'm not."

"Doesn't that bother you?"

"That I'm not going to hell?" She giggled.

"We have to be real adult about this," I said.

"Yes we do. We absolutely have to be totally adult. We have to walk around as if everything is normal. This is *not* normal. I mean, it isn't like I'm saying it's abnormal in the sense of—you know."

"Like making it with a goat."

Kirsten said, "I wonder if there's a word for it . . . making it with an Episcopal bishop. Bishopric. Tim told me that word."

"Bishop prick?"

"No, bishop *ric*. You're not pronouncing it right." We had to hold onto each other to keep from falling; neither of us could stop laughing. "It's the place he lives or something. Oh, God." She wiped the tears of laughter from her eyes. "Always be sure you pronounce it bishop *ric*. This is terrible. We really are going to go to hell, straight to hell. You know what he let me do?" Kirsten leaned close to me to whisper in my ear. "I tried on some of his robes and his miter; you know, the shovel hat. The first lady bishop."

"You may not be the first."

"I looked great. I looked better than he does. I want you to see. We're getting an apartment. For Christ's sake, don't say anything about this part especially, but he's paying for it out of his Discretionary Fund."

"Church money?" I stared at her.

"Listen." Kirsten looked solemn again, but she could not maintain her expression; she hid her face in her hands.

"Isn't that illegal?" I said.

"No, it's not illegal. That's why it's called the Bishop's Discretionary Fund; he gets to do with it what he wants. I'm going to go to work for him as—we haven't decided, but some kind of general secretary, like a booking agent or something, to handle all the speeches and traveling he does. His business affairs. I can still stay on with the organization . . . FEM, I mean." She was silent a moment and then she said, "The problem is going to be Bill. I can't tell him because he's nuts again. I shouldn't say that. Deep autistic fugal withdrawal with impaired ideation compounded with delusions of reference, plus alternating catatonic stupor and excitement. He's down at Hoover Pavilion, at Stanford. Mostly for diagnosis. In terms of diagnosis, they're the best on the West Coast. They use something like four psychiatrists for diagnosis, three from the hospital itself and one from outside."

"I'm sorry," I said.

"The Army thing did it. Anxiety about being drafted. They accused him of malingering. Well, I guess it's part of life. He had to drop out of school anyhow. He would have had to drop school anyhow, is what I'm trying to say. His episodes always begin the same way—he starts crying and he doesn't take out the trash. The crying part doesn't bother me; it's the goddamn trash. It just piles up, trash and garbage. And he doesn't bathe. And he stays in his apartment. And he doesn't pay his utility bills, so they cut off his gas and electricity. And he starts writing letters to the White House. This is one area Tim and I haven't discussed. I really don't discuss it with very many people. So I would estimate that I can keep our affair—my affair with Tim —secret because I've had practice keeping things secret. No, pardon me; it doesn't begin with him crying—it begins with him not being able to drive his car. Driving phobia; he's afraid he'll veer off the road. First it has to do with the Eastshore

Freeway and then it spreads to all the other streets, and then he winds up afraid to walk to the store, so as a result he can't shop for food. But that doesn't matter because by that time he isn't eating anything anyhow." She lapsed into silence. "There's a Bach cantata about it," she said finally, and I saw her try to smile. "A line in the 'Coffee Cantata.' About having trouble with your children. They're a hundred thousand miseries, something like that. Bill used to play the goddamn thing. Few people know Bach wrote a cantata about coffee, but he did."

We walked in silence.

"It sounds as if—" I said.

"It's schizophrenia. They use him to try out every new phenothiazine that comes along. He goes in cycles, but the cycles get worse. He's sick longer and he's more sick. I shouldn't have brought it up; it's not your problem."

"I don't mind."

Kirsten said, "Maybe Tim can effect a deep spiritual cure. Didn't Jesus cure mentally ill people?"

"He sent the evil spirits into a bunch of pigs," I said. "And they all rushed over a cliff."

"That seems like a waste," Kirsten said.

"They may have eaten them anyhow."

"Not if they were Jews. Anyhow, who would want to eat a pork chop that had an evil spirit in it? I shouldn't joke about this, but—I will talk to Tim about it. But not for a while. I think Bill got it from me. I'm screwed up, God knows. I'm screwed up and I screwed him up. I keep looking at Jeff and noticing the difference between them; they're about the same age and Jeff has such a good grip on reality."

"Don't bet on it," I said.

Kirsten said, "When Bill gets out of the hospital, I'd like him to meet Tim. I'd like him to meet your husband, in fact; they never have met, have they?"

"No," I said. "But if you think Jeff can serve as a role-model, I'm really not—"

"Bill has very few friends. He's not outgoing. I've talked about you and your husband; you're both his age."

Thinking about it, I perceived down the pipe of time Kirsten's lunatic son messing up our lives. That thought surprised me. It was utterly devoid of charity and it had in it an essence of fear.

I knew my husband and I knew myself. Neither of us was ready to take on the job of amateur therapy. Kirsten, however, was an organizer. She organized people into doing things, good things but things not necessarily to their own benefit.

I had, at that instant, a keen intuition that I was being hustled. At the Bad Luck, I had essentially witnessed Bishop Archer and Kirsten Lundborg hustle each other in an intricate transaction, but it was, apparently, a transaction that benefited them both, or anyhow they both thought so. This, with her son Bill, looked to me like a purely one-way matter. I didn't see what we had to gain.

"Let me know when he's out," I said. "But I think that Tim, because of his professional training, would be a better—"

"But there's the age difference. And you get the element of the father-figure."

"Maybe that would be good. Maybe that's what your son needs."

Glaring at me, Kirsten said, "I've done an excellent job of raising Bill. His father walked out of our lives and never looked back."

"I didn't mean—"

"I know what you meant." Kirsten stared at me, and now, really, she had changed; she was angry and I could see hatred on her face. It made her look older. It made her look, in fact, physically ill. She had a bloated quality and I felt uncomfortable. I thought, then, of the pigs that Jesus had cast the evil spirits into, the pigs that rushed over the cliff. This is what you do when an evil spirit inhabits you, I thought. This is the sign, this look: the stigma. Maybe your son did inherit it from you.

But now we had an altered situation. Now she was my father-in-law's *pro tem* lover, potentially his mistress. I couldn't tell Kirsten to go fuck herself. She was family—in an illegal and unethical way. I was stuck with her. All of the curses of family, I thought, and none of the blessings. And I arranged it. The idea of introducing her and Tim had been mine. Bad karma, I thought, come back from the other side of the barn. As my father used to say.

Standing there in the grass near the San Francisco Bay, in the midafternoon sunlight, I felt uncomfortable. This is really in some respects a reckless and savage person, I said to myself.

She dabbles in the life of a famous and respected man; she has a psychotic son; pins bristle from her as from an animal. Bishop Archer's future depends on Kirsten not flying into a rage one day and phoning up the *Chronicle*—his future depends on her unending goodwill.

"Let's go back to Berkeley," I said.

"No." Kirsten shook her head. "I have yet to find a dress I can wear. I came to the City to shop. Clothes are very important to me. They have to be; I'm seen in public a lot and I expect to be seen much more, now that I'm with Tim." Rage still showed on her face.

I said, "I'll go back by BART." I walked away.

"She's a very attractive woman," Jeff said that night when I told him. "Considering her age."

"Kirsten is on reds," I said.

"You don't know that."

"I suspect it. Her mood-changes. I've seen her take them. Yellow jackets. You know. Barbiturates. Sleeping pills."

"Everybody takes something. You smoke grass."

I said, "But I'm sane."

"You may not be when you get to be her age. It's too bad about her son."

"It's too bad about your father."

"Tim can manage her."

"He may have to have her killed."

Eying me, Jeff said, "What a strange thing to say."

"She's out of control. And what happens when Bounding Bill the Dingaling finds out?"

"I thought you said—"

"He'll be out. It costs thousands of dollars to be in Hoover Pavilion. You stay about four days. I've known people who passed in their front door and out the back. Even with all the financial resources of the Episcopal Diocese of California, Kirsten can't keep him in there. He'll bound out on kangaroo-spring shoes one of these days, his eyes rolling around in their sockets —that's all Tim needs. First she has me introduce her to Tim; *then* she tells me about her son the madman. Tim'll be preaching a sermon some Sunday morning at Grace Cathedral, and all of a sudden this lunatic will stand up and God will grant him the gift of tongues and that'll be the end of the most famous bishop in America."

"Life is a risk."

I said, "That's probably what Dr. King said that last morning of his life. They're all dead but Tim anyhow; Dr. King is dead; Bobby Kennedy and Jack Kennedy are dead—I've set up your father." I knew it that evening as I sat with my husband in our little living room. "He stops bathing; he stops taking out the garbage; he writes letters; what more do you need to know? He's probably writing a letter to the pope right now. Martians probably walked through the wall of his room and told him about his mother and your father. Christ. And I did it." I reached around under the couch for my beer can of grass.

"Don't get loaded. Please."

You worry about me, I thought, when madness rules our friends. "One joint," I said. "Half a joint. I'll toke up. A puff. I'll look at the joint. I'll pretend to look at the joint." I fished the empty beer can out. I guess I moved my stash, I said to myself. To a safer place. I remember; in the middle of the night, I decided that monsters were going to rip me off. Mad Margaret from *Ruddigore* enters, the picture of theatrical madness, or however Gilbert put it. "Maybe I smoked it all up," I said. And I don't remember, I thought, because that's what mary jane does to you: fucks up your short-term memory. Probably I smoked it up five minutes ago and already I've forgotten.

"You're borrowing trouble," Jeff said. "I like Kirsten. I think it'll work out. Tim misses my mother."

Tim misses getting his rocks off, I said to myself. "That is a truly kinky lady," I said. "I had to come home by snail train. It took two hours. I'm going to talk to your father."

"No you're not."

"I will. I'm responsible. My stash is behind the stereo tuner. I'm going to get totally wasted and phone Tim and tell him that—" I hesitated, and then futility crushed me; I felt like crying. Seating myself, I got out a Kleenex. "Goddamn it," I said. "Fry the bacon is not a game bishops are supposed to play. If I had known he felt that way—"

" 'Fry the bacon'?" Jeff said wonderingly.

"Pathology frightens me. I sense pathology. I sense highly professional, responsible people wrecking their lives in exchange for a warm body, a temporarily warm body. I don't even sense the bodies staying warm, for that matter. I sense everything getting cold. You're only supposed to get into such limited time-binding if you're on junk and think in hours; these people are supposed to think in terms of decades. Lifetimes. They meet in a restaurant run by Fred the Hatchetman, which is ill-omen incarnate, the ghost of Berkeley coming back to get us all, and when they leave they have each other's phone number and it's all accomplished. What I wanted to do was help a women's lib group, but then everyone queeged out on me, you included. You were there; you watched it happen. *I* watched it happen. I was as crazy as the rest of you; I suggested that Fred the Soviet narc get photographed with the Bishop of the Diocese of California—they should have been in drag, according to my logic. The trouble with seeing ruin coming is that—" I wiped at my eyes. "Please, God, let me locate my mary jane. Jeff, look behind the tuner. It's in a Carl's Junior bag, a white bag. Okay?"

"Okay." Obligingly, Jeff rummaged behind the tuner. "I found it. Calm down."

"You can see ruin but you can't see what direction it's coming from. It just sort of hangs there, like a cloud. Who was that character in *Li'l Abner* who had the cloud following him around? You know, this was the stuff the FBI was trying to hang on Martin Luther King. Nixon loves this shit. Maybe Kirsten is a government agent. Maybe I am. Maybe we're programmed. Pardon me for playing Cassandra in our collective movie, but I see death. I thought Tim Archer, your father, was a spiritual person. Does he dive into—" I broke off. "My metaphor is offensive. Forget it. Does he go after women like this normally? I mean, is this just merely the fact that I know about it and arranged it? Remind me not to go to Mass, not that I ever do. There's no telling where the hands that hold out the chalice—"

"That's enough."

"No, I get to be crazy along with Bong-Bong-Bill and Creepy Kirsten and Tim the No-Longer-Torpid. And Jeff the Jerk, you jerk. Is there a joint already rolled, or do I have to chew up grass like a cow? I can't roll a joint right now; look." I held out my hands; they shook. "This is called a *grand mal* seizure. Get somebody in here. Get up to the Avenue and score me some tranks. I will tell you what is coming: somebody's life is going to get destroyed because of all this, not 'this' that I'm doing right now but 'this' that I did at the Bad Luck, appropriately named. When I die, I will have a choice: head up in shit or head down in shit. Shit is the word for it, what I did." I had begun to gasp. Crying and gasping, I reached for the joint my husband held. "Light it for me," I said, "you fool. I really can't chew it up; it's a waste. You have to chew up half a lid to get off, or at least I do. God knows about the rest of the world; maybe they can get off anyhow, any time. Head down in shit and never able to get loaded again—exactly what I deserve. And if I could call it all back, if I knew any way to call it back, I would. I am cursed with total insight. I see and—"

"You want to go to Kaiser?"

"The hospital?" I stared at him.

"I mean, you're out of control."

"That's what total insight does for you. Thanks." I took the joint, which he had lit, and inhaled. At least now I could no longer talk. And pretty soon I would no longer know or think. Or even remember. Put on *Sticky Fingers*, I said to myself. The Stones. "Sister Morphine." Hearing about all those bloody sheets calms me. I wish there was a comforting hand placed on my head, I thought. I'm not the one who's going to be dead tomorrow, although I should be. Let us by all means name the most innocent person possible. That will be the one. "The bitch made me walk home. From San Francisco."

"You took—"

"That's walking."

Jeff said, "I like her. I think she's a good friend. I think she will be—and probably is already—good for Dad. Has it occurred to you that you're jealous?"

"What?" I said.

"That's right. I said jealous. You're jealous of the relationship. You wish you were part of it. I see your reaction as an insult to me. I should be—our relationship should be—enough for you."

"I'm going for a walk."

"Suit yourself."

"If you had eyes in the front of your head—let me finish. I'll be calm. I'll say it calmly. Tim is not just a religious figure; he speaks for thousands in the church and outside the church, maybe more so outside. Do you grasp it? If he tumbles, we all take a fall. We all are doomed. He is almost the last one left; the others are dead. The thing about this is, it isn't necessary. It's like he decided. He saw it and he walked right at it; he didn't duck and he didn't fight—he embraced it. You think this— what I feel—is because I had to come home on the train? One by one, they got every public figure and now Tim hands over the keys, hands them over under his own power, without a fight."

"And *you* want to fight. Me, if necessary."

I said, "I see you as stupid. I see everyone as dumb. I see stupidity winning. This is not something the Pentagon is doing. This is dumb. This is walking right at it and saying, 'Take me, I'm—'"

"Jealousy," Jeff said. "Your psychological motivation is all over this house."

"I have no 'psychological motivation.' I just want to see someone there when the firing ends, someone who isn't—" I broke off. "Don't come around later and say this was done to us, because it wasn't. And don't tell me it was a complete surprise. A bishop who has an affair with a woman he meets in a restaurant—this is a man who just finished backing over a gasoline pump and drove happily away. And the pump came after him. That's how it works: you flatten some joker's pump and he runs until he catches up with you. You're in a car and he's on foot, but he seeks you out and then, all of a sudden, there he is. This is that; this is someone chasing us down and he will catch up; he always does. I saw that pump jockey; he was mad. He was going to keep running. They never give up."

"And you see that now. Due to one of your best friends."

"That's the worst kind."

Grinning, Jeff said, "I know that story. It's a W. C. Fields story. There's this director—"

"And she isn't running any more," I said. "She caught up with him. They're renting an apartment. All it takes is one nosy neighbor. What about this redneck bishop prosecuting Tim for heresy? What would he do with this? If someone is after you for heresy, do you bang the next broad you meet for lunch? And then go shopping for an apartment? Look." I walked over to my husband. "Where do you go after being a bishop? Is Tim tired of that already? He got tired of everything else he ever did. He even got tired of being an alcoholic; he's the only hopeless drunk who sobered himself up out of boredom, out of a short attention span. People generally will their own misfortune. I see us doing that now. I see him getting bored and subconsciously saying, 'What the hell; it's dull putting on these funny clothes every day; let's stir up some human misery and see what comes out of it.' "

Laughing, Jeff said, "You know what—who—you remind me of? The witch in Purcell's *Dido and Aeneas*."

"What do you mean?"

" 'Who, like dismal ravens crying, Beat the windows of the dying.' I'm sorry but—"

"You fool Berkeley intellectual," I said. "What horse's ass world do you inhabit? Not the same as me, I hope. Quoting some old verse—that's what did us in. They will report when they dig up our bones—your dad quoted the Bible in the restaurant the same way you're doing now. You ought to hit me or me you. I'll be glad when civilization ends. People babble out bits of books. Put on *Sticky Fingers*—put on 'Sister Morphine.' I can't be trusted with the stereo at this moment. You do it for me. Thanks for the joint."

"When you've calmed down—"

"When you've woken up," I said, "it'll all be over."

Jeff bent to search for the record I wanted to hear. He said nothing. Finally he had become angry. A dollar short and a day late, I thought, and at the wrong person. Like with me. Destroyed by our giant intellects: reasoning and pondering and doing nothing. Nitwits rule. We squabble. The sorceress in *Dido*; you are right. "*Thy hand, Belinda, darkness shades me; on thy bosom let me rest: more I would, but Death invades me*—" And what else does she say? "*Death is now a welcome guest.*" Shit, I thought. It is relevant. He's right. Absolutely right.

Fiddling with the stereo, Jeff put the Stones' record on.

The music calmed me. A little. But I still cried, thinking about Tim. And all because they are stupid. It goes no deeper than that. And that is the worst of it all, that it is that simple. That there is no more.

*

A few days later, after thinking about it and making up my mind, I phoned Grace Cathedral and got an appointment to see Tim. He met me in his office, which was large and beautiful, in a building separate from the cathedral itself. After greeting me with a hug and kiss, he showed me two ancient clay vessels which, he explained, had been used as oil lamps in the Near East over four thousand years ago. As I watched him handling them, the thought came to me that the lamps probably—in fact, certainly—did not belong to him; they belonged to the Diocese. I wondered what they were worth. It was amazing that they had survived all these years.

"It's nice of you to give me some of your time," I said. "I know how busy you are."

The expression on Tim's face told me that he knew why I had shown up in his office. He nodded absently, as if, in fact, giving me as little of his attention as he could manage. I had seen him tune out that way several times; a part of his brain listened, but the greater part had sealed itself off already.

When I had finished delivering my set little speech, Tim said gravely, "Paul, you know, had been a Pharisee. For them a strict observance of the minutiae of the Torah—the Law—was everything. That particularly involved ritual purity. But later—after his conversion—he saw salvation not in the Law but in *zadiqah*, which is the state of righteousness that Jesus Christ brings. I want you to sit down with me here." He beckoned me over, opening a very large leatherbound Bible. "You're familiar with Romans, four through eight?"

"No, I'm not," I said. But I sat down beside him. I could see it coming, the lecture. The sermon. Tim had met me prepared.

"Romans five states Paul's basic premise, that we are saved through grace and not by works." He read, then, from the Bible he held open on his lap. " 'So far then we have seen that, through our Lord Jesus Christ, by faith we are judged righteous and at peace with God—' " He glanced up at me; his gaze was keen and sharp. This was Timothy Archer the lawyer. " '—since it is by faith and through Jesus that we have entered this state of grace in which we can boast about looking forward to God's glory.' Let's see." He ran his fingers down the page, his lips moving. " 'If it is certain that through one man's fall so many died, it is even more certain that divine grace, coming through the one man, Jesus Christ, came to so many as an abundant free gift.' He looked further on, turning pages. "Yes; ah. Here. 'But now we are rid of the Law, freed by death from our imprisonment, free to serve in the new spiritual way and not the old way of a written law.'" Again he looked further along. "'The reason, therefore, why those who are in Christ Jesus are not condemned, is that the law of the spirit of life in Christ Jesus has set you free from the law of sin and death.'" He glanced up at me. "This goes to the heart of Paul's perception. What 'sin' really refers to is hostility toward God. Literally, it means 'missing the mark,' as if, for example, you shot an arrow and it fell short, too low, or went too high. What mankind needs, what it requires, is righteousness. Only God has that and only God can provide it to men . . . men and women; I don't mean—"

"I understand," I said.

"Paul's perception is that faith, *pistis*, has the power, the absolute power, to kill sin. Out of this comes freedom from the Law; one is not required to believe that by following a formal stipulated code—code-ethics, it's called—one is saved. That position, that one is saved by following a very intricate, complex system of code-ethics, is what Paul rebelled against; that was the position of the Pharisees and that's what he turned from. This really is what Christianity, faith in our Lord Jesus Christ, is all about; righteousness through grace, and grace coming through faith. I'm going to have you read—"

"Yes," I said, "but the Bible says you're not supposed to commit adultery."

Instantly, Tim said, "Adultery is sexual unfaithfulness on the part of a married person. I am no longer married; Kirsten is no longer married."

"Oh," I said, nodding.

"The Seventh Commandment. Which pertains to the sanctity of marriage." Tim set down his Bible and crossed the room to the vast bookshelves; he lifted down a blue-backed volume. As he returned, he opened the book and searched its pages. "Let me quote to you what Dr. Hertz said, the late Chief Rabbi of the British Empire. In connection with the Seventh Commandment. Exodus, twenty thirteen. 'Adultery. Is an execrable and god-detested wrong-doing.' Philo. This Commandment against infidelity warns husband and wife alike against profaning the sacred Covenant of Marriage.'" He read further silently, then shut the book. "I think you have enough common sense, Angel, to understand that Kirsten and I are—"

"But it's risky," I said.

"Driving on the Golden Gate Bridge is risky. Do you know that Yellow Cabs are not allowed—I mean, not allowed by Yellow Cab, not the police—to drive in the fast lane on the Golden Gate Bridge? What they call 'suicide lane.' If a driver is caught driving in that lane he is fired. But people drive in the fast lane on the Golden Gate Bridge constantly. Maybe that's a poor analogy."

"No, it's a good one," I said.

"Do you drive in the fast lane on the Golden Gate Bridge?"

After a pause I said, "Sometimes."

"What if I came to you and sat you down and started lecturing you about it? Wouldn't you think I was treating you as a child, not an adult? Do you follow what I'm saying? When an adult does something you don't approve of, you discuss the matter with him or her. I'm willing to discuss my relationship with Kirsten with you because, for one thing, you're my daughter-in-law, but much more important, you're someone I know and care about and love. I think that's the salient term, here; it's the key to Paul's thinking. *Agape* in the Greek. Translated into Latin, it's *caritas*, from which we get the word 'caring,' to be concerned about someone. As you're concerned about me now, myself and your friend Kirsten. You care about us."

"That's right," I said. "That's why I'm here."

"Then for you, caring is important."

"Yes," I said. "Obviously."

"You can call it *agape* or you can call it *caritas* or love or caring about another person, but whatever you call it—let me read from Paul." Bishop Archer again opened his big Bible; he flipped through the pages rapidly, knowing exactly where he was going. "First Corinthians, chapter thirteen. 'If I have the gift of prophecy, understanding—'"

"Yes, you quoted that at the Bad Luck," I interrupted.

"And I will quote it again." His voice was brisk. "'If I give away all that I possess, piece by piece, and if I even let them take my body to burn it, but am without love, it will do me no good whatever.' Now listen to this. 'Love does not come to an end. But if there are gifts of prophecy, the time will come when they must fail; or the gift of languages, it will not continue for ever; and knowledge—for this, too, the time will come when it must fail. For our knowledge is imperfect and our prophesying is imperfect, but once perfection comes, all imperfect things will disappear. When I was a child, I used to talk like a child, and think like a child, and argue like a child, but now I am a man, all childish ways are put behind me.'"

The phone on his big desk rang, then.

Looking annoyed, Bishop Archer set down his Bible, open. "Excuse me." He went to get the phone.

As I sat, waiting for him to finish his phone conversation, I looked over the passage he had been reading. It was a passage familiar to me, but in the King James translation. This Bible, I saw, was the Jerusalem Bible. I had never seen it before. I read on past the point at which he had stopped.

His phone conversation finished, Bishop Archer returned. "I have to be off. There's an African bishop waiting to see me; they just brought him here from the airport."

"It says," I said, putting my finger on the passage in his big Bible, "that all we see is a dim reflection."

"It also says, 'In short there are three things that last: faith, hope and love; and the greatest of these is love.' I would point out to you that that sums up the *kerygma* of our Lord."

"What if Kirsten tells people?"

"I think she can be counted on to be discreet." He had already reached the door of his office; reflexively, I rose to my feet and followed after him.

"She told me."

"You're my son's wife."

"Yeah, well—"

"I'm sorry I have to run off like this." Bishop Archer shut and locked his office door behind us. "God bless." He kissed me on the forehead. "We want to have you over when we're set up. Kirsten found an apartment today, in the Tenderloin. I haven't seen it. I'm leaving that up to her." And off he strode, leaving me standing there. He got me on a technicality, I realized. I had adultery confused with fornication. I keep forgetting he was a lawyer. I entered his large office with something to say and never said it; I went in smart and came out stupid. With nothing in between.

Maybe if I didn't smoke dope I could argue better. He won; I lost. No: he lost; I lost; we both lost. Shit.

I never said love was bad. I never knocked *agape*. That was not the point, the fucking point. Not getting caught is the point. Bolting your feet down to the floor is the point, the floor we call reality.

As I started toward the street, I thought: I am passing judgment on one of the most successful men in the world. I will never be known as he is known; I will never influence opinion. I did not put away my pectoral cross for the duration of the Vietnam War as Tim did. Who the fuck am I?

4

Not long thereafter, Jeff and I received an invitation to visit the Bishop of California and his mistress at their hideout in the Tenderloin. It turned out to be a sort of party. Kirsten had fixed canapés and hors d'oeuvres; we could smell food cooking in the kitchen . . . Tim had me drive him to a nearby liquor store to get wine; they had forgotten. I chose the wine. Tim stood blankly, as if abstracted, while I paid the clerk. I guess when you've been a member of AA, you learn to phase out in a liquor store.

Back at the apartment, in the medicine cabinet of the bathroom, I found a vast bottle of Dexamyl, the size bottle they give you when you're going on a long trip. Kirsten doing speed? I asked myself. Making no noise, I took down the bottle. The bishop's name was on the prescription label. Well, I thought. Off booze and onto speed. Aren't they supposed to warn you about that in AA? I flushed the toilet—so as to create some sound—and while the water gurgled I opened the bottle and stuck a few of the Dex tablets in my pocket. This is something you automatically do if you live in Berkeley; no one thinks anything about it. On the other hand, no one in Berkeley leaves their dope in the bathroom.

Presently, the four of us sat around the modest living room, relaxing. Everyone but Tim held a drink. Tim wore a red shirt and permapress slacks. He did not look like a bishop. He looked like Kirsten Lundborg's lover.

"This is a really nice place," I said.

On the way home from the liquor store, Tim had talked about private detectives and how they go about finding you. They sneak into your apartment while you're gone and go through all the dresser drawers. The way you catch on to this is by taping a human hair to every outer door. I think Tim had seen that in a movie.

"If you come back and find the hair gone or broken," he informed me as we walked from the car to the apartment, "you know you're being watched." He narrated, then, the history of the FBI in regard to Dr. King. It was a story everyone in Berkeley knew. I listened politely.

In the living room of their hideout that evening, I first heard about the Zadokite Documents. Now, of course, you can buy the Doubleday Anchor book, the Patton, Myers and Abré translation, which is complete. With the Helen James introduction dealing with mysticism, comparing and contrasting the Zadokites with, for example, the Qumran people, who presumably were Essenes, although that has really never been established.

"I feel," Tim said, "that this may prove more important than even the Nag Hammadi Library. We already have a fair working knowledge of Gnosticism, but we know nothing about the Zadokites, except for the fact that they were Jews."

"What is the approximate date on the Zadokite scrolls?" Jeff asked.

"They have made a preliminary estimate of about two hundred B.C.E.," Tim said.

"Then they could have influenced Jesus," Jeff said.

"It's not likely," Tim said. "I'll be flying over there to London in March; I'll have a chance to talk to the translators. I wish John Allegro were involved, but he's not." He talked for a while about Allegro's work in connection with the Qumran scrolls, the so-called Dead Sea Scrolls.

"Wouldn't it be interesting," Kirsten said, "if the—" She hesitated. "Zadokite Documents turned out to contain Christian material."

"Christianity is, after all, based on Judaism," Tim said.

"I mean specific sayings attributed to Jesus," Kirsten said.

"There is not that clear a break in the rabbinical tradition," Tim said. "You find Hillel expressing some of the ideas we consider basic to the New Testament. And of course Matthew understood everything that Jesus did and said as a fulfillment of Old Testament prophecies. Matthew wrote to Jews and for Jews and, essentially, as a Jew. God's plan set forth in the Old Testament is brought to completion by Jesus. The term 'Christianity' was not in use at his time; by and large, apostolic Christians simply spoke of 'the Way.' Thus they stressed its naturalness and universality." After a pause he added, "And you find the expression 'the word of the Lord.' That appears in Acts, six.

'The word of the Lord continued to spread; the number of disciples in Jerusalem was greatly increased.'"

"What does 'Zadokite' derive from?" Kirsten asked.

"Zadok, a priest of Israel, about the time of David," Tim said. "He founded a priestly house, the Zadokites. They were of the house of Eleazar. There is mention of Zadok in the Qumran scrolls. Let me check." He rose to go get a book from a still-unpacked carton. "First Chronicles, chapter twenty-four. 'These also, side by side with their kinsmen the sons of Aaron, cast lots in the presence of Kind David, Zadok—' There he is mentioned." Tim shut the book. It was another Bible.

"But I guess now we're going to find out a lot more," Jeff said.

"Yes, I hope so," Tim said. "When I'm in London." He now, as was his custom, abruptly shifted mental gears. "I'm commissioning a rock mass to be given at Grace this Christmas." Scrutinizing me he said, "What is your opinion about Frank Zappa?"

I was at a loss for an answer.

"We would arrange for the actual service to be recorded," Tim continued. "So it could be released as an album. Captain Beefheart has also been recommended to me. And there were several other names offered. Where could I get a Frank Zappa album to listen to?"

"At a record store," Jeff said.

"Is Frank Zappa black?" Tim asked.

"I don't see that that matters," Kirsten said. "To me, that is inverse prejudice."

Tim said, "I was just curious. This is an area I know nothing about. Does any of you have an opinion about Marc Bolan?"

"He's dead," I said. "You're talking about T. Rex."

"Marc Bolan is dead?" Jeff said. He looked amazed.

"I could be wrong," I said. "I suggest Ray Davies. He writes the Kinks' stuff. He's very good."

"Would you look into it for me?" Tim said, speaking both to Jeff and me.

"I wouldn't know how to go about doing that," I said.

Kirsten said quietly, "I'll take care of it."

"You could get Paul Kantner and Gracie Slick," I said. "They just live over at Bolinas in Marin County."

"I know," Kirsten said, nodding placidly and with the air of total confidence.

Bullshit, I thought. You don't even know who I'm talking about. Already you're in charge, just from being set up in this apartment. It isn't even that much of an apartment.

Tim said, "I would like Janis Joplin to sing at Grace."

"She died in 1970," I said.

"Then whom do you recommend in her place?" Tim asked. He waited expectantly.

" 'In Janis Joplin's place,' " I said. " 'In Janis Joplin's place.' I'll have to think that over. I really can't come up with a name off the top of my head. That will take some time."

Kirsten regarded me with a mixture of expressions. Mostly disapproval. "I think what she's trying to say," Kirsten said, "is that no one can or ever will take Joplin's place."

"Where would I get one of her records?" Tim said.

"At a record store," Jeff said.

"Would you do that for me?" his father said.

"Jeff and I have all her records," I said. "There aren't that many. We'll bring them over."

"Ralph McTell," Kirsten said.

"I want all these suggestions written down," Tim said. "A rock mass at Grace Cathedral is going to attract a good deal of attention."

I thought: There is no such person as Ralph McTell. From across the room Kirsten smiled at me, a complicated smile. She had me; I couldn't be sure one way or another.

"He's on the Paramount label," Kirsten said. Her smile increased.

"I had really hoped to get Janis Joplin," Tim said, half to himself. He seemed puzzled. "They were playing a song with her—perhaps she didn't write it—on the car radio this morning. She's black, isn't she?"

"She is white," Jeff said, "and she is dead."

"I hope somebody is writing this down," Tim said.

My husband's emotional involvement with Kirsten Lundborg did not begin at one particular moment on a certain day, at least so far as I could discern. Initially, he maintained that Kirsten was good for the bishop; she had enough practical realism to keep both of them anchored, not floating endlessly upward. It is necessary, in evaluating these things, to distinguish your awareness from that of which you are aware. I can say when I noticed it but that is all I can say.

Considering her age, Kirsten still managed to emit tolerable amounts of sexually stimulating waves. That was how Jeff saw her. From my standpoint she remained an older female friend who now, by virtue of her relationship with Bishop Archer, outranked me. The degree of erotic provocativeness in a woman has no interest for me; I do not swing both ways, as the expression goes. Nor for me is it a threat. Until, of course, my own husband is involved. But the problem is with him, then.

While I worked at the law office and candle shop, seeing to it that drug dealers got out of trouble as fast as they got in, Jeff bothered his head with a series of extension courses at the University of California. We in Northern California had not quite reached the point of offering survey courses in how to compose your own mantras; that belonged to the Southland, totally despised by everyone in the Bay Area. Jeff had enrolled in a serious project: tracing the ills of modern Europe back to the Thirty Years War which had devastated Germany (circa 1648), caused the collapse of the Holy Roman Empire, and culminated in the rise of Nazism and Hitler's Third Reich. Above and beyond the courses pertaining to this, Jeff now advanced his own theory as to the root of it all. Upon reading Schiller's *Wallenstein Trilogy*, Jeff leaped to the intuitive insight that had the great general not gotten involved with astrology the imperial cause would have triumphed, and, as a result, World War Two would never have come into being.

The third play in Schiller's trilogy, *The Death of Wallenstein*, profoundly affected my husband. He regarded the play as equal to any of Shakespeare's and a whole lot better than most. Moreover, no one had read it—at least insofar as he could tell—except himself. To him, Wallenstein loomed as one of the ultimate enigmas of Western history. Jeff noted that Hitler, like Wallenstein, relied in times of crisis on the occult rather than on reason. In Jeff's view this all added up to something significant, but he could not fathom just what. Hitler and Wallenstein had had so many traits in common—Jeff maintained—that the resemblance bordered on the uncanny. Both were great but eccentric generals and both had utterly wrecked Germany. Jeff hoped to do a paper on the coincidences, extracting from the evidence the conclusion that the abandoning of Christianity for the occult opened the door to universal ruin. Jesus and Simon Magus (as Jeff saw it) stood as the bipolarities, absolute and distinct.

I couldn't have cared less.

You see, this is what going to school forever and ever does to you. While I slaved away at the law office and candle shop, Jeff read everything in the U.C. Berkeley Library on, for instance, the Battle of Lützen (November 16, 1632) at which time and place Wallenstein's fortunes were decided. Gustavus II Adolphus, king of Sweden, died at Lützen, but the Swedes won anyhow. The real significance of this victory lay, of course, in the fact that at no time again would the Catholic powers be in a position to crush the Protestant cause. Jeff, however, viewed it all in terms of Wallenstein. He reread and reread Schiller's trilogy and tried to reconstruct from it—and from more accurate historical accounts—the precise moment when Wallenstein lost touch with reality.

"It's like with Hitler," Jeff said to me. "Can you say he was always crazy? Can you say he was crazy at all? And if he was crazy but not always crazy, when did he become crazy and what caused him to become crazy? Why should a successful man who holds really an enormous amount of power, a staggering amount of power, power to determine human history—why should he drift off like that? Okay; with Hitler it was probably paranoid schizophrenia and those injections that quack doctor was giving him. But neither factor was involved in Wallenstein's case."

Kirsten, being Norwegian, took a sympathetic interest in Jeff's preoccupation with Gustavus Adolphus' campaign into Central Europe. In between telling Swede jokes she revealed great pride in the role that the great Protestant King had played in the Thirty Years War. Also, she knew something about all this, which I did not. Both she and Jeff agreed that the Thirty Years War had been, up until World War One, the most dreadful war since the Huns sacked Rome. Germany had been reduced to cannibalism. Soldiers on both sides had regularly skewered bodies and roasted them. Jeff's reference books hinted at even more abominations too dreadful to detail. Everything connected with that period in time and place had been dreadful.

"We are still paying the price today," Jeff said, "for that war."

"Yeah, I guess it really was dreadful," I said, seated by myself in a corner of our living room reading a current issue of *Howard the Duck*.

Jeff said, "I don't think you're particularly interested."

Glancing up, I said, "I get tired from bailing out heroin dealers. I'm always the one they send over to the bail bondsman. I'm sorry if I don't take the Thirty Years War as seriously as you and Kirsten do."

"Everything hinges on the Thirty Years War. And the Thirty Years War hinged on Wallenstein."

"What are you going to do when they go to England? Your father and Kirsten."

He stared at me.

"She's going, too. She told me. They've got that agency set up, Focus Center, where she's his agent or whatever."

"Jesus Christ," Jeff said bitterly.

I went back to reading *Howard the Duck*. It was the episode where space people turn Howard the Duck into Richard Nixon. Reciprocally, Richard Nixon grows feathers while addressing the nation on network TV. Likewise the top brass at the Pentagon.

"And they're going to be gone how long?" Jeff said.

"Until Tim figures out the meaning of the Zadokite Documents and how they pertain to Christianity."

"Shit," Jeff said.

"What's 'Q'?" I said.

"'Q,'" Jeff echoed.

"Tim said that preliminary reports, based on fragmentary translations of some documents—"

"'Q' is the hypothetical source for the Synoptics." His voice was brutal and rough.

"What are the Synoptics?"

"The first three Gospels. Matthew, Mark and Luke. They supposedly come from one source, probably Aramaic. Nobody's ever been able to prove it."

"Well," I said, "Tim told me on the phone the other night while you were in class that the translators in London think that the Zadokite Documents contain—not just Q—but the material Q is based on. They're not sure. Tim sounded more excited than I ever heard him sound before."

"But the Zadokite Documents date from two hundred years before Christ."

"That's probably why he was so excited."

Jeff said, "I want to go along."

"You can't," I said.

"Why not?" Raising his voice, he said, "Why don't I get to go if she gets to go? I'm his son!"

"He's straining the Bishop's Discretionary Fund as it is. They're going to be staying several months; it's going to cost a whole lot."

Jeff walked out of the living room. I continued reading. After a time, I realized I was hearing a strange sound; I lowered my copy of *Howard the Duck* and listened.

In the kitchen, in the darkness, by himself, my husband was crying.

One of the strangest and most perplexing accounts I ever read concerning my husband's suicide was that he, Jeff Archer, Bishop Timothy Archer's son, killed himself because he was afraid he was a homosexual. Some book written a number of years after his death—after all three of them had died—mangled the facts so thoroughly that, when you had finished reading it (I don't even remember the title or who wrote it) you knew less about Jeff and Bishop Archer and Kirsten Lundborg than before you started. It is like information theory; it is noise driving out signal. But it is noise posing as signal so you do not even recognize it as noise. The intelligence agencies call it disinformation, something the Soviet Bloc relies on heavily. If you can float enough disinformation into circulation you will totally abolish everyone's contact with reality, probably your own included.

Jeff held two mutually exclusive views toward his father's mistress. On the one hand she sexually stimulated him, so he felt strongly but wickedly attracted to her. On the other hand he loathed her and hated her and resented her for—he supposed—replacing him in terms of Tim's interest and affections.

But it did not end even there . . . although I didn't discern the rest until years had passed. Beyond and above being jealous of Kirsten, he was jealous of—well, Jeff had it all screwed up; I can't really untangle it. One has to bear in mind the special problems in being the son of a man whose picture has appeared on the cover of *Time* and *Newsweek* and who gets interviewed by David Frost, shows up on the Johnny Carson program, gets political cartoons in major newspapers devoted to him—what in Christ's name do *you* do, as the son?

For one week Jeff joined them in England, and regarding that week I know little; Jeff came back mute and withdrawn, and that was when he headed for the hotel room in which he shot himself in the face one late night. I am not going to go into my feelings about that as a way of killing yourself. It did bring the bishop back from London within a matter of hours, which, in a certain sense, the suicide was all about.

In a very real sense, it also had to do with Q, or rather the source of Q, now referred to in the newspaper articles as U.Q., which is *Ur-Quelle* in German: Original Source. Behind Q lay the *Ur-Quelle*, and this is what led Timothy Archer to London and several months in a hotel with his mistress, ostensibly his business agent and general secretary.

No one had ever expected the documents behind Q to reappear in the world; no one had known that U.Q. existed. Since I am not a Christian—and never will be, after the deaths of the people I loved—I am not now and was not then particularly interested, but I suppose it is theologically important, especially so inasmuch as the date assigned to U.Q. is two hundred years before the time of Jesus.

5

WHAT I remember most, in the first newspaper articles to come out, the first intimation we had, anybody beyond the translators had, that this was an even more important find than the Qumran scrolls, was (the articles said) a particular Hebrew noun. They spell it two different ways; sometimes it showed up as *anokhi* and sometimes *anochi*.

The word shows up in Exodus, chapter twenty, verse two. This is a terribly moving and important section of the Torah, for here God Himself speaks, and he says:

> *"I am the Lord thy God, who brought thee out of*
> *the land of Egypt, out of the house of bondage."*

The first Hebrew word is *anokhi* or *anochi* and it means "I" —as in "I am the Lord thy God." Jeff showed me what the official Jewish commentary is on this part of the Torah:

> "The God adored by Judaism is not an impersonal Force, an It, whether spoken of as 'Nature' or 'World-Reason.' The God of Israel is the Source not only of power and life, but of consciousness, personality, moral purpose and ethical action."

Even for me, a non-Christian—or I should say a non-Jew, I guess—this shakes me; I am touched and changed; I am not the same. What is expressed here, Jeff explained to me, is, in this single word, one letter of the English alphabet, the unique self-consciousness of God:

> "As man towers above all the other creatures by his will and self-conscious action, so God 'rules over all as the one completely self-conscious Mind and Will. In both the visible and the invisible realms, He manifests Himself as the absolutely free personality, moral and spiritual, who allots to everything its existence, form and purpose.'"

That was written by Samuel M. Cohon, quoting Kaufmann Kohler. Another Jewish writer, Hermann Cohen, wrote:

"God answered him thus: 'I am that which I am. So shalt thou say to the children of Israel: *"I am"* has sent me to you.' There is probably no greater miracle in the history of the spirit than that revealed in this verse. For here, a primeval language which is as yet without any philosophy, emerges and haltingly pronounces the most profound word of all philosophy. The name of God is 'I am that which I am.' This signifies that God is Being, that God is the I, which denotes the Existing One."

And this is what turned up at the *wadi* in Israel, dating from 200 B.C.E., the *wadi* not far from Qumran; this word lay at the heart of the Zadokite Documents, and every Hebrew scholar knows this word, and every Christian and Jew should know it, but there at that *wadi* the word *anokhi* was used in a different way, a way no living person had ever seen it employed before. And so Tim and Kirsten stayed in London twice as long as they had intended to stay, because the very core of something had been located, the core in fact, of the Decalogue, as if the Lord had left tracings in his own autograph, which is to say, his own hand.

While these discoveries took place—in the translating stage —Jeff wandered around the U.C. Berkeley campus learning about the Thirty Years War and Wallenstein, who had cut himself off progressively from reality during the worst war, perhaps, of all wars, except for the total wars of this century; I am not going to say that I have ascertained which particular drive killed my husband, which thrust from the mix got to him, but one did or they all did in chorus—he is dead and I wasn't even there at the time, nor did I expect it. My expectation came initially when I learned that Kirsten and Tim had gotten involved in an invisible affair. I said what I had to say then; I took my best shot—I visited the bishop at Grace Cathedral and found myself outargued with little effort on his part: little effort and professional skill. It was an easy verbal victory for Tim Archer. So much for that.

If you intend to kill yourself you don't require a reason, in the usual sense of the term; just as, to the contrary, when you intend to stay alive, no verbal, articulated, formal reason is necessary, one you can seize on if the issue comes up. Jeff had been left out. I could see that his interest in the Thirty Years War really had to do with Kirsten; his mind, or some portion of it, had noted her Scandinavian origin, and another part of his mind had perceived and recorded the fact that the Swedish army was the victor and heroic power of that war; his emotional pursuits and his intellectual pursuits wove together, which was, for a time, to his advantage, and then when Kirsten flew to England he found himself wrecked by his own cleverness. Now he had to confront the fact that he didn't really give a good goddamn about Tilly and Wallenstein and the Holy Roman Empire; he was in love with a woman his mother's age who was sleeping with his father—and doing that eight thousand miles away, and above and beyond everything else the two of them, to his exclusion, participated in one of the most exhilarating archeological theology discoveries in history, on a day-to-day basis as the translations became available, as the documents got patched and pasted together and the words emerged, one by one, and again and again the Hebrew word *anokhi* manifested itself, in unusual contexts, baffling contexts: new contexts. The documents spoke as if *anokhi* were present at the *wadi*. It or he was referred to as *here*, not there, *now*, not then. *Anokhi* was not something the Zadokites thought about or knew about; *it was something they possessed*.

It is very hard to read your library books and listen to a Donovan record, no matter how good, when a discovery of that magnitude is going on in another part of the world, and if your father and his mistress, both of whom you love and at the same time furiously hate, are involved in that unfolding discovery— what drove me frantic was Jeff playing and replaying Paul McCartney's first solo album; he liked "Teddy Boy" in particular. When he left me to go live alone in the hotel room—the room where he shot himself—he took the album with him, although he had, it turned out, nothing to play it on. He wrote me a number of times, telling me that he was still active in anti-war happenings. Probably he was. I think, though, by and large he just sat alone in the hotel room trying to figure out how he felt about his father and, even more important, how he felt about Kirsten. So that would be 1971, since the McCartney album came out in 1970. But see, that left me alone, too, in our house. I got the house; Jeff died. I told you not to live alone but I am speaking, really, to myself. You can do any goddamn thing you want but I am never going to live alone again. I'll take in street people before I let that happen to me, that isolation.

Just don't play any Beatles albums around me. That's the main thing I ask. I can take Joplin, because I still think it's funny that Tim thought Joplin was alive and black instead of dead and white, but I do not want to hear the Beatles because they are linked to too much pain in me, inside me, in my life, in what happened.

I am not quite rational myself when it comes down to it, to, specifically, my husband's suicide. I hear in my mind a mélange of John and Paul and George—with Ringo thumping away in the rear somewhere—with fragments of tunes and their words, critical terms pertaining to souls suffering a great deal, although not in a way I can pin down except, of course, for my husband's death and then Kirsten's death, and finally, Tim Archer's death—but I suppose that is enough. Now, with John Lennon shot, everyone is pierced as I have been, so I can fucking well stop feeling sorry for myself and join the rest of the world, no better off than they are, no worse off either.

Often, when I look back to Jeff's suicide, I discover that I rearrange dates and events in sequences more syntonic to my mind; that is, I edit. I condense, cut bits out, do a fast number myself so that—for example—I no longer recall viewing Jeff's body and identifying it. I have managed to forget the name of the hotel where he stayed. I don't know how long he stayed there. As near as I can make out, he didn't hang around the house very long after Tim and Kirsten flew to London; one early letter came from them, typed: signed by both of them but almost certainly written by Kirsten. Possibly Tim dictated it. The first hint of the magnitude of the find showed up in that letter. I didn't recognize what the news implied but Jeff did. So, perhaps, he left right after that.

What surprised me the most was to grasp, all at once, that Jeff had wanted to go into the priesthood, but what point was there, in view of his father's role? But this left a vacuum. Jeff did not want to do anything else either. He *could* not become a priest; he did not care about any other profession. So he remained what we in Berkeley called a "professional student"; he never stopped going to Cal. Maybe he left and came back. Our marriage hadn't been working for some time; I have blank spots back to 1968, perhaps a full year missing in all. Jeff had emotional problems that I later repressed any knowledge of. We both repressed it. There is always free psychotherapy in the Bay Area and we took advantage of it.

I don't think Jeff could be called—could have been called—mentally ill; he simply wasn't terribly happy. Sometimes it is not a drive to die but a failure of a subtle kind, a failing of the sense of joy. He fell out of life by degrees. When he came across someone he genuinely wanted she became his father's mistress, whereupon they both flew to England, leaving him to study a war he didn't care about, leaving him stranded back where he had started from. He started out not caring; he wound up not caring. One of the doctors did say he believed that Jeff started taking LSD during that period after he left me and before he shot himself. That is only a theory. However, unlike the homosexual theory, it may have been true.

Thousands of young people kill themselves in America each year, but it remains the custom, by and large, to list their deaths as accidental. This is to spare the family the shame attached to suicide. There is, indeed, something shameful about a young man or woman, maybe an adolescent, wanting to die and achieving that goal, dead before in a certain sense they ever lived, ever were born. Wives get beaten by their husbands; cops kill blacks and Latinos; old people rummage in garbage cans or eat dog food—shame rules, calling the shots. Suicide is only one shameful event out of a plethora. There are black teenagers who will never get a job as long as they live, not because they are lazy but because there are no jobs—because, too, these ghetto kids possess no skills they can sell. Children run away, find the strip in New York or Hollywood; they become prostitutes and wind up with their bodies hacked apart. If the impulse to slay the Spartan runners reporting the battle results, the outcome at Thermopylae, rises in you, by all means slay them. I am those runners and I report what you do not want, most likely, to hear. Personally, I report only three deaths, but three more than were necessary. This is the day John Lennon died; you wish to slay those who report that, too? As Sri Krishna says when he assumes his true form, his universal form, that of time:

> *"All these hosts must die; strike, stay your hand— no matter.*
> *Seem to slay. By me these men are slain already."*

It is an awful sight. Arjuna has seen what he cannot believe exists.

> *"Licking with your burning tongues,*
> *Devouring all the worlds,*
> *You probe the heights of heaven*
> *With intolerable beams, O Vishnu."*

What Arjuna sees was once his friend and charioteer. A man like himself. That was only an aspect, a kindly disguise. Sri Krishna wished to spare him, to hide the truth. Arjuna asked to see Sri Krishna's true form and he got to see it. He will not now be as he was. The spectacle has changed him, changed him forever. This is the true forbidden fruit, this kind of knowledge. Sri Krishna waited a long time before he showed Arjuna his actual shape. He wanted to spare him. The true shape, that of the universal destroyer, emerged at last.

I would not want to make you unhappy by detailing pain, but there is a crucial sort of difference between pain and the narration of pain. I am telling you what happened. If there is vicarious pain in knowing, there is actual peril in not knowing. In aversion lies a colossal risk.

When Kirsten and the bishop had returned to the Bay Area —not permanently but, rather, to deal with Jeff's death and the problems raised by it—I could upon seeing them again notice a change in both of them. Kirsten looked worn and wretched, and this did not seem to me to emanate from the shock of Jeff's death alone. Obviously she was in ill health in purely physical terms. On the other hand, Bishop Archer seemed even more animated than when I had last seen him. He took complete charge of the situation regarding Jeff; he selected the burial spot, the kind of gravestone; he delivered the eulogy and all other rites, wearing full robes, and he paid for everything. The inscription on the gravestone came as a result of his inspiration. He chose a phrase which I found quite acceptable; it is the motto or basic statement of the school of Heraclitus: NO SINGLE THING ABIDES; BUT ALL THINGS FLOW. I had been taught in philosophy class that Heraclitus himself invented that, but Tim explained that this summation came after Heraclitus, by those of his school who followed him. They believed that only flux, which is to say change, is real. They may have been right.

The three of us joined together after the graveside service; we returned to the Tenderloin apartment and tried to make ourselves comfortable. It took a while for any of us to say anything.

Tim talked about Satan, for some reason. Tim had a new theory about Satan's rise and fall that he apparently wanted to try out on us, since we—Kirsten and I—were the closest people at hand. I presumed at the time that Tim intended to include his theory in the book he had begun working on.

"I see the legend of Satan in a new way. Satan desired to know God as fully as possible. The fullest knowledge would come if he became God, was himself God. He strove for this and achieved it, knowing that the punishment would be permanent exile from God. But he did it anyhow, because the memory of knowing God, really knowing him as no one else ever had or would, justified to him his eternal punishment. Now, who would you say truly loved God out of everyone who ever existed? Satan willingly accepted eternal punishment and exile just to know God—by becoming God—for an instant. Further, it occurs to me, Satan truly knew God, but perhaps God did not know or understand Satan; had He understood him, He would not have punished him. That is why it is said that Satan rebelled—which means Satan was outside of God's control, outside God's domain, as if in another universe. But Satan did I think welcome his punishment, for it was his proof to himself that he knew and loved God. Otherwise he might have done what he did for the reward . . . had there been a reward. 'Better to rule in hell than to serve in heaven' *is* an issue, here, but not the true one: which is the ultimate goal and search to know and be: fully and really to know God, in comparison to which all else is really very little."

"Prometheus," Kirsten said absently. She sat smoking and gazing.

Tim said, "Prometheus means 'Forethinker.' He was involved in the creating of man. He was also the supreme trickster among the gods. Pandora was sent down to Earth by Zeus as a punishment to Prometheus for stealing fire and bringing it to man. In addition, Pandora punished the whole human race. Epimetheus married her, he was Hindsight. Prometheus warned him not to marry Pandora, since Prometheus could foresee the consequences. This same kind of absolute foreknowledge is or was considered by the Zoroastrians to be an attribute of God, the Wise Mind."

"An eagle ate his liver," Kirsten said remotely.

Nodding, Tim said, "Zeus punished Prometheus by chaining him and sending an eagle to eat his liver, which regenerated itself endlessly. However, Hercules released him. Prometheus was a friend to mankind beyond any doubt. He was a master craftsman. There is an affinity to the legend of Satan, certainly. As I see it, Satan could be said to have stolen—not fire—but true knowledge of God. However, he did not bring it to man, as Prometheus did with fire. Perhaps Satan's real sin was that upon acquiring that knowledge he kept it to himself; he did *not* share it with mankind. That's interesting . . . by that line of reasoning, one could argue that we could acquire a knowledge of God by way of Satan. I've never heard that theory put forth before." He became silent, apparently pondering. "Would you write this down?" he said to Kirsten.

"I'll remember." Her tone was listless and drab.

"Man must assault Satan and seize this knowledge," Tim said, "and take it from him. Satan does not want to yield it up. For concealing it—not for taking it in the first place—he was punished. Then, in a sense, human beings can redeem Satan by wresting this knowledge from him."

I said, "And then go off and study astrology."

Glancing at me, Tim said, "Pardon?"

"Wallenstein," I said. "Off casting horoscopes."

"The Greek words which our word 'horoscope' is based on," Tim said, "are *hora*, which means 'hour,' and *scopos*, which means 'one who watches.' So 'horoscope' literally means 'one who watches the hours.'" He lit a cigarette; both he and Kirsten, since their return from England, seemed to smoke constantly. "Wallenstein was a fascinating person."

"So Jeff says," I said. "Said, I mean."

Cocking his head alertly, Tim said, "Was Jeff interested in Wallenstein? Because I have—"

"You didn't know?" I said.

Looking puzzled, Tim said, "I don't think so."

Kirsten regarded him steadily, with an inscrutable expression.

"I have a number of very good books on Wallenstein," Tim said. "You know, in many ways Wallenstein resembled Hitler."

Both Kirsten and I remained silent.

"Wallenstein contributed to the ruin of Germany," Tim said. "He was a great general. Friedrich von Schiller, as you may know, wrote three plays about Wallenstein, whose titles are: *Wallenstein's Camp*, *The Piccolominis* and *The Death of Wallenstein*. They are profoundly moving plays. This brings up, of course, the role of Schiller himself in the development of Western thought. Let me read you something." Setting his cigarette down, Tim went over to the bookcase for a book; he found it after a few minutes of hunting. "This may shed some light on the subject. In writing to his friend—let me see; I have the name here—in writing to Wilhelm von Humboldt, this was toward the very end of Schiller's life, Schiller said, 'After all, we are both idealists, and should be ashamed to have it said that the material world formed us, instead of being formed by us.' The essence of Schiller's vision was, of course, freedom. He was naturally absorbed in the great drama of the revolt of the Lowlands—by that I mean Holland—and—" Tim paused, thinking, his lips moving; he gazed absently off into space. On the couch, Kirsten sat in silence, smoking and staring. "Well," Tim said finally, leafing through the book he held, "let me read you this. Schiller wrote this when he was thirty-four years old. Perhaps it sums up much of our aspirations, our most noble ones." Peering at the book, Tim read aloud. "'Now that I have begun to know and to employ my spiritual powers properly, an illness unfortunately threatens to undermine my physical ones. However, I shall do what I can, and when in the end the edifice comes crashing down, I shall have salvaged what was worth preserving.'" Tim shut the book and returned it to the shelf.

We said nothing. I did not even think; I merely sat.

"Schiller is very important to the twentieth century," Tim said; he returned to his cigarette, stubbed it out. For a long time, he stared down at the ashtray.

"I'm going to send out for a pizza," Kirsten said. "I'm not up to fixing dinner."

"That's fine," Tim said. "Ask them to put Canadian bacon on it. And if they have soft drinks—"

"I can fix dinner," I said.

Kirsten rose, made her way to the phone, leaving Tim and me alone together.

Earnestly, Tim said to me, "It is really a matter of great importance to know God, to discern the Absolute Essence, which is the way Heidegger puts it. *Sein* is his term: Being. What we have uncovered at the Zadokite Wadi simply beggars description."

I nodded.

"How are you fixed for money?" Tim said, reaching into his coat pocket.

"I'm fine," I said.

"You're working, still? At the real estate—" He corrected himself. "You're a legal secretary; you're still with them, then?"

"Yes," I said. "But I'm just a clerk-typist."

"I found my career as a lawyer taxing," Tim said, "but rewarding. I'd advise you to become a legal secretary and then perhaps you can use that as a jumping-off platform and go into law, become an attorney. It might even be possible for you to be a judge, someday."

"I guess so," I said.

Tim said, "Did Jeff discuss the *anokhi* with you?"

"Well, you wrote to us. And we saw newspaper and magazine articles."

"They used the term in a special sense, a technical sense— the Zadokites. It could not have meant the Divine Intelligence because they speak of having it, literally. There is one line from Document Six: '*Anokhi* dies and is reborn each year, and upon each following year *anokhi* is more.' Or greater; more or greater, it could be either, perhaps lofty. It's extremely puzzling but the translators are working on it and we hope to have it during the next six months . . . and, of course, they're still piecing together the fragments, the scrolls that became mutilated. I

672 THE TRANSMIGRATION OF TIMOTHY ARCHER

have no knowledge of Aramaic, as you probably realize. I studied both Greek and Latin—you know, 'God is the final bulwark against non-Being.'"

"Tillich," I said.

"Beg pardon?" Tim said.

"Paul Tillich said that," I said.

"I'm not sure about that," Tim said. "It was certainly one of the Protestant existential theologians; it may have been Reinhold Niebuhr. You know, Niebuhr is an American, or rather was; he died quite recently. One thing that interests me about Niebuhr—" Tim paused a moment. "Niemöller served in the German navy in World War One. He worked actively against the Nazis and continued to preach until 1938. The Gestapo arrested him and he was sent to Dachau. Niebuhr had been a pacifist originally, but urged Christians to support the war against Hitler. I feel that one of the significant differences between Wallenstein and Hitler—actually it is a very great similarity—lies in the loyalty oaths that Wallenstein—"

"Excuse me," I said. I went into the bathroom, opened the medicine cabinet to see if the bottle of Dexamyls was still there. It was not; all the medicine bottles were gone. Taken to England, I realized. Now in Kirsten's and Tim's luggage. Fuck.

When I came out, I found Kirsten standing alone in the living room. "I'm terribly, terribly tired," she said in a faint voice.

"I can see that," I said.

"There is no way I am going to be able to keep down pizza. Could you go to the store for me? I made a list. I want boned chicken, the kind that comes in a jar, and rice or noodles. Here; this is the list." She handed it to me. "Tim'll give you the money."

"I have money." I returned to the bedroom, where I had put my coat and purse. As I was putting on my coat, Tim appeared from behind me, anxious to say something more.

"What Schiller saw in Wallenstein was a man who colluded with fate to bring on his own demise. This would be for the German Romantics the greatest sin of all, to collude with fate, fate regarded as doom." He followed me from the bedroom, down the hall. "The whole spirit of Goethe and Schiller and—the others, their whole orientation was that the human will could overcome fate. Fate would not be regarded as inevitable but as something a person allowed. Do you see my point? To the Greeks, fate was *ananke*, a force absolutely predetermined and impersonal; they equated it with Nemesis, which is retributive, punishing fate."

"I'm sorry," I said. "I have to go to the store."

"Aren't they bringing the pizza?"

"Kirsten's not feeling well."

Standing close to me and speaking in a low voice, Tim said, "Angel, I'm very concerned about her. I can't get her to go to a doctor. Her stomach—either that or her gall bladder. Maybe you can convince her to undergo a multiphasic. She's afraid of what they'll find. You know, don't you, that she had cervical cancer a number of years ago."

"Yes," I said.

"And a hysterocleisis."

"What is that?"

"A surgical procedure; the mouth of the uterus is closed. She has so many anxieties in this area, that is, pertaining to this topic; it's impossible for me to discuss it with her."

"I'll talk to her," I said.

"Kirsten blames herself for Jeff's death."

"Shit," I said. "I was afraid of that."

Coming from the living room, Kirsten said to me, "Add ginger ale to the list I gave you. Please."

"Okay," I said. "Is the store—"

"Turn right," Kirsten said. "It's four blocks straight and then one block left. It's a Chinese-run little grocery store but they have what I want."

"Do you need any more cigarettes?" Tim said.

"Yes, you might pick up a carton," Kirsten said. "Any of the low-tar brands; they all taste the same."

"Okay," I said.

Opening the door for me, Tim said, "I'll drive you." The two of us made our way down the sidewalk to his rented car, but, as we stood, he discovered that he did not have the keys. "We'll have to walk," he said. So we walked together, saying nothing for a time.

"It's a nice night," I said finally.

"There's something I've been meaning to discuss with you," Tim said. "Although technically it's not within your province."

"I didn't know I had a province," I said.

"It's not an area of expertise for you. I'm not sure who I should talk to about it. These Zadokite Documents are in some respects—" He hesitated. "I would have to say distressing. To me personally, is what I mean. What the translators have come across is many of the Logia—the sayings—of Jesus predating Jesus by almost two hundred years."

"I realize that," I said.

"But that means," Tim said, "that he was not the Son of God. Was not, in fact, God, as the Trinitarian doctrine requires us to believe. That may pose no problem for you, Angel."

"No, not really," I agreed.

"The Logia are essential to our understanding and apperception of Jesus as the Christ; that is, the Messiah or Anointed One. If, as would now seem to be the case, the Logia can be severed from the person Jesus, then we must reevaluate the four Gospels—not just the Synoptics but all four . . . we must ask ourselves what, then, we indeed do know about Jesus, if indeed we know anything at all."

"Can't you just assume Jesus was a Zadokite?" I said. That was the impression I had gotten from the newspaper and magazine articles. Upon the discovery of the Qumran Scrolls, the Dead Sea Scrolls, there had been an enormous flurry of speculation that Jesus came from or was in some way connected with the Essenes. I saw no problem. I could not see what Tim was concerned about, as the two of us walked slowly along the sidewalk.

"There is a mysterious figure," Tim said, "mentioned in a number of the Zadokite Documents. He's referred to by a Hebrew word best translated as 'Expositor.' It is this shadowy personage to whom many of the Logia are attributed."

"Well, then Jesus learned from him, or anyhow they were derived from him," I said.

"But then Jesus is not the Son of God. He is not God Incarnate, God as a human being."

I said, "Maybe God revealed the Logia to the Expositor."

"But then the Expositor is the Son of God."

"Okay," I said.

"These are problems over which I've agonized—although that is rather a strong term. But it bothers me. And it should bother me. Here we have many of the parables related in the Gospels now extant in scrolls predating Jesus by two hundred years. Not all the Logia are represented, admittedly, but many are, many crucial ones. Certain cardinal doctrines of resurrection are also present, those being expressed in the well-known 'I am' utterances by Jesus. 'I am the bread of life.' 'I am the Way.' 'I am the narrow gate.' These simply cannot be separated from Jesus Christ. Just take that first one: 'I am the bread of life. Anyone who does eat my flesh and drink my blood has eternal life, and I shall raise him up on the last day. For my flesh is real food and my blood is real drink. He who eats my flesh and drinks my blood lives in me and I live in him.' Do you see my point?"

"Sure," I said. "The Zadokite Expositor said it first."

"Then the Zadokite Expositor conferred eternal life, and specifically through the Eucharist."

"I think that's wonderful," I said.

Tim said, "It was always the hope, but never the expectation, that we would someday unearth Q, or unearth something that would permit us to reconstruct Q, or parts of Q; but no one ever dreamed that an *Ur-Quelle* would manifest itself pre-dating Jesus, and by two centuries. Also, there are peculiar other—" He paused. "I want to obtain your promise not to discuss what I'm going to say; not to talk about it with anyone. This part hasn't been released to the media."

"May I die horribly."

"Associated with the 'I am' statements are certain very peculiar additions not found in the Gospels and apparently not known to the early Christians. At least, no written record of their knowing these things, believing these things, has passed down to us. I—" He broke off. "The term 'bread' and the term used for 'blood' suggest literal bread and literal blood. As if the Zadokites had a specific bread and a specific drink that they prepared and had that constituted in essence the body and blood of what they call the *anokhi*, for whom the Expositor spoke and whom the Expositor represented."

"Well," I said. I nodded.

"Where is this store?" Tim looked around.

"Another block or so," I said. "I guess."

Tim said earnestly, "Something they drank; something they

ate. As in the Messianic banquet. It made them immortal, they believed; it gave them eternal life, this combination of what they ate and what they drank. Obviously, this prefigures the Eucharist. Obviously it's related to the Messianic banquet. *Anokhi*. Always that word. They ate *anokhi* and they drank *anokhi* and, as a result, they became *anokhi*. They became God Himself."

"Which is what Christianity teaches," I said, "regarding the Mass."

"There are parallels found in Zoroastrianism," Tim said. "The Zoroastrians sacrificed cattle and combined this with an intoxicating drink called *haoma*. But there is no reason to assume that this resulted in a homologizing with the Deity. That, you see, is what the Sacraments achieve for the Christian communicant: he—or she—is homologized to God as represented in and by Christ. Becomes God or becomes one with God, unified with, assimilated to, God. An apotheosis, is what I'm saying. But here, with the Zadokites, you get precisely this with the bread and the drink derived from *anokhi*, and of course the term '*anokhi*' itself refers to the Pure Self-Awareness, which is to say, Pure Consciousness of Yahweh, the God of the Hebrew people."

"Brahman is that," I said.

"I beg your pardon? 'Brahman'?"

"In India. Brahmanism. Brahman possesses absolute, pure consciousness. Pure consciousness, pure being, pure bliss. As I recall."

"But what," Tim said, "is this *anokhi* that they ate and drank?"

"The body and blood of the Lord," I said.

"But what *is* it?" He gestured. "It's one thing to say glibly, 'It's the Lord,' because, Angel, that is what in logic is called a *hysteron proteron* fallacy: what you are trying to prove is assumed in your premise. Obviously, it's the body and blood of the Lord; the word '*anokhi*' makes that clear; but it doesn't—"

"Oh, I see," I said, then. "It's circular reasoning. In other words, you're saying that this *anokhi* actually exists."

Tim stopped and stood, gazing at me. "Of course."

"I understand. You mean it's real."

"God is real."

"Not really real," I said. "God is a matter of belief. It isn't real in the sense that that car—" I pointed to a parked TransAm— "is real."

"You couldn't be more wrong."

I started to laugh.

"Where did you ever get an idea like that?" Tim said. "That God isn't real?"

"God is a—" I hesitated. "A way of looking at things. An interpretation. I mean, He doesn't exist. Not the way objects exist. You couldn't, say, bump into Him, like you can bump into a wall."

"Does a magnetic field exist?"

"Sure," I said.

"You can't bump into it."

I said, "But it'll show up if you spread iron filings across a piece of paper."

"The hieroglyphs of God lie all about you," Tim said. "As the world and in the world."

"That's just an opinion. It's not my opinion."

"But you can see the world."

"I see the world," I said, "but I don't see any sign of God."

"But there cannot be a creation without a creator."

"Who says it's a creation?"

"My point," Tim said, "is that if the Logia predate Jesus by two hundred years, then the Gospels are suspect, and if the Gospels are suspect, we have no evidence that Jesus was God, very God, God Incarnate, and therefore the basis of our religion is gone. Jesus simply becomes a teacher representing a particular Jewish sect that ate and drank some kind of—well, whatever it was, the *anokhi*, and it made them immortal."

"They believed it made them immortal," I corrected him. "That's not the same thing. People believe that herbal remedies can cure cancer, but that doesn't make it true."

We arrived at the little grocery store and stood momentarily.

"I take it you're not a Christian," Tim said.

"Tim," I said, "you've known that for years. I'm your daughter-in-law."

"I'm not sure I'm a Christian. I'm now not sure there in fact is such a thing as Christianity. And I've got to get up and tell people—I have to go on with my ministerial and pastoral duties. Knowing what I know. Knowing that Jesus was a teacher and not God, and not even an original teacher; what he taught was the aggregate belief-system of an entire sect. A group product."

I said, "It could still have come from God. God could have revealed it to the Zadokites. What else does it say about the Expositor?"

"He returns in the Final Days and acts as Eschatological Judge."

"That's fine," I said.

"That's found in Zoroastrianism also," Tim said. "So much seems to go back to the Iranian religions . . . the Jews developed a distinct Iranian quality to their religion during the time . . ." He broke off; he had turned inward, mentally, oblivious, now, to me, to the store, our errand.

I said, trying to cheer him up, "Maybe the scholars and translators will find some of this *anokhi*."

"Find God," he echoed, to himself.

"Find it growing. A root or a tree."

"Why do you say that?" He seemed angry. "What would make you say that?"

"Bread has to be made out of something. You can't eat bread unless it's made from something."

"Jesus was speaking metaphorically. He did not mean literal bread."

"Maybe he didn't, but the Zadokites apparently did."

"That thought crossed my mind. Some of the translators are proposing that. That a literal bread and a literal drink is signified. 'I am the gate of the sheepfold.' Jesus certainly did not mean he was made of wood. 'I am the true vine, and my father is the vinedresser. Every branch in me that bears no fruit he cuts away, and every branch that does bear fruit he prunes to make it bear even more.'"

"Well, it's a vine, then," I said. "Look for a vine."

"That's absurd and carnal."

"Why?" I said.

Tim said savagely, "'I am the vine, you are the branches.' Are we to assume that a literal plant is referred to? That this is a physical, not a spiritual, matter? Something growing in the Dead Sea Desert?" He gestured. "'I am the light of the world.'

Are we to assume you could read a newspaper by holding it up to him? Like this streetlight?"

"Maybe so," I said. "Dionysos was a vine, in a manner of speaking. His worshippers got drunk and then Dionysos possessed them, and they ran over the hills and fields and bit cows to death. Devoured whole animals alive."

"There are certain resemblances," Tim said.

Together, we continued on into the little grocery store.

6

BEFORE Tim and Kirsten could return to England, the Episcopal Synod of Bishops convened to look into the matter of his possible heresies. The jerk-off—I should say, I suppose, conservative; that is the more polite term—bishops who stood as his accusers proved themselves idiots in terms of their ability to mount a successful attack on him. Tim emerged from the Synod officially vindicated. It made the newspapers and magazines, of course. Never at any time had this subject worried him. Anyhow, due to Jeff's suicide, Tim had plenty of public sympathy. He had always had that, but now, because of the tragedy in his personal life, he had it even more.

Somewhere Plato says that if you are going to shoot at a king you must be sure you kill him. The conservative bishops, in failing to destroy Tim, left him as a result even stronger than ever, which is the way with defeat; we say about such a turn of events that it has backfired. Tim knew now that no one within the Episcopal Church of the United States of America could bring him down. If he were to be destroyed, he would have to do it himself.

As for myself, in regard to my own life, I owned the house that Jeff and I had been buying. Jeff had made out a will, due to his father's insistence. I did not acquire much, but I acquired what there was. Since I had supported Jeff and myself, no financial problems confronted me. I continued to work at the law office and candle shop. For a time I believed that, with Jeff dead, I would gradually lose touch with Tim and Kirsten. That did not turn out to be the case. Tim seemed to find in me someone he could talk to. After all, I was one of the few people who knew the story about his relationship with his general secretary and business agent. And, of course, I had brought him and Kirsten together.

Beyond that, Tim did not jettison people who had become his friends. I amounted to much more than that anyhow; a great deal of love existed between the two of us, and out of that had come an understanding. We were, literally, good friends, in a sort of traditional way. The Bishop of California who held so many radical views and advanced such wild theories was, in his immediate life, an old-fashioned human being, in the best sense of the term. If you were his friend, he became loyal to you and stayed loyal to you, as I informed Ms. Marion years later, long after Kirsten and Tim were, like my husband, dead. It is a forgotten matter about Bishop Archer, that he loved his friends and stuck with them, even if he had nothing to gain in the sense that they had, or did not have, some power to advance his career, to enhance his station or advantage him in the practical world. All I amounted to in that world was a young woman working as a clerical secretary in a law office, and not an important law office. Tim had nothing to gain strategically by maintaining our relationship, but he maintained it up until his death.

Kirsten, during this period following Jeff's death, showed progressive symptoms of a deteriorating physical condition which, finally, the doctors diagnosed correctly as peritonitis, from which you can die. The bishop paid all her medical expenses, which came to a staggering sum; for ten days she languished in the intensive care unit of one of the best hospitals in San Francisco, complaining bitterly that no one visited her or gave a good goddamn. Tim, who flew all around the United States lecturing, saw her as often as he could, but it was not nearly often enough to suit her. I came over to the city to see her as frequently as possible. With me, as with Tim, it was (in her opinion) far too inadequate a response to her illness. Most of the time I spent with her amounted to a one-way diatribe in which she complained about him and about all else in life. She had aged.

It strikes me as semi-meaningless to say, "You are only as old as you feel" because, in point of fact, age and illness are going to win out, and this stupid statement only resonates with people in good health who have not undergone the sort of traumas that Kirsten Lundborg had. Her son Bill had disclosed an infinite capacity to be crazy and for this Kirsten felt responsible; she knew, too, that a major factor in Jeff's suicide had been her relationship with his father. That made her bitterly severe toward me, as if guilt—her guilt—goaded her into chronically abusing me, the chief victim of Jeff's death.

We really did not have much of a friendship left, she and I.

Nevertheless, I visited her in the hospital, and I always dressed up so that I looked great, and I always brought her something she could not eat, if it was food, or could not wear or use.

"They won't let me smoke," she said to me one time, by way of a greeting.

"Of course not," I said. "You'll set your bed on fire again. Like you did that time." She had almost suffocated herself, a few weeks before going into the hospital.

Kirsten said, "Get me some yarn."

" 'Yarn,' " I said.

"I'm going to knit a sweater. For the bishop." Her tone withered the word; Kirsten managed to convey through words a kind of antagonism one rarely encountered. "The bishop," she said, "needs a sweater."

Her animosity centered on the fact that Tim had proved able to handle his affairs quite well in her absence; at the moment, he was all the way up in Canada somewhere, delivering a speech. It had been Kirsten's contention for some time that Tim could not survive a week without her. Her confinement in the hospital had proven her wrong.

"Why don't Mexicans want their children to marry blacks?" Kirsten said.

"Because their kids would be too lazy to steal," I said.

"When does a black man become a nigger?"

"When he leaves the room." I seated myself in a plastic chair facing her bed. "What's the safest time to drive your car?" I said.

Kirsten gave me a hostile glance.

"You'll be out of here soon," I said, to help her cheer up.

"I'll never be out of here. The bishop is probably—never mind. Grabbing ass in Montreal. Or wherever he is. You know, he had me in bed the second time we met. And the first time was at a restaurant in Berkeley."

"I was there."

"So he couldn't do it the first time. If he could have, he would have. Doesn't that surprise you about a bishop? There are a few things I could tell you . . . but I won't." She ceased speaking, then, and glowered.

"Good," I said.

"Good what? That I'm not going to tell you?"

"If you start telling me," I said, "I will get up and leave. My therapist told me to set clear limits with you."

"Oh, that's right; you're another of them. Who's in therapy. You and my son. You two ought to get together. You could make clay snakes in occupational therapy."

"I am leaving," I said; I stood up.

"Oh Christ," Kirsten said irritably. "Sit down."

I said, "What became of the Swedish mongoloid cretin who escaped from the asylum in Stockholm?"

"I don't know."

"They found him teaching school in Norway."

Laughing, Kirsten said, "Go fuck yourself."

"I don't have to. I'm doing fine."

"Probably so." She nodded. "I wish I was back in London. You've never been to London."

"There wasn't enough money," I said. "In the Bishop's Discretionary Fund. For Jeff and me."

"Oh, that's right; I used it all up."

"Most of it."

Kirsten said, "I got to go nowhere. While Tim hung around those old faggot translators. Did he tell you that Jesus is a fake? Amazing. Here we find out two thousand years later that somebody else entirely made up all those Logia and all those 'I am' statements. I never saw Tim so downcast; he just sat and stared at the floor, in our flat, day after day."

To that I said nothing.

"Do you think it matters?" Kirsten said. "That Jesus was a fake?"

"Not to me it doesn't," I said.

"They haven't really published the important part. About the mushroom. They're keeping that secret for as long as they can. However—"

"What mushroom?"

"The *anokhi*."

I said, incredulous, "The *anokhi* is a mushroom?"

"It's a mushroom. It was a mushroom back then. They grew it in caves, the Zadokites."

"Jesus Christ," I said.

"They made mushroom bread out of it. They made a broth from it and drank the broth; ate the bread, drank the broth.

That's where the two species of the Host come from, the body and the blood. Apparently the *anokhi* mushroom was toxic but the Zadokites found a way to detoxify it, at least somewhat, enough so it didn't kill them. It made them hallucinate."

I started laughing. "Then they were a—"

"Yes, they turned on." Kirsten, too, now laughed, in spite of herself. "And Tim has to get up every Sunday at Grace and give Communion knowing that, knowing they were simply getting off on a psychedelic trip, like the kids in the Haight-Ashbury. I thought it was going to kill him when he found out."

"So then Jesus was in effect a dope dealer," I said.

She nodded. "The Twelve, the disciples, were—this is the theory—smuggling the *anokhi* into Jerusalem and they got caught. This just confirms what John Allegro figured out . . . if you happened to see his book. He's one of the greatest scholars *vis-à-vis* Near Eastern languages . . . he was the official translator of the Qumran scrolls."

"I didn't see his book," I said, "but I know who he is. Jeff used to talk about him."

"Allegro figured out that the early Christians were a secret mushroom cult; he deduced it from internal evidence in the New Testament. And he found a fresco or wall-painting . . . anyhow, a picture of early Christians with a huge *amania muscaria* mushroom—"

"*Amanita muscaria*," I corrected. "It's the red one. They are terribly toxic. So the early Christians found a way to detoxify it, then."

"That's Allegro's contention. And they saw cartoons." She began to giggle.

"Is there actually an *anokhi* mushroom?" I said. I knew something about mushrooms; before I married Jeff, I had gone with an amateur mycologist.

"Well, there probably was, but nobody today knows what it would be. So far, in the Zadokite Documents, there's no description. No way to tell which one it was or if it still exists."

I said, "Maybe it did more than cause hallucinations."

"Like what?"

A nurse came over to me, at that point. "You'll have to leave, now."

"Okay." I rose, gathered up my coat and purse.

Kirsten said, "Bend over." She waved me toward her; in a whisper directly into my ear she said, "Orgies."

After kissing her good-bye, I left the hospital.

When I arrived back in Berkeley and had made my way by bus to the little old farmhouse that Jeff and I had been living in, I saw, as I walked up the path, a young man crouched over in the corner of the porch; I halted warily, wondering who he was.

Pudgy, with light-colored hair, he bent stroking my cat Magnificat, who had curled up happily against the front door of the house. I watched for a time, thinking: Is this a salesman or something? The young man wore trousers too large for him, and a brightly colored shirt. On his face, as he petted Magnificat, was the most gentle expression I had ever seen on a human face; this kid, who obviously had never encountered my cat before, radiated a kind of fondness, a kind of palpable love, that in fact was something new to me. Some of the very early statues of the god Apollo reveal that sweet smile. Totally absorbed in petting Magnificat, the kid remained oblivious to me, to my nearby presence; I watched, fascinated, because for one thing Magnificat was a rough-and-tumble old tomcat who normally did not allow strangers to get near him.

All at once the kid glanced up. He smiled shyly and rose awkwardly to his feet. "Hi."

"Hi." I walked toward him, carefully, very slowly.

"I found this cat." The kid blinked, still smiling; he had guileless blue eyes, absent of any cunning.

"It's my cat," I said.

"What's her name?"

"It's a tomcat," I said, "and he's named Magnificat."

"He's very beautiful," the kid said.

"Who are you?" I said.

"I'm Kirsten's son. I'm Bill."

That explained the blue eyes and the blond hair. "I'm Angel Archer," I said.

"I know. We've met. But it was—" He hesitated. "I'm not sure how long ago. They gave me electroshock . . . my memory isn't very good."

"Yes," I said. "I guess we did meet. I just came from the hospital visiting your mom."

"Can I use your bathroom?"

"Sure," I said. I got my keys from my purse and unlocked the front door. "Excuse the mess. I work; I'm not home enough to keep it neat. The bathroom is off the kitchen, in the back. Just keep on going."

Bill Lundborg did not close the bathroom door behind him; I could hear him urinating loudly. I filled the tea kettle and put it on the burner. Strange, I thought. This is the son she derides. As she derides us all.

Reappearing, Bill Lundborg stood self-consciously, smiling at me anxiously, quite obviously ill at ease. He had not flushed the toilet. I thought, then, very suddenly: He has just come out of the hospital, the mental hospital; I can tell.

"Would you like coffee?" I said.

"Sure."

Magnificat entered the kitchen.

"How old is she?" Bill asked.

"I have no idea how old he is. I rescued him from a dog. After he had grown, I mean, not as a kitten. He probably lived somewhere in the neighborhood."

"How is Kirsten?"

"Doing really well," I said. I pointed to a chair. "Sit down."

"Thanks." He seated himself; placing his arms on the kitchen table, he interlocked his fingers. His skin was so pale. Kept indoors, I thought. Caged up. "I like your cat."

"You can feed him," I said; I opened the refrigerator and got out the can of cat food.

As Bill fed Magnificat, I watched the two of them. The care he took in spooning out the food . . . systematically, his attention deeply fixed, as if it were very important, what he had become involved in; he kept his gaze intent on Magnificat, and as he scrutinized the old cat he smiled again, that smile that so touched me, so made me start.

Batter me, oh God, I thought, remembering for some strange reason. Batter and kill me; they have injured this sweet kind baby until there is almost nothing left. Burned his circuits out as a pretense of healing him. The fucking sadists, I thought, in their sterile coats. What do they know about the human heart? I felt like crying.

And he will be back in, I thought, as Kirsten says. In and out of the hospital the rest of his life. The fucking sons of bitches.

> *Batter my heart, three person'd God; for, you*
> *As yet but knocke, breathe, shine, and seeke to mend;*
> *That I may rise, and stand, o'erthrow mee, and bend*
> *Your force, to breake, blowe, burn and make me new.*
> *I, like an usurpt towne, to'another due,*
> *Labour to'admit you, but Oh, to no end,*
> *Reason your viceroy in mee, mee should defend,*
> *But is captiv'd, and proves weake or untrue.*
> *Yet dearely' I love you, and would be loved faine,*
> *But am betroth'd unto your enemie:*
> *Divorce mee, untie, or breake that knot againe,*
> *Take mee to you, imprison mee, for I*
> *Except you enthrall mee, never shall be free,*
> *Nor ever chaste, except you ravish mee.*

My favorite poem of John Donne's; it came up into me, into my mind, as I watched Bill Lundborg feed my worn old cat.

And I laugh at God, I thought; I make no sense out of what Tim teaches and believes, and the torment he feels over these various issues. I am fooling myself; in my own labored way, I do understand. Look at him serve that ignorant cat. He—this child—would have been a veterinarian, if they hadn't maimed him, shredded up his mind. What had Kirsten told me? He is afraid to drive; he stops taking out the garbage; he will not bathe and then he cries. I cry, too, I thought, and sometimes I let the trash pile up, and one time I nearly got sideswiped on Hoffman and had to pull over. Lock me up, I thought; lock up us all. This, then, is Kirsten's affliction, having this boy for her son?

Bill said, "Is there anything else I can feed her? She's still hungry."

"Anything you see in the fridge," I said. "Would you like something to eat?"

"No thanks." Again he stroked the awful old cat—a cat who never gave the time of day to any person. He has made this animal tame, I thought, as he himself is: tame.

"Did you come here on the bus?" I said.

"Yes." He nodded. "I had to surrender my driver's license. I used to drive, but—" He became silent.

"I take the bus," I said.

"I had a real great car," Bill said "A '56 Chevy. A stick shift with an eight, the big eight they made; it was only the second year Chevrolet made an eight; the first year was '55."

"Those are very valuable cars," I said.

"Yes; Chevrolet had changed to that new body-style. After the old higher, shorter body-style they used so long. The difference between a '55 and a '56 Chevy is in the front grille; if the grille includes the turn-signal lights, you can tell it's a '56."

"Where are you living?" I said. "In the City?"

"I'm not living anywhere. I got out of Napa last week. They let me out because Kirsten is sick. I hitched down here. A man gave me a ride in his Stingray." He smiled. "You have to take those 'Vettes out on the freeway every week or they build up carbon deposits in the mill. He was blowing carbon out the whole way. What I don't like about a 'Vette is the fiberglass body; you can't really repair it." He added, "But they certainly are good-looking. His was white. I forget the year, although he told me. We got it up to a hundred, but the cops pace you a lot when you're in a 'Vette, hoping you'll exceed the limit. We had a Highway Patrol after us part of the way but he had to turn his siren on and take off; an emergency of some kind, somewhere. We flipped him off as he went by. He was real disgusted but he couldn't cite us; he was in too much of a hurry."

I asked him, then, as tactfully as I could, why he had come to see me.

"I wanted to ask you something," Bill said. "I met your husband one time. You weren't home; you were working or something. He was here alone. Was his name Jeff?"

"Yes," I said.

"What I wanted to know is—" Bill hesitated. "Could you tell me why he killed himself?"

"There are a lot of factors involved in something like that." I seated myself at the kitchen table, facing him.

"I know he was in love with my mother."

"Oh," I said. "You do know that."

"Yes, Kirsten told me. Was that the main reason?"

"Perhaps," I said.

"What were the other reasons?"

I was silent.

"Would you tell me one thing," Bill said, "one particular thing? Was he mentally disturbed?"

"He had been in therapy. But not intensive therapy."

"I've been thinking about it," Bill said. "He was mad at his father because of Kirsten. A lot of it had to do with that. See, when you're in the hospital—a mental hospital—you know a lot of people who've tried suicide. Their wrists are all sawed on. That's always the way you can tell. The best way, when you do that, is up the arm in the direction the veins run." He showed me his bare arm, pointing. "The mistake most people make is cutting at right angles to the vein, down at the wrist. We had this one guy, he laid open his arm for like about seven inches and—" He paused, calculating. "Maybe as much as a quarter inch wide. But they still were able to sew it up. He had been in for months. He said one time in group therapy that all he wanted to be was a pair of eyes bugging out from the wall, so he could see everyone but no one could see him. Just an observer, not a part of what was going on, ever. Just watching and listening. He would have to be a pair of ears, too, to do that."

For the life of me I could think of nothing to say.

"Paranoids have a fear of being looked at," Bill said. "So invisibility would be important to them. There was this one lady, she couldn't eat in front of anyone. She always took her tray off to her room. I guess she thought eating was dirty." He smiled. I managed to smile back.

How strange this is, I thought. An eerie conversation, as if it is not actually taking place.

"Jeff was real hostile," Bill said. "Toward his father and toward Kirsten both, and maybe toward you, but I don't think as much; toward you, I mean. We talked about you that day I came over. I forget when that was. I had a two-day pass. I hitched down then, too. It's not that hard to hitch. A truck picked me up, even though it had a NO RIDERS sign posted. It was carrying some kind of chemicals, but not the toxic kind. If they're carrying flammable material or toxic material they know not to give you a ride, because if there is an accident and you're killed or poisoned then sometimes it voids their insurance."

Again I could think of nothing to say; I nodded.

"The law," Bill said, "in case of an accident where a hitch-hiker is injured or killed, is that it's presumed he rode at his own risk. He took the chance. So because of that when you hitch if something happens you can't sue. That's California law. I don't know how it is in other states."

"Yes," I said. "Jeff felt a lot of anger toward Tim."

"Do you feel animosity toward my mother?"

After a pause, after I had thought it over, I said, "Yes. I really do."

"Why? It wasn't her fault. Any time a person kills himself, he has to take full responsibility. We learned that. You learn a lot in the hospital. You know a whole bunch of things that people on the outside never find out. It's a crash course in reality, which is the ultimate—" He gestured. "Paradox. Because the people there are there because, presumably, they don't face reality, and then they wind up in the hospital, the mental hospital, a state hospital like Napa, and have to face a whole lot more reality all of a sudden than other people ever have to do. And they face it very well. I've seen things I have been very proud of, patients helping other patients. One time this lady— she was like about in her fifties—said to me, 'Can I confide in you?' She swore me to secrecy. I promised not to say anything. She said, 'I'm going to kill myself tonight.' She told me how she was going to do it. This was not a locked ward. She had her car parked out in the lot and she had an ignition key they didn't know she had; they—the staff—thought they had all her keys but she kept this one back. So I thought it over, about what I should do. Should I tell Dr. Gutman? He was in charge of the ward. What I did was, I sneaked outside onto the lot—I knew which car was hers—and I removed the coil wire that runs—well, you wouldn't know. It runs between the coil and the distributor. There's no way you can start an engine with that wire missing. It's easy to do. When you park your car in a really rough neighborhood and you're afraid someone will steal it, you can pull out that wire; it comes out real easy. She cranked it until the battery ran down and then she came back in. She was furious but later on she thanked me." He pondered and then said, half to himself, "She was going to ram an on-going car on the Bay Bridge. So I saved him, too; the other car. It might have been like a station wagon full of kids."

"My God," I said faintly.

"It was a decision I had to make in a hurry." Bill said. "Once I knew she had that key, I had to do something. It was a big Merc. Silver-colored. Almost new. She had a lot of money. In a situation like that if you don't act, it's the same as helping them."

I said, "It might have been better to tell the doctor."

"No." He shook his head. "Then she would have—well, it's hard to explain. She knew that I did it to save her life, not to get her in trouble. If I had told the staff—especially if I had told Dr. Gutman—she would have interpreted that as me just trying to get her kept there another couple of months. But this way they never knew, so they didn't hold her any longer than they originally intended to. When I got out—she got out before I did—one time she came by my apartment . . . I gave her my address; anyhow, she came by—she was driving that same Merc; I recognized it when she pulled up—and she wanted to know how I was getting along."

"How were you getting along?" I said.

"Not good at all. I didn't have money to pay my rent; they were going to evict me. She had a whole lot of money; her husband was rich. They owned a bunch of apartment buildings up and down California, as far down as San Diego. She went back to her car and came back and handed me a roll of what I thought were nickels. You know; a roll of coins. After she left, I opened the roll at one end and they were gold coins. She told me later she kept a lot of her money in the form of gold. It was from some British colony. She told me when I sold them to a coin dealer to specify that they were 'B.U.' That stands for 'bright uncirculated.' It's a dealers' term. A bright uncirculated coin is worth more than whatever the opposite would be. I got about twelve dollars a coin, when I sold them. I kept one, but I lost it. I got something like six hundred dollars for the roll, with that one coin missing." Turning, he scrutinized the stove. "Your water's boiling."

I poured the water into the Silex coffee pot.

"Unboiled coffee," Bill said, "filtered coffee, is a lot better for you than the percolated kind, where it shoots back up to the top and starts all over again."

"That's true," I said.

Bill said, "I've been thinking a lot about your husband's death. He seemed like a really nice person. Sometimes that's a problem."

"Why?" I said.

"Much mental illness stems from people repressing their hostility and trying to be nice, too nice. The hostility can't be repressed forever. Everybody has it; it has to come out."

"Jeff was very calm," I said. "It was hard to get him to fight. Marital quarrels; I was usually the one who got mad."

"Kirsten says he had been dropping acid."

"I don't think that's true," I said. "That he dropped acid."

"A lot of people who get messed up get messed up from drugs. You see a lot of them in the hospital. They don't always stay that way, contrary to what you hear. Most of it is due to malnutrition; people on drugs forget to eat and, when they do eat, they eat junk food. The muscles. Everyone who does drugs gets the munchies, unless, of course, they're taking amphetamines, in which case they don't eat at all. Much of what looks like toxic brain psychosis in speed freaks is in fact a deficiency in their galvanic electrolytes. Which are easily replaced."

"What sort of work do you do?" I said. He seemed less ill at ease, now. More confident in what he was saying.

"I'm a painter," Bill said.

"What artist is your work—"

"Car painting." He smiled gently. "Spray painting. At Leo Shine's. In San Mateo. 'I'll spray your car any color you want it for forty-nine-fifty and give you a written six-month guarantee.'" He laughed and I laughed, too; I had seen Leo Shine's commercials on TV.

"I loved my husband very much," I said.

"Was he going to be a minister?"

"No. I don't know what he was going to be."

"Maybe he wasn't going to be anything. I'm taking a course in computer programming. Right now I'm studying algorithms. An algorithm is nothing but a recipe, like when you bake a cake. It is a sequence of incremental steps sometimes utilizing built-in repeats; certain steps have to be reiterated. One primary aspect of an algorithm is that it be meaningful; it's very easy to unintentionally ask a computer a question it can't answer, not because it's dumb but because the question really has no answer."

"I see," I said.

"Would you consider this a meaningful question," Bill said. "Give me the highest number short of two."

"Yes," I said. "That's meaningful."

"It's not." He shook his head. "There is no such number."

"I know the number," I said. "It's one-point-nine-plus—" I broke off.

"You would have to carry the sequence of digits into infinity. The question is not intelligible. So the algorithm is faulty. You're asking the computer to do something that can't be done. Unless your algorithm is intelligible, the computer can't respond, but it will attempt to respond, by and large."

"Garbage in," I said, "garbage out."

"Right." He nodded.

"I'm going to ask you a question," I said. "In return. I'm going to give you a proverb, a common proverb. If you are not familiar with the proverb—"

"How much time will I have?"

"This isn't timed. Just tell me what the proverb means. 'A new broom sweeps clean.' What does that mean?"

After a pause, Bill said, "It means that old brooms wear out and you have to throw them away."

I said, " 'The burnt child is afraid of fire.' "

Again he was silent a moment, his forehead wrinkling. "Children easily get hurt, especially around a stove. Like this stove here." He indicated my kitchen stove.

" 'It never rains but it pours.' " But I could tell already. Bill Lundborg had a thinking impairment; he could not explain the proverb: instead he repeated it back in concrete terms, the terms in which it itself had been phrased.

"Sometimes," he said haltingly, "there's a lot of rain. Especially when you don't expect it."

" 'Vanity, thy name is woman.' "

"Women are vain. That's not a proverb. It's a quotation from something."

"You're right," I said. "You did fine." But in truth, in very truth, as Tim would say, as Jesus used to say, or the Zadokites said, this person was totally schizophrenic, according to the Benjamin Proverb Test. I felt a vague, haunting ache, realizing this, seeing him sit there so young and physically healthy, and so unable to desymbolize, to think abstractly. He had the classic schizophrenic cognitive impairment; his ratiocination was limited to the concrete.

You can forget about being a computer programmer, I said to myself. You will be spray-painting low-rider cars until the Eschatological Judge arrives, and frees us, one and all, from our cares. Frees you and frees me; frees everyone. And then your damaged mind will, presumably, be healed. Cast into a passing pig, to be run over the edge of a cliff, to doom. Where it belongs.

"Excuse me," I said. I walked from the kitchen, through the house, to the farthest point from Bill Lundborg possible, leaned against the wall with my face pressed into my arm. I could feel my tears against my skin—warm tears—but I made no sound.

I VIEWED myself as Jeff, weeping off by myself in the margins of the house, weeping over someone I cared about. Where is this going to end? I wondered. It has to end. And it seems not to have an end; it just goes on: a sequence of explosions, like Bill Lundborg's computer trying to figure out what the highest number less than an integer is, a hopeless task.

Not long thereafter, Kirsten came out of the hospital; she gradually recovered from her digestive ailment, upon which cure having happened, she and Tim returned to England. Before they left the United States, I found out from her that her son Bill had gone to jail. The U.S. Postal Service had hired him and then fired him; his response to being fired had been to smash the plate glass windows of the San Mateo substation. He smashed them with his bare knuckles. Obviously he was crazy again. If it could be said at any time that he was ever not.

So I lost track of everyone: I did not see Bill again after that day he visited me; I saw Kirsten and Tim a number of times— Kirsten more often than Tim—and then I found myself alone, and not very happy, and wondering and speculating about the sense underlying the world, assuming that any sense existed. Like Bill Lundborg's periods of sanity, it was a dubitable thing.

The law office and candle shop, one day, ceased to be in business. My two employers got busted on drug charges. I had foreseen it. More money could be made in the sale of cocaine than in the sale of candles. Cocaine at that time did not enjoy the fad popularity that it enjoys now, but the demand even so amounted to an inducement that my employers could not refuse. The authorities managed to accommodate them in their inability to say no to big bucks: each man got a five-year prison term. I drifted for a few months, drawing unemployment compensation, and then I squeezed in as a retail record clerk at the Musik Shop on Telegraph Avenue near Channing Way, which is where I work now.

Psychosis takes many forms. You can be psychotic about everything or you can concentrate on one particular topic. Bill represented ubiquitous dementia; madness had infiltrated every part of his life, or so I presume.

The fixed idea kind of madness is fascinating, if you are inclined toward viewing with interest something that is palpably impossible and yet nonetheless exists. *Over-valence* is a notion about possibilities in the human mind, possibilities of something going wrong, that did it not exist it could not be supposed. I mean by this simply that you have to see an over-valent idea at work fully to appreciate it. The older term is *idée fixe*. Over-valent idea expresses it better, because this is a term derived from mechanics and chemistry and biology; it is a graphic term and it involves the notion of *power*. The essence of valence is power and that is what I am talking about; I speak of an idea that once it comes into the human mind, the mind, I mean, of a given human being, it not only never goes away, it also consumes everything else in the mind so that, finally, the person is gone, the mind as such is gone, and only the over-valent idea remains.

How does such a thing begin? When does it begin? Jung speaks somewhere—I forget which of his books it is mentioned in—but anyhow he speaks in one place of a person, a normal person, into whose mind one day a certain idea comes, and that idea never goes away. Moreover, Jung says, upon the entering of that idea into the person's mind, nothing new ever happens to that mind or in that mind; time stops for that mind and it is dead. The mind, as a living, growing entity has died. And yet the person, in a sense, continues on.

Sometimes, I guess, an over-valent idea enters the mind as a problem, or imaginary problem. This is not so rare. You are getting ready for bed, late at night, and all of a sudden the idea comes into your mind that you did not shut off your car lights. You look out the window at your car—which is parked in your driveway in plain sight—and you can see that it shows no lights. But then you think: Maybe I left the lights on and they stayed on so long that they ran the battery down. So to be sure, I must go out and check. You put on your robe and go out, unlock the car door, get in and pull on the headlight switch. The lights come on. You turn them off, get out, lock up the car and return to the house. What has happened is that you have gone crazy; you have become psychotic. Because you have discounted the testimony of your senses; you could see out the window that the car lights were not on, yet you went out to check anyhow. This is the cardinal factor: you saw but you did not believe. Or, conversely, you did not see something but you believed it anyhow. Theoretically, you could travel between your bedroom and the car forever, trapped in an eternal closed loop of unlocking the car, trying the light-switch, returning to the house—in this regard you herewith are a machine. You are no longer human.

Also, the over-valent idea can arise—not as a problem or imaginary problem—but as a solution.

If it arises as a problem, your mind will fight it off, because no one really wants or enjoys problems; but if it arises as a solution, a spurious solution, of course, then you will not fight it off because it has a high utility value; it is something you need and you have conjured it up to fill this need.

There exists very little likelihood that you will travel in a loop between your parked car and your bedroom for the rest of your life, but there is a very great possibility that if you are tormented by guilt and pain and self-doubt—and vast floods of self-accusations that hit every day without fail—that a fixed idea as solution will, once it is happened upon, remain. This is what I next saw with Kirsten and with Tim, upon their return to the United States from England, their second return, after Kirsten got out of the hospital. During the period that they lived in London that second time, an idea, an over-valent idea, one day came into their minds, and that was that.

Kirsten flew back several days before Tim. I did not meet her at the airport; I met her at her room on the top floor of the St. Francis, on the same noble hill of San Francisco that Grace Cathedral itself enjoys. I found her busily unpacking her many bags, and I thought: My God, how young she looks! In contrast to the last time I saw her . . . she glows. What has happened? Fewer lines marred her face; she moved with deft flexibility, and, when I entered the room, she glanced up and smiled at me, with none of the sour overtones, the various latent accusations I had become familiar with.

"Hi," she said.

"Boy, do you look great," I said.

She nodded. "I quit smoking." She lifted a wrapped package

from a suitcase open before her on the bed. "I brought you a couple of things. More are on the way by surface mail; I could only fit these in. Do you want to open them now?"

"I can't get over how good you look," I said.

"Don't you think I've lost weight?" She went over to stand before one of the suite's mirrors.

"Something like that," I said.

"I have a huge steamer trunk coming by ship. Oh, you've seen it. You helped me pack. I've got a lot to tell you."

"On the phone, you hinted—"

"Yes," Kirsten said. She seated herself on the bed, reached for her purse, opened it and took out a package of Player's Cigarettes; smiling at me, she lit a cigarette.

"I thought you quit," I said.

Reflexively, she put out the cigarette. "I still do it now and then, out of habit." She continued to smile at me, in a wild, yet veiled, mysterious way.

"Well, what is it?" I said.

"Look over there on the table."

I looked. A large notebook lay on the table.

"Open it," Kirsten said.

"Okay." I picked the notebook up and opened it. Some of the pages showed nothing but most of them had been scribbled on, in Kirsten's handwriting.

Kirsten said, "Jeff has come back to us. From the other world."

Had I said, then, at that moment: Lady, you are totally crazy —it would have made no difference, and I do not castigate myself because I failed to say it. "Oh," I said, nodding. "Well; what do you know." I tried to read her handwriting but I could not. "What do you mean?" I said.

"Phenomena," Kirsten said. "That's what Tim and I call them. He sticks needles under my fingernails at night and he sets all the clocks to six-thirty, which was the exact moment he died."

"Gee," I said.

"We've kept a record," Kirsten said. "We didn't want to tell you in a letter or over the phone; we wanted to tell you face-to-face. So I waited until now." She raised her arms in excitement. "Angel, he came back to us!"

"Well, I'll be fucked," I said mechanically.

"Hundreds of incidents. Hundreds of the phenomena. Let's go down to the bar. It started right away after we got back to England. Tim went to a medium. The medium said it was true. We knew it was true; nobody had to tell us but we wanted to be really certain because we thought possibly—just possibly—it was only a poltergeist. But it isn't! It's Jeff!"

"Hot damn," I said.

"Do you think I'm joking?"

"No," I said, with sincerity.

"Because we both witnessed it. And the Winchells saw it, too; our friends in London. And now that we're back in the United States, we want you to witness it and record it, for Tim's new book. He's writing a book about it, because this has meaning not just for us but for everyone, because it proves that man exists in the other world after he dies here."

"Yes," I said. "Let's go down to the bar."

"Tim's book is called *From the Other World*. He's already gotten a ten-thousand-dollar advance on it; his editor thinks it'll be his bestselling book by far."

"I stand before you amazed," I said.

"I know you don't believe me." Her tone, now, had become wooden, and edged with anger.

"Why would it enter my head not to believe you?" I said.

"Because people don't have faith."

"Maybe after I read the notebook."

"He—Jeff—set fire to my hair sixteen times."

"Wow."

"And he shattered all the mirrors in our flat. Not once but several times. We would get up and find them broken but we didn't hear it; neither of us heard anything. Dr. Mason—he's the medium we went to—said that Jeff wants us to understand that he forgives us. And he forgives you, too."

"Oh," I said.

"Don't be sarcastic with me," Kirsten said.

"I'll really truly try not to be sarcastic," I said. "It is as you can see a great surprise to me. I am left without words. I'll certainly recover, later on." I moved toward the door.

Edgar Barefoot, in one of his lectures on KPFA, discussed a form of inferential logic developed in India by the Hindu school. It is very old and has been much studied, not just in India but also in the West. It is the second means of knowledge by which man obtains accurate cognition and is called *anumana*, which is Sanskrit for: "Measuring along some other thing, inference." It has five stages and I will not go into it because it is difficult, but what is important about it is that if these five stages are correctly carried out—and the system contains safeguards by which one can determine precisely whether he has indeed carried them out—one is assured of going from premise to correct conclusion.

What especially dignifies *anumana* is step three, the illustration (*udaharana*); it requires what is called an invariable concomitance (*vyapti*, literally "pervasion"). The *anumana* form of inferential reasoning will only work if you can be absolutely certain that you indeed possess a *vyapti*; not a concomitance but an invariable concomitance (for example, late at night you hear a loud, sharp, echoing popping sound; you say to yourself, "That must be an auto backfiring because when an auto backfires, such a sound is created." This precisely is where inferential reasoning—reasoning, that is, from effect back to cause—breaks down. This is why in the West many logicians feel that inductive reasoning as such is suspect, that only deductive reasoning can be relied on. The Indian *anumana* strives for what is called a sufficient ground; the illustration requires an actual—not assumed—observation at all times, holding that no concomitance can be assumed *which fails to be exemplified*). We in the West have no syllogism exactly equal to the *anumana* and it is a shame that we do not, because had we such a rigorous form by which to check our inductive reasoning, Bishop Timothy Archer might well know of it, and had he known of it he would have known that his mistress waking up to find her hair singed does not, in fact, prove that the spirit of his dead son has returned from the other world, from, in essence, beyond the grave. Bishop Archer could and did fling around such terms as *hysteron proteron* because that logical fallacy is known in Greek—which is to say, Western—thought. But the *anumana* is from India. The Hindu logicians distinguished a typical fallacious ground that wrecked the *anumana*; they called it *het-vabhasa* ("merely the appearance of a ground") and this deals with only one step in the *anumana* out of five. They found all sorts of ways to fuck up this five-stage structure, any one of which a man with Bishop Archer's intelligence and education would have—or should have—been able to follow. That he could believe that a few weird unexplained events proved that Jeff was not only still alive (somewhere) but communicating with the living (somehow) shows that, like Wallenstein with his astrological charts during the Thirty Years War, the faculty of accurate cognition is variable and depends, in the final analysis, on what you want to believe, not what is so. A Hindu logician living centuries ago could have seen at a glance the basic fallacy in the reasoning that argued for Jeff's immortality. Thus the will to believe chases out the rational mind, whenever and wherever the two come into conflict. This is all I can assume, based on what I now was seeing.

I suppose we all do it, and do it often; but this was too glaring, too basic, to ignore. Kirsten's lunatic son, palpably schizophrenic, could show why asking a computer for the largest number short of two is an unintelligible request, but Bishop Timothy Archer, a lawyer, a scholar, a sane adult, could see a pin on the bedsheet beside his mistress and leap to the conclusion that his dead son was communicating with him from another world; moreover, Tim was writing it all up in a book, a book that would first be published and then read; he not only believed nonsense, he believed it in a public way.

"Wait'll the world hears about this," Bishop Archer and his mistress declared. Winning the heresy confrontation perhaps had convinced the bishop that he could not err; or, if he erred, no one could pull him down. He was wrong in both respects: he could err and there were people who could pull him down. He could pull himself down, for that matter.

I saw all this clearly as I sat with Kirsten at one of the bars in the St. Francis Hotel that day. And there was nothing I could do. Their fixed idea, being not a problem but a solution, could not be reasoned away, even though, finally, it amounted to a further problem on its own. They had tried to solve one problem with yet another. That is not how you do it; you do not solve one problem with another, greater problem. This is how Hitler, who uncannily resembled Wallenstein, had tried to win World War Two. Tim could admonish me about *hysteron proteron* reasoning to his heart's content—and then fall victim to the merely occult nonsense-stuff of popular paperback books. He might as well have believed that Jeff had been brought back by ancient astronauts from another star system.

I hurt, thinking about this. I hurt in my legs; I hurt throughout. Bishop Archer, who *hysteron-proteron*ed me up and down the street, he being a bishop, I being a young woman with a B.A. from Cal in liberal arts—I had one night heard Edgar Barefoot talk about this *anumana* Hindu thing and I knew more or could do more than the Bishop of California; and it didn't matter because the Bishop of California was not going to listen to me any more than he was going to listen to anybody else, over and beyond his mistress, who, like himself, was so steeped in guilt and so messed up by intrigue and deceit— emanating from their invisible relationship—that they had long since ceased to be able to reason properly. Bill Lundborg, shut up in jail now, could have set them straight. A taxi driver picked at random could have told them they were calculatedly destroying their lives—not just by believing this, although that alone was sufficiently destructive, but by deciding to publish it. Fine. Do it. Wreck your goddamn life. Cast charts of the stars, cast horoscopes while the most destructive war in modern times is raging. It will earn you a place in the history books—as a dunce. You get to sit on the tall stool in the corner; you get to wear the conical cap; you get to undo all the social activist shit you ever engineered in concert with some of the finest minds of the century. For this, Dr. Martin Luther King, Jr., died. For this you marched at Selma: to believe—and to say publicly that you believe—that the ghost of your dead son is pushing pins under the fingernails of your mistress while she is asleep. By all means publish it. Be my guest.

The logical error, of course, is that Kirsten and Tim reasoned backward from effect to cause; they did not see the cause —they saw only what they called "phenomena"—and from these phenomena they inferred Jeff as the secret cause operating in or from "the other world." The *anumana* structure shows that this inductive reasoning is not reasoning at all; with the *anumana* you begin with a premise and work through the five steps to your conclusion, and each step is airtight in relation to the step before it and the step after it, but there is no airtight logic involved in inferring that broken mirrors and singed hair and stopped clocks and all that other crap reveals and, in fact, proves another reality in which the dead are not dead; what it proves is that you are credulous and you are operating at a six-year-old level mentally: you are not reality-testing, you are lost in wish fulfillment, in autism. But it is an eerie kind of autism because it revolves around a single idea; it does not invade your general field, your total attention. Outside of this one spurious premise, this one faulty induction, you are clear-headed and sane. It is a localized madness, allowing you to speak and act normally the rest of the time. Therefore no one locks you up because you can still earn a living, take baths, drive a car, take out the trash. You are not crazy in the manner that Bill Lundborg is crazy, and in a certain sense (depending on how you define "crazy") you are not crazy at all.

Bishop Archer could still perform his pastoral chores. Kirsten could still buy clothes at the best stores in San Francisco. Neither of them would smash the windows of a U.S. Postal Service substation with their bare fists. You cannot arrest someone for believing that his son is communicating to this world from the next, or believing, for that matter, that there *is* a next world. Here the fixed idea shades off into religion generally; it becomes part of the other-worldly orientation of the revealed religions of the world. What is the difference between believing in a God you can't see and your dead son whom you can't see? What distinguishes one invisibility from another invisibility? Nonetheless, there is a difference, but it is tricky. It has to do with the general opinion, a slippery area; many people believe in God but few people believe that Jeff Archer sticks pins under Kirsten Lundborg's fingernails while she is asleep—that is the difference, and when put that way the subjectivity of it is plain. After all, Kirsten and Tim have the goddamn pins, and the burned hair, and the broken mirrors, not to mention the stopped clocks. But the two of them are making a logical error, for all that. Whether the people who believe in God are making an error I don't know, since their belief-system cannot be tested one way or another. It simply is faith.

Now I had been formally asked to sit in as a hopeful specta-tor to further "phenomena," and were they to occur I could, along with Tim and Kirsten, vouch for what I witnessed and add my name to Tim's forthcoming book—a book that, his editor had said, would undoubtedly outsell all his previous books based on less sensational material. But I could not be disinterested. Jeff had been my husband. I loved him. I wanted to believe. Worse, I sensed the psychological motor driving Kirsten and Tim to believe; I did not want to shoot their faith —or credulity—down because I could see what cynicism would do to them: it would leave them with nothing—leave them, once more, with staggering guilt, a guilt neither could cope with. I found myself, then, in a position where I had to comply, at least *pro forma*. I had to allege belief, allege interest, allege excitement. Neutrality would not be enough: enthusiasm was required. The damage had been done in England, before I was brought in on this. The decision was already made. If I said, "It's bullshit," they would continue on anyhow, but bitterly. Fuck the cynicism, I thought to myself as I sat with Kirsten that day at the St. Francis bar. There is nothing to be gained and a lot to lose, and anyhow it doesn't matter; Tim's book is going to get written and published—with or without me.

That is bad reasoning. Just because something bears the aspect of the inevitable one should not, therefore, go along willingly with it. But that was my reasoning. I saw this: if I told Kirsten and Tim how I felt, I could look forward never to seeing either of them again; they would cut me off, lop me away and discard me, and I would have my job at the record shop—my friendship with Bishop Archer would be a thing of the past. It meant too much to me; I could not let it go.

That was *my* faulty motivation, my wish. I wanted to keep on seeing them. And so I arranged to collude and *knew* that I was colluding. I decided that day in the St. Francis; I kept my mouth shut and my opinions to myself and I agreed to log the expected phenomena, and so I came to be a part of something that I knew was silly. Bishop Archer wrecked his career and not once did I try to talk him out of it. After all, I had tried to talk him out of his affair with Kirsten, to no avail. This time, he would not merely out-argue me; he would drop me. The cost, to me, would be too great.

I did not share their fixed idea. But I did as they did and talked as they talked. I'm mentioned in Bishop Archer's book; he gives me credit for "invaluable assistance" in "noting and recording the day-to-day manifestations of Jeff," of which there were none. I guess this is how the world is run: by weakness. It all goes back to Yeats' poem where he speaks of "the best lack all conviction" or however he phrases it. You know the poem; I don't have to quote it to you.

"When you shoot at a king you must kill him." When you plan to tell a world-famous man that he is a fool, you must face the fact that you will lose what you cannot bring yourself to lose. So I kept my fucking mouth shut, drank my drink, paid for my drink and Kirsten's, accepted the presents she had brought me from London, and promised to watch for fast-breaking phenomena, for all new developments.

And I would do it again, if I had the opportunity, because I loved the two of them very much, both Kirsten and Tim. I loved them far more than I cared about my own probity. Friendship loomed large; the importance of probity—hence, probity itself—dwindled and at last vanished entirely. I said good-bye to my integrity and kept my friendships alive. Somebody else will have to judge if I did the right thing, for I am still not disinterested; I still see only two friends, just returned from months abroad, friends I had longed for, especially with Jeff dead . . . friends I could not survive without, and, deep inside me, a subtle factor urged me on, a factor I did not admit to that day; I took pride in the fact that I knew a man who had marched with Dr. King at Selma, a famous man whom David Frost interviewed, whose opinions helped shape the modern intellectual world. There you have it, the essence of it. I defined myself to myself—my identity—in terms of being Bishop Archer's daughter-in-law and friend.

This is an evil motivation and it pinned me; it had me caught fast. "I know Bishop Timothy Archer," my mind uttered to itself in the darkness of the night. It whispered these words to me, bolstering my self-esteem; I, too, felt guilt over Jeff's suicide, and by participating in the life and times, the customs and habits of Bishop Archer, I lost my own self-doubts—or, at least, felt them diminish.

But there is a logical error in *my* reasoning—as well as an ethical one—and I had not perceived it; through his credulity and superstitious folly, the Bishop of California intended to barter away his influence, his power to control public opinion, the very power that drew me to him. Had I been able to time-bind adequately that day at the St. Francis, I would have foreseen this—and done differently. He would not long be a great man; he connived to transform himself from authority to crank. Thus, much of what drew me to him would soon vanish. So, in this respect, I stood in as deluded a state as he. This failed to register on my mind that day. I saw him only as he was then, not as he would be in a few years. I, too, was operating at a six-year-old level. I did not do any real harm, but I did not do any real good, and I debased myself really for nothing; no good came out of it, and when I look back I long bitterly for the insight I have now, long to have had it then. Bishop Archer swept us along with him because we loved him and believed in him, even when we knew he was wrong, and this is a terrible realization, a matter that should incite moral and spiritual dread. It does that, in me, now; but it did not then; my dread came too late; it came as hindsight.

This may be tiresome prattle to you, but it is something else to me: it is my heart's despair.

8

THE authorities did not keep Bill Lundborg in jail long. Bishop Archer arranged for his release—based on Bill's history of chronic mental illness—and presently a day came when the boy showed up at their apartment in the Tenderloin, wearing a wool sweater Kirsten had knitted for him, and his baggy pants, his pudgy face bland.

It personally gladdened me to see him. I had thought about him a number of times, wondering how he was doing. Jail did not seem to have done him any harm. Perhaps he did not distinguish it from his periodic confinements in the hospital. For all I knew, not that much difference existed; I had been confined in neither.

"Hi, Angel," he said to me as I entered the apartment; I had been forced to move my new Honda to keep from getting a ticket. "What is that you're driving?"

"A Honda Civic," I said.

"That's a good engine in that," Bill said. "It doesn't overrev like most mills that small. And it's sprung well. Do you have the four-speed or the five?"

"Four." I took off my coat and hung it in the hall closet.

"For that short a wheel-base, it rides really good," Bill said. "But on impact—if an American car hits you—you'd be wiped out. You'd probably roll."

He told me, then, the statistics on fatalities in single-car accidents. It presented a gloomy picture insofar as small foreign cars were concerned. My chances were nothing like, say, with a Mustang. Bill spoke with enthusiasm about the new front-wheel drive Oldsmobile, which he depicted as a major engineering advance in terms of traction and road-handling. It was evident that he believed I should get a larger car; he exhibited concern for my safety. I found this touching, and, moreover, he knew what he was talking about. I had lost two friends to a single-car accident involving a VW Beetle, the rear wheels of which had cambered in, causing the car to roll. Bill explained that that design had been successfully modified, starting in 1965;

after that, VW utilized a fixed rather than swing axle. It limited toe-in.

I think I have these terms right. I am dependent on Bill for this kind of information about cars. Kirsten listened with apathy; Bishop Archer revealed at least simulated attention, although I had the impression that this was a pose. It seemed impossible to me that he either cared or understood; for the bishop such matters as toe-in were as metaphysical matters are to the rest of us: mere speculation, and a frivolous one at that.

When Bill disappeared into the kitchen for a can of Coors, Kirsten's lips formed into a word directed at me.

"What?" I said, cupping my ear.

"Obsession." She nodded solemnly and with distaste.

Returning with the beer, Bill said, "Your life depends on the suspension of your car. A transversal torsion-bar suspension provides—"

"If I hear anything more about cars," Kirsten interrupted, "I am going to begin shrieking."

"Sorry," Bill said.

"Bill," Bishop Archer said, "if I were to buy a new car, what car should I get?"

"How much money—"

"I have the money," the bishop said.

"A BMW," Bill said. "Or a Mercedes-Benz. One advantage with a Mercedes-Benz is that nobody can steal it." He explained, then, about the astoundingly sophisticated locks on the Mercedes-Benz. "Even car repossessors have trouble getting into them," he finished. "A thief can rip off six Caddies and three Porsches in the time it takes to get into a Mercedes-Benz. So they tend to leave them alone; that way, you can leave your stereo in the car. Otherwise, with any other car, you have to lug it around with you." He told us, then, that it had been Carl Benz who had engineered and built the first practical automobile propelled by an internal combustion engine. In 1926 Benz had merged his company with Daimler-Motoren-Gesellschaft to form Daimler-Benz from which had come the Mercedes-Benz cars. The name "Mercedes" was that of a little girl whom Carl Benz had known, but Bill could not remember if Mercedes had been Benz's daughter, grandchild or what.

"So 'Mercedes' was not the name of an auto designer or

engineer," Tim said, "but, rather, the name of a child. And now that child's name is associated with some of the finest automobiles in the world."

"That's true," Bill said. He told us another story about automobiles that few people knew. Dr. Porsche, who had designed both the VW and, of course, the Porsche, had not invented the rear-engine, air-cooled design; he had encountered it in Czechoslovakia in an auto firm there when the Germans took over that country in 1938. Bill could not remember the name of the Czech car, but it had been eight-cylinder, not four, a high-powered, very fast car that rolled so readily that German officers were finally forbidden to drive them. Dr. Porsche had modified the eight-cylinder high-performance design at Hitler's personal order. "Hitler wanted an air-cooled engine utilized," Bill said, "because he expected to use the VWs on *autobahns* in the Soviet Union after Germany took it over, and because of the weather, because of the cold—"

"I think you should get a Jaguar," Kirsten interrupted, speaking to Tim.

"Oh, no," Bill said. "The Jaguar is one of the most unstable, trouble-prone cars in the world; it's far too complex and requires you to have it in the shop all the time. However, their terrific double-overhead cam engine is maybe the finest high-performance mill ever built, excepting the sixteen-cylinder touring cars of the Thirties."

"Sixteen cylinders?" I said, amazed.

"They were very smooth," Bill said. "There was a huge gap between the flivvers of the Thirties and the expensive touring cars; we don't have that gap now . . . there is a complete spread from, say, your Honda Civic—which is basic transportation—up to the Rolls. Price and quality go in small increments, now, which is a good thing. It's a measure of the change in society between then and now." He started to tell us about steam cars and why that design had failed; Kirsten, however, rose to her feet and glared at him severely.

"I think I'll go to bed," Kirsten said.

Tim said to her, "What time am I speaking at the Lions' Club tomorrow?"

"Oh God, I don't have that speech finished," Kirsten said.

"I can improvise," Tim said.

"It's on the tape. All I have to do is transcribe it."

"You can do that in the morning."

She stared at him.

"As I say," Tim said, "I can improvise."

To Bill and me, Kirsten said, " 'He can improvise.' " She continued to stare at the bishop, who shifted about uncomfortably. "Christ," she said.

"What's wrong?" Tim said.

"Nothing." She walked toward the bedroom. "I'll finish transcribing it. It wouldn't be a good idea if you—I don't know why we have to keep going into this. Promise me you won't launch into one of your tirades about the Zoroastrians."

Faintly but firmly, Tim said, "If I'm to trace the origins of Patristic thought—"

"I don't think the Lions want to hear about the desert fathers and the monastic life in the second century."

"Then that is exactly what I should talk about," Tim said. To Bill and me he said, "A monk was dispatched to a city carrying with him medicine for an ailing saint . . . the names are not necessary. What must be understood is that the ailing saint was a very great saint, one of the most beloved and revered in the north of Africa. When the monk reached the city, after a long journey across the desert, he—"

"Good night," Kirsten said, and disappeared into the bedroom.

"Good night," we all said.

After a pause, Tim continued, speaking in a low voice to Bill and me. "When he entered the city, the monk did not know where to go. Stumbling about in the darkness—it was night— he came across a beggar lying in the gutter, quite ill. The monk, after pondering the spiritual aspects of the issue, ministered to the beggar, applying the medication to him, with the result that the beggar soon showed signs of mending. However, now the monk had nothing to take to the great ailing saint. He therefore returned to the monastery from which he had come, dreadfully afraid of what his abbot would say. When he had told the abbot what he had done, the abbot said, 'You did the right thing.' " Tim fell silent, then. The three of us sat, none of us speaking.

"Is that it?" Bill said.

Tim said, "In Christianity no distinction is made between the humble and the great, the poor and the not-so-poor. The monk, by giving the medication to the first sick man he saw, instead of saving it for the great and famous saint, had seen into the heart of his Savior. There was a term of contempt used in Jesus' time for the ordinary people . . . they were dismissed as the *Am ha-aretz*, a Hebrew term meaning, simply, 'the people of the land,' meaning that they had no importance. It was to these people, the *Am ha-aretz*, that Jesus spoke, and with whom he mingled, ate and slept, that is, slept in their houses— although he did sleep occasionally in the houses of the rich, for even the rich are not excluded." Tim seemed somewhat downcast, I noticed.

" 'The bish,' " Bill said, smiling. "That's what Kirsten calls you behind your back."

Tim said nothing to that. We could hear Kirsten moving about in the other room; something fell and she cursed.

"What makes you think there's a God?" Bill said to Tim.

For a time Tim said nothing. He seemed quite tired, and yet I sensed him trying to summon a response. Wearily, he rubbed his eyes. "There is the ontological proof . . ." he murmured. "St. Anselm's ontological argument, that if a Being can be imagined—" He broke off, lifted his head, blinked.

"I can type up your speech," I said to him. "That was my job at the law office; I'm good at that." I rose. "I'll go tell Kirsten."

"There is no problem," Tim said.

"Wouldn't it be better if you were speaking from a written transcript?" I said.

Tim said, "I want to tell them about the—" He ceased speaking. "You know, Angel," he said to me, "I really love her. She has done so much for me. And if she hadn't been with me after Jeff's death . . . I don't know what I would have done; I'm sure you understand." To Bill, he said, "I am terribly fond of your mother. She is the person closest to me in all the world."

"Is there any proof of God's existence?" Bill said.

After a pause, Tim said, "A number of arguments are given. Perhaps the best is the argument from biology, advanced for instance by Teilhard de Chardin. Evolution—the existence of evolution—seems to point to a designer. Also there is Morrison's argument that our planet shows a remarkable hospitality toward complex forms of life. The chance of this happening on a random basis is very small. I'm sorry." He shook his head. "I'm not feeling well. We'll discuss it some other time. I would say, however, in brief, that the teleological argument, the argument from design in nature, from purpose in nature, is the strongest argument."

"Bill," I said, "the bishop is tired."

Opening the bedroom door, Kirsten, who now had on her robe and slippers, said, "The bishop is tired. The bishop is always tired. The bishop is too tired to answer the question, 'Is there any proof of the existence of God?' No; there is no proof. Where is the Alka-Seltzer?"

"I took the last packet," Tim said, remotely.

"I have some in my purse," I said.

Kirsten closed the bedroom door. Loudly.

"There are proofs," Tim said.

"But God doesn't talk to anybody," Bill said.

"No," Tim said. He rallied, then; I saw him draw himself up. "However, the Old Testament gives us many instances of Yahweh addressing his people through the prophets. This fountain of revelation dried up, finally. God no longer speaks to man. It is called 'the long silence.' It has lasted two thousand years."

"I realize God talked to people in the Bible," Bill said, "in the olden days, but why doesn't he talk to them now? Why did he stop?"

"I don't know," Tim said. He said no more; there he ceased. I thought: You should not stop there. That is not the place to come to the end.

"Please go on," I said.

"What time is it?" Tim said; he looked around the living room. "I don't have my watch."

Bill said, "What's this nonsense about Jeff coming back from the next world?"

Oh God, I said to myself; I shut my eyes.

"I really wish you would explain it to me," Bill said to Tim. "Because it's impossible. It's not just unlikely; it's impossible." He waited. "Kirsten has been telling me about it," he said. "It's the stupidest thing I ever heard of."

"Jeff has communicated with the two of us," Tim said.

"Through intermediary phenomena. Many times, in many ways." All at once, he reddened; he drew himself up and the authority that lay deep in him rose to the surface: he changed as he sat there from a tired, middle-aged man with personal problems into force itself, the force of conviction contrived into, formed into, words. "It is God Himself working on us and through us to bring forth a brighter day. My son is with us now; he is with us in this room. He never left us. What died was a material body. Every material thing perishes. Whole planets perish. The physical universe itself will perish. Are you going to argue, then, that nothing exists? Because that is where your logic will carry you. It isn't possible right now to prove that external reality exists. Descartes discovered that; it's the basis of modern philosophy. All you can know for sure is that your own mind, your own consciousness, exists. You can say, 'I am' and that's all. And that is what Yahweh tells Moses to say when the people ask who he has talked to. 'I am,' Yahweh says. *Ehyeh*, in Hebrew. You also can say that and that is all you can say; that exhausts it. What you see is not world but a represen-tation formed in and by your own mind. Everything that you experience you know by faith. Also, you may be dreaming. Had you thought of that? Plato relates that a wise old man, probably an Orphic, said to him, 'Now we are dead and in a kind of prison.' Plato did not consider that an absurd state-ment; he tells us that it is weighty and something to think about. 'Now we are dead.' We may have no world at all. I have enough evidence—your mother and I—for Jeff returning to us as I have that the world itself exists. We do not suppose he has come back; we experience him as coming back. We have lived and are living through it. So it is not our opinion. It is real."

"Real for you," Bill said.

"What more can reality give?"

"Well, I mean," Bill said, "I don't believe it."

"The problem does not lie with our experience in this matter," Tim said. "It lies with your belief-system. Within the confines of your belief-system, such a thing is impossible. Who can say, truly say, what is possible? We have no knowledge of what is and isn't possible; we do not set the limits—God sets the limits." Tim pointed at Bill; his finger was steady. "What one believes and what one knows depend, in the final analysis, on God: you can't will your own consent or refusal to consent; it is a gift from God, an instance of our dependence. God grants us a world and compels our assent to that world; he makes it real for us: this is one of his powers. Do you believe that Jesus was the Son of God, was God Himself? You don't believe that, either. So how can I prove to you that Jeff returned to us from the other world? I can't even demonstrate that the Son of Man walked this Earth two thousand years ago for us and lived for us and died for us, for our sins, and rose in glory on the third day. Am I not right about that? Do you not deny that also? What do you believe, then? In objects you get into and drive around the block. There may be no objects and no block; someone pointed out to Descartes that a malicious demon may cause our assent to a world that is not there, may impress a forgery onto us as an ostensible representation of the world. If that happened, we would not know. We must trust; we must trust God. I trust in God that he would not deceive me; I deem the Lord faithful and true and incapable of deceit. For you that question does not even exist, for you will not grant that He exists in the first place. You ask for proof. If I told you this minute that I have heard God's voice speaking to me—would you believe that? Of course not. We call people who speak to God pious and we call people to whom God speaks lunatics. This is an age where there is little faith. It is not God who is dead; it is our faith that has died."

"But—" Bill gestured. "It doesn't make any sense. Why would he come back?"

"Tell me why Jeff lived in the first place," Tim said. "Then perhaps I can tell you why he came back. Why do you live? For what purpose were you created? You do not know who created you—assuming anyone did—and you do not know why, assuming there is a why. Perhaps no one created you and perhaps there is no purpose to your life. No world, no purpose, no Creator, and Jeff has not come back to us. Is that your logic? Is that how you live out your life? Is that what Being, in Heidegger's sense, is to you? That is an impoverished kind of inauthentic Being. It strikes me as weak and barren and, in the end, futile. There must be something you can believe, Bill. Do you believe in yourself? Will you grant that you, Bill Lundborg, exist? You will grant that; fine. Good enough. We have a start.

Examine your body. Do you have sense organs? Eyes, ears, taste, touch and smell? Then, probably, this percept-system was designed to receive information. If that is so, it is reasonable to assume that information exists. If information exists, it probably pertains to something. Probably, there is a world—not certainly but probably, and you are linked to that world through your sense organs. Do you create your own food? Do you out of yourself, out of your own body, generate the food that you need in order to live? You do not. Therefore it is logical to assume that you are dependent on this outer world, of whose existence you possess only probable knowledge, not necessary knowledge; world is for us only a contingent truth, not an ineluctable one. What does this world consist of? What is out there? Do your senses lie? If they lie, why were they caused to come into being? Did you create your own sense organs? No, you did not. Someone or something else did. Who is that someone who is not you? Apparently you are not alone, the sole existent reality; apparently there are others, and one of them or several of them designed and built you and your body the way Carl Benz designed and built the first motorcar. How do I know there was a Carl Benz? Because you told me? I told you about my son Jeff returning—"

"Kirsten told me," Bill corrected him.

"Does Kirsten normally lie to you?" Tim said.

"No," Bill said.

"What do she and I gain by saying that Jeff has returned to us from the other world? Many people will not believe us. You yourself do not believe us. We say it because we believe it is true. And we have reasons to believe it is true. We have both seen things, witnessed things. I don't see Carl Benz in this room but I believe he once existed. I believe that the Mercedes-Benz is named after a little girl and a man. I am a lawyer; I am a person familiar with the criteria by which data is scrutinized. We—Kirsten and I—have the evidence of Jeff, the phenomena."

"Yeah, but that phenomena you have, all of them—they don't prove anything. You're just assuming Jeff caused it, caused those things. You don't know."

Tim said, "Let me give you an example. You look under your parked car and you find a pool of water. Now, you don't *know* that—the water—came from your motor; that is something you have to assume. You have evidence. As an attorney, I understand what constitutes evidence. You as an auto-mechanic—"

"Is the car parked in your own parking slot?" Bill said. "Or is it in a public parking lot, like at the supermarket."

Slightly taken aback, Tim paused. "I don't follow you."

"If it's your own garage or parking slot," Bill said, "where only you park, then it's probably from your car. Anyhow, it wouldn't be from the motor; it'd be from the radiator or the water pump or one of the hoses."

"But this is something you assume," Tim said. "Based on the evidence."

"It could be power-steering fluid. That looks a lot like water. It's sort of pinkish. Also, your transmission, if you have an automatic transmission, uses the same kind of fluid. Do you have power steering?"

"On what?" Tim said.

"On your car."

"I don't know. I'm speaking about a hypothetical car."

"Or it could be engine oil," Bill said, "in which case, it wouldn't be pink. You have to distinguish whether it's water or whether it's oil, if it's from the power-steering or the transmission; it could be several things. If you're in a public place and you see a puddle under your car, it probably doesn't mean anything because a lot of people park where you're parked; it could have come from the car parked there before you. The best thing to do is—"

"But you're only able to make an assumption," Tim said. "You can't know it came from your car."

"You can't know right away, but you can find out. Okay; let's say it's your own garage and no one else parks there. The first thing to figure out is what kind of fluid it is. So you reach under the car—you may have to back it out first—and dip your finger in the fluid. Now, is it pink? Or brown? Is it oil? Is it water? Let's say it's water. Well, it could be normal; it could be overflow from the relief system of your radiator; after you turn off an engine, the water gets hotter sometimes and blows out through the relief pipe."

"Even if you can determine that it is water," Tim said, doggedly, "you can't be sure it came from your car."

"Where else would it come from?"

"That's an unknown factor. You're acting on indirect evidence; you didn't see the water come from your car."

"Okay—turn the engine on, let it run, and watch. See if it drips."

"Wouldn't that take a long time?" Tim said.

"Well, you have to know. You should check the level in the power-steering system; you should check your transmission level, your radiator, your motor oil; you should routinely check all those things. While you're standing there, you can check them. Some of them, like the level of fluid in the transmission, have to be checked while the motor's running. Meanwhile, you can also check your tire pressure. What pressure do you carry?"

"In what?" Tim said.

"Your tires." Bill smiled. "There're five of them. One in your trunk; your spare. You probably forget to check that when you check the others. You won't find out you've got no air in your spare until you get a blowout someday and then you'll find out if you have air in your spare. Do you have a bumper jack or an axle jack? What kind of car are you driving?"

"I think it's a Buick," Tim said.

"It's a Chrysler," I said quietly.

"Oh," Tim said.

After Bill departed for his trip back to the East Bay, Tim and I sat together in the living room of the Tenderloin apartment, and Tim talked openly and candidly to me. "Kirsten and I," he said, "have been having a few difficulties." He sat beside me on the couch, speaking in a low voice so that Kirsten, in the bedroom, would not hear.

"How many downers is she taking?" I said.

"You mean barbiturates?"

"Yes, I mean barbiturates," I said.

"I really don't know. She has a doctor who gives her all she wants . . . she gets a hundred at one time. Seconal. And also she has Amytal. I think the Amytal is from a different doctor."

"You better find out how many she's taking."

Tim said, "Why would Bill resist the realization that Jeff has come back to us?"

"Lord only knows," I said.

"The purpose of my book is to provide comfort to heart-broken people who have lost loved ones. What could be more reassuring than the knowledge that there is a life beyond the trauma of death, just as there is life beyond the trauma of birth? We are assured by Jesus that an afterlife awaits us; on this the whole promise of salvation depends. 'I am the Resurrection. If anyone believes in me, even though he dies he will live, and whoever lives and believes in me will never die.' And then Jesus says to Martha, 'Do you believe in this?' to which Martha responds, 'Yes, Lord. I believe that you are the Christ, the Son of God, the one who was to come into this world.' Later, Jesus says, 'For what I have spoken does not come from myself; no, what I was to say, what I had to speak, was commanded by the Father who sent me, and I know that his commands mean eternal life.' Let me get my Bible." Tim reached for a copy of the Bible which lay on the end table. "First Corinthians, fifteen, twelve. 'Now if Christ raised from the dead is what has been preached, how can some of you be saying that there is no resurrection of the dead? If there is no resurrection of the dead, Christ himself cannot have been raised, and if Christ has not been raised then our preaching is useless and your believing it is useless; indeed, we are shown up as witnesses who have committed perjury before God, because we swore in evidence before God that he had raised Christ to life. For if the dead are not raised, Christ has not been raised, and if Christ has not been raised, you are still in your sins. And what is more serious, all who have died in Christ have perished. If our hope in Christ has been for this life only, we are the most unfortunate of all people. But Christ has in fact been raised from the dead, the first-fruits of all who have fallen asleep.'" Tim closed his Bible. "That says it clearly and plainly. There can be no doubt whatsoever."

"Guess so," I said.

"So much evidence turned up at the Zadokite Wadi. So much that sheds light on the whole *kerygma* of early Christianity. We know so much, now. In no way was Paul speaking metaphorically; man literally rises from the dead. They had the techniques. It was a science. We would call it medicine today. They had the *anokhi*, there at the *wadi*."

"The mushroom," I said.

He eyed me. "Yes, the *anokhi* mushroom."

"Bread and broth," I said.

"Yes."

"But we don't have it now."

"We have the Eucharist."

I said, "But you know and I know that the substance is not there, in the Eucharist. It's like the cargo cults where the natives build fake airplanes."

"Not at all."

"How is it different?"

"The Holy Spirit—" He broke off.

"That's what I mean," I said.

Tim said, "I feel that the Holy Spirit is responsible for Jeff coming back."

"So then you reason that the Holy Spirit does still exist and always existed and is God, one of the forms of God."

"I do now," Tim said. "Now that I've seen evidence. I did not believe it until I saw the evidence, the clocks set at the time of Jeff's death, Kirsten's burned hair, the broken mirrors, the pins stuck under her fingernails. You saw her clothes all disarranged that time; we had you come in and see for yourself. We didn't do that. No living person did that; we wouldn't manufacture evidence. Do you believe we would do that, contrive a fraud?"

"No," I said.

"And the day that those books leaped out of the bookshelf and fell to the floor—no one was there. You saw that with your own eyes."

"Do you think the *anokhi* mushroom still exists?" I asked.

"I don't know. There is a *vita verna* mushroom mentioned in Pliny the Elder's *Historia Naturalis, Book Eight*. He lived in the first century . . . it would be about the right time. And this citation was not something he derived from Theophrastus; this was a mushroom he saw himself, from his direct knowledge of Roman gardens. It may be the *anokhi*. But that's only a guess. I wish we could be sure." He changed the subject, then, as was his custom; Tim Archer's mind never stayed on one topic for long. "It's schizophrenia that Bill has, isn't it?"

"Yep," I said.

"But he can earn a living."

"When he's not in the hospital," I said. "Or spiraling into himself and on the way to the hospital."

"He seems to be doing fine right now. But I note—an inability to theorize."

"He has trouble abstracting," I said.

"I wonder where and how he'll wind up," Tim said. "The prognosis . . . it's not good, Kirsten says."

"It's zero. For recovery. Zilch. Zip. But he's smart enough to stay off drugs."

"He does not have the advantage of an education."

"I'm not sure an education is an advantage. All I do is work in a record store. And I wasn't hired for that because of anything I learned in the English Department at Cal."

"I've been meaning to ask you which recording of Beethoven's *Fidelio* we should buy," Tim said.

"The Klemperer," I said. "On Angel. With Christa Ludwig as Leonora."

"I am very fond of her aria," Tim said.

"*'Abscheulicher! Wo Eilst Due Hin?'* She does it very well. But no one can match Frieda Leider's recording years ago. It's a collectors' item . . . it may have been dubbed onto an LP; if so, I've never seen it. I heard it once over KPFA, years ago. I never forgot it."

Tim said, "Beethoven was the greatest genius, the greatest creative artist the world has ever seen. He transformed man's conception of himself."

"Yes," I said. "The prisoners in *Fidelio* when they're let out into the light . . . it is one of the most beautiful passages in all music."

"It goes beyond beauty," Tim said. "It involves an apprehension of the nature of freedom itself. How can it be that purely abstract music, such as his late quartets, can without words change human beings in terms of their own awareness of themselves, in terms of their ontological nature? Schopenhauer believed that art, in particular music, had—has—the power to cause the will, the irrational, striving will, to somehow turn back onto and into itself and cease to strive. He considered this a religious experience, although temporary. Somehow art, somehow music especially, has the power to transform man from an irrational thing into some rational entity that is not driven by biological impulses, impulses that cannot by definition ever be satisfied. I remember when I first heard the final movement of the Beethoven *Thirteenth Quartet*—not the 'Grosse Fuge' but the allegro that he added later in place of the 'Grosse Fuge.' It's such an odd little bit, that allegro . . . so brisk and light, so sunny."

I said, "I've read that it was the last thing he wrote. That little allegro would have been the first work of Beethoven's fourth period, had he lived. It's not really a third-period piece."

"Where did Beethoven derive the concept, the entirely new and original concept of human freedom that his music expresses?" Tim asked. "Was he well-read?"

"He belonged to the period of Goethe and Schiller. The *Aufklärung*, the German Enlightenment."

"Always Schiller. It always comes back to that. And from Schiller to the rebellion of the Dutch against the Spanish, the War of the Lowlands. Which shows up in Goethe's *Faust, Part Two*, where Faust finally finds something that will satisfy him, and he bids the moment stay. Seeing the Dutch reclaiming land from the North Sea. I translated that passage, once, myself; I wasn't satisfied with any of the English translations available. I don't know what I did with it . . . that was years ago. Do you know the Bayard Taylor translation?" He rose, approached a row of books, found the volume, brought it back, opening it as he walked.

> " '*Below the hills, a marshy plain*
> *infects what I so long have been retrieving:*
> *that stagnant pool likewise to drain*
> *were now my latest and my best achieving.*
> *To many millions let me furnish soil,*
> *though not secure, let free for active toil:*
> *green, fertile fields, where men and herds go forth*
> *at once, with comfort, on the newest earth,—*
> *all swiftly settled on the hill's firm base,*

> *raised by a bold, hard-working populace.*
> *In here, a land like Paradise about:*
> *up to the brink the tide may roar without,*
> *yet though it gnaw, to burst with force the limit,*
> *by common impulse all men seek to hem it.*
> *Yes! to this thought I hold with firm persistence,*
> *this wisdom's ultimate and true:*
> *he only earns his freedom and existence—'"*

I said, "'Who daily conquers them anew.'"

"Yes," Tim said; he closed the copy of *Faust, Part Two.* "I wish I hadn't lost the translation I made." He then opened the book again. "Do you mind if I read the rest?"

"Please do," I said.

> "'Thus here, by dangers girt, shall glide away
> of childhood, manhood, age, and vigorous day.
> And such a throng I fain would see,—
> stand on free soil among a people free!
> Then dared I hail the Moment fleeting,
> "Ah, linger still—thou art so fair!"'"

"At that point God has won the bet in heaven," I said.

"Yes," Tim said, nodding.

> "'The traces cannot, of mine earthly being,
> in aeons perish: they are there!—
> Anticipating here such lofty bliss,
> I now enjoy the highest Moment,—this.'"

"That's a very beautiful and clear translation," I said.

Tim said, "Goethe wrote *Part Two* just a year before his death. I remember only one German word from that passage: *verdienen. Earns.* 'Earns his freedom.' I suppose that would be *Freiheit, freedom.* Perhaps it went, *'Verdient seine Freiheit—'"* He broke off. "That's the best I can do. 'Earns his freedom who daily conquers it—them, freedom and existence—anew.' The highest point in German Enlightenment. From which they so tragically fell. From Goethe, Schiller, Beethoven to the Third Reich and Hitler. It seems impossible."

"And yet it had been prefigured in Wallenstein," I said.

"Who picked his generals by means of astrological prognostications. How could an intelligent, educated man, a great man, really, one of the most powerful men of his times—how could he begin to believe in that?" Bishop Archer said. "It is a mystery to me. It is an enigma that perhaps will never be solved."

I saw how tired he was, so I got my coat and purse, said good night, and departed.

My car had been ticketed. Shit, I said to myself as I pulled the ticket from the wiper-blade and stuck it into my pocket. While we're reading Goethe, Lovely Rita Meter-Maid is ticketing my car. What a strange world, I thought; or, rather, strange worlds —plural. They do not come together.

9

BISHOP TIMOTHY ARCHER conceived in his mind after much prayer and pondering, after much application of his brilliant analytical faculties, the notion that he had no choice but to step down as Bishop of the Episcopal Diocese of California and go—as he phrased it—into the private sector. He discussed this matter with Kirsten and me at length.

"I have no faith in the reality of Christ," he informed us. "None whatsoever. I cannot in good conscience go on preaching the *kerygma* of the New Testament. Every time I get up in front of my congregation, I feel that I am deceiving them."

"You told Bill Lundborg that night that Christ's reality is proven by Jeff coming back," I said.

"It's not," Tim said. "It fails to. I have exhaustively scrutinized the situation and it fails to."

"What does it prove, then?" Kirsten said.

"Life after death," Tim said. "But not the reality of Christ. Jesus was a teacher whose teachings were not even original. I have the name of a medium, a Dr. Garret living in Santa Barbara. I will be flying down there to consult him, to try to talk to Jeff. Mr. Mason recommends him." He examined a slip of paper. "Oh," he said. "Dr. Garret is a woman. Rachel Garret. Hmmm . . . I was certain it was a man." He asked if the two of us wished to accompany him to Santa Barbara. It was his intention (he explained) to ask Jeff about Christ. Jeff could tell him, through the medium, Dr. Rachel Garret, if Christ were real or not, genuinely the Son of God and all the rest of that stuff that the churches teach. This would be an important trip; Tim's decision as to whether to resign his post as bishop hinged on this.

Moreover, Tim's faith was involved. He had spent decades rising within the Episcopal Church, but now he seriously doubted whether Christianity was valid. That was Tim's term: "valid." It struck me as a weak and trendy term, falling tragically short of the magnitude of the forces contending within Tim's heart and mind. However, it was the term he used; he spoke in a calm manner, devoid of any hysterical overtones. It was as if he were planning whether or not to buy a suit of clothes.

"Christ," he said, "is a role, not a person. It—the word—is a mistransliteration from the Hebrew 'Messiah,' which literally means the Anointed One, which is to say the Chosen One. The Messiah, of course, comes at the end of the world and ushers in the Age of Gold which replaces the Age of Iron, the age we now live in. This finds its most beautiful expression in the *Fourth Eclogue* of Virgil. Let me see . . . I have it here." He went to his books as he always did in time of gravity.

"We don't need to hear Virgil," Kirsten said in a biting tone.

"Here it is," Tim said, oblivious to her.

"*'Ultima Cumaei venit iam carminis aetas; magnus—'*"

"That's enough," Kirsten said sharply.

He glanced at her, puzzled.

Kirsten said, "I think it's insanely foolish and selfish of you to resign as bishop."

"Let me translate the eclogue for you, at least," Tim said. "Then you'll understand better."

"I understand that you're destroying your life and mine," Kirsten said. "What about me?"

He shook his head. "I'll be hired on at the Foundation for Free Institutions."

"What the hell is that?" Kirsten said.

"It's a think tank," I said. "In Santa Barbara."

"Then you're going to be talking with them while you're down there?" Kirsten said.

"Yes." He nodded. "I have an appointment with Pomeroy, who's in charge of it—Felton Pomeroy. I'd be their Consultant in Theological Matters."

"They're very highly thought of," I said.

Kirsten gave me a look that would have withered trees.

"There's been nothing decided," Tim said. "We are going to see Rachel Garret anyhow . . . I see no reason why I shouldn't combine the two in a single trip. That way, I'll have to fly down there only once."

"I'm supposed to set up your appointments," Kirsten said.

"Actually," Tim said, "this will be a purely informal discussion. We'll have lunch . . . I'll meet the other consultants. I'll see their buildings and gardens. They have very lovely gardens. I saw the Foundation's gardens several years ago and still remember them." To me he said, "You'll love them, Angel. Every kind of rose is represented, especially Peace. All the five-star patented roses are there, or however it is roses are rated. May I read the two of you the translation of Virgil's eclogue?

> " 'Now comes the final age announced in the
> Cumaen Sibyl's chant; the great succession
> of epochs is born anew. Now the Virgin
> returns, the reign of Saturn returns; now
> a new race descends from heaven on high.
> O chaste Lucina, goddess of births! smile
> upon the boy just born, in whose time the
> race of iron shall first cease, and a race
> of gold shall arise throughout the world.
> Thine own Apollo is now king.' "

Kirsten and I looked at each other. I saw Kirsten's lips move but I heard no sound. Heaven only knows what she was saying and thinking at that moment, as she witnessed Tim shoot down his career and life out of conviction—more properly, lack of conviction: faith in the Savior.

The problem for Kirsten was, simply, that she could not see the problem. To her, Tim's dilemma was a phantom dilemma, manufactured for bookish reasons. According to her reasoning, he had the option to shed the problem any time he saw fit; her analysis was, simply, that Tim had become restive in his job as bishop and wanted to move on; asserting a loss of faith in Christ was his way of justifying his career move. Since it was a stupid career move, she did not approve. After all, she gained so very much from his status; as she had said, Tim was not thinking about her: he thought only of himself.

"Dr. Garret is highly recommended," Tim said, almost in a plaintive voice, as if appealing to one or the other of us for support.

"Tim," I said, "I really think—"

"You think with your crotch," Kirsten said.

"What?" I said.

"You heard me. I know about your little conversations, that you two have, after I go to bed. When you're alone. And I know you've been meeting."

"Meeting what?" I said.

"Each other."

"Christ," I said.

"'Christ,'" Kirsten echoed. "Always Christ. Always the summoning of the Almighty Son of God to justify your selfishness and what you're up to. I find it disgusting; I find both of you disgusting." To Tim she said, "I know you visited her goddamn record store last week."

"To buy an album," Tim said. "Of *Fidelio.*"

"You could have gotten it here in the City," Kirsten said. "Or I could have picked it up for you."

Tim said, "I wanted to see what she had—"

"She doesn't have anything I don't have," Kirsten said.

"The *Missa Solemnis,*" Tim said faintly; he seemed dazed; appealing to me, he said, "Can you reason with her?"

"I can reason with myself," Kirsten said. "I can reason out exactly what's going on."

"You better knock off taking those downers, Kirsten," I said.

"And you better stop turning on five times a day." Her look carried such furious hate that I could not credit my senses. "You smoke enough grass to—" She broke off. "More than the San Francisco Police Department uses in a month. I'm sorry; I'm not feeling well. Excuse me." She walked into the bedroom; the door shut silently after her. We could hear her stirring around. Then we heard her go into the bathroom; water ran: she was taking a pill, probably a barbiturate.

To Tim, who stood inert and amazed, I said, "Barbiturates cause that kind of personality change. It's the pills talking, not her."

"I think—" He rallied. "I really want to fly down to Santa Barbara and see Dr. Garret. Do you think it's the fact that she's a woman?"

"Kirsten?" I said. "Or Garret?"

"Garret. I could swear it was a man; I just now noticed the first name. I may have gotten it wrong. Maybe that's what's upsetting her. She'll calm down. We'll go together. Dr. Mason said that Dr. Garret is elderly and infirm and semiretired, so she won't pose any threat to Kirsten, once she sees her."

To change the subject, I said, "Did you play the *Missa Solemnis* that I sold you?"

"No," Tim said vaguely. "I haven't had time."

"It's not the best recording," I said. "Columbia uses a peculiar microphone placement; they have microphones scattered around throughout the orchestra, with the idea of bringing out the individual instruments. The idea is good, but it does away with hall ambiance."

"It bothers her that I'm stepping down," Tim said. "As bishop."

"You should think about it longer," I said. "Before you do it. Are you sure it's this medium that you want to consult? Isn't there someone in the church you go to when you have a spiritual crisis?"

"I will be consulting Jeff. The medium acts as a passive agent, much in the fashion that a telephone acts." He went on, then, to explain how misunderstood mediums are; I half-listened, neither impressed nor caring. Kirsten's hostility had upset me, even though I had become used to it; this amounted to more than her chronic bitchiness. I can tell a red freak when I see one, I said to myself. The personality change, the hair-trigger response. The paranoia. She is crapping out on us, I said to myself. She is going down the drain. Worse, she is not going down the drain alone; her nails are dug deep in us and we go perforce along. Shit. This is just dreadful; a man like Tim Archer should not have to put up with this. *I* should not have to.

Kirsten opened the bedroom door. "Come in here," she said to Tim.

"I will in a minute," Tim said.

"You will come in here now."

I said, "I'll take off."

"No," Tim said, "you will not take off. I have further things to discuss with you. Is it your contention that I should not step down as bishop? When my book comes out about Jeff, I will have to step down. The church will not allow me to publish a controversial book of that sort. It is too radical for them; put another way, they are too reactionary for it. It is ahead of its time and they are behind the times. There is no difference between my stand on this issue and my stand on the Vietnam War; I bucked the Establishment on that, and I should—theoretically—be able to buck the Establishment on the issue of life beyond the grave, but with the war I have support from the youth of America. But in this matter, I have support from no one."

Kirsten said, "You have my support but that doesn't matter to you."

"I mean public support. The support of those in power, those who control human minds, unfortunately."

"My support means nothing to you," Kirsten repeated.

"It means everything to me," Tim said. "I could not—I would not—have dared to write the book without you; I would not even have *believed* without you. It is you who gives me my strength. My capacity to understand. And from Jeff, when we have contacted him, I will learn about Jesus Christ one way or another. I will learn if the Zadokite Documents do, in fact, indicate that Jesus spoke only secondhand of what he had been taught . . . or possibly Jeff will tell me that Christ is with him, or he with Christ, in the other world, the upper realm, where we all go eventually, where he is now, reaching across to us as best he can, God bless him."

I said, "You see this business with Jeff, then, as a sort of opportunity. To clear up your doubts one way or another about the meaning of the Zadokite—"

"I think I have made that clear," Tim interrupted, peevishly. "That is why it is so crucial. To talk to him."

How strange, I thought. To use his son—make calculated use of his dead son—to determine an historical issue. But it is more than an historical issue: it is Tim Archer's entire corpus of faith, the summation, for him, of belief itself. Belief or the falling away of belief. What is at stake here is belief versus nihilism . . . for Tim to lose Christ is for Tim to lose everything. And he has lost Christ; his statements to Bill that night may have been Tim's last defense of the fortress before that fortress fell. It may have fallen then, or perhaps before then; Tim argued from memory, as if from a page. A written speech spread out before him, as when, in the celebration of the Last Supper, he reads from the Book of Common Prayer.

The son, his son, my husband, subordinated to an intellectual matter—I could never, myself, view it that way. This amounts to a depersonalization of Jeff Archer; he is converted into an instrument, a device for learning; why, he is converted into a talking book! Like all these books that Tim forever reaches for, especially in moments of crisis. Everything worth knowing can be found in a book; conversely, if Jeff is important he is important not as a person but as a book; it is books for books' sakes then, not knowledge, even, for the sake of knowledge. The book is the reality. For Tim to love and appreciate his son, he must—as impossible as this may seem—he must regard him as a kind of book. The universe to Tim Archer is one great set of reference books from which he picks and chooses as his restless mind veers on, always seeking the new, always turning away from the old; it is the very opposite of that passage from *Faust* that he read; Tim has not found the moment where he says, *"Stay"*; it is still fleeing from him, still in motion.

And I am not much different, I realized; I, who graduated from the English Department at U.C. Berkeley—Tim and I are of a kind. Has it not been the final canto of Dante's *Commedia* that struck off my identity when I first read it that day when I was in school? Canto Thirty-three of *Paradiso*, for me the culmination, where Dante says:

> *"I beheld leaves within the unfathomed blaze*
> *Into one volume bound by love, the same*
> *That the universe holds scattered through its maze.*
> *Substance and accidents, and their modes, became*
> *As if fused together, all in such wise*
> *That what I speak of is one simple flame."*

The superb Laurence Binyon translation; and then C. H. Grandgent comments on this passage:

> "God is the Book of the Universe."

To which another commentator—I forget which one—said, "This is a Platonist notion." Platonist or otherwise, this is the sequences of words that framed me, that made me what I am: this is *my* source, this vision and report, this view of final things. I do not call myself a Christian but I cannot forget this view, this wonder. I remember the night I read that final canto of *Paradiso*, read it—truly read it—for the first time; I had that infected tooth and I hurt hideously, unbearably, so I sat up all night drinking bourbon—straight—and reading Dante, and at nine A.M. the next day I drove to the dentist's without phoning, without an appointment, showed up with tears dripping down my face, demanding that Dr. Davidson do something for me . . . which he did. So that final canto is deeply impressed onto and into me; it is associated with terrible pain, and pain that went on for hours, into the night, so there was no one to talk to; and out of that I came to fathom the ultimate things in my own way, not a formal or official way but a way nonetheless.

> "He who learns must suffer. And even in our sleep pain that cannot forget falls drop by drop upon the heart, and in our own despair, against our will, comes wisdom to us by the awful grace of God."

Or however it goes. Aeschylus? I forget, now. One of the three of them who wrote the tragedies.

Which means that I can say with all truthfulness that for me the moment of greatest understanding in which I knew spiritual reality at last came in connection with emergency root-canal irrigation, two hours in the dentist chair. And twelve hours drinking bourbon—bad bourbon at that—and simply reading Dante without listening to the stereo or eating—there was no way I could eat—and suffering, and it was all worth it; I will never forget it. *I am no different, then, from Timothy Archer.* To me, too, books are real and alive; the voices of human beings issue forth from them and compel my assent, the way God compels our assent to world, as Tim said. When you have been in that much distress, you are not going to forget what you did and saw and thought and read that night; I did nothing, saw nothing, thought nothing; I read and I remember; I did not read *Howard the Duck* or *The Fabulous Furry Freak Brothers* or *Snatch Comix* that night; I read Dante's *Commedia*, from *Inferno* through *Purgatorio*, until at last I arrived in the three colored rings of light . . . and the time was nine A.M. and I could get into my fucking car and shoot out into traffic and Dr. Davidson's office, crying and cursing the whole way, with no breakfast, not even coffee, and stinking of sweat and bourbon, a sorry mess indeed, much gaped at by the dentist's receptionist.

So for me in a certain unusual way—for certain unusual reasons—books and reality are fused; they join through one incident, one night of my life: my intellectual life and my practical life came together—nothing is more real than a badly infected tooth—and having done so they never completely came apart again. If I believed in God, I would say that he showed me something that night; he showed me the totality: pain, physical pain, drop by drop, and then, this being his dreadful grace, there came understanding . . . and what did I understand? That it is *all* real; the abscessed tooth and the root-canal irrigation, and, no less and no more:

> *"Three circles from its substance now appeared,*
> *Of three colors, and each an equal whole."*

That was Dante's vision of God as the Trinity. Most people when they try to read the *Commedia* get bogged down in *Inferno* and suppose his vision to be that of a chamber of horrors: people head up in shit; people head down in shit; and a lake of ice (suggesting Arabic influences; that is the Muslim hell), but this is only the beginning of the journey; it is how it starts. I read the *Commedia* through to the end that night and then shot up the street for Dr. Davidson's office, and was never the same again. I never changed back into what I had previously been. So books are real to me, too; they link me not just with other minds but with the *vision* of other minds, what those minds understand and see. I see their worlds as well as I see my own. The pain and the crying and the sweating and stinking and cheap Jim Beam Bourbon was my *Inferno* and it wasn't imaginary; what I read bore the label "Paradiso" and *Paradiso* it was. This is the triumph of Dante's vision: that all the realms are real, none less than the others, none more than the others. And they blend into each other, by means of what Bill would call "gradual increments," which is indeed the proper term. There is a harmony in this because, like automobiles of today in contrast to autos of the Thirties, no sharp break exists.

God save me from another night like that. But goddamn it, had I not lived out that night, drinking and crying and reading and hurting, I would never have been born, truly born. That was the time of my birth into the real world; and the real world, for me, is a mixture of pain and beauty, and this is the correct view of it because these are the components that make up reality. And I had them all there that night, including a packet of pain-pills to carry home with me from the dentist's, after my ordeal had ended. I arrived home, took a pill, drank some coffee, and went to bed.

And yet—I feel that this was what Tim had not done; he had

either not integrated the book and the pain, or, if he had, he had got it wrong. He had the tune but not the words. More correctly, he had the words but those words pertained not to world but to other words, which is termed by philosophy books and articles on logic "a vicious regress." It is sometimes said in such books and articles that "again a regress threatens," which means that the thinker has entered a loop and is in great danger. Usually he does not know it. A critical commentator with a mind that is keen and an eye that is keen comes along and points this out. Or doesn't. For Tim Archer I could not serve as that critical commentator. Who could? Dingaling Bill had taken a good shot at it and had been sent back to his East Bay apartment to think better of it.

"Jeff has the answers to my questions," Tim said. Yes, I should have said, but Jeff does not exist. And very likely the questions themselves are irreal as well.

That left only Tim. And he was busily preparing his book dealing with Jeff's return from the next world, the book that Tim knew would finish off his career in the Episcopal Church—and, moreover, deal him out of the game of influencing public opinion. That is a high price to pay; that is a very vicious regress. And indeed it threatened. It was, in fact, at hand; the time for the trip to Santa Barbara to visit Dr. Rachel Garret, the medium, had come.

Santa Barbara, California, strikes me as one of the most touchingly beautiful places in the country. Although technically (which is to say, geographically) it is a portion of Southern California, spiritually it is not; either that or else we in the north supremely misunderstand the Southland. A few years ago, antiwar students from the University of California at Santa Barbara burned down the Bank of America, to everyone's secret delight; the town, then, is not cut off from time and world, not isolated, although its lovely gardens suggest a tame persuasion rather than a violent one.

The three of us flew from the San Francisco International Airport to the small airport at Santa Barbara; we had to go by two-motor prop plane, that airport being too short of runway length to accommodate jets. Law requires that the city's adobe character, which is to say, Spanish Colonial-style, be preserved.

As a cab took us to the house where we would stay, I noted the overwhelmingly Spanish design of everything, including arcade-type shopping centers; to myself I said, This is a place where I reasonably might live. If I ever depart the Bay Area.

Tim's friends, with whom we stayed, made no impression on me: they consisted of retractile, genteel, well-to-do people who stayed out of our way. They had servants. Kirsten and Tim slept in one bedroom; I had another, a rather small one, obviously made use of only when the other rooms had filled up.

The next morning, Tim and Kirsten and I set forth by cab to visit Dr. Rachel Garret, who would—no doubt—put us in touch with the dead, the next world, heal the sick, turn water into wine, and perform whatever other marvels were necessary. Both Tim and Kirsten seemed excited; I felt nothing in particular, perhaps only a dim consciousness of what we planned, what lay ahead; not even curiosity: only what a starfish living at the bottom of a tidal pond might feel.

We found Dr. Garret to be a rather lively small elderly Irish lady wearing a red sweater over her blouse—even though the weather was warm—and low-heeled shoes, and the sort of utility skirt suggesting that she performed all her own chores.

"And who are you, again?" she said, cupping her ear. She could not even figure out who stood before her on her porch: Not an encouraging beginning, I said to myself.

Presently, the four of us sat in a darkened living room, drinking tea and hearing from Dr. Garret a narration, delivered with enthusiasm, of the heroism of the IRA to which—she told us proudly—she contributed all the money she took in via her séances. However, she informed us, "séance" was the wrong word; it suggests the occult. What Dr. Garret did belonged within the realm of the perfectly natural; one could rightly call it a science. I saw in a corner of the living room among the other archaic furniture a Magnavox radio-phonograph of the Forties, a large one, the kind with two identical twelve-inch speakers. On each side of the Magnavox, stacks of 78 records—albums of Bing Crosby and Nat Cole and all the other trash of that period could be discerned. I wondered if Dr. Garret still listened to them. I wondered if, in her supernatural fashion, she had learned about long-playing records and the artists of today. Probably not.

To me Dr. Garret said, "And you're their daughter?"

"No," I said.

"My daughter-in-law," Tim said.

"You have an Indian guide," Dr. Garret said to me brightly.

"Really," I murmured.

"He's standing just behind you, to your left. He has very long hair. And behind you on your right side stands your great-grandfather on your father's side. They are always with you."

"I had a feeling that was the case," I said.

Kirsten gave me one of her mixed looks; I said no more. I settled back against the couch with all its pillows, noted a fern growing in a huge clay pot near the doors leading to the garden . . . I noted assorted uninstructive pictures on the walls, including several famous loser pictures of the Twenties.

"Is it about the son?" Dr. Garret said.

"Yes," Tim said.

I felt as if I had found my way into Gian Carlo Menotti's opera *The Medium*, which Menotti describes in his album-liner notes for Columbia Records as set in "Mme. Flora's weird and shabby Parlor." That is the trouble with education, I realized; you have been everywhere before, seen everything, vicariously; it has all already happened to you. We are Mr. and Mrs. Gobineau visiting Mme. Flora, a fraud and lunatic. Mr. and Mrs. Gobineau have been coming to Mme. Flora's séances—or, rather, scientific sessions—every week for nearly two years, as I recall. What a drag. Worst of all, the money Tim will be paying her goes to kill British soldiers; this is a fund-raiser for terrorists. Great.

"What is your son's name?" Dr. Garret asked. She sat in an ancient wicker chair, leaning back, her hands clasped together, her eyes slowly shutting. She had begun to breathe through her mouth, as the very ill do; her skin resembled that of a chicken, with bits of hair here and there, little tufts like minor scarcely watered plants. The whole room and everything in it now possessed a vegetable quality, totally lacking in vitality. I felt myself drained and being drained, my own energy taken away. Perhaps the light—or lack of light—gave me this impression. I did not find it pleasant.

"Jeff," Tim said. He sat alert, his eyes fixed on Dr. Garret. Kirsten had gotten a cigarette from her purse but did not light it; she merely held it; she also scrutinized Dr. Garret, with evident expectations.

"Jeff has passed across to the distant shore," Dr. Garret said.

As the newspapers reported, I said to myself.

I had expected a lengthy preamble from Dr. Garret, to set up the scene. I was wrong. She launched into it at once.

"Jeff wants you to know that—" Dr. Garret paused as if listening. "You should feel no guilt. Jeff has been trying to reach you for some time. He wanted to tell you that he forgives you. He has tried one means after another to attract your attention. He has stuck pins into your fingers; he has broken things; he has left notes to you—" Dr. Garret opened her eyes wide. "Jeff is highly agitated. He—" She broke off. "He took his own life."

You are batting a thousand, I thought acridly.

"Yes, he did," Kirsten said, as if Dr. Garret's statement was a revelation or else confirmed in a startling way something up to now only suspected.

"And violently," Dr. Garret said. "I get the impression that he used a gun."

"That's correct," Tim said.

"Jeff wants you to know that he is no longer in pain," Dr. Garret said. "He was in a great deal of pain when he took his own life. He didn't want you to know. He suffered from great doubts about the worth of living."

"What does he say to me?" I said.

Dr. Garret opened her eyes long enough to fathom who had spoken.

"He was my husband," I said.

"Jeff says that he loves you and prays for you," Dr. Garret said. "He wants you to be happy."

That and fifty cents, I thought, will get you a cup of coffee.

"There is more," Dr. Garret declared. "A great deal more. It's all coming in a rush. Oh my. Jeff, what is it you're trying to tell us?" She listened silently for a time, her face showing agitation. "The man at the restaurant was a Soviet what?" Again she opened her eyes wide. "My goodness. A Soviet police agent."

Jesus, I thought.

"But there's nothing to worry about," Dr. Garret said,

then, showing relief; she leaned back. "God will see that he is punished."

I glanced questioningly at Kirsten, trying to catch her eye; I wanted to know what—if anything—she had said to Dr. Garret; Kirsten, however, sat staring fixedly at the old lady, apparently dumbfounded. So it would seem I had my answer.

"Jeff says," Dr. Garret said, "that it is a matter of utmost joy to him that—that Kirsten and his father have each other. This is a great comfort to him. He wants you to know that. Who is 'Kirsten'?"

"I am," Kirsten said.

"He says," the old lady continued, "that he loves you."

Kirsten said nothing. But she listened with more intensity than I had ever seen her display before.

"He felt it was wrong," Dr. Garret said. "He says he's sorry . . . but he couldn't help it. He feels guilty about it and he would like your forgiveness."

"He has it," Tim said.

"Jeff says that he can't forgive himself," Dr. Garret said. "He also felt anger toward Kirsten for coming between him and his father. It made him feel cut off from his father. I get the impression that his father and Kirsten went on a long trip, a trip to England, and left him behind. He felt very badly about that." Again the old lady paused. "Angel is not to smoke any more drugs," Dr. Garret said, then. "She smokes too much . . . what is it, Jeff? I can't pick this up clearly. 'Too many numbers.' I don't know what that means."

I laughed. In spite of myself.

"Does that make any sense to you?" Dr. Garret said to me.

"In a way," I said, paying out as little line to her as possible.

"Jeff says he's glad about your job at the record store," Dr. Garret said. "But—" She laughed. "You're not being paid enough. He liked it better when you worked at the—shop kind of shop. A bottle shop?"

"Law office and candle shop," I said.

"Strange," Dr. Garret said, puzzled. "'Law office and candle shop.'"

"It was in Berkeley," I said.

Dr. Garret said, "Jeff has something very important to say to

Kirsten and his father." Her voice, now, had become faint, almost reduced to a rasping whisper. As if coming from a vast distance away. Traveling over invisible wires strung between stars. "Jeff has some dreadful news he wants to convey to the two of you. This is why he has been trying so badly to get through to you. This is why the pins and the burning and the breaking and the disordering and the smearing. He has a reason, a dreadful reason."

Silence, then.

Leaning toward Tim, I said, "This is a judgment call, but I want to leave."

"No," Tim said. He shook his head. His face showed unhappiness.

10

WHAT a peculiar mixture of nonsense and the uncanny, I thought as we waited for elderly Dr. Rachel Garret to go on. Mention of Fred Hill, the KGB agent . . . mention of Jeff disapproving of my turning on. Scraps derived obviously from newspapers: how Jeff had died and his probable motivations. *Lumpen* psychoanalysis and scandal-sheet garbage, and yet, stuck in here and there, a fragment like a tiny shard that could not be explained.

Beyond doubt Dr. Garret had easy access to most of the knowledge she had divulged, but there remained a creepy residuum: defined as, "That which remains after certain deductions are made," so this is the right term, and I have had a long time, many years, to mull over it. I have mulled and I can explain no part of it. How could Dr. Garret know about the Bad Luck Restaurant? And even if she knew that Kirsten and Tim had met originally at that place, how could she have known about Fred Hill or what we supposed was the case with Fred Hill?

It had been the joke passed endlessly between Jeff and me, that the owner of the Bad Luck Restaurant in Berkeley had been a KGB agent, but this fact wasn't printed anywhere; no one had ever written it down, except perhaps in the computers of the FBI and of course at KGB GHQ in Moscow, and it was only speculation anyhow. The issue of my turning on could be a shrewd guess, since I lived and worked in Berkeley, and, as everyone in the world knows, all the people in Berkeley do dope regularly—in fact, do it to excess. A medium is traditionally one who relies on a potpourri of hunches, common knowledge, clues unknowingly delivered by the audience itself, delivered unintentionally and then handed back . . . and, of course, the standard bullshit, such as "Jeff loves you" and "Jeff isn't in any more pain" and "Jeff felt a lot of doubt," generalizations available to anyone at any time, given the known facts.

Yet an eerie sensation held me, even though I knew that this old Irish lady who gave money—or said she gave money—to the Irish Republican Army was a fraud, that we three collectively were being fleeced out of our money, fleeced, too, in the sense that our credulity was being pandered to and manipulated—by someone in the business of doing this: a professional. The primary medium—it sounded like the medical term for cancer: "the primary cancer"—Dr. Mason had undoubtedly passed on everything *he* had learned and knew; this is how mediums work it, and we all know this.

The time to have left was before the revelation came, and now it was going to come, dumped on us by an unscrupulous old lady with dollar signs in her eyes and a clever ability to fathom the weak links in human psyches. But we didn't leave, and so it followed as the night the day that we got to hear from Dr. Garret what had so agitated Jeff, causing him to come back to Tim and Kirsten as the occult "phenomena" that they logged each day for Tim's forthcoming book.

It seemed to me as if Rachel Garret had become very old as she sat in her wicker chair, and I thought about the ancient sibyl—I could not remember which sibyl it had been, the one at Delphi or at Cumae—who had asked for immortality but had neglected to stipulate that she remain young; whereupon she lived forever but got so old that eventually her friends hung her up on the wall in a bag. Rachel Garret resembled that tattered wisp of skin and fragile bones, whispering out of the bag nailed to the wall; what wall in what city of the Empire I do not know—perhaps the sibyl is still there; perhaps this being who faced us as Rachel Garret was, in fact, that same sibyl; in any case, I did not want to hear what she had to say: I wanted to leave.

"Sit down," Kirsten said.

I realized, then, that I had stood without intending to. Flight reaction, I said to myself. Instinctive. Upon experiencing close adversaries. The lizard part of the brain.

Rachel Garret whispered, "Kirsten." But now she pronounced it correctly: *Shishen*, which I did not do, nor had Jeff, nor did Tim. But that was how she pronounced it herself, and gave up on getting anyone else to, at least in the States.

At this, Kirsten gave a muffled gasp.

The old lady in the wicker chair said:

> " *Ultima Cumaei venit iam carminis aetas;*
> *magnus ab integro saeclorum nascitur ordo.*

any reason for staying any longer." She reached for her purse and coat.

Tim paid Dr. Garret—I did not see how much, but it took the form of cash, not a check—and then phoned for a cab. Ten minutes later, the three of us rode back down the winding hillside roads to the house where we had accommodated ourselves.

Time passed and then, half to himself, Tim said, "That was the same eclogue of Virgil that I read to you. That day."

"I remember," I said.

"It seems a remarkable coincidence," Tim said. "There is no way she could have known it is a favorite of mine. Of course, it is the most famous of his eclogues . . . but that would scarcely account for it. I have never heard anyone else quote it but myself. It was as if I were hearing my own thoughts read back to me aloud, when Dr. Garret lapsed into Latin."

And I—I, too, had experienced that, I realized. Tim had expressed it perfectly. Perfectly and precisely.

"Tim," I said, "did you say anything to Dr. Mason about the Bad Luck Restaurant?"

Eying me, Tim said, "What is the 'Bad Luck Restaurant'?"

"Where we met," Kirsten said.

"No," Tim said. "I don't even remember the name of it. I remember what we had to eat . . . I had abalone."

"Did you ever tell anybody," I said to him, "anybody at all, at any time, anywhere, about Fred Hill?"

"I don't know anybody by that name," Tim said. "I'm sorry." He rubbed his eyes wearily.

"They read your mind," Kirsten said. "That's where they get it. She knew my health was bad. She knows I'm worried about the spot on my lung."

"What spot?" I said. This was the first I had heard about it. "Have you been in for more tests?"

When Kirsten did not answer, Tim said, "She showed a spot. Several weeks ago. It was a routine X-ray. They don't think it means anything."

"It means I'm going to die," Kirsten said bitingly, with palpable venom. "You heard her, the old bitch."

"Kill the Spartan runners," I said.

Furiously, Kirsten lashed at me, "Is that one of your Berkeley educated remarks?"

"Please," Tim said in a faint voice.

I said, "It's not her fault."

"We pay a hundred dollars to be told we're both going to die," Kirsten said, "and then on top of that, according to you, we should be grateful?" She scrutinized me with what struck me as psychotic malice, exceeding anything I had ever seen in her or in anyone else. "You're okay; she didn't say anything was going to happen to you, you cunt. You little Berkeley cunt— you're doing fine. I'm going to die and you get to have Tim all to yourself, with Jeff dead and now me. I think you set it up; you're involved; goddamn you!" Reaching, she took a swing at me; there in the back of the Yellow Cab she tried to hit me. I drew back, horrified.

Grabbing her with both hands, Tim pinned her against the side of the cab, against the door. "If I ever hear you use that word again," he said, "you are out of my life forever."

"You prick," Kirsten said.

After that, we drove in silence. The only sound was the occasional racket of the cab company's dispatcher, from the driver's two-way radio.

"Let's stop somewhere for a drink," Kirsten said, as we approached the house. "I don't want to have to deal with those awful mousy people; I just can't. I want to shop." To Tim she said, "We'll let you off. Angel and I'll go shopping. I really can't take any more today."

I said, "I don't feel like shopping right now."

"Please," Kirsten said tightly.

Tim said to me in a gentle voice, "Do it as a favor to both of us." He opened the cab door.

"Okay," I said.

After giving Kirsten money—all the money he had with him, apparently—Tim got out of the cab; we shut the door after him, and, presently, arrived at the downtown shopping district of Santa Barbara, with all the many lovely little shops and their various handcrafted artifacts. Soon Kirsten and I sat together in a bar, a nice bar, subdued, with low music playing. Through the open doors we could see people strolling around in the bright midday sunlight.

"Shit," Kirsten said as she sipped her vodka collins. "What a thing to find out. That you're going to die."

"Dr. Garret worked backward from Jeff's return," I said.

"How do you mean?" She stirred her drink.

"Jeff had come back to you. That's the given. So Garret summoned up a reason to explain it, the most dramatic reason she could find. 'He returned for a reason. That's why they return.' It's a commonplace. It's like—" I gestured. "Like the ghost in *Hamlet*."

Gazing at me quizzically, Kirsten said, "In Berkeley there is an intellectual reason for everything."

"The ghost warns Hamlet that Claudius is a murderer, that he murdered him, Hamlet's father."

"What's Hamlet's father's name?"

"He's just called 'Hamlet's father, the late king.'"

Kirsten, an owlish expression on her face, said, "No, his father is named Hamlet, too."

"Ten bucks says otherwise."

She extended her hand; we shook. "The play," Kirsten said, "instead of being called *Hamlet* should properly be called *Hamlet, Junior*." We both laughed. "I mean," Kirsten said, "this is just sick. We're sick going to that medium. Coming all this way—of course, Tim is meeting with those double-domed eggheads from the think tank. You know where he really wants to work? Don't ever say this to anyone, but he'd *like* to work for the Center for the Study of Democratic Institutions. This whole business about Jeff coming back—" She sipped her drink. "It's cost Tim a lot."

"He doesn't have to bring out the book. He could drop the project."

As if thinking aloud, Kirsten said, "How do those mediums do it? It's ESP; they can pick up your anxieties. Somehow the old biddy knew I have medical problems. It goes back to that damn peritonitis . . . that's public knowledge that I had that. There's a central file they keep, mediums of the world. Media, I guess, is the plural. And my cancer. They know I'm plagued with a second-rate body, sort of a used car. A lemon. God sold me a lemon for a body."

"You should have told me about the spot."

"It's none of your business."

"I care about you."

"Dike," Kirsten said. "Homo. That's why Jeff killed himself, because you and I are in love with each other." Both of us had begun laughing, now; we bumped heads, and I put my arm around her. "I have this joke for you. We're not supposed to call Mexicans 'greasers' any more; right?" She lowered her voice. "We're supposed to call them—"

"Lubricanos," I said.

She glanced at me. "Well, fuck you."

"Let's pick up somebody," I said.

"I want to shop. You pick up somebody." In a more somber tone she said, "This is a beautiful city. We may be living down here, you realize. Would you stay up in Berkeley if Tim and I moved down here?"

"I don't know," I said.

"You and your Berkeley friends. The Greater East Bay Co-Sexual Communal Free Love Exchange-Partners Enterprise, Unlimited. What is it about Berkeley, Angel? Why do you stay there?"

"The house," I said. And I thought: Memories of Jeff. In connection with the house. The Co-op on University Avenue where we used to shop. "I like the coffee houses on the Avenue," I said. "Especially Larry Blake's. One time, Larry Blake came over to Jeff and me; downstairs in the Ratskeller—he was so nice to us. And I like Tilden Park." And the campus, I said to myself. I can never free myself of that. The eucalyptus grove, down by Oxford. The library. "It's my home," I said.

"You'd get accustomed to Santa Barbara."

I said, "You shouldn't call me a cunt in front of Tim. He might get ideas."

"If I die," Kirsten said, "would you sleep with him? I mean, seriously?"

"You're not going to die."

"Dr. Spooky says I am."

"Dr. Spooky," I said, "is full of it."

"Do you think so? God, it was weird." Kirsten shivered. "I felt she could read my mind, that she was tapping it, like you tap a maple tree. Reading my own fears back to me. Would you sleep with Tim? Answer me seriously; I need to know."

"It would be incest."

"Why? Oh; okay. Well—it's already a sin, a sin for him; why

not add incest? If Jeff is in heaven and they're preparing a place for me, apparently I'm going to go to heaven. That's a relief. I just don't know how seriously to take what Dr. Garret said."

"Take it with the entire output of salt from the Polish salt mines for one full calendar year."

"But," Kirsten said, "it is Jeff coming back to us. Now we have it confirmed. But if I'm going to believe that, don't I have to believe the other, the prophecy?"

As I listened to her, a line from *Dido and Aeneas* entered my head, both the music and the words:

> *"The Trojan Prince, you know, is bound*
> *By Fate to seek Italian ground;*
> *The Queen and he are now in chase."*

Why had that come to mind? The sorceress . . . Jeff had quoted her or I had; the music had been a part of our lives, and I was thinking about Jeff, now, and the things that had bound us together. Fate, I thought. Predestination; doctrine of the church, based on Augustine and Paul. Tim had once told me that Christianity as a Mystery Religion had come into existence as a means of abolishing the tyranny of fate, only to reintroduce it as predestination—in fact, double predestination: some predestined to hell, some to heaven. Calvin's doctrine.

"We don't have fate any more," I said. "That went out with astrology, with the ancient world. Tim explained it to me."

Kirsten said, "He explained it to me, too, but the dead have precognition; they're outside of time. That's why you raise the spirits of the dead, to get advice from them about the future: they know the future. To them, it's already happened. They're like God. They see everything. Necromancy; we're like Dr. Dee in Elizabethan England. We have access to this marvelous supernatural power—it's better than the Holy Spirit, who also grants the ability to foresee the future, to prophesy. Through that wizened old lady we get Jeff's absolute knowledge that I'm going to kick off in the near-future. How can you doubt it?"

"Readily," I said.

"But she knew about the Bad Luck Restaurant. You see, Angel, we either reject it all or accept it all; we don't get to pick and choose. And if we reject it then Jeff didn't come back to us, and we're nuts. And if we accept it he did come back to us, which is fine as far as that goes, but then we have to face the fact that I'm going to die."

I thought: And Tim, too. You've forgotten about that, in your concern for yourself. As is typical of you.

"What's the matter?" Kirsten said.

"Well, she said Tim would die, too."

"Tim has Christ on his side; he's immortal. Didn't you know that? Bishops live forever. The first bishop—Peter, I imagine—is still alive somewhere, drawing a salary. Bishops live eternally and they get paid a lot. I die and I get paid almost nothing."

"It beats working in a record store," I said.

"Not really. Everything about your life is out in the open, at least; you don't have to skulk around like a second-story-man. This book of Tim's—it's going to be clear as day to everyone who reads it that Tim and I are sleeping together. We were in England together; we witnessed the phenomena together. Perhaps this is God's revenge against us for our sins, this prophecy by that old lady. Sleep with a bishop and die; it's like 'See Rome and die.' Well, I can't say it's been worth it, I really can't. I'd rather be a record clerk in Berkeley like you . . . but then I'd have to be young like you, to get the full benefits."

I said, "My husband is dead. I don't have all the breaks."

"And you don't have the guilt."

"Balls," I said. "I have plenty of guilt."

"Why? Jeff—well, anyhow, it wasn't your fault."

"We share the guilt," I said. "All of us."

"For the death of someone who was programmed to die? You only kill yourself if the DNA death-strip tells you to; it's in the DNA . . . didn't you know that? Or it's what they call a 'script,' which is what Eric Berne taught. He's dead, you know; his death-script or -strip or whatever caught up with him, proving him right. His father died and he died, the exact same age. It's like Chardin, who desired to die on Good Friday and got his wish."

"This is morbid," I said.

"Right." Kirsten nodded. "I just heard a while ago that I'm doomed to die; I feel very morbid, and so would you, except that you're exempt, for some reason. Maybe because you don't have a spot on your lung and you never had cancer. Why doesn't

that old lady die? Why is it me and Tim? I think Jeff's malicious, saying that; it's one of those self-fulfilling prophecies
you hear about. He tells Dr. Spooky I'm going to die and as a
result I die, and Jeff enjoys it because he hated me for sleeping
with his father. The hell with both of them. It goes along with
the pins stuck under my fingernails; its hate, hate toward me. I
can tell hate when I see it. I hope Tim points that out in his
book—well, he will because I'm writing most of it; he doesn't
have the time, and, if you want to know the truth, the talent
either. All his sentences run together. He has logorrhea, if you
want to know the blunt truth—from the speed he takes."

I said, "I don't want to know."

"Have you and Tim slept together?"

"No!" I said, amazed.

"Bull."

"Christ," I said, "you're crazy."

"Tell me it's due to the reds I take."

I stared at her; she stared back. Unwinkingly, her face taut.

"You're crazy," I said.

Kirsten said, "You have turned Tim against me."

"I *what?*"

"He thinks that Jeff would be alive if it hadn't been for me,
but it was his idea for us to get sexually involved."

"You—" I could not think what to say. "Your mood-swings
are getting greater," I said finally.

Kirsten said in a fierce, grating voice, "I see more and more
clearly. Come on." She finished her drink and slid from her
stool, tottered, grinned at me. "Let's go shop. Let's buy a
whole lot of Indian silver jewelry imported from Mexico; they
sell it here. You regard me as old and sick and a red freak, don't
you? Tim and I have discussed it, your view of me. He considers
it damaging to me and defamatory. He's going to talk to you
about it sometime. Get prepared; he's going to quote canon
law. It's against canon law to bear false witness. He doesn't
consider you a very good Christian; in fact, not a Christian at
all. He doesn't really like you. Did you know that?"

I said nothing.

"Christians are judgmental," Kirsten said, "and bishops even
more so. I have to live with the fact that Tim confesses every
week to the sin of sleeping with me; do you know how that

feels? It is quite painful. And now he has me going; I take Communion and I confess. It's sick. Christianity is sick. I want him to step down as bishop; I want him to go into the private sector."

"Oh," I said. I understood, then. Tim could then come out in the open and proclaim her, his relationship with her. Strange, I thought, that it never entered my mind.

"When he is working for that think tank," Kirsten said, "the stigma and the hiding will be gone because they don't care. They're just secular people; they're not Christians—they don't condemn others. They're not saved. I'll tell you something, Angel. Because of me, Tim is cut off from God. This is terrible, for him and for me; he has to get up every Sunday and preach knowing that because of me he and God are severed, as in the original Fall. Because of me, Bishop Timothy Archer is recapitulating the primordial Fall in himself, and he fell voluntarily; he chose it. No one made him fall or told him to do it. It's my fault. I should have said 'no' to him when he first asked me to sleep with him. It would have been a lot better, but I didn't know a rat's ass about Christianity; I didn't comprehend what it signified for him and what, eventually, it would signify for me as the damn stuff oozed out all over me, that Pauline doctrine of sin, Original Sin. What a demented doctrine, that man is born evil; how cruel it is. It's not found in Judaism; Paul made it up to explain the Crucifixion. To make sense out of Christ's death, which in fact makes no sense. Death for nothing, unless you believe in Original Sin."

"Do you believe in it now?" I asked.

"I believe I've sinned; I don't know if I was born that way. But it's true now."

"You need therapy."

"The whole church needs therapy. Old Dr. Batshit could take one look at me and Tim and know we're sleeping together; the whole media-news network knows it, and when Tim's book comes out—he *has* to step down—it has nothing to do with his faith or lack of faith in Christ: it has to do with me. I'm forcing him out of his career, not his lack of faith; I'm doing it. That cracked old lady only read back to me what I already knew, that you can't do what we're doing; you can do it but you have to pay for it. I'd just as soon be dead, I really would.

This is no life. Every time we go somewhere, fly somewhere, we have to get two hotel rooms, one for each of us, and then I slip up the hall into his room . . . Dr. Batshit didn't have to be a psychic to ferret it all out; it was written on our faces. Come on; let's shop."

I said, "You're going to have to lend me some money. I didn't bring enough along to shop."

"It's the Episcopal Church's money." She opened her purse. "Be my guest."

"You hate yourself," I said; I intended to add the word unfairly, but Kirsten interrupted me.

"I hate the position I'm in. I hate what Tim has done to me, made me ashamed of myself and my body and being a woman. Is this why we founded FEM? I never dreamed I'd ever be in this situation, like a forty-dollar whore. Sometime you and I should talk, the way we used to talk before I was busy all the time writing his speeches and making his appointments—the bishop's secretary who makes sure he doesn't reveal in public the fool that he is, the child that he is; I'm the one who has all the responsibility, and I'm treated like garbage."

She handed me some money from her purse, grabbed out at random; I accepted it, and felt vast guilt; but I took the money anyhow. As Kirsten said, it belonged to the Episcopal Church.

"One thing I have learned," she said as we left the bar and emerged into the daylight, "is to read the fine print."

"I'll say one thing for that old lady," I said. "She certainly loosened up your tongue."

"No—it's being out of San Francisco. You haven't seen me out of the Bay Area and Grace Cathedral before. I don't like you and I don't like being a cheap whore and I don't particularly like my life in general. I'm not sure I even like Tim. I'm not sure I want to continue with this, any of this. That apartment —I had a much better apartment before I met Tim, although I suppose that doesn't count; it's not supposed to, anyhow. But I had a very rewarding life. But I was programmed by my DNA to get mixed up with Tim and now some old skuzz-bag rails at me that I'm going to die. You know what my feeling is about that, my real feeling? It no longer matters to me. I knew it anyway. She just read my own thoughts back to me and you know it. That is the one thing that sticks in my mind from this séance or whatever we're supposed to call it: I heard someone express my realizations about myself and my life and what's become of me. It gives me courage to face what I have to face and do what I have to do."

"And what is that?"

"You'll see in due time. I've come to an important decision. This today helped clear my mind. I think I understand." She spoke no further. It was Kirsten's custom to cast a veil of mystery over her connivings; that way, she supposed, she added an element of glamour. But in fact she did not. She only murked up the situation, for herself most of all.

I let the subject drop. Together, then, we sauntered off, in search of ways to spend the church's wealth.

We returned to San Francisco at the end of the week, laden with purchases and feeling tired. The bishop had secured, covertly, not for publication, a post with the Santa Barbara think tank. It would be announced presently that he intended to resign from his post as Bishop of the Diocese of California; the announcement would be coming ineluctably, his decision having been made, his new job arranged for: nailed down. Meanwhile, Kirsten checked into Mount Zion Hospital for further tests.

Her apprehension had made her taciturn and morose; I visited her at the hospital but she had little to say. As I sat beside her bed, ill at ease and wishing I were elsewhere, Kirsten fussed with her hair and complained. I left dissatisfied, with myself, basically; I seemed to have lost my ability to communicate with her—my best friend, really—and our relationship was dwindling, along with her spirits.

At this time, the bishop had in his possession the galleys for his book dealing with Jeff's return from the next world; Tim had decided on the title *Here, Tyrant Death*, which I had suggested to him; it is from Handel's *Belshazzar*, and reads in full:

"Here, tyrant Death, thy terrors end."

He quoted it in context in the book itself.

Busy as always, over-extended and preoccupied with a hundred and one major matters, he elected to bring the galleys to Kirsten in the hospital; he left them with her to proofread and at once departed. I found her lying propped up, a cigarette in one hand, a pen in the other, the long galley-pages propped up on her knees. It was evident that she was furious.

"Can you believe this?" she said, by way of greeting.

"I can do them," I said, seating myself on the edge of the bed.

"Not if I throw up on them."

"After you're dead you'll work even harder."

Kirsten said, "No; I won't work at all. That's the point. As I read over this thing I keep asking myself, Who is going to believe this crap? I mean, it *is* crap. Let's face it. Look." She pointed to a section on the galley-page and I read it over. My reaction tallied with hers; the prose was turgid, vague and disastrously pompous. Obviously, Tim had dictated it at his rush-rush, speeded-up, let's-get-it-over-with velocity. Equally obviously, he had never once looked back. I thought to myself, The title should be *Look Backward, Idiot.*

"Start with the final page," I said, "and work forward. That way, you won't have to read it."

"I'm going to drop them. Oops." She simulated dropping the galleys onto the floor, catching them just in time. "Does the order matter on these? Let's shuffle them."

"Write in stuff," I said. "Write in, 'This really sucks.' Or, 'Your mother wears Army boots.'"

Kirsten, pretending to write, said, "'Jeff manifested himself to us naked with his pecker in his hand. He was singing "The Stars and Stripes Forever."'" Both of us were laughing, now; I collapsed against her and we embraced.

"I'll give you one hundred dollars if you write that in," I said, almost unable to talk.

"I'll just turn it over to the IRA."

"No," I said. "To the IRS."

Kirsten said, "I don't report my earnings. Hookers don't have to." Her mood changed, then; her spirit palpably ebbed away. Gently, she patted me on the arm and then she kissed me.

"What's that for?" I said, touched.

"They think the spot means I have a tumor."

"Oh, no," I said.

"Yep. Well, that's the long and the short of it." She pushed me away, then, with stifled—ill-stifled—anger.

"Can they do anything? I mean, they can—"

"They can operate; they can remove the lung."

"And you're still smoking."

"It's a little late to give up cigarettes. What the hell. This raises an interesting question . . . I'm not the first to ask it. When you're resurrected in the flesh, are you resurrected in a perfect form or do you have all the scars and injuries and defects you had while alive? Jesus showed Thomas his wounds; he had Thomas thrust his hand into his—Jesus'—side. Did you know that the church was born from that wound? That's what the Roman Catholics believe. Blood and water flowed from the wound, the spear wound, while he was on the cross. It's a vagina, Jesus' vagina." She did not seem to be joking; she seemed, now, solemn and pensive. "A mystical notion of a spiritual second birth. Christ gave birth to us all."

I seated myself on the chair beside the bed, saying nothing. The news—the medical report—stunned and terrified me; I could not respond. Kirsten, however, looked composed.

They have given her tranks, I realized. As they do when they deliver this sort of news.

"You consider yourself a Christian now?" I said finally, unable to think up anything else, anything more appropriate.

"The fox hole phenomenon," Kirsten said. "What do you think of the title? *Here, Tyrant Death.*"

"I picked it," I said.

She gazed at me, with intensity.

"Why are you looking at me like that?" I said.

"Tim said he picked it."

"Well, he did. I gave him the quotation. One among a group; I submitted several."

"When was this?"

"I don't know. Some time ago. I forget. Why?"

Kirsten said, "It's a terrible title. I abominated it when I first saw it. I didn't see it until he dumped these galleys in my lap, literally in my lap. He never asked—" She broke off, then stubbed her cigarette out. "It's like somebody's idea of what a book title ought to consist of. A parody of a book title. By

someone who never titled a book before. I'm surprised his
editor didn't object."

"Is all this directed at me?" I said.

"I don't know. You figure it out." She began, then, to scru-
tinize the galleys; she ignored me.

"Do you want me to go?" I said awkwardly, after a time.

Kirsten said, "I really don't care what you do." She continued with her work; presently, she halted a moment to light up
another cigarette. I saw, then, that the ashtray by her bed overflowed with half-smoked, stubbed-out cigarettes.

11

I LEARNED of her suicide by hearing it from Tim on the phone. My little brother had come over to the house to visit me; it was on Sunday, so I didn't have to go to the Musik Shop that day. I had to stand there and listen to Tim telling me that Kirsten had "just slipped away"; I could see my little brother, who had really been fond of Kirsten; he was assembling a balsawood model of a Spad Thirteen—he knew the call was from Tim but, of course, he didn't know that now Kirsten, along with Jeff, was dead.

"You're a strong person," Tim's voice sounded in my ear. "I know you will be able to stand up to this."

"I saw it coming," I said.

"Yes," Tim said. He sounded matter-of-fact but I knew his heart was breaking.

"Barbiturates?" I said.

"She took—well, they're not sure. She took them and timed herself. She waited. Then she walked in and told me. And then she fell. I knew what it was." He added, "Tomorrow she was supposed to go back to Mount Zion."

"You called—"

"The paramedics came," Tim said, "and they took her right to the hospital. They tried everything. What she had done was build up the maximum amount in her system already, so that what she took as the overdose—"

"That's how it's done," I said. "That way pumping her stomach doesn't help; it's already in the system."

"Do you want to come over here?" Tim said. "To the City? I would really appreciate your being here."

"I have Harvey with me," I said.

My little brother glanced up.

To him I said, "Kirsten died."

"Oh." He nodded, and, after a moment, returned to his balsawood Spad. It's like *Wozzeck*, I thought. Exactly like the end of *Wozzeck*. There I go: Berkeley intellectual, viewing everything in terms of culture, of opera, of novel, oratorio and poem. Not to mention play.

"Du! Deine Mutter ist tot!"

And Marien's child says:

"Hopp, hopp! Hopp, hopp! Hopp, hopp!"

It will break you, I thought, if you keep this up. The little boy assembling a model airplane and not understanding: double horror, and both happening to me now.

"I'll come over there," I said to Tim. "As soon as I can find someone to take care of Harvey."

"You could bring him," Tim said.

"No." Reflexively, I shook my head.

I got a neighbor to take Harvey for the rest of the day, and, shortly, I was on my way to San Francisco, driving over the Bay Bridge in my Honda.

And still the words of Berg's opera percolated obsessively through my mind.

> *"The huntsman's life is gay and free,*
> *Shooting is free for all!*
> *There would I huntsman be,*
> *There would I be."*

I mean, I said to myself, George Büchner's words; he wrote the damn thing.

As I drove, I cried; tears ran down my face; I turned on the car radio and pressed button after button, station after station. On a rock station I picked up an old Santana track; I turned up the volume and, as the music rebounded throughout my little car, I screamed. And I heard:

"You! Your mother is dead!"

I narrowly missed rear-ending a huge American car; I had to swerve into the lane to my right. Slow down, I said to myself. Fuck this, I thought; two deaths are enough. You want to make it three? Then just keep driving the way you're driving: three plus the people in the other car. And then I remembered Bill. Dingaling Bill Lundborg, off in an asylum somewhere. Had Tim called him? I should tell him, I said to myself.

You poor miserable fucked-up son of a bitch, I said to myself, remembering Bill and his gentle, pudgy face. That air of sweetness, like new clover, about him, him and his dumb pants and dumb look, like a cow, a contented cow. The Post Office is in for another round of their windows smashed, I realized; he will walk down there and start hitting the great plate glass windows with his fists until blood runs down his arms. And then they'll lock him up again in one place or another; it doesn't matter which because he doesn't know the difference.

How could she do it to him? I asked myself. What malice. What abysmal cruelty, toward us all. She really hated us. This is our punishment. I'll always think I'm responsible; Tim will always think he's responsible; Bill likewise. And of course none of us is, and yet in a sense all of us are, but anyhow it is beside the point, after the fact, null and moot and void, totally void, as in "the infinite void," the sublime non-Being of God.

There is a line somewhere in *Wozzeck* that translates out to, roughly, "The world is awful." Yes, I said to myself as I shot across the Bay Bridge not giving a fuck how fast I drove, that sums it up. That is high art: "The world is awful." That says it all. This is what we pay composers and painters and the great writers to do: tell us this; from figuring this out, they earn a living. What masterful, incisive insight. What penetrating intelligence. A rat in a drain ditch could tell you the same thing, were it able to talk. If rats could talk, I'd do anything they said. Black girl I knew. Not rats with her; it's rats for me—for her, she said, it was spiders; *viz*: "If spiders could talk." That time she got the runs while we were up in Tilden Park and we had to drive her home. Neurotic lady. Married to a white guy . . . what was his name? Only in Berkeley.

Viz, a short form of Visigoths, the noble Goths. Visitation, as in, Visitation from the dead, from the next world. That old lady bears some real responsibility for this; if any one single person done did it she done did it. But that's killing the Spartan runners; now they have me doing it myself, after all the warnings. WARNING: THIS LADY IS NUTS. Get out of my way. May you all be fucked forever, all of you in your washed big cars.

I thought: "*Destructive War, thy limits know; here, tyrant Death, thy terrors end. To tyrants only I'm a foe, to virtue and her friends, a friend.*" And then it says it again: "*Here, tyrant Death.*" It's a great title; it's not a parody. That's what did it,

Tim using my title and, of course—in his usual chickenshit fashion—not bothering or remembering to tell her. In fact, telling her that *he* thought of it. He probably thinks so. Every valuable idea in the history of the world was thought into being by Timothy Archer. He invented the heliocentric solar system model. We'd still have the geocentric one if it hadn't been for him. Where does Bishop Archer end and God begin? Good point. Ask him; he'll tell you, quoting from books.

No single thing abides; and all things are fucked up, I thought. That's how it should have been worded. I'll suggest that to Tim for Kirsten's gravestone. Teaching school in Norway, the Swedish cretin. A million nasty things I said to her, in the guise of play. Her brain recorded them and played them back to her, late at night when she couldn't sleep, while Tim snoozed on; she couldn't sleep and took more and more downers, those barbiturates that killed her; we knew they would: the only issue was whether it would be an accident or a purposeful overdose, assuming there is a difference.

My instructions required me to meet with Tim at the Tenderloin apartment before going on with him, then, to Grace Cathedral. I had expected to find him red-eyed and distraught. However, to my surprise, Tim looked stronger, more powerfully put-together, even in a literal sense larger, than I had ever seen him before.

He said, as he put his arms around me and hugged me, "I have a terrible fight on my hands. From here on in."

"You mean the scandal?" I said. "It'll be in the papers and on the news, I guess."

"I destroyed part of her suicide note. The police are reading what's left. They've been here. Probably they'll be coming back. I do have influence but I can't keep the news quiet. All I can hope for is to keep it retained as speculation."

"What did the note say?"

"The part I destroyed? I don't remember. It's gone. It had to do with us, her feelings about me. I had no choice."

"Guess so," I said.

"As to it being suicide, there is no doubt. And the motive is, of course, her fear that she had cancer again. And they're aware that she was a barbiturate addict."

"Would you describe her that way?" I said. "An addict?"

"Certainly. That's not disputed."

"How long have you known?"

"Since I met her. Since I first saw her taking them. You knew."

"Yes," I said. "I knew."

"Sit down and have some coffee," Tim said. He left the living room for the kitchen; automatically, I seated myself on the familiar couch, wondering if any cigarettes could be found anywhere in the apartment.

"What do you take in your coffee?" Tim stood at the kitchen doorway.

"I forget," I said. "It doesn't matter."

"Would you rather have a drink?"

"No." I shook my head.

"Do you realize," Tim said, "that this proves Rachel Garret right."

"I know," I said.

"Jeff wanted to warn her. Warn Kirsten."

"So it would seem."

"And I'm going to die next."

I glanced up.

"That's what Jeff said," Tim said.

"Guess so," I said.

"It will be a terrible fight but I will win. I am not going to follow them, follow Jeff and Kirsten." His tone rang with harshness, with indignation. "This is what Christ came to the world to save man from, this sort of determinism, this rule. The future can be changed."

"I hope so," I said.

"My hope is in Jesus Christ," Tim said. " 'While you still have the light, believe in the light and you will become sons of light.' John, twelve, thirty-six. 'Do not let your hearts be troubled. Trust in God still, and trust in me.' John, fourteen, one. 'Blessings on him who comes in the name of the Lord!' Matthew, twenty-three, thirty-nine." Breathing heavily, his great chest rising and falling, Tim, gazing at me, pointed at me saying, "I'm not going that way, Angel. Each of them did it intentionally, but I will never do it; I will never go like that, like a sheep to slaughter."

Thank God, I thought. You are going to fight.

"Prophecy or no prophecy," Tim said. "Even if Rachel were the sibyl herself—even then I wouldn't walk toward it willingly, like a dumb animal, to have my throat cut, to be offered up." His eyes blazed, hot with intensity and fire. I had seen him this way sometimes at Grace Cathedral when he preached; this Tim Archer spoke with the authority vested in him by the Apostle Peter himself: through the line of apostolic succession, unbroken in and for the Episcopal Church.

As we drove to Grace Cathedral in my Honda, Tim said to me, "I see myself falling into Wallenstein's fate. Catering to astrology. Casting horoscopes."

"You mean Dr. Garret," I said.

"Yes, I mean her and Dr. Mason; they're not doctors of any kind. That wasn't Jeff. He never came back from the next world. There is no truth in it. Stupidity, as that poor boy said; her son. Oh Lord; I haven't called her son."

I said, "I'll tell him."

"It will finish him off," Tim said. "No, maybe it won't. He may be stronger than we give him credit for. He could see through all that nonsense about Jeff coming back."

"You get to tell the truth," I said, "when you're schizophrenic."

"Then more people should be schizophrenic. What is this, a matter of the emperor's new clothes? You knew, too, but you didn't say."

I said, "It's not a matter of knowing. It has to do with evaluation."

"But you never believed it."

After a pause, I said, "I'm not sure."

"Kirsten is dead," Tim said, "because we believed in nonsense. Both of us. And we believed because we wanted to believe. I have not that motive now."

"Guess not."

"If we had ruthlessly faced the truth, Kirsten would be alive now. All I can hope is to put an end to it here and now . . . and accompany her at some later date. Garret and Mason could see that Kirsten was sick. They took advantage of a sick, disturbed woman and now she's dead. I hold them responsible." He paused and then said, "I had been attempting to get Kirsten to go into the hospital for drug detox. I have several friends who're in that field, here in San Francisco. I was well aware of her addiction and I knew that only professionals could help her. I had to go through this myself, as you know . . . with alcohol."

I said nothing; I merely drove.

"It's too late to stop the book," Tim said.

"Couldn't you phone your editor and—"

"The book is their property now."

I said, "They're a totally reputable publishing house. They would listen to you if you instructed them to withdraw the book."

"They've sent out promotional prepublication material. They've circulated bound galleys and Xerox copies of the manuscript. What I'll do—" Tim pondered. "I'll write another book. That tells about Kirsten's death and my reevaluation of the occult. That's the best avenue for me to pursue."

"I think you should withdraw *Here, Tyrant Death*."

His mind, however, had been made up; he shook his head vigorously. "No; it should be allowed to come out as planned. I've had years of experience with these matters; you should face up to your own folly—my own, I am referring to, of course —and then, after you've faced up to it, set about correcting it. My next book will be that correction."

"How much was the advance?"

Glancing swiftly at me, Tim said, "Not much, considering its sales potential. Ten thousand on my signing the contract; then another ten thousand when I delivered the completed manuscript to them. And there will be a final ten thousand when the book is released."

"Thirty thousand dollars is a lot of money."

Half to himself, reflecting, Tim said, "I think I'll add a dedication to it. A dedication to Kirsten. In memoriam. And say a few things about my feeling for her."

"You could dedicate it to both of them," I said. "Both Jeff and Kirsten. And say, 'But for the grace of God—'"

"Very appropriate," Tim said.

"Add me and Bill," I said. "While you're at it. We're part of this movie."

"'Movie'?"

"A Berkeley expression. Only it's not a movie; it's the opera *Wozzeck* by Alban Berg. They all die except the little boy riding his wooden horse."

"I'll have to phone in the dedication," Tim said. "The galleys are already back in New York, corrected."

"She finished, then? Her job?"

"Yes," he said, vaguely.

"Did she do it right? After all, she wasn't feeling too well."

"I assume she did it correctly; I didn't look them over."

"You're going to have a Mass said for her, aren't you?" I said. "At Grace?"

"Oh, yes. That's one of the reasons I'm—"

"I think you should get Kiss," I said. "It's a group, a very highly thought of rock group. After all, you had been planning a rock mass anyhow."

"Did she like Kiss?"

"Second only to Sha Na Na," I said.

"Then we should get Sha Na Na," Tim said.

We drove for a time in silence.

"The Patti Smith Group," I said suddenly.

"Let me ask you," Tim said, "about several things regarding Kirsten."

"I am here to answer any question," I said.

"At the service, I want to read poems that she loved. Can you give me the names of a few?" He got from his coat pocket a notebook and gold pen; holding them, he waited.

"There is a very beautiful poem about a snake," I said, "by D. H. Lawrence. She loved it. Don't ask me to quote it; I can't quote it just now. I'm sorry." I shut my eyes, trying not to cry.

12

A T the service, Bishop Timothy Archer read the D. H. Lawrence poem about the snake; he read it wonderfully and I saw how moved the people were, although not many mourners had shown up. Not that many people knew Kirsten Lundborg. I kept seeking to locate her son Bill somewhere in the cathedral.

When I had phoned him to tell him the news, he had showed little response. I think he foresaw it. At this time, the hospital and the house of many slammers held no power over him; Bill had earned his freedom to walk around or to paint cars or whatever he did. However he currently amused himself in his earnest fashion.

The cobwebs departed Bishop Archer's mind when Kirsten killed herself, so, it would seem, her death had served a useful purpose, although a purpose unequal to our loss. It amazes me: the sobering power of human death. It outweighs all words, all arguments; it is the ultimate force. It coerces your attention and your time. And it leaves you changed.

How Tim could derive strength from death—the death of a person he loved—baffled me; I could not fathom it, but this was the sort of quality in him that made him good: good at his job, good as a human being. The worse things got, the stronger he became; he did not like death but he did not fear it. He comprehended it—once the cobwebs left. He had tried out the bullshit solution of séances and superstition and that hadn't worked; it simply brought on more death. So now he shifted gears and tried out being rational. He had a profound motive: his own life had been placed on the line, like bait. Bait to tempt what the ancients called "a sinister fate," meaning premature death, death before its time.

The thinkers of antiquity did not regard death per se as evil, because death comes to all; what they correctly perceived as evil was premature death, death coming before the person could complete his work. Lopped off, as it were, before ripe, a hard, green little apple that death took and then tossed away, as being of no interest—even to death.

Bishop Archer had by no means completed his work and by no means did he intend to be lopped off, severed from life. He now correctly perceived himself sliding by degrees into the fate that had overtaken Wallenstein: first the superstition and credulity, then run through with a halberd by an otherwise historically undistinguished English captain named Walter Devereux (Wallenstein had pleaded in vain for quarter; when the halberd is in the foe's hand, it is usually too late to plead for quarter). At that final instant Wallenstein, roused from sleep, had probably also been roused from his mental stupor; I would guess that the swift realization came to him as the enemy soldiers broke into his bedroom that all the astrological charts and all the horoscopes in the world had been of no use to him, for he had not foreseen this, and was caught. The difference between Wallenstein and Tim, however, was great and crucial. First, Tim had the advantage of Wallenstein's example; Tim got to see where folly led great men. Second, Tim was fundamentally a realist, for all his double-domed, educated flow of twaddle. Tim had entered the world with a wary eye, a keen sense of what benefited him and what worked to his disadvantage. At the moment of Kirsten's death he had cannily destroyed part of her suicide note; no fool he, and he had been able—amazingly —to conceal their relationship from the media and from the Episcopal Church itself (it all came out later, of course, but by then Tim was dead and probably did not care).

How an essentially pragmatic—even, it could be argued, opportunistic—man could involve himself in so much self-defeating nonsense is, of course, amazing, but even the nonsense had a sort of utility in the larger economy of Tim's life. Tim did not wish to be bound by the formal strictures of his role; he did not really define himself as a bishop any more than he had previously let himself be defined as an attorney. He was a man, and he thought of himself that way; not a "man" in the sense of "male person," but "man" in the sense of human being who lived in many areas and spread out into a variety of vectors. In his college days, he had learned much from his study of the Renaissance; once he had told me that in no way had the Renaissance overthrown or abolished the Medieval world: *the Renaissance had fulfilled it,* whatever T. S. Eliot might imagine to the contrary.

Take, for example, (Tim had said to me) Dante's *Commedia*. Clearly, in terms of brute date of composition, the *Commedia* emanated from the Middle Ages; it summed up the Medieval worldview absolutely: its greatest crown. And yet (although many critics will not agree) the *Commedia* has a vast span of vision that in no way can be bipolarized to, say, the view of Michelangelo, who, in fact, drew heavily on the *Commedia* for his Sistine Chapel ceiling. Tim saw Christianity reaching its climax in the Renaissance; he did not view that moment in history as the ancient world revived and overpowering the Middle Ages, the Christian Ages; the Renaissance was not the triumph of the old pagan world over faith but, rather, the final and fullest flowering of faith, specifically the Christian faith; therefore, Tim reasoned, the well-known Renaissance man (who knew something about everything, who was, to use the correct term, a polymath) was the ideal Christian, at home in this world and in the next: a perfect blend of matter and spirit, matter divinized, as it were. Matter transformed but still matter. The two realms, this and the next, brought back together, as they had been joined before the Fall.

This ideal Tim intended to capture for himself, to make it his own. The complete person, he reasoned, does not lock himself into his job, no matter how exalted that job. A cobbler who views himself only as one who repairs shoes is circumscribing himself viciously; a bishop, by the same reasoning, must therefore enter regions occupied by the whole man. One of these regions consisted of that of sexuality. Although the general opinion ran contrary to this, Tim did not care, nor did he yield. He knew what was apt for the Renaissance man and he knew that he himself constituted that man in all his authenticity.

That this trying out of every possible idea to see if it would fit finally destroyed Tim Archer can't be disputed. He tried out too many ideas, picked them up, examined them, used them for a while and then discarded them . . . some of the ideas, however, as if possessing a life of their own, came back around the far side of the barn and got him. That is history; this is an historical fact. Tim is dead. The ideas did not work. They got him off the ground and then betrayed him and attacked him; they dumped him, in a sense, before he could dump them. One thing, however, could not be obscured: Tim Archer could tell when he was locked in a life-and-death struggle and, upon perceiving this, he assumed the posture of grim defense. He did not—just as he had said to me the day Kirsten died—surrender. Fate, to get Tim Archer, would have to run him through: Tim would never run himself through. He would not collude with retributive fate, once he spotted it and what it was up to. He had done that, now: discerned retributive fate, seeking him. He neither fled nor cooperated. He stood and fought and, in that stance, died. But he died hard, which is to say, he died hitting back. Fate had to murder him.

And, while fate figured out how to accomplish this, Tim's quick brain was totally engaged in sidestepping through every mental gymnastic move possible that which perhaps held in it the force of the inevitable. This is probably what we mean by the term "fate"; were it not inevitable, we would not employ that term; we would, instead, speak of bad luck. We would talk about accidents. With fate there is no accident; there is intent. And there is relentless intent, closing in from all directions at once, as if the person's very universe is shrinking. Finally, it holds nothing but him and his sinister destiny. He is programmed against his will to succumb, and, in his efforts to thrash himself free, he succumbs even faster, from fatigue and despair. Fate wins, then, no matter what.

A lot of this Tim himself told me. He had studied up on the topic as part of his Christian education. The ancient world had seen the coming into existence of the Greco-Roman Mystery Religions, which were dedicated to overcoming fate by patching the worshipper into a god beyond the planetary spheres, a god capable of short-circuiting the "astral influences," as it had been called in those days. We ourselves, now, speak of the DNA death-strip and the psychological-script learned from, modeled on, other, previous people, friends and parents. It is the same thing; it is determinism killing you no matter what you do. Some power outside of you must enter and alter the situation; you cannot do it for yourself, for the programming causes you to perform the act that will destroy you; the act is performed with the idea that it will save you, whereas, in point of fact, it delivers you over to the very doom you wish to evade.

Tim knew all this. It didn't help him. But he did his best; he tried.

Practical men do not do what Jeff did and Kirsten did; practical men fight that drift because it is a romantic drift, a weakness. It is learned passivity; it is learned giving up. Tim could ignore his son's death as unique—reasoning that no contagion was involved—but when Kirsten went the same way, Tim had to change his mind, return to Jeff's death and reappraise it. He saw in it, now, the origins of later disaster, and he saw that disaster shaping up for himself. This caused him immediately to jettison all the claptrap notions that he had picked up beginning with Jeff's death, all the weird and shabby ideas associated with the occult, to borrow Menotti's apt phrase. Tim suddenly realized that he had seated himself at the table in Mme. Flora's parlor, for the purpose of contacting the spirits—for the purpose, really, of delivering himself over to folly. He now did what characterized him throughout his life: he abandoned that route and sought another; he dumped that malicious cargo and reached around for something more stable, more durable and sound, to replace it. If the ship is to be saved, cargo must sometimes be flung overboard; when something is jettisoned, it is dumped calculatedly—heaved away, to float off, leaving the ship intact. This moment only comes when the ship is in trouble, as Tim now was. Dr. Garret had pronounced doom on both himself and Kirsten, beginning with Kirsten. The first prophecy had come true. He could expect, then, to be next. These are emergency procedures. They are employed by the desperate and the smart. Tim was both. And out of necessity. Tim knew the difference between the ship (which was not expendable) and the cargo (which was). He viewed himself as the ship. He viewed his faith in spirits, in his son's return from the next world, as cargo. This clear distinction was his advantage, inasmuch as he could discern it. Throwing away his beliefs did not compromise him, nor did it vitiate him. And there existed a slight chance that it might save him.

I rejoiced in Tim's newfound lucidity. But I felt deeply pessimistic. I viewed his clearheadedness as a surfacing of his basic determination to survive. This is a good thing. You cannot fault the drive to endure. The only question that frightened me was: had it come soon enough? Time would tell.

When the ship is saved—if it is saved—necessary jettison gives the right of general salvage to the owner or owners of the

goods. This is an international rule of the seas. This is an idea
basic to human beings, of whatever place of origin. Tim consciously or unconsciously understood this. In doing what he
was doing, he partook of something venerable and universally
accepted. I understood him; I think anybody would. This was
not the time to whine over lost battles involving the issue of
whether or not his son had returned from the next world; this
was the time for Tim to fight for his life. He did so, and he did
the very best he could. I watched, and where possible I helped.
It failed in the end, but not for want of effort, not for a failure
of trying, a decline of nerve.

This is not expedience. This is rousing oneself to a final defense. To view Tim in his final days as a cheap man devoted to
animal survival at all costs—abandoning all moral conviction—
is to misunderstand totally; when your life is at stake, you act
in certain ways if you are smart, and Tim acted in those ways:
he dumped everything that could be dumped, should have
been dumped—he bared his dog-tooth and offered to bite,
and that is what a man does in the sense of man the creature
who is determined to survive, and to hell with the cargo. Upon
Kirsten's death, Tim stood in danger of imminent death himself and he understood it, and for you to understand him in
that final period you must take his realization into consider-
ation and you must also understand that his perception, his
realization, was correct. He was, as the therapists put it, in
touch with the reality situation (as if there is some kind of distinction between "situation" and "reality situation"). He desired to live. So do I. Presumably, so do you. Then you should
be able to figure out what Bishop Archer had in mind during
the period following Kirsten's death and preceding his own,
the first a given, the second an ominous but dubitable possibility, not a reality, not then, at least, although from our standpoint now, as hindsight, we can comprehend it as inevitable.
But this is the famous nature of hindsight: to it everything is
inevitable, since everything has already happened.

Even if Tim regarded his own death as inevitable, willed by
prophecy, willed by the sibyl—or by Apollo, speaking through
the sibyl as a mouthpiece—he was determined to confront that
fate and put up the best fight he could manage. I think that is
quite remarkable and to be lauded. That he jettisoned a whole

lot of claptrap that he once believed in and preached is of no importance; should he have hugged all that crap and died in a curled-up abreactive posture, his eyes shut, his dog-tooth not bared? I am of firm conviction in this; I saw it; I fathomed it. I saw the cargo go. I saw it heaved overboard the instant Dr. Garret's first prophecy came true. And I said, Thank God.

I think, though, he should have withdrawn that goddamn book from publication, that *Here, Tyrant Death*, as I had titled it. But he did have thirty thousand dollars riding on it, and perhaps this determination to let it get into print was simply further evidence of his practicality. I don't know. Some aspects of Tim Archer remain a mystery to me, even to this day.

It simply was not Tim's style to abort a mistake before it happened; he let it happen and then—as he put it—he filed a correction in the form of an amendment. Except insofar as his physical survival was involved; there he calculated activity in advance. There he looked ahead. The man who had run through his own life, outpacing himself, outdistancing himself as if urged on by the amphetamines he daily swallowed—that man now all at once ceased to run, turned instead, gazed at fate and said, as Luther is supposed to have said but did not, "Here I stand; I can do not otherwise (*Hier steh' Ich; Ich kann nicht anders*)." The German ontologist Martin Heidegger has a term for that: the transmutation of inauthentic Being to true Being or *Sein*. I studied that at Cal. I didn't think I would ever see it happen, but it did and I did. And I found it beautiful but very sad, because it failed.

Within my mind I conceived of the spirit of my dead husband penetrating my thoughts and being highly amused. Jeff would have pointed out to me that I viewed the bishop as a cargo ship, a freighter, baring its dog-tooth, a mixed metaphor which would have kept Jeff in a state of rapture for days; I would never have heard the end of it. My mind had begun to go, due to Kirsten's suicide; at work, comparing the content of shipments to the listings on the invoices, I barely noticed what I did. I had withdrawn. My fellow workers and my boss pointed this out to me. And I ate little; I spent my lunch hour reading Delmore Schwartz, who, I am told, died with his head in a sack of garbage that he had been carrying downstairs when he suffered his fatal heart attack. A great way for a poet to go!

The problem with introspection is that it has no end; like Bottom's dream in *A Midsummer Night's Dream*, it has no bottom. From my years at Cal in the English Department, I had learned to make up metaphors, play around with them, mix them, serve them up; I am a metaphor junkie, over-educated and smart. I think too much, read too much, worry about those I love too much. Those I loved had begun to die. Not many remained here; most had gone.

> *"They are all gone into the world of light!*
> *And I alone sit lingring here;*
> *Their very memory is far and bright,*
> *And my sad thoughts doth clear."*

As Henry Vaughan wrote in 1655. The poem ends:

> *"Either disperse these mists, which blot and fill*
> *My perspective (still) as they pass,*
> *Or else remove me hence unto that hill,*
> *Where I shall need no glass."*

By "glass" Vaughan means a telescope. I looked it up. The seventeenth century minor metaphysical poets constituted my specialty, during my school years. Now, after Kirsten's death, I turned back to them, because my thoughts had turned, like theirs, to the next world. My husband had gone there; my best friend had gone there; I expected Tim to go there, soon, and thus he did.

Unfortunately, I began now to see less of Tim. This for me acted as the worst strike of all. I really loved him but now the ties had been severed. They got severed from his end. He resigned as Bishop of the Diocese of California and moved down to Santa Barbara and the think tank there; his book, which in my eternal opinion should have been suppressed, had come out to indict him as a fool; this combined with the scandal about Kirsten: the media, despite Tim's tampering with evidence, had caught on to their secret relationship. Tim's career with the Episcopal Church ended suddenly; he packed up and left San Francisco, surfacing in (as he had put it) the private sector. There he could relax and be happy; there he could live his life without the repressive strictures of Christian canon law and morality.

I missed him.

A third element had blended in to terminate his relationship with the Episcopal Church, and that of course consisted of the goddamn Zadokite Documents, which Tim simply could not leave alone. No longer involved with Kirsten—she being dead —and no longer involved with the occult—since he recognized that for what it was—he now concentrated all his credulity on the writings of that ancient Hebrew sect, declaring as he did in speeches and in interviews and articles that here, indeed, lay the true origins of the teachings of Jesus. Tim could not leave trouble behind him. He and trouble were destined to join company.

I kept abreast of developments concerning Tim by reading magazines and newspapers; my contact came secondhand; I no longer had direct, personal knowledge of him. For me this constituted tragedy, more perhaps than losing Jeff and Kirsten, although I never told anyone that, even my therapists. I lost track, too, of Bill Lundborg; he drifted out of my life and into a mental hospital, and that was that. I tried to track him down but, failing, gave up. I was either batting zero or a thousand, whichever way you want to compute it.

Whichever way you want to compute it, the results came out to this: I had lost everyone I knew, so the time had arrived to make new friends. I decided that retail record selling was more than a job; for me it amounted to a vocation. Within a year, I had risen to the post of manager of the Musik Shop. I had unlimited powers to buy; the owners put no ceiling on me, none at all. My judgment alone determined what I ordered or did not order, and all the salesmen—the representatives of the various labels—knew it. That earned me a lot of free lunches and some interesting dates. I started coming out of my shell, seeing people more; I wound up with a boyfriend, if you can abide such an old-fashioned term (it would never be employed in Berkeley). "Lover" I guess is the word I want. I let Hampton move into my house with me, the house Jeff and I had bought, and began what I hoped was a fresh, new life, in terms of my involvements.

Tim's book, *Here, Tyrant Death*, did not sell as well as had been expected; I saw remaindered copies at the different bookstores near Sather Gate. It had cost too much and rambled on too long; he would have done better to shorten it, insofar as he had written it—most of it, when I finally got around to reading it, struck me as Kirsten's work; at least she had done the final draft, no doubt based on Tim's bang-bang dictation. That was what she had told me and probably it was the case. He never followed it up with an amending sequel, as he had promised me.

One Sunday morning, as I sat with Hampton in our living room, smoking a joint of the new seedless grass and watching the kids' cartoons on TV, I got a phone call—unexpectedly—from Tim.

"Hi, Angel," he said, in that hearty, warm voice of his. "I hope this isn't a bad time to call you."

"It's fine," I managed to say, wondering if I really heard Tim's voice or if, due to the grass, I was hallucinating it. "How are you? I've been—"

"The reason I'm calling," Tim interrupted, as if I had not been speaking, as if he did not hear me, "is that I'll be in Berkeley next week—I'm attending a conference at the Claremont Hotel—and I'd like to get together with you."

"Great," I said, immensely pleased.

"Can we get together for dinner? You know the restaurants in Berkeley better than I do; I'll let you pick whichever one you like." He chuckled. "It'll be wonderful to see you again. Like old times."

I asked him, haltingly, how he had been.

"Everything down here is going fine," Tim said. "I'm extremely busy. I'll be flying to Israel next month; I wanted to talk to you about that."

"Oh," I said. "That sounds like a lot of fun."

"I'm going to visit the *wadi*," Tim said. "Where the Zadokite Documents were found. They've all been translated, now. Some of the final fragments proved extremely interesting. But I'll tell you about that when I see you."

"Yes," I said, warming to the topic; as always Tim's enthusiasm was contagious. "I read a long article in *Scientific American*; some of the last fragments—"

"I'll pick you up Wednesday night," Tim said. "At your house. Be formally dressed, if you would."

"You remember—"

"Oh, of course; I remember where your house is."

It seemed to me he was speaking ultra-rapidly. Or had the grass affected me? No, the grass would slow things down. I said, in panic, "I'm working at the store on Wednesday night."

As if he hadn't heard me, Tim said, "About eight o'clock; I'll see you then. Good-bye, dear." Click. He had rung off.

Shit, I said to myself. I'm working until nine Wednesday night. Well, I will just have to get one of the clerks to fill in for me. I am not going to miss having dinner with Tim before he leaves for Israel. I wondered, then, how long he would be over there. Probably for some time. He had gone once before, and planted a cedar tree; I remembered that: the news media had made quite a bit of it.

"Who was that?" Hampton said, seated in jeans and a T-shirt before the TV set, my tall, thin, acerbic boyfriend, with his black-wire hair and his glasses.

"My father-in-law," I said. "Former father-in-law."

"Jeff's father," Hampton said, nodding. A crooked grin appeared on his face. "I have an idea as to what to do with people who suicide. I think it should be a law that when they find someone who's suicided, they should dress him up in a clown suit. And photograph him that way. And print his picture in the newspaper like that, in the clown suit. Such as Sylvia Plath. Especially Sylvia Plath." Hampton went on, then, to recount how Plath and her girlfriends—according to Hampton's imagination —used to play games in which they'd see who could stick their head in the oven of the kitchen stove the longest, meanwhile all of them going "tee-hee," giggling and breaking up.

"You're not funny," I said, and walked from the room, into the kitchen.

Hampton called after me, "You're not sticking your head in the oven, are you?"

"Go fuck yourself," I said.

"—with a big red rubber bulb for a nose," Hampton was droning on, mostly to himself; his voice and the racket of the TV set, the kids' cartoons, assailed me; I put my hands over my ears to shut out the noise. "Head out of the oven!" Hampton yelled.

I walked back into the living room and shut off the TV set; turning to face Hampton I said, "Those two people were in a lot of pain. There's nothing funny about someone who's in that much pain."

Grinning, Hampton rocked back and forth, seated curled up on the floor. "And big floppy hands," he said. "Clown hands."

I opened the front door. "I'll see you. I'm going for a walk." I shut the door after me.

The front door swung open. Hampton came out on the porch, cupped his hands to his mouth and called, "Tee-hee; I'm going to stick my head in the oven. Let's see if the baby-sitter gets here in time. Do you think she'll get here in time? Anybody want to make a bet?"

I did not look back; I kept on going.

As I walked along, I thought about Tim and I thought about Israel and what it must be like there, the hot climate, the desert and the rock, the *kibbutzim*. Tilling the soil, the ancient soil that had been worked for thousands of years, farmed by Jews long before the time of Christ. Maybe they would direct Tim's attention to the ground, I thought. And away from the next world. Back to the real; back to where it belonged.

I doubted it, but perhaps I was wrong. I wished, then, that I could go with Tim—quit my job at the record store, just take off and go. Maybe never return. Stay in Israel forever. Become a citizen. Convert to Judaism. If they'd have me. Tim could probably swing it. Maybe in Israel I'd stop mixing metaphors and remembering poems. Maybe my mind would give up trying to solve problems in terms of recycled words. Used phrases, bits ripped from here and there: fragments from my days at Cal in which I had memorized but not understood, understood but not applied, applied but never successfully. A spectator to the destruction of my friends, I said to myself; one who records on a notepad the names of those who die, and did not manage to save any of them, not even one.

I will ask Tim if I can go with him, I decided. Tim will say no—he has to say no—but nonetheless, I will ask.

To root Tim in reality, I realized, they will first have to get his attention, and if he is still on the Dex it will not be possible for them to do that; his mind will be tripping and freewheeling and spinning forever out into the void, conceiving the great models of the heavens . . . they will try and, like me, they will fail. If I go with him, maybe I can help, I thought; the Israelis and I maybe could do what I never could do alone; I will direct their attention to him and they, in turn, will direct his attention to the soil under their feet. Christ, I thought; I have to go with him. It's essential. Because they will not have time to notice the problem. He will skim his way across their country, be first here, then there, never lighting, never coming to rest long enough, never letting them—

A car honked at me; I had wandered out onto the street, crossing unconsciously, without looking.

"Sorry," I said to the driver, who glared at me.

I am no better than Tim, I realized. I'd be no help in Israel. But even so, I thought, I wish I could go.

13

O N Wednesday night, Tim picked me up in a rented Pontiac. I wore a black strapless gown and carried a little beaded purse; I wore a flower in my hair, and Tim, gazing at me as he held the car door open, remarked that I looked lovely.

"Thank you," I said, feeling shy.

We drove to the restaurant on University Avenue, just off Shattuck, a Chinese restaurant that had recently opened. I had never been there, but customers at the Musik Shop had told me it was the great new place to eat in town.

"Have you always worn your hair up like that?" Tim asked, as the hostess led us to our table.

"I got it done for tonight," I explained. I showed him my earrings. "Jeff got me these years ago. I usually don't wear them; I'm afraid I'll lose one."

"You've lost a little weight." He held my chair for me and I nervously seated myself.

"It's the work. Ordering far into the night."

"How is the law firm?"

I said, "I manage a record store."

"Yes," Tim said. "You got me that album of *Fidelio*. I haven't had much chance to play it . . ." He opened his menu, then; absorbed, he turned his attention away from me. How easily that attention waned, I thought. Or, rather, alters its focal point. It isn't the attention that changes; it is the object of that attention. He must live in an endlessly shifting world. Heraclitus' flux world personified.

It pleased me to see that Tim still wore his clericals. Is that legal? I asked myself. Well, it's none of my business. I picked up my menu. This was Mandarin-style Chinese food, not Cantonese; it would be spiced and hot, not sweet, with lots of nuts. Ginger root, I said to myself; I felt hungry and happy, and very glad to be back with my friend again.

"Angel," Tim said, "come with me to Israel."

*

Staring at him, I said, "What?"

"As my secretary."

Still staring, I said, "Take Kirsten's place, you mean?" I began, then, to tremble. A waiter came over; I waved him away.

"Would either of you like a drink?" the waiter said, ignoring my gesture.

"Go away," I said to him, with menace in my voice. "The goddamn waiter," I said to Tim. "What are you talking about? I mean, what sort of—"

"Just as my secretary. I don't mean any personal involvement; nothing of that sort. Did you think I was asking you to become my mistress? I need someone to do the job Kirsten did; I find I can't manage without her."

"Christ," I said. "I thought you meant as your mistress."

"That's out of the question," Tim said, in the stern, firm tone that meant he was not joking. That, in fact, he disapproved. "I think of you still as my daughter-in-law."

"I run the record store," I said.

"My budget permits a fairly good outlay; I can probably pay you as well as your law office—" He corrected himself. "As the record store pays."

"Let me think about it." I beckoned to the waiter to come over. "A martini," I said to him. "Extra dry. Nothing for the bishop."

Tim smiled wryly. "I'm no longer a bishop."

"I can't," I said. "Come to Israel. I have too many ties here."

In a quiet voice, Tim said, "If you don't come with me, I will never—" He broke off. "I saw Dr. Garret again. Recently. Jeff came across from the next world. He says that unless I take you to Israel with me, I'll die there."

"That is pure nonsense," I said. "Pure, absolute bilge. I thought you gave all that up."

"There have been more phenomena." He did not elaborate; his face, I saw, looked strained and pale.

Reaching, I took Tim's hand. "Don't talk to Garret. Talk to me. I say, Go to Israel and the hell with that old lady. It isn't Jeff; it's her. You know that."

"The clocks," Tim said. "They've been stopped at the time Kirsten died."

"Even so—" I began.

"I think it may be both of them," Tim said.

"Go to Israel," I said. "Talk to the people there, to the people of Israel. If ever any people was embedded in reality—"

"I won't have much time. I've got to get right to the Dead Sea Desert and find the *wadi*. I have to be back in time to meet with Buckminster Fuller. I think it's Buckminster I'm supposed to meet with." He touched his coat. "It's written down." His voice trailed off.

"It was my impression that Buckminster Fuller is dead," I said.

"No, I'm sure you're wrong." He gazed at me; I gazed back, and then, by degrees, we both began to laugh.

"See?" I said, still holding the bishop's hand in mine. "I wouldn't be any help to you."

"They say you would," Tim said. "Jeff and Kirsten."

"Tim," I said, "think of Wallenstein."

"I have a choice," Tim said in a low but clear voice, a voice of brisk authority, "between believing the impossible and the stupid—on the one hand—and—" He ceased speaking.

"And not believing," I said.

"Wallenstein was murdered," Tim said.

"No one will murder you."

"I am afraid," Tim said.

"Tim," I said, "the worst thing is the occult crap. I know. Believe me. That's what killed Kirsten. You realized that when she died; remember? You can't go back to that stuff. You will lose all the ground—"

" 'Better a live dog,' " Tim grated, " 'than a dead lion.' By that I mean, Better to believe in nonsense than to be realistic and skeptical and scientific and rational and die in Israel."

"Then simply don't go."

"What I need to know is there at the *wadi*. What I need to find. The *anokhi*, Angel; the mushroom. It's there somewhere and that mushroom is Christ. The real Christ, whom Jesus spoke for. Jesus was the messenger of the *anokhi* which is the true holy power, the true source. I want to see it; I want to find it. It grows in the caves. I know it does."

I said, "It once did."

"It is there now. Christ is there now. Christ has the power to break the hold of fate. The only way I'm going to survive is if someone breaks the hold of fate and releases me; otherwise, I will follow Jeff and Kirsten. That's what Christ does; he unseats the ancient planetary powers. Paul mentions that in his *Captivity Letters* . . . Christ rises from sphere to sphere." Again his voice trailed off, bleakly.

"You're talking about magic."

"I'm talking about God!"

"God is everywhere."

"God is at the *wadi*. The Parousia, the Divine Presence. It was there for the Zadokites; it is there now. The power of fate is, in essence, the power of world, and only God, expressed as Christ, can burst the power of world. It's inscribed in the Book of the Spinners that I will die, except that Christ's blood and body save me." He explained, "The Zadokite Documents speak of a book in which the future of every human is written from before Creation. The Book of the Spinners; it's something like Torah. The Spinners are fate personified, like the Norns in Germanic mythology. They weave men's fortunes. Christ, alone, acting for God here on Earth, seizes the Book of the Spinners, reads it, carries the information to the person, informs him of his fate, and then, through his absolute wisdom, Christ instructs the person on the way his fate can be avoided. The road out." He was silent, then. "We'd better order. There are people waiting."

I said, "Prometheus stealing fire for man, the secret of fire; Christ seizing the Book of the Spinners, reading it and then carrying the information to man to save him."

"Yes." Tim nodded. "It's roughly the same myth. Except that this is no myth; Christ really exists. As a spirit, there at the *wadi*."

"I can't go with you," I said, "and I'm sorry. You'll have to go by yourself and then you'll see that Dr. Garret is pandering to your fears the way she pandered to—and viciously exploited —Kirsten's fears."

"You could drive me."

"There are drivers there in Israel who know the desert. I don't know anything about the Dead Sea Desert."

"You have an excellent sense of direction."

"I get lost. I am lost. I'm lost now. I wish I could go with you but I have my job and my life and my friends; I don't want to leave Berkeley—it's my home. I'm sorry but that's God's truth. Berkeley is where I've always lived. I'm just not ready to leave it at this time. Maybe later." My martini came; I drank it down, all at once, in a spasmodic gulp that left me panting.

Tim said, "The *anokhi* is the pure consciousness of God. It is, therefore, Hagia Sophia, God's Wisdom. Only that wisdom, which is absolute, can read the Book of the Spinners. It can't change what is written, but it can discern a way to outwit the Book. The writing is fixed; it will never change." He seemed defeated, now; he had begun to give up. "I need that wisdom, Angel. Nothing less will do."

"You are like Satan," I said, and then realized that the gin had hit me in a rush; I had not meant to say that.

"No," Tim said, and then he nodded. "Yes, I am. You're right."

"I'm sorry I said that," I said.

"I don't want to be killed off like an animal. If the writing can be read, then an answer can be figured out; Christ has the power to figure it out, Hagia Sophia—Christ. They're homologized from the Old Testament hypostasis to the New." But, I could see, he had given up; he could not budge me and he knew it. "Why not, Angel?" he said. "Why won't you come?"

"Because," I said, "I don't want to die there in the Dead Sea Desert."

"All right. I'll go alone."

"Someone should survive all this," I said.

Tim nodded. "I would want you to survive, Angel. So stay here. I apologize for—"

"Just forgive me," I said.

He smiled wanly. "You could ride on a camel."

"They smell bad," I said. "Or so I've heard."

"If I find the *anokhi* I will have access to God's wisdom. After it has been absent from the world for over two thousand years. That is what the Zadokite Documents speak of, that wisdom that we once had open to us. Think what it would mean!"

The waiter approached our table and asked us if we were ready to order. I said I was; Tim glanced about him in confusion, as if just now aware of his surroundings. It made my heart ache to see his bewilderment. But I had made up my mind. My life, as it was constituted, meant too much for me; most of all,

I feared involvement with this man: it had cost Kirsten her life, and, in a subtle way, my husband's. I wanted that all behind me; I had started over; I no longer looked back.

Wanly, without enthusiasm, Tim told the waiter what to bring him; he seemed oblivious of me, now, as if I had faded into the surroundings. I turned to my own menu, and saw there what I wanted. What I wanted was immediate, fixed, real, tangible: it lay in this world and it could be touched and grasped; it had to do with my house and my job, and it had to do with banishing ideas finally from my mind, ideas about other ideas, an infinite regress of them, spiraling off forever.

The food, when the waiter brought it, tasted wonderful. Both Tim and I ate with pleasure. My customers had been right.

"Mad at me?" I said, after we had finished.

"No. Happy because you will survive this. And you will stay as you are." He pointed at me, then, with a commanding expression on his face. "But if I find what I am after, *I will change.* I will not be as I am. I have read all the documents and the answer isn't in them; the documents point to the answer and they point to the location of the answer, but the answer is not in them. It is at the *wadi.* I am taking a risk but it's worth it. I am willing to take the risk because I may find the *anokhi* and just knowing that makes it worth it."

I said suddenly, with insight, "There haven't been any more phenomena."

"True."

"And you didn't go back to Dr. Garret."

"True." He did not seem contrite or embarrassed.

"That was to get me to come with you."

"I want you along. So you can drive me. Otherwise—I'm afraid I won't find what I'm looking for." He smiled.

"Shit," I said. "I believed you."

"I have had dreams," Tim said. "Disturbing dreams. But no pins under my fingernails. No singed hair. No stopped clocks."

I said, falteringly, "You wanted me to come with you that badly." For a moment I felt a surge in me, a need to go. "You think it would be good for me, too," I said, then.

"Yes. But you won't come. That's clear. Well—" He smiled his old familiar, wise smile. "I tried."

"Am I in a rut, then? Living in Berkeley?"

"Professional student," Tim said.

"I run a record store."

"Your customers are students and faculty. You're still tied to the university. You haven't broken the cord. Until you do, you will not fully be an adult."

"I was born the night I drank bourbon and read the *Commedia*. When I had that abscessed tooth."

"You *began* to be born. You knew about birth. But until you come to Israel—that is where you will be born, there in the Dead Sea Desert. That is where the spiritual life of man began, at Mt. Sinai, with Moses. *Ehyeh* speaking . . . the theophany. The greatest moment in the history of man."

"I would almost go," I said.

"Go, then." He reached out his hand.

I said, simply, "I'm afraid."

"That's the problem," Tim said. "That's the heritage of the past: Jeff's death and Kirsten's death. That's what it's done to you, done permanently. Left you afraid to live."

" 'Better a live dog—' "

"But," Tim said, "you are not genuinely alive. You are still unborn. This is what Jesus meant by the Second Birth, the Birth in or from the Spirit; the Birth from Above. This is what lies in the desert. This is what I will find."

"Find it," I said, "but find it without me."

" 'He who loses his life—' "

"Don't quote the Bible to me," I said. "I've heard enough quotations, my own and others'. Okay?"

Tim reached out and we solemnly, without speaking, shook hands. He smiled a little, then; after a bit he let my hand go and then examined his gold pocket-watch. "I'm going to have to get you home. I've still got one appointment left this evening. You understand; you know me."

"Yes," I said. "It's okay. Tim," I said, "you are a master strategist. I watched you when you met Kirsten. You brought it all to bear on me, here, tonight." And you almost persuaded me, I said to myself. In a few more minutes—I would have given in. If you had kept up just a little longer.

"I am in the business of saving souls," Tim said enigmatically. I could not tell if he spoke in irony or if he meant it; I simply could not tell. "Your soul is worth saving," he said, then, as he rose to his feet. "I'm sorry to rush you, but we do have to go."

You always were in a hurry, I said to myself as I also got up. "It was a wonderful dinner," I said.

"Was it? I didn't notice; I'm preoccupied, apparently. I have so many things to finish before I fly to Israel. Now that I don't have Kirsten to arrange everything for me . . . she did such a good job."

"You'll find someone," I said.

Tim said, "I thought I found you. The fisherman, tonight; I fished for you and didn't get you."

"Some other time, maybe."

"No," Tim said. "There will be no other time." He did not amplify. He did not have to; I knew that it was so, for one reason or another: I sensed it. Tim was right.

When Timothy Archer flew to Israel, the NBC network news mentioned it briefly, as they would mention a flight of birds, a migration too regular to be important and yet something the viewers should be told about, by way (it would seem) of a reminder that Episcopal Bishop Timothy Archer still existed and was still busy and active in the affairs of the world. And then we, the American public, heard nothing for a week or so.

I got a card from him, but the card arrived after the big news coverage, the late-breaking sensational story of Bishop Archer's abandoned Datsun found, its rear end up off the little rutted winding road, up on a jutting rock, the gas station map still on the right-hand front seat where he had left it.

The government of Israel did everything possible and did it swiftly; they had troops and—shit. They employed everything they had, but the news people knew that Tim Archer had died in the Dead Sea Desert because you cannot live out there, crawling up cliffs and down into ravines; you cannot survive, and they did eventually find his body and it looked as if, one of the reporters on the scene said, as if he knelt praying. But, in fact, Tim had fallen, a long way, down a cliff-side. And I drove, as usual, to the record store and opened it up for business and put money in the register and this time I did not cry.

Why hadn't he taken a professional driver? the news people

asked. Why had he ventured out on the desert alone with a gas station map and two bottles of soda pop—I knew the answer. Because he was in a hurry. Undoubtedly getting hold of a professional driver took, in his view, too much time. He could not wait around. As with me in the Chinese restaurant that night, Tim had to get moving; he could not stay in one place; he was a busy man, and he rushed on, he rushed out into the desert in that little four-cylinder car that isn't even safe on California freeways, as Bill Lundborg had pointed out; those subcompact cars are dangerous.

I loved him the most of all of them. I knew it when I heard the news, knew it in a different way than I had known it before; before it had been a feeling, an emotion. But when I realized he was dead, that knowledge made me into a sick person that limped and cringed, but drove to work and filled the register and answered the phone and asked customers if I could help them; I wasn't sick as a human is sick or an animal is sick; I became ill like a machine. I still moved but my soul died, my soul that, Tim had said, had never been fully born; that soul, not yet born, but born a little and wishing to be born more, born fully, that soul died and my body mechanically continued on.

The soul I lost during that week did not ever return; I am a machine now, years later; a machine heard the news of John Lennon's death and a machine grieved and pondered and drove to Sausalito to sit in on Edgar Barefoot's seminar, because that is what a machine does: that is a machine's way of greeting the horrible. A machine doesn't know any better; it simply grinds along, and maybe whirrs. That is all it can do. You cannot expect more than that from a machine. That is all it has to offer. That is why we speak of it as a machine; it understands, intellectually, but there is no understanding in its heart because its heart is a mechanical one, designed to act as a pump.

And so it pumps, and so the machine limps and coasts on, and knows but does not know. And keeps up its routine. It lives out what it supposes to be life: it maintains its schedule and obeys the laws. It does not drive its car over the speed limit on the Richardson Bridge and it says to itself: I never liked the Beatles: I found them insipid. Jeff brought home *Rubber Soul* and if I hear . . . it repeats to itself what it has thought and heard, the simulation of life. Life it once possessed and now has lost; a life now gone. It knows it knows not what, as the philosophy books say about a confused philosopher; I forget which one. Locke, maybe. "And Locke believes he knows not what." That impressed me, that turn of phrase. I look for that; I am attracted to clever phrases, which are to be regarded as good English prose style.

I am a professional student and will remain one; I will not change. My opportunity to change was offered to me and I turned it down; I am stuck, now, and, as I say, know but know not what.

14

Facing us, smiling a moon-wide smile, Edgar Barefoot said, "What if a symphony orchestra was intent only on reaching the final coda? What would become of the music? One great crash of sound, over as soon as possible. The music is in the process, the unfolding; if you hasten it, you destroy it. Then the music is over. I want you to think about that."

Okay, I said to myself. I'll think about it. There is nothing on this particular day I'd prefer to think about. Something has happened, something important, but I do not wish to remember it. No one does. I can see it around me, this same reaction. My reaction in the others, here on this cushy houseboat at Gate Five. Where you pay a hundred dollars, the same sum, I believe, that Tim and Kirsten paid that crank, that quack psychic and medium, down in Santa Barbara, who wrecked us all.

One hundred dollars appears to be the magic sum; it opens the door to enlightenment. Which is why I am here. My life is devoted to seeking enlightenment, as are the other lives around me. This is the noise of the Bay Area, the racket and din of meaning; this is what we exist for: to learn.

Teach us, Barefoot, I said to myself. Tell me something I don't know. I, being deficient of comprehension, yearn to know. You can begin with me; I am the most attentive of your pupils. I trust everything you utter. I am the perfect fool, come here to take. Give. Keep on with the sounds; it lulls me and I forget.

"Young lady," Barefoot said.

With a start, I realized he was speaking to me.

"Yes," I said, rousing myself.

"What's your name?" Barefoot asked.

"Angel Archer," I said.

"Why are you here?"

"To get away," I said.

"From what?"

"Everything," I said.

"Why?"

"It hurts," I said.

"John Lennon, you mean?"

"Yes," I said. "And more. Other things."

"I was noticing you," Barefoot said, "because you were asleep. You may not have realized it. Did you realize it?"

"I realized it," I said.

"Is that how you want me to perceive you? As asleep?"

"Let me alone," I said.

"Let you sleep, then."

"Yes," I said.

" 'The sound of one hand clapping,' " Barefoot quoted.

I said nothing.

"Do you want me to hit you? Cuff you? To wake you up?"

"I don't care," I said. "It doesn't matter to me."

"What would it take to awaken you?" Barefoot said.

I did not answer.

"My job is to wake people."

"You are another fisherman."

"Yes; I fish for fish. Not for souls. I do not know of 'soul'; I only know of fish. A fisherman fishes for fish; if he thinks he fishes for anything else, he is a fool; he deludes himself and those he fishes for."

"Fish for me, then," I said.

"What do you want?"

"Not ever to wake up."

"Then come up here," Barefoot said. "Come up and stand beside me. I will teach you how to sleep. It is as hard to sleep as it is to wake up. You sleep poorly, without skill. I can teach you that as easily as I can teach you to wake up. Whatever you want you can have. Are you sure you know what you want? Maybe you secretly want to wake up. You may be wrong about yourself. Come on up here." He reached out his hand.

"Don't touch me," I said as I walked toward him. "I don't want to be touched."

"So you know that."

"I am sure of that," I said.

"Maybe what is wrong with you is that no one has ever touched you," Barefoot said.

"You tell me," I said. "I have nothing to say. Whatever I had to say—"

"You have never said anything," Barefoot said. "You have been silent all your life. Only your mouth has talked."

"If you say so."

"Tell me your name again."

"Angel Archer."

"Do you have a secret name? That no one knows?"

"I have no secret name," I said. And then I said, "I am traitor."

"Who did you betray?"

"Friends," I said.

"Well, Traitor," Barefoot said, "talk to me about your bringing your friends to ruin. How did you do it?"

"With words," I said. "Like now."

"You are good with words."

"Very good," I said. "I am a sickness, a word-sickness. I was taught it by professionals."

"I have no words," Barefoot said.

"Okay," I said. "Then I will listen."

"Now you begin to know."

I nodded.

"Do you have any pets at home?" Barefoot said. "Any dogs or cats? An animal?"

"Two cats," I said.

"Do you groom them and feed them and care for them? Are you responsible for them? Do you take them to the vet when they're ill?"

"Sure," I said.

"Who does all that for you?"

"For me?" I said. "No one."

"Can you do it for yourself?"

"Yes, I can," I said.

"Then, Angel Archer, you are alive."

"Not intentionally," I said.

"But you are. You don't think so but you are. Under the words, the disease of words, you are alive. I am trying to tell you this without using words but it is impossible. All we have is words. Sit down again and listen. Everything I say from now on, today, is directed at you; I am speaking to you but not with words. Does that make any sense to you?"

"No," I said.

"Then just sit down," Barefoot said.

I reseated myself.

"Angel Archer," Barefoot said, "You are wrong about yourself. You are not sick; *you are starved*. What is killing you is hunger. Words have nothing to do with it. You have been starved all your life. Spiritual things will not help. You don't need them. There are too many spiritual things in the world, far too many. You are a fool, Angel Archer, but not a good kind of fool."

I said nothing.

"You need real meat," Barefoot said, "and real drink, not spiritual meat and drink. I offer you real food, for your body, so it will grow. You are a starving person who has come here to be fed, but without knowing it. You have no idea why you came here today. It is my job to tell you. When people come here to listen to me speak, I offer them a sandwich. The foolish ones listen to my words; the wise ones eat the sandwich. This is not an absurdity that I tell you; it is the truth. This is something none of you has imagined, but I give you real food and that food is a sandwich; the words, the talking, is only wind—is nothing. I charge you one hundred dollars but you learn something priceless. When your dog or cat is hungry, do you talk to him? No; you give him food. I give you food, but you do not know it. You have everything backward because the university has taught you that; it has taught you wrong. It has lied to you. And now you tell yourselves lies; you have learned how to do it and you do it very well. Take the sandwich and eat; forget about the words. The only purpose in the words was to lure you here."

Strange, I thought. He means it. Some of my unhappiness began, then, to ebb away. I felt a peacefulness come over me, a loss of suffering.

Someone from behind me leaned forward and touched me on the shoulder. "Hi, Angel."

I turned around to see who it was. A pudgy-faced youth, blond-haired, smiling at me, his eyes guileless. Bill Lundborg, wearing a turtleneck sweater and gray slacks and, I saw to my surprise, Hush Puppies.

"Remember me?" he said softly. "I'm sorry I didn't answer any of your letters. I've been wondering how you've been doing."

"Fine," I said. "Just fine."

"I guess we better be quiet." He leaned back and folded his arms, intent on what Edgar Barefoot was saying.

At the end of his lecture, Barefoot walked over to me; I still sat, unmoving. Bending, Barefoot said, "Are you related to Bishop Archer?"

"Yes," I said. "I was his daughter-in-law."

"We knew each other," Barefoot said. "Tim and I. For years. It was such a shock, his death. We used to discuss theology."

Coming up beside us, Bill Lundborg stood listening, saying nothing; he still smiled the same old smile I remembered.

"And then John Lennon's death today," Barefoot said. "I hope I didn't embarrass you, bringing you up front like that. But I could see something was wrong. You look better now."

I said, "I feel better."

"Do you want a sandwich?" Barefoot indicated the people gathered around the table at the rear of the room.

"No," I said.

Barefoot said, "Then you weren't listening. To what I told you. I wasn't joking. Angel, you can't live on words; words do not feed. Jesus said, 'Man does not live by bread alone'; I say, 'Man does not live by words at all.' Have a sandwich."

"Have something to eat, Angel," Bill Lundborg said.

"I don't feel like eating," I said. "I'm sorry." I thought, I'd rather be left alone.

Bending down, Bill said, "You look so thin."

"My work," I said remotely.

"Angel," Edgar Barefoot said, "this is Bill Lundborg."

"We know each other," Bill said. "We're old friends."

"Then you know," Barefoot said to me, "that Bill is a *bodhisattva*."

"I didn't know that," I said.

Barefoot said, "Do you know what a *bodhisattva* is, Angel?"

"It has something to do with the Buddha," I said.

"The *bodhisattva* is one who has turned down his chance to attain *Nirvana* in order to turn back to help others," Barefoot said. "For the *bodhisattva* compassion is as important a goal as wisdom. That is the essential realization of the *bodhisattva*."

"That's fine," I said.

"I get a lot out of what Edgar teaches," Bill said to me. "Come on." He took me by the hand. "I'm going to see that you eat something."

"Do you consider yourself a *bodhisattva*?" I said to him.

"No," Bill said.

"Sometimes the *bodhisattva* does not know," Barefoot said. "It is possible to be enlightened without knowing it. Also, it is possible to think you are enlightened and yet not be. The Buddha is called 'the Awakened One,' because 'awakened' means the same as 'enlightened.' We all sleep but do not know it. We live in a dream; we walk and move and have our lives in a dream; most of all we speak in a dream; our speech is the speech of dreamers, and unreal."

Like now, I thought. What I'm hearing.

Bill disappeared; I looked around for him.

"He's getting you something to eat," Barefoot said.

"This is all very strange," I said. "This whole day has been unreal. It is like a dream; you're right. They're playing all the old Beatles songs on every station."

"Let me tell you something that happened to me once," Barefoot said; he seated himself in the chair beside me, bent over, his hands clasped together. "I was very young, still in school. I attended classes at Stanford, but I did not graduate. I took a lot of philosophy classes."

"So did I," I said.

"One day I left my apartment to mail a letter. I had been working on a paper—not a paper to turn in but a paper of my own: profound philosophical ideas, ideas very important to me. There was one particular problem I couldn't figure out; it had to do with Kant and his ontological categories by which the human mind structures experience—"

"Time, space and causation," I said. "I know. I studied that."

"What I realized as I walked along," Barefoot said, "was that, in a very real sense, I myself create the world that I experience; I both make that world and perceive it. As I walked, the correct formulation of this came to me, suddenly, out of the blue. One minute I didn't have it; the next minute I did. It was a solution I'd been striving for over a period of years . . . I had read Hume, and then I had found the response to Hume's criticism of causation in Kant's writing—now, suddenly, I had a response, and a correctly worked-out response to Kant. I started hurrying."

Bill Lundborg reappeared; he held a sandwich and a cup of

fruit punch of some sort; these he held out to me. I accepted them reflexively.

Continuing, Barefoot said, "I hurried back up the street toward my apartment as fast as I could go. I had to get the *satori* down on paper before I forgot it. What I had acquired, there on that walk, out of my apartment where I had no access to pen and paper, was a comprehension of a world conceptually arranged, a world not arranged in time and space and by causation, but a world as idea conceived in a great mind, the way our own minds store memories. I had caught a glimpse of world not as my own arrangement—by time, space and causation—but as it is in itself arranged; Kant's 'thing-in-itself.' "

"Which can't be known, Kant said," I said.

"Which normally can't be known," Barefoot said. "But I had somehow perceived it, like a great, reticulated, arborizing structure of interrelationships, everything organized according to meaning, with all new events entering as accretions; I had never before grasped the absolute nature of reality this way." He paused a moment.

"You got home and wrote it down," I said.

"No," Barefoot said. "I never wrote it down. As I hurried along, I saw two tiny children, one of them holding a baby-bottle. They were running back and forth across a street. A lot of cars came along very fast. I watched for a moment and then I went over to them. I saw no adult. I asked them to take me to their mother. They didn't speak English; it was a Spanish neighborhood, very poor . . . I didn't have any money in those days. I found their mother. She said, 'I don't speak English' and closed the door in my face. She was smiling. I remember that. Smiling at me beatifically. She thought I was a salesman. I wanted to tell her that her children would very soon be killed and she shut the door in my face, smiling angelically at me."

"So what did you do?" Bill said.

Barefoot said, "I sat down on the curb and watched the two children. For the rest of the afternoon. Until their father came home. He spoke a little English. I was able to get him to understand. He thanked me."

"You did the right thing," I said.

"So I never got my model of the universe down on paper," Barefoot said. "I just have a dim memory of it. Something like that fades. It was a once-in-a-lifetime *satori*. *Moksa*, it is called in India; a sudden flash of absolute comprehension, out of nowhere. What James Joyce means by 'epiphanies,' arising from the trivial or without cause at all, simply happening. Total insight into world." He was silent, then.

I said, "What I hear you saying is that the life of a Mexican child is—"

"Which way would you have taken?" Barefoot said to me. "Would you have gone home and written down your philosophical idea, your *moksa*? Or would you have stayed with the children?"

"I would have called the police," I said.

"To have done that," Barefoot said, "would have required you to go to a phone. To do that you would have had to leave the children."

"It's a nice story," I said. "But I knew someone else who told nice stories. He's dead."

"Maybe," Barefoot said, "he found what he went to Israel to find. Found it before he died."

"I very much doubt that," I said.

"I doubt it, too," Barefoot said. "On the other hand, maybe he found something better. Something he should have been looking for but wasn't. What I am trying to tell you is that all of us are unknowing *bodhisattvas*, unwilling, even; unintentional. It is something forced on us by chance circumstance. All I wanted to do that day was rush home and get my great insight down on paper before I forgot it. It really was a great insight; I have no doubt of that. I did not want to be a *bodhisattva*. I did not ask to be. I did not expect to be. In those days, I hadn't even heard the term. Anyone would have done what I did."

"Not anyone," I said. "Most people would have, I guess."

"What would you have done?" Barefoot said. "Given that choice."

I said, "I guess I would have done what you did and hoped I'd remember the insight."

"But I did not remember it," he said. "And that is the point."

Bill said to me, then, "Can I hitch a ride with you back to the East Bay? My car got towed off. It threw a rod and I—"

"Sure," I said; I stood up, stiffly; my bones ached. "Mr. Barefoot, I've listened to you on KPFA many times. At first, I thought you were stuffy but now I'm not so sure."

"Before you go," Barefoot said, "I want you to tell me how you betrayed your friends."

"She didn't," Bill said. "It's all in her mind."

Barefoot leaned toward me; he put his arm around me and drew me back to my chair, reseating me.

"Well," I said, "I let them die. Especially Tim."

"Tim could not have avoided death," Barefoot said. "He went to Israel in order to die. That's what he wanted. Death was what he was looking for. That's why I say, Maybe he found what he was looking for or even something better."

Shocked, I said, "Tim wasn't looking for death. Tim put up the bravest fight against fate I ever saw anybody put up."

"Death and fate are not the same," Barefoot said. "He died to avoid fate, because the fate he saw coming for him was worse than dying there on the Dead Sea Desert. That's why he sought it and that's what he found; but I think he found something better." To Bill he said, "What do you think, Bill?"

"I'd rather not say," Bill said.

"But you know," Barefoot said to him.

"What was the fate you're talking about?" I asked Barefoot.

Barefoot said, "The same as yours. The fate that has overtaken you. And that you're aware of."

"What is that?" I said.

"Lost in meaningless words," Barefoot said. "A merchant of words. With no contact to life. Tim had advanced far into that. I read *Here, Tyrant Death* several times. It said nothing, nothing at all. Just words. *Flatus vocis*, an empty noise."

After a moment I said, "You're right. I read it, too." How true it was, how terribly, sadly true.

"And Tim realized it," Barefoot said. "He told me. He came to me a few months before his trip to Israel and told me. He wanted me to teach him about the Sufis. He wanted to exchange meaning—all the meaning he'd piled up in his lifetime—for something else. For beauty. He told me about an album of records that you sold him that he never got a chance to play. Beethoven's *Fidelio*. He was always too busy."

"Then you knew who I was already," I said. "Before I told you."

"That's why I asked you to come up front with me," Barefoot said. "I recognized you. Tim had shown me a picture of you and Jeff. At first, I wasn't sure. You're a lot thinner now."

"Well, I have a demanding job," I said.

Together, Bill Lundborg and I drove back across the Richardson Bridge to the East Bay. We listened to the radio, to the endless procession of Beatles songs.

"I knew you were trying to find me," Bill said, "but my life wasn't going too well. I've finally been diagnosed as what they call 'hebephrenic.'"

To change the subject I said, "I hope the music isn't depressing you; I can turn it off."

"I like the Beatles," Bill said.

"Are you aware of John Lennon's death?"

"Sure," Bill said. "Everybody is. So you manage the Musik Shop now."

"Yes, indeed," I said. "I have five clerks working under me and unlimited buying power. I've got an offer from Capitol Records to go down to the L.A. area, to Burbank, I guess, and go to work for them. I've reached the top in terms of the retail record business; managing a store is as far as you can go. Except for owning the store. And I don't have the money."

"Do you know what 'hebephrenic' means?"

"Yes," I said. I thought, I even know the origin of the word. "Hebe was the Greek goddess of youth," I said.

"I never grew up," Bill said. "Hebephrenia is characterized by silliness."

"Guess so," I said.

"When you're hebephrenic," Bill said, "things strike you as funny. Kirsten's death struck me as funny."

Then you are indeed hebephrenic, I said to myself as I drove. Because there was nothing funny about it. I said, "What about Tim's death?"

"Well, parts of it were funny. That little boxy car, that Datsun. And those two bottles of Coke. Tim probably had shoes on like I have on now." He lifted his foot to show me his Hush Puppies.

"At least," I said.

"But by and large," Bill said, "it was not funny. What Tim was looking for wasn't funny. Barefoot is wrong about what Tim was looking for; he wasn't looking for death."

"Not consciously," I said, "but maybe unconsciously he was."

"That's nonsense," Bill said. "All that about unconscious motivation. You can posit anything by reasoning that way. You can attribute any motivation you want, since there's no way it can be tested. Tim was looking for that mushroom. He sure picked a funny place to look for a mushroom: a desert. Mushrooms grow where it's moist and cool and shaded."

"In caves," I said. "There are caves there."

"Yes, well," Bill said, "it wasn't actually a mushroom anyhow. That, too, is a supposition. A gratuitous assumption. Tim stole that idea from a scholar named John Allegro. Tim's problem was that he didn't really think for himself; he picked up other people's ideas and believed they had come out of his own mind, whereas, in fact, he stole them."

"But the ideas had value," I said, "and Tim synthesized them. Tim brought various ideas together."

"But not very good ones."

Glancing at Bill, I said, "Who are you to judge?"

"I know you loved him," Bill said. "You don't have to defend him all the time. I'm not attacking him."

"It sure sounds like it."

"I loved him, too. A lot of people loved Bishop Archer. He was a great man, the greatest we'll ever know. But he was a foolish man and you know that."

I said nothing; I drove and I half-listened to the radio. They were now playing "Yesterday."

"Edgar was right about you, however," Bill said. "You should have dropped out of the university and not finished. You learned too much."

With bitterness I said, " 'Learned too much.' Christ. The *vox populi*. Distrust of education. I get sick and tired of hearing that shit; I am glad of what I know."

"It's wrecked you," Bill said.

"You can just go take a flying fling," I said.

Bill said calmly, "You are very bitter and very unhappy. You are a good person who loved Kirsten and Tim and Jeff and you haven't gotten over what happened to them. And your education has not helped you cope with this."

"There is no coping with this!" I said, with fury. "They all were good people and they are all dead!"

" 'Your fathers ate manna in the desert and they are all dead.' "

"What's that?"

"Jesus says that. I think it's said during Mass. I attended Mass a few times with Kirsten, at Grace Cathedral. One time, when Tim was passing the chalice around—Kirsten was kneeling at the rail—he secretly slipped a ring around her finger. No one saw but she told me. It was a symbolic wedding ring. Tim had on all his robes, then."

"Tell me about it," I said, bitterly.

"I am telling you about it. Did you know—"

"I knew about the ring," I said. "She told me. She showed it to me."

"They considered themselves spiritually married. Before and in the eyes of God. Although not according to civil law. 'Your fathers ate manna in the desert and they are all dead.' That refers to the Old Testament. Jesus brings—"

"Oh, my good God," I said, "I thought I'd heard the last of all this stuff. I don't want ever to hear any more. It didn't do any good then and it won't ever do any good. Barefoot talks about useless words—*those* are useless words. Why would Barefoot call you a *bodhisattva*? What is all this compassion and wisdom you have? You attained *Nirvana* and came back to help others, is that it?"

"I could have attained *Nirvana*," Bill said. "But I turned it down. To return."

"Forgive me," I said, with weariness. "I don't understand what you're talking about. Okay?"

Bill said, "I came back to this world. From the next world. Out of compassion. That is what I learned out there in the desert, the Dead Sea Desert." His voice was calm; his face showed a deep calm. "That is what I found."

I stared at him.

"I am Tim Archer," Bill said. "I have come back from the other side. To those I love." He smiled a vast and secret smile.

15

AFTER a moment of silence, I said, "Did you tell Edgar Barefoot?"

"Yes," Bill said.

"Who else?"

"Almost no one else."

I said, "When did this happen?" And then I said, "You fucking lunatic. It will never end; it goes on and it goes on. One by one, they go mad and die. All I want to do is run my record store and turn on and get laid now and then and read a few books. I never asked for this." My car's tires squealed as I swerved to pass a slow-moving vehicle. We had almost reached the Richmond end of the Richardson Bridge.

"Angel," Bill said. He put his hand on my shoulder, tenderly.

"Get your goddamn hand off of me," I said.

He withdrew his hand. "I have come back," he said.

"You have gone crazy again and belong back in the hospital, you hebephrenic nut. Can't you see what this is doing to me, to have to listen to more of this? You know what I thought about you? I thought: There, in a certain real sense, is the only sane one among us; he is labeled as a nut but he is sane. We are labeled as sane and we are nuts. And now you. You are the last one I would have expected this from, but I guess—" I broke off. "Shit," I said. "It's out of control, this madness process. I always said to myself: Bill Lundborg is in touch with the real; he thinks about cars. You could have explained to Tim why one does not drive out on the Dead Sea Desert in a Datsun with two bottles of Coke and a gas station map. And now you are as crazy as they were. More crazy." Reaching, I turned up the radio; the sound of the Beatles filled the car—Bill at once shut the radio off, entirely off.

"Please slow down," Bill said.

"Please," I said, "when we get to the toll gate, get out of the car and hitch a ride with somebody else. And you can tell Edgar Barefoot to go stick his—"

"Don't blame him," Bill said sharply. "I only told him; he didn't tell me. Slow down!" He reached for the ignition key.

"Okay," I said, putting my foot on the brake.

"You will roll this sardine can," Bill said, "and kill us both. And you don't even have your seat belt fastened."

"On this day of all days," I said. "The day they murder John Lennon. I have to hear this right now."

"I did not find the *anokhi* mushroom," Bill said.

I said nothing; I simply drove. As best I could.

"I fell," Bill said. "From a cliff."

"Yes," I said. "I read that, too, in the *Chronicle*. Did it hurt?"

"By that time, I had become unconscious from the sunlight and the heat."

"Well," I said, "apparently you are just not a very bright person, to go out there like that." And then, suddenly, I felt compassion; I felt shame, overwhelming shame at what I was doing to him. "Bill," I said, "forgive me."

"Sure," he said, simply.

I thought through my words and then I said, "When did— what am I supposed to call you? Bill or Tim? Are you both, now?"

"I'm both. One personality has been formed out of the two. Either name will do. Probably you should call me Bill so that people won't know."

"Why don't you want them to know? I would think something as important and unique as this, as momentous as this, should be known."

Bill said, "They'll put me back in the hospital."

"Then," I said, "I will call you Bill."

"About a month after his death, Tim came back to me. I didn't understand what was happening; I couldn't figure it out. Lights and colors and then an alien presence in my mind. Another personality much smarter than me, thinking all sorts of things I never thought. And he knows Greek and Latin and Hebrew, and all about theology. He thought about you very clearly. He had wanted to take you with him to Israel."

At that, I glanced sharply at him and felt chilled.

"That night at the Chinese restaurant," Bill said, "he tried to talk you into it. But you said you had your life all planned out. You couldn't leave Berkeley."

Taking my foot from the gas pedal, I allowed the car to slow down; it moved more and more slowly until it came to a stop.

"It's illegal to stop on the bridge," Bill said. "Unless you're having motor trouble or run out of gas, something of that sort. Keep on driving."

Tim told him, I said to myself. Reflexively, I down-shifted, into low; I started the car up again.

"Tim had a crush on you," Bill said.

"So?" I said.

"That was one reason he wanted to take you to Israel with him."

I said, "You speak of Tim in the third person. So, in point of fact, you do not identify yourself with Tim or as Tim; you are Bill Lundborg talking about Tim."

"I am Bill Lundborg," he agreed. "But also I am Tim Archer."

"Tim wouldn't tell me that," I said, "about being sexually interested in me."

"I know," Bill said, "but I am telling you."

"What did we have for dinner that night at the Chinese restaurant?"

"I have no idea."

"Where was the restaurant?"

"In Berkeley."

"Where in Berkeley?"

"I don't remember."

I said, "Tell me what *hysteron proteron* means."

"How would I know that? That's Latin. Tim knows Latin; I don't."

"It's Greek."

"I don't know any Greek. I pick up Tim's thoughts and now and then he's thinking in Greek but I don't know what the Greek means."

"What if I believe you?" I said. "What then?"

"Then," Bill said, "you are happy because your old friend is not dead."

"And that's the point of this."

He nodded. "Yes."

"It would seem to me," I said carefully, "there would be a larger point involved. This would be a miracle of staggering importance, to the entire world. It is something that scientists should investigate. It proves there is eternal life, that a next world does exist—everything that Tim and Kirsten believed is, in fact, true. *Here, Tyrant Death* is true. Don't you agree?"

"Yes. I suppose so. That's what Tim is thinking; he thinks that a lot. He wants me to write a book, but I can't write a book; I don't have any writing talent."

"You can act as Tim's secretary. The way your mother did. Tim can dictate and you can write it all down."

"He rattles on and on a mile a minute. I've tried to write it down but—his thinking is fucked. If you'll pardon the expression. It's all disorganized; it goes everywhere and nowhere. And I don't know half the words. In fact, a lot of it isn't words at all, just impressions."

"Can you hear him now?"

"No. Not right now. It's usually when I'm alone and no one else is talking. Then I can sort of tune in on it."

" '*Hysteron proteron*,' " I murmured. "When the thing to be demonstrated is included in the premise. So it's all in vain, the reasoning. Bill," I said, "I've got to hand it to you; you have me tied up in a knot, you really have. Does Tim remember backing over the gas pump? Never mind; fuck the gas pump."

Bill said. "It's a presence of mind. See, Tim was in that area —the word 'presence' reminded me; he uses that word a lot. The Presence, as he calls it, was there in the desert."

"The Parousia," I said.

"Right." Bill emphatically nodded.

"That would be *anokhi*," I said.

"Would it? What he was looking for?"

"Apparently he found it," I said. "What did Barefoot say to all this?"

"That's when he told me—when he realized—I was a *bodhisattva*. I came back. Tim came back, I mean, out of compassion for others. For those he loves. Such as you."

"What is Barefoot going to do with this news?"

"Nothing."

" 'Nothing,' " I echoed, nodding.

"There's no way I can prove it," Bill said. "To skeptical minds. Edgar pointed that out."

"Why can't you prove it? It should be easy to prove it. You have access to everything Tim knew; like you said—all the theology, details of his personal life. Facts. It should be the most simple matter on Earth to prove."

"Can I prove it to you?" Bill said. "I can't even prove it to you. It's like belief in God; you can know God, know he exists; you can experience him, and yet you can never prove to anyone else that you've experienced him."

"Do you believe in God now?" I said.

"Sure." He nodded.

"I guess you believe in a lot of things now," I said.

"Because of Tim in me, I know a lot of things; it isn't just belief. It's like—" He gestured earnestly. "Having swallowed a computer or the whole *Britannica*, a whole library. The facts, the ideas, come and go and just whizz around in my head; they go too fast—that's the problem. I don't understand them; I can't remember them; I can't write them down or explain them to other people. It's like having KPFA turned on inside your head twenty-four hours a day, without cease. In many respects, it's an affliction. But it's interesting."

Have fun with your thoughts, I said to myself. That is what Harry Stack Sullivan said schizophrenics do: they have endless fun with their thoughts, and forget the world.

There is not much you can say when someone unveils an account such as Bill Lundborg's—assuming that anyone ever unveiled such a narration before. It did, of course, resemble what Tim and Kirsten had revealed to me (that is the wrong word) when they returned from England, after Jeff's death. But that had been minor compared with this. This, I thought, consists of the ultimate escalation, the monument itself. The other narration was only the marker pointing to the monument.

Madness, like small fish, runs in hosts, in vast numbers of instances. It is not solitary. Madness does not remain content; it fans out across the landscape, or seascape, whichever.

Yes, I thought; it is like we are under water: not in a dream—as Barefoot says—but in a tank, and being observed, for our bizarre behavior and our more bizarre beliefs. I am a metaphor junkie; Bill Lundborg is a madness junkie, unable to get enough of it: he possesses a boundless appetite for it and will obtain it by whatever means possible. Just when it seemed, too, as if madness had passed out of the world. First John Lennon's death and now this; and, for me, on the same day.

I could not say, and yet he is so plausible. Because Bill was not plausible; it is not a plausible matter. Probably, even Edgar Barefoot recognized that—well, however a Sufi phrases such *moksa* to himself, that someone is sick and needs help, but is touchingly appealing, is guileless and not going to do any harm. This madness arose from pain, from the loss of a mother and what almost certainly amounted to a father in the true sense of the word. I felt it; I feel it; I always will feel it, as long as I live. But Bill's solution could not be mine.

Any more than mine—managing the record store—could be his. We each must find our own solution, and, in particular, we each must solve the sort of problem that death creates—creates for others; but not death only: madness also, madness leading to final death as its end-state, its logical goal.

When my original anger at Bill Lundborg's psychosis had subsided—it did subside—I began to view it as funny. The utility of Bill Lundborg, not just for himself but, as I viewed it, to all of us, consisted in his grounding in the concrete. This, precisely, he had lost. His showing up at Edgar Barefoot's seminar disclosed the change in Bill; the kid I had known, formerly known, would never have set foot in such surroundings. Bill had gone the way of the rest of us, not the way of all flesh but the way of our intellects: into nonsense and the foolish, there to languish without a trace of anything redemptive.

Except, of course, Bill could now emotionally deal with the assortment of deaths that had plagued us. Was my solution any better? I worked; I read; I listened to music—I bought music in the form of records; I lived a professional life and yearned to move into the A & R Division of Capitol Records down in Southern California. There my future lay, there were the tangible things that records had become for me, not something to enjoy but something to first buy and then sell.

That the bishop had returned from the next world and now inhabited Bill Lundborg's mind or brain—that couldn't be, for obvious reasons. One knows this instinctively; one does not debate this; one perceives this as absolute fact: it cannot happen. I could quiz Bill forever, trying to establish the presence in him of facts known only to me and to Tim, but this would lead nowhere. Like the dinner Tim and I had eaten at the Chinese restaurant on University Avenue in Berkeley, all data became suspect because there are multiple ways that data can arise within the human mind, ways more readily acceptable and explained than to assume that one man died in Israel and his psyche floated halfway across the world until it discriminated Bill Lundborg from all the other people in the United States and then dove into that person, into that waiting brain, and took up residence there, to sputter with ideas, thoughts and memories, half-baked notions; in other words, the bishop as we had known him, the bishop himself, like a sort of plasma. This does not lie within the domain of the real. It lies elsewhere; it is the invention of derangement, of a young man who grieved over the suicide of his mother and the sudden death of a father-figure, grieved and tried to understand, and one day into Bill's mind came—not Bishop Timothy Archer— but the *concept* of Timothy Archer, the notion that Timothy Archer was there, in him, spiritually, a ghost. There is a difference between the notion of something and that something itself.

Still, upon the lessening of my original anger, I felt sympathy toward Bill because I understood why he had gone this route; he had not willed it out of perversity: it did not consist of, so to speak, optional madness but, rather, madness compelled on him, thrust onto him forcibly, whether he liked it or not. It had simply happened.

Bill Lundborg, the first of us to be crazy, had become now the last of us to be crazy; the only genuine issue could best be phrased this way: could anything be done about it? Which raises a deeper question: *should* anything be done about it?

I pondered that during the next couple of weeks. Bill (he told me) had no major friends; he lived alone in a rented room in East Oakland, eating his meals at a Mexican café. Perhaps, I said to myself, I owe it to Jeff and Kirsten and Tim—to Tim, especially—to straighten Bill out. That way, there would be a survivor. That is, of course, in addition to myself.

Indubitably, I had survived. But survived, as I had for some time realized, as a machine; still, this is survival. At least my mind had not been invaded by alien intelligences who thought in Greek, Latin and Hebrew and used terms I could not comprehend. Anyhow, I liked Bill; it would not be a burden on me to see him again, to spend time with him. Together, Bill and I could summon back the people we had loved; these were the same people we had known, and our pooled memories would yield up a great crop of circumstantial details, the little bits that made of memory the semblance of the veridical . . . which is an ornate way of saying that my seeing Bill Lundborg would make it possible for me to experience Tim and Kirsten and Jeff again because Bill, like me, had once experienced them and would understand who I was talking about.

Anyhow, we both were attending Edgar Barefoot's seminar; Bill and I would run into each other there, for better or worse. My respect for Barefoot had climbed, due, of course, to the personal interest he had taken in me. I had warmed to that; I needed that. Barefoot had sensed it.

I interpreted Bill's statement that the bishop had been interested in me sexually as an oblique way of saying that he himself was interested in me sexually. I pondered that and came to the conclusion that Bill was too young for me. Anyhow, why get involved with someone classified as a hebephrenic schizophrenic? Hampton, who had had traces—rather more than traces—of paranoia and hypomania had been enough trouble, and it had been difficult to rid myself of him. In fact, it was not demonstrable that I had gotten rid of him; Hampton still phoned me, complaining aggressively that when I kicked him out of my house I had kept certain choice records, books and prints that, in truth, belonged to him.

What bothered me about my getting involved with Bill lay in my sense of the ferocity of madness. It can consume its owner, leave him, look around for more. If I was a rickety machine, I stood in danger of that madness, for I was not all that psychologically intact. Enough people had gone mad and died already; why add myself to the list?

And, perhaps worst of all, I discerned the kind of future that awaited Bill. He had no future. Someone with hebephrenia has dealt himself out of the game of process, growth and time; he simply recycles his own nutty thoughts forever, enjoying them even though, like transmitted information, they degenerate. They become, finally, noise. And the signal that is intellect fades out. Bill would know this, having planned at one time to become a computer programmer; he would be familiar with Shannon's information theories. This is not the sort of thing you want to tie into.

Bringing my little brother Harvey along, I picked up Bill on my day off and drove up into Tilden Park, by Lake Anza and the clubhouse and barbecue stoves; there the three of us broiled hamburgers, and we tossed a Frisbie around and had a hell of a time. We had brought a Ghetto-blaster with us—one of those super sophisticated two-channel two-speaker combination radio and tape deck masterpieces that Japan turns out—and we listened to the rock group Queen and we drank beer, except for Harvey, and ran around and then, when it didn't seem anyone was watching or cared, Bill and I shared a joint. Harvey, while we did that, tried out all the heat-sensor controls of the Ghetto-blaster and then concentrated on picking up Radio Moscow on its shortwave.

"You can go to jail for that," Bill told him. "Listening to the enemy."

"Bull," Harvey said.

"I wonder what Tim and Kirsten would say," I said to Bill, "if they could see us now."

"I can tell you what Tim is saying," Bill said.

"What does he say?" I said, relaxed by the marijuana.

Bill said, "He says that—he's thinking that—it is peaceful here and he has finally found peace."

"Good," I said. "I could never get him to smoke grass."

"They smoked it," Bill said. "Him and Kirsten, when we weren't around. He didn't like it. But he likes it now."

"This is very good grass," I said. "They probably had local stuff. They wouldn't know the difference." I pondered over what Bill had said. "Did they really turn on? Is that true?"

"Yes," Bill said. "He's thinking about that now; he's remembering."

I regarded him. "In a way, you're lucky," I said. "To find your solution. I wouldn't mind having him in me. In my brain, I mean." I giggled; it was that kind of grass. "Then I wouldn't be so lonely." And then I said, "Why didn't he come back to me? Why to you? I knew him better."

After a moment of reflection, Bill said, "Because it would have wrecked you. See, I'm used to voices in my head and thoughts that aren't my own; I can accept it."

"It's Tim that's the *bodhisattva*, not you," I said. "It was Tim who came back, out of compassion." And then I thought with a start: My God; do I believe it, now? When you're high on good grass, you can believe anything, which is why it sells for as much as it does, now.

"That's right," Bill said. "I can feel his compassion. He sought wisdom, the Holy Wisdom of God, what Tim calls Hagia Sophia; he equates it with *anokhi*, God's pure consciousness. And then, when he got there and the Presence entered him, he realized that it was not wisdom that he wanted but compassion . . . he already had wisdom but it hadn't done him or anyone else any good."

"Yes," I said, "he mentioned Hagia Sophia to me."

"That's some of the Latin he thinks in."

"Greek."

"Whatever. Tim thought that with Christ's absolute wisdom he could read the Book of the Spinners and untangle the future for Tim, so Tim could figure out a way to evade his fate; that's why he went to Israel."

"I know," I said.

"Christ can read the Book of the Spinners," Bill said. "The fate of every human is inscribed in it. No human being has ever read it."

"Where is this book?"

"All around us," Bill said, "I think, anyhow. Wait a sec; Tim is thinking something. Very clearly." He remained silent and withdrawn for a time. "Tim is thinking, 'The last canto. Canto Thirty-three of *Paradiso*.' He's thinking, ' "God is the book of the universe" ' and you read that; you read it the night you had the abscessed tooth. Is that right?" Bill asked me.

"That's right," I said. "It made a great impression on me, that whole last part of the *Commedia*."

"Edgar says that the *Divine Comedy* is based on Sufi sources," Bill said.

"Maybe so," I said, wondering about what Bill had said, the statements about Dante's *Commedia*. "Strange," I said. "The things you remember and why you remember them. Because I had an abscessed tooth—"

"Tim says that Christ arranged that pain," Bill said, "so the final part of the *Divine Comedy* would impress itself on you in a way that would never wear off. 'One simple flame.' Oh, shit; he's thinking in a foreign language again."

"Say it out loud," I said, "as he thinks it."

Bill haltingly said:

> " '*Nel mezzo del cammin di nostra vita*
> *Mi ritrovai per una selva oscura,*
> *Che la diritta via era smarrita.*' "

I smiled. "That's how the *Commedia* begins."

"There's more," Bill said.

> " '. . . *Lasciate ogni speranza, voi ch' entrate!*' "

" 'Abandon all hope, you who enter here,' " I said.

"He wants me to tell you one thing more," Bill said. "But I'm having trouble catching it. Oh; now I have it—he thought it again very clearly for me:

> " '*La sua voluntate è nostra pace* . . .' "

"I don't recognize that," I said.

"Tim says it's the basic message of the *Divine Comedy*. It means, 'His will is our peace.' Meaning God, I guess."

"I guess so," I said.

"He must have learned that in the next world," Bill said. "He certainly didn't learn it here."

Approaching us, Harvey said, "I'm tired of the Queen tapes. What else did we bring?"

"Did you manage to pick up Radio Moscow?" I asked.

"Yeah, but the Voice jammed it. The Russians switched to another frequency—probably, the thirty-meter band—but I got tired of looking for it. The Voice always jams it."

"We'll be going home soon," I said, and passed the remains of the joint to Bill.

16

IT became necessary to rehospitalize Bill sooner than I had expected. He entered voluntarily, accepting this as a fact of life—a perpetual fact of his life, anyhow.

After they had signed Bill in, I met with his psychiatrist, a heavyset middle-aged man with a mustache and rimless glasses, a sort of portly but good-natured authority-figure who at once read me my mistakes, in order of descending importance.

"You shouldn't be encouraging him to use drugs," Dr. Greeby said, the file on Bill open before him across the surface of his desk.

"You call grass 'drugs'?" I said.

"For someone with Bill's precarious mental balance, any intoxicant is dangerous, however mild. He goes into the trip but he never really comes out. We have him on Haldol now; he seems able to tolerate the side effects."

"Had I known the harm I was doing," I said, "I would have done otherwise."

He glanced at me.

"We learn by erring," I said.

"Miss Archer—"

"Mrs. Archer," I said.

"The prognosis on Bill is not good, Mrs. Archer. I think you should be aware of that, since you seem to be the one closest to him." Dr. Greeby frowned. "'Archer.' Are you related to the late Episcopal Bishop Timothy Archer?"

"My father-in-law," I said.

"That's who Bill thinks he is."

"Sufferin' succotash," I said.

"Bill has the delusion that he has become your late father-in-law due to a mystical experience. He does not merely see and hear Bishop Archer; he is Bishop Archer. Then Bill actually knew Bishop Archer, I take it."

"They rotated tires together," I said.

"You are a very smart-assed woman," Dr. Greeby said.

I said nothing to that.

"You have helped put Bill back in the hospital," the doctor said.

I said, "And we had a couple of good times together. We also had some very unhappy times together, having to do with the death of friends. I think those deaths contributed more to Bill's decline than did the smoking of grass in Tilden Park."

"Please don't see him any more," Dr. Greeby said.

"What?" I said, startled and dismayed; a rush of fear overcame me and I felt myself flush in pain. "Wait a minute," I said. "He's my friend."

"You have a generally supercilious attitude toward me and toward the world in all aspects. You obviously are a highly educated person, a product of the state university system; I'd guess that you graduated from U.C. Berkeley, probably in the English Department; you feel you know everything; you're doing great harm to Bill, who is not a worldly-wise, sophisticated person. You're also doing great harm to yourself, but that is not my concern. You are a brittle, harsh person, who—"

"But they were my friends," I said.

"Find somebody in the Berkeley community," the doctor said. "And stay away from Bill. As Bishop Archer's daughter-in-law, you reinforce his delusion; in fact, his delusion is probably an introjection of you, a displaced sexual attachment acting outside his conscious control."

I said, "And you are full of recondite bullshit."

"I've seen dozens like you in my professional career," Dr. Greeby said. "You don't faze me and you don't interest me. Berkeley is full of women like you."

"I will change," I said, my heart full of panic.

"That I doubt," the doctor said, and closed up Bill's file.

After I left his office—ejected, virtually—I roamed about the hospital, at a loss, stunned and afraid and also angry—angry mostly at myself for lipping off. I had lipped off because I was nervous, but the harm was done. Shit, I said to myself. Now I've lost the last of them.

I go back now to the record store, I said to myself, and check the back orders to see what did and didn't arrive. There will be a dozen customers lined up at the register and the phones will be ringing. Fleetwood Mac albums will be selling; Helen Reddy albums will not be. Nothing will have changed.

I can change, I said to myself. Lard-butt is wrong; it isn't too late.

Tim, I thought; why didn't I go to Israel with you?

As I left the hospital building and walked toward the parking lot—I could see my little red Honda Civic from afar—I spotted a group of patients trailing along behind a psych tech; they had gotten off a yellow bus and were now returning to the hospital. Hands in the pockets of my coat, I walked toward them, wondering if Bill was among them.

I did not see Bill in the group, and I continued on, past some benches, past a fountain. A grove of cedar trees grew on the far side of the hospital, and several people sat here and there on the grass, undoubtedly patients, those with passes; those well enough to exist for a time outside of stern control.

Among them Bill Lundborg, wearing his usual ill-fitting pants and shirt, sat at the base of a tree, intent on something he held.

I approached him, slowly and quietly. He did not look up until I had almost reached him; suddenly, aware of me now, he raised his head.

"Hi, Bill," I said.

"Angel," Bill said, "look what I found."

I knelt down to see. He had found a stand of mushrooms growing at the base of the tree: white mushrooms with—I discovered when I broke one off—pink gills. Harmless; the pink gilled and brown-gilled mushrooms are, by and large, not toxic. It is the white-gilled mushrooms that you must avoid, for often they are the *amanitas*, such as the Destroying Angel.

"What have you got?" I said.

"It is growing here," Bill said, in wonder. "What I searched for in Israel. What I went so far to find. This is the *vita verna* mushroom that Pliny the Elder mentions in his *Historia Naturalis*. I forget which book." He chuckled in that familiar good-humored way that I knew so well. "Probably *Book Eight*. This exactly fits his description."

"To me," I said, "it looks like an ordinary edible mushroom that you see growing this time of year everywhere."

"This is the *anokhi*," Bill said.

"Bill—" I began.

"Tim," he said, reflexively.

"Bill, I'm taking off. Dr. Greeby says I wrecked your mind. I'm sorry." I stood up.

"You never did that," Bill said. "But I wish you had come to Israel with me. You made a major mistake, Angel, and I did tell you that night at the Chinese restaurant. Now you're locked into your customary mind-set forever."

"And there's no way I can change?" I said.

Smiling up at me in his guileless way, Bill said, "I don't care. I have what I want; I have this." He carefully handed me the mushroom that he had picked, the ordinary harmless mushroom. "This is my body," he said, "and this is my blood. Eat, drink, and you will have eternal life."

I bent down and said, speaking with my lips close to his ear so that only he could hear me, "I am going to fight to make you okay again, Bill Lundborg. Repairing automobile bodies and spray-painting and other real things; I will see you as you were; I will not give up. You will remember the ground again. You hear me? You understand?"

Bill, not looking at me, murmured, "I am the true vine, and my Father is the vinedresser. Every branch in me that bears no fruit he cuts away, and every—"

"No," I said, "you're a man who spray-paints automobiles and fixes transmissions and I will cause you to remember. A time will come when you leave this hospital; I will wait for you, Bill Lundborg." I kissed him, then, on the temple; he reached to wipe it away, as a child wipes a kiss away, absently, without intent or comprehension.

"I am the Resurrection and the life," Bill said.

"I will see you again, Bill," I said, and walked away.

The next time I attended Edgar Barefoot's seminar, Barefoot noted Bill's absence and, after he had finished talking, he asked me about Bill.

"Back inside looking out," I said.

"Come with me." Barefoot led me from the lecture room to his living room; I had never seen it before and discovered with surprise that his tastes ran to distressed oak rather than to the Oriental. He put on a *koto* record which I recognized—that is my job—as a rare Kimio Eto pressing on World-Pacific. The record, made in the late-Fifties, is worth something to collectors. Barefoot played "*Midori No Asa*," which Eto wrote himself. It is quite beautiful but sounds not at all Japanese.

"I'll give you fifteen bucks for that record," I said.

Barefoot said, "I'll tape it for you."

"I want the record," I said. "The record itself. I get requests for it every now and then." I thought to myself: And don't tell me the beauty is in the music. The value to collectors lies in the record itself; this is not a matter that need be opened to debate. I know records: it is my business.

"Coffee?" Barefoot said.

I accepted a cup of coffee and together Barefoot and I listened to the greatest living *koto* player twang away.

"He's always going to be in and out of the hospital, you realize," I said, when Barefoot turned the record over.

"Is this something else you feel responsible for?"

"I've been told that I am," I said. "But I'm not."

"It's good that you realize that."

I said, "If somebody thinks Tim Archer came back to him, that somebody goes into the hospital."

"And gets Thorazine," Barefoot said.

"It's Haldol now," I said. "A refinement. The new antipsychotic drugs are more precise."

Barefoot said, "One of the early church fathers believed in the Resurrection 'because it was impossible.' Not 'despite the fact that it was impossible' but 'because it was impossible.' Tertullian, I think it was. Tim talked to me about it one time."

"But how smart is that?" I said.

"Not very smart. I don't think Tertullian meant it to be."

"I can't see anybody going through life that way," I said. "To me that epitomizes this whole stupid business: believing something because it's impossible. What I see is people becoming mad and then dying; first the madness, then the death."

"So you see death for Bill," Barefoot said.

"No," I said, "because I am going to be waiting for him when he gets out of the hospital. Instead of death, he is going to get me. How does that strike you?"

"As much better than death," Barefoot said.

"Then you approve of me," I said. "Unlike Bill's doctor, who thinks I helped put him in the hospital."

"Are you living with anyone right now?"

"As a matter of fact, I'm living alone," I said.

Barefoot said, "I'd like to see Bill move in with you when he gets out of the hospital. I don't think he has ever lived with a woman except with his mother, with Kirsten."

"I'd have to think a long time about that," I said.

"Why?"

"Because that's how I do things like that."

"I don't mean for his sake."

"What?" I said, taken by surprise.

"For your sake. That way, you would find out if it really is Tim. Your question would be answered."

I said, "I have no question; I know."

"Take Bill in; let him live with you. Take care of him. And maybe you'll find you're taking care of Tim, in a certain real sense. Which—I think—you always did or anyhow wanted to do. Or if you didn't, should have done. He is very helpless."

"Bill? Tim?"

"The man in the hospital. Who you care about. Your last tie to other people."

"I have friends. I have my little brother. I have the people at the store . . . and my customers."

"And you have me," Barefoot said.

After a pause, I said, "You, too; yes." I nodded.

"Suppose I said I think it may be Tim. Actually Tim come back."

"Well, then," I said, "I'd stop coming to your seminars."

He eyed me intently.

"I mean it," I said.

"You are not readily pushed around," Barefoot said.

"Not really," I said. "I've made certain serious mistakes; I stood there doing nothing when Kirsten and Tim told me that Jeff had returned—I did nothing and as a result they are now dead. I wouldn't make that mistake again."

"You genuinely foresee death for Bill, then."

"Yes," I said.

"Take him in," Barefoot said, "and I tell you what; I'll give you the Kimio Eto record we're listening to." He smiled. "'*Kibo No Hikari*,' this song is called. 'The Light of Hope.' I think it's appropriate."

"Did Tertullian actually say he believed in the Resurrection because it is impossible?" I said. "Then this stuff started a long time ago. It didn't begin with Kirsten and Tim."

Barefoot said, "You're going to have to stop coming to my seminars."

"You do think it's Tim?"

"Yes. Because Bill talks in languages he doesn't know. In the Italian of Dante, for instance. And in Latin and—"

"Xenoglossy," I said. The sign, I thought, of the presence of the Holy Spirit, as Tim pointed out that day we met at the Bad Luck Restaurant. The very thing Tim doubted existed any more; he doubted that it had ever existed, probably. According to what he, anyhow, could discern; to the best of his ability. And now we have it in Bill Lundborg claiming to be Tim.

"I'll take Bill in," Barefoot said. "He can live with me here on the houseboat."

"No," I said. "Not if you believe that stuff. I'll bring him to my house in Berkeley, rather than that." And then it came to me that I had been maneuvered and I gazed at Edgar Barefoot; he smiled and I thought: Just the way Tim could do it— control people. In a sense, Bishop Tim Archer is more alive in you than he is in Bill.

"Good," Barefoot said. He extended his hand. "Let's shake on it, to close the deal."

"Do I get the Kimio Eto record?" I asked.

"After I've taped it."

"But I do get the record itself."

"Yes," Barefoot said, still holding onto my hand. His grip was vigorous; that, too, reminded me of Tim. So maybe we do have Tim with us, I thought. One way or another. It depends on how you define "Tim Archer": the ability to quote in Latin and Greek and Medieval Italian, or the ability to save human lives. Either way, Tim seems to be still here. Or here again.

"I'll keep coming to your seminars," I said.

"Not for my sake."

"No; for my own."

Barefoot said, "Someday perhaps you'll come for the sandwich. But I doubt that. I think you will always need the pretext of words."

Do not be that pessimistic, I said to myself; I might surprise you.

We listened to the end of the *koto* record. The last song on the second side is called "*Haru No Sugata*," which means, "The Mood of Early Spring." We listened to that last and then Edgar Barefoot returned the record to its cover and handed it to me.

"Thank you," I said.

I finished my coffee and then left. The weather struck me as good. I felt a lot better. And I could probably get almost thirty dollars for the record. I had not seen a copy in years; it has long been out of print.

You must keep these things in mind when you operate a record store. And acquiring it that day amounted to a sort of prize: for doing what I intended to do anyhow. I had outsmarted Edgar Barefoot and I felt happy. Tim would have enjoyed it. Were he alive.

BIBLIOGRAPHY

Aeschylus. *Agamemnon*. Quoted in *Bartlett's Familiar Quotations*, Fifteenth Edition. Boston: Little, Brown, 1980.

Aristophanes. *Lysistrata*. Jack Lindsay, trans. New York: Bantam, 1962.

Bible, the. *The Jerusalem Bible*. Garden City, New York: Doubleday & Co., 1966.

Büchner, Georg. *Wozzeck*. Alfred A. Kalmus, trans. by arrangement with Universal Edition of Eric Blackall and Vida Harford. 1836.

Cohen, Hermann. In *Contemporary Jewish Thought: A Reader*. Simon Noveck, ed. New York: B'nai B'rith Department of Adult Jewish Education, 1963.

Dante. *The Divine Comedy*. Laurence Binyon, trans., with notes by C. H. Grandgent. In *The Portable Dante*. New York: The Viking Press, 1947.

Donne, John. "Batter my Heart, three person'd God." Holy Sonnet XIV. In *The Complete Poetry and Selected Prose of John Donne*. New York: The Modern Library, 1952.

Geothe, Johann Wolfgang von. *Faust: Part Two*. Bayard Taylor, trans. Revised and edited by Stuart Atkins. New York: Collier Books, 1962.

Hertz, Dr. J. H. *The Pentateuch and Haftorahs*. London: Soncino Press, 5729 [1967].

Huxley, Aldous. *Point Counter-Point*. New York: Harper & Row, 1965.

Jennens, Charles. *Belshazzar* [text of Handel oratorio]. 1744.

Kohler, Kaufmann. Quoted by Samuel M. Cohon in *Great Jewish Thinkers of the Twentieth Century*. Simon Noveck, ed. New York: B'nai B'rith Department of Adult Jewish Education, 1963.

Menotti, Gian Carlo. Liner notes to Columbia recording of Menotti's *The Medium*. Undated.

Plato. In *From Thales to Plato*. T. V. Smith, ed. Chicago: University of Chicago Press, 1934.

Prabhavananda, Swami, and Isherwood, Christopher. *The Song of God: Bhagavad-Gita*. New York: NAL/Mentor, 1944.

Schiller, Friedrich. In *The New Encyclopedia Britannica*. Chicago: Encyclopedia Britannica, 1973.

Shakespeare. *Hamlet.* 1601.

Sonnleithner, Joseph, and Treitschke, Friedrich. *Fidelio* [text of Beethoven opera]. 1805.

Tate, Nahum. *Dido and Aeneas* [text of Purcell opera]. 1689.

Tertullian. Quoted in *Psychological Types, or The Psychology of Individuation* by C. G. Jung. London: Routledge & Kegan Paul, 1923.

Tillich, Paul. *A History of Christian Thought.* New York: Simon and Schuster, 1967.

Vaughan, Henry. "They are all gone into the world of light." 1655.

Virgil. Quoted in *Caesar and Christ* by Will Durant. New York: Simon and Schuster, 1944.

Yeats, W. B. "The Second Coming" and "The Song of the Happy Shepherd." *The Collected Poems of W. B. Yeats.* London: Macmillan, 1949.

CHRONOLOGY

NOTE ON THE TEXTS

NOTES

Chronology

1928   Born Philip Kindred Dick on December 16 at home in Chicago, Illinois—six weeks premature, with twin sister Jane Charlotte Dick—to Dorothy Kindred Dick, an editorial secretary and Joseph Edgar Dick, a World War I veteran working at the Department of Agriculture. Mother, suffering from chronic kidney disease, finds nourishing twins difficult and receives poor support from doctor; neither child thrives.

1929   On January 26, both babies, severely dehydrated and undernourished, rushed to hospital; sister dies en route. Philip is nursed to health in incubator until reaching the weight of five pounds. (Haunted by his twin's death, later writes: "She fights for her life & I for hers, eternally. . . . My sister is *everything* to me. I am damned always to be separated from her/& with her, in an oscillation.") Father is granted a transfer from Department of Agriculture to posting in San Francisco. Family travels to Fort Morgan, Colorado, for vacation, and Dorothy and Philip remain, staying with relatives while awaiting father's transfer. Sister is buried in Fort Morgan cemetery. Family moves to the Bay Area in California, first to Sausalito, then the peninsula, at last to Alameda.

1930   Father promoted to director, Western Division National Recovery Act posting in Reno, Nevada. Family settles in Berkeley; father commutes, remaining in Reno during work week.

1931   Attends the University of California Institute of Child Welfare experimental nursery school, where he tests high in memory, language, and manual coordination. Praised for his musical ability.

1933–34   Mother asks father for divorce and parents separate. Mother and son live with maternal grandparents and Aunt Marion. Dorothy begins to work full time, leaving Philip in the care of his warmly loving grandmother, "Meemaw." Attends kindergarten at Bruce Tatlock School, a progressive nursery. Develops loving relationship with Aunt

Marion, despite her psychological difficulties including occasional institutionalization.

1935–37   After parents' divorce is final, mother moves with Philip to Washington, D.C. Father remarries. Begins to experience asthma and tachycardia. Doctor recommends Philip be sent away to boarding school. Attends Country Day School for children with behavior difficulties. There he first experiences fear of vomiting; cannot swallow and is unable to eat in public. Sent home after six months and sees first therapist. Attends Friends Quaker day school, then attends public school through second grade. Philip experiences isolation; struggles in school begin pattern of absenteeism. ("There then followed a long period in which I did nothing in particular except go to school—which I loathed—and fiddle with my stamp collection . . . plus other boyhood activities such as marbles, flipcards, bolo bats, and the new invented comic books. . . .") Experiences a spontaneous vision of peace and empathy he will later refer to in interviews as a childhood "Satori" experience. First attempts at writing encouraged by mother.

1938   With mother, returns to Berkeley. After three year separation, visits father. Introduces himself at new public school as "Jim Dick," but soon reverts to Phil. Creates a personal newspaper, "The Daily Dick," with local news items and comic strips.

1940–43   Discovers passion for classical music and opera, a lifelong pursuit. Reads *The Little Prince*, *The Hobbit*, *Winnie the Pooh*, and the *Oz* books. Discovers and begins avidly collecting science-fiction magazines (*Astounding*, *Amazing*, *Unknown*), which he begins to emulate by both drawing and writing. Teaches himself to type. Follows World War II through radio broadcasts, frequently discussing war progress with his friends. Begins second self-published newspaper, "The Truth," featuring a comic-strip hero "Future-Human": "Using his super-science for the welfare of humanity, he pits his strength against the underworld of the future." Completes first novel, *Return to Lilliput*, now lost. Regularly publishes stories and poems in the *Berkeley Gazette*. Attends Garfield Junior High public school and California Prep boarding school in Ojai. Continued difficulties overcoming emotional illnesses. Demonstrates intimate knowledge of psychiatry and psychiatric testing to classmates. (In 1974 he writes to his daughter Laura, "In a sense, the better you adapt to school the less your chances are of later adapting to the actual world. So I figure, the worse you adapt to school, the better you will be able to handle reality when you finally manage to get loose at last from school, if that ever happens. But I guess I have what in the military they call a 'poor attitude,' which means 'shape up or ship out.' I always elected to ship out.") Agoraphobia and panic attacks increase.

1944–47   Begins high school at Berkeley High. Studies German. Begins reading Jung. Bouts of dizziness leave him intermittently bedridden. Attends weekly psychotherapy at Langley Porter Clinic in San Francisco, where he is treated by a Jungian analyst, for whom he eventually develops a thoroughgoing intellectual contempt. Begins working as a sales clerk at University Radio, then later at Art Music, two music shops selling records, sheet music, and electronics, as well as offering repairs. Herb Hollis, the charismatic and demanding owner of the shops, becomes a mentor and father figure (and will become a model for many warmly tyrannical "boss" figures in his fiction). Dick's anxiety recedes while he is employed by Hollis, but so cripples him at school that he is forced to complete his senior year working at home with a tutor. The following autumn, leaves home and moves to a group apartment in a converted warehouse with writers and poets Robert Duncan, Jack Spicer, and Philip Lamantia, among others. The bohemian, writerly—and largely homosexual—contingent of roommates becomes another source of Dick's autodidactical intellectual growth. Briefly attends UC Berkeley, where he majors in philosophy; dislikes mandatory ROTC training, experiences further agoraphobic attacks, and by November withdraws permanently. Maintains later that he was expelled from university for refusing to re-assemble his rifle in ROTC.

1948–49   Knowing of Dick's lack of experience with women, the manager of Art Music arranges a sexual liaison with a young woman in the finished basement of the store. Meets and quickly marries Jeanette Marlin and moves into a Berkeley apartment, where they live in clumsy distress for six months, and divorce before the year's end. Reconnects with his father. Begins fragmentary novel *The Earthshaker* (lost).

1950   Marries second wife, Kleo Apostolides, in June. Buys a
        small house on Francisco Street in Berkeley. Sees father for
        last time. Enters the orbit of Anthony Boucher (Anthony
        White), an editor, reviewer, and writing teacher in the
        fields of crime and SF (science fiction). Under Boucher's
        influence begins to write a spate of SF stories. (Dick later
        recalled, "I discovered that a person could be not only
        mature, but matured and educated, and still enjoy SF.")
        Lives in a condition of extreme poverty (as later described
        in his 1980 introduction to *The Golden Man*: "The horse-
        meat they sell at Lucky Dog Pet Store is only for animal
        consumption. But Kleo and I are eating it ourselves. . . .
        It's called poverty . . .").

1951–52 Sells first story, "Roog," to *The Magazine of Fantasy and
        Science Fiction*. Loses job at Art Music over a breach of
        loyalty to Hollis. First published story, "Beyond Lies the
        Wub," appears in *Planet Stories*. Is represented by the
        Scott Meredith Literary Agency. Writes first realist novels
        Voices From the Street (published 2007) and *Mary and the
        Giant* (published 1987), but agency fails to sell them dur-
        ing his lifetime. (Later writes, "I made my first sale in No-
        vember of 1951, and my first stories were published in
        1952. At the time I graduated from high school I was writ-
        ing regularly, one novel after another. None of which, of
        course, sold. I was living in Berkeley, and all the milieu-
        reinforcement there was for the literary stuff. I knew all
        kinds of people who were doing literary-type novels. And
        I knew some of the very fine avant-garde poets in the Bay
        area. They all encouraged me to write, but there was no
        encouragement to sell anything. But I wanted to sell, and
        I also wanted to do science fiction. My ultimate dream was
        to be able to do both literary stuff *and* science fiction.")

1953–54 Sells first SF novels *Solar Lottery* (published 1955), *The
        World Jones Made* (published 1956), and fantasy novel *The
        Cosmic Puppets* (published 1957), along with realist novel
        Gather Yourselves Together (published 1994). Briefly works
        for Tupper and Reed, another music store, where he again
        experiences panic attacks, agoraphobia, and claustropho-
        bia. Begins taking amphetamines prescribed for phobias
        and depression. Writes many dozens of stories and places
        the majority of them, becoming one of the most prolific
        writers in science fiction (30 of his stories appear in pulp
        magazines in 1953 alone). Visited and gently interrogated

by a pair of FBI investigators, inspiring the lifelong sense that he was under surveillance. Despite both ambivalence about assuming the identity of an SF writer and agoraphobic tendencies, visits an SF convention for the first time and meets A. E. Van Vogt, whose fiction is highly influential on Dick's early SF novels. With proceeds from sale of short stories and the help of his wife's salary from a variety of part-time jobs, pays off his mortgage and enjoys brief period of financial stability. Aunt Marion dies. Mother marries Marion's widower, Joe Hudner, and adopts eight-year-old twins.

1955   First published novel, *Solar Lottery*, is published in U.S. by Ace Books, as a paperback original. First published short-story collection, *A Handful of Darkness*, is brought out in England by Rich & Cowan. Dick writes novels *The Man Who Japed* (published 1956) and *Eye in the Sky* (published 1957).

1956–57   In renewed effort at literary respectability, writes realist novels *A Time for George Stavros* (lost), *Pilgrim on the Hill* (lost), *The Broken Bubble of Thisbe Holt* (published 1988), and *Puttering About in a Small Land* (published 1985). With Kleo, takes two road trips, touring the country as far east as Arkansas. *The Variable Man and Other Stories*, an expanded version of *A Handful of Darkness*, is published by Ace as a paperback original. Briefly breaks with Scott Meredith Agency, but returns.

1958   Dick applies his realist motifs to a science-fiction novel for the first time; the result, *Time Out of Joint*, is accepted for publication by Lippincott (1959). It is his first hardcover in the U.S., marketed not as SF but as a "Novel of Menace." Writes realist novels *In Milton Lumky Territory* (published 1985) and *Nicholas and the Higs* (lost). Learns that short story "Foster, You're Dead" has been published without permission in a magazine in USSR. Corresponds with Soviet scientist Alexander Topchiev on the subject of Einstein's theory of relativity; CIA reads this correspondence (as Dick learns after submitting a Freedom of Information Act request in 1970s). Moves with Kleo in September to Point Reyes Station, in Marin County. Meets Anne Rubenstein, a widow, in October, and begins a tumultuous romance. In December, asks Kleo for a divorce.

1959   Divorces Kleo, who leaves Point Reyes Station to return
          to Berkeley. Moves in with Anne and her three daughters
          (Hatte, Jayne, and Tandy), assuming the role of stepfather;
          they raise fowl and sheep, and live primarily on Anne's
          child-support settlement from her deceased husband's
          family in St. Louis. Begins to see Anne's psychiatrist, with
          whom he will consult intermittently until 1971. Marries
          Anne on April Fool's Day, in Ensenada, Mexico. Seeking
          income, reworks two earlier novellas into SF novels, each
          to be published in 1960 as half of an Ace "double": *Dr.
          Futurity* and *Vulcan's Hammer*. Writes realist novel *Con-
          fessions of a Crap Artist*, based largely on his fresh divorce
          from Kleo and romance with Anne, and which is nearly
          accepted for publication by both Knopf and Harcourt.
          On the strength of the near-miss, is offered advance from
          Harcourt for his next realist novel. Anne is pregnant. Con-
          tinues taking prescription amphetamine, Semoxydrine.

1960   First child, a daughter, Laura Archer Dick, is born on
          February 25. The Harcourt prospect goes unrealized, as
          the publisher during a merger fumbles two realist novels
          in turn when the editor goes on leave, *The Man Whose
          Teeth Were All Exactly Alike* and *Humpty Dumpty in Oak-
          land*, a rewrite of *A Time for George Stavros*. In autumn
          Anne becomes pregnant again. Fearing financial hardship
          she has an abortion, over Dick's initial objections.

1961   Works briefly in Anne's handcrafted jewelry business. Dis-
          covers the *I Ching*, the Chinese *Book of Changes*, the
          oracular advice of which he will consult for the next two
          decades. Retreats to what he calls "the hovel," a cabin he
          equips with his typewriter, stereo, and books. There be-
          gins writing *The Man in the High Castle*, plotted partly
          with the assistance of the *I Ching*.

1962   *The Man in the High Castle* is published by Putnam as a
          thriller, to positive reviews but few sales. Putnam sells the
          rights to the Science Fiction Book Club. Dick writes *We
          Can Build You*, which is serialized as "A. Lincoln, Simu-
          lacrum" in 1969–70 in *Amazing*, and *Martian Time-Slip*,
          which is serialized the following year in *Worlds of Tomor-
          row* as "All We Marsmen." (Dick later recalls: "With *High
          Castle* and *Martian Time-Slip*, I thought I had bridged
          the gap between the experimental mainstream novel and
          science fiction. Suddenly I'd found a way to do every-
          thing I wanted to do as a writer.")

1963   In July, Meredith Agency returns 10 or more manuscripts of the realist novels as unsaleable. Financially strapped, considers mortgaging Anne's house to finance a record store. In September, *The Man in the High Castle* wins the Hugo Award for best novel, SF's highest honor. Marriage degenerates; Dick claims to friends that his wife is trying to kill him. During a protracted marital fight, arranges to have Anne committed to Ross Psychiatric Hospital, where she consents to two weeks of observation at Langley Porter Clinic. In an attempt to save marriage they begin attending Episcopal church services, where Dick is baptized. Maren Hackett, a fan, arranges to meet Dick through a friend. She and her stepdaughters are Episcopalian. Fueled by amphetamines, writes *Dr. Bloodmoney, or How We Got Along After the Bomb*, *The Game-Players of Titan* (published by Ace that year), *The Simulacra, Now Wait for Last Year*, and begins *Clans of the Alphane Moon* and *The Crack in Space*. While walking to his writing shack, experiences devastating vision of a cruelly masked human face in the sky, which he will later incorporate into *The Three Stigmata of Palmer Eldritch*.

1964   Visits to Berkeley become frequent. Writes *The Three Stigmata of Palmer Eldritch*, which he delivers to his agent in March. On March 9, files for divorce, and briefly moves in with his mother. Enters the lively Bay Area SF social scene, spending time with writers Poul Anderson, Marion Zimmer Bradley, Ron Goulart, and Ray Nelson. Begins and abandons a sequel to *The Man in the High Castle*. Writes *The Crack in Space*, *The Zap Gun* (serialized that year as "Project Plowshare"), and *The Penultimate Truth* (published that year), and begins *The Unteleported Man*. Begins epistolary romance with Grania Davidson (later to publish fiction as Grania Davis), the separated wife of SF writer Avram Davidson. In July, Dick flips his car, resulting in serious injuries. Suffers major depression and loss of writing impetus. Attends the 1964 World Science Fiction convention, held in Oakland, which is marked by a proliferation of drug use. Friends Jack and Margo Newkom move into the Oakland house. In December, begins courting the 21-year-old Nancy Hackett, stepdaughter of Maren Hackett: "I want you to move in here for my sake, because otherwise I will go clean out of my balmy wits, take more and more pills . . . and do no real writing. . . . I need you as a sort of incentive and muse."

1965   In March, Hackett moves in. Domesticity, agoraphobia, and writing resume. Dick takes LSD twice, leading to uncomfortable visions. ("I perceived Him as a pulsing, furious, throbbing mass of vengeance-seeking authority, demanding an audit [like a sort of metaphysical IRS agent].") In "Drugs, Hallucinations, and the Quest for Reality," essay for fanzine *Lighthouse*, writes: "One doesn't have to depend on hallucinations. One can unhinge one-self by many other roads." Completes *The Unteleported Man*. Gains rewarding friendship with James Pike, the Episcopal bishop of California, who had taken Maren Hackett, Nancy's stepmother, as his secret lover while she was employed as his secretary. In conversation with Pike becomes increasingly involved in theological speculation and research into the early origins of Christianity. Moves with Nancy to San Rafael. Works on *The Ganymede Takeover* with Ray Nelson. Writes *Counter-Clock World*.

1966   Completes *The Ganymede Takeover*, and writes *Do Androids Dream of Electric Sheep?*, *Ubik*, and *The Glimmung of Plowman's Planet*, a children's story (published in 1988 in the United Kingdom as *Nick and the Glimmung*). In July, marries Nancy. Despite skepticism, participates with Bishop Pike, Maren Hackett, and Nancy in a séance conducted by a medium, with the intention of making contact with Pike's son Jim, who had committed suicide. *Now Wait for Last Year*, *The Unteleported Man*, and *The Crack in Space* published.

1967   Second daughter, Isolde (Isa) Freya Dick, born March 15. Writes treatment for television show *The Invaders*, which goes unsold. *Counter-Clock World*, *The Zap Gun*, and *The Ganymede Takeover* published as paperback originals. In June, Maren Hackett commits suicide. IRS demands payment of overdue back taxes, penalty and interest, devastating already fragile household finances. Short story "Faith of Our Fathers" is published in Harlan Ellison's *Dangerous Visions* anthology; Dick falsely leads Ellison to believe and claim in his introduction that the story was written under the influence of LSD.

1968   Signs "Writers and Editors War Tax Protest" petition published in February issue of *Ramparts* magazine, aggravating his conflict with the IRS. With Nancy, attends the 1968 SF Baycon, a science-fiction convention known anecdotally as "Drug Con." Meets Roger Zelazny, with whom he will begin collaborative novel *Deus Irae*. *Do Androids Dream of Electric Sheep?* published as hardcover original. Sells first film option, for *Androids*. Writes *Galactic Pot-Healer* and *A Maze of Death*. Anthony Boucher, Dick's longtime mentor, dies. Writes unpublished biographical statement: ". . . Married, has two daughters and young, pretty, nervous wife . . . Spends most of his time listening to first Scarlatti and then the Jefferson Airplane, then 'Gotterdammerung,' in an attempt to fit them all together. Has many phobias . . . Owes creditors a fortune, which he does not have. Warning: don't lend him any money. In addition he will steal your pills."

1969   Writes *Our Friends from Frolix 8*. The paperback original *Galactic Pot-Healer* and hardcover *Ubik* are published. Receives phone call from Timothy Leary who is attending John Lennon and Yoko Ono's "bed-in" in a Montreal hotel. Leary puts Lennon and Ono on phone; they discuss their admiration for his novel *The Three Stigmata of Palmer Eldritch* and their desire to adapt it to film. Visited by journalist Paul Williams. Marriage increasingly strained by escalating prescription drug use, particularly Ritalin. Hospitalized in an emergency intervention for pancreatitis and near-kidney failure, the result of compulsive amphetamine abuse. In September, Bishop Pike dies in the Judean desert, searching for proof of the historical Jesus.

1970   Begins *Flow My Tears, the Policeman Said*, and, contrary to his usual method, rewrites it several times between March and August. Nancy's brother, Michael Hackett, in the midst of a divorce, moves in. Dick takes mescaline and experiences a vision of radiant love, which he incorporates into *Flow My Tears*. Applies for food stamps in July. *The Preserving Machine*, a story collection, is published. *Our Friends from Frolix 8* is published as a paperback original and *A Maze of Death* in hardcover. In September, Nancy leaves with Isa, beginning a period for Dick of communal living characterized by extensive drug use (adding illegal street drugs to the mix), late-night amphetamine-fueled conversation, paranoia, and bohemian squalor. Dick does little writing, working intermittently on *Flow My Tears, the Policeman Said*. In October Tom

Schmidt moves in. (In a November letter, Dick writes: "We all take speed and we are all going to die, but we will have a few more years . . . and while we live we will live it as we are: stupid, blind, loving, talking, being together, kidding, propping one another up.")

1971   Places unfinished manuscript of *Flow My Tears, the Policeman Said* into the care of his attorney for protection from the chaos of his home life. Mike Hackett leaves house as a stream of young hippies, bikers, and addicts pass through. In May, Dick is committed by a friend to the psychiatric ward of Stanford University Hospital. In August, he is admitted to both Marin General Psychiatric Hospital and Ross Psychiatric Clinic. Asserts belief that he is probably under surveillance by the FBI or CIA. Purchases gun. In November, the house is violently broken into, leaving file cabinets apparently blown up, windows and doors smashed, and personal and financial papers stolen. (Theories as to responsibility for the break-in preoccupy Dick for years to come; suspects include government agents, religious fanatics, Black Panthers, himself.) Dick abandons the house.

1972   Visits Vancouver, Canada, SF Con in February, as guest of honor. Delivers well-received convention speech ("The Android and the Human"), and declares intention to remain in Canada. Rapidly becomes disenchanted with Vancouver and seeks another destination; writes to Ursula K. Le Guin in Portland, asking for permission to visit, and to Cal State Fullerton professor Willis McNelly, asking if Fullerton would be a good place to relocate. (Letter-writing increases dramatically at this point and continues until his death. In addition to Le Guin, he regularly corresponds with other writers including James Tiptree, Stanislaw Lem, John Brunner, Norman Spinrad, Thomas Disch, Bryan Aldiss, Robert Silverberg, Theodore Sturgeon, and Philip José Farmer.) In March, makes his first suicide attempt. Enters X-Kalay rehabilitation center, a facility primarily for heroin addicts, where he participates in confrontational group therapy. Ends decades-long abuse of prescription amphetamines. Professor McNelly and his students write to invite him to Orange County. Dick settles in Fullerton, living with a series of roommates, and surrounds himself with young friends, including aspiring writer Tim Powers. McNelly arranges paid guest lecturer position and houses bulk of Dick's papers at the California State University at Fullerton's library. Assembles personal letters and dream notes, creating *The Dark-Haired Girl* (expanded and published 1988). Assists in the selection of stories for collection *The Best of Philip K. Dick*, published that year. In July, meets 18-year-old Leslie (Tessa) Busby, and they soon move in together. In September, Dick attends Los Angeles SF Worldcon. In October, travels with Tessa to Marin County to finalize divorce from Nancy Hackett, who is awarded full custody of Isa. Corresponds with Stanislaw Lem, who arranges for Polish translation of *Ubik*. Completes work on *Flow My Tears, the Policeman Said*, and writes "A Little Something for Us Tempunauts."

1973   Resumes full-time writing. From February to April, writes *A Scanner Darkly*. Is interviewed by BBC and French documentarians. In April, marries Tessa. Son Christopher Kenneth Dick born on July 25. Visited by Jean-Pierre Gorin, then a doctoral student, who tells Dick commentators on French television have proposed him for Nobel Prize. Is interviewed by the London *Daily Telegraph*. Money and health worries continue. United Artists reacquires film option on *Do Androids Dream of Electric Sheep?*

1974   *Flow My Tears, the Policeman Said*, published in hardcover in February, is his best-received novel since *The Man in the High Castle*, gaining nominations for the Hugo and Nebula awards, and winning, in 1975, the John W. Campbell Memorial Award. Dick dreads upcoming April tax period, fearing retribution for signing the *Ramparts* petition. In February, after oral surgery for an impacted wisdom tooth, during which he is given sodium pentothal, experiences the first of a sequence of overwhelming visions that will last through and intensify during March, then taper intermittently throughout the year. Interpretation of these revelations, which are variously ascribed to benign and malign influences both religious and political (including but not limited to God, Gnostic Christians, the Roman Empire, Bishop Pike, and the KGB), will preoccupy Dick for much of his remaining life. "It hasn't spoken a word to me since I wrote *The Divine Invasion*. The voice is identified as Ruah, which is the Old Testament word for the Spirit of God. It speaks in a feminine voice and tends to express statements regarding the messianic expectation. It guided me for a while. It has spoken to me sporadically since I was in high school. I expect that if a crisis arises it will say something again. . . ." He begins writing speculative commentary on what he comes to call "2-3-74"; these writings are eventually assembled into a disordered manuscript of approximately 8,000 mostly handwritten pages, and which Dick will call the *Exegesis* (excerpts from which are published posthumously, though the whole remains unpublished and largely unread). Fires and within the week rehires the Meredith Agency after they agree to move contract for *Flow My Tears, the Policeman Said* from Doubleday to DAW. Is hospitalized for five days for extremely high blood pressure and possibly a minor stroke. Dick is visited again by French film director Jean-Pierre Gorin, who negotiates an out-of-pocket film option for *Ubik*, with Dick to write the screenplay. Writes *Ubik* screenplay in one month (never produced, but published in 1985). Is visited by two different screenwriters who have worked on adapting *Do Androids Dream of Electric Sheep?* (filmed as *Blade Runner*). Is interviewed by Paul Williams for *Rolling Stone*, a conversation dominated by a recounting and analysis of the 1971 break-in.

1975   Injures shoulder, and following surgery, dictates notes on novel-in-progress *Valisystem A* (the material eventually to bifurcate into *Radio Free Albemuth*, published posthumously, and *VALIS*, published in 1981) into a portable tape recorder but resumes typing within two weeks. *The New Yorker* publishes a two-part interview in successive issues in January and February in the "Talk of the Town" section, calling Dick "our favorite science fiction writer." Last flares of visionary experience occur in January and February. Works nightly on the *Exegesis*, fueled by readings on Gnosticism, Zoroastrianism, and Buddhism. *Confessions of a Crap Artist* published, the only one of the early realist novels to be published during his lifetime. Receives visit from cartoonist Art Spiegelman. Dick becomes increasingly enamored of an earlier friend and a trainee for Episcopal priesthood, Doris Sauter. In May, Sauter is diagnosed with cancer. Has a falling-out with Harlan Ellison. *Deus Irae* is completed, with collaborator Roger Zelazny. Dick earns somewhat better income for the year, largely due to foreign royalties. During a brief flush period, thanks to the release of foreign royalties, purchases a used sports car and an *Encyclopedia Britannica*, but within months is reduced to borrowing funds from idol and mentor Robert Heinlein. Finishes revisions on *A Scanner Darkly*. In November, *Rolling Stone* magazine publishes Paul Williams's long profile, billing Dick as "The Most Brilliant SF Mind on Any Planet."

1976   Dick asks Doris Sauter to marry him; she refuses, not wanting to interfere with his family. In February, Christopher is hospitalized for hernia. Later that month Dick and Tessa separate. Within hours Dick attempts suicide by simultaneous multiple methods. He is hospitalized at Orange County Medical Center, where he is soon transferred to the psychiatric ward, and stays for 14 days, under observation. Afterward, Tessa briefly returns, but Dick ends the relationship and moves in with Sauter, in a Santa Ana apartment where he will live for the remainder of his life. (The relationship remains platonic.) In May, Bantam acquires three novels for reprint—*Palmer Eldritch*, *Ubik*, and *A Maze of Death*—and offers an advance for the 2-3-74–based novel-in-progress, still called *Valisystem A*. In September Sauter decides to move into the apartment next door. Depressed again and fearful of suicidal impulses, Dick checks into the mental ward of St. Joseph's Hospital in October. Near the year's end, editor at Bantam requests minor revisions to *Valisystem A*, which triggers a re-drafting of the book so different that it becomes another novel, *VALIS*. (*Valisystem A*, in the form submitted in 1976, will be published in 1985 as *Radio Free Albemuth*.) *Deus Irae* is published.

1977   Dick adjusts to living alone for the first time. Tessa and Christopher become regular visitors. In February, divorce from Tessa becomes final. *A Scanner Darkly* is published. Friendship with Tim Powers is at its height, and evenings with Powers, K. W. Jeter, and James Blaylock, all destined for SF writing careers, become a regular occasion. Powers and Jeter, with whom he recounts and debates the 2-3-74 visions, will become models for characters in the still-gestating, highly autobiographical *VALIS* manuscript. Novels *Ubik*, *The Three Stigmata of Palmer Eldritch*, and *A Maze of Death* republished by Bantam, with blurb from *Rolling Stone* article and endorsements from contemporaries acknowledging Dick as a major American writer. In

April, meets Joan Simpson, a 32-year-old social worker. After three weeks together in Orange County, Dick follows Simpson to Sonoma, where he spends part of the summer. Dick is plagued by bouts of fierce depression. Travels to France for the Metz Festival, where he is guest of honor. The overseas travel represents a personal triumph over phobia. His speech, "If You Find This World Bad, You Should See Some of the Others," is received with bewilderment due to heavy religious content and difficulties with simultaneous translation. On return, suffers a split with Simpson over his unwillingness to permanently relocate to Northern California. Continues to work on *Exegesis*. Short story "We Can Remember It For You Wholesale" optioned for film adaptation (later released as *Total Recall*).

1978   With new version of *VALIS* overdue at Bantam, continues work on *Exegesis* instead. Mother dies in August. Is thrilled when daughters Laura and Isa finally meet. In September, struggling to find appropriate fictional form for 2-3-74 experiences, writes in *Exegesis*: "My books (& stories) are intellectual (conceptual) mazes. & I am in an intellectual maze in trying to figure out our situation . . . because the *situation* is a maze, leading back to itself. . . ." New Meredith Agency contact Russell Galen provides encouragement by aggressively marketing titles for reprint, and by proposing a book of nonfiction, a suggestion that at last triggers an effective approach to the *VALIS* material. Writes *VALIS* in two weeks in November, dedicating the book to Galen.

1979   Daughters Laura and Isa each visit several times. *A Scanner Darkly* wins the Grand Prix du Festival at Metz, France. Works with tremendous devotion on the *Exegesis*, which he remarks may be his most significant work. Russell Galen places new short stories in high-paying markets: *Playboy* and *Omni*. Dick and Galen finally meet in person when he visits Orange County, but Galen finds the resultant all-night talk marathon exhausting. When his building is converted to condominiums, Dick purchases his apartment. Doris Sauter, unable to afford purchasing her own, is forced to move. The separation causes great distress. Fictionalizes his attachment to Sauter in the short story "Chains of Air, Webs of Aether." Short story "Second Variety" optioned (premieres in 1995 as *Screamers*).

1980   Incorporating "Chains of Air, Webs of Aether," completes *The Divine Invasion*, conceived as a sequel to *VALIS*, by late March. Continues efforts on *Exegesis*, but does little other writing for remainder of year. Outlines several novels that remain unwritten. Increasingly anxious about the cessation of visionary inspiration, experiences flash of revelation in late November, from which he infers that he should stop working on the *Exegesis*. After writing a five-page concluding parable, on December 2 types the words "End" and creates a title page (*THE DIALECTIC: God against Satan, & God's Final Victory foretold & shown/ Philip K. Dick/AN EXEGESIS/Apologia Pro Mia Vita*). Ten days later, resumes compulsive writing of *Exegesis*.

1981   In February, *VALIS* is published. Falls out painfully from friendship with Ursula K. Le Guin but quickly reconciles. Concerned by loss of energy, takes up dieting and quickly loses weight. Director Ridley Scott begins work on *Blade Runner*, a film adaptation of *Do Androids Dream of Electric Sheep?*, written by Hampton Fancher and David Peoples. Dick's reaction to the production is alternately jubilant and disdainful. The film's financiers seek a novelization of the screenplay, but Russell Galen insists that *Androids* should be released in conjunction with the film instead (*Androids* is reissued under the film's title in 1982). Accepts offer from Simon & Schuster editor David Hartwell for a realist novel and a SF novel. In April and May writes *The Transmigration of Timothy Archer*, a fictionalization of the events surrounding Bishop James Pike's death, and the first non-SF work he has written since the final rejection of his realist novels by the Meredith Agency in 1963. Dick tells Galen, in a June letter, that exclusion from non-genre publication "has been the tragedy—and a very long-term tragedy—of my creative life." Two months later, contemplating *The Owl in Daylight*, his proposed next SF novel, writes: "Yes, I think I will continue to write SF novels. It's in my blood. . . ." Finds himself depleted and unable to begin writing. On September 17, receives a nighttime vision of a savior named "Tagore," who he is convinced is alive and living in Ceylon, and from whom he begins to feel he is receiving instruction. Drawn by the possibility of family life, considers remarriage with Tessa. In November is invited to Hollywood to a screening of a reel of special effects from the early cut of *Blade Runner*. Invited to return to Metz Festival, he begins to make plans to travel. Begins series of interviews with Gregg Rickman; invites Rickman to be his official biographer. Writes two (wholly different) outline proposals for "Owl in Daylight."

1982   In January, becomes enthusiastic about the prophecies of a British mystic, Benjamin Creme, who predicts the coming of a future Buddha called Maitreya. Continues interviews with Rickman, to whom Dick confesses uncertainty and weariness with spiritual matters. In what was likely his final interview, Dick is interviewed by Doris Sauter's friend Gwen Lee for a college paper. He reveals details about "Owl in Daylight," which he does not live to write. On February 18, Dick suffers a stroke alone in his apartment, where he is found unconscious by neighbors. In hospital recovers consciousness but not speech, and remains paralyzed on left side. Dies in hospital of further strokes and heart failure on March 2. Buried in a twin grave beside sister Jane in Fort Morgan, Colorado. *The Transmigration of Timothy Archer* is published after his death. Dedicated to Dick's memory, the film *Blade Runner* premieres in May. Philip K. Dick Award, awarded annually for distinguished science fiction published in paperback original form in the United States, is established.

Note on the Texts

This volume contains four novels by Philip K. Dick: *A Maze of Death* (1970), *VALIS* (1981), *The Divine Invasion* (1981), and *The Transmigration of Timothy Archer* (1982).

In September 1968 Dick reported in a letter to Larry Ashmead, science fiction editor at Doubleday, that he had begun work on the novel eventually published as *A Maze of Death*. An early typescript of the book, now at Bowling Green State University, bears the title "The Hour of the T.E.N.C.H."; in late October, when he sent his literary agent a completed draft, his working title was "A Maze with Death." Doubleday accepted the novel for publication in November. In January 1970—the title having been changed in the interim to "In a Maze of Death"—Doubleday editor Judith M. Glaushanok suggested "Maze of Death" as an alternative title. Dick offered "*The Maze of Death* (or possibly *A Maze of Death*)" instead; he also sent a revised manuscript page to replace revisions made by the publisher. Doubleday published *A Maze of Death* in hardcover in July 1970. Dick was not involved in subsequent paperback editions of the novel, except to receive royalties. The text of the present volume is taken from the 1970 Doubleday edition.

Dick wrote his novel *VALIS* in a mere two weeks, in November 1978, but its composition had a longer foreground. He had received an advance from Bantam Books in May 1976 for a novel to be titled "VALISystem A," originally conceived in 1974 and then written in the summer of 1976. Dick abandoned "VALISystem A" after Bantam editor Mark Hurst requested extensive revisions, and it was not published until after Dick's death (as *Radio Free Albemuth* [New York: Arbor House, 1985].) "Valis," a science-fiction film depicted in the novel *VALIS*, recapitulates elements of "VALISystem A." Dick first used the title *VALIS* to describe a new project in September 1977, but sketched out a plot and characters different from those that appear in the published book. *VALIS* also incorporated material Dick had rehearsed in his "Exegesis," an extensive journal project to which he gave a title in March 1974 and which is referred to and quoted from in the novel. (Dick's "Exegesis" has never been published in its entirety, but the posthumous *In Pursuit of VALIS: Selections from the Exegesis*, ed. Lawrence Sutin [Lancaster, Pennsylvania: Underwood-Miller, 1991] presents representative and significant passages.) Bantam Books published *VALIS* in paperback in February 1981; the 1981 Bantam Books edition contains the text printed here.

Dick planned a sequel to *VALIS*, with the working title "VALIS Regained," soon after he completed *VALIS* in 1978, but he did not begin writing the new novel until March 1980. Retitled *The Divine Invasion*, the sequel was completed in less than a month. Its opening chapters drew on a short story Dick had written in the interim, "Chains of Air, Web of Aethyr," subsequently published in *Stellar #5: Science Fiction Stories*, ed. Judy-Lynn del Rey (N.Y.: Ballantine, 1980). Simon & Schuster published *The Divine Invasion* in hardcover in May 1981; the text presented here has been taken from the Simon & Schuster first edition.

In April 1981, Dick entered into an agreement with Simon & Schuster editor David Hartwell—also his editor on *The Divine Invasion* —to write two new novels, "The Owl in Daylight" and "Bishop Timothy Archer." He turned to the latter first, having already mentally outlined the book in what Hartwell later recalled as "enormous detail," and finished writing during April and May. Simon & Schuster published *The Transmigration of Timothy Archer* in hardcover in May 1982, soon after Dick's death; this volume presents the text of the Simon & Schuster first edition.

In 1990, the Book of the Month Club published *VALIS*, *The Divine Invasion*, and *The Transmigration of Timothy Archer* in a single volume as *The VALIS Trilogy*. Dick referred to the three novels as "the VALIS trilogy" in interviews just prior to his death, but their publication under this title was planned without his involvement, and on other occasions he envisioned other groupings and arrangements for his novels. The present volume includes the three novels in Dick's "trilogy" but withholds the posthumous title *The VALIS Trilogy*.

This volume presents the texts of the original printings chosen for inclusion here, but it does not attempt to reproduce nontextual features of their typographic design. The texts are presented without change, except for the correction of typographical errors. Spelling, punctuation, and capitalization are not altered, even when inconsistent or irregular. The following is a list of typographical errors corrected, cited by page and line number: 30.28–29, pentabarbital; 32.32, fatigue; 84.8, learned; 137.8, himself.; 176.21, Glora; 180.14, corrolation; 190.11, 14, 31, Pyrric; 214.11, now; 219.16, hospital; 223.25, Paramenides; 231.7, verbals; 238.31,).; 239.1, commond; 239.40, anti-freeeze; 249.11, all—' "; 270.23, 32, pentathol; 274.16, Parsival; 279.29, pentathol; 313.27, solice; 316.22, VALIS; 318.23, inscrutible; 334.18–19, goat," Linda said, "and; 347.2, master."; 352.22, *are*; 354.14, afraid?"; 369.34, dieties; 370.31, large,; 451.27, Pythagorias; 456.8, back. He; 471.33, replacement; 475.28, *And . . . verse.*; 499.29, off—"; 529.40, D.C. zoo; 536.23, said.; 542.36, The; 593.20, warmth.'"; 648.38, Lets's; 678.16, up.; 688.17, 19, 23, 'Vette; 801.37, there there.

Notes

In the notes below, the reference numbers denote page and line of this volume (the line count includes chapter headings). No note is made for material included in the eleventh edition of *Merriam Webster's Collegiate Dictionary*. Biblical quotations are keyed to the King James Version. Quotations from Shakespeare are keyed to *The Riverside Shakespeare*, ed. G. Blakemore Evans (Boston: Houghton Mifflin, 1974). For further background, see: Lawrence Sutin, *Divine Invasions: A Life of Philip K. Dick* (New York: Harmony Books, 1989); *The Shifting Realities of Philip K. Dick: Selected Literary and Philosophical Writings*, edited by Lawrence Sutin (New York: Pantheon, 1995); Gregg Rickman, *To the High Castle: Philip K. Dick, A Life, 1928–1982* (Long Beach, CA: Fragments West / The Valentine Press, 1989).

The editor of the present volume wishes to thank Laura Leslie and Isa Hackett for their assistance in researching the Chronology.

A MAZE OF DEATH

3.3   William Sarill] A graduate student in physics, Sarill (b. 1942) lived with Dick briefly in 1968.

3.6   Bishop James A. Pike] Pike (1913–1969), an Episcopal bishop and a prominent and controversial liberal theologian, had been Dick's longtime friend and later provided the inspiration for the title character of *The Transmigration of Timothy Archer* (1982).

10.37   old epic] *The Lord of the Rings* (1954–55), by J.R.R. Tolkien (1892–1973).

15.18–19   that was the long and the short of it] See *Princess Ida* (1884), comic opera by W. S. Gilbert (1836–1911) and Arthur Sullivan (1842–1900): "And I'm a peppery kind of King / Who's indisposed to parleying / To fit the wit of a bit of chit / And that's the long and the short of it!"

33.27   T.A.T. test] The Thematic Apperception Test, first developed in 1935, consists of a series of cards featuring images of human figures in various ambiguous situations, of which the test subject is asked to devise narrative explanations.

74.26   *Granada*] A popular song (1932) by Mexican composer Agustín Lara (1897–1970).

79.10   Person-from-Porlock] An unexpected visitor, on business from the nearby town of Porlock, interrupted the visionary state in which Samuel

Taylor Coleridge composed his poem "Kubla Khan" (according to Coleridge's 1816 introduction to the poem); the "person from Porlock" has since become a commonplace image of thwarted creative concentration.

126.3   "Agnus Dei . . . mundi."]   "Lamb of God who takes away the sins of the world." This and subsequent Latin quotations on pages 126–27 are taken from the Requiem Mass of Roman Catholic liturgy.

126.9–15   "Lacrymosa . . . dona eis requiem."]   "Mournful that day, when from the ashes shall rise again sinful man to be judged. Therefore pardon him, Oh God. Merciful Lord Jesus, give them rest."

126.18   "Libera me . . . aeterna!"]   "Deliver me, Lord, from eternal death."

126.23   "Salve pietatis,"]   "Save me, fount of mercy."

127.13–14   "Mors stupebit . . . responsura."]   "Death and nature will be astounded, when all creation rises again to answer the judge."

VALIS

172.1   Russell Galen]   Galen (b. 1954), working for the Scott Meredith Agency, was Dick's literary agent from 1977 until Dick's death and continues to represent his estate.

177.15   the Synanon Building]   A large residential facility operated by Synanon (1958–1991), a drug-rehabilitation program that had degenerated into sometimes violent cultism.

184.10–11   *I Ching*]   "Book of Changes," ancient Chinese book used as the basis for a system of divination.

186.28   Fraunhofer Lines]   Dark lines in the solar spectrum first described by German physicist Joseph von Fraunhofer (1787–1826).

188.1–2   "exegesis,"]   The title also of Dick's journals; see "Note on the Texts," page 839 in this volume.

189.24   "Desarts . . . Eternity"]   See "To His Coy Mistress" (c. 1651) by Andrew Marvell (1621–1678).

195.8–28   "And can I think . . . dark to me!"]   Richard Lewis (1914–1990), an English tenor, recorded arias by Georg Friedrich Handel (1685–1759) from *Jeptha* (1752) and *Samson* (1743) in 1957.

196.13   when Sandoz LSD–25 . . . acquired]   LSD produced by Sandoz Laboratories in Switzerland as an experimental psychiatric drug, reputedly more potent than later illegal production.

197.9   Q]   In the higher or historical criticism of the New Testament, a hypothetical source-text underlying the gospels of Matthew and Luke, written most probably in Greek.

198.25–26   The T-34 tank . . . Soviet Union's salvation] The T-34 medium tank first saw combat in the summer of 1941, shortly after the German invasion of the Soviet Union. It proved technically superior to, or the equal of, the German tanks it encountered in 1941–42, although its advantages in armament, armor protection, and mobility were reduced by poor crew visibility, inadequate radio equipment, and a cramped two-man turret, as well as by the superior training and tactics of German tank crews. The T-34 weighed 32 tons, had a four-man crew, a maximum speed of 34 mph, sloping armor 45 mm. thick, and was armed with a 76.2 mm. gun; 35,000 T-34s were produced between 1940 and 1944. An improved model with an 85 mm. gun and a three-man turret was introduced in 1944, and almost 17,000 T-34/85s were manufactured before the end of the war.

198.30   At Kursk] In an attempt to regain the strategic initiative following their defeat at Stalingrad, the Germans attacked the Kursk salient on July 5, 1943, but were unable to break through the carefully prepared Soviet defenses and were forced to abandon the offensive on July 17.

198.31   Porsche Elefants] Also known as the Ferdinand, the Elephant was a German assault gun (i.e., a tank with an armored superstructure, but without a traversing turret) that first saw action during the battle of Kursk, where it proved vulnerable to mechanical breakdown, mines, and close-range attacks by Soviet infantry. The Elephant weighed 71 tons, had a six-man crew, a maximum speed of 19 mph, frontal armor 200 mm. thick, and was armed with an 88 mm. gun; only 90 were ever produced.

198.32   Fourth Panzer Army] The Fourth Panzer Army attacked the southern side of the Kursk salient.

198.35–36   Zhukov . . . Vatutin] Marshal Georgi Zhukov (1896–1974), the leading Soviet commander in World War II, supervised the defense of the northern side of the Kursk salient until July 12, when he began planning a Soviet counteroffensive along the southern side. General Nikolai Vatutin (1901–1944) commanded the Voronezh Front, which was deployed along the southern side of the salient. He successfully led his command (later renamed the 1st Ukrainian Front) until February 29, 1944, when he was fatally wounded by partisans of the nationalist Ukrainian Insurgent Army in an ambush near Rivne (Rovno).

198.38   Tiger tank . . . Panthers] The Tiger tank, which entered service in late 1942, weighed 61 tons, had a five-man crew, a maximum speed of 23 mph, frontal armor 100 mm. thick, and was armed with an 88 mm. gun; only 1,350 were produced. The Panther, which first saw combat in the battle of Kursk, weighed 47 tons, had a five-man crew, a maximum speed of 28 mph, sloping frontal armor 80 mm. thick, and was armed with a high-velocity 75 mm. gun; 6,000 were produced. Although both the Tiger and the Panther were superior to the T-34 in armament and armor protection, they were its inferiors in regards to mobility and mechanical reliability.

199.1–2   General Koniev . . . March twenty-sixth.]   Ivan Koniev (1897–1973) commanded the 2nd Ukrainian Front during the Soviet offensive in the western Ukraine in March 1944, during which his troops advanced 150 miles in three weeks.

199.9   movie *Patton*]   The film, starring George C. Scott and Karl Malden and directed by Franklin J. Schaffner, was released in 1970.

199.39   Pinto]   The Ford Motor Company's subcompact model Pinto, built from 1970 to 1980, became notorious for a defect in the design of its fuel system, which made an explosion more likely in the event of a rear-end collision.

202.17–18   Elijah . . . murmuring voice]   See 1 Kings 19:1–21.

208.10   PAT]   Paroxysmal atrial tachycardia, a condition typified by an irregular and sometimes rapid heartbeat.

210.7–8   Yeats's . . . dying animal']   See Yeats's "Sailing to Byzantium" (1928): "Consume my heart away; sick with desire / And fastened to a dying animal / It knows not what it is."

214.13   *Parsifal* . . . space."]   From the first act of *Parsifal* (1882), an opera by Richard Wagner (1813–1883).

239.28   Bishop Pike . . . Sea?"]   See note 3.6.

241.6–7   his study . . . Reik]   See *Masochism in Modern Man* (1941). Born in Vienna, Reik (1888–1969) studied psychoanalysis with Sigmund Freud; he immigrated to the U.S. in 1938, and later founded the National Psychological Association for Psychoanalysis.

245.9–10   SNCC and CORE]   The Student Nonviolent Coordinating Committee and the Congress of Racial Equality, activist groups that played a leading role in the African-American civil rights movement.

257.39   Melodyland]   MelodyLand, a 3,000 seat theater-in-the-round in Anaheim, California, near Disneyland, became the MelodyLand Christian Center, an evangelical megachurch, in 1969.

280.27–29   A sufficiently . . . pointed that out.]   See *Profiles of the Future* (1962), by Arthur C. Clarke (1917–2008).

287.17–21   a wonderful passage . . . the stall."]   Malachi 4:1–3.

296.35–297.9   "So everything . . . Schopenhauer.)]   See *The World As Will and Idea* (*Die Welt als Wille und Vorstellung*, 1819; R.B. Haldane, tr.), by German philosopher Arthur Schopenhauer (1788–1860). The same work is the source of "the cat which you see playing in the yard" in the paragraph that follows.

327.21–22   Paul Williams . . . the writer."]   Williams (b. 1948), writer and founder of the pop music magazine *Crawdaddy*, managed Timothy Leary's 1968 campaign for U.S. President and was selected by Dick as his literary executor. In May–June 1969 he joined Leary and John Lennon in Montreal, where Lennon and Yoko Ono staged their second "Bed-In for Peace" protest.

338.10   What happened at Jonestown] On November 18, 1978, over 900 members of the Peoples Temple, a California cult, committed mass suicide at their settlement, Jonestown, in rural Guyana.

343.20–21   *The Cosmic Trigger . . .* Wilson says] In his *Cosmic Trigger: The Final Secret of the Illuminati* (1977), Robert Anton Wilson (1932–2007), an American novelist and esoteric philosopher, pursues metaphysical and historical conspiracy theories.

377.7   Jim Jones] Jones (1931–1978) founded the Peoples Temple and led its members to mass suicide; see note 338.10.

396.16   **48.**] The repeated "48" in this numbered list, a possible typographical error, has been left uncorrected in the present volume.

THE DIVINE INVASION

403.13–14   *Fiddler on the Roof*] 1964 Broadway musical with music by Jerry Bock (b. 1928) and lyrics by Sheldon Harnick (b. 1924).

406.4–5   'Matchmaker, Matchmaker'] A musical number from *Fiddler on the Roof* (1964).

408.9   Cathy Berberian . . . *Ulysses*?] An American mezzo-soprano and composer, Berberian (1925–1983) read from *Ulysses* for her husband Luciano Berio's 1958 *Thema (Omaggio a Joyce)*, which experimentally alters the sounds of the spoken text.

424.5–10   C. S. Lewis's . . . *Letters.*] *The Problem of Pain* (1940), a work of Christian apologetics; *Out of the Silent Planet* (1938), a science-fiction novel; and *The Screwtape Letters* (1942), an epistolary Christian satire, by Anglo-Irish writer C.S. Lewis (1898–1963).

444.21–22   X Fretensis . . . Seventy-three C.E.] In 73 CE, the Roman tenth legion occupied the Zealot fortress at Masada, in Judea, after a lengthy siege.

450.26   Hepplewhite] Furniture in the style of English cabinetmaker George Hepplewhite (1727?–1786).

452.4   Chinvat] In Zoroastrianism, the bridge between the mortal and immortal realms, to be crossed after death; its width depended on the moral fitness of the deceased.

462.37–463.6   Go, stranger . . . we lie.] An epigram by Simonides (c. 556–468 BCE) inscribed on the burial mound of the Spartans at Thermopylae, in translations by George Rawlinson (1812–1902) and William Lisle Bowles (1762–1850).

465.17–29   How you have fallen . . . and ponder]   Isaiah 14:12.

469.8–9   Hartshorne . . . defense of Anselm]   See *Man's Vision of God* (1941), by Charles Hartshorne (1897–2000), and *Knowledge and Certainty* (1963) by Norman Malcolm (1911–1990); both philosophers revived interest in and further investigated ontological arguments for the existence of God proposed in the *Proslogion* (c. 1077–1078) of Anselm of Canterbury (1022–1109).

471.25–27   Penderecki . . . "Magnificat"]   Polish composer Krzysztof Penderecki (b. 1933) completed his choral "Magnificat" in 1973–74. The Magnificat is a Christian canticle derived from Luke 1:46–55; in part, it lists the Lord's works ("quia fecit," he has done).

481.28   Graf Egemont]   Lamoral, Count of Egmont (1522–1568), a Flemish general whose execution helped to precipitate the Dutch Revolt against Spanish rule.

508.6–9   I will betroth . . . love the Lord.]   Hosea 2:19–20.

508.24–33   I know a bank . . . fairy in.]   *A Midsummer Night's Dream*, II.i.249–56.

516.21–517.1   For He is like . . . from the stall.]   See Malachi 3:2–4:2.

517.14–16   I will break you . . . vessel.]   Psalm 2:9.

529.4   *Sepher Yezirah*]   *The Book of Creation* or *Book of Formation*, a foundational text (c. 200–300?) of Jewish esoteric tradition.

542.36–543.7   The woods of Arcady . . . sooth.]   The opening and closing lines of Yeats's "The Song of the Happy Shepherd" (1889).

552.11–12   *Silver Pennies*   . . . fairy land.']   The prefatory poem in Blanche Jennings Thompson's *Silver Pennies: A Collection of Modern Poems for Boys and Girls* (1925) reads: "You must have a silver penny / To get into Fairyland."

567.35–36   We are spirits . . . care.]   From *The Indian Queen*, a 1695 semi-opera by Henry Purcell (c. 1659–1695).

568.4–7   Come, all ye . . . the good.]   From *The Fairy-Queen*, Henry Purcell's 1692 semi-opera.

584.7   *South Pacific*]   1949 musical with music by Richard Rodgers (1902–1979) and lyrics by Oscar Hammerstein II (1895–1960).

605.18–19   Herman W. Mudgett . . . history,]   Mudgett (1860–1896), also known as Dr. Henry Howard Holmes, was an American serial killer.

THE TRANSMIGRATION OF TIMOTHY ARCHER

616.1   *him*]   Ben Jonson (c. 1572–1637), English poet and dramatist.

618.34–37   "*The best* . . . Yeats."]   See Yeats's poem "The Second Coming" (1919).

621.8–9   Arthur Koestler . . . *Janus*]   Koestler (1905–1983), a Hungarian-born British novelist and political philosopher, turned late in his career to studies of crypto-scientific paranormal subjects, including *Janus: A Summing Up* (1978).

621.26–27   Emily Dickinson . . . kindly Death"]   See Emily Dickinson, #479 (c. 1862): "Because I could not stop for Death—/He kindly stopped for me—".

624.35   Spad Thirteen]   The SPAD (Société pour l'Aviation et ses Dérivés) 13 was a French biplane first built in 1917.

626.5–8   "And still I dream . . . Yeats put it.]   See "The Song of the Happy Shepherd" (1889) by W. B. Yeats.

627.35   CP-USA]   The Communist Party of the United States of America.

631.34–38   '*Quod si hoc* . . . Terence]   See *Heauton Timorumenos* (*The Self-Tormentor*), a play by Terence (c. 195/185–159 BCE): "Start that way? That's no go. Or that? No go either."

635.14–15   Malebranche . . . in me.']   See *Dialogues on Metaphysics* (1688), by Nicolas Malebranche (1638–1715).

643.21   *Ruddigore*]   *Ruddigore; or, The Witch's Curse* (1887), comic opera by W. S. Gilbert (1836–1911) and Arthur Sullivan (1842–1900).

644.21–23   that character in *Li'l Abner* . . . around?]   Joe Btfsplk—"the world's worst jinx," followed by a perpetual rain cloud—is a minor character in *Li'l Abner*, a comic strip (1934–1977) created by Al Capp (1909–1979).

645.20–21   *Sticky Fingers* . . . bloody sheets]   See "Sister Morphine" by Mick Jagger, Keith Richards, and Marianne Faithfull, from The Rolling Stones' album *Sticky Fingers* (1971): "Yeah and you can sit around yeah and you can watch / all the clean white sheets turn red."

654.22   John Allegro]   Allegro (1923–1988) was a British biblical scholar whose controversial studies into the origins of Christianity included *The Sacred Mushroom and The Cross* (1970) and *The Dead Sea Scrolls and the Christian Myth* (1979).

655.17–656.21   Frank Zappa . . . Ralph McTell]   The performers recommended to Archer include experimental rock musicians Frank Zappa (1940–1993) and Captain Beefheart (b. Dan Van Vliet, 1941); Marc Bolan (1947–1977), of the glam-rock band T. Rex, who had died in a car accident;

Ray Davies (b. 1944), lead singer of The Kinks; Paul Kantner (b. 1941) and Grace Slick (b. 1939) of Jefferson Starship; and folk singer/songwriter Ralph McTell (b. 1944).

659.5–6   *Howard the Duck*] A comic book based on a character created in 1973 by writer Steve Gerber (1947–2008) and artist Val Mayerik (b. 1950); the first series was published by Marvel Comics from 1976 to 1979.

667.4–11   *"All these hosts . . . Vishnu."*] Arjuna's battle with Vishnu appears in the *Bhagavad Gita* (c. 500–200 BCE), chapter 11, verse 30.

672.11   Niemöller] Martin Niemöller (1892–1984), a German pastor and theologian, became a prominent spokesman for pacifism after his release from incarceration in Nazi concentration camps.

687.5–19   *Batter my . . . Donne's*] Holy Sonnet XIV (1633), by John Donne (1572–1631).

694.3   Benjamin Proverb Test] See John D. Benjamin, "A Method for Distinguishing and Evaluating Formal Thinking Disorders in Schizophrenia," in J. S. Kasanin, ed., *Language and Thought in Schizophrenia* (1944).

720.19–21   which recording . . . Ludwig] Otto Klemperer (1885–1973) conducted the Philharmonia Orchestra and Chorus, and mezzo-soprano Christa Ludwig (b. 1928), in a performance of Beethoven's 1814 opera *Fidelio* for Angel Records (S 3625) in 1962.

720.24   'Abscheulicher! . . . Hin?'] "Vile one! Where are you rushing off to?"

747.9   *Dido and Aeneas*] 1689 opera by English baroque composer Henry Purcell (c. 1659–1695) and librettist Nahum Tate (1652–1715).

747.29–30   Dr. Dee . . . England] John Dee (1527–c. 1608), an English alchemist and scholar.

748.31   Eric Berne . . . dead] Berne (1910–1970), a Canadian-American psychiatrist responsible for "transactional analysis" and author of *Games People Play* (1964), died of a heart attack.

748.34–35   Chardin . . . his wish."] French Jesuit philosopher Pierre Teilhard de Chardin (1881–1955) died following a heart attack suffered on Good Friday.

763.27   poem . . . D. H. Lawrence] See "Snake" (1923), by D. H. Lawrence (1885–1930).

780.4   *Captivity Letters*] Those of Paul's Epistles written while he was under house arrest in Rome, including Colossians, Philemon, Ephesians, and Philippians, are sometimes referred to as his "Captivity Letters" or "Prison Letters."

797.17   John Allegro]   See note 654.22.

803.20–21   Harry Stack Sulllivan . . . the world.]   Sullivan (1892–1949) was known for his pioneering clinical work with schizophrenic patients; his *Schizophrenia as a Human Process* was published posthumously in 1962.

809.9–11   '*Nel mezzo . . . smarrita.*']   In the middle of the journey of our life / I found myself in a dark wood / For the straight way was lost.

813.38–814.2   *koto* record . . . *Asa*,"]   "Midori no Asa" ("Bright Morning") appears on the LP *Koto Music* (WP-1278, 1959) by Kimio Eto (b. 1924?). The koto is a traditional Japanese string instrument.

THE LIBRARY OF AMERICA SERIES

The Library of America fosters appreciation and pride in America's literary heritage by publishing, and keeping permanently in print, authoritative editions of America's best and most significant writing. An independent nonprofit organization, it was founded in 1979 with seed money from the National Endowment for the Humanities and the Ford Foundation.

To subscribe to the series or to order individual copies,
please visit www.loa.org or call (800) 964.5778.

This book is set in 10 point Linotron Galliard,
a face designed for photocomposition by Matthew Carter
and based on the sixteenth-century face Granjon. The paper
is acid-free lightweight opaque and meets the requirements
for permanence of the American National Standards Institute.
The binding material is Brillianta, a woven rayon cloth made
by Van Heek-Scholco Textielfabrieken, Holland. Compo-
sition by Dedicated Business Services. Printing by
Malloy Incorporated. Binding by Dekker Book-
binding. Designed by Bruce Campbell.